Beauty from Ashes

NOVELS BY EUGENIA PRICE

ST. SIMONS TRILOGY

Lighthouse

New Moon Rising

The Beloved Invader

FLORIDA TRILOGY

Don Juan McQueen

Maria

Margaret's Story

SAVANNAH QUARTET

Savannah

To See Your Face Again

Before the Darkness Falls

Stranger in Savannah

GEORGIA TRILOGY

Bright Captivity

Where Shadows Go

Beauty from Ashes

DOUBLEDAY
New York   London   Toronto
Sydney   Auckland

Beauty from Ashes

Eugenia Price

Pri
cl

PUBLISHED BY DOUBLEDAY

a division of Bantam Doubleday Dell Publishing Group, Inc.
1540 Broadway, New York, New York 10036

D O U B L E D A Y *and the portrayal of an anchor with a dolphin*
are trademarks of Doubleday, a division of
Bantam Doubleday Dell Publishing Group, Inc.

Book design by Marysarah Quinn

Library of Congress Cataloging-in-Publication Data
Price, Eugenia.
Beauty from ashes / Eugenia Price.—1st ed.
p. cm.
Sequel to Where shadows go.
1. Georgia—History—Fiction. I. Title.
PS3566.R47B33 1995
813'.54—dc20
94-38912
CIP

ISBN 0-385-26703-7
ISBN 0-385-42314-4 (large print)
Copyright © 1995 by Eugenia Price
Printed in the United States of America
May 1995

1   3   5   7   9   10   8   6   4   2

First Edition

For
Frances Stubinger Daugherty

. . . to give unto them beauty for ashes,
the oil of joy for mourning, . . .

ISAIAH 61:3

PROLOGUE

July 19, 1845

JERKED FROM A SOUND SLEEP, ANNE FRASER SAT bolt upright in bed and listened. The darkness outside her thick-walled tabby cottage at Lawrence Plantation on the north end of St. Simons Island was silent as a tomb. Still, something—was it a wild animal's scream?—had roused her, and the old, sickening fear of being alone made her shudder. As she had done for the past six years, she stretched her arm all the way to the far side of the empty bed searching in half sleep for her dead husband, John.

"Eve?"

No answer. Eve had not come yet. Night after night for the six long years since John left her, Anne's bright-skinned, insistently faithful servant, Eve, had spent a part of each night in Anne's room, curled on a straw mattress on the floor beside the bed where her mistress slept alone. "Ain't nobody can help you through the first hours when you hab to climb into that empty bed without Mausa John," Eve said again and again, "but Eve be here eber time the pain hit you when you wakes up." Anne had tried to convince Eve to spend the nights beside her own husband, June, so they would not miss waking up together when dawn came. "June, he know zactly how to cook his own breakfus," Eve would remind her, as usual leaving no room for argument.

"You aren't here, are you, Eve?" So that she would not wake the children, Anne was whispering into the shadowy room. Her daughter Pete, who would be twenty in November, had probably heard the same wild sound that woke her mother. But Fanny, thirteen, John Couper, twelve, and Selina, eight, were surely asleep. Still clutching a light blanket around her shoulders even though the July night was warm and airless, she tried to help herself by giving thanks that Pete and Fanny and John Couper were old enough for adult conversation. Selina had been too young, only two, when her father died and couldn't "figure for sure" that she really remembered much about John. There was an odd solace in that the child seemed not to miss him as sharply as did everyone else.

"Eve! Eve, where are you?" Anne's voice sounded like a croak. If only Mama's big clock downstairs would strike, she would at least have an idea when Eve might get here to help her. What could Eve do anyway? What could anyone do now that John was gone? Now that her blessed firstborn, Annie, had died on a cool September morning some two years later trying to give Paul Demere a child. Not only Annie but Anne's only sister, Belle, had also died in childbirth, just eight months before Annie.

Unshed tears seemed about to choke her and she cried out, "No! No, Mama, *I don't want you to be dead, too.* You can't be dead, too!" The dam of pent-up tears broke, and unmindful of her sleeping children, Anne began to cry aloud—wrenching, hard, loud sobs torn from somewhere deeper than her very heart. The heart that had been so smashed, so broken, so torn that restraint of any kind was beyond her. . . .

PETE HAD HALF HEARD THE WILD COON'S SCREAM, BUT SLEEP overcame her so that when the unmistakable sound of her mother's helpless, almost primitive weeping roused her again, she ran halfway down the narrow upstairs hall before she came fully awake.

When the girl burst into her mother's room, loosed red hair tousled because her nightcap had, as usual, fallen off, she made herself stop running, tried to catch her breath in the hope of offering some comfort. But all she could do was throw herself on the bed beside her parent and grab her in her arms. Holding Mama seemed not to help at all. The harsh, racking sobs only grew louder, and for once, Pete felt no response. She had come often through the years since Papa died, sometimes right, sometimes wrong in thinking she'd heard her mother crying. There was no mistaking what she'd heard tonight. The still-slender, still-pretty aging woman in her arms was a total stranger in her heavy grief— grief that revealed itself in almost as wild a cry as the coon's.

"Mama," she gasped. "Mama, did the coon wake you? I heard it, too, but I'm afraid I—I went back to sleep. Oh, Mama, how do you keep walking around all day doing things that have to be done? So many in our family have—died. So much grief! Too much. I don't like God at all anymore. I not only don't like Him, I don't trust Him either!"

Still feeling like a stranger in Pete's arms, her mother seemed to make no effort to stem the weeping. "Mama, can't you stop? Can't you even slow down?"

A voice Pete had never heard before groaned, "No! And don't you try to stop me. Get out of my way, Rebecca, so I can get out of this house!"

"Mama, *what?* You haven't called me Rebecca in—in years. Only when you're out of sorts with me. What did I do? Did I make you mad because I said I didn't trust God? Well, I don't. How could I trust a God who could send all this sorrow and heartbreak down on you? One person dying right after another!"

Her mother was pushing her away, pushing her roughly to one side so that she could crawl out of bed. Without even grabbing her voile summer robe, the bent woman, who by now didn't look like Mama, stumbled across the bedroom floor, out the door, and down the cottage steps. The front door banged and just as young John Couper appeared, eyes wide, young face distorted with fear, Pete heard the hard, helpless weeping all the way from the front yard. Mama was running out there in the dark toward their landing— toward Lawrence Creek!

"Pete, where's Mama going?" John Couper whispered.

When she could only stand there like a pine stump, her brother repeated, "Where's Mama going? She could—Pete, she could drown out there if she took a wrong step off the dock. It's pitch dark on that dock at this hour." The words were no sooner out of his mouth than the big clock downstairs struck five times. "Where's Eve, Pete? Isn't it about time for Eve to be here?"

Without giving her a chance to answer, John Couper turned and ran down the stairs. Even before he slammed the front door, she heard their mother's frantic voice almost screaming Eve's name— screaming from far off. It was plain that Mama was all the way across the big front yard, past the giant oaks, and down to the water's edge.

In seconds, finally able to make her legs move again, Pete was also racing across the yard. In the black, starless, moonless night, she hurried to where they both stood, John Couper clutching Mama's shoulders as though holding her back.

Suddenly Pete realized that Mama was no longer sobbing, no longer letting out that terrible wail. The woman who had come to be the one solid part of all their lives—the one person they had left to them on St. Simons—was just standing there, facing them in stark silence. Silence that was almost worse than the sound of her helpless sobs.

John Couper said nothing but continued to grip Mama's shoulders. Pete could think of nothing to say either, so the three simply stood there wordless in the velvet night.

Finally, Pete, never comfortable with silence, said, "Mama? Mama, I'm so glad you could stop crying."

"I'm sure you are, dear," her mother said, her voice still thick. And then, in the now barely perceptible first light, they saw their mother turn away from them. For what seemed another eternity, she just stood there, forced back her shoulders, lifted her chin, and fluffed at the stringy curls on her neck as though mindful for the first time of how she must look to her children.

After a long, long time, holding her rigid posture, still facing the water and the marshes, Mama whispered hoarsely, "Will one of you run for Eve? Then both of you go back to bed. I need Eve. I'll be too glad to have her with me to give her a piece of my mind for being so late getting here, but I do need to talk with her. I think suddenly I feel different. It just could be that I've made a big leap ahead in the past few minutes."

"What kind of leap, Mama?" Pete asked, her own voice timid, especially for her. "I have to know. John Couper, you run for Eve. I have to stay here with Mama as long as—as long as she'll let me. Did you hear me, John Couper? Scat."

When her brother had hurried up the lane toward the cabin Eve shared with June, Pete wondered helplessly if she dared ask Mama if she knew the date today. It was July 19, and the day had come and gone last year without a mention that on July 19, 1839, they'd buried Papa in the churchyard. Last July 19 had, for Pete, been a ghastly day, not only because of her own distressing memories but because, more than anyone else, Pete did suffer from silence around her. She'd far rather be fussed at or scolded or allowed to weep than to endure everyone she loved, including Mama, moving through any day as though made of wood. For the first four anniversary years, they had all gone in the carriage to Christ Church with flowers and they had all cried until their eyes ached and to Pete, that had been far, far better than ignoring the date. Surely Mama remembered what day it was. But in all the six years Papa had been gone, Pete had never known her mother to act the way she was acting now. What on earth did Mama mean when, out of the blue, she mentioned a leap ahead? What could Eve do to help her that Pete couldn't do?

For as long as she could bear it, Pete waited, then said, "I know you wish I were Annie, Mama. She would think of some way to help you. I want to. I really want so much to help you."

"Don't do that, Pete!"

"Don't do—what, Mama? I am just standing here like a lump and I do want to do something for you."

Still staring out over the marshes as Lawrence Creek reflected a hint of the clear, pink dawn now beginning to light the sky, her mother said, "You don't know, do you, dear Pete? As grown-up and wise as you're getting to be, you still don't know."

"Don't talk in riddles, Mama! Please don't. I know perfectly well that you do need to be with Eve now and I also know you and Annie were always so close that you wouldn't have called out for Eve if Annie had been here. I've always known I'm a tomboy and not as good as Annie was."

Now her mother whirled around to face her. "I never want to hear you say such a thing again as long as I live! Do you hear me? Never. I'm doing my very best to grab on to the fact that I seem to have made some kind of good leap ahead after I carried on the way I did earlier. There's some kind of *relief* inside me, but if you even hint that you're not one of my really solid rocks these days, I may go to pieces again." Holding both hands out to her beseechingly, Mama begged just above a whisper, "Help me, Pete. Help me—not to do that again. I must not ever let myself go like that again. We all have to go on living."

Eve, always light on her feet, startled even Pete by seeming to appear out of the dawn mists as though she'd been there a long time.

"Miss Anne," Eve gasped. "You havin' a hard time, Miss Anne? I done sleep too long. But Eve's here now. Come on, you 'n' me go back to the house to get you some breakfus. You too, Pete. Take her by the other arm. Mina not be t'work yet, but Eve can cook. Grab her arm, Pete. We take her home."

"This be the day," Eve said, serving Anne a second cup of coffee after Pete had impulsively galloped down the lane on her white horse, Cotton, pretending she wasn't a bit hungry. "It ain't like Pete not to want to eat nothin'," Eve went on while she creamed and sweetened the steaming coffee. "Petey be mad 'bout somepin?"

"No, not angry. Hurt. And I hurt her by needing you more than anyone else. Where were you? I know I fuss because you insist on sleeping part of the night upstairs in my room, but a noise woke me early—a horrible, wild scream of some kind. Didn't you and June hear it?"

"No'm, we just laid there sleepin' like two hound dogs, both of us."

"No wonder. You were still ironing curtains for my parlor until late last night. Why do you have to go on being so absolutely essential to me?"

With a half grin Eve returned the cream pitcher to its silver holder. "I knows what *essential* mean now. You done taught me. It mean you hab—have—to have me on the place. And that's good, 'cause you got me. What you reckon you hear in the night?"

"A coon fight, I suppose."

"Coons sound meaner than panters—panthers."

"You're really trying to speak correctly, aren't you? I'm proud of you."

"It's hard to remember to talk good to you when I kin still talk like me to June." She stood ramrod straight. "You does—do—know this be the day?"

"Yes."

"That all you kin say?"

"Six years ago today, we—buried John."

Eve almost hated herself because tears were again streaming down Miss Anne's tired, sorrowful face, but her mistress needed to learn to say Mausa John's name out loud. It would help someday. Maybe not yet today, but someday.

"Oh, Eve, what I wouldn't give if I could *feel* him close to me just once! If I could only have a sense now and then of his presence with me. I dream about him some. I wake up reaching for him. But do you suppose anyone will ever be able to explain to me why it is that my blessed Annie seems to stay nearby? I know John's been gone longer, but not much longer. I wasn't good at all with Annie when she married Paul Demere."

"You done fine at her wedding. You sit right beside her bed the morning she die."

"But she and I weren't close the way John and I were at the end. I didn't like Paul Demere. I didn't want her to marry him. I still don't like him, but a day hasn't passed since Annie went away that I haven't caught myself talking to her."

"Do—does—Annie she say anything to you?"

Eve watched her mistress closely for any sign that talk about her dead loved ones may be helping. No one had told Eve it would help, but deep down she knew it could, if Miss Anne found some way to open up to it. It might be hard for her, and the last thing Eve wanted was to see Miss Anne hurt anymore. Too much hurt had already come her way, but it might help swallow some of all the sorrows—first her man, Mausa John; then just a year and a half later her young sister, Miss Belle; then, God have mercy, the very same year she done lose her firstborn, sweet Annie.

Eve turned away. Miss Anne must not see tears in her eyes, because not much more than three months ago, Miss Anne's mama, Miss Rebecca, she die too. Almost nobody mentioned that, though, like it was one sorrow too many. Bad. Look like her mama dyin' sealed her lips. Oh, Eve had stood in the church aisle beside her while poor, heartbroken Revern Bartow, he preach Miss Becca's funeral with tears for Miss Belle pourin' down his own face while he talk. But except for worryin' out loud some about her papa, ole Mausa John Couper, livin' now over at Hopeton with Mausa James Hamilton an' his family, Miss Anne, she clam up tight. Lord, it must seem to her they all gone but me an' her younguns. She do need to talk some an' not keep it all shut up.

Eve repeated her question. "Does Annie ever say anything back to you when you talks to her?"

"No, but she's found a way to stay close."

"Yo' mama, Miss Becca? Be she ever close to you?"

Miss Anne jumped to her feet. "That's enough. You're talking too much. Not another word. I don't want another bite to eat and no more coffee, either. It must be full sunrise outside now. You help Mina in the kitchen. I'm going out again. I dare not miss the sunrise, especially if it's as beautiful today as I need it to be. Go, do you hear me? I have work to do."

"What work you got to do?"

"That's my business. Oh, Eve, someday you'll know for yourself that grieving is the hardest work there is. It just has to be done, though. There's no other way."

YOUNG JOHN COUPER HAD BEEN HIDING IN THE AZALEA BUSHES near the Lawrence front porch when he saw his mother and Eve enter the cottage. He had obeyed his mother, as he surely always meant to do, but he had no intention of going inside yet. From his hiding place, an idea was forming. Today was Saturday. If Nathaniel Twining had kept his schedule bringing the Island mail from Savannah, most likely he'd already stopped at Frederica. Mr. Horace Gould was postmaster now and he may have picked it up late yesterday. With all his eager heart, the boy needed to do something to help his mother. He could ride down to Black Banks, the second tabby house old Mr. Gould had built on his property. It now belonged to Mr. Horace, who would live there when he married pretty Miss Deborah Abbott in November. Of course, there may not be any mail for the Frasers, but his mind was made up. The famous English lady Mrs. Fanny Kemble Butler wrote to his mother sometimes. So did Cousin Willy Maxwell. Other friends in Darien and Savannah also wrote, knowing, as did most people up and down their part of the coast, how much grief Mama had to bear these days.

Mr. Horace Gould never failed to mention John Couper's papa, too, the boy thought as he galloped south toward the Black Banks Plantation. He liked that. There were times when he'd give almost anything if Pete would talk more often about Papa. Selina did, but sweet and good as his sister was most of the time, she was only eight and mainly just wished she could hear Papa sing again, which always made tears come to Mama's eyes. To Pete's eyes, too. The older John Couper became, the more he missed his father. Almost every night, he went to sleep wishing the two of them could have a man-to-man talk, for in December he would be thirteen. Only six and a half when Papa died, he did not then understand or even need to understand so much of what he'd like to discuss with him now.

Today, even though Mr. Horace Gould had liked Papa a lot, John Couper meant not to stay long at Black Banks because he would need to get back to Mama as soon as possible. Especially if there were letters for her to read.

WITH THREE PIECES OF MAIL TUCKED IN HIS SHIRT POCKET, JOHN Couper galloped almost all the way home from Black Banks, smiling to himself because he was bringing not only a letter from the famous English actress Fanny Kemble Butler and one from Aunt Frances Anne Wylly Fraser—living now part-time in Savannah with her two children—but also an always welcome letter from Cousin Willy Maxwell, Lord Herries. His mother would have to be pleased. Heart pounding, he rounded the turn in the Lawrence lane and trotted toward their dock, where he could see Mama sitting by herself. Good, he thought, and took a moment to realize what a long, long time it had been since he'd known anything resembling happiness. He felt almost happy now despite how much he missed his father, Annie, Aunt Belle, and now Grandmama Couper. Sometimes, he reflected, it was as though they'd been burying close family members in the sandy ground behind Christ Church for most of his life. This minute as he neared the hitching post, he felt abruptly grown-up. He could sense a vague but new purpose. He would bend every effort from now on, not trying to take Papa's place—no one could do that—but doing his level best to make things a little cheerier every day for Mama. No better way to begin, he thought, as he swung to the ground and hurried with the letters toward where she was sitting.

ANNE HAD HEARD THE BOY RIDE UP, BUT FOR A REASON EVEN SHE could not have explained, she did not turn around to smile at him. Through the years she had always made a point of giving her children a bright greeting. John Couper probably deserved her smile above them all, but so much was taking place down inside her—so much that was nameless and fragile—she was almost afraid to speak, even to this sensitive, strong boy who was daily becoming her special stay. She wouldn't have burdened the child by telling him, but despite her growing dependence on Pete, another, almost mystical bond held her to her son, John Couper.

"Mama? I won't stay," he said softly, standing now right beside her, "but I have a surprise for you. Mr. Horace Gould was saving these letters to hand to you tomorrow at church, but I've got 'em right here."

Now she turned to face him. "Letters, Son? Did you ride to Black Banks hoping you might find some mail for us?"

"Yes, ma'am. And it couldn't be better. There's one from Mrs. Butler and one from Aunt Frances and even one from Cousin Willy Maxwell! All people you love to hear from."

Anne took the letters, looking first at the one from Cousin Willy. "I wonder where he was when he wrote this. Probably back in Scotland by now. Our Cousin Willy's been in China, you know, for almost a year."

"Do you wish we could travel to China, Mama?"

On a weak laugh, she answered, "No, I do not. I want to be right here at Lawrence, exactly where we are."

"Even with one end of our porch caving in? June says he'll find time to fix the porch. It—it seems funny to have anything in our house in such bad shape, doesn't it? I know Grandfather Couper would have sent his carpenters a long time ago if he still lived at Cannon's Point."

"Our little cottage would never have gotten so dilapidated if he still lived nearby."

"But shouldn't it make us feel good knowing Grandpapa's with Uncle James over at Hopeton, where there are so many people to look after him? We have to think of Grandfather first. Especially—now."

"I do think of him. I probably think of him too much. Oh, John Couper, I think too much about far too many things, but you do know I'm trying, don't you?"

His radiant smile both cheered and strengthened her. "Mama, yes! And you're doing fine—just about all the time. I really think that."

She held up the letters. "Would you like to read these aloud to me? Your tutor, Pete, vows you were born a good reader."

"Old Pete's a good teacher."

"That girl goes on surprising me in a lot of ways." With a half smile, she added, "Isn't that an odd thing for me to be telling Pete's young brother when she's almost twenty?"

Still giving her his buoyant smile, the boy said, "I think you'd much rather read your mail yourself, by yourself, Mama. Anyway, I like Mr. Horace so much I stayed talking to him longer than I meant to, especially when I promised Eve and Pete I'd chop kitchen firewood for Mina's oven in time for dinner. Today I'm just your postmaster, Mrs. Fraser. Read your letters in peace and I'll tell Eve not to let Fanny or Selina bother you out here."

🦋 🦋

FOR A TIME AFTER HER SON LEFT, ANNE SAT THERE, THE LETTERS unopened. Her fingers traced a splintered, weathered plank in the dock. Smiling a little, she remembered how proud John had been that he had actually driven the nails that still held the once clean, replacement boards. That was years ago, before they moved their family to live down at Hamilton Plantation. Back when all of life had seemed too good, too right, too happy to last. Back before the dark, dark shadows had begun to fall, one after another, across that nearly perfect life. Back before she'd lost John or Isabella or their blessed, blessed Annie—and now, as in an unreal dream, Mama was also lying still and dead in the ground behind Christ Church. Before the shadows began to fall across the days, Anne had anticipated each letter bearing her name by making a nervous game of forcing herself to wait before breaking the seal. Sorrow upon sorrow since had choked the life from almost any anticipation.

"God, why have I known so much sorrow?" she cried aloud. "Will the blows stop falling on me? Will they ever stop?"

Did God even hear her cry? Did Annie hear? John? Mama?

"Well, I heard," she said to herself now, sternly. "I heard myself and that must be the end of it!" Her scolding voice actually seemed to help some. "No wonder my own son didn't stay." She spoke aloud now to the black, rippling water below her feet. Slowly the river water lapped at the pilings in mute, neutral response. "No wonder I'm here alone. I'm dreadful company these days. And that's going to end! Only minutes ago I felt something like new hope. What happened to it? Where did it go? Annie, are you here? I don't feel that you are this time. But I'm sure you're ashamed of me."

She drew in an unsteady, deep draft of air already muggy now that the sun rode high in the sky, pouring down its July heat. July. "July nineteenth." She was speaking aloud again. "John, *John?*" She had actually called him by name for the first time in months and months! Then, almost clutching the unopened letters, she sat up straight and listened.

Beautiful Anne . . . beautiful Anne.

"John? John, did you actually say something to me? Darling, I need you to tell me I'm going to be—all right again. I know you're here! John, where have you been all this time? Were you here when our wonderful son came to bring me these letters? Were you out here waiting when I left the house a while ago because I needed to be alone? Were you here when I felt so sure that something almost new and hopeful was taking place down inside me? When I began to hope that I'd someday find room not only to grieve for my own mother, but to allow God to turn my grief into something useful? You're with Him now. Tell me, is He a redeemer God, darling? Can He redeem even my tears and despair and failure? I've been failing everyone, even you, because I've been so helpless against all this onslaught of grief—*one loved one after another, John.* Now Mama's gone, too. Have you seen Mama yet? Where you are? Will you ask God to help me find room to grieve for her, too? To grieve so that I can begin to be me again? How can I possibly help poor Papa with his loss when I'm so numb all over?"

As though afraid to stop talking to John for fear he'd be gone again, she hurried to break the seal on the one-page letter from Fanny Kemble Butler and explained to him that they'd heard not only from Fanny but from Willy Maxwell, too, and from dear, courageous Frances Anne, who was still trying to live without John's brother, William.

Fanny Kemble Butler's letter was sent from Philadelphia and dated three weeks ago.

> My dear Anne . . .
> I'm writing from a dark mood mainly to let you know that from now on, I should be addressed at the newly remodeled Walnut Street house. Should you find time to write, I could not bear to miss receiving a letter from you. I pass my days mostly alone, though, in a near total, locked silence. My husband, Pierce, in conspiracy with the children's efficient but hateful governess, has laid down such brutal rules for me that I am permitted, due to my rank misbehavior over slavery, as he terms it, to spend only one hour a day with my daughters, who need me so much. If I chance to meet her with my two girls anywhere in the house, I am not allowed to speak to them, so obedient is the governess to her benefactor since she knows I am penniless without Pierce's dole to me. Anne, I am ashamed to add to your already unbearable sorrow even by telling you that for love of my children and for love of this shallow, selfish man, I literally begged him to allow me to live again in the same house with them. Dear Anne, does this help you in your own black grief? Does it help you at all that your memories of the late, handsome John Fraser are of a love that now can never die or even tarnish? You have that much. Oh, at least you have that much!

There were a few more agonized lines, but Anne stopped reading. Gifts from God, she knew, did not always arrive in sweetness and beauty. Had God sent Fanny's pathetic, tragic plaint in order to stiffen Anne's own sagging spirit? Had she been truly grateful that all her memories of John would, through all eternity, be beautiful and good?

Staring out over the creek and the marshes, she could almost feel the ugly, old skin of self-pity begin to peel away as though it had literal substance—as though her body were shedding it. For long, anxious minutes, she sat there on the dock and felt naked, exposed, afraid, because self-pity, she realized only now, had become a protective cloak; had caused her sense of failure before her own children, who needed her as desperately as the Butler girls needed Fanny. Pete and John Couper and Fanny and Selina needed Anne to be their mother again, needed her to smile and laugh with them. Needed her to help them find a way to bridge the very real grief they all suffered at losing not only their adored teacher, Isabella, but their sister Annie, their beloved, laughing father—and now Grandmother Couper.

"I'm not the only one who misses John," she said aloud. "I'm not the only one who misses Isabella and Annie, and I'm certainly not the only one who misses my mama."

The words were barely spoken into the cloudless, hot day when tears began to flow again, and until her first hard weeping for her dead mother slowed, she couldn't have seen well enough to finish Fanny Kemble Butler's unhappy letter if she'd tried. Nor had she noticed that her grown daughter had tiptoed onto the dock and was standing silently behind where she sat.

"Pete! How long have you been standing there?"

"All the time you've been sobbing your heart out," the tall young woman said in an almost matter-of-fact voice. "You were crying for Grandmama Couper, weren't you?"

"I—I think I was. And for the first time since she left us in April. I guess I haven't had any tears left for her until now. I'm ashamed of myself, but until a few minutes ago, I don't think I really believed that she's gone, too."

"And you knew Grandmama would understand that."

Anne reached for Pete's hand, pulled her down beside her on the dock. "I'm not sure. You may be right, but I don't think I'd reached the place where I even considered what your grandmother might be thinking of my dry eyes. I've been dwelling only on myself. Can you ever forgive me?"

"You bet," Pete said in her tomboy way. "After all, you were never quite as close to Grandmama as you are to Grandpapa."

"What?"

"I just said I've known for years that you and Grandmama kind of had to work on being close the way a mother and daughter are supposed to be. At least in books—and in the minds of people who don't know them very well."

Anne studied Pete's always expressive face. "I wonder if I've ever known exactly what you've been thinking about—anything, darling."

Now Pete was grinning her father's own devilish, somewhat cocky grin. "It may be just as well that you haven't known everything I thought, Mama," she said, the grin broadening. "We're not talking about you and me, though. We're talking about you and Grandmama Couper. I knew you hadn't let it hit you quite yet that she's really gone. Are you surprised that you hadn't?"

"Yes! Yes, I am. Surprised and—ashamed."

"That's silly."

"Silly?"

"I don't want us ever to have to work on being close. I've wanted to ask you a hundred times since Grandmama died why you hadn't cried, but I didn't ask."

"And do you know why you didn't?"

"I just told you. I don't ever want us to have to work on being friends. I just want our friendship to happen."

"Pete, I've never told anyone this before. Not even your father. But I'll never forget the day it dawned on your grandmother that she and I needed to start right then and there to be friends instead of only mother and daughter. It was the very day Mrs. Fanny Kemble Butler left for the North."

"Well, did the friendship work better than being just mother and daughter?"

"Yes. I have to believe it did."

"John Couper said he brought you a letter from Mrs. Butler today."

"He did. I haven't quite finished reading it, but I'm afraid she's anything but happy these days. Oh, Pete, do you think I'm being too optimistic in feeling some new hope? Do you suppose I may be right to have this sense that today—after my ghastly outburst of weeping earlier and after Mrs. Butler's reminder that at least all my memories of your father are beautiful—I might be able to act more like myself again? That I might be a decent, unselfish mother to you and Fanny and Selina and John Couper—the way I've always meant to be?"

"Do *you* feel that outburst of weeping may have helped?"

"I hope so. Oh, I hope so, Pete."

"I didn't ask what you hoped for. I asked how you actually felt when the weeping ended. The weeping just now for Grandmama, too."

"I feel as though it all helped—some. As though something tight may have been loosed a little. I don't want to go on acting as though I'm the only person who's grief-stricken. I need to be comforting all of you, to be comforting poor Grandpapa. Just think what it's like for him to wake up every morning in a strange room over at Hopeton, without Mama beside him."

"Is it harder to lose the person you marry, Mama, than anyone else?"

"Harder? Oh, darling, each grief is different. For a time I believed losing Annie was the worst of all because she seemed to stay so close to me." Anne got to her feet. "This doesn't sound right at all, but for months after Annie went away, I thought my grief over her was even harder to bear than losing your father."

Pete got up slowly and looked straight at her mother. In the terse, direct tone that had almost chastened Anne once or twice since Pete had grown up, she asked, "And how is it now, Mama? Are you still more heartbroken because my sister Annie is dead? I doubt it, frankly. I think you'll always miss Papa more than anyone else who will ever die before you do. You just think your sorrow over Annie is worse because you could never bring yourself to like the man she married. You must carry some guilt about that."

For an instant, Anne reacted as though her daughter had struck her. "Don't be impudent!"

"I'm not being. I know better than anyone else that I can be impudent, but I also know when I'm being that way. Can't you face it yet, Mama, that you didn't really fool any of us where Paul Demere is concerned? Don't you think I know you hate the idea that Annie's only child, little John Fraser Demere, isn't still here with us? That he's with his father, Paul, and Paul's new wife? Doesn't it help at all that Annie and Paul agreed together to name the boy for my papa? Annie didn't name him John Fraser all by herself, Mama. You know that."

"Do you have some wild idea that you're helping by preaching at me?" Anne demanded, turning away from Pete.

As though their roles had suddenly been reversed, Anne grudgingly looked at Pete's earnest, oddly stern face. The blue eyes—not pale blue like Anne's eyes but deeper like Papa Couper's—were not shaming her. They seemed almost to be pleading. Pleading firmly, a no-nonsense look only Pete knew how to give, but still begging her own mother to listen to reason.

When Anne said nothing, Pete asked, "How do you know Annie's spirit isn't trying to get through to you about Paul every time she seems to be closer to you than Papa is? We're Christians. Don't we believe Annie and Papa and Aunt Belle and Grandmama Couper are all still alive with God? Don't you think they know about us down here?"

"Pete, yes!"

"And don't you think Annie wishes you could stop the upheaval between our family and the Demeres that's gone on now for over three years? Ever since Paul Demere began to court the Sinclair woman? Mama, Paul's married again and there isn't a thing we can——"

"I know he's married again! I also know he desecrated the sweet memory of my Annie by marrying so soon after she died."

"What can we do about that, Mama? Paul was left with a tiny baby. Don't you think he needed someone to look after the baby?"

"I kept Annie's child right here until he went galloping off to the altar and took little John Fraser away from me."

Now Pete turned away. "I'm here to state that's something *I* will never do!"

"What? What won't you ever do?"

"Get married. It just causes sorrow and heartache. I don't expect ever to fall in love. That's by far the safest way."

Anne reached for the slender young woman, now at least two

inches taller than her mother. "Pete, Pete, no! Don't ever say a thing like that. Your father gave me enough joy and beauty and happiness to last me for the remainder of my days!"

Without looking at her, Pete asked almost gently, "Then, why don't you act like it? Oh, Mama, forgive me! Would you—would you mind if I put my arms around you?"

"Have I ever minded that? Hold me, Pete. Please hold your complaining mother. I know she needs to be spanked, but hold her instead, will you?"

With Pete's strong arms around her, Anne wept again, but not for long this time. Another load had seemed to lift. In a way only Pete could have managed, her red-haired, tomboy daughter had brought Anne to her senses. Had forced her to face the bitterness to which she still clung. John and Annie and Belle and Mama *were* all dead. Paul Demere, with or without a valid excuse, was married to another woman. He was now the father of this other woman's child, as well as of little John Fraser Demere. There wasn't one single thing Anne could do about any of it, so what choice did she have but to let go of her bitterness if she was not to go on scarring the valuable young lives of her own children. And Papa! No wonder she'd made the boat trip only once to Hopeton on the mainland, where her heartbroken father now lived with James's family to comfort him. She had gone just once since her mother's funeral back in April because she knew perfectly well that instead of comforting Papa the one time they'd been alone, she had demanded comfort of him.

Was she truly beginning to shed the ugly skin of her self-pity as she'd thought? Or was that another selfish figment of her imagination?

"Mama?"

"Yes, dear."

"Wouldn't you like to read the end of Mrs. Butler's letter? You said you hadn't finished it."

"That's right, I haven't. Your precious brother brought letters from Aunt Frances in Savannah and from Cousin Willy Maxwell too." A weary smile played at the corners of her mouth as she looked down at the letters she still held. "I never knew myself to forget to read letters. Not ever before in my long life!" She handed them to Pete. "You read the end of Mrs. Butler's and then Frances Anne's, please."

Hesitating a little, Pete took the letters. "Are you sure you wouldn't rather be alone to read them for yourself?"

"I'm sure."

"All right, if you say so. Where did you stop reading Mrs. Butler's letter?"

"I'd only begun what's on the back. Begin at the top. I know she's allowed to live under the same roof with her husband and two little girls but is permitted only one hour a day with the children."

Pete snorted. "That's one lady who should never have married!"

"Just read, Pete. Don't comment."

"All right."

"With all my heart, I hope to make my time with my girls one of laughter and beauty, but most days I fail. Oh, Anne, dear friend Anne, no matter how tragic your life, keep your children uppermost in your mind and your heart. I cannot for the life of me, I cannot for the love of God in my heart, imagine that I could have done other than write of their plight and try to ease the pain and hardship of the dusky folk Pierce owns, but had there been another way to avoid quarreling with him, for the sake of my beloved girls, I would have tried. Do your best to live in the sheltering fold of that 'amazing grace' we share in our mutual worship of the God who is love. By that grace, He will help you find a way to smile again—for John's sake, for your own sake, and for the sake of your four remaining offspring. Don't scar their minds as I fear I have caused the minds of my girls to be scarred. I will try to write more cheerfully when again I reach for your understanding heart.

Your still devoted friend,
Fanny Kemble Butler"

After a long silence during which a cardinal made its ticking sound from the branches of the nearest oak at the foot of their cottage path, Anne said, "Don't comment, Pete. Don't say one word about what Fanny Butler wrote. Just open Aunt Frances's letter and read, please."

"I didn't plan to say a word," Pete muttered, breaking the seal. "Aunt Frances dated hers four days ago and this is all she wrote."

"My Dearest Anne,

I have just heard some Darien gossip, which prompts this brief letter. I'm sure you have visited Anna Matilda King many times since the financial devastation which befell her adored husband nearly three years ago now, but when excellent traits of character such as she shows in the midst of her trouble become reason for gossip, I felt the urge to beg you to visit Anna Matilda again soon in case you are still in a dark state of mind. Anna Matilda has also known sorrow—deep sorrow at the loss of both parents within months and then her adored son William. Everything was lost to Mr. King but Retreat Plantation, which was left to her, so I know she is on St. Simons to stay. I feel so certain that Anna Matilda can help you, beloved friend."

"That's all she wrote, Mama, except to send her love by name to us all."

"Thank you, Pete. There's still Cousin Willy's letter. Read it, please."

"Does he know Grandmama Couper died, too?" Pete asked.

"I wrote to him while he was still in China. Maybe he got my letter. Maybe not. Read, just read."

"Cousin Willy wrote from Caerlaverock Castle in Scotland. It's dated the first of last month."

"Beloved Anne,

Your last letter sent to me at my Peking address in China reached me the day before my ship sailed. My excuse for the long silence since is due to my own grief at the news that my dear cousin Rebecca Couper has died, too. I must admit that my own sorrow at the steadily forthcoming news of your loved ones leaving you one after another has almost overcome me. How, dearest Anne, do you manage to keep living through your days? Your nights? I have never said this to you, but it is true and from the depths of my heart: Should you need anything, just anything, which my means might provide, you have only to let me know. Should you, because your father had to close Cannon's Point except for occasional visits to the Island, find yourself in need of anything money can buy, you have only to inform me. With all my helpless heart, I wish I could write more—anything to lift your blessed spirits. I cannot, but as long as I live on this earth, you need only to turn to me.

Your devoted Willy, Lord of Herries"

"What a strange letter. Does it strike you as strange, Pete?"

"Am I allowed to comment now?" Pete was grinning.

With her first real smile of the day, Anne reached for her daughter's hand. "Your sense of humor gets more like your father's every minute, and I'm praying right now that it will be still more like his so that you can go on saving me the way he always did." She pressed a kiss into the palm of Pete's hand. "Now, comment, please. Comment to your heart's content."

"Are you going to visit your old friend Anna Matilda King after Sunday dinner tomorrow?"

"That's a question, not a comment."

"My comment is that I think Aunt Frances Anne had a rip-roaring idea. I'll go with you if you like, but I know it will break Big Boy's heart if he can't ride with you the way he always has when you visit at Retreat."

"Yes, I'm going to visit Anna Matilda tomorrow and yes, Big Boy will take me. But Pete, don't you have any comment about Cousin Willy's generous offer?"

"Only that it's exactly like him and that he should know our cottage is falling down around us."

"Shame on you!"

"Shame on *me?* It isn't my fault that the corner of the porch plus the railing is collapsing. I think it would make Cousin Willy happy if you told him we do need some money to have the house repaired. John Couper's too much like Papa to be much of a carpenter and Uncle James Hamilton's using all of Grandpapa's carpenters over at Hopeton right now. There's no one left at Cannon's Point who knows how to fix porches, and everybody's too much in debt to hire carpenters."

"Listen to me, young lady." Hoping to make her smile again, Anne knew, Pete leaned toward her and cupped a hand around her ear. To show her gratitude for Pete's playful efforts, Anne tried to smile. "All right, I'm convinced you're listening. And this is what you must remember. You and John Couper and Fanny and Selina and I will make it on our own, somehow. We'll start today to pray for help with our porch."

"And the railing. Don't forget the railing."

"And the railing. But I'd have to be in far worse straits than we are now before I'd ever, ever take advantage of Willy Maxwell's great heart. Is that clear?"

"Yep. Clear as mud."

"Young ladies of almost twenty do not say 'yep.' "

"Sometimes this one does."

"I know. And you must know you're perfectly welcome to go with me tomorrow to Retreat. Big Boy can take us both."

The half-devilish, teasing smile vanished from Pete's face. "I know I'm welcome. But do you remember when I said before that I'm never going to get married? Well, the main reason I said it, so far as I know, is that I still love William Page King better than any grown man who will ever draw breath. I know his sister Hannah is happy as a clam married to Uncle William Audley Couper now. I also know Reverend Bartow was awfully happy with Aunt Belle— like you and Papa. Like Aunt Frances Anne and Uncle William Fraser. I'd go anywhere if you really needed me, Mama, except to Retreat when I really don't have to. I still miss William too much."

Anne stared at her. "As long as we've been mother and daughter, you've never stopped knocking the wind out of me! You—you were just a child when William died. I'll never forget the day you and I rode from Hamilton to Retreat together, but Pete, you weren't quite eight then."

Pete was half grinning now. "What difference does that make?

Eve would say, 'Where is it written down in law that a woman has to be any special age?' "

"Nowhere. It isn't written down anywhere, darling." With a deliberate smile, she added, "Pete, we're becoming friends, I think, don't you?"

"Yep. In fact, I feel pretty sure we are. I feel so sure that I'm going to find June and tell him that in a week or so after you visit Miss Anna Matilda, you and I—the other children if you like—and Eve will need him to scrounge up a crew of oarsmen so he can take us all over to Hopeton for a few days." Pete smiled. "I'm commenting, I know, but they're worthy comments. Aunt Frances is usually right about things, and if a visit with Miss Anna Matilda helps you the way she thinks it will, I believe you'll be able to help Grandpapa Couper."

"Don't push me."

"I'm not pushing. I'm encouraging. Mama, I can honestly see us starting to rock right along living our lives again someday—not exactly in the same old carefree way but maybe almost the same."

Anne looked down at the weathered boards of the dock John had helped build with his own dear hands. And then she smiled up at her daughter. "Look," she said, pointing with the toe of her slipper at an old, rusty, bent nail. "Papa must have driven that one. It's pretty crooked."

When Anne said nothing further, Pete peered at her. "Are you really smiling, Mama?"

"Yes, darling. I am. But repeat what you said just before I happened to look down at Papa's handiwork."

"I think I said I can see us living our lives again someday if not in the same old way, then in a new, good way we'll all find together. A way we can all manage."

"Oh, Pete, remind me of that over and over until I can believe it too, please?"

PART I

March 7, 1849–
April 5, 1849

Chapter 1

PAPA COUPER'S OLD BUT WELL-PRESERVED PLANTA-
tion boat, the *Lady Love,* moved with a steady, rocking motion out into Buttermilk Sound en route to the
South Branch of the Altamaha River, where James
Hamilton Couper's Hopeton mansion stood on its
rise of land beside a broad canal. At home early this
morning, in her diary Anne had written the date,
March 7, 1849, then scribbled that she and Eve and
the girls were leaving for the mainland to celebrate
her father's ninetieth birthday two days later. By co-
incidence, Papa and Anne's little niece, Rebecca Isabella, shared the same birth date, March 9, and Anne
knew the child would feel extra special. There had
been little time to write more than that she felt almost
excited to be going to Hopeton again. "Papa, in spite
of how much he misses Cannon's Point, is cheerful
and we've been so blessed to have had him with us all
this time. How can I not be excited? If only I knew
that my wonderful son, John Couper, could leave his
new position in Savannah long enough to join us for
Papa's Big Day, I'd be beside myself with joy. He's
just begun work as a clerk, though, with the firm of
McCleskey and Norton, so I know hoping is false,
but how I miss that boy! I even miss his father more
than ever without John Couper nearby."

During the four years just past, a few difficult

things had become possible without her adored husband, and Pete, twenty-three, had seen to it that Anne counted now and then the ways in which she was learning how to live life without him. For example, she could again bear to play her pianoforte, to listen while Fanny played, as long as no one ever played the song she and John had shared almost from the first moment of their love. Thanks to Pete, not one of the children ever sang, whistled, or even hummed "Drink to Me Only with Thine Eyes." The song was never mentioned, although Papa had hinted once that hearing it might bring her some relief from the stress of avoiding the inevitable first pain. "So many love the tune, Anne," Papa had said, "it's just not possible to go through your entire life without hearing it somewhere—somehow."

But her daughter Pete knew, as did young John Couper and Eve, that it was still too soon. She disliked being treated like a child by her servant and her own offspring, but even after ten endless years without John, she saw no hope that she could ever bear to hear their song again.

A soft, spring breeze off the water brushed her face. She exchanged an easy smile with Eve, seated as usual on the boat seat beside her, watchful of her every change of expression. "You be safe wif the songs the people sings, Miss Anne," Eve often assured her. "Dey don' even know any white music." Eve understood. For all the years of both their lives, Eve had proved her friendship for her mistress, and somehow Anne felt sure that even her own mother, wise now with the wisdom of heaven, finally accepted the irrevocable fact of that friendship. The subject of whether Mama would approve seldom came up anymore, but when it did, Eve always laughed a little, no longer seeming to mind at all. Oh, Eve could still be overly attentive. She bossed Anne too much, but Anne felt no more uneasiness that Mama would think she allowed Eve too many liberties, gave her too much freedom of choice, unwisely permitted her to believe that she and Anne were friends. Well, they were. They had always been. During recent years as grief piled upon grief, both women seemed convinced that Rebecca Couper, in heaven now, saw things more clearly, more as they had always been. "She see more'n my little bit darker skin now," Eve would say with a sly grin.

Deep in thought, Anne had only half listened to the steady slap of water against the cypress sides of the dugout, the rhythm of the water an accompaniment to the familiar cadence of her oarsmen's rowing songs. Six of Anne's people from Lawrence, her beloved but now dilapidated plantation adjoining Papa's old home, Cannon's Point, were pulling the heavy oars of the *Lady Love,* which Papa had left behind for her use. After Mama's death, nearly four years ago during a visit to Hopeton, the aging, heartbroken laird of Cannon's Point had been forced to make his home permanently with his son James Hamilton and his large family on the mainland. Rowing the heavy, brass-trimmed boat were Big Boy, young Cuffy, Rollie, Tiber, Peter, and George. None had been trained as oarsmen, but under June's steady steering, they all did fine. Tiber, Peter, Rollie, and George were the first men John bought at the Savannah slave market. It had been such a disturbing ordeal for him that Anne knew he didn't forget it until his dying day years later. Her slave-owning father was not in favor of the South's system, but Anne had never known anyone who loathed it as did John—except her friend Fanny Kemble Butler.

John. How many times during the course of every day his name moved through her mind. For months she had avoided speaking that name, but she could do it more freely now. Not only because John had been gone nearly ten years, but because her sensitive, dependable son, John Couper, had helped so much by urging her to talk to him about his father. The boy, six and a half when John left them, had even then been her stay. She depended on him far more now. His every letter from Savannah seemed so happy and proud because he could earn money to send her, and heaven knew they needed it. But except for his father, she had never missed anyone as she missed young John Couper—every hour of every day.

Somehow Anne felt deep in her bones that only Eve truly knew how much she depended on John Couper. Pete and Fanny and Selina adored their only brother, too, and not once did any of them show a single sign of jealousy because their mother leaned so hard on him. Papa knew also and genuinely rejoiced for her that she had such a son to watch over her into old age. But no one seemed to understand as did her half-white servant, Eve, and Anne counted on that in an odd way even she was relieved not to have to explain or even fully understand.

Eve had been there right beside her through the terrifying agony of John's final illness. She was beside her today as they all headed through the bright spring sunlight toward what would surely be a joyous event once the *Lady Love* entered the quarter-mile canal that would take them from the wide Altamaha to James Hamilton's large, well-built dock. Eve would be right beside her in joy as she had been in grief.

"They be singin' your favorite song, Miss Anne," Eve said, a disarming smile lighting her face as she tapped her long, graceful fingers to the rhythm. "They be singin' 'Five Fingers in the Boll'! Leastways, it's one of your favorites. How come you ain't singin' too?"

"I know what they're singing and I'm listening."

"You know somepin?"

"I know one or two things. But what in particular?"

"It jus' come to me that you might like African songs better'n you does them slow, sad ones they sings at Christ Church of a Sunday mornin'."

"Oh, they're not all slow and sad. But I do feel so, so much at home with the people's music. Your people's music. I think I always have, but what's wrong with that? Why even compare the way the congregation sings at Christ Church with the way the men are singing now? Are you trying to start something?"

"Why I wanta do that? I hate that white man fo' what he done to my sweet mama, but I'm half his child. So how come I don' like them white songs at all? Honest, I ain't in a fussin' state. I done come with you today 'cause I be partial to your ole papa, Mausa John Couper, too. I be happy to be at he ninetieth birfday party! I done bring a present for Mausa Couper!"

"You did? What?"

"That's for you to guess and me to know," Eve teased.

"Did you paint a picture for him?"

Eve's merry laughter caused Pete and Fanny to turn around from their seat in front of them to find out what was going on. Happy-natured Selina, now twelve, simply joined in Eve's laughter as usual.

"I can't tell you girls why Eve's so amused," Anne said, "but I'm sure she can."

"Yo' mama, she ax me effen I paint a pitcher for you Gran'papa's birfday." Still giggling, Eve added, "What else I gonna do? Take a steamboat to Savannah an' buy him a gilsey gol' gif' in one ob dem fancy, high-price stores?"

"You think that's funny, do you?" Anne wanted to know.

"Don' you, Miss Anne? Don' that make you laugh, too?"

"No, because I wanted so much to be able to do just that for him, Miss Smarty. Right now, I don't have any more cash than you have to walk into one of those fine shops and buy a present even half good enough for my father."

"Shame on you, Mama," Pete said in her firm way, again squelching her own mother a little by acting more sensibly. "You know all Grandpapa Couper wants for his birthday is for us to be there with him—all of us."

"Of course I know that, Pete. And I'd give almost anything if I thought there was a chance that your brother could come too."

"Are you absolutely, positively certain John Couper won't be there?" Pete asked almost impishly.

So impishly, Anne's hopes shot up a little. "Pete! Don't you dare tease me about a thing like that!"

"No, Pete," Eve snapped. "I come to see that nothin' upset yo' mama, you hear me?"

"Who's teasing?" Pete asked with her most innocent look.

So excited that she tried to stand up on the boat seat until Eve pushed her back down, Selina cried, "Pete, do you know but just aren't telling us that our brother might be coming down from Savannah for Grandpapa's nonagenarian birthday?"

"What word she say?" Eve asked, genuinely puzzled.

"*Nonagenarian,*" Pete explained. "But that's not quite the right use of it, Selina. Grandpapa Couper isn't having his nonagenarian birthday. *He* is going to be a nonagenarian day after tomorrow when he turns ninety."

"I've already turned twelve," Selina said. "What am I called?"

"That's enough, Selina," Anne said. "Settle back down beside Fanny because June is about to steer the boat toward Uncle James's canal. We're almost there."

"Ain't nobody kin steer a boat like my June, is they?" Eve asked.

"Is there," Anne corrected. "But I agree. June's the very best. Won't it seem strange—doesn't it always seem strange—that Papa's too old to be down on the dock to greet us when we reach Hopeton?"

"It sure do," Eve said.

On impulse, Anne almost reached out to grab Eve's hand, then drew back. She had never held Eve's hand in all their years together. Her mother would have disapproved. Instead, Anne said, "I—I need you on this trip, Eve. I need your encouragement."

"You 'fraid Mausa Couper he gonna die soon, ain't you?"

They were both whispering now. "Of course I'm afraid. The old darling's going to be ninety years old day after tomorrow. Why wouldn't I be afraid? I—I don't even know for sure that I could go on living on St. Simons without him."

"Grandpapa Couper always used to meet us at the dock," Selina piped. "Does having your nonagenarian birthday mean you can't walk good enough to come all the way down the path from Uncle James's veranda?"

"Something like that," Anne answered absently.

Half turned in her seat, Pete grinned. "And because dear old Grandmama Couper's in heaven and can't, or maybe wouldn't, even think of fussing at you and him anymore, Mama?"

Anne bit her lip in silence for a minute, then deciding that today was no time for anything but happy exchanges, said with a smile, "You're too smart sometimes, Pete."

"Sometimes, because she happens to be our tutor, she thinks she's smarter than anybody," Fanny said.

"No grumbling today, Fanny," Anne said, keeping her voice pleasant. "Just be glad you have such a brainy sister."

"I don't see anything wrong with my brain," Fanny said. "I just don't talk a lot. At least not compared with Pete." With a short laugh, Fanny patted her older sister on the shoulder. "The truth is, Pete, I wish I had your gift of gab sometimes. No matter what anyone says to you, you always seem to think of something to say back. Don't you ever feel shy? I do."

With a grin, Pete answered, "Being a shy young lady becomes you, Sister dear. I must say, though, you just made quite an impressive speech. Don't you think so, Mama?"

"I do indeed," Anne replied, then added, "I will also say I've rather enjoyed not having to scold Fanny because she yelled during the years she was growing up."

Pete's grin widened. "I know I yelled when I was a young squirt. Sometimes I miss getting by with it now that I'm an old woman."

"I don't think it matters at all how old any of us may be," Selina said in her newly mature manner. "Nothing else is important now but that our Grandpapa Couper is going to be ninety. Isn't that so, Mama?"

On a long sigh, Anne said, "Yes, Selina. Grandpapa Couper is the star on this trip. Along with little Rebecca Isabella, of course. She'll be six on the same day. But all of us must find ways to make Grandpapa laugh and enjoy himself the whole time we're at Hopeton. I'm sure birthdays get to be very important at ninety."

"I wish my papa had lived to be ninety," Selina said, her face as wistful as her voice. "Pete, you did tell me, didn't you, that Papa sometimes called me Eena?"

"Yes, I told you that."

"I wish I remembered how he sounded when he said Eena," the girl said to no one in particular.

"I—I know it's ridiculous, Selina," Anne said softly, "but it's still so, so hard for me to believe you don't remember more about your father."

"Should I try harder?" Selina asked.

"No, dear. There are times, though, when I—I almost wish I didn't remember him quite so—clearly."

June signaled the oarsmen to move the big boat in at the north side of the Hamilton landing, and as though he had been holding a watch on their arrival, exactly at the moment they bumped against the sturdy pilings, James hurried out onto the dock's platform, alone except for three of his people who would secure the boat and carry its contents.

It was never a surprise to Anne when her brother James Hamilton acted precisely by his watch. She did feel a bit of concern, though, because he came alone this time. "And a good day to you, Brother," she called after he'd given them his formal bow and what seemed a guardedly pleasant greeting. "No one's ill, I hope. We thought you and Caroline and all your children except your Yale scholar, Hamilton, would be out here to welcome us. Is everyone all right? Papa's well as usual, isn't he?"

"Everyone's fine," James laughed, reaching to help them, one after another, from the *Lady Love* while June, who climbed ashore first, pulled Eve after him up onto the sturdy dock.

"But where's Margaret?" Selina wanted to know. "And Robert and James Maxwell and Alexander and John Lord and Rebecca Isabella and little William? I thought I'd have all of them to play with—especially Margaret."

"There's bound to be a good reason why Uncle James came alone," Pete said. "So, why don't we just hold our horses until he's ready to tell us?"

Anne, the last to be helped out of the boat, was giving Eve instructions about where bags and valises should be taken when she saw Eve nod emphatically toward James Hamilton. "I think Eve is urging me to pin you down, Brother," Anne said, hoping her lingering anxiety about the whereabouts of the other family members didn't show. "So I'll just repeat my question. You're sure, James, that Papa's well? That no one's sick?"

"Eve knows you better than I do," James said easily. "The last time I saw you, Sister, I felt sure you'd stopped being such a worry-wart. Everyone is in good health and our father is as excited as a boy at the prospect of his birthday celebration. Of course, so is my daughter Becca Belle. So, put a wide smile on your face and make them both still happier. Have I made myself clear? You'll all find out soon enough why I've met you alone."

"Can't you give us even a small hint?" Anne begged.

"Only one, madam," James Hamilton said in his most grandiose manner. "And that is that immediately on entering my entrance hall, you will find our father waiting for you—arms wide, face aglow—but as part of the plan, he will be alone too."

Holding her brother's arm as they walked up the landscaped path toward the Hopeton mansion, Anne kept nagging him. "You're just not the kind of person to plan surprises, James. Anyway, it isn't my birthday. Your aging sister has already had her fifty-second earlier this year."

Smiling down at her, James asked, "Who said anything about a surprise for you, Anne? And I beg to differ that I'm not a man to plan surprises. Our father's oldest and dearest friend, now that Mr. James Hamilton is dead, informed me this week by the post that he will indeed be able to attend Papa's birthday celebration day after tomorrow. That's going to be a surprise and I arranged it."

"Mr. Thomas Spalding is coming from Sapelo Island? Oh, James, that will please Papa no end! But I thought Mr. Spalding was too feeble to travel."

In as proud a tone as he ever allowed himself, her brother replied, "I've arranged to send one of my schooners for the old fellow. It—it could be the last time he and our father will actually have time for a good, long talk together." Smiling down at her again, he added, "But I'm sure I haven't said a word about a surprise for my sister Anne."

Chapter 2

IT SEEMED TO OLD JOCK COUPER, FURTHER PAINING his stiff back by trying to sit up straight on one of James Hamilton's highly polished Queen Anne chairs in the Hopeton entrance hall, that Anne and her brood would never get there. For a man nearing his ninetieth birthday, he felt fairly well, he supposed. As ready for the excitement of being the guest of honor at such a memorable occasion as a man could expect, but for him, waiting had never been easy.

He squared his bent shoulders and tried to sit erect for the anticipated moment when the apple of his eye, his daughter Anne, and her children trooped through the gracious front door of his son's fine plantation house. How can it be, he thought, that my Anne is now a lady of fifty-two years! To his fading old eyes she was as lovely as ever. A bit thicker at the waist, perhaps, but there were advantages even to old age and dimming eyesight: Anne, to her doting father, looked as bonnie as ever. Bonnier than any of her three sweet daughters would ever be. Pete, always his favorite if he were to tell the truth—which, of course, he meant never to do—could talk her way out of any predicament she might be likely to encounter. Jock Couper, himself a facile talker, relished the trait in her. Like her tall, handsome father, Couper's lamented late son-in-law, Pete seemed at times to talk too much, but the lass never failed to speak with content and remarkable wisdom for her age.

Pete, he believed, was somehow different from other young ladies of her years. He'd never forget the day he'd urged her to tell her mother that she meant not to marry because she still felt bonded to her dead young playmate, William, Anna Matilda King's boy. How, he often wondered, had Anne received such a decision by her eldest living daughter when she had been so deeply attached to Pete's splendid father, John Fraser? One thing about which Jock Couper felt absolutely certain was the plain fact that Anne's youngest, Selina of the long, dark curls, had been born to fall in love and mother young ones. And Fanny? How old was Fanny now? Seventeen, he thought, and like his own late daughter, sweet Isabella, not precisely what a mon would term lovely to look upon. Never one to settle for mere hoping when he could pray, Jock Couper prayed often that there would be another lad, as perceptive and kind as was Isabella's Theodore Bartow, ready to marry Fanny despite her shy plainness and because of her deep-down inner worth.

Any minute now, he should, even if his old ears did feel much of the time as though they were stopped up, hear laughter and good talk from outside. If Anne and her girls had boarded the *Lady Love* early this morning as James Hamilton had instructed them to do, they should be nearing Hopeton by now unless the same sunny, clear skies that hung here above the mainland had thickened closer to the shore where they embarked from his large Cannon's Point dock. The *Lady Love* drew too much water for Anne's little Lawrence Creek. He sighed heavily. Lawrence. What dreams he'd held for Anne and John, living in the well-remodeled little Lawrence cottage on their return from London with blessed little Annie and Anne carrying Pete, their second child. He'd seen some of his dreams come true, too. Tall, restless young John Fraser had worked so hard trying to learn how to become a successful planter—had worked and sweated and turned his fine mind to what must always have seemed to John the rather dull lessons every prosperous planter needed to know. The lad had succeeded, too, despite his love of travel and adventure, despite his sense of failure because his old regiment no longer needed his brilliant military skills.

My advanced age, Couper thought, when again he felt his eyes sting with tears as they did with almost every memory of the son-in-law who had left them in his late forties. "I loved John Fraser like a son," he said aloud. "And I'm talking too much aloud to myself these days. My beloved Rebecca would be teasing me unmercifully were she not gone from us. One good thing," he went on conversing with himself: "I won't have to wait much longer to see Becca again." He reached for the corner of a lamp table in order to pull his stiff body up from the hard, wooden chair. "Aye, it's been too long now without her. Four lonely years come April."

Anne and the children couldn't get there soon enough. Waiting tired him. His hands shook, his breath came harder. But dread seemed to wear him away more than did any other emotion. Dread today when Anne could arrive at any moment? Aye, he deeply dreaded what he'd be forced to tell Anne face-to-face.

"Lord, how many contradictory feelings can this old ram contain?" He was speaking aloud again—to God, his most frequent conversationalist. "Somehow I thought only You could find a way to encompass two such different emotions, Lord. When you look down in love and see us in cruelty, we expect You to know exactly how to deal with both contradictions at once. But I? Teach me how to manage the joy over the arrival of my beloved visitors from St. Simons along with the downright *dread* I feel at having to tell precious Anne the bad news about Lawrence. She loves that place so much, Lord, but You know my choices have been taken away— all gone with my money. All gone with James Hamilton's money."

Couper stopped for a moment before the tall, ornate mirror in the Hopeton entrance hall and studied his long, lined face, flicked at the gray in his still-red sideburns, and tried to laugh at the image he saw. "St-r-raighten your shoulders, old goat! I vow you've shrunk a foot in height. Do you want to startle your adored Anne, who's gone through her life believing her father has st-r-rength for any vicissitude? Stand straight! Walk steadily across the veranda when you hear their happy voices! And don't even *think* of telling her about Lawrence until well after the birthday dinner is fully enjoyed and past."

ANNE, EVE, AND THE CHILDREN HAD JUST BEGUN THE WALK FROM the Hopeton dock toward the house when she saw the handsome front door open and her father shuffle slowly toward them across the veranda. Not once since so many of their loved ones had died had she failed to be stunned by how frail and shrunken Papa looked each time they met. He had been eighty when Anne's dear ones began to leave, and, of course, he was showing his age then. But year after year the continuing deaths somehow magnified the frightening truth that one day she would lose Papa, too.

As though reading Anne's thoughts again, Eve, who walked up the path on her right, Pete on her left, called over to Pete: "Yo' gran'papa, he look good, don't he, Pete?"

"To me, he's even sprightlier than the last time we were here," Pete said in her firm, decisive way. "Mama, I honestly think Grandpapa's growing backward. Don't you think he looks younger, stronger, more like himself? Almost as tall as he used to be!"

"No," Anne said softly. "No, Pete, I think he looks older, more stooped—but sweeter, kinder than ever. How could he look anything but old? The man's going to be ninety day after tomorrow!"

"But look at he smile, Miss Anne," Eve persisted. "That man so glad to see yo' face, it show on his. He smile jus' the same as always."

"Eve, don't say 'he smile.' It's *his* smile. But thank you both for trying. I'm doing the best I can to prepare myself for losing him someday. Neither of you helps, you know, by treating me as though I were Selina's age. I'm going to lose—my papa. I need to be ready. I—I need at least to try to be ready."

"You won't ever be, though, Mama. I know that. I know just what you're saying. Don't pay any attention to Pete and Eve." Normally shy, quiet Fanny took them all by surprise.

Eve would always try to protect Anne's feelings. Pete would

always find a way to speak the bald truth. Anne knew them both and trusted their instincts about her. Now, after Fanny's surprising remark, she felt a touch of guilt because she'd honestly never thought one way or the other about the extent of Fanny's wisdom or maturity. Just that Fanny was always there to help, however quietly, and at least almost always willingly.

Well, she would weigh her own reactions to her two older daughters later. She already knew what prompted Eve to protect her. Protecting her mistress, proving that their friendship went deeper than most such relationships, had come to be Eve's mission in life. Perhaps had always been.

They had almost reached the veranda when James Hamilton hurried ahead to steady their father down the four front steps so that the old gentleman wouldn't have to wait a second longer than necessary to embrace Anne. The instant Papa's feet touched the ground, his arms opened to her, and as she'd done through her whole life, Anne rushed into them.

"Happy birthday, Papa! A blessed, blessed, *happy* birthday!"

"Anne, Anne, Anne," he murmured. "How good it is to have you here where I can look at you—where my creaky old arms can hold you again!" In response to Selina's jumping up and down and tugging at his jacket sleeve, he reached to pat her head, hung with the long curls everyone so admired. He gave Anne one more endearing embrace, then hugged Pete and Fanny and added a whimsical, exaggerated bow for Eve, whose lovely face lit with her proudest smile.

"Not every gentleman about to celebrate a birthday is honored by such a boatload of charming ladies, eh, Father?" James Hamilton asked with, for him, a surprisingly easy smile. "There's more excitement to come, Sister," he added, turning to Anne. "The plan is quite definite, in fact. You are all to follow Papa and me into the house with bated breath."

"I expect detailed instructions from you, Brother mine," Anne laughed, "but what more could there be inside your mansion? Where in the world is Caroline?"

"I've told you all I mean to right now," James Hamilton said.

"But where's my favorite, little William, Uncle James?" Selina, more and more attracted to younger children, looked genuinely disappointed.

"Now, no more questions, Selina. You'll see my youngest son, William, in due time. His nurse, Polly, may be feeding him his noon meal now. I'm not sure. But everyone is inside the house and Father and I are in the process of carrying out our carefully laid plans."

"What, *what*, Uncle James?" Selina wanted to know.

"Sh! I've told you there's more excitement ahead, and for now, just quietly follow your grandfather and me." Helping his parent again, James mounted the steps with Papa slowly, carefully, the others trooping after them.

"Now then," Jock said, puffing from the short climb, "are we all here? And is everyone's breath bated as my son James Hamilton decreed?"

"As bated as we can manage, knowing so little of these mysterious plans." Pete grinned at her grandparent. "It's your birthday we're here to celebrate. Isn't it peculiar for the two of you to be surprising us with some secret mischief?"

"No mischief at all," the old fellow said innocently. "Can you believe Pete would conjure up such an accusation about us, Son?"

"She's your granddaughter, Papa," Anne teased. "What do you expect? Especially since no one but Pete inherited your red hair." On the veranda just before entering the gracious entrance hall, Anne again threw both arms around her father. "Papa! Oh, Papa, your birthday party is going to be glorious. If your namesake, my son, could only be here, I think I'd be too happy to keep both feet on the ground."

Returning her hug, Papa said, "But my dear Anne, the boy's doing so well in his new position with my friends McCleskey and Norton in Savannah, we must only rejoice for him. McCleskey promised me in his latest letter that John Couper would be the very fir-rst new cler-rk to be given time off from his duties. Now, doesn't that make you proud?"

INSIDE THE ELEGANT ENTRANCE HALL, A SLANT OF SUNSHINE piercing the fanlight so that her mother's face seemed lovelier than usual, Pete watched the lady—to her, the beautiful lady who was her mother. There was plainly something afoot. Grandpapa and Uncle James had hatched a scheme of some description, and Pete's almost unfailing instinct told her it had to do with her mother. As usual, Eve stood just behind Mama and when Pete caught Eve's eye, she knew the bright-skinned woman, who loved the very ground under Anne Fraser's feet, was also aware that something unexpected was up. When Eve gave Pete her knowing smile, Pete was sure they had both guessed the elaborately kept secret.

A clatter at the top of the graceful, winding stair announced the rehearsed arrival of Uncle James's family. His always pretty wife, Aunt Caroline Wylly Couper, began to descend the stair ahead of her entire brood of children—all there except Pete's oldest cousin, Hamilton, who was away at Yale College. Peering up the slightly shadowy stair, Pete looked for her only brother. They hadn't exchanged one word, but she was sure she and Eve had guessed Grandpapa's secret surprise: By some means, he'd arranged for John Couper to leave his new work in Savannah to attend the birthday celebration! Pete could see Eve looking for him, too. Eve's instincts were even sharper than Pete's. Both could not be wrong. But so far, no sign of her gentle, good-looking brother.

If this had been an ordinary visit, all seven younger Couper children would have come pushing and tumbling down the stair to hug every visitor. Not today. Pete's sense of humor began to get the best of her, because despite Uncle James's noble efforts to enter into the spirit of the festive occasion (she had never seen him smile so often), he had obviously given his usual precise instructions. Aunt Caroline was holding young William's hand as he took the big steps required to stay even with his mother in the procession. Rebecca Isabella, nearing six, was all but marching down the carpeted steps, side by side with pretty ten-year-old Margaret, followed by James Maxwell, almost twelve, and John Lord, who must be close to fourteen by now. Bringing up the rear were Robert, eight, and Alexander, sixteen—a self-conscious age at best, Pete remembered.

When Aunt Caroline embraced Pete's mother at the foot of the stairs, everyone began to chatter and laugh. Little William, who struck Mama as always shouting as much as Pete had when she was young, had to be shushed by his father's hand over his mouth because the small boy was yelling to his Aunt Anne that he knew "a big, fat secret."

"We will settle for shaking Aunt Anne's hand and you may even try out the bow I'm teaching you," Uncle James told the boy firmly, "but not one word. Do you understand, William? We all made a promise—in fact, you and I made a gentleman's agreement, remember? Not one word to Aunt Anne about—anything. Just be polite and silent."

"Caroline, for heaven's sake, what is going on in this house?" Pete's mother demanded. "Don't let my brother bully you! He and Papa both look terribly guilty to me—about something. What is it? What's this strange behavior all about?"

Pete saw her aunt, smiling as she did it, make a locking gesture as though she'd inserted a key between her own lips and then pretended to toss the key into the corner of the entrance hall.

"No one's going to give us even one clue, Mama," Pete said. "We might just as well go along with the game. Somehow I think Grandpapa's behind the whole thing. Look at his crinkled-up face. He's having a dreadful time trying not to look too smug."

"What is it we're supposed to do, Grandpapa?" Selina asked. "We'll play Grandpapa's game, won't we, Fanny?"

Fanny laughed sharply, then said, "Of course we will. What's next, Grandpapa?"

The old man bowed as deeply as he could while gesturing for everyone to follow him into Uncle James's large, beautifully furnished parlor. "Follow me, all of you—that is, all of you except my daughter Anne."

"And why, sir, am I being kept out of whatever this is you and

James have cooked up? I don't think I like it. You know I never like being left out of a game."

A finger over his lips for Mama to say no more, Grandpapa took Pete's arm, gesturing for the others to come too. They literally marched into the parlor, leaving poor Mama standing alone in the entrance hall.

"You don't think you're being mean, Grandpapa?" Pete asked, entering into his game fully by helping him herd all the younger ones inside the large room so that Uncle James could close the heavy mahogany sliding doors—of which he was so proud. Pete even pulled Eve inside the parlor a little against her will. Exchanging grins with Eve, Pete was now positive the faithful servant had also guessed the happy truth of the surprise planned for Mama.

Chapter 3

FOR AN UNDECIDED MOMENT, AS INSTRUCTED, ANNE stood alone in the entrance hall, not sure whether to laugh or compose a cross little speech to deliver to both her father and her brother. Actually, she felt almost embarrassed. "Being embarrassed after all the jokes Papa and I have played on each other is just plain silly," she whispered to herself.

Then for no apparent reason, she went quickly to the tall looking glass to examine her hair. For goodness' sake, why? she thought to herself. Everyone's shut up in the parlor. Who's going to see me who hasn't already?

At first sure she'd only imagined she heard a voice, she turned quickly to peer up the stairway. No doubt that she'd heard a footstep in the upstairs hall —at least a floorboard creaked, then a shadow moved across the wall of the stairwell, and the sound of two or three steps came plainly from the second floor. Anne gasped.

"Hello, Mama!"

"Oh, darling boy, it's really you! John Couper, how did you—how did you manage to leave your work?"

Halfway down the curving flight of stairs stood the slender, altogether handsome young man who was her only son. He was smiling at her. Then he began to laugh softly. How she'd always loved his laughter—so like his father's.

He bounded lightly down the remaining steps, swept her entirely off her feet, and whirled her around until even her heavy dark blue travel skirt made circles of joy.

"Grandpapa did surprise you, didn't he?" John Couper asked, still half laughing. "Mama, the old gentleman will be so proud of himself that even Uncle James's most elaborate birthday celebration will have to take second place!"

"The old gentleman?"

"Grandpapa!"

Then it was Anne's turn to laugh. "Do you know I never think of him that way?"

"I know, because you've told me a hundred times that you and Grandpapa always called Uncle James Hamilton the Old Gentleman —even when he was still a boy."

"Look at us, standing here like bumps on a log. When did you know you could come for Papa's ninetieth birthday party? I thought Mr. McCleskey said you couldn't get away quite yet."

"He did. And even I didn't know I could come until Mr. Mc-Cleskey informed me himself—after he got Grandpapa's letter, of course."

"What letter?"

John Couper took her arm and led her toward the closed parlor doors. "Let's have him tell you. He deserves to squeeze the last drop out of his excellent performance in our behalf, don't you think?"

"Yes. But first I have to know how long you can stay."

"Until the day after the celebration. Grandpapa persuaded my employers to give me four full days."

Anne shook her head and smiled. In her smile she let her son see into the fathomless depths of the singular respect and adoration she'd always held for her own father, who had never failed to find a way to make everything right. "John Couper, your father and I gave you an honored name."

"I know, Mama. I'll never be able to live up to it, but I'll certainly try."

Anne grabbed his hand in a tight grip. "How—how will I be able to endure losing him too?"

His arms around her, John Couper said nothing for a moment. He just held her close. And as she struggled against tears, her mind went back to the afternoon on the Cannon's Point veranda only an hour or two after they'd buried John. The strong young man holding her now was six and a half then, but he had helped her believe that once they moved back to Lawrence, the sunrise *would* somehow push away the shadows nearly suffocating her that frightening day. He'd been right. She had lived almost ten years believing in the promise of the Lawrence sunrise. At least most of the time she'd believed in it—thanks to young John Couper. This minute, as he stood holding her in his arms, there was no need for words spoken in his grown-up, man's voice. She could still hear her boy child as he had spoken to her that helpless, long-ago afternoon: *"I guess maybe when there's enough light, Mama, the shadows just sort of go away, don't they?"*

Then, the gentle, tender man's voice asked, "Does the Lawrence sunrise still help, Mama?"

John Couper had done it for her again. She lifted her head from his shoulder and took one step back so that she could look straight up at him. "Yes, Son. The sunrise still helps. Even on a rainy morning, I know it's there. It will help when—when we lose Grandpapa too. Thank you for reminding me. Anyway, your grandfather's right here—right in the parlor gloating, I'm sure, unable to wait a second longer to revel in his perfect surprise."

"It's hard to believe, but he will be ninety years old day after tomorrow," John Couper said. "If there's any way I can help you get ready for the possibility that this could be his last birthday, tell me, please."

"You've already helped me—again, Son. Just go on being the finest son a mother ever had and forgive me for borrowing more sorrow." She made herself smile up at him. "I do still live at dear Lawrence with that sunrise, you know. Don't worry about your fretting mother. The last thing she ever means to do is to trouble you." Her smile widened. "Or to lean too hard against you. Don't let me lean too hard, John Couper. Not ever."

"Do you think we're supposed to wait for Grandpapa to slide open the doors? Or should I do it?"

"You open them. Papa won't be able to stand the suspense much longer, I'm sure."

Chapter 4

ALTHOUGH THERE WASN'T A SINGLE STRANGER IN the spacious Hopeton parlor, Fanny, always more at ease observing than talking, stood with her back to one of the high front windows that looked out onto the greening lawn to the canal. She watched them all, a contented smile on her plain, smooth young face. Even if she thought of something to say, Fanny was sure she couldn't be heard above the din of laughter and merriment filling the room. Most of all, she was watching her pretty mother. I declare, Fanny thought, Mama hasn't looked this young or this pretty since Papa went away. How she loves and depends on John Couper! Here it was supposed to be a big birthday celebration for Grandpapa, and as usual, he pulled one of his merry pranks by keeping it a secret that John Couper's new employers in Savannah would, after all, let him leave his work for four whole days to be with us for this happy time.

The last any of the Frasers had heard, John Couper would not be able to be there. No one had told her so, but Fanny's hunch was very strong that Grandpapa had written one of his most persuasive letters to Mr. McCleskey, his young friend. Mr. Mc-Cleskey had relented and John Couper now stood beaming down at Mama, who still clung to his arm, then across the room at Grandpapa, then around the big room at the whole family. No wonder shouts and talk and laughter rang. There were five Frasers and Eve, all but one of Uncle James's big brood, plus Grandpapa.

The contented smile left Fanny's face when suddenly, despite the throng of close family members, she felt her father's absence—and Annie's, Aunt Isabella's, and Grandmama's—so painfully she had to blink back tears. This was certainly no time for sorrow. At least it was no time to let the sorrow show. But how proud Papa would be if he could see his only son giving so much support and strength to Mama! Maybe he could see—maybe he could see them all. Maybe Papa and Annie and Aunt Belle and Grandmama Couper were together this minute, enjoying the gathering of the clan, as Grandpapa would call it, right there in the beautiful Hopeton parlor. As Christians that's what they were all supposed to believe. It was just so hard when no one had yet found a way to prove it. "Faith has nothing whatever to do with proof," Pete went on reminding her. "It has only to do with whether you think God is truthful or not. Didn't He say the night before they killed Him that where He went, there we would be also? Either we believe Him or we don't, Fanny."

How did Pete get to be so sure about everything?

Every single night of their lives, the two sisters had shared a room. Fanny, for the first few years after Papa went away, cried herself to sleep most nights. She'd cried, too, when their oldest sister, Annie, died and also Grandmama Couper, even though she had never lived in the same house with her grandmother. Not once had she caught Pete weeping. When did she do it? Pete always appeared to be in charge, but her heart, Fanny knew, was tender. She must have cried a lot, especially on those sweet but strained evenings after Mama got so she could bear to play her pianoforte again without Papa there to sing. Six years separated the two sisters. Pete wasn't all that much more grown-up than Fanny. I'm seventeen, she thought. How could Pete be so much more mature? And why did Pete seem not to care a fig about falling in love? Heaven knew, Fanny cared. But where did she ever go to meet eligible young men? Their little cottage at Lawrence was so rundown that Mama wouldn't dream of entertaining, and evidently because of the financial panic all over the country, no one, not even Grandpapa or Uncle James Hamilton, had any money to fix it up.

Mama couldn't bear to live anywhere else. Everyone knew that. No one who knew Mama believed she could make it through her days without the almost daily beauty of the sunrise over the marshes. Fanny hadn't said much about it, but when Pete wasn't looking, she too went first thing to their bedroom window, hoping as Mama must have hoped every morning for either clear skies or just enough clouds to heighten the beauty. Would Pete have made fun of her if she'd seen Fanny checking the sunrise? No. Pete did it too. Being Pete, she just went in plain view of Fanny or anyone else who happened to be nearby. Pete did everything that way, always seeming sure that if she did it, whatever it was, it would work out just fine.

Look at Pete now, Fanny thought, wondering what on earth her sister found to discuss so vehemently with Uncle James's two sons, James Maxwell and John Lord Couper. After all, they were only about twelve and fourteen. How could Pete find such an animated subject for conversation with either of them?

In some ways I'm better with grown-ups, though, Fanny reminded herself. At least, Mama says I am. "I never have to worry about what startling thing Fanny might blurt out before people," Mama often told Pete. "I wish you'd think for two or three seconds before you say whatever it is you're thinking, Pete. You are a young lady now."

When Aunt Caroline, holding four-year-old William by one hand and little Rebecca Isabella by the other, hurried to the window Fanny had been standing near during the excited hubbub in the room, her aunt was laughing. Then her still very pretty face abruptly took on a look of concern. "Fanny, my dear, is something the matter? Why are you over here all by yourself when the others —me included—are acting like silly children about to open Christmas presents?"

Fanny took care to give her an especially cheerful smile. "Oh, you're just not with me much anymore, Aunt Caroline. I'm—I'm the dull, quiet one in our family. I just enjoy watching instead of taking part. Nothing's the matter. Honest." Fanny looked around the handsomely furnished room. "If I lived here at Hopeton, I think I'd never leave this glorious parlor of yours. What a beautiful house you keep for Uncle James!"

Aunt Caroline laughed again. "My dear girl, you know perfectly well your uncle selects every stick of furniture, every candlestand, every piece of tapestry and damask for every chair."

"But you really adorn his house. Some people think he's stiff and—well, difficult because he's so precise and careful about everything, but you're happy with him, aren't you? And you've always been fun-loving."

"I declare, Fanny, you should talk more often. You've a golden tongue—like your handsome father always had."

At that moment Fanny saw little Rebecca's laughing face turn serious. To get her attention, the child pulled at the end of Fanny's best silk scarf. "Cousin Fanny, does it feel just terrible having your father dead?"

"Rebecca, what a dreadful thing to ask our cousin!"

"No," Fanny said. "I think it's a perfectly plausible question. Yes, Rebecca. Sometimes it feels really terrible. Especially in the evenings when I miss the way he used to sing for us while Mama played."

When Eve, who had gone to the Hopeton kitchen to help out, came to serve them a glass of blackberry juice from an ornate silver tray, she said, "Miss Rebecca Isabella, I 'spect Fanny she miss her papa's laughin' more'n she miss almos' anything."

"How come you take part in our parlor talk, Eve? Our servants aren't allowed to do that," young Rebecca stated.

All Fanny could think to say was "Eve's—Eve's different, Rebecca. That's all. Families do things differently. You'll find that out someday."

"Why?" young William piped.

"Never mind why," Aunt Caroline said. "Look! Look over there, Son. Your grandpapa's motioning for you to come stand beside his chair. He may have something very important to tell you."

When the small boy raced across the room, Rebecca said thoughtfully, "Papa forbids servants to chatter. Is it because my father doesn't laugh a lot, the way people say?"

"But when Papa does laugh," Aunt Caroline put in, "it's a wonderful sound. Don't you think it is, Becca?"

"Are you calling her Becca now?" Fanny asked.

"Yes," the young girl answered quickly. "Grandpapa started to call me Becca because that's what he always called our grandmother. I'm named for her and he misses her, so he calls me Becca. Grandmama's dead, too, you know."

"Yes, Becca, I know. Do you remember our grandmother?"

"I—I think so," the child said. "She died while she and Grandpapa were here on a visit. Mama says it was just a few months after Uncle William Audley and Aunt Hannah King got married."

"I might have known William Audley and Hannah wouldn't get here until tomorrow," Aunt Caroline said, relieved at the change of subject. "William's working so hard at Hamilton these days. He's really trying to live up to the fine precedent your father set, Fanny."

Before Fanny could think of anything to say, little Becca pulled her scarf again and asked, "Don't a lot of people die? At least a lot of people we know have died, haven't they, Cousin Fanny?"

"Becca, today is no time for such talk. We're supposed to be having a happy day in Grandpapa's honor. When anyone lives to be ninety years of age, it's cause for celebration. Now, run over to where he's sitting and tell him you're there to wish him a cheerful, happy birthday! After all, the day after tomorrow will be *your* birthday too."

When the girl scampered off, Fanny gave Aunt Caroline her most loving smile. "Did you ever realize that I love you a lot, Aunt Caroline? You didn't need to send Rebecca Isabella away. It's all right for her to let me know she even noticed that—four members of our family died so close together."

"You're very sensible and strong, aren't you, Fanny?"

"I am?"

"I overheard Becca talking to Pete about all the deaths we've experienced, and she made a joke to distract the child. I could tell Pete couldn't face talk of it with such a young girl. Pete seems so strong and in command, too."

"And I don't because I'm quiet a lot, is that it?"

"I don't know exactly. I do know I'm relieved to have discovered such poise and strength in you, my dear. Now, it *is* time for more merriment or Grandpapa Couper is going to explode. I can't imagine what's preventing Lydia from clanging her dinner bell. It's past time for us to dine." Laughing, Aunt Caroline said, "In fact, I'll give your Uncle James exactly two minutes before he comes striding across this room to inquire of me why she's all of seven minutes late!"

Fanny laughed too. "I've always heard from Mama that you put up with Uncle James's strict ways by making jokes right to his face."

"Your mama is exactly right. But he's so kind and good to the children and to me, making him laugh at himself has come to be one of my favorite things to do."

"And does he really laugh at himself?"

Aunt Caroline smiled. "Well, let me just say that the dear man laughs just often enough to keep me on my toes. I've taught myself to enjoy the challenge."

Chapter 5

ABOUT NOON THE DAY BEFORE THE BIRTHDAY FES-
tivities, Jock's son William Audley, his daughter-in-
law Hannah, and two of their three children reached
Hopeton with Hannah's mother's old nurse, Haynie,
to look after the young ones.

Soon after breakfast Jock had settled in his
favorite veranda chair to watch for them and was
delighted to see they'd at least brought their two
older children to help celebrate his big day tomorrow.
Three-year-old Anna was named, of course, for
her grandmother, Anne's lifelong friend Anna Matilda Page King. The child scrambled on her chubby
legs up the front steps and threw herself into the old
man's lap, shouting "Grandpapa! Grandpapa!"
at the top of her lungs. Tall, wide-shouldered William Audley, finer appearing and more adept at
running a big plantation like Hamilton than his father had dared hope, followed with his only son,
two-year-old William Page Couper, in his
arms. It had been months since they'd visited Hopeton, but in no time the small boy was fighting for
space on Jock's lap, too, even though everyone
knew he didn't remember seeing his grandfather
before.

"It's that Scottish charm, Papa Couper," Hannah
said, brushing an unruly lock of hair back from Wil-

liam Page's forehead. "He just might remember you. After all, you're unforgettable and everyone along the Georgia and South Carolina coast will attest to that."

"Which, of course, is the reason you're so smitten with me, his son," William Audley joked. "Give us a nod when you've had enough of both squirming offspring, Papa. Haynie came with us, you know. She'll take them off your hands when you say the word."

Still smiling, Jock Couper looked up at William Audley. Despite the determined smile, tears stood in his old eyes. "Aye, I'll say the word, Son, when they've tired me. Right now, all I can think is that my memorable birthday is complete because all my family will be around me to cheer me on toward the century mark! All, that is, but your blessed mother, Becca, your equally blessed sister Isabella, your sweet niece Annie, and my fine son-in-law John Fraser."

At that moment Rebecca Isabella, James's girl, burst onto the veranda and yelled, "I heard that through the parlor window, Grandpapa, and came as fast as I could get here to remind you it's my birthday, too! And you still have both Rebecca and Isabella because my name is Rebecca Isabella and I'm right here. Does that make you happier?"

Before he could collect himself to answer, the little girl was busily wiping tears from his cheeks with her pinafore.

"Anne told me when we first got here," William Audley said, "that you'd made her the central recipient of attention yesterday by surprising her with young John Couper, but something tells me you're going to be center stage from now on, Papa. And"—he hugged his father's neck—"well you should be. After all, how many men does God honor with such a long, full life?"

Tears were coming again. They embarrassed Jock, almost angered him. He'd been crying too often lately and knew it was because of his advanced age. "Aye, Son, I'm grateful for my every year. Except for these infernal tears that keep spilling down me face as though I were an—an ancient lass!"

EARLY ON FRIDAY, MARCH 9, ANNE FOUND THE AGING CAN-
non's Point butler, Johnson, in a narrow connecting hall that led to
the Hopeton kitchen, built separately from the main house in case
of a cooking fire. As she thought, her brother James, born to handle
most details, had neglected Papa's music for the day.

"Oh, Miss Anne," the gentlemanly Johnson said, his face alight,
"I shoulda known you'd remember! Mausa John Couper, he be
discomforted like a man at the table without his dinner jacket if they
ain't no music fo' his ninetieth birthday."

"Of course he'd be miserable, and you and I are going to see to
it that he's happy. I'll play the Hopeton pianoforte while everyone
waits for dinner to be served, and then, on a signal from me, my
son, John Couper, and William Audley will lead Papa into the
dining room *to your piping*."

Johnson beamed. "You reckon it be all right if I plays the bagpipes for the celebration, Miss Anne? Don' forget Mausa Thomas
Spalding, he be here, too."

"I know Papa's day wouldn't be complete without his oldest
friend, Mr. Spalding, and I also know he despises music of any
kind, but this is Papa's birthday—not his. There's going to be music and lots of it. Fanny's getting to be quite good on the pianoforte, and I might even persuade her to wait for her dinner and play
through most of our meal. Don't you think Papa would like
that?"

Johnson's low, mellow chuckle had always been like music to
Anne, and she joined him now in a good laugh at Thomas Spalding's expense. "Might be Mausa Spalding get a bad bout of indi-
gestion, but Miss Fanny, she so sweet and obliging, she agree to
play long as you wants her to."

"Now, we know all of Papa's favorite piping tunes. Can you
still play them?"

"Yes, ma'am, I kin. But I knows his mos' favorite be the 'Maxwell March.' That be good to play while everybody go to the table,

but you reckon it make Mausa Couper miss his wife, Miss Rebecca, too much?"

"Oh, Johnson," Anne said, her voice tender. "It should not be a secret to anyone why Papa has always favored you. You're so considerate—and you do know him, don't you."

"Me an' Mausa Couper, we been friends a long time, Miss Anne. You reckon 'Maxwell March' might spoil his joy in this day? I knows he so partial to it cause Miss Rebecca, she be a Maxwell, but we want his day to be the bes'."

"It will be. I think the 'Maxwell March' would be perfect. After all, Papa's good sense tells him that at age ninety, it can't be too long until they're together again. But, oh, Johnson, what will we ever do without him?"

WHILE JOHNSON PIPED THE ROUSING STRAINS OF THE "MAXWELL March," tears streamed again down Jock's smiling face as John Couper and William Audley led him into the dining room, followed by his old friend Thomas Spalding—on the arm of his own butler, who made the boat trip from Sapelo Island to look after his master. All the other dinner guests, except the young children, formed a merry procession into the long room, the table gleaming with silver, china, and crystal. As planned with Johnson, Anne had played softly while the guests waited in the parlor for dinner to be served, and as they sat down at the table, she smiled her pleasure when obedient, willing Fanny took over the keyboard.

Anne was seated between Pete and little Rebecca Isabella Couper, the child flushed and excited because today she had turned six and was permitted to sit at the grown-up table. On Papa's right, in the place of honor, was Thomas Spalding, his now almost toothless mouth working as he made a real effort not to show downright displeasure because his good friend Jock seemed unable to function without all that noisy music.

"Why do you think Mr. Spalding's making such faces all the time?" Rebecca Isabella whispered to Anne.

"He just doesn't care for music, I'm afraid. But bless his heart, he's so fond of your grandfather, he wouldn't have missed this day for anything."

"Mr. Spalding really hates music? Even Johnson's good loud bagpipes?"

"I should imagine especially Johnson's good loud bagpipes."

Of course, Caroline and James Hamilton had planned a superb menu, and under their watchful eyes it was being served flawlessly. After the soup bowls had been cleared, silver covered dishes of vegetables were brought in, and as though someone had slipped into the parlor to give her a signal, Fanny struck up a grand flourish on the keyboard as Johnson entered, followed by none other than Papa's longtime chef, Sans Foix himself. On the great entrée platter Johnson carried with such care and elegance was her father's favorite of all Sans Foix's culinary masterpieces from the old days when the Couper chef reined supreme at Cannon's Point: a completely boned, crisp, browned turkey looking exactly as though its skeleton were still in place!

Anne began the applause, which then spread around the long table while everyone gasped and exclaimed and wondered aloud how James Hamilton managed to keep Sans Foix's presence a secret. No one had even seen him arrive from Darien, where he'd lived since Jock left Cannon's Point four years ago, after Becca's death.

Grandfather Couper, smiling broadly, lost no time in commending his friend. "The wor-r-ld's greatest chef, my old friend of many years, Mr. Cassamene Sans Foix, who, though a free person of color, served my every gastronomic need for more year-rs than either he or I care to recall. Hail to you, old friend. Hail to you, old friend!"

For the first time on this celebratory day, tears stood in Anne's eyes. She had known—oh, she had known painfully since the day of her mother's death—of Papa's heartbreak because at such an advanced age he could not live out his days at his beloved Cannon's Point. She had known as surely as anyone except Papa himself that in the night silences he lay alone in his empty bed at Hopeton wondering, perhaps even worrying, about the welfare of this or that Cannon's Point olive tree, this or that sago palm, his orange groves. Of course, he worried less because skillful June, Eve's husband, lived at Anne's place on adjoining Lawrence Plantation and not only tended Papa's trees and flowers, but made regular trips to Hopeton to report on them. No one but June knew every bush and tree so intimately—almost as intimately as did Papa himself. But however frail his old body, the Couper brain had remained sharp, and Papa was fully aware that Cannon's Point could never be its old, flourishing self again. He knew well that with cotton prices so low, James Hamilton had undoubtedly been selling off slaves from both Cannon's Point and Lawrence. As far as Anne knew, no one had actually told Papa, but he of all people understood the pervasive financial pinch of dropping cotton prices in Liverpool, and he of course worried.

Did he know, she wondered, the somehow terrifying fact that eighteen people from both places, under the persuasion of other Island Negroes who learned through their grapevine of the rising unrest on some mainland plantations, had already run away under the cover of darkness? The news had terrified Anne because such a large part of her mind still believed that she *knew* their people were, each one, loyal to the Coupers and the Frasers.

In normal times James Hamilton would already have arranged for the runaway slaves to be hunted down and returned under the Fugitive Slave Act—a "dastardly law" according to Fanny Kemble Butler—in effect in the United States since the Constitutional Convention in 1787, when it had also been decreed that a Negro was only three-fifths of a person.

Anne's eyes met Eve's as Eve stood at the foot of the table, watching the sheer pleasure on Mausa Couper's face as he eagerly anticipated San Foix's turkey. Anne did not return Eve's smile. She forced her thoughts back to Papa as she watched him happily hand the huge silver knife and carving fork over to young John Couper because his old hands trembled so much. What, she wondered, did Papa really think of those old constitutional laws? What, for that matter, did James think of them? Anne herself had never given thought to any of that until Fanny Kemble Butler regaled her one afternoon during her stay on St. Simons Island about the evil injustice of slavery and all laws that protected it.

Why am I thinking of that now, of all times, she asked herself. This is Papa's big day, his big celebration, and I'm allowing dear Fanny Butler's extreme ideas to upset me. Were they extreme? Of course. But as Anne's tender John used to say, "Some extremes are to be treasured, my dear. Can you honestly say you believe there is an extreme where goodness is concerned? Consideration for our fellow man? Isn't June a man? Isn't Eve a woman? Can we possibly be too humane?"

"You're frowning, Aunt Anne," Rebecca Isabella, her dinner partner, said for the second time before Anne really heard, because her mind had leaped so far away. "Is something wrong, Aunt Anne? How did Grandpapa's old cook, Sans Foix, get all that turkey's bones out and still make it look whole the way a real roasted turkey looks?"

"Listen to me, Rebecca. I've wondered about that for my entire life—since before I was as old as you are now. I'm fifty-two and I'm still wondering. Sans Foix doesn't even allow the other people in the kitchen to find out. He works his magic under a clean white tablecloth and even Grandpapa doesn't know how he does it!"

"Are you teasing me?"

"I am not teasing you. I'm telling you the truth. In fact, I'm sure your grandpapa doesn't even want to know how his old friend does his magic deboning. That would spoil his fun!"

"I'm glad Grandpapa likes to have fun."

"Did I ever tell you, or did your father ever tell you, that when I was young like you, your grandfather and I used to march around the big Cannon's Point porch every time there was a huge rainstorm?"

"No! You did? Didn't you both get awfully wet?"

"Of course we got wet—soaked. In fact, your papa always thought my papa and I were a little crazy, I think. We got even with him, though. We both called him the Old Gentleman, even when he was just a young boy like your brothers Robert and James Maxwell."

"Lean down so I can whisper something to you, Aunt Anne, will you, please?"

"Why, yes. What is it?"

"Sometimes my papa acts a lot older than Grandpapa Couper."

Whispering back in the same conspiratorial manner, Anne said, "Oh, I agree! I agree one hundred percent. And do you mind that your father is so—so well behaved compared with Grandfather Couper?"

"Oh no, I don't mind at all. Papa's awfully kind, but it's a lot more fun to be with Grandpapa."

"And will you just look at how Grandpapa's enjoying his birthday dinner? He's eating and eating and he's asked Johnson to refill his claret glass again. I hope he doesn't overdo."

Pete, who had been deep in conversation with Aunt Caroline, now turned to Anne. "Mama, I know my submissive little sister must be starving. Could I be excused long enough to invite Fanny to stop playing and join us before the food's all cold?"

With a somewhat shamefaced grin, Anne said, "By all means, bring dear Fanny to the table. I've been so occupied with my attractive partner here, I almost forgot her!"

"What does it feel like to be a mother, Aunt Anne?" Rebecca asked after Pete had gone for Fanny.

"Oh, it feels wonderful, Rebecca. You'll find out someday when you're a mother."

"I hope I'm as pretty as my mother, don't you?"

Anne laughed. "Well, your mother is a beautiful woman. I certainly know that."

"Is she a lot younger than you, Aunt Anne?"

"Oh yes! And she looks even younger than she is."

"Are you old?"

"Old? Some days, yes, I am. I look older by far than your mother, not only because I am, but because—because—"

"I know."

"You do?"

"You've had to cry so much since so many people you love have died."

The bright child had dumbfounded Anne. Better just to wait and hope the conversation would shift again or that Pete would return soon with Fanny. For a long moment, Rebecca Isabella said nothing. In fact, after so much laughing and talking, there was near silence around the table as everyone's attention turned to Anne's father, who surprised them all by pulling himself to his feet without help.

"What's Grandpapa going to do?" Rebecca asked as Pete and Fanny sat down. "He's smiling. He must feel all right."

"Of course he feels fine," Pete said as Johnson took Fanny's plate and began at once to serve her meal. "He's got that look of half mischief and half determination. Grandpapa has something up his sleeve, Rebecca. Listen and we'll all find out."

When, to get their full attention, Papa tapped his knife against his half-filled wineglass, every eye was on him.

For a reason she definitely did not understand at all, Anne felt abruptly nervous. Anxious. Papa was up to something.

On his feet, her father picked up the wineglass, bowed first to his old friend Thomas Spalding, and in a thick Scottish accent said with a bow, "I'm cer-rtain that my esteemed fr-riend and neighbor, Thomas Spalding, is vastly relieved that I have not instructed Johnson or my talented granddaughter Fanny to torment his delicate ears further with more of their splendid music." He lifted the glass toward Fanny. "Your old grandfather commends you for the pleasure you've given us all, Fanny—except for my esteemed friend and neighbor, who was, alas, born without an ear for music." Turning to Spalding, glass raised again, he added, "And I'd be remiss, Thomas, if I did not express all our gratitude for your admirable patience with those of us who revel in rhythm and melody."

He bowed again to Thomas Spalding, who, though still seated, returned the courtesy with a deep nod and a smile.

"And now, beloved friends and members of my family, I would like, with your permission, to propose a toast."

Unexpectedly, John Couper got abruptly to his feet and in a

firm voice said, "Sorry, Grandpapa, but you do not have our permission at all. At least, not mine."

Because he was normally rather reserved, the boy surprised not only his mother but everyone else at the table. John Couper went on in such a determined way that no one said a word or even coughed or cleared a throat. "I admit, sir, that it is indeed you who normally proposes the first toast, but today is a day unlike any other. You have done what few men ever do. You have, strewing laughter and joy and good gifts and love along your way, reached your ninetieth birthday. And so it is with a great deal of happiness and some surprise at my own forwardness that I lift my glass, along with your guests who have come to honor you as the pillar of our entire family, the source of our humor and security, and the best playmate any child or grandchild ever had! To your continued health and happiness and to your very real sense of God!"

All around the table, everyone—even Rebecca Isabella, who raised her glass of water—drank to Anne's father, to Anne's sturdy rock, to the gentleman her John loved above all men.

John.

She had spoken his name aloud first thing this morning, even before she opened her eyes, before Pete, with whom she shared a Hopeton guest room, had come awake. Today, Papa's ninetieth birthday, would have been the happiest of Anne's life if only John could have been there to share it with her—with them all. If only he had been there to stand tall and handsome beside her at Caroline's pianoforte to sing for Papa as she played. This morning, sitting up in bed, she would have given almost anything—almost everything—if only for five seconds or so John could stand just inside the bedroom door, blotting out the strangeness she still felt everywhere except at Lawrence in the safe shelter of their own little home. Even at Cannon's Point the few times James Hamilton and his family had brought Papa for a few weeks' visit, Anne had felt strange because John couldn't be there ever again.

Even at this moment with her heart reaching toward Papa and swelling with pride in her own articulate, handsome son, the strangeness was there in the midst of her remaining family, at the festive table of her brother James Hamilton.

Little Rebecca's light tug at the sleeve of Anne's gown brought her attention back to Papa. He was hugging his grandson and namesake, John Couper, in gratitude for the boy's excellent toast and again holding his own glass in midair, ready, Anne knew, to make another try at a speech or at least a toast.

The thin, lined old face broke into an even wider smile as he began to speak. Anne, who had indeed always loved Papa's speeches, was still aware, not only of the persistent strangeness even after the years without John, but of the wave of anxiety that had swept her when Papa first got to his feet before John Couper's tasteful interruption. *There was no reason for anxiety.* Everyone seemed well and happy. Papa, especially, was having the time of his long life, but the nervousness held. Almost like a nameless dread.

Because a light chatter had begun to circle the table, Papa once more tapped his silver table knife on the wineglass he was still holding. Then, bowing elaborately in the direction of his grandson John Couper, he began: "With the kind permission of my handsome and already successful grandson John Couper Fraser, I will once more attempt to speak my piece."

In response, on a musical laugh so like John's it caught at Anne's heart, her son began to applaud his grandfather with such love and respect that the applause spread noisily around the table. Papa was still standing, bowing again, looking so frail and shrunken that Anne's heart squeezed. But the old man was beaming like a Lawrence sunrise, and after a slight cough, he cleared his throat and began to speak.

"Seldom at a loss for words, today I find myself fumbling a bit, but the conviction concerning what I want to say is so strong, I believe I must try, at least, to let all of you know—my cherished old friend Thomas Spalding and each member of my treasured family—that it is *not* my advanced age causing me to imagine there are four more blessed members of my family here gathered with us than merely those we can see. My wife, Rebecca, is here, my daughter Isabella is here, my grandchild Annie is here, and so close I can hear the singing of his silver voice is also my son-in-law John Fraser. The song he is singing is 'Drink to Me Only with Thine Eyes,' my Anne's favorite."

Anne could feel the silence pushing hard against her. For much of the decade since John had been gone—out of her sight, out of her hearing—she had struggled against even the memory of his voice singing their song: "Drink to Me Only." On any morning when she chanced to awaken with the haunting melody running through her mind, she had forced herself at once to hum another tune. The grief remained too sharp, too keen a reminder of the agony of those early days and weeks without him when she had done well just to keep walking around. Surely, dear Papa had not meant to bring back that pain, but he had done it just the same and it took every ounce of strength she had to stay seated quietly in her chair.

"It just could be," Papa went on, "that at age ninety—ten years shy of the century mark—I am so close to our absent and still sorely missed loved ones, I am enabled by Almighty God to sense their presence here with us. Either way, their presence brings me all joy and so I felt compelled to share it with you whose faces I can see even with my dimming old eyes. The kindest way I know to show all of you my devotion and my gratitude for this festive occasion is to assure you, with the same strong certainty I now experience, that even on that still-unknown day when I too take my leave of you, there will be no reason to weep, no reason to grieve. I will still be with you and the earthly parting will be brief, the reunion sure. As I stand here, bracing myself on the sturdy back of this dining chair, I want you to believe that I am at this minute here with you and also there with our loved ones, who have simply gone ahead to see that our rooms are ready."

"Grandpapa, you're making Mama cry!"

Pete's voice, almost as shrill as when she used to shout nearly every sentence as a young girl, startled everyone around the table except Jock Couper. Anne watched her father turn his attention slowly, lovingly, to Pete. In all the years of her life, she had never seen Papa smile as he was smiling now at his red-haired, often feisty granddaughter who, as a boisterous child, had been dubbed Pete by her father, John, because he liked the nickname.

"I knew I'd make your lovely mother cry if I shared my certainty, dear Pete, but now and then a mon knows the time has come. The time has come today for me to do all in my feeble power to set my beloved Anne straight—to set all of you straight. To set you on what just could turn out to be an entirely new course. A fresh way of seeing life, a fresh way of tackling the hard things life often brings. A fresh, sure way of seeing death as inseparably a part of life."

For the first time since Papa had begun his strange but altogether gentle speech, Anne was aware of her nails biting into the palms of both hands. She had been sitting there in such a tight wad of pain and misery and rebellion at what her parent had been saying, both hands had become white-knuckled fists. Now, slowly, her fingers began to loosen, the fists to open. Both hands freed the blood to begin coursing again, and without realizing it, she had allowed each hand to drop to her lap—almost at ease.

Papa's blue eyes, now faded with age, were too dim for him to have seen the change in her fingers, in her hands, but Eve, standing in the doorway, would surely insist that the old man was reading Anne's mind because he was addressing Anne alone now.

"Anne, blessed Anne—firstborn daughter to your mother and to me—you have lived these grief-scarred ten years just past through sheer grit and determination; through *forcing* yourself to fill the emptiness of losing John and our other loved ones by attending even more lovingly and more doggedly to the needs of those of us left to you. You have done it nobly and well, Daughter. I know your mother agrees. She and I are proud, pr-roud of you and so is John. So too is your sweet sister, Isabella, and your sensitive daughter Annie. I can promise all this to you. We are all of us poppin' with pride and esteem for you. But we also begin, as of this moment, to beg you to ease off a little. You will miss your loved ones no less, but God has a generous dollop of extra strength and wisdom to give you once you can open your clenched hands and heart to receive it."

Involuntarily, as though a strong arm had lifted her from the chair, Anne stood up. There were no strangers around the table. Heaven knows dear old Mr. Spalding had been like an uncle for all her long life. She felt no embarrassment that she had gotten so abruptly to her feet. She simply wondered what she intended to do next.

"If I've upset you, Daughter, forgive me, but somehow as these minutes pass right now, I see you beginning to turn . . . ever so slowly perhaps . . . but you will turn, you are turning, beloved Anne. The clenched fist will become the open hand. Life for you will go on after the turning, and at least some of the pain I saw lacerate you when I mentioned John's silver voice just now will carve room for new joy you want so much to share with your fine, fine bairns—the children of the love you still hold for that splendid man who chose you to be his wife. In a very real sense I can assure you—all of you—that our loved ones are here, cheering for us to believe that God can and will bring beauty from the ashes that must never be allowed to smother us again."

No longer perplexed by what she meant to do next, Anne simply stood there for a few seconds, her pale blue eyes moving slowly, lovingly, from one concerned face to another. And then, with no effort whatever, she felt herself begin to light from within by her own smile.

The next thing she knew, she had begun to applaud her father's words as did John Couper. When one after another joined in, none seemed at all surprised that the Birthday Boy, old Jock Couper himself, was also clapping his hands.

Chapter 6

THE BIRTHDAY FESTIVITIES TOOK PLACE ON FRIDAY. Jock Couper, accustomed throughout his long life to waking up no later than five in the morning, surprised himself by sleeping soundly on Saturday until after seven. He might not have aroused even then had not a soft, rapid knock sounded at his bedroom door at Hopeton.

Feeling a bit less stiff than usual on awaking, he pulled on his frayed damask dressing gown—a gift from Becca on his sixtieth birthday—and opened the door to find the other birthday person, six-year-old Rebecca Isabella.

"Well, good morning, fair lady," he said, rubbing his eyes. "To what do I owe this unusual surprise visit?"

"To our birthdays, I guess," the girl said, still standing in the hallway outside his room. "I hope I didn't wake you, but I just had to know something."

"And what is that, Becca Belle? Would you like to come in my mussed-up room?"

"No. I just had to know if you feel any older today. I don't."

What the child asked struck his funny bone. He bent to give her a big hug. "Not a minute older! Are you sure you don't want to come in? At least I'm not too old to remember my manners."

"Thank you, Grandpapa, but Mama told me not to disturb you, so I'd better go back downstairs. I—I don't want you to be old enough to die. I see you're not, so I'll go now."

After another hug and a kiss on her forehead, Couper climbed back into his rumpled bed to wait for Johnson, who would surely josh him for oversleeping but would just as surely be there any minute, armed with a sharpened razor, soap, and hot water. He stretched his old body under the light bedcover, still smiling over his early-morning visitor. He fully intended to smile as long as possible, because today he would be forced to tell his adored Anne that even he had not been able to think of a way to keep her very life from being torn apart again.

"I'm a blessed old goat," he told Johnson as the well-mannered, faithful servant dried and rubbed Couper's back after a good, soapy bath and then began to shave him. "I occupy the best room in my son's house and his kindness to me in my infirmity is almost as tender as that of his beautiful wife, Caroline, and every one of his children. Am I not blessed, Johnny?"

"Yes, sir. An' now that my wife, she lef' me for heaven, too, I be blessed right along wif you, Mausa Couper. What I do effen you didn't need me here to Hopeton to look after you?"

"What would I do if you didn't look after me? You must be getting on too, Johnson. Do you know how old you are?"

Chuckling, Johnson answered, "I be older than dat riber out there, sir, but not quite as old as you. Scuse me, Mausa, but I couldn' help oberhearin' what your lil granddaughter ax you awhile ago. She jus' had to know was you feelin' any older today?"

"Aren't you about through shaving me? I need to talk," Couper said, his long face abruptly serious.

"Jus' let me get dis one place under yo' chin, sir. Dere." Johnson rinsed off the last of the lather, then dried his master's cheeks and forehead. "Now, what you got to talk 'bout, sir?"

"Before my breakfast tray arrives, I need to ask you to pray for me, Johnny, and I want you to put your knees to the floor if they aren't too stiff and pray as hard as you can. In my own strength, I know I can't do what I have to do an hour or so from now."

"Miss Anne? You gonna tell her after dey finish breakfus downstairs?"

"That's right. My son James offered to give her the bad news, but James Hamilton has never been known to deliver any kind of news gently—with feeling. And that's the way Anne must learn this. Oh, Johnson, it's going to be a dreadful blow to her. James is doing all the caring, considerate things for her and her family, but I —I feel I'll—"

"You'll let it come down on her easy."

"I'll try. Oh, I'll try."

WHEN JOHNSON LEFT JOCK'S ROOM, BEARING THE HEAVY PORCElain washbowl, wet cloths, and used towels, he went straight to the kitchen, where he hoped to find Miss Anne's woman, Eve. No one had given him permission to tell Eve what lay ahead for her mistress, but Johnson had long known how close the two were, and if Mausa Couper had thought about it, he'd agree for sure that once Anne heard what she had to face, no one could comfort her as Eve could.

He'd failed to ask Mausa Couper exactly when he expected Miss Anne to come to his room, so to make certain that Eve knew well ahead of time, he quickly left the bathing paraphernalia on a shelf in the roofed walkway outside the main house and headed for the kitchen, hoping to find her.

"Where you think I be?" Eve asked in her pert way when Johnson motioned for her to join him in the yard just outside the kitchen door. "You think I be takin' my ease on the veranda wif de white folks? Ain't you looked around at the crowd of guests in dis house, Johnny? Poor ole Lydia 'bout cooked herself to death tryin' to keep up. I jus' got to lend her a han'. What you want wif me? Ain't nothin' wrong wif Mausa Couper today, is they?"

"He be good as 'spected wif what he got to do next."

"What he got to do nex'?"

"Sit down here on the steps, Eve," Johnson instructed her as though she were a small girl.

"I ain't tired. Why I have to sit down?"

"Because I aim to, an' it gonna take me a while to git it all tol'."

As though noticing for the first time, Eve said, "You—you mus' be most as ole as Mausa Couper, I guess."

"You guess right," Johnson said with a weary smile. "But my bein' so old ain't why it take me some time to tell you what I got to tell you. It be the badness of what I got to say. Knowin' how you takes to Miss Anne, an' how she takes to you, I'se got to tell you ahead of her findin' out from Mausa Couper that she got to break up her lil family an' stop livin' at Lawrence."

Eve jumped as though he'd struck her, but she said not one word and made it no easier by sitting there on the kitchen step wiping tears from her eyes as Johnson talked. Finally Johnson put a question to her: "Ain't you eben gonna ax why Miz Anne got to break up her family an' leave her home she loves so much?"

Johnson, knowing Eve, wasn't surprised that she began to fuss and fume at him in her effort to get hold of herself, plainly torn by what he had said. "Why I ax what I already knows? You think June an' me's so dumb we don't know Miss Anne's Lawrence house is fallin' down 'roun' her ears? It be a wonder to me dat her an' Fanny an' Pete an' Selina ain't sick from sleepin' under dat leaky ole roof. An' come summer when the hard rains start, they be so much dampness on the walls de mildew turn the whole house green!" She gave both eyes a good hard rub with her apron and turned to look straight at Johnson. "What I don' know is why, the way she cling to dat lil house since Mausa John be gone, de mens don' fix it up for her. Why her papa an' her almighty brother Mausa James Hamilton let it fall down on her? Why dey let it git so bad? You kin tell me that much, Johnny."

Johnson tried to straighten his stooped shoulders. "No, Eve, I can't tell you. I knows, but a person's got loyalty in his heart for mens like Mausa Couper an' Mausa James. Leastways, dis man's got loyalty in he heart."

"What do you owe to Mausa James Hamilton? You more'n pays fo' yo' keep lookin' after he papa like you does."

"He the son ob the gent'man I respect more'n any other gent'man on the whole, wide earth, that why. Eve, I tol' you 'bout the talk Miss Anne's got to hab wif her papa 'cause I knows you got the same kind ob loyalty to her. She gonna need you when she walk outa the old gent'man's room afterwhile. She gonna need a friend."

On her feet, Eve almost glared down at him. "Leavin' Lawrence gonna break her heart near like losin' Mausa John an' Annie," she snapped. "But where you think I gonna be? You think I fixin' to take a trip across the ocean? It be bad enough that she got to tell young John Couper good-bye down at the dock when they finish eatin' breakfus. Hearin' bad news from her own papa gonna grind her heart. But one thing be sure. When de time come fo' me to help Miss Anne, Eve be right there!"

THROUGHOUT BREAKFAST WITH CAROLINE AND JAMES HAMILTON, William Audley and his likable wife, Hannah—daily growing more like her mother, Anna Matilda—Anne sat memorizing the incredibly handsome features of John Couper, who would be leaving her in minutes. She had forced herself to laugh during their meal, determined to send her son back to his fine new work in Savannah in a happy mood, not dragged down by the memory of a struggling, lonely mother left behind. Laughing had not been too difficult, despite the lingering dread she'd been conscious of since Papa's birthday celebration yesterday. She had lain awake last night trying vainly to understand why she felt dread. Papa had seemed to enjoy himself, to feel fairly well. The reunion of their family had been as pleasant for Anne as she supposed anything would—could—ever be pleasant again without John, without Annie. Tomorrow or at least the next day, she and her girls would be able to go back to the warm, cozy, familiarity of Lawrence, bedraggled as the sweet little house was these days. John Couper was obviously doing extremely well in his new position as clerk in the Savannah firm of McCleskey and Norton. She could feel only proud that at sixteen her boy had already carved such a promising niche for himself in a successful mercantile house. Oh, he'd tried to make funny stories of the "dumb things" he'd done with bills of lading and shipment files during his first weeks as clerk. The boy, while a bit quieter and less talkative than his father had been, without doubt had inherited John's gift of gab, his penchant for making a good story of almost any incident. Unlike Anne's brother William Audley at this age, John Couper was already a man—strong, decisive, energetic, responsible. Of course, William Audley had finally grown up, although he still took evident pleasure in poking fun at his staid, brilliant brother, James Hamilton, for whom he had worked as manager of Hamilton Plantation since John went away. Even with the cotton market so bad, William Audley had managed somehow to break even at Hamilton. James seemed pleased with him if only because William had harvested crops profitable enough to feed his own family and his Hamilton people. At least he'd run up no debt, and that could be said for few planters in the financially depressed year 1849. Even James Hamilton had no cash. No means of expanding his own huge operations. And poor, humorless James, as brilliant as he surely was, never seemed to catch on when William was unable to suppress teasing him. Anne longed for Papa to be having breakfast with them today because William Audley was in fine form. Anne laughed at every opportunity, wanting each last golden moment with her son to be just that—golden, despite her heavy heart at losing him again so soon. Still, finding a means to do the impossible was becoming almost a way of life for her. Perhaps Papa's little talk last evening about his own conviction that John and Annie and Isabella and Mama were really still there with them, in spirit, had helped more than she thought at the time. Somehow this very morning, when she first opened her eyes, John had seemed closer than he had in years.

"This is all a part of the maturing process," Mama would say, were she still there to say it.

"How I wish I could smooth your path, dear Anne. Make all things easy for you," Papa would say, and he *was* still there.

As soon as she'd given John Couper one final hug at the Hopeton dock, she would head straight for her father's room as he'd asked at the end of the dinner party last night. Papa was too frail to join the family at breakfast these days, but he was still here and he'd never failed to find a way to help.

Chapter 7

Unashamed of the tears still wet on her cheeks from her last sight of John Couper at the Hopeton dock, Anne hurried to her father's room. She found him alone, waiting—bathed, dressed, shaved—in his favorite old Cannon's Point rocker by the high front window from which he'd obviously been watching the family tell John Couper good-bye.

His arms were out. She rushed into them.

"Papa, oh Papa, what would I do without you? How do I manage to live for such long periods at my beloved Lawrence with you all the way over here on the mainland? I miss you! I miss John Couper. I—I even miss his father more when the boy's at work in Savannah."

"I know, Daughter. I know."

"You do, don't you? You always know everything. Papa, it's so good to be with you again. Even my blessed Lawrence cottage seems lonely sometimes now that the Cannon's Point house is empty." She freed herself from his arms enough to look straight at his face. "Do you ever think how dear and generous you were to give Lawrence to John and me? Do you have any idea how—how rescued I feel living there even now?"

He grabbed her again, his frail arms trembling. "Oh, Anne, don't say that!"

She tried a little laugh. "And why not, sir? If you only knew how much more Lawrence means to me than Hamilton ever did, you'd never doubt how completely at home I am there. Even with the whole end of the roof over the porch rattling every time we get a good blow off the water." She smoothed his red hair, marveling at how little gray there was for a man who had just turned ninety. "Do you ever get one of our old urges to march around James Hamilton's veranda when it's storming? The way you and I always marched the Cannon'a Point porches?" She laughed again. "I should probably ask if my pompous brother allows you even the urge to march!"

His arms tightened around her and Papa buried his face in her breast as she leaned above his chair. "Anne," he said in a voice so thin and cracked, he sounded like a stranger. "Anne darling, this old goat can't even respond to your—joke about James Hamilton this time."

"Papa! Papa, is something wrong?"

"Have you ever known me not to be ready for a good joke? A playful poke at your fine, stiff brother James? Can you ever forgive me for being such a—dud? Tr-ruly, I'm sor-ry, Annie."

He was weeping. Papa weeping! And she couldn't think of one thing to say. Not one single word of comfort. She was too puzzled, too confused, so ended up with only a helpless plea. "Papa, try to —try to explain to me! What did I say to make you cry?"

Wiping hard at his eyes, he struggled with even a crooked half smile. "It's not what you said, lass. It's—it's what I find I don't have cour-r-age enough to say to you. I tell you, Daughter, your papa's a a useless old mon. A very useless, very old mon. Sometimes I can almost hear my bones rattle, but until now I took what cour-rage I own for granted. I—I've lost my cour-r-age, Annie!"

He was clutching the sleeves of her morning dress, peering up into her eyes, pleading for her to help him. All she could think to say was feeble at best. Something that undoubtedly would make him feel even worse. "Don't, Papa! Don't—be *old*. Be—you. Be the same as you've always been! I know there's God to trust, but I can't see Him. I couldn't have gone on breathing with John gone, if

I hadn't had you. I refuse to let you get any older. I couldn't—I couldn't—" She cut off her own words.

I am making everything worse for him, she thought, so ashamed of herself, she too battled tears. And then she did what they'd always done in any tight place. She smiled, lifted his wattled old chin, and smiled still more. "Are you really looking at me?"

"Aye."

"Then why aren't you smiling? Since when have we been able to look at each other without laughing, even when something might be terribly wrong or irritating? Since when, Papa?"

A mere hint of the familiar, slightly devilish grin flicked at the corners of his nearly toothless mouth. He looked almost like her papa again. This was her papa. Nothing must ever happen that could tarnish the singular humor that had always rescued them both. She and Papa were together—together in a room all by themselves—and any second now, one of them would find a way to laugh at the other, *with* the other.

"Which one of us is going to be the first to think of something funny to say?"

"You, Annie," he whispered hoarsely.

"I don't know how funny this is, but I can ask you a question. A silly question, really. One that came to me in the middle of that stormy night last week. I was just lying there in my Lawrence bed, thinking about our great, noble, giggly marches up and down the long Cannon's Point porch, and suddenly I yearned to know if ever, since the beginning of time, any other father and daughter marched as we did, even in the face of all those scoldings from Mama and James Hamilton. Have you ever wondered that? Every time there's a storm, do you think about us in the old days, Papa? Can you sometimes still hear them both scolding us through the open parlor windows?"

Anne patted his cheek. Not only was he looking at her through the tears standing in his blue eyes, he was smiling almost the way he'd always smiled when each had inevitably known the very moment when humor was about to spring forth of its own accord.

When he cleared his throat, jerked back his bent shoulders, and began his gallant apology for keeping her standing all this time while he sat, she quickly pulled up a straight chair, perched on the edge of it, and took both his hands. "You're about to make one of your little speeches, aren't you?" she asked.

"Aye. The hardest speech I've made in my long life, and the only way I know to do it is to begin, say it fast, and—and—"

"And what, Papa?"

"It's about Lawrence, Annie . . . *you'll have to leave Lawrence.*"

She jumped to her feet. "Don't tease about that, please!"

"I'm not teasing, lass. Lawrence is falling down around you. One more storm like the one last week, and that whole porch roof that's banging in the wind now will blow off into the marsh."

"No, it won't! I won't let it."

"You've wrapped your old papa ar-round your finger all your life, but even you can't control a dilapidated house." His hands shook as they reached for hers. "I'd rather cut off both my hands than say this, Annie, but your proud old Scottish father's a pauper. Too old to manage his own land any longer, taking the very nourishment for his ancient body itself from the charitable hand of James Hamilton."

"But I—I own some people yet! I have John's small widow's pension. The children and I own the Lawrence land free and clear. I can borrow enough money to fix my flapping porch roof if it really bothers you. I'm not a pauper and neither are you!"

"We're both the same as paupers, Daughter. Even James Hamilton has no cash to repair an old cottage on land no longer productive because so many of your people are here at Hopeton, down helping William Audley at Hamilton, or shamefully rented out. James can't borrow a dollar anywhere. William's eking out just enough to feed and clothe his people and his own family, but *no profit* at all through the sale of several crops. James and I have settled the matter, my dear. Do you think if he could avoid it, he'd be leasing Cannon's Point to those folks from South Carolina? He is, you know. My tongue feels like a poison adder telling you what I know will deaden your soul, but Annie, you and your family—

because there is no other way, no means of making your house livable—will have to leave Lawrence and move over here to Hopeton to live with us."

For a long moment Anne just stood there beside his chair, not daring to look at him—fearing the defeat in Papa's heart, fighting utter defeat in her own. In what seemed at this dark minute a complete irrelevance, her thoughts flew back over the decade past to the day she found the strength to leave John, to walk away from his grave, to leave her reason for living there alone in the sandy churchyard ground. Would it be any more painful for her and her little family to pack only their clothes and personal belongings and leave the crumbling Lawrence cottage to which she still clung?

"I live in fear and trembling," Papa was saying, "that the very next storm could injure all of you. Every storm is fiercer at Lawrence and Cannon's Point, so near the sea. James and Caroline will try to make room for you and your three girls here, and from time to time, so will William Audley and Hannah. You know you'll be more than welcome. Oh-h, Annie, help me—a little!"

Still she stood there, unable to speak one word of comfort to her own adored father.

"You've never lied to me, Annie," Jock went on, his voice weak and helpless. "I know you're all deathly afraid every time a storm strikes. Can you look me in the eye and tell me you're not? Can you look me in the eye and tell me you don't believe me when I say that neither I nor your brothers can lay hands on one penny for repairs until cotton prices go up again? Because you're forced to rent out so many of your people now just to make ends meet, Lawrence can no longer be productive. I've tried to shield you from the pain of any financial hardship throughout the years of your life, Daughter. I'd give my old right arm if I could shield you now. I can't. I—can't. Annie, speak one word to me that shows me you at least understand. I know how it will hurt you to leave your home— to live on the charity of your brothers. But we face an irrevocable fact, my child. Please? Just one word to—help me?"

"I—I don't have any words," she said, her voice sounding hard. "I need—time. If I began to talk to you now, I'd break your heart.

I knew conditions in the market were bad, but—give me some time! Even for you, I'm not going to pretend this isn't almost as hard as losing John or Annie."

Unable to help herself, she was hurting him. So, without another word, she ran from the room, down the curving stair, and out into the vast, perfectly landscaped Hopeton yard, with no thought of where she meant to go except away from that elegant, always orderly mansion where she would now be forced to live for only God knew how long.

True, she would be living right in the same house with Papa, but she was no longer a girl, not even a young woman. Certainly she could never again run to the frail old man who was her father and expect him to fix her problems, to kiss the skinned knee. Nothing could ever be right again if she had to leave Lawrence, and she *did* have to leave Lawrence for a humiliating, crushing reason John would have been unable to endure for her. Not until now, even inside her own thoughts, had she been able to admit that except for Lawrence, he'd left her poorly fixed—a wretchedly small widow's pension from his Royal Marines and debts she'd managed, with Papa's help, to pay off only four years ago. John had left her Lawrence, though, and now she was losing even that.

Once outside, she had run until her knees ached and her heart pounded so hard, breathing hurt. Why was she running as though desperate to find something? What? Anything, she supposed, anything *not* neatly in order but wild, unkempt. One little crooked scrub tree would help. Something homey, not perfect in the way that everything her brother James Hamilton owned was perfect.

When she came on a clump of bullis grapevines at the opening of a pinestraw path she thought must lead to James Hamilton's woods, from which his sawyers cut logs for cooking and heating, she plunged onto the path and into the woods. Woods were what she needed now—a plain old tangled stand of woods. Hurrying along the path, relieved that not even one of the Hopeton people was anywhere in sight, she went deeper into the thicket, searching for one blessedly crooked, scraggly little tree. She was glad there was no one to ask why she needed a crooked, wild tree, except that most of her own woods at Lawrence were not what anyone could call tidy. Besides, her heart ached for any living thing that resembled her own cluttered, snarled, untidy thoughts.

Still rushing along, peering right and left as she went, aloud she said, "I'm as crazy as Heriot Wylly! John . . . John, did you hear me? I just said I'm as peculiar as dear Heriot for needing a plain, crooked little tree to cling to."

And then she saw it. Unmistakably a sweet gum, its bent trunk leaning toward her from behind a big hickory. Anne braced herself against the huge hickory's trunk and swung her body around the gum, encircled the bent, plain, lopsided scrub tree with both arms, and began to cry harder than she remembered crying since the morning she'd roused the children in her unleashed need for John to be in the bed beside her. And that had been years ago.

A Lord God Bird, the huge, awkward, red-crested woodpecker who had been her childhood friend, sounded his tin-horn call from somewhere above her head in the top of the tall hickory. Lord God Birds squawked often, but normally at a distance. She had never heard one so close.

And then footsteps were coming toward her—running footsteps breaking twigs and dead branches as they came. Who in the world would dare to crash unasked into her solitary agony? Pete? Had her impetuous daughter seen her run from the house? That Pete would dare she had no doubt, but surely Pete would be yelling her name. Even in her twenties Pete yelled at the drop of a hat. And then Anne knew . . .

A hoarse, desperate whisper—as desperate as Anne felt facing the loss of the only house that had ever been truly hers—told her beyond doubt that Eve had found her.

"Lord have mercy, Miss Anne! Sweet Jesus, have mercy . . ."

As though floodgates had been lowered, Anne's sobs broke out again. Her careful breeding, Mama's teaching that ladies found a way to control themselves, were as nothing at all to Anne as she clung to the crooked little tree. Two strong arms were suddenly around her, but still she clung.

"Miss Anne, you knows! Mausa Couper, he done tol' you, ain't he? It's Eve, Miss Anne. Leggo dat little scrub tree an' look at me!"

"Go away!"

If you allow them too much liberty, Anne, they'll invade your privacy. They'll gossip about you—tell lies. In their efforts to prove their standing with the mistress, they'll go to all lengths at times. . . .

Was Mama actually talking to her from the grave? "I'm crazy as Heriot Wylly ever thought about being!" she cried out. "Eve! I always thought—and so did John—that Heriot Wylly was just odd. Now I don't know. Now, I don't know anything."

"Miss Anne, hush. Hush now."

"Let go of me!"

With Anne still grasping the tree trunk, Eve was trying to rock her anyway—back and forth. Anne was standing there seemingly fastened to the tree, but Eve went on trying to rock her as though she were a child.

"I'm not a child! Let go of me. Do you hear?"

"I hears, but sometimes a frien' knows better—kin help get things untangled."

"Then tell me if I'm losing my mind! Is this what it's like to go out of your mind? I can't find anything, anywhere, to hold on to but this tree."

Anne could almost feel the earth slide under her as she stood there peering through tears at the agonized, strangely beautiful face of the half-black woman who honestly seemed to love her at times more than she loved herself. Maybe, Anne thought fearfully, even more than she loved June! A different kind of love, surely, but despite the near fierceness of Eve's attachment to June, she had never once allowed it to take her away from Anne when her mistress needed her. Did Eve know her better than she knew herself? Did Eve know her as she really was?

On impulse, Anne stepped back to look straight into Eve's expressive eyes. "Do you know me as I really am? And if you do, what—am I?"

"What you feel like you is, Miss Anne?"

"Lost! Eve, Eve, I just found out I have to—to leave—Lawrence forever."

"I knows."

Anne stared at her. "You *know*?"

"Johnson he done tol' me an' I done tol' June. Him 'n' me goes with you. Anywhere you eber goes, Eve be there to help you. We do it all together, you 'n' me. We packs up, we goes, an' we lives our days side by side. You believe what I say? You gonna *do* what I say?"

Eve had grabbed both her shoulders and stood waiting for Anne's answer. "Answer me, Miss Anne!"

Her voice loud and shrill, Anne cried, "Can't you tell I—I don't know what to say? I don't even know how, without my own house, I'm ever going to sleep through another night, how I'll ever find a way to swallow a bite of food. Take your hands off me. Do you hear?"

"I hears, but I don' heed an' if you don' believe Eve's gonna shake you till you tell me you trust me enough to do what I say, I'se gonna shake you till you does an'—" Eve's chin lifted. "Eve not one bit afraid to shake you neither. Even if you got a few white pockets lef' in you dat don' trust me, I trusts me to be the way you needs me to be an' I ain't plannin' to wait forever to start shakin'."

For what seemed a long, long time, the two women who had played together as children, who had quarreled and laughed together through tears and happiness, stood looking, looking deep into each other's eyes.

At last, with a hint of a smile, Eve let go of Anne's shoulders and said gently, "Maybe I don' got to shake you—now. Maybe you comin' to yo' senses, Miss Anne."

Anne failed an attempt at a smile, but as though the last worn, rusty chain that held her to her primary role as mistress of this remarkably perceptive servant had been broken, she allowed herself to fall back against the crooked little gum tree.

"You're smiling, Eve. What's so funny?"

"Don' have to be funny, Miss Anne. Smiles come outa relief."

"Relief?"

"Did you eber feel so much relief as dis minute?"

"How did you know I was out here in the woods—needing you?"

"For near fifty years I been tellin' you I'se your frien'."

"Am I—your friend?" Anne asked simply.

"Why you ax me dat?"

"I don't know."

"I does."

"The word is *do,* not *does.*"

"Do, does. Part ob tryin' to prove to you dat I be you frien', that I be more'n jus' you slabe, is the way I been tryin' to talk better lately. When I all tore up inside ober you, though, I forgets to talk good. You know what I be sayin' anyway. Is I more'n jus' your slabe?"

Anne covered her face with both hands. "Oh, Eve, how do I know? I can't think even one whole thought right now, knowing I'll have to live the remaining years of my life visiting among my relatives and living off their charity." When, after a long silence, Eve said nothing, Anne, in an almost accusing voice, said, "You've never called yourself my slave before."

"Well, I is."

"Yes. But all this talk of our being friends seems a funny time to bring that up for the first time in over half a century. Are you trying some kind of trick?"

Eve grinned. "You sound more like Miss Anne now. Smart aleck."

Feeling more helpless than ever before in her whole life, Anne, because she could think of nothing to say, reached to grab Eve's hand.

Eve took a step closer to where Anne stood, gripping Eve's fingers. She looked at her mistress's white hand clinging to her darker one, appeared to think a minute, then clasped Anne's hand hard in both of hers.

"You'll—you'll go with me, won't you?" Anne whispered. "You and June?"

"I done tol' you we would. We hab to go effen you say we do." Tears were now streaming down Eve's face. "Me an' June's yo' property."

Feeling as though Eve had stabbed her, Anne just stood there.

Finally, taking another step nearer, Eve begged, "You *is* orderin' me an' June bof to go where you go, ain't you, Miss Anne? Sweet

Jesus, order me, Miss Anne! Order bof June an' me to leave Lawrence whenever you leaves."

"But what if I don't *want* to order you?"

"I begs you! Could you stand to leave dat pore lil tumbledown place wifout Eve 'longside you?"

"I don't know how I'll leave it even with you! But am I taking too much for granted, because of what happened between us just now, to expect you'll be going with me because we're friends?"

A quick, puzzled frown creased Eve's light brown forehead. "What happen wif us—just now?"

"You always know everything about me first. I'm surprised you haven't reminded me that the very last barrier to our being truly friends just fell down."

"When you think it fall?"

"Probably when I suddenly reached for your hand. Who knows? Who cares? It's gone, Eve! And Mama was wrong. She was wrong about *you* anyway. You'll never go to all lengths to trick or mislead me. What took me fifty-two years to realize that my nearly perfect, sweet mother could possibly be dead wrong?"

"Yes'm, she be wrong 'bout me, but I ain't all them other peoples, Miss Anne. Don' you trus' no nigger but June till you ax Eve first. Eve just be Eve." Slowly, but not unkindly, Eve loosed Anne's fingers, dropped her hand, and stood very straight. "Two things I got to tell you. First thing is dat ain't nobody, not even young John Couper or Pete, is gonna know plain as Eve knows what pain it bring you to walk fo' de las' time outa yo' lil Lawrence house."

"I know that—now," Anne said in a scant whisper.

"I'se not through yet. Second thing is my grapevine's got it dat niggers is runnin' away here an' dere all ober the South. Right here in Gawja too. Dey say someday we all gonna be free. Mos' likely it be grapevine foolishness, but eben if it ain't foolishness, Eve don' wanta be free or anything else dat take her away from you. June an' me, we done settle all dat. June, he got it all plan out how to keep watch on ole Mausa Couper's trees an' groves an' flower beds at Cannon's Point an' still lib two, three nights a week ober here at Hopeton with you an' me when we comes here to lib."

Anne could only stare at her, unbelieving. "You and June would live apart except for two or three nights a week? Just so you could be here at Hopeton with the children and me?"

"Yes'm."

"I don't think real friends say yes'm to each other!"

Eve grinned again. "Now you does sound more like yo'self, Miss Anne. Smartin' off."

"I'm serious. As long as June is still on this earth with you, I won't have you living that way."

"We all lib the way we got to lib 'cause you hab to leave Lawrence. Miss Anne, yo' papa be a tenderhearted gent'man. He make sure Johnson know right off 'cause Mausa Couper, he know Johnson tell me. I tell June. Mausa Couper he know eberthing be better for you—even sompin as bitter as leavin' Lawrence—effen June an' Eve be ready to help you." The smile Eve gave her was only kind now and compassionate. "Me an' June an' Mausa Couper gonna do all we kin to help. Ain't one ob us wants to see you suffer no more. You gonna be lost wifout yo' own lil nest to shelter you. Wifout yo' own private place to run to when the day's gone. Look to me like the least you kin do is help us by not fightin' us off when we tries to ease yo' way."

With all her being, Anne longed to cry again, to feel the cleansing flow of tears at such love pouring over her from this woman who had, even when Anne didn't realize it or know how to accept it, probably always been her best friend.

No tears came. She had cried all her tears. But she had also seen the last barrier between her and Eve fall, and dry-eyed, she said, "Eve, I need to be hugged. Oh, how I need to be hugged, right now. Don't say a word, but will you please just hug me?"

Chapter 8

FOR ANNE, WHO HAD TOLD HER FATHER THAT SHE needed time, every hour of the next two days dragged by in near silence. She did the expected things a guest does. She helped Caroline cut out some dresses for the quarters children, did her best to make small talk at the table, but the one thing to which she'd always clung for dear life—good, long talks with Papa—she found impossible.

"You're doing the obvious, Sister," James Hamilton said repeatedly. "You're blaming the messenger for the bad news. Surely you know that if it were within his power, our father would give the few remaining months of his own life to spare you such misery. Can't you buck up, act a bit more normal for the Old Gentleman's sake?"

For all the years of her life, if anything could have drawn her to Papa, one of James Hamilton's stuffy lectures would surely have done it. Instead, every word he uttered, every chagrined look he gave her, drove her closer to total despair. Not once in her fifty-two years had Anne gone to sleep with anything but the warmest, coziest feelings toward Papa. Papa, her rock. Papa, her rescuer. Even twelve-year-old Selina knew something was terribly wrong between her mother and her grandfather. Insofar as Anne knew, no one, certainly not she, had said one word to Selina, Pete, or Fanny to indicate that they were going to have to break up what was left of their little family, abandon the beauty and simplicity and sweet familiarity of Lawrence, and traipse from relative to relative, friend's house to friend's house, with never the solace of knowing they could eventually go home—back to their own house.

Papa had said James and Caroline could make room for them. In the tumbling chaos of Anne's mind, she had tried to figure out how this could be done without adding an extra room even to the ample mansion her brother had built. If he could add a whole room onto his house, why couldn't he find funds for a few nails and boards and two or three men to make her own house livable?

And then the chilling thought struck as Anne sat rocking alone on the wide Hopeton veranda the day before they were to leave for home to pack. Could it be true, she thought frantically, that her own family expected her and the three girls to live apart, under different roofs? Not everyone they visited would have room for all four of them! Hadn't she been asked already, by a God she could no longer even find, to live without John? Without Annie? Where would they hang the very clothes off their backs? Would Pete have to pack boxes and valises when it came her turn to live somewhere other than in the same house with her own mother? Would Fanny? Anne had no intention of allowing young Selina, just entering womanhood, to live anywhere without her, but the two older girls would be expected—expected by Anne's own once protective family—to take shelter wherever they might find it.

Again as she'd done so often since Papa had broken the tragic news, she longed for someone stronger than she to help her, to tell her which way to turn, even how to act in the smothering presence of once cherished family members who, in their separate ways, had been there to support her when each new blow fell, but who now made her feel only burdensome. No one could act naturally with her. Even the Couper children gave her the impression they were keeping their voices down, their laughter hushed. She was sure she had never lived through days in which she, Anne Couper Fraser, forced those nearby to tiptoe around her nettlesome personality.

Only Pete, who seldom acted intimidated by anything, was behaving in any way approaching the usual.

In the flickering light of the one candle burning in their shared Hopeton room on the night before they were to leave, Anne could tell that her daughter was up on her elbow in the bed, peering down at her mother lying beside her but turned away to avoid talking. She couldn't see Pete's face but knew that her daughter was scrutinizing her. Knowing Pete as she did, she also knew the girl was concocting something firm and persuasive to say to her. *If she pities me, sympathizes with me, tries to convince me that things won't be as bad as I imagine, I'll have no choice but to shut her up, order her to be quiet and allow me some sleep,* Anne thought. *One person Pete had better not mention is Papa. Sleep is the last thing I'll get tonight if I'm hounded one more time about being the reason he hasn't left his room for a day and a half.* She already felt too much guilt at being unable to talk to her father. Then Anne surprised herself by asking, "Do you suppose there's any way we could send for Eve tonight? I need Eve! Where does she sleep over here at Hopeton? Do you know?"

"In Lydia's cabin, I think," Pete said so calmly her mother wanted to shake her. "The only way I know to reach her is for me to get dressed and walk way over by the river to the quarters. Are you really asking me to do that, Mama?" Pete spoke so quietly, with such feigned patience, Anne buried her own face in the pillow. "I can do that, Mama, but it could help a lot if you'd take a minute to think how such a thing might sound to—even to your own daughter. What can Eve do for you that I can't do?" Anne felt Pete's firm hand on her shoulder. "Are you thinking about how that really sounded at this time of night? Can you tell me, Mama?"

"No! No, Rebecca, I can't tell you—anything. I can't tell you anything because I don't know anything. Not one thing about how I'm going to make it through one more day, to say nothing of day after day for the rest of my life."

"It's all right that you're angry with me, Mama."

"Who said I was angry with you?"

"You called me Rebecca. It isn't right, though, for you to be angry, to shut yourself away from poor old Grandpapa. But you know that, don't you?"

"You're being more than ridiculous! I've never been angry with my father in all my born days!" For a long time neither spoke. Then Anne said, "The old darling is just all worn out from his big birthday celebration. I know he's been in his room almost the whole time since, but it hasn't one thing on earth to do with me."

No one needed to tell her how feeble, how false, that sounded.

"Pete, I'm acting like a six-year-old, aren't I?"

"Yes, you are."

"It looks as though you could give me a little argument on that. Am I—am I really being so childish? If I am, it's only because I'm so scared. So . . . lost."

And then the realization came—indirectly at least—that she was talking to Pete about a subject she hadn't mentioned before. Anne had not told any of her three daughters that they were going to have to leave Lawrence!

"Pete, am I losing my mind?"

"No. You do have a big wide river to cross, though, and so far you don't have a boat, Mama. There is one, though. There's got to be a boat somewhere and I'd like to help you find it."

"Why do you say that? Has someone told you what we're going to be forced to do?"

"Yes. Grandpapa told me. He called me to his room. Mama, you've got to go see him. Give him a chance. His old heart is broken over you. Over the fact that for the first time he can't do anything to fix things for you. Grandmama Couper told me that he'd spoiled you all your life, but only because he loves you. I'm glad my papa wasn't rich the way Grandpapa Couper has been most of the time. Papa had no choices to make about spoiling me. Do you know why you thought you needed Eve before?"

"No. I just know she always tries to help me."

"And don't you think it's time for *you* to start to try to help all of us who love you so much? Selina and Fanny know we have to get out of Lawrence, because I told them just as soon as Grandpapa told me. They deserve to know. I've written to John Couper, too.

He should get my letter tomorrow in Savannah. Go ahead and be angry with me. Scold. Tell me I'm a nosy busybody. I may be, but you're the only mother I have and I don't intend to see you drown in self-pity if I can, by any means, pull you out of it. Mama, will you—will you promise me you'll talk to dear Grandpapa first thing tomorrow morning right after breakfast? Early enough so that the two of you can get everything patched up before we have to pile into the *Lady Love* and head for home?"

"Are you quite finished?"

"Except to ask you to forgive me if I've overstepped my bounds as a mere daughter." In an almost roughhouse gesture, Pete took Anne in her arms and held her so hard, Anne felt almost frantic. "Promise, Mama? You always keep your promises. We all count on that. Promise you'll visit Grandpapa just as soon as we're sure he's awake in the morning?"

Anne was clinging to Pete now. Weak, helpless, she was cling-ing to her eldest living daughter as though they'd changed places. She had cried all her tears. She was weeping inside, but in a surpris-ingly steady voice she said, "I promise, Pete. And thank you. I'd never, ever forgive myself if anything happened to Papa before I could see him again—try to tell him I'll do my best. Oh, dear girl, I do thank you."

"It's all right. I did all I know how to do—just say it right out. I wish I could be Annie for you. I told Grandpapa I did, and he convinced me that Annie knows all about everything. Mama, do you really believe my sister Annie knows about the two of us in this bed, holding on to each other because there's no one else to hold on to?"

Anne waited. "Yes. I have to believe she—knows."

"She'd think of a way to break through to you, to reach you in your agony over leaving Lawrence. I do know that."

"Annie might think of another way, Pete, but if you can just give me a little more time, I'll prove to you that you found a way too."

Chapter 9

THE MEMORY OF THE NEAR MIRACLE OF HER VISIT with Papa the morning after Pete had managed to bring her to her senses would, Anne prayed, never leave her. Once she'd recovered from the shock of her first sight of him, grown gaunt and hollow-eyed in the day and a half they'd been apart, the first semblance of peace came. A soft, bright, dependable grace fell on them both, and the few verbal exchanges they'd shared would stay in her memory for as long as she lived. Not the exact words they spoke to each other. Their true message lay beneath and above their conversation. For every future hour she lived on this earth, she would cling to that unexpressed exchange. A grace melded their two hearts that spring morning at Hopeton in her father's room, and Anne knew it would have to hold her through all the years she would be forced to live away from Lawrence and without Papa.

That he already had one foot in heaven that morning was plain. Especially when he smiled his nearly toothless grin and whispered in a rolling Scottish burr, "Ya stayed away from me because ya had to, Annie, lass. I disappointed you for the first time in your sweet life. I had to tell you so that James Hamilton wouldn't, but I did not do it well. Lying here since, I see I should have given you hope, at least, that you dinna have to leave Lawrence right away."

She stared at him. "I—don't, Papa?"

"Oh, you do have to leave, child. But coastal stor-rms are not always bad ones and people have lives and hearts to consider as well as gales off the water. We bend our lives to the winds and the rains to the extent we can. Beyond that, we're gamblers. The hateful words were no sooner out of my mouth when I saw plain as you see the long, Scottish nose on my face that you'd break if you made the effort to obey me without time to prepare *yourself*. You even tried to tell me you needed—time. I was too tor-r-n up to listen."

"But James Hamilton will never agree for us to spend another stormy season at Lawrence. I don't need to tell you he's already been lecturing me since I was here with you last."

"But turning ninety should give a mon a bit of an edge, even with James Hamilton. I'll try everything to persuade him. I'll even beg for his pity. I live on his charity, too, Anne."

"Papa, you've done so much through the years for James Hamilton. I can't bear to think that you might have to humble yourself with him in order to help me."

"I've only tried the best I could for all my bairns," he said as the familiar, nearly devilish smile lit his sagging, folded face. "But now I mean to try out an adage I've heard used by other aging folk. 'Tis said the older a mon comes to be, the more eccentric he has a right to be."

"I'm not sure I know what you mean."

"Simply, that if my daughter Annie wants to take her sweet time leaving Lawrence, I mean to demand it of your brother, the Old Gentleman! Let him think what he will of me for it."

She dared a half smile. "He'll think you eccentric, to say the least. But let's try it. Even James Hamilton can't do anything more than refuse. And if you win with him and he agrees to allow me to stay a little longer, you mustn't worry about us if a storm comes."

"We will be taking a big risk daring to think the old Lawrence cottage will withstand even one more buffeting. Perhaps you may ready your sweet self before a really bad one str-rikes. But you and

I always reveled in a bit of a game of chance. Every time we mar-r-ched in a bad storm, we dared the lightning to str-r-ike us!"

"I know, but I also know that every time we marched, James scolded us. Papa, I don't think he'll agree at all. I'm not afraid at Lawrence. It's the only place I haven't been afraid since John went away. But my brother won't think us just eccentric, he'll think us insane! And I don't want you upset."

"Let your old father decide that, Annie, lass. I'll send for James and do the best I can."

"Beggars can't be choosers," she murmured. "Oh, Papa, I don't like for either of us to be beggars! I hate it. And there is another way. I haven't told you this before because I was too afraid your Scottish pride would get in our way, but Mama's cousin, Willy Maxwell, has offered to look after me. With no strings attached at all, he seems really to want to help me should I ever need it. He has ample funds. He's a good man. Willy's honest and his offer was freely made. Could you buy enough time from James Hamilton for me to write to Willy—to tell him of my dreadful need of house repairs? I vowed I'd never accept such an offer, but Papa, I can't see how I'll live away from Lawrence!"

He stiffened, his brow furrowed. "Daughter, I'll thank you never to mention such a thing again. As dear and generous as your mother was, she and Willy were well-born Maxwells, socially my betters. No Couper man would ever allow his daughter to accept a farthing under such circumstances. Now, don't puddle up on me. I'll do my very best to convince James Hamilton. To get him to let you wait at least a few months before you uproot your family, but not a farthing will we ever accept from a Maxwell! Is that clear?"

Anne waited. He was growing so agitated, so pale, she could say only, "All right. All right, Papa. I'll do as you say."

"And don't tuck into your mind the thought that once I'm dead and in my grave in the churchyard you can ever dream of doing a deed like that. Do ya hear-r me, lass? Never, never, *never!*"

Chapter 10

J AMES H AMILTON WATCHED HIS FATHER CLOSELY
throughout dinner that day, sensing somehow that
Jock was working hard at charming him. Papa
seemed even more frail than usual, his once ruddy
face pale, but he'd insisted on being helped downstairs to dine with the family. He not only repeated
two or three boyhood incidents from his childhood
back in Lochwinnoch, Scotland, but laughed more
often than seemed indicated, since he must have remembered telling them the same stories often in the
years past. While dessert was being served, James
was not at all surprised when his father cheerfully
urged that the two of them—father and son—retire
alone to the parlor to enjoy their flaky berry pie.

Of course, James agreed, and when Eve had
served them and gone, he waited patiently for Papa's
next move. That his parent intended to ask some
enormous favor James had no doubt. But instead, the
old man launched into still another often-told story
about the day he'd been caught throwing snowballs at
his Scottish father's parishioners as they left church.
Two or three sentences into the yarn, James interrupted.

"Father," he said in his courteous but no-nonsense way, "I do believe you've told that tale so often
I could repeat it to you word for word. There's

something far different on your mind, and since I do allot only forty minutes out of my day's schedule for family dinner, I'd appreciate it if you'd come to the point of what it is you mean to ask of me."

After savoring a huge bite of pie, his father gave him a long, almost pleading look. "James Hamilton, through all the years of your successful, accomplished life, I've borne a double burden—all the pride a father could ever have in a son and along with it, the almost equal burden of feeling inadequate beside you. You have contributed to the fields of horticulture, architecture, botany, conchology, and certain aspects of engineering to the extent that one day, even long after you're gone, teachers in great universities will refer to your work, your name will appear in textbooks to be used by young men seeking to follow in your matchless footsteps, and—"

"Thank you, Father. I'm pleased if anything I've done makes you proud, but if I'm not mistaken, there's something else on your mind."

"And you seldom are mistaken, Son. Aye. There is something else. 'Tis about your sister and her children and the rundown condition of the Lawrence house. You know, I'm sure, that the once sturdy cottage at Lawrence has been—still is—the one place Anne has ever felt belonged to her. And so, deep in my bones I believe that fertile brain of yours could, if you'd set yourself to do it, think of a way that our blessed Annie could stay on in the place that has so tenderly sheltered her since the dark, deep-shadowed day she lost her beloved husband, John. Son, you and I must find a way to allow your sister to remain—"

On his feet, towering above his shrunken father, who was balancing his berry pie on his lap, James Hamilton again broke into the long speech his parent was trying to make. "Interrupting a gentleman as revered and respected as yourself, Papa, goes against every ounce of breeding you and my late, esteemed mother bestowed on me, but interrupt I must and forcefully. I haven't mentioned it to you because I wanted to spare you any shred of worry until she and her daughters are safely out of the Lawrence house.

But I've had it inspected carefully, and to have permitted her to stay as long as I have was a foolhardy act on my part. Carpenter ants have eaten away—are, at this moment, eating away—at the very supports under the room where Anne sleeps at night!"

The crestfallen old face tugged at James's heart. "Son, ar-re ya sure? I know the porch roof is half off, I know the wooden shutters are loose and banging even in a breeze off Lawrence Creek, but James, are you su-r-re? If you are, even a small gale could bring Annie's bedroom crashing to the downstairs!"

"I am sure, Father. As sure as that I am the most embarrassed of men not to be able financially to repair the house for my dear sister. Since there's no one to make the land productive, it would be foolish in the extreme to spend a penny on repairing the cottage for any reason except the high regard we all feel for Annie, but she must pack at once and be over here on a permanent basis within two weeks. I can see I've startled you. I am also well aware that you have done everything in your power to spoil my sister for all of her fifty-two years. I know you long to dissuade me, but it can't be done. My mind is made up and it was made up for me by the simple expedient of facing facts. Anne and her daughters could be seriously hurt—even killed—were we to have anything resembling a severe storm."

His father leaned toward him, started to speak, and then sank back in his chair. "And I all but gave Annie my word that I'd convince you to give her at least several months to prepare her dear heart for living out her life with no place to call home."

"You didn't make such a rash promise, did you?"

"Well, all but a promise. Have you thought about how crowded you and Caroline and your family will be when Annie and her three girls move in here to stay?"

"You know in your heart that they would always be welcome in my home. But as plain as the realization that they have to get out of Lawrence is that for at least certain periods of time, she and her daughters will have to visit around among friends and relatives. Of course, the instant I can see my way clear to adding a room here, I will most certainly do so, but—"

"James, you're not a hard man. You're brilliant, astute, but I never considered you hard."

"If I'm hard, sir, it is only because I treasure the very lives of my only living sister and her children. While young John Couper was here with us, I had a letter waiting for him in Savannah. Captain James Frewin was kind enough to bring the boy's answer today. He agrees with me entirely."

"You'd made up your mind before the boy even arrived for the holiday with us, eh?"

"I had indeed. I wrote to him the same day I told you."

"Couldn't bring yourself to tell the lad such ugly news to his face during his visit with us?"

"Taking potshots at me will not help a whit, Father."

Tears brimmed in his faded blue eyes, but all the fight had not yet gone out of him. "I find it difficult to believe the boy agrees with you about forcing his mother to live from pillar to post."

"He has no choice. That is, unless he wants to chance growing into manhood as an orphan." James felt his own heart about to break, but he forced himself to speak firmly. "We are talking of taking a chance on my sister's very life, Father."

"I know. I know. And I know my grandson, John Couper, does agree with you, James. A letter was, of course, the best way to tell him."

For a moment neither spoke. Then James said, "I'll spare you the pain of telling Anne, Papa. I'll tell her myself this afternoon after I've inspected the work being done on my barn."

"James, you're right as always. For Annie's sake, because I'm the only one who knows how crushed she'll be that all hope is gone, I should be the one to tell her." He sighed heavily. "But your old papa's not only older than the marshes, he's also weak. You'll have to tell her. I find I haven't the strength or the courage."

Chapter 11

By a little after 9 a.m., some three weeks later, Papa's old plantation boat, the *Lady Love,* was again moving with a steady, rocking motion, water slapping its worn cypress sides, out into Buttermilk Sound. The early April breeze held a slight chill as it touched Anne's face, but she scarcely noticed and was only half listening to the familiar rhythm of her oarsmen's rowing song. The odd African beat had, from her childhood, been a part of her, but this morning she could barely sense the jagged, almost drumlike rhythm. Mostly she was numb. This was no ordinary visit over the waters that separated St. Simons Island from the mainland, where Anne's brother James Hamilton lived in his mansion at Hopeton. In tow behind the *Lady Love* was a flatboat piled with boxes, valises, trunks filled with personal belongings, and a few pieces of furniture—her favorite bedroom rocker and John's old kneehole desk— things she couldn't bear to have out of her sight. She and her three daughters were leaving Lawrence forever on Thursday, April 5, 1849, to live off the charity of relatives and friends.

The tall, handsome desk sent from London by John's father still stood in a corner of the Lawrence cottage hall—out of place, dwarfing the small empty house with its heavy, dark elegance. How Anne longed to have it moved to Hopeton! But she'd kept the longing to herself, knowing how set in his ways her brother was. If there had been a proper spot for such a cabinet, James Hamilton would have had one of his own.

"Miss Anne?"

Eve, as always, sitting beside her on the wooden boat seat, peered into Anne's face.

"What is it, Eve?"

"You so still. Your face so sad. Effen Eve could think of somepin to do to help, you know she'd do it, don't you?"

Anne gave her the merest smile. "Yes, I know you would. But you're doing all anyone can do—under these ghastly circumstances. You're here with me."

"You know Eve always be here—right here."

"I hope you know I'm going to do all I can to persuade my brother to arrange for you and June to have your own cabin at Hopeton, too. I have absolutely no influence with him, but I'm going to try."

"June, he hab to come back to Lawrence for another month anyway. He dead set on movin' dem new lil trees from Lawrence to Cannon's Point for Mausa Couper. June be hardheaded. He gonna steer us all to Hopeton an' help us unload, den head back across the water to our Lawrence cabin all by hisself."

Anne touched Eve's forearm. "And you're willing to be away from him because of me. I'll find a way to thank you. I will. Your faithfulness is my one bright spot these days. Your faithfulness and the fact that my dear papa is still alive."

"You an' me gonna work some at findin' more bright spots, too," Eve said with a determined smile. "An' I jus' thought of somepin dis minute. The room you an' Pete gonna sleep in at Hopeton, don' it face east?"

"Yes, I guess it does. What on earth does that have to do with anything?"

"You don' think the same sun show when it come up of a mornin' as we used to watch from your room at Lawrence? De sky's big, Miss Anne. De sun, he come up at Hopeton too an' we's gonna watch for him eber day! Maybe not as clear or as close, but he gonna show his face jus' the same."

"Eve, you're not going to be with me when the sun comes up! For the time being anyway, you'll have to sleep in Lydia's cabin. You know that."

"Dat don' mean I can't slip ober to the big house every day before the sun come up. I done dat when Mausa John, he lef' you all alone in yo' bed at Lawrence."

"But Pete will be with me from now on. There's no space even at my brother's place for her to have a room of her own. What really worries me is Fanny sleeping in that hot, stuffy attic!"

"But dat where Fanny she want to sleep. She done tol' me."

"I know, I know. She volunteered to sleep up there because she's Fanny. Fanny is always going to do the unselfish thing. You know that."

"You wouldn't want young S'lina up there by herself, would you? She be better off in the room with your niece Miss Margaret Couper. They mos' of an age."

"Do we have to go on talking about such sad things? It's all I can do to keep control of myself without your stirring it all up again. Eve, it's different, but I'm almost as miserable and lost this minute as I was when John and Annie left me!"

PART II

September 18, 1849– March 24, 1850

Chapter 12

THROUGHOUT THE HOT SUMMER AND WELL INTO the damp month of September, Anne, when she wasn't worrying about frail, reserved Fanny trying to sleep alone in the attic room at Hopeton, lay awake many nights beside Pete in their shared bed and worried about her father. Allowing only enough time to do some sewing with her daughters and keep up her end of courteous conversations with her sister-in-law Caroline Couper, Anne spent most days in her father's room, doing her level best to stay cheerful and still weather the increasing scoldings from both Pete and Eve for what she was doing with her time.

"I'm perfectly aware that I annoy you by my constant nagging, Mama," Pete said one sticky September afternoon as the two sat together darning, "but—"

"Yes, Pete, you do annoy me. It seems to me that it's my business if I choose to spend all my waking hours with my father, especially at his age. I can see a difference in him every single day. He's growing weaker and weaker. Do you realize he hasn't left his room even to dine with us except once in the more than five months we've been living at Hopeton?"

"Yes, I do. And I hope you realize how hard I'm trying, especially with John Couper too far away to help make things better for you. The air cools a little around seven in the evening. If you don't want my company, why don't you try taking a short walk out by the river with poor Selina? With Fanny? I don't think Fanny's a bit well either."

"Pete, I'm her mother. Is anyone better equipped to know that Fanny has never been really strong? Not since she had measles at seven and certainly not since her bout with fever two years after your father went away."

Pete's abrupt laughter at first infuriated Anne. Then, because she and Papa and John had always believed firmly in the healing power of humor, she began to laugh a little too. "Listen to us! Will you just listen to the way we must sound? You're my mainstay, Pete. Why on earth am I taking my misery out on you?"

"Are you keeping your diary these days? Have you written in it at all since we moved to Hopeton?"

"No, I am not keeping my diary and I have not written a line because whatever I might set down would make anyone who happened to read it—vomit!"

Smiling her father's mischievous smile, Pete said quickly, "Then, for heaven's sake, don't write a line. There's something else you could do, though, and I know it would be good for you and maybe for all the rest of us."

Anne cocked her head in suspicion. "What now?"

"Visit Aunt Frances Anne Fraser in Savannah. You know she wants you, that when she's up there she rents a place with plenty of room for you."

"Pete, you're every bit as distracted as I am! When you dropped off to sleep last night, I was telling you that Frances Anne's mother isn't well and that she's already back on St. Simons at the Village, the Wylly home. I will work out a way to get to the Island soon and visit her, though. Big Boy can take a boat across to Hamilton with me and ride along up to the Village. Uncle William Audley has my horse, Gentleman. It would be like old times."

Sighing as she tossed her sewing aside, Pete said, "Well, I hope you go somewhere soon, just to give yourself a little change."

"But what if something were to happen to Papa while I'm away?"

"He'd be surrounded by family. We'd all do everything we could for him. You know Johnson never leaves him for an hour once it begins to get dark."

"I know all that. And my dear girl, I appreciate everything you try to do. You are a help. With John Couper away and Papa so weak he tires even with a short conversation, I don't see how I'd make it without you. I almost don't make it anyway. I feel as though I'm lost in a big, dark forest. I want so desperately to go home!"

"Does it help at all that so many of our people from Lawrence are here now? Eve's grandmother and mother, ole Sofy and Fanny, Cuffy, Robert, Rollie, Tiber, Peter, George, good old Big Boy, and June. And Mama, I know Uncle James Hamilton seems too strict, but I thought he was very sensitive about bringing both June and Eve here. Even he knew you could never make it without Eve."

Laying aside her own darning, Anne looked straight at her eldest daughter. "And I couldn't. Only God knows better than I that I can never make it without Eve nearby. Your Grandmother Couper didn't really approve, but no matter how hard I tried to keep the proper mistress-servant distance between Eve and me just to please Mama, I couldn't do it. Mainly, I think, because I didn't want to."

"You don't have to now."

"That's right. I no longer have to try. Eve and I can even laugh about how hard it was on Mama—how she worried that Eve and I were friends."

With a surprised look, Pete asked, "You and Eve actually *talk*— even laugh—about dear old Grandmama's strict rules on handling servants?"

"We do. Any objections?"

"Me? Not on your life. I like the whole idea. Why not?"

"I don't know why not. I just know I didn't question Mama's word on it for years, but now, especially after listening to your father and, of course, to my friend Fanny Kemble Butler when she visited here all those years ago, I have begun to have questions about the whole subject of our people. Lots of questions, most still unanswered." Anne got to her feet. "We'll go on with our little discussion later, Pete. I need to look in on Papa now. You understand, don't you?"

"Yep. I surely do."

"I wish you wouldn't say 'yep.' "

"I know you do, but I like to sometimes. Go pay Grandpapa a visit." While she gathered up her sewing, Pete asked, "Do you want to know something, Mama?"

"Of course. What?"

"Since I've grown up, I often think that maybe Grandpapa Couper never really felt comfortable in the role of slave owner. Do you think he did during all those years as the Cannon's Point master?"

"What a strange thing to say."

"Strange or not, I've thought about it a lot. Have you ever come right out and asked him?"

"No. No, I haven't, I guess. For me, his owning people has just always been a part of being his daughter."

W<small>HEN</small> A<small>NNE</small> <small>REACHED THE DOOR TO</small> P<small>APA'S</small> <small>BEDROOM AND SAW</small> Johnson just outside, an involuntary shudder of alarm went through her. What was Papa's man, Johnson, doing in her father's room at this hour of the day?

"Johnson," she whispered sharply. "What are you doing here? Did Papa send for you? Is he—is he feeling worse than usual?"

The reassuring smile on the old Negro's face calmed some of her fear. "No'm, Miss Anne, Mausa Couper don' send for me. I just come on my own. It help me to stay nearby enough to look in on him a tech more often these days." The reassuring smile widened. "He be glad to see you. It be a mite early for you to visit him, too."

"Yes, but he has been sleeping most of the mornings. Sometimes until early afternoon lately." Anne's nervous laugh sounded silly. "I'm sure none of that explained anything, did it? I'm—I'm just here, that's all. Pete and I were darning, talking away downstairs in the parlor, when suddenly I felt I had to see my father. Was he asleep when you were in there just now?"

"No'm. He ain't sleepin'. He just layin' there lookin' up at the ceiling. Seems to be thinkin' pretty hard 'bout somepin. Not sayin' much. I know he be glad you come."

She nodded gratitude as Johnson held open the door for her and shuffled down the shadowy upstairs hall to retake his usual daytime post in a chair close enough to his master to hear if he jangled the little bell beside his bed.

For several seconds Anne stood just inside the sunlit bedroom and looked at the shriveled, wrinkled face of her once tall, vital father. His graying hair was still definably red, but oh, his thin, shrunken form under the light coverlet tore at her heart. Johnson had shaved his sagging old face, his still-thick hair was brushed, but above the cover she could see that the scrawny, once muscular shoulders were clad only in a nightshirt. He hadn't felt like dressing today.

"Papa? Good morning! It's Anne. Do you want to open your eyes and prove me right? Or are you too sleepy? I didn't come to tire you with a lot of talk. I just came to look at you. To tell you how much more I love you today than yesterday. . . ."

The blue eyes opened slowly, and as always when he looked at Anne, his eyes held a smile for her. "Aye," he said just above a whisper, " 'tis my bonnie Anne. My bonnie, bonnie daughter Anne. And did you gr-r-eet me with a good morning? Isn't it a tad early for you to be paying me the honor of a visit?"

"Well, it's still morning. Almost eleven o'clock. Anyway, don't I have the right to look in on you every time I get the urge to see my wonderful father?"

"But Pete said the two of you would be darning a gallon of socks this morning."

Surprised, Anne asked, "Pete's already been here to visit you? She didn't say one word about it to me. Papa, I don't think I'll ever catch up with her. There is just no way to guess five minutes ahead of time what the girl might do next. Did Pete have a particular reason for coming to your room so early?"

He smiled a little. "And did she need one? She's my very own gr-r-andaughter, now, isn't she? But no, lass. She had no special reason beyond asking me a rather blunt question—from over there at the doorway just as she was about to take her leave." He tossed one pale, slender hand toward the closed door to his room. Then, looking straight at Anne, he added, "Pete is a handful all right. Seems to me no one will ever be sure just what the gir-rl might think of next."

"Do you want to tell me what she asked you?"

"If you like. She gave me almost no time to answer, since she was on her way out, but she asked me straight out if I really— down in my heart—approve of being a slave owner."

"Papa! Pete—asked you that?"

"Aye."

"This morning?"

"Aye. And I'm sure you want to know how I responded to the lass."

Anne nodded yes.

"Not fairly, I'm afraid. I resorted to a trick I'd known Pete to use. I answered by asking her a question. A tricky one, I fear. Two questions, in fact."

"Well, are you going to tell me what you asked her?"

"These may not be my exact words, but close. I asked, 'And what do you think, Pete?' When she said firmly that she had thought for a long time that I did *not* approve of owning other people, I then asked my trickiest of her: 'And Granddaughter, what choice do you think I had even if I disliked the evil system?'"

"Well, did Pete just go on out the door then?"

"She did indeed. Should I have called her back to discuss it with her more fully? Was I wicked?"

Anne leaned over to kiss his forehead. "You're too sweet and generous and dear to be wicked, ever. Now I've worn you out with so much talk. How about a nap? Johnson's right outside in the hall if you need anything. And I'll come back soon to visit my most favorite gentleman."

Her hand clutched tightly in his, the old man squinted up at her, brow furrowed. "Oh, Annie, lass, you do know how my heart aches for you? With no home of your own?"

"Sh! None of that matters nearly as much as long as I have my handsome, cheerful father close enough for real conversation. Papa, you do know how important you are to me, don't you? How important you've always been? And can you forgive me for letting it show so much when my heart breaks? I'm trying hard to learn to be strong, to live my days drawing courage from deep inside myself, from God. Really, it helps so much just knowing that when the girls and I have to spend a while in someone else's house, you'll be here waiting for us when we come back."

"That's the har-r-dest part, isn't it? All your visits to Savannah, to the Kings' Retreat, to your brother William Audley at Hamilton, and to Frances Anne over at the Village on St. Simons. I'm sure you know that you're most welcome everywhere you go, but the har-r-dest part must be not being able to go home—back to your own home when the visit's done."

She stood straight, her eyes turned away. "Don't talk about any of that, please! I can't bear it yet. I—sometimes I don't think I'll ever learn to bear never being able to go home again."

"And does it ease you some spending time with the others in their homes?"

She tried hard to smile. She failed. "No. If I'm truthful and I've always meant to be with you—no. It doesn't help. It's just a different way to pass the time until—"

"Until what, Annie?"

"I don't know! Can't you see that's the trouble? I spend time—days, weeks, months—waiting for nothing. Oh, someday John Couper will be given time off to visit me again. I can visit Savannah to try to let the boy fill my heart full enough to last until our next visit, but mostly I live through days and nights because there's nothing else to do."

"Annie, Annie . . . if only I could make it all happy for you again, I could die in perfect peace. Should I have one more talk with the Old Gentleman, James Hamilton, in one last effort to convince him that he and William Audley could manage to spare a few people to look after you so that you and the gir-r-ls could live in a part of old Cannon's Point? Just cancel the lease? It was once you-r home."

Ashamed to the depths of her being that she'd allowed herself to pour so much of her heartache onto her feeble, helpless father, Anne determined to make herself smile—say something that would bring a smile to the sunken old lips. She did force what felt, at least, like a real smile. "Now, sir, I'm smiling and that's your cue to smile right back at me. No, I don't want to *think* about living in two or three of those blessed Cannon's Point rooms because my memories of when I did live there as a girl are too bright and too happy. Do you hear me? I don't want you ever to mention such a thing again. If you'll really try, I know you'll understand all the way to your toes why I won't—couldn't—bear to spoil what I can keep always of Cannon's Point the way it used to be. Tell me the truth. Could you endure living in a dusted-out corner of that beloved old place? Even if there were enough people to tend everything? Isn't it better, strange as things are sometimes, to be over here—away from the Island—on the *foreign* mainland in James's house? You've been here for nearly five years now." She made herself smile still more. "If you can visit—without a home of your own—for five years, don't you think I'm strong enough too? I *am* your daughter, you know."

Later, standing alone in the upstairs hallway outside his room, she almost despised herself because she'd even tried to lie to Papa. She was *not* strong enough to live all the remainder of her days without the sanctuary of her own home. She would never be.

Chapter 13

PAPA SEEMED UNCHANGED WHEN THE END OF SEP-
tember rolled around, and as he did more and more
often, he urged her to "pay a little visit" to someone.
Anne had been as careful as she knew how not to
sadden him again by allowing him even one more
clear glimpse into the agony of her heart, into the
depths of the constant, quiet desperation she felt. At
the conclusion of no "little visit" she made was there
ever the solace of going home.

During the early part of September, when Pete
and Fanny had spent two weeks in Savannah at the
home of Miss Eliza Mackay and her daughters, Kate
and Sallie, Anne had shared their letters with Papa,
hoping they'd written something funny or interesting.

Along with the ever-present pain of being homeless, Anne was also struggling to prepare herself for
the inevitable. She wouldn't have Papa for very much
longer. People, even healthy, strong-minded, steady,
optimistic people like Jock Couper, did die of old age.
Few men ever lived past seventy. In only half a year's
time, her father would be ninety-one! That he no
longer enjoyed living was plain even to Anne, who
knew too well that when Papa went away, the very
last shred of home, as it once was, would be gone for
her too. As long as the two of them could reminisce
together about the fun they once shared out in the

sun-shot, leaf-shadowed beauty of St. Simons, they could both cherish the memories—relive them, rehear the voices. Together, they could speak of John's singing, the lilting way he could laugh at himself during the years in which he was working so hard to learn how to become a coastal planter of Sea Island cotton.

❧ ❧

"DON'T MY CHILDREN MATTER ENOUGH TO ME?" SHE ASKED HER lifelong friend, Anna Matilda King, during a month's visit in November to Retreat on the blessed Island they both loved.

"Of course they matter enough, Anne. Fanny and Selina and Pete and your sweet, good-looking son, John Couper, are your reasons for waking up in the morning, but they weren't here—weren't even born—during those happy, carefree days you and your father love so to relive. Those memories and your children are two separate experiences. Don't forget, I know a little of what you suffer day after day. Except for the children still living here on the Island with me, I'm mostly alone, too, you know."

"I do know, Anna Matilda. I do know and I try to remember." She sighed deeply. "At least, barring an accident or a sudden illness, you can count on Thomas Butler King's coming home to you from California someday. Thank you, though, for trying to feel—what I try to feel."

"What you *try* to feel?"

"Yes. Some days I'm just numb. Some days I count on just being—numb. Inside and out. Does it ever make you wonder that your husband is away so much? Oh, I don't mean to question his devotion to you, but northern California! Must he always pick such a distant place to go?"

"Evidently. I nag him in letters for leaving me with the burden of running this big plantation. I shouldn't, but I do. Not in every letter. I love the man too much. I want him home too terribly to chance overnagging, but I do complain."

"He seems quite involved in all that goes on back here at Retreat during the periods he's home. Women aren't supposed to understand how men think, why they think as they do, but sometimes do you rather console yourself because Thomas may think that since all this land and property belong to you by inheritance, he owes it to you to let you make the big decisions, handle the people, plan the crops?"

Anna Matilda actually laughed. "I used to be consoled some by such circuitous thinking. I'm not sure anymore. I just go about my duties, go on missing him as much as, maybe more than ever as we both get older. Are you really going back to Hopeton tomorrow, Anne? I love having you here with me. Georgia and Virginia are so fond of you. My people all feel as though they belong to you, too, you know. If Caroline's coming over in the family schooner with James Hamilton to get you tomorrow, can't we think of a way to persuade them to stay another week or so? That way I won't lose you again quite so soon."

Sitting beside her in a porch rocker, Anne reached to pat her friend's hand. "Thank you for wanting me. Truthfully, I'd as soon stay as go back to Hopeton, but I'm sure James and Caroline will need to return no later than day after tomorrow. And while I'm here, I really should visit with dear, troubled Frances Anne. Her mother is quite unwell. So unwell that Frances Anne, even with two months' rent paid in advance on her rooms in Savannah, thought she had to come home to see to her. Because her twin, Anne Frances, has died, and dear, fey Heriot is still being dear, fey Heriot, Mrs. Wylly needs Frances Anne."

"At least you know your blessed father will still be there."

"No. I never know, when I kiss him good-bye to leave on one of my wanderings from friend to relative, that I'll ever be able to talk to him again on this earth."

With the affectionate humor family friends often used when speaking of Jock Couper, Anna Matilda laughed softly. "But you know your papa better than that. He'd never pull such a trick on you! Not you. He worships the—"

"The ground I walk on," Anne finished for her. "Everyone has always said that, and in a way I know it's true. I've been hard for him this past year. I try to keep my lostness to myself, but for as long as I've been on this earth, the easiest thing has always been to pour out my troubles to Papa. He's too old now. Too frail." Anne smiled a little. "Sometimes I wish he weren't so smart—still so quick in his mind. Even when I'm closemouthed about having no home, he still knows I'll be lost as long as I have to roam the earth without a place of my own to run to. Anna Matilda, I know how you long for Thomas to come home to stay and try to recoup his losses. And I know that you want to rebuild this old cottage, but think, think, think before you do that. This beloved house—just the way it is—has been your refuge for so many years. It's even a blessing to me. Compared with Hopeton, as elegant as it all is, I walk in this cottage and feel I can almost pull its dear walls around me for sheer comfort. Believe me, it's no fun feeling like a helpless bird out of its nest, fluttering like a crazy thing in the dead leaves on the ground, with no way to get back to what was familiar. Anna Matilda, you're so fortunate to have a place where you really feel at home. Don't ever do anything to change that!"

THERE COULD HAVE BEEN NO BETTER GIFT FOR ANNE AT CHRIST-mas 1849 than a surprise three-day visit from John Couper. It had been weeks since she'd seen him during a visit to Savannah with Miss Eliza Mackay in early December, and except for the humiliation that such a fine, mature young gentleman should be forced to sleep on a pallet at Hopeton for lack of room, her joy knew no bounds. Pete did her best to console her mother by reminding her that her brother had no false sense of his own importance and would only make a lark of bedding himself down in the corner of James Hamilton's library. Pete's words helped some, but to Anne, her only son deserved the best. To John Couper's mother, his re-markably swift success in being made head clerk at the prominent firm of McCleskey and Norton in Savannah, his stunning good looks, his always pleasant, encouraging, gentlemanly manner, should have gained him special treatment anywhere he went, and, of course, James Hamilton would have offered more had his home not already been running over with his own family and Frasers.

Her son's easy, lighthearted acceptance of such meager hospitality so charmed his mother, the already strong bond between them seemed even stronger.

"No one makes friends by being a burden," John Couper had said, laughing as he reached the breakfast table after his first night on the floor pallet. "I'm here to enjoy a happy holiday with my family and I don't want to hear one more word, Mama, about whether or not I slept. I did. Like a puppy dog."

About midmorning of his first day at Hopeton, Anne clung to the boy's strong arm as they walked together in the mild December sunlight beside the canal. His occasional smile seemed to reassure her that although it seemed impossible, she was really not a burden to John Couper. The boy's acute sensitivity to her grief, to her misery at being uprooted from all she counted on, could so easily have caused him to find excuses not to visit, not to write so often. He had never given her one clue that in any way she was a burden to him. He must know how desperately she needed him, would always need him, but instead of dragging him down, her need of him seemed to buoy her son. Was she overreassuring herself that she was not a burden? Did this handsome, highly intelligent young man truly enjoy being his mother's solace? As they walked in silence for a time, her thoughts flew to poor Frances Anne, whose elder son, James, let his mother know he had all he could handle with his own restless, troubled life. "When something troubles me," Frances Anne had once told Anne, "I keep it away from James. I simply could not endure being a burden to the boy. We've never been as close as his younger brother, Menzies, and I have always been, but I mean to keep what little I have of his confidence."

Anne would have given almost anything if John Couper lived nearby, but he was only an overnight water trip away. In their hearts, neither mother nor son were ever really apart. This was her solace. More than solace. John Couper gave her a security that often caused her to think of the place her own father had held in her life when they were all younger—in the early days when it was all right to run to Papa not only when any large or small thing went wrong, but when it was expected of her.

For some time, mother and son walked along in close, easy

silence. Then John Couper slipped an arm around her waist and said, "Do you know my mother is excellent company?"

Anne laughed. "That's nice to hear, but I haven't said a word in nearly five minutes."

"That's part of what I mean. When two people are really as much of one mind as you and I, constant talk isn't necessary."

"I know. And it's unusual. Do you think it's because so many people aren't really as close as they think they are? Or as they think they should be?"

"Maybe. But we know about us, don't we, Mrs. Fraser?"

"Yes, Son. We know about us. Could I interpret that to mean that your old mother isn't a burden to you after all?"

Now the boy laughed. Maybe the two of them were of the same mind about many things, but his laughter was so like his father's, she still choked back mixed emotions when something struck him funny. "I don't know what I'd give if I didn't have to live so far away, Mama."

"Me too. But I'm so, so proud of your almost instant success. Your papa would be so proud, too, he'd be hard to shush. You know that, don't you?" She squeezed his firm, young arm. "What I wouldn't give to hear him boast about your rapid advancement with McCleskey and Norton! Your father, you know, was prone to a bit of exaggeration at times, but he'd have no need of it in bragging about his only son."

"Do you still have bad times over Papa?" the boy asked.

"Yes. I don't get overcome the way I once did, but I miss him terribly some evenings when it begins to get dark. When those times come, I concentrate my thoughts on you."

"My cousin Menzies says his mother still misses Uncle William very much, too. The two Fraser brothers must have been hard men to lose."

"They were. Not at all alike, either, in appearance or in personality, but they captured far more than a Georgia coastal island when they first came here as Royal Marines. They captured Aunt Frances Anne and me, too—entirely. Have you heard from your aunt lately?"

"No, but Menzies did write from school up in Cobb County that he and his mother are still trying to sell the Darien house."

"Dear Frances could never bring herself to live in it again after William died."

"I know, and although I mean nothing deprecatory about her, I'm secretly quite proud that my mother had the courage and the strength to go back to the Lawrence cottage where we were all so happy with Papa."

"You seldom mention your other cousin, Menzies's brother, James."

"I don't, do I? Well, no two brothers could ever be as different as those two."

"There are about ten years between their ages, you know."

"James is on the high seas so much, I doubt that he and Menzies have had a chance to get to know each other as adults. Poor old James is so restless, constantly dissatisfied, it's a good thing, I guess, that he's a seaman. Life aboard ship and in foreign ports is probably all he could cope with anyway. I always rather liked the fellow."

Even John Couper's short laugh sounds like John's, Anne thought.

"But I couldn't keep up with James. For one thing, the man swears too much for me. I don't think I'm prudish about his language. It just strikes me as showing a streak of—helplessness, uncertainty about himself down inside. I hope you don't think me critical."

Again, she hugged his arm. "Critical? I think you are inordinately wise for a young man who just had his seventeenth birthday. Do you think poor James swears so because he feels he has to prove his manhood?"

"Something like that. Menzies is just the opposite. Oh, he's a real man, even though he's ten years younger than James, but he seems to have a different idea of what being a man means."

"What do you think it means to him, Son?"

"A grasp on certain manly values—maybe even virtues—although he's really funny and lots of fun. James seems to believe he needs to make people quake when he walks into a room. Menzies is satisfied to make people feel good all over. I don't mean to make him sound like a budding parson, but he's—I don't know—I sometimes think of the word *noble* when I think of my cousin Menzies."

"Then it's no wonder I've always thought that his mother depends on him much the way I depend on you, young as you both are. John Couper, do I lean too hard?"

He laughed. "The only danger I see is that I might get a big head from being proud that you do. And I pray every day I don't disappoint you." The boy stopped walking to look at her. "The truth is, I feel any little thing I can do for you, I'm also doing for Papa. I know I'll never be able to take his place, but I can be the best person I'm able to be and hope with all my heart to help you."

Anne hugged him. "John Couper, listen to me. The girls are truly dear to me. Pete, especially, is strong when I need her to be, but if I didn't have you, there are times when I—I feel I might stop trying at all."

"I vowed I wouldn't bring this up, Mama," he said when they'd begun to walk slowly ahead again, "but somehow I want you to know that the hardest times for me are when it comes all over me that you, my mother, who loved our little home at Lawrence so much, can't ever go back there again. Right now, although I was recently promoted to head clerk for Mr. McCleskey, there's no way I can rescue you, but I mean to find a way to get you another house someday. I know that sounds young and boyish now, but wait and see. I'm going to do it."

"How can it be true that you sense so deeply, understand so much, at barely seventeen? What manner of boy are you anyway? I was really making some progress in my grieving, I think, when I had to leave Lawrence. I know there's a sunrise over here at Hopeton, too, and everyone in my brother's family is kind to me, but—Son, do you remember the whole family sitting together over on the Cannon's Point veranda the day—the day we buried your father?"

"I was just a boy, but I'll never forget that day."

"You, above all the others, seemed to understand what moving back to Lawrence might do for me. You, at six and a half years, somehow knew I'd be helped by the Lawrence sunrises."

"I remember that, too."

"Well, I was. Oh, I was helped by them. Over here on the mainland, the sunrise just seems so far away."

"Poor Aunt Frances Anne hasn't found a place where she feels at home either, I guess. I know it worries Menzies a lot. He tells me she's about to make up her mind to move permanently to Savannah to be near him. He'll be starting in business somewhere in Savannah at the end of next year, I think. He's been studying business, and the Burroughs firm is interested in him."

Impressed, Anne said, "Any mother would be proud to have her son work for the Burroughs firm." She was silent a moment, then asked, "You know I'd love nothing better than being near you."

"Who knows, Mama? Maybe someday I'll be successful enough for you and all three of my sisters to live in Savannah, too. I've already thought of that, but could you really be contented away from St. Simons Island? Any more contented than here at Hopeton on the mainland?"

"We're both dreaming, Son. And right now, if the truth were known, I can't imagine being really contented anywhere except at Lawrence." She forced a small laugh. "You see how spoiled your mother is?"

"Dear lady," he said quite solemnly, "you're anything but spoiled. You're a woman of true, true courage and spirit."

"Oh, am I? Do I actually seem that way to you now and then?"

"I know everyone used to say on St. Simons that Grandpapa Couper spoiled you, but there isn't a man anywhere at any age who could possibly be prouder of his mother than I. I wish I could think of a way to tell you that there have been times since Papa went away, since Annie left us, when I could almost see you grow wiser, stronger. Not only do I love you with all my heart, Mama, I admire you more every day. You're always so straightforward, so honest with me. With all of us."

"You almost convince me. And I want to be convinced. I want desperately to be the kind of mother you and your sisters need me to be. I long to believe your father is proud of me, too."

Once more he stopped walking and took her hand. "We just have to be patient a while longer. Leaving you again in a couple of days will be harder than ever, but you and I are going to find a way to free you of being a rootless vagabond."

Anne smiled up at him. "And while we wait, I'll try hard not to *act* homeless. Do you believe me, John Couper?"

"I believe everything you tell me, milady. I always have and I always will. And Mama, you can believe what I tell you, too."

Chapter 14

AFTER A HUG IN THE MIDDLE OF THEIR SPOTLESS Hopeton cabin floor and a patient, almost halfhearted kiss of the kind June might have given one of the quarters children who had asked him to do something he had some doubts about, he laughed into Eve's up-turned face.

"You gonna be the death ob me, woman. What you want axin' me to leave my fieldwork before buttermilk time to meet you here?"

Eve pulled his face down close enough to give him a proper kiss, then said, "Dat better'n any ole buttermilk dey gonna bring de fiel' hands, now ain't it?"

Her heart squeezed at the low, velvety sound of his laugh, and she thought how to this day Miss Anne must miss Mausa John laughin' and wondered how she could even try to live anywhere on this old earth should something happen to June.

"What you want special, Eve?" he asked. "A kiss like dat befo' buttermilk time mean somepin good or somepin bad."

She stepped back to look him straight in the face. "Eve, she got one ob her knowin's. Like ole Gran'maum Sofy git. Wouldn't s'prise me none effen Gran'maum Sofy, she got the same knowin' dis very day!"

"Be your knowin' good or bad?"

"You an' me, we done got it settled, ain't we, dat we goes ever'where Miss Anne an' her girls goes to lib?"

"She own us, don' she? Look like Miss Anne, she be de one to settle where we libs."

Hands on hips, Eve took still another step back from him and flared. "You hush yo' smart mouthin' wif me, Mistah June! Ain't I done tol' you Miss Anne an' me, we be more'n mistress an' slabe these days? Ain't I been tellin' you her an' me be friends for longer dan she eben knows? Dat we talks to each other like reg'lar womens?"

He snickered a little. "You done tol' me till I knows it by heart."

Eve tossed her elegant head. "An' what Eve tell you be true! Miss Anne, she knows as good as I knows now dat her mama, Miss Rebecca, she be dead wrong when she think—"

"I knows, I knows. Miss Rebecca, she be dead wrong when she think you like any other slabe woman anywhere on the face ob dis ole earth. She dead wrong cause you an' Miss Anne you done decided she be wrong."

"Don' josh me, man! Jus' listen. I gotta knowin' dat say one day —maybe not anytime soon, but one day not far off—you an' me an' the girls an' Miss Anne, we git us a house fo' her to lib in again all her own an' we all might jus' find dat house way off from Sn Simons Islan'!"

His smile melted her momentary annoyance with him. "You done read me outa the Good Book dat 'where you goes, I goes too.' Don' you 'member readin' dem words to me, Eve?" His arms were out to her and she moved into them, her own arms circling his waist. "If you got a knowin', dat be good enuf for June, Sweets."

With one fist she gave him a quick, loving thump on his deep chest. "You knows I turns to jelly when you calls me Sweets an' you ain't called me Sweets for how long?" Pressing her whole self hard against him, she asked again, "How long, June?"

"You knows June don't keep records, Sweets. Dat be Mausa James Hamilton dat keep all dem fancy records, but lif' up yo' heart, woman. In my way, I'm fastened onto Miss Anne's happiness as much as you eber was. It be pert near more'n ole June kin stan' to hab to row dat pore lil woman off away from her papa to lib offa some other kin or frien'. Me an' her papa spend a lot ob time talkin'. She always been his favorite. It be killin' 'im now to see her homeless like him."

"Least Mausa Couper's got a big, sunny room ob his own at Hopeton an' he ben ninety years an' more an' my poor Miss Anne, she got to keep runnin' here an' runnin' there so's not to crowd up the Hopeton family too long at a time. Oh, my knowin' be a good one, June. One day Miss Anne an' you an' me an' de girls, we all gonna hab a place to call home again!"

"You sure dat's all your knowin' say, Eve? Don' it say *where?*"

"No. Not where. Not eben how we gonna find a house for her, but she tell me today she gettin' sick an' tired libin' off charity an' she eben talk about it to John Couper when he done visit her. Miss Anne, she changin' eber day. She not Mausa Couper's spoiled girl no more. But one thing won't change 'bout her, an' dat be when she make up her mind to somepin she find a way."

He kissed her forehead. "An' when my Eve, she get a knowin', it come to pass." On another low chuckle, June added, "I sure be glad you born wif a veil ober yo' face, wife. Sometime it be mighty good to know ahead of somepin happenin', but June, he be glad dey ain't nuffin ober dat face now." He held her to him, his big, wide hand caressing her back. "It be too fine to see plain de face I love. Oh, Eve, you got de face I love. . . ."

Chapter 15

BIG BOY HAD ALWAYS RIDDEN ALONG WITH ANNE, turning in his saddle now and then to lift his giant hand in assurance that all was well. Today, though, the huge, gentle Ebo was fishing with Anne's girls, and part of her, at least, was glad for the solitary gallop on Gentleman in and out of the shadows cast by a clear February winter sun. On this spur-of-the-moment visit from Hopeton to the Village, Frances Anne's family home, Anne felt little of her usual dread. Oh, she knew poor Mrs. Wylly would be as pathetic as she had been for the months of what must surely be her final illness, but the compulsion to have a good talk with Frances had grown until Anne was almost excited to be going.

Even if Frances Anne's mood was as dark as the last time, Anne felt somehow that today she would be able to help. With no concrete reason, she also felt Frances Anne might help her. There probably wasn't a part of the coast between St. Simons and Savannah Frances hadn't scoured for a home of her own once she decided she could never again live in the Darien house without her husband, Dr. William Fraser. Of course, Anne could probably afford only to rent, not buy, but at last she was ready to talk about it.

When Anne reined Gentleman off the Couper Road and into the leaf-shadowed lane that led back to the Wylly house, into her mind flashed the always painful memory of the day she had been forced, because of a shortage of money, to sell John's splendid mare, Ginger. The memory of seeing a mere acquaintance of her father's ride out of sight on the horse that had carried her late husband so faithfully still brought a rush of pain. More pain than on the day she'd had to leave her own horse, Gentleman, in her brother William Audley's care at Hamilton.

But the first glimpse of Frances Anne's younger sister, Heriot, cutting huge, pink camellia blossoms from the garden, helped dim the pain. Any encounter with the oddly attractive, but strange, young woman no one was quite ready to call crazy, but who was inevitably unpredictable, required concentration. Anne liked her. John especially had been downright fond of Heriot and said again and again that the girl merely saw things from a different angle than did most people.

Without doubt, Heriot could hear Gentleman's trot along the lane toward her home, but as always, she pretended she didn't. She stood straight in a narrow path between the lush, dark green foliage of the camellias, peering intently into the sheer beauty of one huge blossom she held in her hand instead of dropping it into the basket on the ground beside her.

"I thought I'd just take this one separately—not include it in the camellia chain I'm making to hang around my mother's neck," Heriot said as Anne reined Gentleman to a stop on the lane nearby. The tone of Heriot's voice, that she went right on looking into the fresh, velvety beauty of the flower as though she and Anne had, together, been talking and already enjoying the winter flowers, in no way surprised Anne. It was simply Heriot Wylly being herself.

"So, you're making a camellia chain for your mother, eh?" Anne asked, still mounted on Gentleman. "Does she feel better today? Well enough to enjoy such a breathtaking gift?"

"Oh, only Mama knows how she feels, of course," Heriot said, counting the blooms in the basket with the free hand not holding the prize specimen. "I just take something from outside to her every day, Miss Anne. And by the way, I think I'll stop calling you *Miss* Anne, since come April 1, I'll be forty-two years of age. Mama taught us always to call our elders Miss, but forty-two is a mature age. I'll be calling you Anne from now on."

On a slight laugh, Anne said, "Fine, Heriot. That way I don't feel so ancient. Is Frances Anne with Mrs. Wylly upstairs?"

"Oh, I've been outside with my posies for more than an hour. I really don't know where Frances is, but definitely in the house—shut away from the real world—tending poor Mama's every need and complaint. Isn't it sad to see the way Mama looks now? I don't allow it to bother me too much, though, because I go on seeing her as she's always been. The most stately and lovely woman I ever saw. Even when she turned seventy and seventy-five, I still saw her as elegant, dressed in the same style black silk gown my father adored on her. Do you remember? Black silk with a kerchief of the snowiest cambric crossed over her breast. Her white, white hair, long and thick, coiled about her beautifully shaped head and topped with a cap of wide lapels. She was dignity itself and all of us held her in the utmost respect."

"I do remember, Heriot. No one could forget Margaret Wylly, your wellborn mother—British to the core."

Heriot laughed. "I'm an American and proud of it, but my mother never forgave the Americans for winning independence from the British Crown. If she could get downstairs now, she'd still be showing us all the portraits of Nelson and Wellington in our drawing room, declaring them 'the greatest men of the nineteenth century.' "

"Even in her present state of such dreadful illness, she's still 'the lady of the manor.' It will be all right, won't it, if I ride up to the house? I do want to talk with Frances."

"That's good, because she's so bowed down these days. I doubt you can talk with Mama, but Frances Anne? Yes."

AS ANNE DISMOUNTED AND HANDED GENTLEMAN OVER TO ONE of the Wylly groomsmen, Frances Anne appeared on the front ve-randa, seeming not even to notice that her other sister, Margaret

Matilda, was sitting in one corner of the shaded porch. As usual, Matilda was peering through her telescope toward Frederica Road, hoping against hope to glimpse someone—anyone—riding by. Anne knew this was Matilda's favorite way to pass her time and that she frowned on being interrupted, so with only a cheerful wave, she hurried to embrace Frances.

"Oh, Anne, how good to see you!" Frances said with a smile that seemed not even to lessen the almost permanent furrows in her brow. "I'm starving for conversation and it is a relief not to have to explain either Matilda or Heriot to a caller."

"I hope I'm not just a caller, Frances Anne."

"Far from it. But let's go inside. Heriot and Matilda don't seem to notice there's a chill in the air today. I'm sure one of our people has laid a fire in the drawing room."

Seated across from each other beneath the famous portraits of Nelson and Wellington, the two women, after one of the expertly trained Wylly women served them tea, just sat looking at the fire for a moment. Then Anne asked, "Your mother, Frances. Is she all right without you for an hour or so? I do long to talk."

Frances Anne shrugged. "I wish I thought the poor dear lady might be left to rest for an hour, Anne. But I know what Heriot's doing out in the camellia bed."

"She's busily gathering blossoms for a camellia chain to hang around your mother's neck, she says."

"How well I know what she's doing! Poor Mama. Such an offering scratches her thin, tender old skin, and yet she goes right on being kind and gracious to Heriot. She'll vow deep gratitude and endure the scratching until Heriot wanders back outside again." Frances set her teacup on the table beside her chair. "Anne, I'm *so* glad to see you! We haven't seen each other in over two weeks and—" Unable to finish her sentence, Anne's sister-in-law began to weep.

On impulse, Anne started to jump to her feet, then sat down. "You—you probably need to do exactly what you can't help doing this minute," she said. "There are times when the load grows so heavy, only the relief of tears helps at all. You know I understand that. Pay no mind to me—unless you'd like me to hold you while you cry."

Stiff and straight in her chair, Frances Anne's whole body showed the struggle against more tears to be painful. "I dare not let myself weep, Anne," she said, taking out a handkerchief. "Mama always knows and it agitates her terribly. She feels so guilty anyway. Feels she's a burden to me because she knows Heriot and Matilda never really learned how to be responsible."

"Perhaps they both know—in their own ways. Matilda's very good with the meals. She runs a splendid household. Heriot does what she believes in doing."

"Doesn't she though? You've always been so kind to Heriot, Anne. I'm grateful for that. I love her very much. I don't understand her at all, but I do love her."

" 'Heriot understands herself,' John used to say. Perhaps that's what matters. Wherever it is that Heriot lives her interior life, she knows it well. Is at home in it. John was fond of her."

"I know. So was my William." After blowing her nose and drying tears from her cheeks, Frances Anne asked, "Will we—you and I—ever learn how to live without the Fraser brothers, Anne?"

"No. If you mean will we ever be the same women we were when we had them with us, no, we won't be. But do you remember the times I've told you what Miss Eliza Mackay explained to me when she lost her handsome, dashing Robert Mackay so long ago?"

"I remember your telling me, but tell me again, please. I'm so tired physically, I guess, I don't think very straight. Would you please tell me once more?"

"As with most things in Miss Eliza's life, this is not easy, but it is simple. I can still see the way she looked at me when she said, 'Anne, I began to have some hope for myself the day I saw for the first time that I could live the remainder of my life without Robert *only*—only if I lived each day as though I were living the *second half of my married life.*' Those may not be her exact words, but I could tell it was a credo with her. She knew she'd never love another man as she loved Robert Mackay. You know you'll never love another man the way you loved William. I know I'll never love any man but John. Living through all the dreadful adjustments—all the fresh waves of missing the little and big things—seems somehow possible as long as we're doing it as the second half of the great adventures we shared with them. I can't explain it. Neither could Miss Eliza, but Frances, it's true. Making our way through each day, even by means of this seemingly thin connection with William and John, is possible. It *is* the second half of our married lives. There's a connection still there. In however nebulous a way, there's still a connection with them."

As though a tight cord had loosed at least a little, Anne could see Frances's weary body sag against her chair back. "Yes. I—I'll try this time to remember what Miss Eliza said." After a long moment spent staring into the snapping fire, Frances added, "You know I want terribly to sell the Darien house."

"John Couper told me you were trying to when he was at Hopeton at Christmas."

"Our lives run parallel in a lot of ways, don't they? You know I care so deeply about my older son, James. You also know I depend on Menzies above everyone else on earth now that his father's gone."

"As I depend on John Couper. Do we lean too hard, do you think?"

"I don't know. But doesn't each bring out dependence in us? Were there ever two boys like Menzies and John Couper, Anne?"

With an almost sad smile, Anne said, "I don't think so. Do—do you see James often? I know he's at sea now, but when he's here on the Island staying with the Ben Caters, does he ride up here often? Am I being nosy?"

"Certainly not. Except for Menzies, who sometimes seems a thousand miles away up in north Georgia at his Marietta school, you're the person closest to me, Anne. Ask me anything, only don't expect satisfactory answers all the time because I'm afraid I know very few answers myself these days. It's ghastly watching one's own once magnificent mother—die. I know your father's nearly ninety-one, but at least he can talk with you when you're together." She paused. "But isn't it dreadful having no home to run to?"

Anne shuddered. "That's almost the worst part of all. I honestly don't know how you endure watching your dear mother worsen every day, but it would help so much if you just had your own home to go to now and then. And Frances, you've looked and looked for a house!"

"I know. I don't know that I would realize it if I *had* found my place by now, though. Anne, I know you asked how much I see of James. I didn't answer. He rides up off and on when he's in port, but even when we're in a room together, we aren't—together. Menzies is more like William each time I see him. They're the same build and height, same manners—all gentility, sensitive to my every thought. And like William, Menzies seems to have nothing to prove. James, on the other hand, is—well, even if I am his mother, I can tell you the boy's almost crude at times. I'm sure you've heard that."

Anne said nothing.

"I've tried to tell myself he takes after his Grandfather Fraser, merely a little hard-shelled, uncommunicative. I honestly don't know why the boy seems so set on *pushing* his way through this life instead of making some small effort to get into the rhythm of it. Menzies was born knowing. I don't love Menzies more. I just know where I stand with him."

For a time, both women sat in silence, looking at the fire. Finally, Anne said, "Frances, I don't think either of us is going to find anything resembling contentment until we find homes of our own. My blessed papa can't be with us much longer. Nor can your mother. I'm so lost at times I—I've even dared to think I might do something I never, never believed I'd even think about."

"Anne! What are you saying?"

"Have you thought we might both get a fresh beginning if we left our lifetime sanctuaries here on St. Simons Island and started all over again in a new place?"

Frances stared at her, then said, "I—don't know! Darien was fine, but it was fine because William was there. Are you—are you financially able to leave the area, Anne?"

"No," she said almost lightly. "I'm certainly not financially able to do anything but accept charity from friends and relations, but lately it doesn't keep me from dreaming. When does Menzies finish at Reverend White's school in Marietta? How long will he be up there?"

"Another year. Marietta must be an almost heavenly climate and they tell me the scenery is breathtaking. I suppose you've decided you and I should move to Marietta! Wouldn't that be awfully far from John Couper?"

Now they both managed a laugh. "I haven't decided anything, but doesn't it sound exciting—even daring to do a little dreaming? Do you think our children aren't going to have homes and families of their own one day? Isn't it time you and I began to get acquainted with—ourselves? As women? As women alone in the world who need desperately to be closely acquainted with someone? Isn't it rather exciting, if slightly crazy, to dare to think that you and I could find a way to dig ourselves out of the holes we're in?"

"But Anne, widows just don't pull up roots and leave their families, do they?"

"Who said anything about leaving our families? You couldn't make it without at least an occasional visit with Menzies! I'd never make it without seeing John Couper now and then. Other families separate sometimes, but people visit each other, Frances, and write letters. When John Couper was with me at Christmas, he vowed that he and I would find a way to free me of being a rootless vagabond. Those were his very words, and Frances, I believe the boy."

"Oh, I know you do. I do too. And Anne, thanks for your plucky attempt to cheer me a little today. I really can't think straight, though. With Mama so ill, needing so much care, I guess I simply get up in the morning praying for enough grace to push me through one day at a time. You did make me laugh a little and for that I'm grateful. You and your wild ideas of our leaving St. Simons!"

"Did I go too far? I know I'm changing some. Eve notices too, but I do wonder if I'm changing in the right direction? We both have heavy family responsibilities now. Papa can no longer walk more than a few feet across his bedroom even with help from Johnson. Your mother has been bedfast for weeks. Still, we do have time to think things through."

Frances gave her a quizzical look, as though taking her seriously for the first time. "Anne, you're not just chattering, are you? You're not just trying to cheer me up."

"I don't know the answer to that any more than you do. I'm sure of only one thing and that is my need to stay near Papa as long as I have him. Dr. Holmes says he could last another year or he could be gone within weeks, even days. And here I am all the way over here on St. Simons, not knowing!" She paused. "Do you sometimes seem to hit peaks and valleys, Frances? I mean, does hope come to all of us in little spurts, do you suppose? I had myself really hoping—dreaming—a few minutes ago. Now I'm suddenly half sick with worry over Papa."

Chapter 16

WHEN MARCH FIRST ROLLED AROUND, ANNE called her three girls to her room at Hopeton for a little talk. Pete, as usual, had already guessed her reason.

"In nine days Grandpapa will be ninety-one," Pete said.

"But he's too sick, I think," Selina said, "for another big birthday party."

"Yes," Anne said. "But we'll make Grandpapa's heart feel fine just because he'll be able to see us all on his birthday."

"Mama," Selina said out of the blue, "John Couper told me we'd have our own home again someday."

Surprised, Anne asked, "John Couper told *you* that, too, Selina?"

"Yes, Mama. He said he thought a little girl my age needed to be sure she'd have a home of her own again someday. What does being thirteen have to do with it?" Selina wanted to know. "I'd be happy if we had a home again even if I was an old woman like Fanny or Pete!"

Anne laughed softly. "Or an ancient woman like your mother."

"I certainly do have a wise brother, don't I?" Pete asked with a grin.

"Me too," Selina piped.

"Don't you think you also have a wise brother, Fanny?" Anne asked her middle daughter.

"Yes, ma'am," Fanny said. "If John Couper doesn't think he'll get Selina's hopes too high. Is there something happening we don't know about, Mama? Do you and John Couper know something you haven't thought it's wise to tell us yet? Even Pete?"

"We don't know anything at all definite," Anne said, a slight frown creasing her forehead, "but your brother has started me dreaming again. He has a way of instilling faith in me. At times even enough faith to believe we just might have a place we can call our home again."

"Mama? I certainly do like it when we have meetings like this with nobody here but—us," Selina said.

"So do I," Anne whispered, untangling one of Selina's long, thick, dark curls. "And we'll have other meetings, dear. Lots of them. Right now, I need to have a meeting with Eve. Send her up here, please?"

"Which means," Pete muttered, "that we, dear Sisters, are being dismissed. Eve hopes we have a place of our own someday, too. She told me yesterday she'd be happy anywhere if June was there. Mama, why do you suppose we never think about whether the colored might be in love with each other, like other people?"

"For goodness' sake, Pete," Selina said with emphasis. "I never thought about it at all until this minute!"

"And it isn't going to be the subject of another meeting because I know you're stalling, Eena."

"Sometimes I think about the times you and Pete told me my papa often called me Eena," the girl said.

Anne hugged her youngest daughter, who remembered so little about John. "He certainly did call you Eena, child. But if he were here with us now, he'd be suggesting in no uncertain terms that you quit thinking up ways to extend our meeting and bring Eve to me. I need to talk to her. I do have Grandpapa Couper on my mind."

"Do you think he's—dying, Mama?" Selina asked.

"No, I don't think that at all. I just know we're going to be with him when he turns ninety-one, and this is the very last time I'm going to tell you to send Eve to me. Now, scoot, all of you."

A FEW MINUTES LATER, WHEN EVE SLIPPED QUIETLY INTO THE Hopeton bedroom Anne shared with Pete, Anne thought she looked worried.

"You're here," Anne said. "And is that a frown on your face? Did Selina blab to you about why I sent for you?"

"She jus' tell me you worried 'bout Mausa Couper cause it be nearly his ninety-first birthday."

"Eve, pull up that rocker and sit down with me a minute."

"Eve sit down to talk to you, Miss Anne?"

"Yes. What's so strange about that? I need to ask you something important."

"Yes'm."

"This is no time for a noncommittal yes'm. Don't just stand there. Sit down with me."

Not quite certain that this, after all the years they'd been together, was the first time she'd ever asked Eve to sit down, Anne was determined not to allow Eve to dwell on it—one way or another. "What else did Selina tell you?"

"Nuffin. But I woke up with a new knowin' dis mornin'."

"And what, pray tell, is it that you 'know' now?"

"Eve got a knowin' that your heart be heavy over Mausa Couper."

"You agree, I'm sure, that Papa will want all the family he has left to be right with him on his ninety-first birthday. It—it could be his last one, Eve."

Eve nodded agreement.

"I wanted to see you alone because I have an important question to ask you. How can you be so sure when you have a *knowing* that it's really true? Don't you ever wish for something so hard that it might just seem like a knowing?"

"Oh, yes'm. But dem times I find out it wasn't a knowin' 'cause dem times it don' come true."

"Isn't there any other way you can tell?"

"Why you axin' me dis?"

"I'm just asking because I want to be sure. Isn't there ever a time when you know something so surely that you have a—sign of some sort?"

"Oh, yes'm. When it be true, I feels it in my blood and also in my bones."

"I don't call that a very clear answer, do you?"

"How you gonna git closer to yourself than yo' blood an' bones?" After waiting for an answer from Anne that didn't come, Eve asked, "You got a knowin' 'bout yo' papa, Miss Anne? You ain't neber had no caul ober yo' face, has you?"

"No, and that's why I'm pinning you down this way. I need to know if I'm just so scared my father's going to die soon, I only imagine that I—I *know* one way or another." When Eve said nothing, Anne pressed her. "Can't you tell me something to help me?"

"Not wifout you bein' borned wif a caul."

"Have you had any kind of knowing about my papa? Does your blood or your bones give you even a hint about him?"

"Miss Anne, you is changin'. Dat's fo' sure!"

"Why do you say a thing like that?"

Eve's grin was sly. " 'Cause it not be like you to ax me somepin you admit not to know yo'self."

"Is that really true? If it is, I'm ashamed of myself, but I've asked you now and I beg you for an answer. Do you have a knowing about my father?"

"No'm."

Without meaning to, Anne brightened a little. "You don't? Do you think that means we'll have the sweet old darling around yet awhile, trying to keep us all cheered up?"

"Only de Lawd, He knows a thing like dat, Miss Anne. Sometime a body as old as Mausa Couper's, it gonna wear out."

Anne let herself fall back in her rocker. "Eve, Eve, you are an enigma."

"What be a 'nigma, Miss Anne?"

"In your case it merely means there's no explaining you to any-one, certainly not to me. I did ask an impossible thing of you, though, didn't I? And you could have said 'what is an *enigma*' instead of 'what be a 'nigma.' "

Now they both laughed. "Yes'm, I coulda said that."

When Anne got up, Eve jumped to her feet and laid one hand on Anne's hand already extended to her.

"We are friends, Eve. Could I thank you for that?"

On another musical laugh, Eve said, "You kin eben thank me fo' breathin' if you feel like it, Miss Anne."

Chapter 17

Two full days before Papa's ninety-first birthday on March 9, no plans for any kind of celebration were under way. Anne had only to look at the wasted old body to know her papa would never leave his bed again, but still he tried to greet her with a weakly lifted hand, a crooked smile, and a hoarse, effort-filled whisper of her name.

"Annie, beloved Annie. You're here this morning —in time."

For Anne, no words came at first. She could only sit on the side of his old bed, which James Hamilton had moved from Cannon's Point to the large, sunny room where his father would sleep once it had been decided, right after Mama died, that the old gentleman could never again preside as master of his beloved St. Simons home on the banks of the Hampton River. "He'll be far more comfortable in his own bed," James Hamilton had told Anne then. "We all intend to make his time with us as good as possible with our mother gone."

Kind, good, stuffy James Hamilton, Anne thought as she kept stroking Papa's thin, brown-spotted hand, its dark blue veins so visible there seemed to be no skin over them. Would she ever be able to share the easy, tender affection with her brother that she sensed so clearly, even back then, between her son, John

Couper, and all three of his living sisters? She pushed back the thought. She did know James Hamilton's kind heart and she trusted it. Such almost irrelevant musings were only an excuse to avoid facing what she saw so starkly in her papa's pale, shrunken features.

He was leaving her. Papa, who had always been there, eager to give her his strength, his worldly goods, his laughter, his heart, *was leaving her.*

"Oh, Papa," she said desperately, "you know, don't you, that every minute with you is a treasure to me?"

"Aye, lass," he whispered. "Aye. I've always known about you, my Annie. And"—his faded blue eyes brightened a bit—"dare we hope your fine son will surprise us again this year for my birthday?"

John Couper! She must write to her son at once. The instant she could leave Papa. John Couper would never forgive himself if he didn't reach Hopeton in time. *In time?* This must not be! She re-worded the terrifying thought: John Couper must reach Hopeton in time for Papa's birthday on March 9.

"Annie—Annie." His halting speech was so weak, so feeble, she leaned down nearer his mouth.

"What is it, Papa? I'm right here holding your hand."

"You must find—your own home, gir-rl," he said weakly, but with an authority she'd seldom heard in his natural voice. Papa seemed almost to be ordering her. "And—never stop—dreaming. I dreamed—as a boy back in Scotland. Dreams need wor-rk to come true. They also need—daring. Dare, Annie, lass. And I promise to talk it all over with your John, when I get to where the lad is."

"Papa!"

The barest smile lit his thin face. "John and I always did enjoy —conferring. We'll confer about your own home. And, Annie, you can also count on my namesake, John Couper."

"Did he tell you at Christmas when he was here that he vows he and I will find a place for me that's mine?"

A steady peace almost eased his speech, an unexpected, odd certainty. "No. He did not. But at my time of life, a mon knows."

The skeletal hand to which she clung seemed suddenly to drop, to grow heavy. Peering at his face, she saw him frown. He was struggling with that hand, but not a muscle moved.

"Papa!"

The sunken, nearly toothless mouth fell open.

"Papa!"

Not a word passed his helpless lips. He could no longer speak.

As Anne dashed from the room, faithful Johnson rushed in to be with his master. Anne hurried to find James Hamilton.

OFF AND ON THROUGH THE ENTIRE DAY OF MARCH 9, JOCK Couper's ninety-first birthday, one after another of Anne's girls and each of James Hamilton's children except Alexander and Hamilton, who were away at school, went to their grandfather's bedside to mumble or hurry through some kind of birthday greetings.

"He may not even know they're in the room. He may not even know when you go in, Pete," Anne said to her eldest daughter, "but Dr. Holmes says there's a chance he can hear and still think."

"Fanny swears he can hear us, Mama," Pete assured her mother as they both stood waiting in the hall outside the sickroom. "You know Fanny loves the whole idea of nursing, and she's read a lot of books about people who've had an apoplectic seizure. Grandpapa is partly paralyzed, we know that. He may never talk again, but he just may hear what we say."

"Don't you dare even mention that he won't be able to talk to us again, do you hear me?"

"All right," Pete said in a tone of voice she might have used to a child. "I won't mention it again. But I think it will help you to know that I'm practically inside every thought you have right now, Mama. It's downright scary even to think your father may die. Don't forget, I know how that is, even though I was a lot younger when we lost Papa."

Anne's eyes shot her daughter an almost angry look. How, at a time like this, could Pete even think of bringing up such a thing? And then she reached for the girl's hand. "I'm sorry, but for a second I wanted to smack you. You're right to remind me, though. Of course you know every dread, every thought I'm having. I needed you to say that. Thank you, Pete. I'm trying."

DAY DRAGGED AFTER DAY WITH NO CHANGE IN PAPA'S CONDI-tion. He ate nothing, spoke not one word, moved no part of his body. But thanks to Johnson—himself surely well into his eighties now, Anne thought—Papa was never left alone. When Johnson slept some at night, Pete or Fanny or Anne or Caroline Couper took up a watch by the bedside. Each watcher did his or her best to speak words of comfort or cheer. Sometimes someone just told a joke or repeated any phrase that might grab his attention if, indeed, normally communicative Jock Couper could hear and understand.

Anne slept little but was seldom alone either in her father's room or just outside in the upstairs hall. In a chair pulled up beside Anne's favorite little rocker, brought over from Lawrence when she and her family moved into Hopeton, Eve usually sat beside her, leaving only long enough to bring food and a hot drink for them both. A pattern began to form as the hours wore on through each day and night. When someone left the sickroom, it became only natural to stop long enough by Anne's rocker to tell her what had been said to her father. To shake his or her head sadly in answer to the question in Anne's eyes. Papa had shown no sign of hearing.

"I told Grandpapa about my new litter of rabbits," Fanny said, "and how I'd nursed the scrub of the litter back to health. That I weighed the little fellow this morning and he'd gained half a pound!"

Even young Rebecca Isabella Couper, James Hamilton's daughter, who grew prettier every day, stopped to tell Anne that she had talked and talked about the shared birthday party when she and her grandpapa laughed so much last year the day he turned ninety and she turned six, old enough to eat at the adult table for the first time. "I thought once he might be going to smile," the child said wearily, "but he was just trying to wipe away some spit from the corner of his old mouth. I wiped it away for him, Aunt Anne."

"I'm sure he appreciated that," Anne said, her mind dipping back to Frances Anne's sadness and humiliation for her own ill mother, forced by age and sickness to be stripped of the dignity that had always been hers.

"We try to keep her hair brushed and pinned up a little," Frances Anne had said as tears stood in her eyes, and she shuddered at the way her mother's once perfectly coiffed hair merely hung these days, long and stringy, needing desperately to be washed if anyone had dared try, given her condition.

"I read to Grandpapa," Pete said on Thursday, March 21. "He always liked to hear me read Robert Burns's poetry. I'm not too good with a Scottish brogue, but I tried. One good thing I told him over and over is that his very own namesake, John Couper, will be here from Savannah tomorrow."

"Yes, yes," Anne breathed. "Everything's bound to be better once your brother reaches Hopeton. I've longed for him every minute of our dreadful vigil, haven't you, Pete?"

"Yep. I do my best to be the strong one, Mama, and most of the time I'm fairly satisfied with the way I act, but I know no one helps you the way John Couper does just by being where you can look at him."

"He's my only son."

"Don't worry, I'm not a bit jealous. I did my best, but being a tomboy was as far as I could go."

Anne smiled in response and patted Pete's hand. "I couldn't have gotten through these days without you, Rebecca."

"Well! You called me Rebecca and this time I know you aren't cross with me." Pete laughed. "Mama, I also know I said 'yep' a minute ago and I'm sorry."

"Don't be. It sounded good—and daily. Normal. I find I'm reaching for anything that smacks of the normal these days."

"I don't suppose Dr. Holmes has said anything about how long Grandpapa could just lie there in his coma."

"Not a word. He's a fine doctor, but doctors know only so

much. I wish I had even a hint, though. I'm sure that in his highly responsible position with Mr. McCleskey, John Couper will need to know when he'll be free to return to Savannah. Today is March 21, isn't it?"

"Yep."

Anne gave her red-haired daughter another smile. "I rather like it when you say 'yep' today."

Chapter 18

JOHN COUPER ARRIVED AT HOPETON JUST BEFORE dark the next day, March 22, and for the first time since her father's apoplectic seizure, Anne slept through the night. The boy's very presence under the same roof with her was a balm she would never try to explain even to herself.

As always after a sleep of twenty minutes, an hour, or blessedly now, a night's sleep of six hours, the first face Anne inevitably saw was Eve's. This morning her servant-friend looked so exhausted, so sleepy, Anne sat up quickly in the bed.

"Eve! You haven't slept a wink, have you?"

"No'm, but I feels triumphant 'cause you sure did sleep, Miss Anne. Don' you worry none about Eve. An' before you have to ax, I tell you, Mausa Couper, he be just the same."

"Hasn't said a word, I guess," Anne murmured almost to herself as Eve helped her into a warm robe.

"No'm. Jus' layin' there. John Couper, our boy, he still asleep, I guess. Nothin' would do but he sit beside his grandpapa till past midnight. Johnson run him off to bed."

"Oh, Eve, Eve, help me to dream again. I was

actually beginning to believe—and that's the start of a real dream—that soon we'd have a place of our own."

"We *gonna* hab a place ob our own, Miss Anne. John Couper he tol' me too las' night after you went to bed."

Anne brightened. "He did? He told you too?"

"Ain't got nuffin in sight yet, but eber time I sees dat boy, I sees better why he lif' yo' heart the way he do."

"The way he does," Anne corrected her.

"Yes'm. Jus' befo' you open yo' eyes, Eve hear one ob de Hopeton people set down hot water fo' yo' bath. It be right outside de door. I knows you be itchin' to get in to yo' papa."

While Eve went for the bucket of hot water to slosh into cold already in the washbowl, Anne wondered where Pete slept last night. She had no memory of her daughter's crawling into bed beside her, and only one side of the bed looked slept in.

"Where did Pete sleep, Eve?"

Busy warming the icy water for Anne's sponge bath, Eve said, "She mighta doze some in a chair, but she stay right wif John Couper till after midnight 'longside yo' papa, and de las' I seen her when I leabes to go wif June to our side ob de cabin Mausa James Hamilton let us use, Pete, she be scratchin' away on a piece of paper downstairs in de parlor. Writin' a letter to somebody, I reckon."

"I suppose, but I wonder who? She must be exhausted, too."

DR. HOLMES REACHED HOPETON BY BOAT FROM DARIEN IN THE early afternoon of the next day, Saturday, March 23. Fanny, because she was so good at nursing the sick, whether it was an injured bird or an ill person, was inside the sickroom with the doctor and the ever-faithful Johnson, who hadn't left his master in two whole days and nights.

"I guess we'll know something soon," Anne said, her voice both nervous and weary. "It's good Fanny's the way she is with the sick, isn't it?"

"Fanny has a lot inside her she doesn't show often," John Couper said. "In her quiet way, she's always been devoted to Grandpapa."

"Do you know anyone who isn't?" Pete wanted to know. "I almost envy Fanny, getting to be in there. Just waiting is ghastly."

For a time they stood outside in the hall. John Couper held Anne's hand, trying as always to give her some of his young strength.

Finally, Pete asked, "Mama, can you close your eyes and picture Grandpapa the way he used to be? Tall, broad-shouldered, handsome, red-haired like me, laughing."

"What, Pete?"

"Where are you, Mama?" John Couper asked with a tender, half-teasing smile. His father's smile.

"Where—am I? Halfway between here and nowhere, I guess," Anne murmured, trying to return his smile. "I heard most of what you said, Pete, dear. I work hard trying to remember Papa as I've always known him. It helps some. But will it help once he's gone forever?"

"Try not to think that way, Mama," John Couper said. "Don't you remember when Grandpapa made that little speech at his ninetieth birthday last March? He seemed sure that my father, Annie, Aunt Isabella, and Grandmama were somehow right there with us. He will be, too, for as long as we all live. It sounds a little weird when I say it, but it didn't sound that way when Grandpapa told us. I believed it then. I believe it now, too. In a way we can't understand, his spirit will still be with us."

"I know what you mean to be doing for Mama, John Couper," Pete said firmly, her words even more direct than usual. "You're trying to help her by telling her not to think of Grandpapa as being gone forever. But he's going to be out of our sight, so we won't be able to hear his voice again. That's what Mama's thinking about— not things like spirits. Mama, all of us will just have to work our way to the place where concepts like heaven help us. Mama's worried about—now. The first empty days."

Anne felt her heart sink. "Pete! Pete, are you saying you don't believe your Grandpapa will know about us all down here once he's in heaven? Darling, sometimes I wonder about your faith."

"That's silly, Mama," Pete almost snapped at her. "Of course I believe what Grandpapa said in his little speech, but I also believe in seeing things as they really are—*now*. It isn't going to help any of us when our friends and relatives come up to us in Christ Churchyard and try to comfort us by saying what a long, full, happy life he had! It doesn't help me at all that he's ninety-one years old. I'll miss him because he's—my grandpapa."

Before anyone could answer Pete or even express an opinion, the sickroom door opened and Fanny slipped into their grieving little group.

"Fanny," Anne gasped. "Is—is there any change?"

"No, Mama. No change. But Dr. Holmes wants me to tell you he'll be staying all night. He also said there's only prayer now. And Johnson said he wants us all to know he's praying right along with Dr. Holmes."

"If there's nothing else that can be done for him, why is Dr. Holmes spending the night?" Pete asked, her voice too loud. Then she quickly added, "Oh, Mama, forgive me! I—I blurted, didn't I?"

"Yes, dear, you did. But we each have our own way of reacting at a time like this. We all know what you meant."

"Dr. Holmes says Grandpapa's already—partly there," Fanny said. "In a way, I think, he's waiting, too. We all know how he longs to see Grandmama again. Jesus said we'd all be together with Him someday. Aunt Isabella's sweet husband, Theodore, told me, just before he went up North to live, that we could count on every word Jesus said while He was still on earth. Jesus told His disciples that wherever He went, they would eventually go too. It's right in the Bible: '. . . where I am, there ye may be also.' We all know Jesus wouldn't fib to us."

For a moment no one said a word. Finally Anne saw a sweet

smile light John Couper's face as he looked in some wonder at his usually shy, quiet sister Fanny. But the boy said nothing. Pete was not smiling. Like John Couper, though, she was staring at her sister, who had always done most of her talking inside herself.

As always, Pete could remain silent only so long. For a moment it was as though they were all waiting for whatever she might think to say.

What Pete said was, "You've got a smile on your face, John Couper, but I don't really believe you're laughing at Fanny."

"Far from it," he said softly, his face still glowing. "I'm too grateful to her for that. Thanks, dear Fanny. I'm in awe of what you just said to us."

"Yeah," Pete murmured, tears standing in her blue eyes. "I'm in awe of what you said, too, Sister."

Again there was silence. Then Anne, arms outstretched to her son and her two older daughters, embraced them all warmly, held them to her for a long time. "Thank you, Fanny. Thank you too, Pete, for being exactly as you are. And I thank you, John Couper, for being my son. I know your father's proud of all of you." Tears streamed down her face, but she found a smile. "I'm proud of you, too." She lifted Fanny's face, plain, tear-streaked, but radiant. "I'm especially proud of you, Fanny. And ever so grateful."

John Couper leaned down to kiss Fanny's forehead. "And, little Sister, so is your only brother."

IN A BRIEF VISIT TO HER FATHER'S SICKBED, DURING WHICH EVEN Johnson and Dr. Holmes left her alone with the dying man who had symbolized safety and love through all the days of Anne's life, she kissed his dry, motionless face and told him she loved him, then whispered, "You'll be right with God, Papa, so talk to Him about all of us. Keep Him reminded of us all trying to learn to live without you. Tell Him we do so want you and John and Mama and

Annie and Isabella to be proud of the way we're living, wherever we'll be on this old earth."

For a moment she could only stand there, choking back sobs. Then, despite the odd, unfamiliar way his mouth pulled back at one corner, she saw real peace on his face and made herself give Papa one last smile. "None of it is going to be—easy," she whispered. "You and I never marched in a storm as fierce as the one we're all facing now—without you to hold us."

DAWN HAD NOT QUITE PUSHED AWAY ALL THE DARKNESS WHEN Anne felt Pete's firm hand on her shoulder. The girl shook her lightly, but there was no need.

"Mama? Oh, you're awake."

"Yes, for most of the night. Where did you sleep, Pete?"

"I didn't. Uncle James Hamilton needed me."

"What?"

"I know he seems not to need people much because he's always so in charge, but Mama, Grandpapa is gone!"

The little cry Anne gave came from so deep inside her, it was barely audible.

"I found Uncle James sitting on the bare floor right outside Grandpapa's closed door—all by himself. He even let Johnson show Dr. Holmes out. I don't know how long Uncle James had been sitting there in a heap like that, but he was crying. Sobbing. I know I embarrassed him by just being there, and because I never saw him out of control before in my whole life, I was embarrassed to try to help him."

For a time Anne just lay there, looking up at her daughter in the coming daylight. Then she asked, "Who was—with Papa?"

"Uncle James, Dr. Holmes, and Johnson, of course."

"Of course, Johnson," Anne said in barely a whisper. "Was it—easy? Did Papa have an easy death?"

"Uncle James said he just took a deep breath and—yes. The old darling has been close, for days."

Anne glanced at the spring sunlight showing now around the heavy winter curtains. "This is just about the time Papa woke up every morning in the old days. I wonder what he's waking up to—now?"

"I felt so sorry for Uncle James, Mama. Somehow sorrier for him than I might have if he hadn't always been so—so strong and strict."

"I know, Pete. It's hard on a man to be caught crying. What did you say to him?"

"I can't remember what I said. I know I just sat down on the floor beside him and hugged him hard. He—he hugged me back, too."

"He did? Oh, that's good, isn't it?"

"He kept telling me that you and Fanny and Selina and I never need to worry about a place to live. That Hopeton's our home from now on."

Anne said nothing.

"It's good of him, but it doesn't help much, does it, Mama?"

"We don't have to think about any of that today. I couldn't anyway. Oh, Pete, Pete, I've leaned on your grandfather every day of my life!"

"I know."

"He and I almost breathed together. No one but you and Eve and Fanny and John Couper really knew what happened to my heart when we had to leave Lawrence—except Papa. He gave that dear house to John and me and he—knew."

For long, long minutes, mother and daughter held on to each other and wept together. When at last Eve pulled open the thick curtains before trying to get them both to eat a little, even the clear, late March sunlight made little difference. Papa was gone and the world held only a giant shadow.

"Somepin gonna happen to help, Miss Anne," Eve said, her voice low and tender. "Eve not just sayin' that. You see. Maybe not today—maybe not even dis year—but somepin good gonna happen for you again. Ain't always gonna be so dark."

In a way even Anne could not have described to anyone, one

small thing that did help a little came to her notice when least expected: She looked up through her tears into Eve's creamy brown face and saw that her cheeks were also wet.

"You loved Papa, too, didn't you, Eve?" Anne asked.

"In their way, ain't nobody didn't take to Mausa Couper, Miss Anne."

PART III

September 1850–
January 1851

Chapter 19

IN SEPTEMBER 1850, THE YEAR ANNE'S FATHER died, her sisters-in-law, Frances Anne Wylly Fraser and Caroline Wylly Couper, lost their mother. Of course, Anne and her girls made the boat trip to St. Simons Island with James Hamilton and Caroline to attend the funeral of Mrs. Margaret Wylly at Christ Church. In a brief moment together following the burial, Anne promised Frances Anne to send her own daughter Fanny to spend time with the exhausted Wylly sisters at their St. Simons plantation within a week or so.

"That's so good of you, Anne, but I know how your heart breaks when you have to live apart from any of your family," Frances said as they stood together in the shell road in front of the tiny white church. "I also know something of what I have ahead of me and how much help she'll be, so I'm not going to refuse. Fanny must be head over heels with sewing for all of you, though. You need mourning clothes, too."

"So do you and your sisters," Anne said. "You'll see how fine a seamstress my Fanny really is. Just don't let her strain her eyes too much. Ever since that dreadful bout with measles the winter before John left us, her eyes have been weak." The two women embraced. "You can count on it. Fanny will be over here on the Island in just a few days from now."

"Thank you, thank you! But is there a chance you might come, too, for a good, long visit later this fall, Anne?"

"Yes. There's always a chance." Anne's laugh was halfhearted. "I'm homeless, remember? I feel my place is with dear Caroline at Hopeton for a few days. And with my brother. They have been so kind to us, and James Hamilton has somehow changed since we lost Papa. Of course, he's as proper and strict as ever, but he's also a very tender man. And Frances, I'm still dreaming for us both. For you and for me. Even though I do miss talking to Papa, I'm still believing that somehow, someday, you and I will find a way not to be homeless any longer. We need time together now, more than ever. I believe I'll try to come with Fanny."

FOR ANNE, THE WEEKS SHE AND FANNY SPENT AT THE VILLAGE on St. Simons with the Wylly girls were both sad and interesting. Her own grief over Papa was still fresh, so Anne inevitably felt the lostness and the sorrow of Frances Anne, Margaret Matilda, and Heriot. John, Anne knew, would have been more intrigued than ever by Heriot, who seemed to make the most creative use of her sadness. From morning till night she worked along with two Wylly gardeners, laying out new flower beds in memory of their late mother. Matilda wept almost steadily for the first few weeks and seemed able to dry her eyes only when infuriated enough that Heriot was "enjoying herself frittering with flowers—using Mama's death as an excuse."

"Don't try to make sense of what my sisters say to each other, Anne," Frances Anne warned after the first few arguments overheard from the new flower bed outside the dining-room windows. "Poor Matilda has never learned to accept Heriot as she is, and Heriot is convinced that Matilda's weeping is mainly an alibi for not helping set out new daisy plants. I just hope their bickering doesn't cause you and Fanny to flee St. Simons earlier than you'd planned."

"I hadn't really planned," Anne said. "I've long ago stopped such foolishness." Forcing a small laugh, she added, "These days, Frances Anne, I'm trying to learn to substitute dreaming for anything so definite as a plan."

"Do you realize you've never actually told me why Pete didn't come along with you?" Frances asked as the two friends sat on the Wylly veranda, working at the seemingly interminable task of taking hems out of the parlor draperies that shrank with a recent washing.

"I know," Anne said. "I think I'm a little embarrassed to tell you."

"Why on earth would you be embarrassed?"

"Because I'm all but sure I sent her on a wild-goose chase up to Liberty County."

"I know you and Pete exchanged several letters right after you arrived to spend this time with me, but what kind of wild-goose chase?"

"The girl is house hunting." Anne tossed a length of summer curtain to one side. "Frances Anne, I'm not at all sure how much longer I can go on living from pillar to post. I knew it would be worse with Papa gone, but I didn't, in my scariest nightmare, think it could be this hard!"

"Did you have a particular house in mind up there?"

"Not really. I acted on pure rumor that there just might be a decent cottage available on twenty acres near some of Mama's Maxwell relatives in Liberty County. So far, I haven't heard a word from her. Pete promised to write to me here at your place. Nothing."

For a time, neither woman spoke. Frances Anne went busily ahead picking at a curtain hem. Anne stared into the sun-dappled late November woods where the Wylly south fields, no longer being planted, were going to pines and gums and hickories.

Finally, Frances Anne said, "Heriot and Matilda can't go on here alone. Neither has the faintest idea how to manage crops, or people. Our young overseer is leaving after the cotton is picked next year. I've known things would come to this, but I confess I hadn't faced it. And my dependable brother John lies over there in the churchyard—unable to help, thanks to our neighbor Dr. Thomas F. Hazzard and his hot temper and trigger finger almost twelve years ago."

"Frances, forgive me for complaining. My problems aren't nearly as bad as yours."

"Do you suppose Heriot and Matilda will ever get along living together—just the two of them? Anne, I don't want to share a home with them. My own sisters! I should be ashamed. I'm not."

"Is there the slightest chance that once he's back from this voyage at sea, your son James might see the need for him to take over here?"

"He might see the need, but he'll never settle down. I'm worried about his health, too. He coughs so hard. Had he been going to battle instead of on a cargo ship, I'm sure he'd have been rejected for health reasons."

"I knew he looked thin when I saw him last, but are you really afraid he's seriously ill?"

"I'm afraid about almost everything, Anne. The only comfort I have right now in my whole life, humanly speaking, is Menzies. I'd give almost anything if I were living in Marietta, Georgia, right now. Just to be near enough to his school to see the boy now and then."

"I'm glad you are considering moving permanently to Savannah. He'll be working there once school is finished. Have you thought of that?"

"I've thought of almost nothing else since Mama died except the disruption of facing life shut up in the same house with my sisters."

"Menzies is your—John Couper, isn't he?"

"If you mean I depend on the boy as you depend on young John Couper, yes. Oh, yes! Anne, are we selfish to lean on our two sons as we do?"

"Probably. I, for one, can't help it, though. Although in hundreds of ways I depend on Pete, Fanny, even my youngest, Selina, I still find myself counting on John Couper to rescue me when I most need someone."

"This minute, there's almost nothing I dread more than for you to end your time here on St. Simons with me, but Anne, shouldn't you consider visiting Miss Eliza Mackay in Savannah next? John Couper is living just blocks from her house. Wouldn't it help you to spend some time with the boy? Savannah's so close. My Menzies in Marietta is hundreds of miles north. Miss Eliza and her daughters are always so eager to have visitors."

"I've already imposed on that dear lady enough. Fanny and Pete and I were there twice last year, I think it was. Speaking of my good Fanny, isn't she nearly finished with your Sunday mourning dress—and do you like it, really?"

"Yes, bless her, she's almost through. Just the collar to be stitched on, and the dress is beautiful. Fanny's so talented. And seems really contented with what she does with her days. I expect she's up in the room you two share right now, hard at work basting that collar into place. I wish there was something I could do to show my gratitude to the child."

"You've given us a refuge again." Then Anne surprised herself by asking, "Do you have any idea how much I miss Eve since I've been here? Frances, how do you really feel about—owning people? I know how William and John felt." She tried a halfhearted laugh. "I certainly know how Fanny Kemble Butler felt. But what about you by now? You and William had only three people—none as close to you, I gather, as I am to Eve. I miss her. Is there something wrong with me?"

"Not that I know of. And I know Eve misses you. How in the world did you ever convince her to stay back at Hopeton while you came here?"

"I didn't convince her. She—obeyed me. Reminding me all the while that she had no choice but to obey because I do own her. I could smack her when she brings that up."

"But Anne, you do own Eve—and her husband."

"I know I do!"

"My, you're touchy on the subject."

"Yes. But I honestly thought by now she'd be here. June vows he means to tend that new olive tree he set out right after Papa died until it's strong enough to move to Papa's grave in the churchyard. I thought surely he'd be arriving at Cannon's Point any day to check the olive trees and that Eve would assert herself and come with him, just to be sure Fanny and I are all right."

Now Frances Anne laughed. "You do miss her, don't you? And to answer your question, I don't know—I still don't know—what I think about owning slaves, because I stay too occupied with my own selfish moilings over where I'll go someday and what I'll be doing. It is unusual the way you and Eve are so close. I've been fond of a few of our people—quite fond of old Bess, who raised me —but no one since I've been an adult. I haven't had anyone long enough, I guess. To me, all the people here at the Village are still my parents' property."

"In John Couper's weekly letter, which came yesterday, he seemed to think that the new Compromise introduced by Senator Henry Clay might help calm some of the growing anger between the North and the South over slavery. I admit I don't know much about it. With John and Papa both gone, I know very little about what's going on in Washington City, I'm afraid. I'm sure my brother does, but unlike Papa and John, he thinks women don't understand such things. John Couper told me, though, that Governor George W. Towns is to call a convention when he thinks the troubles over slavery are bad enough. I believe my son said he's called it for next month, December 10, in Milledgeville. I'll find out what happens, I'm sure, since dear old Mr. Thomas Spalding, Papa's closest friend, is to chair the meeting."

"At his age? He must be way up in his seventies. And does he actually write to you, Anne?"

"Now and then I have a letter from him. One of his daughters writes for him. I think he must be nearly seventy-seven. I hope making the trip to Milledgeville won't be too much for the old darling. One thing I know. He'll go if at all possible. Thomas Spalding loves the Union, which, of course, puts him at fiery odds with his friend Mr. Calhoun of South Carolina. I can't help thinking how Papa would relish being at that state convention. He cared as deeply about the Union as Mr. Spalding does."

"I've always heard that down in their hearts your father and Mr. Spalding disapproved of owning slaves, too. Does John Couper think there could be any kind of real trouble over this new Compromise?"

"If men like John C. Calhoun have any say, he does think so, yes. What kind of trouble I'm not sure, but I know my son fairly well. I can even read between the lines of his letters."

"I know there must be a lot of talk about the resentment between the Northern states and those down here, but no one else in this house gives it a thought. Mama's illness and now the mountain of decisions to make are all anyone talks about. Plus Heriot's garden."

"Frances Anne, I've just decided something. If it's convenient for her, I am going to take Fanny and visit Miss Eliza Mackay in Savannah after all! Are you sure you and your sisters won't mind having Fanny and me through Christmas? We may just go right on to Savannah from here early in the new year."

"Haven't I already begged you to stay? If you had any real idea how I dread being alone with only my sisters and their sparring, you'd stay out of the goodness of your heart."

Chapter 20

FRANCES ANNE VOWED THERE WOULD HAVE BEEN no peaceful hours at the Wyllys' home during the holidays had Anne and Fanny not been there as welcome guests. Saying good-bye to Frances Anne was far from easy for Anne when, early on the morning of January 2, she and Fanny boarded one of Captain James Frewin's schooners at Frederica for the water trip to Savannah, with a night spent at the home of friends in Darien en route.

Eliza Mackay had written at once urging them to visit her, and when John Couper surprised his mother and sister by meeting them in Darien for the final leg of the journey with his father's old friend Captain Frewin from St. Simons, Anne felt almost young again, almost excited in a way she hadn't experienced in years.

John Couper surprised them for the second time by having rented a carriage, which was waiting at the Savannah waterfront to take them and their luggage in style to the familiar old Mackay house on East Broughton Street. With Miss Eliza and her two daughters, they enjoyed a deliciously prepared dinner and heard the latest news. That wise, aging Eliza Mackay feared trouble ahead in the country was plain to see. As did most ladies, Miss Eliza deferred to John Couper for his ideas concerning the likelihood that the South would follow Georgia and accept the terms of the much-talked-about Compromise of 1850, as it was known, written in the main by the eminent Senator Henry Clay and designed to reconcile the differences now dividing the antislavery and the proslavery forces of Congress and the nation.

"What do you think, John Couper?" Miss Eliza asked the young man seated in the place of honor at her right. "If the other Southern states follow us, will it settle the troublesome question of whether slavery will be sanctioned or prohibited in the regions acquired during that dreadful Mexican War? And do you agree that now that Georgia has accepted the terms of the Compromise, the other Southern states *will* follow us?"

He laughed—the laugh that never failed to twist Anne's heart because it was so much like John's. "Ladies, I swear to you that I know only what I've read in the newspapers—the same as all of you have. Georgia accepted. I expect the others to follow. But if you want my opinion, I feel sure the passage of one of the resolutions, the Fugitive Slave Law—which, if I understand correctly, is one of the main Compromise concessions to the South—will eventually cause a barrel of trouble in the North. I hate to say this, but the new Compromise may work for a time only, then turn into fertile ground for much more hostility. We can all be thankful, though—that is, those of us who care about preserving the Union —that Grandpapa's best friend, Mr. Thomas Spalding, was chairman of the Georgia convention. Whether it's true the other Southern states mean to follow Georgia, we all know that Spalding is strong for keeping the country together."

Anne wanted to rise from her place at the table and raise a glass to her son. Could this strikingly handsome, maturing, wise young man with the melting eyes and wide shoulders be the same person as the small boy whose grubby little hand had steadied her that long-ago day on the Cannon's Point veranda and who'd spoken the words she'd never, never forget? *"I guess maybe when there's enough light, Mama, the shadows just sort of go away, don't they?"*

Once more now, John Couper had somehow steadied her, was actually shedding light for her just by being there. He was also shedding light on Anne's own growing feelings about keeping the Union together. As with slavery itself, she had never really thought a lot about whether she agreed with Papa and Mr. Spalding about the importance of the Union. She was, thanks to her son, aware today that her scattered political notions were jelling at last. With all her heart, she hoped the Union would hold. *I must write to Fanny Kemble Butler and tell her,* she thought, wishing painfully that she could also tell John. Could somehow let him know that their only son was again shedding light for his mother more surely than had any Lawrence sunrise.

"Old Mr. Thomas Spalding was nominated unanimously from McIntosh County," Sallie Mackay was saying. "It's a great honor, but after all, he's the only person still alive who was present when the Georgia Constitution was drawn up."

"But isn't he awfully old and feeble?" Kate Mackay asked. "I thought after his wife died, he'd gone into seclusion in his big mansion on Sapelo Island."

"Not when he can try to help his country," Anne said, her thoughts running back to her own father's ninetieth birthday party at Hopeton, when Thomas Spalding did indeed strike her as looking far older than Papa. "He isn't the kind of man *not* to act on his principles," she went on. "Papa used to say that Thomas Spalding was as strong and resolute as he was humorless. He didn't have any humor, you know. And unlike Papa, who plagued him during every visit to Cannon's Point by ordering Johnson to play and play the bagpipes, he hated music of any kind!"

"Still, those two were fast friends," Miss Eliza said, her memories of the two planters bringing a smile to her gentle face. "The last time I spoke with Mr. Spalding, he assured me—and I'm not the only person he assured—that before he saw our country broken apart, he would prefer to see himself and all his kin 'slumbering under the load of final monumental clay.' How he does love the word *United* in the name of our beloved land! Almost, I've thought at times, as much as he loves his precious Sapelo Island plantation."

"When he agreed to chair the convention," John Couper said,

"our Savannah *Georgian* quoted him as declaring that his feeble health and declining years would not prevent his attending, even if he died on the road to or from Milledgeville."

"Well, I certainly hope he's safely back on Sapelo again by now," Eliza Mackay said. "Wasn't your wonderful father also present when our Georgia Constitution was drawn up, Anne?"

Anne smiled at her hostess. "Yes, Miss Eliza. Papa was there."

Again, John Couper laughed his father's laugh. "And if I know my grandpapa, his spirit was on hand cheering his old friend Spalding at the Milledgeville convention last month, too. My Scottish grandfather John Couper believed in the union of all our states, didn't he, Mama?"

"He did indeed," she said. "And so did your Scottish father, Son. And I now realize that I believe in the Union, too!"

THE NEXT MORNING JOHN COUPER WANTED TO SHOW OFF HIS mother to his friends at the Exchange Coffee House on Bay Street. Leaving Fanny behind to placate Miss Eliza's longtime cook, Hannah, he escorted Anne proudly into the popular dining room and ordered a lavish breakfast for them both.

After he had introduced her to six or seven of his friends from the mercantile world of Savannah, he reached across the table where they sat in a secluded corner and patted her hand.

"I'm doing well in my position with McCleskey and Norton, Mama," he said, beaming at her, "and I'm fairly proud of the work I do, but far more proud that you're my mother and at last I can let a few important colleagues treat themselves to looking at the most attractive lady in Georgia."

His mother laughed almost merrily. "Normally, you don't exaggerate," she said. "But when you go as far as you went just now, you're exactly like your father."

"I'm proud of that, too."

As he held out a basket of steaming biscuits, John Couper saw the smile leave her still-lovely face, so he wasn't at all surprised when she said softly, "I've learned somehow to find my way through days and weeks and months and years without him, but I miss your father so much!"

Again, he touched her hand. "I know. At least, I try to know. I think about all that far more than I mention to you."

"You're just right with me. You have always been just right with your old mother, John Couper. I can't imagine my life without you in it. Pete, with all her impulsive ways, is far more than merely headstrong; she's turning out to be a truly strong woman. I'm more and more dependent on her. And you know how amenable your sister Fanny is and helpful in every way. Even your baby sister, Selina, is beginning to carry her part of family responsibility so gracefully that I sometimes forget she won't be fifteen until November of this year. But you're my *rock*. I feel safe just knowing you're my son. Our son. How I longed to give your father a son. Finally I did and the handsomest, most intelligent, talented, compassionate son any two people ever had. Don't forget him, John Couper. Don't ever allow what memories you have of your beautiful father to—dim."

"Am I at all like him? I know Papa was far more worldly-wise than I'll ever be. More traveled. Surely more colorful in all ways, but"—he grinned boyishly—"I'd like to think that now and then I make you think of him."

"Your laughter is so like his at times, I feel I can almost reach out and touch him again."

Pleased by that, John Couper said, "Would you like to know the things I remember most about Papa?"

"Yes! Oh, yes, I would."

He stopped buttering a second biscuit, laid it down, and told her as best he could that his most vivid memory of his father was his singing—his command of every pair of listening ears, his singular way of reaching out as though to pull every person in the room to him as the silvery melodies flowed. "I've never known another man who filled every room he entered as Papa did, and without seeming to try at all. That he filled a room was far less important than that he filled our lives with strong, happy energy and light. I remember him from some of our family evenings at Lawrence, Mama, as almost glowing. I also remember he sometimes changed moods abruptly. Was he as much like quicksilver as I think?"

He watched her pale, sky-blue eyes fill with tears, but she was smiling. "Oh, yes! How is it possible that you were sensitive to that when you were such a little boy the last time we were all together with him?"

"I've just always believed he was one of those rare men who have the capacity to scale great heights of joy and excitement and then, maybe because of some secret feeling of inadequacy to be the kind of man you deserved, he would slide down, down, down until no one but you knew how to rescue him."

He could tell that she was listening intently, but when he'd mentioned his father's mercurial moods and a possible reason for them, her eyes had left his and were now staring as into some secret infinity that would always belong only to Anne and John Fraser.

When she spoke at last, her voice was both tender and firm. "I knew it all along, Son," she began, "but now I've just had it confirmed forever that I *can* truly depend on you to understand me, to guide me, to help me hold on to some shred of my real self even in the midst of this ghastly, rootless, *unbelonging* time in my life. When I'm with you, and maybe only when I'm with you, I feel hopeful again. What sense of hope I had left, after your father went away, my own father helped strengthen. Now, thanks to you, I almost belong again." A fleeting smile crossed her face. "Don't worry, don't feel burdened. I'll never consciously be a weight around your neck, but it's all right, isn't it, if I tell you that some indefinable trait in you has made me believe that I will someday— sometime—belong somewhere again? I've lost touch with myself since I had to leave my beloved little Lawrence house. But you knew that, didn't you?"

"Of course I knew it. Nothing that's happened to me as a man has hurt me half as much as seeing my own mother—homeless. I also haven't forgotten that I promised you we'd find a way together to change all that one day. Didn't I?"

"Yes, and if I admitted how wholeheartedly I've leaned on your dream, you'd be ashamed of me."

He laughed. "Mrs. Fraser, I could never be anything but proud of you, and if you've finished with your eggs and biscuits, I have some news that just may make you proud of me. And prove that what I promised is more than a dream."

She looked ten years younger as she leaned forward, her face eager. "What news? Now you're being exactly like your father. Don't make me guess. What's your news? Did you find a house somewhere—any kind of little place without a leaky roof where the girls and I can live to ourselves again?"

"Not so fast," he laughed. "No house. Not yet. But I did receive a rather impressive promotion at work, and beginning this fall, I'll be earning enough salary for us to at least rent a modest cottage somewhere. *If* we can find one you like."

"John Couper, I'd be contented in an empty molasses barrel if at the end of a day or a visit, I could open my own door and sleep again in my own house! But tell me about your promotion."

"Could I order more coffee for you, ma'am?"

"No, no, thank you. Just talk. What will your title be in this new position?"

This time when he laughed, John Couper knew it was like his father's. "I have no idea that there'll even be a new title," he went on, "but my goal in life, Mama, is to have my own mercantile business someday, and Mr. McCleskey will begin this summer to train me to become his assistant. He'll teach me how to order for the planters who deal with our firm, how to make cotton selections on my own, and many other dull-sounding but progressive duties. By fall of this year 1851, or maybe even sooner if I learn quickly, my salary will be almost double what it is now."

"Of course you'll learn quickly. So quickly, Mr. McCleskey's head will swim!"

"There have been indications of something like this in the offing and"—he grinned—"that's one reason you haven't heard from good old Sister Pete as often as you'd hoped. She's now way up in Marietta, Georgia, milady."

She gasped. "Pete's up in Marietta?"

"She is indeed and although you haven't heard from her, I have."

"I'm not sure I like being kept in the dark like this! Who's in Marietta with Pete?"

"Two good Savannah friends of mine. Mr. John R. Wilder and his wife, Drusilla, who've been going to Marietta for long visits for some time. They're both absolutely smitten with the idea of buying property up there in order to live at least part of every year in that marvelous climate, even though John's business is here in Savannah. They like it so much and the future of the town is so promising, he thinks it's wiser to own something rather than just pay hotel rent at the Howard House as they've been doing. The Wilders were going to Marietta anyway, and it seemed to Pete and me a good time for her to make the trip and do a little scouting."

"I gather you and Pete have been discussing this for some time."

"Both of us would give anything if we could really help you, Mama."

"I know that, but if I'm honest, what you've done, you and Pete, with your secret, surprise planning, has me dumbfounded. Oh, I know both your hearts. But Son, I need time to think. Does Fanny know anything of your plans?"

He grinned. "Not yet. I wanted to learn Pete's firsthand opinion of Marietta before I mentioned it to anyone. It can't be news to you that more and more people from down here and from Florida are going to Marietta to escape our heat and dampness. The United States Census Bureau calls it the most perfect climate anywhere. There are breathtaking mountain vistas, healthful mineral waters, and pure freestone drinking water. But what makes it even more attractive as a place to live are the residents. The people of Marietta are said to be unusually congenial, highly cultivated, refined folk." He leaned toward her. "In short, it sounds almost good enough for my mother. Wouldn't you like it if we found a place for you and the girls and let you find out? A place with its own key, its own door, both of which belonged to you? You could try living there for a while—only as a trial—so that you wouldn't feel forced, bound in any way. Mama, I so want you to have the freedom to be yourself again!"

Her face radiant, she whispered, "John Couper, John Couper, you'd really do that for us, wouldn't you? Don't forget, though, your old mother has a little income. There's Papa's small widow's pension. Fanny could do some fancy sewing. Pete's a fine teacher." She laughed softly at herself as she wiped away tears shed unashamedly in public. "But then, you always said you and I would work it out together didn't you?"

"Together," he said. "And it's easy travel by railroad from right here in Savannah. Why not take Fanny, board the Central of Georgia after a good visit with Miss Eliza, and I'll come up as soon as possible and bring Selina with me. What do you think?"

"Don't push, Son. Please don't push. I could have brought Selina when I made my first escape to the Wyllys' before Christmas, but she begged to stay at Hopeton, where there are children more her age. I don't like being away from her for such a long time."

"But Mama, you could tell a lot about Marietta from just a short visit. You can take the Central of Georgia from here. Pete will still be up there to help you inspect the place. It's just a day on the train, with changes at Macon and Atlanta." He grinned. "Around ten dollars for a first-class ticket. I can afford that right now!"

After a long look, she said, "You're *very* like your father, who always wanted decisions made yesterday. But Son, your mother has done what she thought she had to do for so long—packed and unpacked, cleared out for visits, returned again—she can't make up her mind that fast. I'll also need to talk it over at length with Miss Eliza. If ever anyone needed her wisdom, I need it now. Thank you, though, for hatching these frightening, exciting plans! You realize, I do need a few days to try to think clearly about so many things."

"Take all the time you need, milady." He got to his feet. "And if you're quite finished with breakfast, I'll walk you back to East

Broughton Street if the wind isn't too chilly. Shall I hire a carriage? It is January out there."

"The walk will do me good. Clear my head," she said, smiling up at him as he moved her chair. "Anyway, just because you'll be rich in the fall doesn't mean we have money to hire anything extra right now, Mr. John Couper Fraser."

Chapter 21

"YOUR FIRE FEELS GOOD," ANNE SAID AS SHE AND Eliza Mackay took chairs before blazing live oak logs in the Mackay parlor. "John Couper offered to rent a carriage, but I needed the walk after the enormous breakfast he ordered. I do hope your Hannah wasn't too upset that the boy had his heart set on eating out this morning."

"For a few minutes only," Eliza Mackay laughed. "We've all been so eager for you and Fanny to get here. Fanny plainly enjoyed her breakfast, but I think Hannah was disappointed not to cook for you and John Couper—especially John Couper. She knows how he loves her corn cakes and apple butter. You know the woman has always been partial to him."

With a smile, Anne said, "Shall I make a confession? So is John Couper's mother. Miss Eliza, wait till you hear what that boy has in mind for his mother and sisters!"

"From the look on your face, it must be something wonderful."

"I vow I'm so dumbfounded by it that I probably won't be able to tell you all he told me at breakfast in its proper sequence, but be patient with me. I do need your advice. You've lived through so many joys and heartaches. This could involve—both." She bit her lip a moment. "I know I could so easily sound like just another whining widow, when the truth is that James Hamilton and his entire family, the friends and other relatives we've visited, have all been so kind to my girls and me. But, somehow it feels all right to tell you that I'm completely worn out with having no home —no place to go when I'm tired and needing to be private. It's been such a long, long time since our little family has been able to sit down together at a table that's really just ours. My good china, even my everyday dishes, have all been packed since the day we had to leave Lawrence. I've almost forgotten their patterns."

"You really loved that tabby cottage at Lawrence, didn't you?"

"More than any other place I've ever lived, because it was the only home that belonged just to John and me."

"So, in a real sense, you belonged to the cottage, too."

"Yes. Oh, yes! I couldn't bring myself even to visit it when I was right at the Wyllys'. Miss Eliza, you are so wise. I also know you'll be straightforward with me. I not only know this from my parents' long friendship with you, but my husband told me how his friend Mark Browning depends on you. Your own daughters have also made it clear that even when they don't agree with everything you say, they know eventually they'll find out you were right."

Miss Eliza's laugh was infectious, far younger than her seventy-three years. "My daughters actually said that?" She raised her hand. "Never mind what they said. I want to know what your son told you this morning at breakfast that has you so excited."

"Have I said I'm excited?"

"It shows. Anyone could see."

"Maybe the most important part to me as his mother is that John Couper has known so clearly how painful it is for me not to have a home of my own. And now he's found out for certain that Mr. McCleskey means to give him a fine promotion this fall, so there will then be funds to rent or even buy a house for me somewhere—one that is *mine,* a real home again where I can invite guests and plan our meals and sleep at night in my own bed."

"Anne, Anne, what a heartbreaking twelve years these have been since John left you! All those deaths in your immediate family, all that grief on top of grief. Any woman would have a reason to whine, as you said. But don't say it again! You mustn't even imply that you're not one of the strongest, bravest women on earth."

Anne frowned. "Don't just pay me compliments, please. Somehow I have found a way to keep on walking around through all of it, but right now I need guidance, real guidance. John Couper's way ahead of me. I think I told you when I wrote, asking if we could spend some time with you here in Savannah, that Pete was in Liberty County trying to find a house that we can afford. Well, she's no longer in Liberty County. She's in Marietta, Georgia, at John Couper's urging, and, Miss Eliza, this is what has me so excited but also frightened. With his new position paying him almost double his present salary by fall, the dear boy wants to find a place for his sisters and me in Marietta because his Savannah friends, the John Wilders, have convinced him that Marietta, Georgia, is exactly what the people there claim it is—'The Little Gem City of Georgia.' "

"And my dear, the Wilders know! They've been spending time up there and know firsthand that the climate is nearly perfect. So healthy, I'm sure even your frail little Fanny would almost never catch a cold or a sore throat again. You should be so proud of John Couper. Most boys his age would not be forming close friendships with caliber folk like the John Wilders. They must know such a move for you and your family would be beneficial, or they'd never lead John Couper to think of such a thing. The Dix Fletchers have moved to Marietta, too. When his lumber and cabinet-making business burned out here on Factor's Walk, they were headed for St. Louis to live—until they spent a night or two en route in Marietta. Louisa Fletcher, especially, is not easy to please. She's a woman of genuine good taste and opinion. She and Mr. Fletcher have been living in Marietta now for something like two years."

"Miss Eliza, you're frowning suddenly. Is something wrong?"

"Only that I'm wondering how you really feel at the thought of such a big change. Weren't you dreadfully homesick for St. Simons the whole time you and your husband lived in England?"

Anne tried to give her a noncommittal look but knew she had failed. "The truth is, I'm still homesick for *my* St. Simons Island. Even when I'm there visiting Anna Matilda or my brother William

Audley's family at Hamilton or Frances Anne Wylly Fraser, I'm not at home anymore. I'm eating someone else's food, sleeping in someone else's bed, taking walks on someone else's property." Her voice broke. "Miss Eliza, I so need a place to call—home. . . ."

"Tell me, Anne, do you have any response down inside yourself to what your fine son is proposing? Does the idea of beginning life all over again in a new area appeal to you? Or does it frighten or sicken you?"

For perhaps a full minute, Anne sat staring into the fire. "I have to ask you a question before I know how to answer yours. It's personal. May I?"

"Please, yes!"

"Did whole years pass after your Robert died before you felt in your heart that you—knew yourself anymore? Before you could decide what you truly wanted to do next? Can you decide even now? John's been gone almost twelve years. I still feel most of the time that I don't recognize myself at all. Is that the way it's always going to be?"

"It will be thirty-five years in October that my Robert left me. There are still some days when I feel it was only yesterday. I'm not sure I know the answer to your question about how long it takes to learn to decide what the real you wants or needs—because it took me years to reach the place where I didn't cry out, in my heart at least, that all I really needed was to have Robert with me again. Acceptance enters the picture about then, I think. There's a world of difference between mere submission and true acceptance. I only *submitted* to my loneliness and tears for a long, long time. Then, one day I began to realize that I had finally stopped rebelling, because I knew he would never come home again. I wish I could tell you exactly how long that took. I can't. I can only promise you that once you're able to stop fighting John's absence and take a firm hold on the fact that someday you'll be together again, *acceptance* comes. Too slowly, but it comes. And with it an unexplainable peace. And—hope."

"Hope?"

"Yes. We're never whole persons without hope. You have John

Couper. You have Fanny. You have Selina. You have Pete. You can begin, perhaps, by placing your hope in them. But first and foremost, it must be firmly in the fact that God loves you through everything."

"Sometimes I don't feel at all close to God. I don't know why I'm telling you, but sometimes I don't think I even—like Him very much. That's sinful of me, I know."

"It is not! It's merely human. And if you don't think God knows that, then remind yourself that it was God who thought you up in the first place."

Anne said nothing for a time. Then, "What I most need to know is, will it ever seem like home in Marietta, do you think?"

"No one on earth should dare try to tell you that. Do you remember your first feeling when your son told you of his plan this morning?"

"Yes," Anne answered with no hesitation. "Yes, I remember. I was rather excited. Almost the way I used to feel when John and I were setting out on a lark of some kind. Is that terribly immature of me?"

"No. But it well could be a clue. My dear, no one knows better than I that you've been pushing yourself through most of your days. We all need a little excitement. We all need things to look forward to. To give us—hope. Even with hope in God and your children, you still need hope for Anne Couper Fraser. You did say John Couper is suggesting that you go on a trial basis, didn't you? You're not committing yourself to living your life in Marietta. My daughter Eliza Anne Stiles loves it up there. So does Mark Browning's daughter, Natalie. I'm told the climate is exhilarating and it's scenic, especially in Marietta. But unless something is stirring inside *you*, I beg you not to let me influence you. I mustn't influence you one way or another, Anne, because only you can possibly know if the gamble is worth it."

"I guess it is a gamble." She paused. "Miss Eliza, how long did it take you not to be afraid of going places you'd never been with Mr. Mackay? John knew and loved St. Simons in his way. We'd been together here in Savannah. He knew Darien. He even knew

Hopeton. Will it be too awful for me to go to live in a place John never even saw? You see, I keep clinging to the need to get back into the Lawrence house because it was ours. I keep believing that if only I could live there again, it would give me back a little bit of John. That's silly, isn't it?"

"I don't think it's silly at all, and you've hit right on an area where people differ so much. Some people do far better in the old, familiar surroundings where memories and images abound. Others fare better starting over where there aren't so many painful reminders, where they aren't clinging to what *is* no longer. No one traveled more expertly or extensively, from what I understand, than your John. Mark Browning told me once that the man could feel right at home almost anywhere on earth within five minutes!"

Anne knew her face brightened, because she felt the brightness inside. "I just thought of something. For all I know, John might absolutely revel in everything about Marietta!"

On a short laugh, Miss Eliza said, "You know, he just might do exactly that."

Chapter 22

BECAUSE OF TIME LOST FROM WORK DURING THEIR leisurely breakfast yesterday at the Exchange Coffee House, Anne was not surprised that it was nearly sundown the next day before John Couper knocked again at the Mackay door. One look at the boy and she knew something troubling had happened.

"It comes as no surprise to anyone," he said as he hung his top hat and warm cape on the hall tree in the entrance hall, "but I knew I wouldn't sleep well tonight if I didn't know for sure that you ladies had seen the Savannah paper today. Grandpapa's best friend, Mr. Thomas Spalding, is dead. He did what he believed was right at the Milledgeville convention. Pushed through Georgia's vote on the slave state Compromise and started for home. The old gentleman got as far as his big house in Darien—"

"Ashantilly," Miss Eliza said.

"Yes. Now his son's home since Mrs. Spalding's death. The old gentleman died at Ashantilly."

"You and Fanny and I must go to his funeral," Anne said. "He's always been such a part of my childhood on St. Simons. I don't remember a time when our family wasn't making the trip up to Mr. Spalding's Sapelo Island place. Or when his oarsmen weren't bringing him to Cannon's Point. I have to represent the Couper family at his service. Will it be held at St. Andrews church in Darien? I'm sure he'll be buried in the family plot in Darien, won't he?'"

She felt John Couper's hand touch hers. "Thomas Spalding is already buried, Mama," the boy said gently. "He died on January 4. His service was the next day."

Anne felt herself sway a little, then whispered, "Oh."

"I'm almost as stunned as your mother, John Couper," Miss Eliza said. "I forgot my manners. Let's all sit down in the parlor. I know this is a shock for you, Anne. I'll ring for Hannah to bring us some hot tea."

"Tea would be nice," Anne said, "but I'm really—all right, Miss Eliza. You see, in a way dear old Mr. Spalding's leaving us has freed me."

"Freed you, Anne?" Eliza Mackay asked.

"I know this won't make sense—maybe not to either of you— but he was always like an uncle to me. One of the first good laughs I remember Papa and I sharing had to do with Uncle Thomas Spalding's downright dislike of music." With a sad but affectionate smile on her face, she went on remembering. "My father and I could be quite mean, you know. In our teasing, that is. Eventually our 'meanness' turned to my brother James Hamilton, but it really began by being aimed at poor Uncle Thomas Spalding. John Couper, you know how your grandpapa adored music of all kinds. 'A mon cannot be blamed for filling his own house with the lilt of melody, now, can he?' Papa used to argue, tongue in cheek. And then, the old darling would signal Johnson to play his bagpipes until the whole house shook. It was torture for Uncle Thomas, I knew, but I also knew Papa felt free to tease like that because they held each other in such high regard. Anyway, the kind of humor I came by through those pranks of your grandfather's has saved me a thousand times since."

Smiling because she was smiling, Anne knew, her son asked, "And by some means not too clear to Miss Eliza and me, it's saving you now, Mama?"

Overcome by sudden tears edged with a kind of joyful laughter, Anne said, "Forgive me, both of you. I've always been so, so fond of Thomas Spalding. I'll miss just knowing he's waking up to the beauty of his beloved Sapelo Island, but just think where he and Papa are now! They're not only two nearly lifelong friends together again, there's only harmony in heaven. Harmony and the singing of all the heavenly hosts! Do you think I've taken leave of my senses, John Couper? Miss Eliza? Laughing and crying at once?"

Anne caught the quick, puzzled though half-hopeful look her son gave Eliza Mackay, whose sweet, aging face was wreathed in a delighted smile. "Anne, no," Miss Eliza said, her voice firm and sounding young. "You've probably just taken the kind of leap you've needed so desperately to take."

"I have?" Anne asked.

"The leap of—well, I guess I'd call it faith, which we all need. The leap I needed and couldn't take when I lost Robert. The leap you needed when you lost your John and all the other dear ones no longer here on this old earth with us. If we're seeing clearly, through the eyes of God, we should all only give thanks that resolute, strong Mr. Spalding is where he now is. His life, even on his beloved Sapelo Island, was an empty shell since his dear wife left him. Sarah Spalding's gone to where her husband is now, and swirling about them both"—the older woman smiled again— "swirling about them both, undoubtedly under your father's direction, Anne, must be all the music of heaven." Miss Eliza looked at John Couper. "Do you think your dear mother and I have taken leave of our senses together, John Couper?"

"Far from it, Miss Eliza," he said, hugging his mother as he spoke. "Anything that makes my mama laugh or even smile I support wholly!"

"And John Couper," Anne said, interrupting his hug long enough to look him straight in the eyes, *"I have been freed.* The thought had never occurred to me, but I now see that the last remaining tie to this beautiful coast was cut when Papa's best friend died. I know I didn't see Thomas Spalding often, even when Papa was still with us, but the bonds held. All that was good in those bonds will last, but suddenly I think I'm ready to take your Marietta gamble."

"Mama, you are?"

"I want my own home again enough to risk uprooting myself and my whole family. You'll visit us in Marietta, won't you, Miss Eliza? Promise?"

"I promise to try, my dear. And, in a way, it won't be such an uprooting for you. People are moving up there to that marvelous climate often these days. The railroad has changed so much for all of us. And I just know your Fanny will be stronger there."

"She will be, Mama," her son said. "And if I know my sister Fanny, nothing will cheer her as much as seeing our mother smile more often."

"Oh, John Couper, I never meant to drag everyone down! Help me explain what I mean by that, Miss Eliza, please."

"She doesn't need to," the boy said. "I already know."

"You did say Pete likes Marietta, didn't you?"

His lilting laugh came again. "She loves everything about it! I can just see her turning that charm on the defenseless Marietta natives. In typical Pete fashion, she even wrote to me last week that she had yet to meet one person who hadn't fallen under her spell!"

For a moment Anne sat on the edge of her chair, beaming. Then she said, a rare lilt in her voice, "Miss Eliza, John Couper is quite like his father in many ways, but sometimes I honestly think our daughter Pete is getting to be more like him every day."

Neither John Couper nor Miss Eliza said a word, but Anne hadn't really expected a response. It was just too fine a moment— that she seemed able at last to speak naturally about John and with almost no twist of the knife blade in her heart.

EVEN WITH WISE, UNDERSTANDING ELIZA MACKAY UNDER THE same roof, always willing to talk about Anne's difficult days of indecision, there were few times when Anne didn't miss Eve, didn't fidget and fret that to keep Eve from making the initial trip to the Wyllys' with her, Anne had been forced to tell her it was an order that Eve remain at Hopeton. Miss Eliza would have welcomed Anne's servant, but the Wyllys simply didn't have room for her, and when Anne had said good-bye to Eve, no one even dreamed that she would be going straight from St. Simons Island to Savannah. At no other time Anne could remember had Eve been so insistent that she go too. Did her servant have a "knowing" that Anne wouldn't be coming back to Hopeton in a few weeks? And what in the world would Eve think of John Couper's plan for his mother to spend time in Marietta, Georgia?

After she'd told Fanny her plans in the privacy of Miss Eliza's guest room they shared, the thought flashed through Anne's mind that it should make no difference what a servant thought. Not true of Eve, she thought as she lay beside Fanny, wide awake, Eve so much on her mind that she knew sleep was out of the question. Fanny, of course, had accepted the idea that visiting Marietta was a good thing for her mother to do, not only because the girl generally believed her brother was right, but because such a time away from every reminder of grief upon grief would surely be beneficial for Mama. Anne sighed deeply. So happy did Fanny seem for her sake, she was already sleeping soundly, her quiet, plain little face barely visible in the flickering light of one candle. What member of the Fraser or the Couper family, Anne wondered, was submissive Fanny like? She's highly unlike her only brother and her two living sisters. Pete was anything but submissive. John Couper had always been a gentle but strong lad, even as a child. He'd been considerate with his mother in telling her of his Marietta plan, but certainly firm enough. Even Selina, though not headstrong, rushed to pour out her love on everything and everyone from a pretty bird's egg found fallen from a nest to a newborn rabbit.

Only Eve, for all the years Fanny had been with them, had seemed able to know what Anne's quiet daughter was really thinking. "Eve, I hate to admit it," she whispered, "but you were right! I should have brought you with me. For all I know, Fanny hates the idea of going to Marietta. You would know the truth of it. And what makes me even wonder about Fanny, who never, never causes me a lick of trouble about anything? I'm sure she'd rather stay here in Savannah, where she feels at home. I'll tell her so tomorrow morning. I know she'll be relieved."

After another loud sigh, which could easily have wakened Fanny, Anne slipped out of the bed, pulled on her warm robe, and moved the one candle to a small writing desk in a corner of the room. If she'd ever written Eve a letter in her entire life, she had no memory of it, but she was going to now. Heaven knew how long it would be before she saw her again, but it was only fair for Eve to know that a whole new way of life could be beginning for them both. Since the Central of Georgia departed from Savannah, John Couper was certainly right that she should board it while she was already here to go to Marietta. And breathing a silent prayer that her servant would *understand* half as much as she instinctively *knew*, Anne struggled to decide how to begin the letter.

She dipped a quill and pushed back the odd, awkward resentment and unease she felt more and more often because a woman as intelligent and reliable as Eve needed anyone's permission to do anything. Anne's life had certainly been simpler in the old days when she'd given the whole slavery issue almost no thought. John had changed that. John and the fascinating, opinionated British actress Fanny Kemble Butler, who had visited St. Simons Island briefly just before John went away forever. One thing was certain. As soon as a permanent decision had been made about where Anne might be living and receiving mail, she meant to write to Mrs. Butler. More than a year had passed since Anne saw in a Savannah paper that in November 1849 Pierce Butler had divorced Fanny and that the poor woman was now entirely deprived of even seeing either of her adored daughters.

Breathing another silent prayer for the dynamic, deeply spiritual woman, whose abolitionist views on slavery had cost her a slave-owning husband as well as her children, Anne turned her thoughts back to Eve. Because she'd been so hurt when Anne left Hopeton without her, Eve had said good-bye with no sign of a smile when the two last saw each other. Thankful that she'd long ago taught Eve to read and write, Anne began the difficult letter.

Savannah, Georgia
10 January 1851

Dear Eve,

I am writing this letter to you by the light of one candle. It is dark outside and Fanny is sound asleep in our bed at Miss Eliza Mackay's house. I'm sorry not to have written to you when I decided suddenly that I needed a good, long talk with Miss Eliza and so came here straight from the Wyllys' on St. Simons. I hope my brother has told you by now where I am.

Even he doesn't know that John Couper has convinced me to take a train from here when my visit is finished and stay, for a short time anyway, in a place called Marietta, Georgia, where so many people go to get away from the heat and fever on the coast. You may think I'm crazy, but John Couper is a wise boy. And Miss Eliza agrees that the change will do me good. No one had told me, but Pete has been in Marietta for some days now and loves the place. She is hunting a house for us so that the girls and I, you and June, and some of our other people can again have a place of our very own. And Eve, I will not, I cannot, make such a big step without you. We are friends for always, Eve, and I send my best to you. I will write again either from here in Savannah or after we are in Marietta. For another week or so you could write to me here in care of Mrs. Robert Mackay. Mail comes to Savannah every day except Sunday. I trust you to tell Selina my latest news and to begin thinking about packing the few pieces of furniture, clothing, and other personal belongings we brought from Lawrence to Hopeton. I will write to Master James Hamilton myself. I am writing first to you, though, because I wanted you to know the minute I was sure that this is what I should do for now. I hope you are not still cross with me for leaving you there. Do you think you and I are ready for a new experience? Am I ever going to be happy again or at least peaceful without John? I do promise that June will, if I decide to stay in Marietta, be right up there with you. Will I ever be myself away from the coast? Will I miss the coastal light too much? Your mother and grandmother are dead now, too, so neither of us has much to hold us down here. I miss my father. *I need you with me.* I know John Couper and Fanny would want to be remembered to you and June, as do I. Hug Selina for me.

Yr lifelong friend,
Anne Couper Fraser

PART IV

March 1851–
December 1851

Chapter 23

ANNE WAS UP BEFORE DAYLIGHT AFTER HER FIRST night in Marietta, Georgia. The hotel bed without the warmth and completeness of John beside her made her feel as though he'd gone away only yesterday. Not once had she failed to miss him for the first minutes alone in any bed since the day he left her, but this was different. Confusing. More confusing than it should have been simply because she was in a strange place. God knew she had slept in nothing but unfamiliar places for the nearly twelve years she'd struggled to live in some semblance of normalcy without him. The nice room she'd rented at the Howard House on the bustling Square in Marietta wasn't unlike rooms in the English and Scottish inns where she and John had stopped all those years ago. Why was the rhythm of this new, tumbling, uneasy night upsetting her so now? Her tall, definite, strong, loving daughter Pete would be joining her at the Howard House by noon today. The whole tumultuous idea that Anne might benefit by moving away from the bittersweet familiarity of the Georgia coast to entirely new surroundings had struck her son, John Couper, as a way to give her a new, meaningful life. He had formed a friendship with the young John Wilders of Savannah, who, during their frequent visits to the scenic village of Marietta, had already rented a house called Oakton beyond the edge of town. Drusilla Wilder, according to John Couper, was falling in love with the pleasant, increasingly popular resort town in the Georgia up-country some three hundred miles north of the coast. John Wilder, in his midthirties as was Drusilla, owned a thriving business in Savannah, but the attraction for permanent living for them both was Marietta. Of course, thanks to John Couper, Pete had been welcomed and warmly entertained by the Wilders. Soon their driver would be bringing Pete to stay with her mother at the Howard House on the northwest corner of the Square.

I should be only excited, Anne told herself, tucking a bed blanket around her legs and feet as she sat down at a small hotel desk to make a diary entry, her first since she'd said good-bye to the Mackays at the railroad depot in Savannah day before yesterday. Anne had forgotten how many years ago she'd obeyed her mother, Rebecca Couper, and began trying to remember to keep her diary current. Mama had been dead for nearly six years, but even at age fifty-four Anne still felt clear in her conscience when obeying her. Wherever she happened to be staying since forced to leave her own beloved cottage at Lawrence on St. Simons Island, she had packed her diary as regularly as she'd packed nightclothes.

She smiled. Only those times when circumstances made it impossible for Eve to go with her had Anne packed anything. Eve. How had Eve reacted to her letter written from Savannah back in January? In it she tried to explain to Eve why she had gone directly from her visit to Frances Anne at the Wylly home on St. Simons to Savannah without a return trip to Hopeton, where Eve fidgeted through her days, unhappy, Anne was sure, because she didn't know exactly where her mistress was or with whom or why.

The blanket felt good, helping to hold some body warmth around her against the chill of the up-country, early March day just beginning to break. It was still dark enough to need the leaping flame of a brass two-candle stand on the tiny desk. She dipped a quill and began to write.

Wednesday, 12 March 1851

In a peculiar state of goose bumps from the dry, cold, up-country spring weather and almost total uncertainty in my own life, I am trying to make some sense here about what might be about to happen to me. The room I occupy at the Howard House on Marietta's city Square is comfortable, except that there seems to be no servant in sight to build up the fire, and I would give more money than I have for a cup of hot coffee. One thing is certain: If, by the wildest chance I should decide to try to make a new life for my children and me here in the up-country, I will not—I *could* not—face any of it without Eve beside me.

In the letter written to Eve in January, I mentioned that she could come with John Couper, Selina, and Fanny if I decide to settle in Marietta. Knowing Eve, I think she has clamped on to that mere suggestion. Even I do not know what I will decide to do, and yet I sit waiting for the lifting of my spirits all the way up here, so far from all I ever held dear, simply because I know that the sun will rise in Marietta, too. I will know it is rising only because its light will push around the winter curtains covering this one window to the outside. I'm away from the sunrise because the Howard House is on the northwest side of the Square. What nonsense I write! Thank God, Pete will be in that other bed, empty beside mine in this strange room, tomorrow when I awake. With Pete will come activity, at least. My tall, determined, red-haired daughter will generate activity. It is her nature. Like her blessed father, she will charm strangers for me, will lay out a thousand plans for my approval, will laugh if I need laughter, will press me steadily but seldom too much. Pete will help. Oh, yes, Pete will help me find out why I'm really here. But as with her sweet father, I will stay alert, because she is as persuasive as John ever thought of being. One thing I know: Pete and the landlady here at the Howard House, Mrs. Dix Fletcher—Louisa, I believe she said her name is—will certainly take to each other. Both know what they think and neither is afraid to express it, with no mincing of words. Did I really like Louisa Fletcher when I spoke briefly with her as she greeted me and showed me to this room yesterday? Yes. I did like her. As tired as I was from all those hours trying to rest on hard, unrelenting train seats, I remember that I did not want her to leave me in this room alone. Only courtesy and good manners made it possible for me to remember how busy she must be in her efforts to run a bustling hotel. I vowed then, and I repeat now, that I will not resemble those cantankerous guests who keep her longing for the day of their departure. Louisa Fletcher reminds me of someone, and I recall that I did not find it at all difficult to put myself in her place, to imagine the hectic pace of her life, and to wonder if she truly enjoys being a landlady in such a popular place. Or does she love her husband, Mr. Dix Fletcher, enough to endure for his sake? At any rate, she vows she will have Pete and me as her guests for dinner tomorrow here in the hotel dining room and will find time to show us around what appeared last evening to be a prosperous and rather charming little village. I believe she said she and Mr. Fletcher came south from Massachusetts and that when his business burned in Savannah, they started a journey to St. Louis but got no farther than Marietta. Both, as she put it, were captivated by the village and had no trouble agreeing that her husband would accept the position as manager of the Howard House. I must say I rather enjoy her vitality, her Northern way of speaking in clipped accents, and find her altogether pleasing. She is, to say the least, stimulating, and in my fearfully numb, uncertain state of mind, I need stimulation.

I missed John so desperately through last night! I do long to find an end to the pain of grieving, the lostness, the odd, continuing fear of it. I so want to be a new person for the children. Could new surroundings accomplish that? Could they—possibly? Frances Anne vows that someday I will be able to enjoy my memories of John. I have at times. At rare times I have truly enjoyed remembering, but more often the enjoyment dissolves into tears. Somehow, by some means, that must stop. Mrs. Fletcher *does* remind me of—someone. I wonder who?

A POLITE KNOCK AT HER HOTEL ROOM DOOR ABOUT 8 A.M. SO startled Anne that when she rushed to answer, a blob of ink waited to be wiped from the surface of the cluttered desk. Streaks of clear, bright sunlight had just begun to lie in yellow shafts across the wide board floor of the room—a sunrise she'd scarcely noticed, so lost in thought had she been since writing the last line in her diary.

The Wilders, John Couper's friends with whom Pete had been staying in Marietta, lived on the outskirts of the village, so the early-morning knock could not have been Pete's. Anyway, she thought as she hurried across the room, Pete would never knock so quietly. But when Anne opened the door, there stood both Pete and the Howard House landlady, Louisa Fletcher.

"Surprise, Mama!" Pete said, beaming, rushing to hug her. "This nice lady likes you so much, she insisted on bringing me up to our room personally. I might have known you'd already begun to make friends in Marietta."

"Good morning, Mrs. Fraser," Louisa Fletcher said brightly in her Northern way. "I find not only you likable, but your daughter Rebecca as well. You didn't give me any warning about her charm. Or her glorious red hair! May we come in? I do apologize that no one has been here yet to bring coffee or to tidy your room." She swept her wide forehead with the back of one hand in a rather dramatic gesture. "No one—no one can imagine what a burden it is trying to keep these servants in line and serving our guests in a manner they deserve." Mrs. Fletcher's laugh was contagious. "At least some guests deserve superior service and surely you're one of them. And now, you're two. I promise to see that neither of you wants for anything while you're in town gracing the Howard House with your presence."

"Forgive my lack of manners, Mrs. Fletcher, and do follow my somewhat willful daughter right on in."

Pete, as though she'd already been living there, offered their landlady one of the two small armchairs in the boxlike room, her mother the other, then took the straight desk chair where Anne had been sitting. "Are you sure you were all right making the long train trip from Savannah alone, Mama?"

"Don't I look all right, Pete?"

"Don't be shocked, Mrs. Fletcher," Pete laughed. "Everyone

who knows me well calls me Pete. I loved my grandmama, but I don't like her name, Rebecca, so I'm glad for Pete. It still surprises me though, Mama, that my gallant brother allowed you to come by yourself on the train. I'd better get a letter off to him right away before he has a case of apoplexy from worry."

As though Pete had said nothing, Anne turned to Louisa Fletcher. "Too many apologies can be tiresome, I know, Mrs. Fletcher, but I am sorry you've caught me in my oldest but warmest robe. I—I had some writing to do and haven't bathed or dressed yet."

"Forget it, Mrs. Fraser," she said, getting quickly to her feet. "I'm leaving at once so you and"—she gave Pete a glowing smile —"Pete can chatter to your heart's content while I see to the very best the Howard House has to offer in breakfast for you both."

"I've eaten at the Wilders'," Pete said, "but, of course, I'll sit with my mother while she has breakfast. I take it you *were* all right making that long train ride by yourself, Mama," she added pointedly, perched ramrod straight on the small wooden chair.

"Your mother didn't arrive alone," Louisa Fletcher offered. "She came with one of Marietta's most prominent and richest gentlemen, Mr. Edward Denmead. It seems he'd been in Savannah purchasing materials for the splendid new mansion he's building at the edge of town. The Denmeads are at least indirectly responsible for our living in Marietta, as I'm sure you know, Mrs. Fraser."

"Mr. Denmead did tell me at length of the visit he and his wife made to Savannah the time they first heard your golden singing voice, Mrs. Fletcher. I believe he said he'd invited you to sing at your convenience to the Episcopal congregation here. I'm eager to hear you myself. So you see, Miss Pete, your brother put me on the train with a most distinguished gentleman as my escort." Turning again to their unusual landlady, Anne added, "I must say, Mrs. Fletcher, your village of Marietta has no more convincing booster than Mr. Denmead!"

"If I live to be a hundred, I'll never forget the first tour of the town given my husband and me by the Denmeads when first we stopped as guests here at the Howard House, met at their insistence by both Mr. and Mrs. Denmead." She moved toward the door. "But for now, I *am* leaving the two of you alone and I promise you a superior breakfast. Then, I intend to declare two free hours to show the two of you around Marietta myself."

Chapter 24

WITH PETE'S ENERGETIC ASSISTANCE AND FOUR pitchers of both cold and scalding water Louisa Fletcher sent up, Anne bathed and dressed to the compliments of her seemingly lighthearted daughter.

"Why wouldn't I be lighthearted?" Pete wanted to know. "Who else is as sure of as many things as I am and who else has such a talented little sister as Fanny, your seamstress? Mama, you look utterly charming in that black walking dress! How did Fanny know that the very latest style is no collar at all?"

"We do see New York and Washington papers down on the coast, you know," Anne snapped. "I'm absolutely starving for breakfast, but before we go down to the dining room, you have to tell me what it is you're so sure of. You're being oddly mysterious. Have you already made up your mind about something you haven't even told me?"

"Maybe I have and maybe I haven't. Stand over closer to the door so I can get a good look at you. What you need with that nice black woolen dress is a shoulder cape—black velvet. It'll be good, won't it, when you can stop wearing mourning clothes? Grandpapa's been gone a whole year. Fanny could start on a few more cheerful dresses for you now, couldn't she? Grandpapa Couper will never be gone from our hearts, but we're beginning a whole new life, Mama, and in some pretty colors there won't be a more attractive woman in Marietta than you can still be."

Anne stood shaking her head, unable not to smile at her talkative, impetuous daughter, even though she hated being pushed almost more than anything. "Fanny already has paper patterns ordered from New York for the time when I can wear colors again, and it wouldn't surprise me to find out that she and the Mackay sisters have already decided exactly which colors I should try to find. That is, if I think my old dresses aren't good enough for visiting awhile in Marietta."

Pete lifted an eyebrow. "Visiting? I know right now we're only visiting, but as good and helpful as Fanny is, we owe it to her to live here where everything from the air to the drinking water is so healthy. I haven't found a house yet, but we will and you're going to feel like a new woman, too. I guarantee it!"

"You guarantee it? And just how do you do that, Rebecca?"

Pete grinned her most impish John-grin. "Oops. I went a little too far, didn't I? But the word *guarantee* does have a good ring to it."

"What has a better ring to me is—breakfast. Then, as you heard, my new friend, our landlady, Mrs. Fletcher, has offered to show us as much of Marietta as she has time for today. If you'll look through the few things hanging on that wall hook over there, you'll find a splendid new short cape Fanny just finished before I left Savannah. And if you'll notice, it is black velvet. Will you slip it around my shoulders, please?"

Pete's happy eagerness when something pleased her was as unmistakable as her somewhat firm lectures. Anne gave her a big smile and a hug and thanked her warmly before they left the hotel room to head arm in arm downstairs for breakfast.

AFTER A DELICIOUS MEAL OF COFFEE, BISCUITS, EGGS, AND HAM, its serving supervised by Louisa Fletcher herself, Pete followed her mother and Mrs. Fletcher out the front door of the Howard House into the bright spring sunshine flooding the Square, already bustling with people. There were well-dressed ladies inspecting shop displays, servants leading children, horse-drawn carts and buggies, and storekeepers tidying up the board sidewalk for the day's business. Pete had ridden more than once around the Square with John Couper's friend Mrs. Wilder, so observed even more than Louisa Fletcher pointed out as she led them along the south side of the Square. Pete even read aloud some of the grocery store signs— C. C. Bostwick, Stephen M. Satterfield, and up ahead on the southwest corner of the Square, Edge and Wright, selling both dry goods and groceries. One large sign caught her eye and brought a smile: General E. R. Mill's Store, which boasted not only a varied assortment of foods but "Cherry Bounce, Champagne, best London Porter, Claret, Port, Cognac 1834, old Bourbon XXX, Whiskey SUITABLE FOR TABLE USE AND NOT BAD TO TAKE BETWEEN MEALS." Mama and Louisa Fletcher were talking, so Pete, a step or two behind them, said nothing but hoped Mama had seen the sign too. Every smile on her mother's face these days was somehow a small triumph for Pete.

Mrs. Fletcher's time was limited this morning, but there would be chances later for mother and daughter to do their own exploring. When Mama began to show more interest in fashion again, they could spend hours at J. J. Northcutt's shop, where all manner of French and English prints were advertised along with a fine assortment of ladies', misses', and children's gloves and fancy handkerchiefs. How Pete longed for Mama to show her old interest in all of life again! Maybe she would never care as she did when dear Papa was alive, but women also cared what other women thought of their looks, and Mama certainly seemed to be enjoying the company of the Howard House landlady.

Pete too liked Louisa Fletcher, who somehow, because of her thoughtful, deep-set eyes and keen intelligence, did not seem at all short or the least bit plump even to Pete, who was taller than almost any other woman. Drusilla Wilder had certainly made a good choice for Mama. The Howard House was a nice hotel, and without doubt Louisa Fletcher herself added to its attraction. So far so good. Pete's goal was for Mama to want, of her own accord, to leave behind all the sorrow and loss and rootless years they'd all experienced down on the coast and to move to Marietta to live. Most encouraging was that Mama seemed eager to hear Louisa Fletcher sing for them. Since the moment Papa went away, Pete knew she'd avoided hearing anyone sing. A good sign, Pete thought, and was sure that years ago when she was visiting the Mackays in Savannah with her parents, she really did remember hearing Mrs. Fletcher sing at Christ Episcopal Church one Sunday morning. She was even sure she recalled that Papa, who could sing better than anyone else, thought the lady's voice remarkable. Did Mama remember? And should Pete find a chance to warn Louisa Fletcher not to sing her parents' special love song, "Drink to Me Only"? Hearing it again could set Mama back for sure. Even Grandpapa Couper had realized that long before he left them last year.

Pete was taking in the obvious prosperity and charm of Marietta, but she was also keeping an eye on Mama, who went on talking and smiling and sometimes laughing with her new friend, who, after conducting them all around the Square, suggested they turn on Decatur Street toward some of Marietta's nice homes.

"Our puddles from the recent rains aren't so bad in that direction," Louisa Fletcher explained, turning briefly to include Pete, too, "and you are looking for a house, if I'm not mistaken?"

"My daughter certainly is," Pete's mother said pleasantly. "And, yes, I suppose one could say I am too. But a modest one, Mrs. Fletcher. My only son has his heart set on our moving to Marietta. It seems Mrs. Drusilla Wilder and her husband have sold John Couper on the magic climate of your village all the way from Savannah. He sent Pete up here ahead of me to do a bit of reconnoitering."

"Wouldn't you and I both be happier calling each other Anne and Louisa? I know I'd like that."

Pete caught her mother's quick, grateful look at their landlady. "So would I, Louisa. Oh, so would I!"

❧ ❧

LOUISA FLETCHER WAS STROLLING ALONG DECATUR STREET between Anne Fraser and her daughter, an arm hooked into one of theirs, when the idea struck her. "There are no more boardwalks out this way," she said. "Why don't we go back to the Howard House and I'll arrange for a carriage. I've just decided to take you a bit farther than I'd planned. Now, don't tell me not to go to any trouble because I want to do it."

If Anne Fraser needed a friend, a real diversion, some stimulating conversation as much as Louisa sensed she did, there could be no more profitable or considerate way to spend the remainder of the morning. She'd already left orders for the hotel's big meal of the day. There was no reason at all that she shouldn't treat herself to the rare pleasure of intelligent conversation. Her days were so crowded with business chores, guest and help problems, she rarely allowed herself to enjoy free time. Today, she would.

"If you have time," Pete said with enthusiasm, "we'd love to see more nice houses, Mrs. Fletcher. My mother will really get the feel of all Marietta's charm and lovely atmosphere. We do thank you."

Anne Fraser laughed. Knowing her as little as she did at this point, Louisa responded at once to the lilt in her new friend's laughter. "I'm relieved that you're also a spontaneous lady," Anne said. "You'll find the word *spontaneous* fitting my daughter Pete more often than not, I'm afraid. If you're sure it won't overburden you to be away from the hotel for another hour or so, a ride sounds like a splendid idea."

"Good. My husband, Dix, keeps the carriage ready for hotel guests who want to tour our fair village, so we'll go right back and be driven in style." Returning to the Square over the half block or so they'd walked, Louisa laughed, too. "Count on me to help you woo your beautiful mother with every beguiling benefit of Marietta!"

LOUISA FLETCHER SHARED THE COMFORTABLE CUSHIONED CARriage seat with Anne while Pete, insisting that she liked to ride backward as well as forward, faced them in the seat opposite. Both her guests appeared delighted to be riding instead of walking, Louisa thought, and she couldn't help noticing the somewhat puzzled look on Anne's face when she first noticed Elmer, the hotel's skilled, rail-thin driver who spoke little but beamed each time he was called on to take anyone for a ride in the new carriage Mr. Fletcher had recently bought.

"You don't need to worry about Elmer's not being strong enough to handle that spirited team, Anne," Louisa said as the carriage rolled out of the Square and onto Decatur Street, headed south as she had directed. "He's a master with horses and never as happy as when he's holding reins in his skinny hands. The more spirited the team, the better Elmer likes it."

"I'm not at all worried about your driver, Louisa," Anne said. "I will confess, though, I'm a bit surprised that he's— white."

"Think nothing of that, Mrs. Fletcher," Pete put in quickly. "Mama grew up, don't forget, in Sea Island cotton country down on the coast. All our people there are colored. You do have colored people working at the hotel, though. I saw some at breakfast."

"Don't be impertinent, Pete," Anne scolded. "It's certainly Mrs. Fletcher's business if her servants are white *or* Negro!"

"That's not a bit impertinent," Louisa said easily. "My husband and I are from Massachusetts, you know, and I especially do not believe in slavery. Actually your daughter is quite right. Breakfast was served by colored people, and they're both *paid* free persons of color. You see, Anne, I'm a Unitarian, and even though I never had the privilege of hearing him preach, I've read every word the Reverend William Ellery Channing ever wrote—especially about slavery. This—this won't come between us, will it? There are many people in Marietta who own at least two or three slaves. Some more. It's their business, I say. I'm responsible to God only for my own soul."

For a moment, no one spoke.

Finally, Louisa touched Anne's hand. "My dear Anne, I had no intention of rubbing your pretty fur the wrong way. Far from it. I simply am an outspoken woman. I do hold strong opinions, I guess, about almost everything. Please know that I'm aware of who you are, that your late illustrious father, John Couper of Cannon's Point, was one of the most revered men in Georgia. That Mr. James Hamilton Couper, your brother, is considered a bright, creative light in the entire world of science and agriculture. I just don't happen to think one human being has a right to own the very life of another. Have I offended you? Either of you?"

"Not I," Pete said.

"Nor I, Louisa." Anne Fraser gave her a long, direct look with those rather amazing pale, pale blue eyes. Then she said, "In fact, you've relieved me. You see, almost from the first moment I met you, I've been trying to think whom you remind me of so much. I know now."

"Oh?"

"A quite famous lady. One with whom I feel close. Closer possibly than I really am, but I feel that way because I liked her so much and found her so intelligent. Intelligent and deeply spiritual. Her name is Fanny Kemble Butler, the famous British actress who was once married to my father's neighboring plantation owner, Mr. Pierce Butler of Philadelphia. The young Butlers visited St. Simons for several weeks just before—just before my husband died. Fanny and I still correspond now and then. She was a personal friend of the Reverend Channing's and totally agreed with him."

"How marvelous!" Louisa gasped. "I'm not only flattered that I make you think of her, I'm—I'm truly honored. I've tried to keep up with the interesting news this woman generates everywhere she goes and I knew she'd married an American, but—just to think, you know her in person! You know her, too, Pete?"

"Well, not the way Mama did," Pete answered.

"But you do remember Mrs. Butler?"

"Oh, yes. She's unforgettable. It's just that she left the Island before my father died, and I wasn't quite fourteen when he went away. Mrs. Butler didn't talk to me the way she talked to Mama. She was really fond of my mother," Pete bragged.

"I read last year in our newspaper of your esteemed father's death, Anne, so I know you're wearing mourning clothes now for him. But would I be too brash if I asked a personal question? Is your *heart* still in mourning for your husband?"

Louisa waited nervously for Anne's response, more certain that she had asked a dreadfully brash question. And surprisingly, Anne's answer mattered. Something so tender, so brave, so sad and vulnerable about Anne Fraser appealed to her in a way she couldn't quite understand, much less put into words. But there was no one to whom she needed to explain it, so she waited, prayerfully, hoping that she hadn't slammed shut the door that only minutes ago seemed to be opening to what Louisa needed most—a truly intelligent, sensitive woman friend in whom she could confide. Who might trust her with the hidden desires of her own heart.

"Forgive me, Anne," Louisa said when she could wait no longer. "I do apologize if I've asked something—"

"No," Anne interrupted, her voice calm, steady, not at all irritated. "You asked me something difficult to answer, but that it even came to your mind has somehow comforted me. My husband has been gone for nearly twelve years now. I try, oh, how I try not to burden others with my—lostness." She reached over to touch Pete's knee. "Pete can tell you I don't always succeed. Sometimes I know I burden her, but she's patient with me, aren't you, Pete?"

"Mama, you know I've been accused of a lot of things, but never of being patient. I'm not patient with you. I just fail most of the time to understand how lost you still are without Papa because, except for a playmate who died when we were both still children, I can't put myself in a—widow's place."

"You still remember losing that playmate?" Louisa asked, truly interested that such a vital, attractive young woman as Anne's daughter would still remember the loss of a playmate in childhood.

"Yes, ma'am," Pete said evenly. "I still remember William Page King and I still miss him sometimes. I wonder a lot what he would look like as a man. What he would be like as a grown person."

"You're both extremely interesting women. Do you realize that? Or am I the only person you've met in Marietta to be so bold as to say so?"

Anne laughed a little. "You're almost the only person I've met in Marietta, Louisa. Pete's been staying with my son's friends the Wilders, so she'll have to answer for herself. Something I know my daughter to be good at doing."

"I hope we're interesting," Pete said. "More than anything I can think of right now, I want Mama to—to make lots of friends here. So, I may just as well tell you, Mrs. Fletcher, you're an interesting lady, too." The girl's infectious laugh was a relief to Louisa. "I like Mama and me just fine. I'll be twenty-six years old in the fall and I can tell you honestly, my mother has never bored me for a single minute before or after my father went away."

"I swear to you, my dear, to hear my eldest daughter, Georgia, now thirteen, say such a thing about me when she's your age would be the supreme compliment." The smile faded from Louisa's face and she turned to look at Anne on the seat beside her. "You do forgive me for my brash question, don't you, Anne?"

"I haven't really answered it. I should ask *your* pardon. The answer is that no matter where we live or how long I live, I'm resigned to living a half-life without Pete's wonderful father. I do try not to let my heartache show, but the man did fill my life for twenty-three glorious years."

"Mama, look!" Pete was on the edge of her seat, peering off to the left side of the Fletcher carriage, her eyes bright, fixed on a handsome white Greek Revival house nestled behind a picket fence in a grove of trees, its carriage lane leading invitingly toward it off Decatur Street.

"What, Pete? What do you see?" Anne asked, her voice a bit vague, her mind plainly still on her heartache.

"That house! That welcoming, pretty house with a whole second floor and white columns holding up the roof. Don't you just love the look of that big, cozy front porch? Do you know who owns the house, Mrs. Fletcher? Could it possibly be for rent?"

"Pete, for heaven's sake," her mother scolded, half laughing. "Don't be so brash, dear! But it is an inviting place, isn't it? There's an air of—kindness about it."

"I like that," Louisa said. "Not many women would sense kindness in a mere house."

"But it's more than a mere house," Anne breathed. "Would it be rude if we drove up the carriage lane for a clearer look at what's really behind those spring green trees in the front yard? I wouldn't want to disturb whoever lives there, but oh, I would love a clearer view."

"Elmer," Louisa called. "Slow the team and take us up to the Bostwick house."

As usual, Elmer didn't answer, but he lifted one skinny hand in willing obedience, reined the horses into a tree-lined lane so bumpy it almost seemed abandoned, then stopped the carriage.

"Well," Louisa said, "here we are. The house Pete called welcoming and you called kind, Anne, was built by Charles Bostwick, a Marietta merchant, back in the 1840s, but he and his wife live in it only part of the time. They travel extensively."

Still looking at the spacious white frame house, Pete asked, "Do the Bostwicks use this lane often?"

Louisa laughed. "It certainly doesn't seem like it, does it? I believe some of their relatives are here off and on, but it does stand empty for much of the time. Don't forget, this is the first day in weeks I've given myself a respite from that hotel my poor husband manages. I work right along with him. You won't, I fear, learn the latest happenings from me. But there just may be a chance that the 'kind, welcoming' house is empty now. I see the lawn could stand a good, sharp scythe."

"Do you suppose it could be available?" Pete was fairly shouting with excitement. "I can tell Mama loves it!"

"How do you know I love it?" Anne asked.

"Oh, I can tell. It's easy. You always think you're doing a good job of masking the real look in those beautiful eyes of yours, Mama, but you almost never do. Don't you think she loves the house, Mrs. Fletcher?"

"I refuse to be caught between the two of you, but I must say you delight me, Pete."

"I do?"

"We all need to laugh more. Our blessed Lord created facial muscles so that it is far easier to smile than to look sour, so, yes. You delight me, young lady."

"Thank you, ma'am," Pete grinned. "Did you hear that, Mama?"

"I heard. And by the minute, Louisa, my own desire to know whether or not that Bostwick house—the *kind* one—might be available is growing by leaps and bounds as we sit here talking. I do try to be practical, but I'm not really."

"Hooray for you, Mama!" Pete exclaimed. "How can we find out, Mrs. Fletcher? Would your husband know?"

"My husband almost always needs a nudge except to try to get me up and going earlier of a morning, but I'll certainly nudge him to start inquiring this very afternoon." She glanced at the gold watch around her neck. "I'm sorry to say this, but I should be getting back to the Howard House. I do have a three-year-old daughter, and her nurse, who has varying degrees of rheumatism, has to see Dr. Slaughter today. We can always come back over here tomorrow, Anne. And by then, I'll have found out about your kind house. It is a charming place, isn't it? I'd seen it fairly often, of course, but especially on this nice sunny day, it's— it's—I'll use your word this time, Pete. In this sunlight, it's welcoming!"

For a moment they sat looking at the simple, clean lines of the elegant white house. Then Anne said, "It looks to be in reasonably good condition."

"It should be," Louisa offered. "It isn't ten years old."

"I'd want it to be comfortable for us during our stay here," Anne went on dreamily, "but even on a rainy day I know I'll see it as it is right now, with the sun overhead. The truth is, ever since the day we buried my husband, Louisa, a certain kind of light has kept me going. Whether we can ever live in it, I'll see it always in my mind's eye with this high-noon light on it."

Chapter 25

ALMOST A WHOLE WEEK PASSED BEFORE LOUISA Fletcher was able to tell Anne and Pete that the white-light house, as Anne was now calling it, was indeed to be for rent sometime early in the new year, at what seemed the fair figure of thirty dollars a month. There was even the possibility that the Bostwicks would be willing to sell the house with payments of the same amount.

"That long!" Pete exclaimed. "Things move even slower up here than down on the coast, and it won't take us that long to get our things packed and ready to move, Mama. This is March 18. What will we do while we wait all that time?"

"We'll just be about our business as usual, dear," her mother said in that calm, maddening way she had when she was purposely trying not to act excited or too hopeful. "I'll want to spend a few weeks with Anna Matilda King. I'd love to talk and talk with dear Miss Eliza Mackay in Savannah, and by the time I can get to Savannah, Frances Anne may be living there. At least her boy Menzies thinks she will be. Wasn't it thoughtful of him to come by to see us from Reverend White's school yesterday?"

"I'm as fond of old Menzies as you are, but

our subject of conversation right now isn't his courtesy, but how long we'll have to wait before we can move to Marietta to live!"

"Have you been so wretched with the way we've spent our time on the coast since we had to leave our beloved little Lawrence cottage, Pete?"

"Sure. Haven't you been miserable, too, Mama?"

"Oh, Pete, I don't know. I don't seem to know very much of anything these days."

"Except that you do want with all your heart to live with Fanny and Selina and Eve and me in the white-light house, don't you? You aren't going to let this long delay spoil everything, are you? I've been so hopeful about you since we found that house, Mama. And the rent is really fair even if we can't buy it. Please don't crawl back into your shell again!"

"I'm not crawling anywhere. I think I just need to be by myself for a while now. Anyway, Mrs. Wilder's due soon to take you back to Oakton long enough to be sure everything's been packed that you left in your room out there when you came here to the Howard House last week. You'd better hurry upstairs for your cape. It's even chilly in this dining room today." On a long sigh, she added, "Hard to believe how warm and mild it may be on St. Simons in mid-March, isn't it?"

"Stop that, Mama."

"Stop what?"

"Stop comparing the clear, dry, brisk air of Marietta with all that warm, muggy coastal stuff Fanny has such trouble breathing into her poor lungs. And stop dwelling on how homesick you've always been away from the Island. I already know that and if I could wave a magic wand, I'd bring Papa back and Grandpapa and Grandmama and Annie and open up Cannon's Point with Sans Foix in the kitchen, move us back to Lawrence, and make your whole life perfect again. I can't do that. No matter how much John Couper and Fanny and Selina and I all wish we could, we can't. John Couper and I are doing the best we know how to try to help you find a new life up here. One you can take part in. We'll have a handsome house one day that will be *ours*. You'll make more new friends like Mrs. Fletcher and——"

"You're certainly smart enough to know there probably isn't one other woman like Louisa Fletcher in the whole state of Georgia!" Anne took a deep breath and tried to smile. "Did you ever see anyone with eyes as expressive and understanding as hers? She is a most understanding woman, Pete."

"But I'm not. Is that what you're talking in circles about?"

"No, no, no! Far from it. If I'm talking in circles, it's because I'm living in circles. Listen to me. When I lost your sister Annie, I was sure I'd never find anyone else anywhere—in or out of our family—with her sensitive, woman's understanding. The truth is, I have. You, Pete."

With her father's half-wicked grin, Pete said, "You didn't have to go that far, Mama."

For a long moment Anne sat there, her second cup of coffee cooling while she studied her daughter. Finally she said, as though just discovering the truth, "You don't need to be reassured about much of anything, do you, dear? You've always known who you are. You've always known exactly what you think. We've all treated you like an impetuous tomboy and tried to rein you in when you probably knew better than we did—about the things that truly matter."

Attempting, as always, to lighten the moment, Pete pretended to be looking around the dining room—even under the white tablecloth—for the mythical person her mother just might be referring to. Then they both laughed.

"Maybe best of all," Anne said, still smiling, "you're not one bit touchy, are you? Look here, I'll give you a big head if I keep this up, but you're a combination of the best and most lovable in both your papa and your grandpapa. I can't pay you a higher compliment than that, but it was more than a compliment. What I just said is the truth."

In her impetuous way, Pete reached across the small table for her mother's hand and kissed it—right in the public dining room. "To prove I'm sensitive, too, I'm on my way right this minute to our room for my cape, and on the way I'll order another cup of hot coffee for the dearest mother anyone ever had. Maybe you do need to be alone, and that's good because Mrs. Wilder's driver is probably already waiting out in the Square to take me to Oakton to finish collecting my stuff."

In a not very ladylike move, Pete jumped to her feet and strode on her long legs out of the dining room. From the doorway she turned to give Anne another reassuring smile, which declared loudly, as Pete had always preferred to declare everything, that their lives were going to be all right.

LATER, UPSTAIRS ALONE IN THEIR HOTEL ROOM, ANNE SAT BY THE window, sipping the excellent coffee Louisa Fletcher had insisted on sending up to allow her guest to escape the party of travelers just descended on the busy dining room. She meant to spend ample time this morning, while Pete was at Oakton, writing in her neglected diary. Today, somehow, following Mama's instructions to keep the diary current seemed important. Of late, Anne had begun to sort things out with more clarity as she wrote. Wise Mama. At times overly proper and self-contained, but almost always wiser than anyone else at Cannon's Point. Wiser than Papa? Anne smiled to herself. Yes, if she were truthful, because Papa was always impetuous and seldom hesitant to speak his mind with or without much forethought. One of the thousand reasons I felt comfortable with him, adored being with him, she thought. Just before Papa died, though, he confessed to her that it was his Becca who, all those years ago, had accepted John long before he was able to bring himself to do it. John.

"John?" Speaking his name aloud, even discussing matters with him, had recently become almost natural. If only she knew what he thought of the white-light house! She really had no doubt that he would be on Pete's side all the way. Her half smile at the still-vivid memory of his spontaneity turned her thoughts again to their daughter Pete and how much she was like him. Had Anne only this morning seen the surprising extent of Pete's understanding of her? Had Anne ever truly tried to understand her own mother? Could she have understood the wellborn lady Rebecca Maxwell Couper if she'd tried harder?

"I am living in circles, John," she said aloud into the empty hotel room. "I try with our children, but my thoughts circle and circle and usually end exactly where they began, showing little or no movement backward or ahead. If only we could talk, dearest! If only you could say something to me. Anything, just *anything.*"

The coffee finished, she set the cup and saucer on a small table beside the stiff armchair and picked up her diary from the same table. Another smile came when she realized that when they lived at Lawrence, she'd guarded that diary, even from the prying eyes of her own children. From Eve. Still, even though Pete had been sharing her room for almost a week, Anne hadn't given a thought to concealing the small, blue grosgrain-covered book. Pete was—Pete. And being Pete was turning out to be far more laudable than even her mother had suspected. The young woman might always need to be toned down here and there, but Anne could no more imagine Pete's invading someone else's privacy by reading mail or a diary than she could imagine the girl's being a mother! That thought had never struck before. Willing, helpful Fanny? Oh, yes. Fanny would one day be a near-perfect mother. Even young Selina showed signs of the gentle tenderness needed to nurture and guide young lives. Maybe especially Selina. But Pete? One thing certain, if Pete did marry and have children, those children could never take their mother for granted.

"John darling," she said aloud again, "how dreadful for you to miss knowing, enjoying, being surprised by, the differences in our offspring! I'm trying so hard to learn to live cheerfully, creatively, for their sake, but it's still so hard to accept the ugly fact that you're deprived of watching them mature and change, become such distinct personalities."

Seated at the small desk now, Anne uncapped the inkwell and turned to a fresh page in her diary.

Tuesday, 18 March 1851
Howard House
Marietta, Georgia

Once more I have neglected writing in these pages since the day after I reached Marietta by train a week ago. I have no excuse beyond my seeming inability to keep up with all that might be happening. Pete, who has been here for some time at the house of John Couper's Savannah friends the Wilders, is with me, sharing this hotel room and continuing to surprise her muddled mother hourly. She is now on her way back to the Wilders' rented cottage, called Oakton, on the edge of town, and while the girl is striking me as wiser by far than I thought, she is also pushing me to a decision. One I fear I must make rather soon. Mrs. Wilder has done her best to accompany or direct Pete to various small houses in Marietta, which we might at least rent for a time, as blessed John Couper says, to give his mother a chance to sort things out in a place she can at least call a temporary home. The children are all trying so hard in their ways to help me find my balance again, and I grow increasingly guilty because I can't seem to do it.

My landlady, Mrs. Louisa Fletcher, whose husband, Dix, manages the Howard House, could well be my reason for deciding to try life in Marietta—away from my beloved coast—*if* I decide that way. So many *ifs*. So, so many *ifs*. How I need my John Couper to help me make top or bottom of something! The boy vows he will be able, with my help from his father's pension, to pay rent and cover our modest needs. Fanny can take in some sewing, Pete can tutor at least part-time, and I can try to learn how to make our meager means stretch as far as possible. Now, the decision of the moment seems to be mine. With the help of Louisa Fletcher, the highly intelligent, unusually well-read and educated landlady, rapidly becoming a choice friend, Pete and I found a splendid house on nine acres of land off Decatur Street, a few blocks from the town Square. The truth, which I trust only to these pages, is that I already love the house shamefully and am determined to try to buy it! I write the word *shamefully* because I am sure that even thirty dollars a month will be too expensive for us and could work a severe hardship on poor, good John Couper.

The house is at least partly furnished and will not be available to us until early next year. It seems a member of the Bostwick family, who own it, needs it for that length of time, although it is at present empty and Louisa assures me that Pete and I can see inside it this very afternoon. And that there is nothing else available to compare. The house is classic Greek Revival, painted white, with handsome proportions, elegant Doric columns, two complete stories and an attic—and eight rooms plus a detached kitchen. There are three fairly good slave cabins at the far end of the property and two nearly new outbuildings, a stable and a barn, with a nearby chicken coop. Best of all, and I fear most persuasive of all to me, is the clean, shimmering, homelike beauty of the exterior of the house with clear, up-country spring light pouring over it! I have clung to light every minute since John left me, and even more vital than the practicality that the house is less than ten years old, and in excellent condition, is that it lingers this minute in my mind's eye as the one place I long to be—*under that light.*

Oh, a part of me wants only to use what money my son can send and we can scrape together, hie me back to Lawrence, and little by little try to make the dear cottage livable again. An equal, other part of me *knows* that would never work out! Twelve years of losing loved ones have passed; all the grief of those years took place on St. Simons Island, until now my one beloved place. Neither John Couper nor Pete believes I will ever shed the sorrow that goes on dragging them down with me unless I am far removed from the coast.

Can I ever learn to love that white-light house (that's the big white house's name to Pete and me now) as I loved Lawrence? Can I ever learn to feel at home under up-country light as I've always been at home in my Island light?

Before this day is ended, I may at least know what my own mind is telling me to do. For the children's sake, I am trying as hard as I know how to learn to participate in life again. Children can put more pressure on a parent than a weak parent can bear at times. For their sake, I must become strong. I must not stay divided in my heart. I must not allow myself to be afraid. They need their mother and they need her to be a whole person again.

What am I afraid of? Only now, in my midfifties, do I truly see and grasp the fearlessness I showed just by giving myself to their father when I knew so little about what future lay ahead. But now, as then, surely *love still covers*. I love my children, and if the truth be known, a large part of me also loves the white-light house. I hope I'm not getting too like Heriot Wylly, but the truth is, maybe I want to be! Heriot wouldn't dither as I'm dithering. Heriot would know right off!

Chapter 26

"I PROMISE YOU DON'T NEED TO WORRY ABOUT ME, Anne," Louisa Fletcher said as she, Anne, and Pete rocked in the Fletcher carriage along Decatur Street about midafternoon of the same day. "Because I obeyed my practical husband and rose before daylight this morning, all my hotel records are finished and my other duties attended to. The three of us have the remainder of the afternoon for the big occasion. You're about to have your first look inside your new home."

"Hurray for you, Mrs. Fletcher!" Pete said, applauding. Her lace mitts kept the sound at least partially ladylike. "I'm on your side when it comes to wanting Mama to be unable to resist the white-light house once she sees the interior."

"Please don't be shocked at my daughter, Louisa. Pete has always spoken her mind with no frills."

"You can't shock me, Pete." Louisa said. "You and I are of the same mind. And your sweet mother is going to find her new home irresistible. I promise you that too." From her handbag she took a large brass key. "This magic key I hold in my hand will open the door to a brand new, happy life for you, Anne. Shall I promise that, too?"

Anne laughed. "No, Louisa. I don't want you to overpromise on anything." Her laughter faded.

"Could—could I—hold it in my hand, though, just for a minute?"

Louisa pressed the slightly worn key into Anne's outstretched hand and closed her fingers around it.

"You're kind to humor me," Anne said a bit sheepishly. "Could I ask where you came by the key?" she questioned, reluctantly returning it to Louisa.

"Why not? My husband's friend Mr. Fred Bentley, Sr., one of Marietta's most prominent and skillful lawyers, has been put in charge of dealing with—what do you call it?—the white-light house. Mr. Bentley will love the name you've given it, and he seemed genuinely sorry that it won't be available for you to move in right away. I'm sure it will take you a while to get ready to leave the coast anyway."

"Yes," Anne said. "But I have good help down there."

"We're relieved there are at least a few cabins on this property, Mrs. Fletcher," Pete put in. "Mama owns several people, and one couple, her personal maid, Eve, and her husband, June, must have a good tight house to live in up here. We'll need quarters for Mina, our cook, and her daughter, Flonnie, our chambermaid. Also for Rollie and Big Boy, who would just plain cry if we had to hire him out with all the others."

"There you go blabbing again, Pete," Anne said, trying to keep her voice light. "It looks as though you could have let me tell Louisa that I'm—I'm a slave owner." With the words *slave owner* hanging in the sunlit air, Anne added quickly, "My late husband definitely did not approve of owning people, though. He had to, of course, despite his strong feelings. I'm sure you know how the British feel about the uncomfortable subject."

"I do indeed," Louisa said, not unpleasantly, but she was frowning a little. "And how do you feel about owning slaves? Are you comfortable with it, Anne? Or uncomfortable?"

"I think I'm both ways now," Louisa's new friend said in a soft voice. "I grew up with the system, you know. Everyone we knew on St. Simons owned people."

"Mama vows my Grandfather Couper didn't really approve,"

Pete said, "but with all the land he farmed, he had no choice. I guess at one time he owned a hundred or more people. He was awfully good to them. So is my uncle, Mama's brother James Hamilton Couper. He isn't as much fun as my grandpapa was, but he's kind and considerate."

" 'Judge not, that ye be not judged,' " Louisa said almost as to herself. "By the way, we have a much-admired, trusted, scholarly teacher in town who thinks highly of your brother, Anne. In fact, he's in the final stages of finishing a new book, and one of the distinguished gentlemen to whom it will be dedicated is James Hamilton Couper of Hopeton Plantation."

"Oh, that must be Menzies's professor up here, Mama!" Pete exclaimed. "The Reverend George White. He once headed the Savannah Academy, too. Won't Uncle James Hamilton be flattered?"

"I expect so," Anne answered absently, her mind, Louisa could tell, not on kind, gentle George White. "You see, my father gave my late husband and me the plantation adjoining his Cannon's Point —a dear, picturesque place called Lawrence. Since there were more than three hundred acres at Lawrence, John had no choice but to— own people."

"Does calling them people instead of slaves make you feel more at ease about it?" Louisa asked gently.

"I—I suppose so," Anne said. "My parents always taught us to call them that, never slaves."

"I see," Louisa said. "And what did your British husband call them?"

"He tried, for my sake, always to call them people," Anne answered. "I know you're wondering if the word itself ever caused trouble between John and me. No. Not real trouble because he was too sensitive to me."

The team was being deftly reined into the narrow lane that led from Decatur Street to the carriage drive, which would take them straight to the white-columned house.

After a fairly lengthy silence during which she sat looking at what might be her home someday, Anne murmured, "The light's still there, isn't it?"

"Just for you, Mama," Pete answered reassuringly, reaching to squeeze her mother's gloved hand.

"That's right," Louisa said. "Even heaven seems determined that you like your new home, Anne. Could you hope for a lovelier spring day?"

In one quick, graceful leap, Pete was on the ground, reaching for her mother's hand to help her from the carriage, almost before Elmer had fastened the reins at the iron hitching post.

"Welcome to our new home, Mama," the tall young lady called out, even though Anne was standing rather breathlessly on the driveway right beside her. "I wish John Couper could be here to escort you up those wide, gracious front steps. Without my sweet young brother, Mrs. Fletcher," Pete explained, her somewhat sharp, even features glowing with anticipation, "we wouldn't even be here —any of us. He's helping us buy it someday, he vows," Pete boasted. "And he won't be nineteen till December of this year! My brother isn't only smart and responsible, he's probably the hand-somest young man you ever looked at. Isn't he, Mama?"

"I'll look forward to meeting him," Louisa laughed, leading the way up the wooden steps, the brass key again in her hand. "What's more," she added, "I'll be sure to tell him that his sister Pete did her best to give him full credit for this happy, expectant moment." Then Louisa turned to Anne, the key extended. "Wouldn't you enjoy the honor of unlocking your front door for the first time, Anne?"

"Mama, yes! You do it."

For an instant, Louisa saw that she and Pete were the only ones smiling. Anne looked almost trapped.

"Mama?" Pete asked again. "Mama, don't you want to unlock the door yourself?"

The quick smile that came to Anne's face was all the more poignant because Louisa knew she had willed it there for Pete's benefit and hers.

"Of course I want to unlock it," Anne said, her voice wavering only a little as she took the key, inserted it in the big, square brass lock, then gasped audibly when as smooth as silk, the heavy door opened to a white splash of sunlight even inside the wide hall that plainly ran through the house, past the stair, to the back door. Streaks of light marked the wide floorboards around an oriental carpet in the large parlor to their left. French doors, which now stood open as though to welcome them, led into the parlor, but intuitively, Louisa knew that Anne was not taking in any of the furniture left behind by the former occupants, or even the lay of the rooms themselves. She was just standing there in the hallway, gloved hands clasped—the trapped look gone and in its place, a radiance Louisa had never before seen on Anne's face.

"I KNOW I'M BEING RUDE," ANNE TOLD HERSELF, STRUGGLING to believe there could be so much sunlight *inside* any house anywhere, then slowly realizing that it surrounded her because not only were the walls, ceiling, mantles, and woodwork all painted white, but the tall, multipaned windows were large enough to give the illusion, even on a cloudy day, that the light was everywhere.

"Oh," she breathed, then went on marveling in silence as though she were alone in the great room. Of course, there were trees in the yard outside. She'd seen them herself when the carriage stopped in the driveway near the porch. Even the Cannon's Point parlor was often shadowy, from Papa's trees throwing shadows. Her small, cozy Lawrence parlor was downright dark. So dark she'd purposely covered her furniture with bright, splashy colors. This room in the white-light house seemed permeated with a shadowless glow new to her. Why? And then it didn't matter why at all. The white light was there, and to every fiber of her being, it mattered above all else.

"Mama?"

For the first time, in Anne's recent memory anyway, Pete's voice sounded small, tentative. Then silence. The child did need a response, Anne reminded herself. But what? How could anyone explain the effect of that light—that white light?

In a less-tentative voice, showing a touch of alarm, Pete repeated, "Mama!"

"Perhaps," Louisa said just above a whisper, "we should give your mother a little time to think."

"Maybe," Pete said, "but there's nothing wrong, is there, Mama?"

Anne shook her head. "Far from it. I'm just overwhelmed by all the light. It's almost as though we were standing right out in the sunshine, isn't it?"

"I suppose it's at least partly because everything in here is painted white," Louisa said. "I've seen one or two interiors decorated only in white, but not many. Now, across the hall is the dining room with its own charming French doors into the hallway. Along the hall, behind this room, is a bedroom. Then a door at the back of the dining room leads to a splendid butler's pantry, with the separate kitchen connected to the house by a porch. Four good rooms along with the kitchen on the first floor. And every room and hallway—upstairs and down—has a chair rail."

"You must have visited often while the Bostwicks were still living here," Pete said to Louisa.

"Only once to dinner when my husband and I first arrived in town, but Mr. Fred Bentley, Sr., in charge of the property, gave me a detailed description of the house to pass along to you. He's a splendid attorney but also has an eye for beauty and seems to have a particular interest in finding the right person for this house. The man is obviously partial to it." With a smile, she added, "I wish he could see your face this minute, Anne. I don't think I need to ask if you like what you've seen."

Anne gave her a half smile. "Thanks for not asking—yet, Louisa. I'm literally whirling and don't want to say something I shouldn't."

"Say everything you're thinking, Mama," Pete urged. "That's half the fun. If you don't, I will."

"I'm sure you will," Anne laughed.

"Why not? I love it! Just think of the wonderful parties we can give in these good, big rooms. Plenty of space for dancing and tables full of food and—"

"Pete, no. Not yet. Don't push. Please don't push. I'm still staggered by this—marvelous light. Oh, the light, the light . . ."

"Don't you want to see the dining room, Mama?"

"Of course I do, dear. And before you have a nervous breakdown, we'll cross the hall and look."

The tour of the downstairs rooms ended in the large, dirt-floored separate kitchen, reached off a small back porch beside which stood an enormous pecan tree not far from what appeared to be an old, gnarled but healthy walnut tree. Both graced the rear yard, where the well—the "good, clear well," Louisa insisted—was located at the end of a picturesque trellis about to burst into bloom with white clematis.

As they climbed the stair to the second floor, Anne was irrelevantly reminded of the afternoon she and John took Willy Maxwell to see Hamilton Plantation on St. Simons, during dear Willy's one visit to them. Where is Willy now? she wondered, and longed for someone to ask. She should write to her beloved cousin, now an old man of almost seventy-five. He had been long neglected in the chaotic tempo of her own life these days.

"There are four nice rooms up here," Louisa was saying as they reached the upstairs hall. "Mr. Bentley thinks the front bedroom on the north side is the choice one, which you will probably select as your own, Anne. Every room in the house, you'll notice, has a good fireplace—all white mantles to match your precious light—and each hearth is of the same stunning white-veined marble. Oh, and off the end of this upstairs hall, that door leads out to a most attractive cantilevered porch where one can almost always catch a fine breeze of a summer afternoon. I believe Mr. Bentley said it's considered a prized feature of the house."

Anne turned abruptly to Pete and Louisa and said, "Before we finish seeing all the second floor, would I be too rude if I asked to be excused for a few minutes?"

"Do you feel all right, Mama?"

"Yes. I—I just suddenly need a few minutes alone to think."

"Of course," Louisa said cordially, "but before you've had a chance to see the bedrooms?"

"Before I've had a chance to see anything else."

She could feel Louisa's beautiful, perceptive eyes studying her. "I hope you don't think me rude," Anne said again. "Pete knows that now and then I just have to—be alone. I thought I might go out onto the balcony you mentioned. Just a few minutes to sort out my tumbling thoughts."

Louisa pointed to the door, its paned glass trim exactly matching the main entrance downstairs, allowing still more light to pour in. "You won't find a more suitable spot to think, my friend. Try your private upstairs porch—one of the very few to be found in the vicinity. Your daughter and I will be just fine. Take your time. I find Pete good company."

"DON'T WORRY ABOUT MY MOTHER'S GOING OFF BY HERSELF LIKE this, Mrs. Fletcher. It's just Mama. She didn't do that until after my father died. There's a lot different about her—without him."

"I find her so likable now, I can't imagine how attractive she must have been before she lost your father. And, of course, her own father died so recently."

"Mama was always the best company and, to me, really beautiful. I used to hear my papa tell her no woman ever carried herself quite the way she did. He meant to be telling her in private, but sometimes we heard, too." Pete smiled, remembering. "He thought she had a throat that, as he said, really knew what to do with her head—just when to cock it to one side, when to hold it level. Papa must have loved her as much as she still loves him. She's awfully different these days."

"But do you know how blessed you are, my dear, to have grown up with so much real love around you?"

"I think about it a lot. And if it's the last thing I do, I'm going to help Mama begin to act like herself again. Sometimes it almost breaks my heart just to look at her and try to imagine what she's really thinking down inside." Pete fell silent, wondering if she dared tell Louisa Fletcher how many deaths Mama had lived through since Papa went away. She hated gossip. Mama hated it, too, but evidently Mrs. Fletcher knew only that Papa and Grandpapa Couper were dead. With all her heart, she was praying that Mama had found a real Marietta friend in this vital, genteel lady, but it seemed plain that Mama had mentioned losing only Papa. "Mrs. Fletcher? Could I ask you something?"

"Anything, my dear."

"I know you read about my grandfather Couper's death in the Marietta paper and that Mama has told you my father is gone, too, but has she told you about all the other grief she's known in the past few years?"

The quick look of deep compassion on the older woman's good, open face told Pete that it would certainly be safe to tell her how much healing her mother needed.

"Your mother's told me nothing else." Quick tears sprang to her eyes. "But I'm sure she will when we know each other a bit better and when she wants me to know."

"She will. I'm positive she will, because I can tell how much she thinks of you already, but my brother and sisters and I all want so terribly for Mama to find a way to be her real self again. Do you think I'd be blabbing, as Mother says, if I told you now and asked you not to tell her I did?"

"Oh, my dear girl, that's a hard question to answer. Will it worry you, cause you to wonder about my discretion if you do tell me? I'm so, so eager to be your mother's friend, to help you help her in whatever way I can, but I don't want to add to your load. After many years, I well remember the burden I dragged about with me after my father died when I was only six. My sister, Marianna, was younger than I, and yet I endured a heavy obligation to help Mother rear her."

"And you were only six?"

"Yes, but the point I'm making is that even at that young age, I somehow *felt* my mother's grief sharply. Any child needs to lean on a parent. When that parent appears helpless for any reason, the child suffers. My heart not only goes out to you, your brother, and your sisters, I truly understand. I loved my father, but even worse than losing him was my heavy heart for Mother. You may tell me whatever you need to tell me, but you know Anne far better than I do. If you think she'd mind my knowing, feel free not to say a word."

"I'm ashamed of myself, but suddenly I need you to know the whole story of our lives beginning with my papa's death in the year 1839. May I try to tell you before Mama comes back?"

As she listened to Pete's story, Louisa marveled that the young woman was so aware not only of the nearly unbelievable, rare romance between her parents, but of Anne Fraser's tearing grief at losing him. Grief made more poignant because she tried so hard to be a whole person again for the children's sake. Then in less than two years another kind of grief struck. Anne's only sister, Isabella, died in childbirth early in the year 1841, and toward the end of that very same year, the severest blow to any mother's heart, Anne's firstborn daughter, Annie, also left her while bearing her first child.

"My sister Annie was Mama's closest friend outside Grandpapa Couper," Pete explained. "I know I'll never take her place because we were nothing alike, but I just try to do the best I can. Mama and Annie's husband didn't like each other much. Then he married again and took the child to be reared by his new wife. Mama's heart breaks every day because she knows almost nothing about how little John Fraser Demere is getting along."

"Oh, my dear girl," Louisa Fletcher said. "Forgive another personal reference, but before my husband and I moved down South, we lost three small children. Our three girls born down here give us great pleasure, though, and although no child ever takes another's place, they are, in a way, dearer."

"Forgive me, please!"

"For what?" Louisa asked, tears on her face again.

"For causing you to remember your own dreadful losses. I'm ever so sorry."

"Please don't be. Am I right to think your mother has lost both her parents? I'm assuming this because she did tell me no one close, except a few friends, still live down on the coast."

"Grandmama Couper died just a few years after my sister Annie. In our immediate family, Mama has just John Couper, Fanny, Selina, and me. But she does have good friends. It's just that my brother and I agree that she also has too many reminders down on the coast and could be ever so much more like herself again up here." Pete took a step toward Louisa. "And Mrs. Fletcher, my mother's such a wonderful lady and so much fun to be with when she—when she isn't so heavy in her heart."

Just then they heard the balcony door open and both turned to smile at Anne, who had finally decided to rejoin them in the upstairs hallway. Louisa waited for Pete to speak first, but she was struck in her own mind by Anne's almost peaceful look. Peaceful and in a weary, somewhat strained way, strong.

"Mama, you're back," Pete said, her expression hopeful, eager. "It must be a nice view from out there. Is it?"

"Yes," Anne said in a firm voice. "Yes, Pete, it's a lovely view out over the village of Marietta and the mountain. That is Kennesaw Mountain, isn't it, Louisa?"

"It is indeed. I'm so glad you enjoyed your little upstairs porch."

"Should I apologize for staying alone for such a long time?" Anne asked with a somewhat nervous smile. "If so, I do apologize to you both, but I want to put this into words right away: I've made up my mind. The payments on the house can be covered between my British pension and what John Couper vows he can send each month once he's in his new position in Savannah. You see, I now know that, all things considered, it will be best for us to move to Marietta as soon as this kind, kind place is available to us."

"Are you sure?" Pete asked. "Are you sure, Mama?"

"Yes, dear. I'm sure. I want to try to live again, right here in this house. And I will. Oh, I will really try!"

Louisa was not surprised to see Pete rush to embrace her mother. "*We* will all try, too," the young woman promised. "And it's going to work out just fine. You'll see, you'll see!"

"That's right," Anne replied in an almost matter-of-fact way. Turning to Louisa, she added, "We do thank you, my friend, for all you've done. And if Lawyer Bentley is in his Marietta office and not out riding circuit, I'll see him myself and commit us to buying the house—this sheltering place—just as soon as possible. I find myself hoping, frankly, that it may even be available earlier than we first expected. You and I, Pete, will go back to Savannah by train, then have your brother buy tickets for us on a steamer scheduled to stop at St. Simons Island. I've decided I want to see both Mrs. Mackay and Anna Matilda King before we go back to Uncle James's house at Hopeton. They will understand, and both visits will give me the courage to explain to him why I believe I must make such a big move."

On impulse, Louisa Fletcher also embraced Anne. "How can I tell you of my delight in having found a woman friend who actually knows her own mind? I won't even try to tell you how happy I am that you and your family will be living right here in Marietta. In a most definite way, you've handed me the chance for a new life, too."

Chapter 27

Back on St. Simons, the Retreat dogwoods were just beginning to show their pure white spring blooms when Anne and her childhood friend Anna Matilda King took rockers side by side on the shady front porch. For a long moment they just sat there, looking at each other. Anne found it a bit difficult to reorient herself with her friend after so much time had passed since their last visit.

"I thought I had weeks' worth of things to tell you, Anna Matilda," she said with a vague smile, "but now that dinner is over and the children are outside with Pete, I'm almost tongue-tied. Are you sure I'm not keeping you from something important you should be doing?"

"Don't be foolish," her friend said. "Your letter written from dear Mrs. Mackay's house in Savannah reached me three days ago. I knew you were coming back to St. Simons. Do you think I'd have scheduled a single thing to do around the place here that might interrupt us after such a long time apart?"

"Aren't you terribly lonely here without your husband? Hasn't he been out in San Francisco for nearly a year?"

"It seems like a year. Thomas has been gone for six months, three weeks, and two days. He's been appointed Collector of the Port of San Francisco, but he hinted he'd like to be a senator from the new state of California, so who knows how long it will be before I can even look at him again."

"Does that man know how blessed he is to have a wife who can do a man's work here at Retreat Plantation? He'd better know! If I ever find out he doesn't, I'll certainly inform him."

Anna Matilda tried to laugh but failed. "He knows. I'm sure he knows. Most important, I know that he loves me. I married him exactly the way he is and I married him because I couldn't imagine living my life with anyone else. Besides, when he's here, Anne, he's adored by all our people and the children. And so, so respected."

"I'm not doubting that for a minute. I just love you so much and sometimes, even with all the other things I've had to worry about, I worry about you struggling day in and day out to see to all this planting, to the care of so many people, to the care of the children. I know Hannah's nearby at Hamilton and, although she has a new baby, does all she can to help, but—"

"But nothing. I want to hear all about you! Your letter only caused my curiosity to grow by leaps and bounds. What *are* your plans? You know what my life's like and if it's left up to me, I'll always be right here in this old house at Retreat. Tell me about you, Anne. Tell me everything."

For a long moment Anne looked out over the expanse of well-cared-for Retreat lawn toward the water of St. Simons Sound, blue-gray under the spring sunlight. "I know I don't have to tell you that even though John will have been gone twelve years in July, I haven't done well at all without him."

"Does any widow?"

"I don't know. And I still hate it when anyone uses the word *widow!* Even you. But at least I have some hope these days and it's all thanks to two of my children, Pete and John Couper. I probably knew, but I see clearly now that at least part of me had refused to face the plain fact that I was scarring all my children because I was so scarred by my own losses during the past few years. I thought I was trying. At times I thought I was succeeding in learning how to live without John, without Papa, without Mama, without my blessed Annie, without Isabella, the sister I was just coming to know. I wasn't succeeding. I was existing day by day, forcing my children to work at trying to cheer *me* up, to help *me*. Anna Matilda, mothers are supposed to help their children. I was harming mine."

The more she talked, the more she warmed to her subject. Anna Matilda's unbroken silence while she listened intently to Anne's every word was exactly what Anne had been hoping for. Not because she wanted to return in any way to the pride-inducing knowledge that her friend had always shown a flattering deference to her, but because she needed someone she felt entirely comfortable with to listen to her. Needed to be free to say exactly what she was thinking without having to wonder if the listener might even silently be criticizing her. Despite their enforced long separations through the years, Anne could still trust Anna Matilda. And so she talked, trying to make her friend understand everything that had taken place around her and in her since the day Papa had been forced to tell her she would have to leave her beloved Lawrence cottage and spend her days learning to live on the charity and goodwill of family and friends.

When at last she started to tell Anna Matilda about the all-important long walk with John Couper during his surprise visit from his work in Savannah to Hopeton at Christmas 1849, she could feel the last cords of indecision begin to loosen. Not that she didn't mean to pull up her remaining roots still deep in the sandy soil of the Georgia coast, but even the dread of the day, the hour, the moment when she would have to do it seemed to be slipping away. At fifty-four, she was not foolish enough even to think that leaving could be easy, but as the minutes passed, as her words poured out, she began to feel that it just might not be quite as painful as she'd feared.

"You were so kind to send your carriage to bring Pete and me and our luggage from Frederica, where the *Welaka* captain was good enough to let us off the little Florida-bound steamer. I knew even before we took the train in Marietta that I could not go first to my brother's house at Hopeton, that I had to come here to you for courage to face James Hamilton with my now irrevocable decision to move to Marietta to live."

"I don't think he'll like it one bit," Anna Matilda said.

"You're undoubtedly right, but James's concern for the children and for me is genuine. He and I are as different as night and day, but you've been such a good listener, I'm sure I've been able to convince you of how drawn I am to that one house in Marietta. So, I'm far less nervous about telling him than I was when I told Miss Eliza Mackay much the same things I've told you."

Anna Matilda frowned. "And why do you think that's true? I've always thought Miss Eliza knew exactly how to advise everyone about everything."

"That's the answer, I think. Poor lady."

"Sweet, strong, wise Miss Eliza—a poor lady?"

"I'd never given it a thought before, but yes. I actually felt sorry for her when she and I talked at her house before we boarded the boat in Savannah. Now I know why I did. She's given such wonderful counsel all her life, she must believe by now that everyone is just sitting there expecting her to pour out golden words of wisdom and gospel truth, and that makes me sorry for her! I will admit that she didn't actually say much to me at the end of my story. Oh, she let me know how happy she is that I have what she called the courage to make such a big, adventurous move at my time of life, but now that I think back, I guess she decided that this time she'd deprive me of the crutch she's always handed me when I've confided in her, begged her help." Smiling a little now, Anne went on. "I'm right about her, I know. The dear lady said very little beyond sharing her delight in my description of the Marietta house—the white-light house. That's what I call it. Miss Eliza seemed to like the idea that even though it's a different light up there, I knew I belonged in the house because it's so full of light. I'd told her often of how I used to depend on sunrises at Lawrence after John went away." Her smile faded. "Anna Matilda, be thankful that at least you know Thomas will be coming home again someday."

"I am thankful, Anne, even during those sleepless nights when

I'm almost in tears with worry because so many miles separate us. But enough of me. I'm thankful, as thankful as I know how to be anyway, and right now what matters is that you've found a house that will soon be your very own." Reaching for Anne's hand, she added, "I—I don't know how I'll ever be able to say good-bye to you once it really soaks in that you'll be leaving St. Simons Island forever, but I am so, so happy and—"

"My dear friend," Anne exclaimed, "I can't leave for months yet! And anyway, we'll write often and the trains do make travel so easy now. I'll visit you. You must promise to come to Marietta. We won't be saying good-bye forever."

Trying her best to smile, Anna Matilda said, "I know, I know, but even when you've been at Hopeton or someone else's house in recent years, I've always known you were still nearby. That a horseback ride or a reasonable boat trip over to the mainland would bring us face-to-face. You know how silly I can be, Anne. No one needs to tell you that after all this time."

"And no one needs to tell me that there was never a truer, better friend anywhere," Anne said. "Sometimes I think nothing in life is permanent but change, though. One day soon I will be leaving the coast. Heaven only knows what life holds up ahead for us both, but you do think I'm doing the right thing, don't you?"

Anna Matilda squeezed Anne's hand again. "Oh, yes! Yes, I do. And there will be other changes—for us both. What matters, I guess, is that we know, you and I, that whatever comes, we'll go on being friends. And Anne, speaking of friends, does Eve know you're back here now?"

"No. Even James Hamilton doesn't know unless my son wrote to him from Savannah. Pete sent word to John Couper the minute I made up my mind about the white-light house. He begins his new position two months earlier than he expected."

"How proud you must be of that boy!"

Anne gave her a long look. "John Couper's my rock," she said. "I'd be afraid of—everything if I didn't have him."

Chapter 28

KNOWING THAT ANY DAY NOW, JAMES HAMILTON would surely learn of their return to the coast, Anne and Pete stayed only a week with Anna Matilda and toward the end of April returned to Hopeton, where Selina and Fanny, back from Savannah, welcomed them with such joy Anne felt a little guilty at having left them for so long. Her guilt included Eve, too, especially since the first night she and Pete shared their old room at Hopeton, Anne had gone to sleep trying to remember how long it had been since she'd seen tears in Eve's large, liquid brown eyes.

"They be tears of happiness, Miss Anne," the devoted servant told her as she served Anne's breakfast in bed the next morning. "You neber desert me for such a long time befo'."

"But I wrote you a letter from Mrs. Mackay's house in January before I took the train to Marietta. Didn't you get it?"

"Co'se I done got it. What you think? Eve be half dead wif worry wifout dat letter! I 'bout done wore it out."

"You've certainly slipped back into your old way of talking while I was away," Anne scolded, buttering a hot muffin from the breakfast tray across her knees. "Where's Pete? I didn't even hear her leave. And you'll spoil me rotten if you bring breakfast upstairs to me even one more day!"

"I aims to spoil you so's you won' run off an' leabe me no more. Pete, she out takin' a walk wif Miss Caroline. De las' I seen 'em, dey was laughin' an' huggin' one another headed down 'long de riber."

"You know perfectly well there's no *b* in river. Where were they heading?"

Eve's big smile broke the tension in the room. "They headed down toward the river, Miss Anne. Now, you satisfied?"

"Yes, because you and I are about to begin a whole new way of life in a house that will be my very own, and you and June will have the best cabin on the entire nine acres."

"Just nine acres? That be no bigger than yo' hand! How you gonna raise crops on any little ole patch of land no bigger'n nine acres?"

"We're not going to raise any crops to sell. The girls can plant a garden—a good big one—the girls and Big Boy, but most of what we'll be planting will be fancy shrubs and trees and flowers. I've found a truly beautiful place that cries out for a luscious garden. The kind June knows so well how to plant and tend."

"June be busy an' happy lately right here at Hopeton, ever since Mausa James Hamilton turn over all his specimen plants an' trees to his care."

"Oh, you've learned a new word—*specimen!* Good for you. But when did my brother turn over such particular work to June? Is old Jeff too crippled with rheumatism to handle his imported plants these days?"

"You been gone a long time, Miss Anne. Ole Jeff be dead."

"Dead? No one let me know."

"Mausa James ain't likely to be writin' to you, busy as he is, when you don' write none to him, now is he? What you do wif yourself up there in Mar'etta all this time?"

"I was hunting a place for us to live and anyway, I wasn't up there very long. It does take time to travel back and forth, you know, even on our trains. You'll find out when the time comes for us to make the trip. I had to spend time in Savannah with Miss Eliza, too, before I could board the steamboat for St. Simons."

"Why you not come straight here? Why you stop on Sn Simons to see Miss Anna Matilda King before you come here to see us?"

"Because I wanted to. You brought too much food up here. Will you please take the tray now?"

"You don' like Eve's cookin'?"

"I like it fine. You simply brought too much. Don't just stand there holding that tray. Put it down and pull up that little straight chair here by the bed."

"You want me to sit down to talk to you?"

"You did that before I left, don't you remember?"

"Co'se I remember," Eve said, pulling up the chair.

"Don't you like it much better when you're sitting with me instead of having one of our long conversations while you just stand there?"

"Oh, Miss Anne," Eve said, the unfamiliar tears once more in her eyes. "Miss Anne, you know Eve feel like Eve again now you home."

"You and I are going to be really *home* again one of these days! Home just the way we used to be at Lawrence when everything was under our control."

Eve's eyes still glistened with tears, but the flashing smile was back now. "Most everything. I don't 'member we always had the chur'n under our control."

"Eve, we don't have much more time to talk now, but you must not move up to Marietta mispronouncing the word *children*. You're still saying the word *chur'n*, which sounds as though you're talking about a churn for making butter, and children and churn aren't at all alike. I'm so proud of you, but I want you to promise me you'll start now being very careful about the way you speak."

A sly grin on her face, Eve jumped to her feet. "Yes'm. But right now, you best jump outa dat bed so's we kin git you bathed an' dressed for yo' talk with Mausa James Hamilton. That man, he don' like to be kept waitin'!"

"I know. And we're both still living here at Hopeton because of the charity of my illustrious brother. James Hamilton has managed to find exactly thirty-five minutes in which to allow me to explain my future plans to him this morning. I need to present myself in his plantation office downstairs promptly at nine-fifteen. But I want to imprint on your good brain, Eve, that Marietta, Georgia, is a highly cultivated place. It's only a village at the moment, but next year, 1852, it will be incorporated into a real city. The people who live there, most of them, are educated and have splendid taste. Just wait till you see the house we're going to live in up there! It isn't fancy, but it's a big house—eight rooms and a kitchen—and it's a beautiful, simply designed place with big, round, white columns in front." She laughed. "I think even my fussy brother James would approve the clean, good lines of its architecture. But he's not going to like it one bit that I went to Marietta without consulting him first. More than that, he'll be sure his sister has taken leave of her senses for committing herself to buy such a fine house, with everyone's funds so low these days. He'll worry that I'm planning to make my monthly payments with only my husband's small pension from the British government and the help of one son not yet nineteen. Eve, will you pray for me while I'm keeping my appointment with my brother?"

"Pray for you?"

"I'll need your prayers. Master Couper is a truly kind, generous man, but in all my years of life as his sister, I've never, despite how much I admire him and his brilliant mind, been able to understand what really goes on inside the man. I didn't know when he was a little boy. I still don't. He doesn't know me, either. We're born of the same parents, but no two people ever differed more from each other than James Hamilton and I do. Papa knew that. I doubt that he understood how James's mind worked either, but he did know we were nothing alike. Dear Papa and I called him the Old Gentleman, you know, through all my childhood. I love my brother. I want him at least not to worry about me. Even if he thinks I'm crazy, I want him to know how grateful I am that he took us all in as he did when we had to leave Lawrence, but that I have realized at last I can't go on living on his charity or anyone else's."

"I pray for you. In my heart I've already started, Miss Anne. An' Eve, she do understand you. Eve understand you zactly the way you are!"

❧ ❧

AT THE ALLOTTED TIME, ANNE KNOCKED ON THE TALL, CLOSED door of her brother's private office at the rear of the spacious downstairs entrance hall.

"Enter, please," he called in a voice he might well have used were he expecting a business acquaintance.

Anne made sure she was smiling when she opened the heavy, dark door and went toward him with her hand out. "I hope I'm right on time, James," she said, embracing him on impulse instead of shaking his hand as he plainly intended.

"You are indeed, Sister," the tall, handsome man said, checking his gold pocket watch. "I like that."

"Oh, James, I know you do." She found smiling rather easy. Eve must be praying. Not that she didn't dread this interview in one way, but her own mind was at ease. That she was doing the right thing, at this moment at least, she had no doubts whatever.

"I think you'll find that armchair comfortable, Anne," he said, leading her to it, then seating her in his gallant way. After he took his own chair behind the heavy desk, he gave her what, for James, was a cordial smile. "Now then, you've been keeping secrets from your family for quite some time. Are you ready to share them?" James lifted one slender hand. "First, I do want you to know I have no intention of demanding that you explain why it is you failed to keep in touch with me after you left here to visit Frances Anne at the Wylly home on St. Simons well before Christmas of last year. And it's now April. But obviously you had a reason, so we don't need to use up our time on that. I find I would be interested to know why you didn't inform me from Marietta that you were returning to the coast at this time. Your son, John Couper, of course, has told me rather a lot of what you've been up to lately."

"The boy writes to you regularly, I'm sure."

"He does and we had the extreme pleasure of his company overnight right here at Hopeton earlier this month. Just before you returned to the coast, I believe."

"Yes. I knew he was coming. James," she said in an almost solemn voice, her smile replaced by a look that begged her brother to believe her, "I told Anna Matilda King day before yesterday that John Couper is my rock. That I'd be afraid of everything without him."

Instead of the slightly critical, puzzled look James so often gave to those who didn't quite keep up with the speed of his facile mind, he was smiling at her. Smiling broadly and leafing through a neatly stacked sheaf of papers in one of his desk drawers. "As usual, Anne, you express yourself in hyperbole, but where John Couper is concerned, I must say that I fully understand why a mother would be tempted to exaggerate." From the sheaf of papers he took out a single-page letter, leaned back in his chair, and announced that although her son hadn't known the nature of the letter he brought with him from Savannah, James considered the message so unusual, so important, he would now read it aloud to Anne, trusting that it also imparted his own estimation of her only son.

She waited while James Hamilton took out his spectacles, shined them carefully, hooked them over his ears, smoothed the single page more than it needed to be smoothed, and began to read.

"Savannah
2 April 1851

James Hamilton Couper, Esq., Glynn County
Dear Sir:
We embrace the opportunity of the intended visit of your nephew, Mr. John C. Fraser, to his relatives in your part of the country, to perform a most pleasant duty in bearing our unsolicited testimony to his uniform rectitude of conduct while in our employ as clerk and soon to be head clerk. The temptations which beset a person of his years in a community like this have so far had no allurements for him, and with an extraordinary exemption

from every specie of vice, strict attention to his business duties, and a high-toned moral principle, he bids fair to be in an eminent degree, the pride of his family and friends and an ornament to society.

We beg the favor that you will communicate the purport of this letter to his mother and sisters, to whom it would doubtless be a gratification to learn that the conduct of their relative meets the highest approbation of his employers.

> Your Obdt. Servants,
> McCleskey and Norton"

Overcome by the content of the letter, Anne slumped a bit in her chair, a smile lighting her face. "James! Oh, James," she gasped. "How can I ever thank you enough?"

"Ah, it is I who can never thank you, dear Anne, for the high privilege of knowing your splendid son not only as my nephew but as what I trust him to be, my friend as well."

"Have you read the letter to his younger sisters yet?"

"No. I wanted you to know of it first. I did, however, read it to John Couper while he was here with us. Anne, I must urge you to make careful note that the Messrs. McCleskey and Norton, of their own volitions, wrote and sent this letter, even bothering to say in it that it is indeed *unsolicited* by John Couper."

Anne knew her sudden, short laugh surprised her brother, but to her it was downright funny for anyone even to think that the boy would ever solicit such a letter. "Don't be shocked that I laughed, James," she said. "The very thought that a young gentleman like my son would ever dream of doing such a thing is, to his mother, only comical."

Doing his best to smile, too—in fact, Anne thought it her brilliant brother's pathetic best—James said a surprising thing: "I feel you must be aware, Sister, that from boyhood, I've recognized that you and our illustrious father had more or less laughed at most of what I think and do. I take no offense now, surely, but I confess I did not expect you to laugh at me for being so proud of your fine son."

Anne rushed to throw both arms around James's neck and was

more than pleased when he quickly returned the embrace. "Dear, dear Brother," she said, still hugging him. "I know I'm difficult for you and you're right. You can be difficult for me, too, but we do care about each other and I love you more than ever for having saved that wonderful letter for me. Papa would be so proud of you. I'm sure I'll wear it out reading and rereading it, so thank you from my heart. Just—just try to be as sensitive to what I've made up my mind to do with my own life as you're being about the McCleskey and Norton letter. Can you be?"

Almost brusquely, he disengaged her arms from around his neck. That her impetuous gesture had pleased him she had no doubt, but this *was* James Hamilton, a gentleman so strict that even his own children were never allowed to play cards with each other in the Hopeton parlor.

When she was back in the armchair where she'd been sitting, he asked politely, "Now, do you feel you can tell me just what it is you have planned, Anne? I can promise only that I'll be totally honest with you in my reaction to it. I will say that I had a firm conviction when John Couper was here that he already knew what it is you mean to do. He said not one word about it, but I sensed that much." After another check of his watch, he asked, "Do you think you're ready to tell me now? My allotted time is running out."

"Yes, James. I know about your rigid schedule and I also know I'm lucky to have been permitted some of your time today. But will you please just listen to me? Hear me out?" By the time she finished telling him of her own state of helplessness when she left Eliza Mackay's house in Savannah and headed by train for Marietta, of her confusion at the lostness of her own life, too much of her allotted time had passed. But with all her heart, she'd tried to explain to him that even though she appreciated his family's taking her and her children in, giving them a home at Hopeton, she also knew that they had been a disruption to James Hamilton and to his dear, hospitable wife, Caroline, and to the children still living there. She stopped talking for an instant when James failed to disagree with her using the word *disruption*. He did say he'd be totally honest with me, she thought. Well, he is being. I'll just go on, not call his attention to something that could well ruin this already risky conversation.

"I can truthfully tell you, James," she heard herself say, "that I would never have made the trip to Marietta had both Pete and John Couper not pushed me to do it. In fact, John Couper had already sent his sister up there. Pete was house hunting, living at the home of his Savannah friends the John Wilders. At their suggestion I stopped at the Howard House, and from almost the first moment I met the landlady, Mrs. Dix Fletcher—Louisa to me now—I knew I had made my own, my very own new friend. No one even introduced Louisa and me. She was simply the landlady at the hotel where I stayed. She is so much like Fanny Kemble Butler, I found myself drawn to her immediately!"

James made his first utterance since she began talking. He said, "Mrs. Butler, eh? Hm-m."

"I'm not even going to ask you what that means. I truly liked Fanny Kemble Butler. Found her stimulating. She stretched my mind, put me at ease because so many of her ideas and convictions were like John's. *My* John's. She kept me on my toes, but I also felt at home with her. I feel the same with Louisa Fletcher, and somehow I believed her when she told me soon after we met that she also needed a new friend of her very own. Needed someone in whom she could confide, with whom she could be herself with no fears of criticism. Yes, James, like Fanny Kemble, she's against slavery. She's also a Unionist."

"Well, you know, Sister," he interrupted, "that I am certainly against secession of the Southern states from the Union!"

Anne stared at him. "No. No, I didn't know that. How would I know? You and I have never talked about such things together. But I think I'm relieved that you are against such a dangerous idea as leaving the Union, and I thank you for telling me now."

"Not at all," he said and allowed her to continue.

She had a bit more trouble than she expected actually telling him that she had committed herself to buy rather than rent a large, handsomely simple house, even though it would not be easy to meet the payments against the final price of almost five thousand dollars. She quickly pointed out that the house would probably not be available until early 1852 and that John Couper was to receive a sizable raise in salary long before then. And that he seemed to have his heart set on making it possible for her to have a home of her very own in surroundings where she could, by God's grace and her earnest effort, learn how to live again without so many people who had once filled her very life.

"I have known for several years that I'm being a burden to all my children, even Selina," she continued. "It's not fair to them. There have been times when I've actually allowed myself to think that because the three older children have been forced to grieve so much over me, they haven't had a chance to grieve properly for their father, their sister Annie, their grandparents." Sitting on the edge of the armchair, she pleaded with him. "James, James, please do your very best not to be annoyed with what I've done and most especially because I did it without consulting you. But you have your own life to live. If anyone knows your heavy financial responsibilities, I know them. I know I may be doing a foolish thing, but I had to make my own decision, with the help of Pete and John Couper, and I have to begin now to take full charge of my life. You've always been available to help me in all the ways you could. I am sure, even though you and I are as different as two people can be, that I know the depth and quality of your feelings toward me, toward my children. But I had to do this on my own. Do you understand at all what I'm saying?"

For some time he sat behind his large desk in silence, his eyes still on the businesslike script of the letter about John Couper from the owners of McCleskey and Norton. Finally, he said softly, "I've always meant to help you in any way I could, Anne. I've always meant to—to understand you. I'm not at all sure that I do understand you, but I believe you and I accept what you've done without consulting me. I also ask your forgiveness because your brother James Hamilton Couper was—still is, along with most other coastal planters—unable to lay hands on an extra dollar with which to assist you financially. I felt ashamed that due to the nation's economy, I could not repair your house at Lawrence because I was unable to borrow money. Not for repairs, not for enough extra hands to work your land over there on St. Simons. I can assure you that otherwise I would never have leased Cannon's Point to anyone outside the family."

"Oh, James, hush! Don't ever say any of this again. Don't even think it. Just tell me you're glad I even *think* I might have made a good decision for me and my children. Whether or not you believe I have, tell me you're glad *I* believe I have. Can you do that?"

After another check of his watch, James got to his feet. "I can truthfully say I am glad if you believe you've done a wise thing, Sister. But could we go over once more the actual amount of your income from John's military pension?"

"Why, yes, James, but it hasn't changed. Not in pounds at least. I receive forty pounds a year as my widow's pension and until Fanny and Selina are twenty-one, ten pounds a year for each, of them."

"I believe at my last check, one British pound is equivalent to something above four dollars in American currency. Am I correct?"

"As far as I know, yes. And John Couper vows he can send us money each month when his salary goes up."

"The lad means that, too. I'd stake almost anything I own on his faithfulness to you, Anne. It's just that this is an enormous decision for a woman to be forced to make alone."

"I wasn't forced to make it. I made it on my own, Brother."

"The truth is, you're not alone. You'll never be alone as long as you have your splendid son, John Couper." James picked up the letter and handed it to her. "I do thank you for telling me of your plans at last and I want you to have this letter to keep. I also want you to join me in the sure knowledge that our own father would be delirious with joy if he could read this letter about his namesake and grandson. I'm proud of my sister, too, and I want very much for you to believe that and to remember it. Now, our interview must come to an end, Anne. It's five minutes past the time I normally allot to reading poetry in the morning before I ride out to inspect my fields. I'll see you to the door."

Chapter 29

THROUGHOUT THE SOFT, SOMETIMES RAINY, SOME-
times sunny spring back on the coast, Anne and her
three girls packed and unpacked. They made what
she knew to be farewell visits to friends in Darien; to
her brother William Audley's family at Hamilton
on St. Simons, where she and John had spent so
many happy years when their children were growing up; to Anna Matilda's home at Retreat. And
when Frances Anne Fraser came to see her sisters at
the Wylly plantation, the Village, she spent time
there too.

She, Pete, Fanny, and Selina had outwardly fallen
back into the tiresome drifting about from relative's
house to friend's house, almost as though the whole
trip to Marietta had been only a dream. Now and
then her youngest daughter would complain because
so much time had to go by before the Marietta house
would be empty so that they could move into it.

"You haven't even seen our new home, Selina,"
Anne would say to her. "Don't you like it at all down
here on the coast anymore?"

"Oh, Mama, I've always liked it fine here, but that
was when we could go home when it began to get
dark. Home to our own place. Wouldn't it be wonderful to make up our own minds what we want to
eat every day?"

Yes, yes. Anne could not have agreed more surely with her fourteen-year-old daughter, growing prettier, her dark brown hair curlier, with the passing of every day. The dragging passing of every day. What they were all doing during this odd, forced interlude was at times sickeningly like what they'd been doing through the sorrow-filled, helpless weeks, months, and years during which one after another of their loved ones left them. But in Anne's secret heart—and she knew in Pete's, too—the white-light house on its rise of land just off Decatur Street in Marietta was continuing to undergird everything they did to fill these waiting days with a brightness and security yet unknown to Fanny and Selina.

Before Anne and Pete had left Marietta for this indefinite stay among their coastal friends and family, Anne had called on Lawyer Bentley in his office overlooking the courthouse in the Square. She had genuinely liked the tall, energetic man and believed him when he promised to write to her at Hopeton at the earliest possible moment, as soon as he had a firm idea of when the Bostwick relatives would vacate the mansion. The house to Anne—to almost anyone, in fact—was indeed a mansion. She would need time to see to the crating and shipping of what little of her own furniture she'd need to take. Thoughtful Mr. Bentley, along with Louisa Fletcher, had promised to find warehouse space for it if it happened to arrive before Anne and her girls got there. The list of what to ship had been made in her mind so often, there would be no actual need to write it down when the good news finally came. She would want them to have their own beds, although all her furniture, once so cozily tucked into the blessed Lawrence cottage, would look out of place in the larger house. But feathers plucked years ago from Cannon's Point fowl made their mattresses exactly what each one longed to have again. Of course, the high, high, heavy desk, a gift from Father Fraser, which still stood in the small Lawrence hall, must accompany them. In her memory the simple, plank ceilings of their new home were high, but would they be high enough to accommodate Father Fraser's handsome, towering desk?

"I don't think you should try to curb yourself one bit in thinking these things through while there are still months to wait," Anna Matilda told Anne almost every time she visited Retreat. "Give yourself all the room you need to dream, and it's only natural for a woman to wonder about placing furniture. Isn't it a good thing the house is partly furnished? It does seem to me as though God Himself has guided this whole venture for you, Anne."

Spending ten days in June with her sister-in-law Frances Anne Fraser at the Village, Frances's family home near Cannon's Point—the Couper and the Wylly families had been close neighbors and warm friends for all of Anne's young years—had special meaning for Anne because by now she knew she wasn't merely imagining that she and Frances could indeed speak their minds together.

"I suppose you're right," Frances Anne said as they sat on a favorite moss-cushioned, fallen log in the Wylly woods near the old house. "We probably have, simply because of our strict upbringings, mostly talked *around* things together, even when we talked alone. I really tried, knowing how you loved the old gentleman, to conceal some of my own annoyance with Father Fraser back when he and my William were both alive. Especially during our years on the Ridge in Darien, the old fellow got on my nerves and not for any special reason. I just didn't want Father Fraser interrupting the blessed privacy William and I had so cherished. I'm a little ashamed of myself now, but"—she laughed softly—"not very. Just as you're not really ashamed because you complain that you've had to move from one place to another for all these years since John died. And that strangers are living now at Cannon's Point. You're not ashamed, are you?"

"No. If I'm honest, I'm not, and it doesn't have one thing to do with my gratitude to you, to my brother William Audley and his family, to Miss Eliza in Savannah, to Anna Matilda, and certainly to James Hamilton and Caroline. Everyone has been most kind to my girls and me, but isn't it marvelous that even though it's taken us years, you and I no longer need to pretend we're only one way about something? That we can say flat out that we felt, or feel, two ways about lots of things? I wish we could admit that to everyone we know, don't you?"

"My sister Heriot does, you know. She spoke bluntly, even to the point of contradicting herself, to our dear, proper, British mother before she died. Of course, people call Heriot peculiar in her head."

"My John didn't call her that. He used to say any conversation with Heriot Wylly was a relief because it was always so plain that she wasn't trying to fool anyone."

Frances turned to look at Anne. "I'm glad you mentioned John so easily. I've always thought you didn't speak of him often enough for your own sake. Do you know why it's always been hard for you to talk about him?"

"For the first few years, yes. I was afraid I'd burst into tears. After that, basically, I guess, the children. My grief has not been easy for them to carry. They shouldn't have had to carry it. That's one of the big reasons I'm moving to Marietta to live, in case your quick brain hasn't already caught on. *I must stop being a heavy load for them*—for the girls and for John Couper."

"And you're convinced that moving away—that far away from the old, heartbreakingly familiar haunts—will help you lighten their loads?"

"Frances Anne, I have to believe that!"

"You've always been able to convince yourself of almost anything, haven't you, Anne?"

Anne stared at her. "I have?"

"Yes. To me, you have."

"Do you think wanting to leave this dear, beautiful Island and move into my white-light house is fooling myself?"

"I suppose I'm not quite sure."

"Well, I am. Oh, that doesn't mean Pete or Fanny or Selina won't catch me brooding, missing their father, longing to hear him tell me what *he* thinks of our new life up there. Frances, you've looked and looked for another place to buy since you found you could no longer bear being in your Darien house without William. You should know, if anyone knows, that where one lives makes a big difference. You've rented a house in Savannah now where you'll move soon. Don't you feel relieved? Don't you think just being in new surroundings, making new friends, will give you the security you haven't had?"

"I can't seem to sell my Darien house. I have to live somewhere."

"What are you driving at?"

"I think I'm only trying to find out if my dearest friend, Anne Couper Fraser, really wants to leave St. Simons Island. Don't forget, I was one of those who received all those homesick letters from London and Scotland when you were over there. And you had John with you in those days. I'm trying to get you to convince me that this big gamble is one you truly want to take, Anne. I do love you very much. Is that so strange? Have you faced the day you'll be forced to say good-bye forever to the coastal sunrises and sunsets of St. Simons? Have you thought what it might be like never to see, as you've always vowed you could see, the very air above St. Simons turn from yellow gold to white when spring comes each year? Have you faced the day you'll just drive up to Frederica, board a steamer for Savannah, and be gone—maybe forever? Have you wondered at all how hard it might be for you to attend your last service in the little church under the big oaks at Frederica? To take one final look at John's grave? At Annie's? At Isabella's? At your parents' handsome tombstones?"

In a quiet, steady voice, Anne answered, "Yes."

"Is that all you can say—yes?"

She nodded. "And the reason I can say just yes is that otherwise I'd have to return to the same old round of living nowhere that was truly mine. I know I'll be saying good-bye to the one spot I love above all others, Frances Anne, but I'll be going toward something new—something that is going to be all of my own making. I've lost so many persons dear to me, guides for my entire life. At times Annie or John or Papa guided me hour by hour, but they're gone. My girls and John Couper are doing all any children could do to try to take their places, but it *is* my life and I alone am responsible for it. Who knows? I may find that I have a strength I never even dreamed I'd need. The only way to find out is to try myself. Thank you for knowing me well enough to have some idea of what my final good-bye to this blessed place will mean to me, but do believe me when I say I have to do it. Otherwise I'll never again know who I am or why."

Chapter 30

THE HOT, STICKY MONTHS OF JULY AND AUGUST passed somehow, with Anne looking almost daily for a letter from Mr. Fred Bentley, Sr., in hopes of learning something definite about when she and her girls could expect to move into their new place in Marietta. The actual last farewell to her beloved St. Simons Island, its surrounding marshes and serpentine coastal salt rivers and creeks, loomed as full of dread as ever; but the days were rare—especially when the heat and dampness seemed unbearable—when she harbored the slightest doubt that she had made the right choice.

The heat-heavy summer months were spent at Hopeton, and James's wife, Caroline, showed such patience, kindness, and downright good humor with Anne and her brood that she somehow endeared herself to Anne more than ever before. The two became so close that Anne found herself trying to unravel a mystery she had never, never expected to solve. A mystery that certainly was none of her business. Still, she wondered how such a happy-natured young wife had managed all these years not only to get along with a strict, almost humorless, brainy husband, but to keep him adoring her. Everyone praised James Hamilton for his astute mind, his diverse interests, his invaluable contributions to science and agriculture as well as his spreading fame as an amateur architect and a scholar, adept at almost any imaginable subject, while too little attention was paid to Caroline, Anne thought. Highly cultivated guests from all over the east coast as well as from abroad vied with each other to visit James, to learn from him, to make careful studies of the nearly perfect plantation operation that was Hopeton. But who truly felt comfortable with the man except the pretty, dark-haired, even-tempered Caroline? Even his children behaved as though he were their schoolmaster instead of the loving, generous father he surely was.

Anne's one interview with her older brother had seemed to close the subject of her risky move away from the coast to a strange place, but the more time she spent with Caroline, the more she found herself needing to discover, if such a discovery were really possible, just what James Hamilton's view of his sister might be. During that one talk he had told her he was glad to find her happy with her decision and had briefly discussed her finances, but little more. And even though Pete kept trying at meals to find out more of what her uncle truly thought, even she failed.

One late August morning as Anne and Caroline were cutting roses in James Hamilton's prized rose garden, Anne decided to come right out and ask Caroline a nervy question. "If all you want to do is close my mouth when I've asked what I mean to ask you, Caroline, will you just say so? I warn you my question is blunt."

Standing in a row of deep red, fragrant Miranda roses, Caroline looked around at Anne with a warm, affectionate smile on her expressive face. "Have I ever given you the slightest reason to suspect that I'm secretive with you, Anne?"

"No. Otherwise I wouldn't have dared open my mouth in the first place."

Still smiling, Caroline said, "And you hesitated at all to be blunt with me because you've always hesitated to be blunt with your brother James Hamilton."

"You're too smart sometimes," Anne said, returning the open smile. "There are certain occasions, Mrs. Couper, when I give myself the pure pleasure of thinking you just may be a lot smarter than James. At least in the ways that matter most to *people*."

Clipping a long-stemmed rose, Caroline said quite casually, "I'm waiting to hear that blunt question."

"Are you sure?"

"So sure, in fact, that I'm downright curious now," Caroline answered. "Only I do hope it isn't the same old question at least twenty people must already have asked me during the years I've been married to your handsome brother."

"It isn't the same one. I promise. It's surely no news to me that most of our family and friends never stop wondering how it is that you and James Hamilton appear to get along so well when you're not only seventeen years younger than he, but also wholly in love with life and laughter. I know the answer to that one as much as anyone can know it, I think. My question—my probably quite rude question—has to do with the kind of love I still have for John. Caroline, do you really still love James Hamilton so much that when he enters a room, you have to control the very beating of your heart?"

Caroline went on smiling as she dropped another rose into the basket beside her on the perfectly mulched ground. "Anne, I dare any wife to claim the love of a kinder, more generous, more thoughtful husband. In all the years we've been married, James has never spoken a harsh word to me."

"Well, why should he?"

"Because I had so much to learn about *how* to be his wife. And if you think I didn't know your dear father, John Couper, wasn't behind his marrying me while I was so young, you're wrong. That's the old-fashioned, European way. Find a young wife and train her by your own standards."

Anne stared at her. "You knew Papa said that?"

"Of course I knew it."

"*How* did you know?"

"James Hamilton told me while he was proposing to me."

"I suppose he also told you he'd decided long before he fell in love with you that he had selected and written down the exact date he believed was the proper time for him to marry."

"He did. That was also part of the dear man's proposal."

"And you didn't mind that he wasn't declaring his undying love for your charms and beauty?"

"No, because I'd heard for years—all through my childhood—that James Hamilton Couper was the most particular man on earth. Surely, the most particular man on earth wouldn't have selected an ugly, bad-tempered, stupid girl to marry!" Caroline looked Anne straight in the eye. "What you really want to know has more to do with you than with me, doesn't it?"

"What?"

"You heard me. It surely can't be too long before you will hear from your Marietta lawyer. Then, soon after that, you'll be leaving us. I certainly do understand why you asked your question, because I'm sure my dear husband let you find out very little of how he truly feels about your going away from the coast to live."

A slow smile crossed Anne's face. "Are you a mind reader?"

"Maybe. How else would I keep my balance with a husband who, except when he's writing letters to me, tells me almost nothing?"

"So that's how you've gotten along so well as Mrs. James Hamilton Couper all these years? By reading his mind."

"That and the way I imagine almost any woman deciphers her husband. James lives his entire life as the methodical, careful, intellectually superior man he is—except when he's holding me close to him at night."

Anne knew the startled look on her own face must have told Caroline everything, but Anne thought of absolutely nothing to say.

"Have I answered your questions?" her sister-in-law asked.

"I—I'm not sure. Yes, I am sure! You did answer my nosy question and a lot more besides."

When Anne began to frown, Caroline dropped her shears into the rose basket and came to stand beside her. "But I've made you unhappy for some reason. I understand James fairly well, but I honestly have no idea why you suddenly look so puzzled. Is something bothering you, Anne?"

Anne nodded. "I can't help wondering if my John wouldn't

have had a far smoother life had I known how to read his thoughts the way you seem always to have known about James. John sometimes talked too much. James can be as silent and unexpressive as a pine stump. Was I terribly stupid not to have realized more of what might have been going on in John's private thoughts? He did talk a lot, but all I ever gathered was that he either was trying to hide something from me or was—afraid."

Caroline threw both arms around Anne. "My dear friend, listen to me. You've never been stupid in your life! You just happened to marry a demonstrative man. Did John ever hesitate to show his deep affection, even for the children? Did he ever have any trouble showing you how deeply he loved you?"

"I don't think so. No, he was almost always an open book to us all."

"Which, of course, has helped make my dear husband seem more enigmatic and difficult for you as the years go by. James will be sixty in three years. I do my best to remind myself that whatever quirks he may have will probably only grow more pronounced as he gets older. But, Anne, listen to me. He has done his level best to tell me exactly what he thinks about the big risk you're taking to leave the coast and move more than three hundred miles away from your family. And before you ask, yes. I think he did make an effort to let me know because he thought, or at least *hoped,* I'd tell you."

Anne stepped back to look at the younger woman. "And are you going to tell me, Caroline?"

"First, I have to tell you that I've never, never seen James downcast, really ashamed of himself as he has been ever since the day Papa Couper had to tell you that you must leave Lawrence because there was no money anywhere in the family to repair your house there."

"James Hamilton—*ashamed?*"

Caroline nodded. "Even I have to use every bit of my imagination to try to understand how deeply it shamed him that he, who had always found a way to come successfully through every large or small business setback until his dearly beloved sister really needed his help, couldn't give it. I feel a bit guilty telling you this, but I can see you need to know. The last thing the blessed man said, when his tender, deep lovemaking was finished just last night, was that he'd feel his life almost perfect if only he could send you off to Marietta with more than ample money in the bank."

Anne turned away. "I'm the one who should be ashamed, Caroline! And I am. But the last thing he said to me, the one occasion he set aside time for us to talk since I've been back from Marietta, was that our allotted time was up and that he would show me to the door."

When Anne turned to face her again, the good, warm, inclusive smile was back on Caroline's lovely face. "And I'm sure he made that speech in his usual gallant way. Anne, I've always known your brother adored you, worried about the load you've had to carry, felt deep concern that you've been left alone, but he counts on your son, John Couper, as though the boy were his own son. And with all his eccentric, great heart, James wants to find a way to come to your rescue, even if some months pass before the price of cotton makes that possible."

Tears stood in Anne's eyes as she embraced her sister-in-law and said, "Thank you, Caroline. I don't want him to worry about us, but with all my slowly mending heart, I do thank you."

"Nonsense. For what? Now, before the roses we've already cut wilt still more, we'd better get back to work, Anne."

Chapter 31

ANNE REALIZED THAT BECAUSE THE LETTER FROM Lawyer Bentley could reach Hopeton any day now, she must make two remaining, difficult visits before she could leave the coast with anything resembling a peaceful mind. The first was a visit to Lawrence; the second, a visit to Christ Churchyard at Frederica. Both necessitated a boat trip to St. Simons, but June and Big Boy would gladly take her, Eve, and the girls, and as always, Big Boy would beam his delight at riding along with her when she and Eve went alone to the cemetery.

June landed the Hopeton schooner at Hamilton, her brother William Audley's place. Loaded into the Hamilton carriage, the little Fraser family and Eve rode toward Lawrence on the north end of the Island.

The maroon tops were gone from the straight, almost branchless, devil's-walking-sticks, which grew along most St. Simons roadways. Autumn's beauty was at the same instant just arriving and just leaving. There were few wildflowers beyond scraggly clumps of yellow, where she knew black-eyed Susans were beginning to fade. But wild cassina berries and Papa's favorite firethorn, dull orange only a few days ago, were now brilliant red. Beauty was coming and going. As were Anne's memories. How she'd always loved the wild, overgrown St. Simons autumn tangles of color—green smilax hearts twining with dark red creeper around green cedar saplings decorated by the bright gold of bullis grape leaves as they climbed or waved in and around old live oaks and wild palms. Today, for the first time in perhaps nearly fifty years, the memory of her own child voice returned, asking Papa why "God's tangles are so much prettier than man's planted gardens," and of Papa's chuckling response, "Perhaps, lass, because God thought them all up first."

Then, as he reined the team into the narrow, almost never traveled lane that would lead them to Lawrence, she heard Big Boy's velvety voice from his high driver's perch: "Hold on, ladies! Dis ole road done got mighty rutty an' growed up wif weeds—eben some lil ole saplin's."

"Just do the best you can, Big Boy," Anne called.

"I kind of like it," Pete said, "providing the wheels don't come off."

They were all laughing—except Anne, who could only smile, hoping to hide her nervous anxiety when at last they would be close enough to actually see the story-and-a-half cottage where she'd spent her happiest, most carefree years with John and their small children. Would its roof still be intact? Both chimneys? Would the old pinestraw path, which John insisted on tending and weeding himself, still direct them across the wide front lawn toward the wooden steps and up onto the tiny, vine-shaded front porch?

"Oh!" Selina's gasp was almost a cry of pain. "The porch is really caved in!"

"Mama," Fanny said just above a whisper, "do you think we should have come at all? Just look at our poor little Lawrence cottage!"

"I see it, child," Anne said, her voice grim, tears burning her eyes. "I see it, Fanny, dear. You didn't expect it to look the way it always looked, did you?"

"Right, Mama," Pete said, trying, Anne knew, to bolster her mother's spirits by using her most energetic voice. "This may be your birthplace, Fanny, but the ladies in the Society to Honor Fanny Fraser haven't done much to keep it repaired."

"I doubt that Fanny finds that very funny, Pete," Anne said, still trying to keep her smile in place.

"The whole corner of the porch roof's fallen in, Mama," Fanny gasped. "Remember when you used to rock me right in that corner?"

"Of course I remember," Anne said, hoping the quaver in her voice wasn't too noticeable.

"Oh, do I wish John Couper were with us today!" Pete said to no one in particular. "He was born here in this old shack, too, but he'd find something funny about it. Wanna bet?"

"You be born here, too, Miss Petey," Eve said smartly. "You think ob somepin funny!"

"I thought I was," Pete snapped.

"You want I should stop the team now, Miss Anne?" Big Boy asked.

"Yes, please. We'll just sit here a minute and try to decide what to do next," Anne replied, hoping she didn't sound as helpless and lost and stricken as she felt.

"We gonna climb dem rickety steps?" Eve asked.

"Maybe we will and maybe we won't," Anne said.

For what seemed like a long, long time, they just sat there in the carriage and stared at their ruined cottage and kept their thoughts to themselves.

Finally, leaning to whisper in Anne's ear, Eve said, "Eve kin climb up dem steps, Miss Anne, den holler out to tell the rest of you if they be safe. Don' worry 'bout me. I won't fall. I kin be careful when I wants to."

Anne surprised herself by agreeing, after she'd warned Eve that she must not hurt herself. "I'll never make it to Marietta or anywhere else without you!"

Eve wouldn't allow Selina to talk her into letting her climb the steps because she was younger. To Eve, Anne said, "No one's any younger than you—and certainly no one's as stubborn."

"I might be stubborn, Miss Anne," Eve laughed, jumping to the ground from the carriage, "but I kin also git myself up dem steps. You watch."

Watch they did, and after dropping to her hands and knees for the final stretch up onto the porch, Eve waved triumphantly and called, "De steps be bad, an' you ain't eben to try, Miss Anne, but Pete and Selina and Fanny kin git theirselves up here. De four ob us, we tell you eberthing 'bout what's inside."

Lifting her voice, Anne addressed Eve. "All right, Eve, but watch where you walk. You know some of the floorboards were separating before we moved out." After warning Pete and Selina to be careful, too, Anne sat waiting.

Big Boy, who seldom made a move of any kind without being asked, offered to go in case someone fell down. Anne refused to let him because of his enormous weight, and so the time dragged by with not another word from Big Boy.

After what seemed to Anne an unnecessarily long wait, she heard their voices from the far side of the Lawrence house. Then, Selina, running ahead of Eve, Fanny, and Pete, hurried around the house to where Anne sat.

"Mama, we all think you can't go inside at all!"

"And why not?"

"Because all three of us had to crawl on our hands and knees through the old, musty-smelling parlor and the dining room to be sure the floorboards didn't give way under us. We'd try one board at a time with our hands, putting just a little weight, then all our weight down. It's just not safe. Besides, rats and mice and coons and who knows what else have been leaving deposits all over!"

Eve and Pete, who had rushed up behind Selina, heard most of her report. "She's told you the truth, Mama," Pete said, her voice too loud, Anne knew, because she intended to be convincing. "You just must not even try to go inside, so there's no point whatever in your taking a chance on climbing those rotten front steps."

"Selina be right, Miss Anne," Eve put in. "I'm here to look after your *heart* first. You gonna be a lot happier in Mar'etta rememberin' dis ole house wif your purty flowered slipcovers an' nice clean carpets on de floors. Mind me on dat, please, ma'am! Eve, she know dat heart ob yours better'n anybody anywhere!"

"I'm not sure I accept that," Pete said, grinning. "After all, she's my mother, which means I'm her daughter, and the last I heard, you're not even related, Eve. But"—Pete's grin looked as bright as her red hair in the November sunlight—"I guess you do know our mama better than anybody anywhere. Even if you are a whole year younger than she is."

"I don't find that a bit funny, Pete, but we'll forget it for now." Anne turned to Eve. "If *you* have no strenuous objections, Miss Eve, there is something I intend doing."

"What, Mama?" Selina asked.

"As soon as we have our picnic lunch, I have every intention of taking a walk—by myself—into the old woods we always called the Park. Maybe it is better if I don't go inside the house, but I am going out to the Park. And I don't want any back talk from anyone. Big Boy, will you bring the picnic basket and the big jug of lemonade from the carriage rack, please?"

"Where will we spread our picnic, Mama?" Selina asked.

"Where we always used to spread it, dear. Behind the house under that lovely old live oak. Your father's favorite tree at Lawrence."

"I wish I remembered picnics here," Selina said, almost sadly.

"But you do remember Papa's telling you how he loved that old tree, don't you?"

"No, Mama. I don't remember that either." The girl brightened. "But I know it now and I'll think about the tree, and Papa, while we're having our picnic. I hope there are a lot of deviled eggs. I'm starved."

THERE WERE, ANNE WAS RELIEVED TO NOTICE, MORE THAN enough deviled eggs. Considering the undercurrent of sadness because this would undoubtedly be the last time Anne saw Lawrence, the picnic was pleasant, in part because of the late-autumn departure of the pesky deerflies. Eve seemed to be rather comfortable at times about sitting down with Anne when they were alone, but although she picked at the delicious eggs, ham, and biscuits, Anne's invitation for her to sit on the ground with them when she ate was too much for Eve to handle. She helped herself to whatever she wanted to eat, but stood the whole time, passing around plates of this and that from the well-packed basket.

"You be goin' to the Park now, Miss Anne?" Eve asked when Anne declared she couldn't eat another bite.

"I am and it's important that I go alone, so no offers of company, please. Not from any of you. The girls can help you clean up, Eve, and repack the basket. Just be sure you ask Big Boy if he's had enough of everything."

"You gonna be out dere in the woods all by yourself a long time?" Eve pressed.

"How do I know? I don't live on James Hamilton's schedule. I'll be there for as long as I need to be."

"You gonna be out there to think some?"

"Oh, Eve, don't make me cross, please. I don't want to feel cross today of all days. I want to be—me. Is that so hard to believe? If anyone knows how hard it is for me to say good-bye to this place, it should be you."

"It is me. An' all I want to do is remind you that you don' need to say good-bye today. We sleepin' tonight at the Wyllys'. We kin all come back."

Her heart reaching toward Eve more than Anne meant it to do at this difficult moment, she tried to think of something to say that might calm Eve's worry over her. For she surely wasn't going to add to the faithful woman's concern by sparring with her. "I'm sorry, Eve, if I sounded cross. I'm not. Not a bit. You're right, of course. We aren't leaving St. Simons quite yet. I just need time alone out there in those woods where I used to go when—when—"

"When what, Mama?" Selina asked.

"When I needed to give myself a good talking to," Anne said. "I need to do that now, so don't come looking for me. Agreed?"

"Agreed," Pete said. "And I'll see to it that no one does, Mama."

Chapter 32

Anne had no sooner found her favorite old fallen log in the Park and settled herself on its cushion of thick, green moss when memories of another, much earlier visit to this very spot sent her thoughts into the one direction she least needed them to go. To John! To another day when Anne had fled the house, years and years ago, even before they'd all moved down to live at Hamilton. For the life of her, she couldn't remember exactly why she'd thought that day that she needed to give herself a good, spine-straightening talk, but the memory rushed back today, and for an instant she felt downright scared. She could all but hear the same crackle and twig-breaking sound John's boots had made on that earlier day as he hurried this way and that through the trees, calling her name, hunting for her—the sound of his steps wandering because he always had trouble finding her favorite old fallen log.

"*John!*"

Her call to him today was almost a scream. On that long-ago day John had come carrying Lovey in his arms, his happy smile lighting the shadows in the woods. The squirming puppy had yapped, wiggling to get down in the leaf mold and pine cones and fallen twigs. The last memory she cared to experience this minute was his gift of the dear little dog, Lovey, and his joy—even his pride—that the usually arrogant, unsmiling James Hamilton had actually given John the pup.

"The future is what matters now," she said aloud today, her voice sounding as strange and old and stiff as the dead, topless devil's-walking-stick over by the nearest hickory tree. There had been no life in that straight old stick in years. There had seemed to be no life in Anne Fraser, but now she was about to set out on the riskiest venture of all—alone—without John. Without Papa. Even without helpful, always present Lovey. Soon after John went away, a rattlesnake's bite killed Lovey. John lay in the churchyard under a thick slab of granite. He'd been there so long, stains were appearing around the letters that formed his name. Would she—could she—bear one more visit to his grave before she left to live in Marietta, some three hundred miles away from the sun-and-shadow-streaked churchyard where lay so much of her own life?

After fingering the tiny, pale green moss flowers growing on the old log where she sat, she spoke aloud again, her voice no longer dry and stiff: "Stop it! You're here to settle in your own mind once and for all, Anne Couper Fraser, that you *are* going away from this Island to live in a house that will be yours and only yours. To begin a new life. Not to leave behind what you don't have anyway, but to begin again. *To begin again.* You cannot leave John or Papa or Mama or Annie or Isabella or even Lovey behind because they all still love you, and where they are now, they could even be waiting for you in your white-light house when you get there!"

Unable to sit any longer, Anne jumped to her feet and stood, looking around the red and yellow leaf-lit woods, watching the light from the sun pick out this and that familiar St. Simons tree or wild shrub—*looking*. Looking for what? For whom? She had firmly forbidden anyone to search for her and wished suddenly, with all her heart, that she hadn't. "God? God, do I believe John and Papa and Isabella and Annie and Mama live now where they know what's happening to me down here? Do I really believe that? Or am I feeling so frantic because what I really believe is that they're all over there in Christ Churchyard just where we buried them in their separate graves? Do I even believe they're alive somewhere—anywhere? Somewhere in the Bible it says, 'Lord, I believe; help thou mine unbelief.' But do I believe anything except that I'm alone with no one left to help me? With dear ones like Pete and Fanny and Selina and John Couper and Eve here only for me to look after them? To find a way to pretend, for their sake, that I don't miss John anymore? To find a way to smile often and be me again with no one to help me?"

Tears were streaming down her cheeks now, and her voice was the lost voice of one woman crying out—alone—to no one!

When something firm and warm and living gripped her shoulder, she gasped, whirled around, eyes wide with fright. There stood Eve, smiling the tenderest smile Anne had ever seen on the bright-skinned, lovely face.

"Eve don' disobey you often, Miss Anne," she said softly. "Leastways not when she know you gonna fin' out. I disobey you dis time. I done been not ten feet away the whole time you been out here in de Park."

"How dare you go against my wishes?"

"You—you ain't eben a lil bit glad to see me?"

Anne threw both arms around her servant and cried harder, louder than she'd cried in years. Eve said nothing. Her arms tightened only so much around Anne's jerking shoulders, and the two stood there as the last sob exhausted itself.

In the silence that surrounded them when the weeping ended, not even a squirrel barked from far off or nearby. No bird chirped. Not a pine cone fell to the ground. Nothing moved. For one of the few times in both their lives, neither woman heard one single sound in a stand of thick St. Simons woods.

"Eve," Anne whispered at last. "Is this what it's like to be—dead?"

"No'm. It ain't like this."

"How do you know?"

"Because I'm standin' here wif my arms 'roun' you. I knows it's you an' you knows it's Eve. I'se livin', so this ain't what it's like to be dead." Smoothing Anne's hair back off her forehead, Eve whispered, "Ain't you glad Eve come after you out here?"

Anne tried hard to smile. "Yes. Oh, yes, but what are we going to tell the children when we get back to the house? They all heard me forbid anyone to follow me. Even Big Boy heard."

"Oh, dey ain't nobody lef' at Lawrence, Miss Anne."

"What?"

"Eve didn't run after you right when you hightail it away out here to the ole Park. I done talk all ob 'em into believin' it do you an' me good to walk back to the Wyllys'. Jus' take our time an' walk along, so's you won't get tired. The girls agree that the fresh air an' walkin' be good for you. Dey done took the picnic basket an' gone to the Wyllys' with Big Boy."

Anne gave her a quick look. "You did that without consulting me?"

"Yes'm. Me an' you got a new life to lib together. We got to get you feelin' strong an' perky again—soon. Ain't dat right, Miss Anne?"

Part of Anne was cross with Eve for having sent Big Boy and the carriage away. Part of her wanted to hug her again. After her ordeal in the woods, the walk would surely be welcome. The walk and no questions from her daughters.

"I wish I knew myself half as well as you know me," she said. And then realized she was really smiling at the woman whose knowledge of her could always be trusted. The smile came easily. "Don't say a word," Anne went on. "Maybe it's just our odd way, but it seems to me as though, without any effort, you've turned me around so that I can see again—at least a little way ahead. Eve, do you believe that I believe my loved ones are all with God now and that they know, as He does, what's happening to me?"

"If I didn't believe dat about you, Miss Anne, I wouldn't believe it 'bout nobody nowhere!"

"All right, then. How do you like the sound of this? I am certain that the letter from Lawyer Bentley will reach us any day. The letter telling me it's—time."

"Time?"

"Yes. Time to begin our new life in Marietta, in the white-light house I'm expecting to heal me. From Hopeton, after Christmas, we'll go to Hamilton. I was dreading it, but now I think I need to see the place once more. After all, Eve, we were at Hamilton when John left me. We can board a steamer for Savannah from there just as soon as I find out about the Marietta house. Am I making sense? Do you have one of your knowings that Lawyer Bentley's letter will come soon?"

The merest flicker of a frown crossed Eve's face. "Not yet, I don' have. But you makin' good sense, Miss Anne."

"And tomorrow morning, I want you to ride with me in the carriage over to Christ Church. Just you and me. I'll probably bawl like a calf, but I have to tell John good-bye. And Papa and Annie and Isabella and Mama. I have to tell them all good-bye, Eve, so don't try to talk me out of doing it."

"No'm."

"All right, let's start walking."

"I know you feel like a big load done roll off your shoulders, Miss Anne. We walkin' too fast."

"Oh, maybe," Anne said, slowing her steps. "I think hurrying has become a habit with me. Sometimes it's as though I've been rushing ever since John went away. And don't ask me why. I've always believed almost everyone could, if she looked hard enough, find something to be happy about—to look forward to. It's been so long since I've looked forward to—anything, I think I'm hurrying to find a way to be the way I always was."

For a time neither spoke. Eve walked a little ahead and to one side, keeping an eye out, Anne knew, for snakes. Finally, Anne said almost longingly, "I must have told you about the new lady friend I met in Marietta. Her name is Louisa Fletcher. She and her husband run one of the nice hotels there. I felt almost like the old me when I was with Louisa. She makes me think a lot of Mrs. Fanny Kemble Butler. She's a Northerner and owns no—people. Doesn't believe in it. I think she's partial to me, too, even though Pete blurted out that I'd need cabins because I do own—people."

"If I gotta be owned by somebody, I be glad it's you."

"Well, I suppose I should thank you. Instead, I'll tell you a secret, if you promise not to try to trick me with it someday."

A glance at Eve revealed that the good smile was flashing. "Mausa John, he tol' me once he didn't believe niggers tricked white folks any more than white folks tricks niggers—and each other."

Anne began laughing softly. "My John really told you that?"

"As I live an' breathe."

"Eve, I do believe he knows what I'm doing—this minute. Even what I'm thinking. You spoke the words, but the man made me laugh just now, almost the way he used to."

"Mausa John still be good at makin' you laugh, if you only listen."

"Yes. Yes, I guess I do need to listen more. Aren't you curious to know about the secret I mentioned just now?"

"If you wants me to be."

"I do. And this is the secret, if it *is* a secret. I suppose most people who know me already know what I'm about to tell you."

"Tell me anyway, Miss Anne."

"If you're glad it's I who own you, you're not half as glad as I am."

"Why, you reckon?

"Because I honestly don't know what I'd do without you now, or anytime, as long as I live on this earth."

Chapter 33

NOT ONE OF HER DAUGHTERS OBJECTED WHEN Anne announced at breakfast at the Wyllys' that Big Boy would be driving her and Eve to the churchyard —just the two of them.

"I need to say some good-byes," she said. Her voice, she thought, sounded almost as cheerful as she meant it to be. "Eve has agreed to humor me. You see, girls, being at Lawrence again in some way helped free me. I'm already making plans for us to begin our new life in Marietta—just as soon as I know when the white-light house will be ours to live in."

"I wish we could go on to Marietta even before Christmas," Pete said. "Then we might be able to have our first Christmas in that great house."

"You know as well as I, Pete, we have to hear first from Lawyer Bentley."

"What if Fanny and I don't like it as much as you and Mama do?" Selina asked.

On a laugh, Pete answered, "Oh, I'm not a bit worried about that, little Sister. Anyway, Mama loves it and Mama's the one who counts."

"We all count," Anne said. "And if I know Eve and Big Boy, they're out front waiting for me now with the carriage hitched to the team, ready to go."

Eve had already made up her mind to follow Miss Anne's lead on their trip over to the churchyard. If Miss Anne felt like just sitting there on the carriage seat beside her the way she was now, without talking, Eve would keep still too. But keeping still didn't need to keep her from praying to the Lord for this woman beside her who would, during the next hour or so, have to face one of the hardest things she'd ever had to do. Because only the Lord knew when, if ever, they might come back again to visit St. Simons Island, it was certainly no secret to Eve that Miss Anne could be about to pay her last visit to Christ Churchyard, to the graves of her papa, Mausa Couper, Miss Rebecca, pretty, bright Annie, and Miss Isabella—and to the grave of Miss Anne's beloved husband, Mausa John.

Eve caught herself just in time to keep from blurting out: "How you gonna do that, Miss Anne? How you gonna say good-bye to the man you loved more than your own life?"

She did catch herself. Eve didn't speak the words, but she felt almost afraid, almost angry, that she was the one who had to be right there nearby while Miss Anne tried to do what no woman ought ever to have to do—walk away for perhaps the last time from the covered-over hole in the ground where they'd put the body she didn't know how to live without.

I could not live long without feeling the hard, safe strength of June's arms holding me in the night, she thought. I could not. I've learned how to do some mighty hard things. Not that. Why, there's no place a body can run even to feel for the warmth and smoothness of a husband's skin against yours. I even wonder, does she still reach her arm across the bed as she used to tell me she reached, trying to find Mausa John in the dark? This has to be almost the hardest time of all for her, because it's been too long for other people to sit still and listen to her telling about pain like that. It's no less pain, though. Nobody has to tell me that. I know Miss Anne too well. I'd give almost anything in this world *not* to be sure she will need me to say exactly the right things to her when she has to turn around and walk away from his grave today! I don't want to know how much she will need me this time, because even though I almost always know, this time nobody but Miss Anne can tell how much she will need me!

All the way out Couper Road to where it forked into Frederica Road as Big Boy turned the team north toward the churchyard, Eve kept her thoughts to herself. The nearly five-mile trip from the Wyllys' had never seemed so long; Big Boy had never driven so carefully, but his occasional smile back at them and the reassuring wave of his huge hand must have comforted Miss Anne some. It comforted Eve too.

Lord, Eve thought, it just came to me that she will be hurt to say good-bye to Father Fraser too. How Miss Anne loved that old man! She loved the little white church, too, so she will need strength to walk away along that old path when it comes time for us to leave. Pulling up roots, Sweet Jesus, as Miss Anne has to pull them up today, will hurt her far more than pulling a tooth!

In sight of the chapel now, Eve struggled to figure out something of what Miss Anne might be thinking. Close as she felt to her mistress, who had in their childhood been her playmate and was now—both women in their fifties—her friend, Eve felt more than helpless because it wasn't possible that even she could tell for certain just how Miss Anne was making it so far.

And then, if the winter sun hadn't already been out, it would have come out, because Miss Anne turned and gave Eve a smile that would have brought it out!

"I'm—all right, Eve," she said. "So far, I'm all right. I wouldn't be were I in this carriage with anyone else but you and Big Boy, but you're both here and—I'm all right."

With the firm, sure support of Big Boy's giant, brown hand, they stepped down from the carriage, and for only a moment Eve wondered whether she should walk up the path a little behind Miss Anne or right alongside her.

"I'd like it if you took my arm, Eve. We don't need to talk. I don't think there are any words anyway—for either of us. Just be with me, please?"

When a wren called from behind the church—beyond the two rows of graves they'd be visiting—Eve knew God was with them. In early winter most birds scarcely chirped. Wrens were faithful, though. God guided wrens, too.

"Thank you for praying," Miss Anne said as they walked past the north side of the church toward the Couper and Fraser graves.

"How you know I'm prayin', Miss Anne?"

In response, Anne lifted her chin and did her best to smile.

Eve turned briefly to be sure Big Boy was following them, although some distance away; he was there, keeping Miss Anne in sight every minute. Their visits began with the Couper plot after they'd passed John Wylly's broken-column tombstone. Slowly, holding her thoughts quietly inside herself, Miss Anne stopped to say good-bye to her parents, Miss Rebecca and Mausa Jock Couper, to her sister, Isabella, to Father Fraser and Dr. William Fraser, Mausa John's only brother. And then, after she knelt for a long, silent moment near them all, instead of going to her lover's grave, she turned and walked slowly toward the Demere plot on the other side of the church. Eve followed her.

At Annie's wide, thick, flat stone, Miss Anne knelt again, her head bowed. Finally, she reached one hand to touch the letters of Annie's name: Anne R. Demere—the *R.* for Rebecca. Each letter was touched lovingly, slowly, with a tenderness only a mother could show her firstborn child. As far as Eve could tell, Miss Anne had not sobbed once. When she looked up at Eve, holding out her hand to be helped to her feet, a smile Eve hadn't seen since Annie died lifted Eve's heart.

"Now," Miss Anne whispered, "we'll go to—John."

Sweet Jesus, help us, Eve breathed wordlessly. Sweet Jesus, we're both in need of help.

Together they walked back around the tiny white church. Eve held on to Miss Anne's arm for dear life. When they reached the granite slab that lay on the sandy ground, keeping Miss Anne's eyes from ever looking at him again on this earth, they stopped. Miss Anne gently removed Eve's hand from her arm. This time, she did not kneel at once. Instead, she just stood there, swaying a little—all by herself—her eyes fixed on the inscription:

SACRED TO THE MEMORY OF
JOHN FRASER
OF THE ROYAL BRITISH MARINE ARTILLERY

And then, as with Annie, her finger traced each letter of his name—
over and over and over.

Finally, eyes still dry, she looked up at Eve with a surprised
smile on her face. Miss Anne looked almost young again—young,
the way she and Eve used to be.

"Eve! Eve, did you hear—what John just said?"

Not wanting to say the wrong thing, Eve simply shook her head
no, to show she hadn't heard. Then she gave a big smile, too, to
make sure her mistress knew Eve believed that Miss Anne *had*
heard his voice.

"Oh, I was so sure you'd heard it too!"

Eve hesitated only an instant, then asked, "What he say, Miss
Anne? What Mausa John say to you?"

"I'll tell you! I'll tell you exactly what I heard him say. He said,
'Oh, Anne, you're going to love the white-light house!' "

"He say that?"

"I suppose you're thinking I sound like Heriot Wylly."

"I'm only thinkin' how proud I am of you!"

"Proud? But do you believe I *heard* John say that?"

"I believes it an' I'm proud, too, cause you ain't cried one
drop!"

Miss Anne's shoulders slumped a little, but there was only certainty on her face when she said, "I don't have any more tears. I
cried all my tears out in the woods at Lawrence yesterday. *I want so
much for John to go to Marietta with me,* but I'm at peace, Eve. I now
know he's alive—somewhere. And that he knows what's happening
to all of us. Otherwise, how would he have known I call it the
white-light house?"

Chapter 34

A WEEK BEFORE CHRISTMAS DAY, 1851, LOUISA
Fletcher caught her oldest daughter, Georgia, thirteen, trying to slip past her mother at work behind
the counter in the lobby at the Howard House in
Marietta.

"Georgia, dear, I know you're not deaf, so will
you kindly slow down for just one minute, please? I
need you to run an errand."

"But Mama, it's time for me to practice my music
lesson!"

"I'm well aware of that, but all I want you to do
is bring our personal mail to me from our rooms
upstairs. It should be on the dressing table in my
bedroom. Your absentminded father forgot I have to
serve my time behind this hotel counter this morning,
and I know there's a letter for me from my new
friend Mrs. Anne Fraser, down on the coast."

"Oh, Mama, are you sure? I should have begun
practicing fifteen minutes ago."

"I'm sure because your father said it was there.
I've waited and waited to hear from her, so do as I
say, Georgia."

"She's the pretty lady with the red-haired daughter named Pete, isn't she?"

"Exactly," Louisa answered.

"The lady who's going to move up here soon and

live in the Bostwick house. I liked her," Georgia said. "I liked her daughter Pete, too."

"Then I'd be ever so grateful if you could see your way clear to grant me a few moments of your time," Louisa Fletcher said with a smile. "I'm fond of them both, too, and I've been on needles and pins waiting for word. I want so much for Anne Fraser to live here."

"Oh, so do I, Mama. She also has another daughter named Fanny and a younger one nearer my age named Selina. Mrs. Fraser told me all three of her girls will be coming to live here with her."

"That's right and I'm still waiting to read her letter. If you aren't in too much of a hurry to practice your music lesson, I'd be ever so happy to share the letter with you, but you will have to get it for me. You know I'm chained to this counter."

Georgia left in a hurry, calling back, "I'm going, I'm going."

WITHIN MINUTES, GEORGIA WAS FLYING BACK DOWN THE HOTEL stair, waving her mother's letter. "Here it is, Mama. Papa's right, it's from Mrs. Fraser!"

After a cordial though somewhat hurried good-bye to some departing hotel guests, during which she made full use of her cultivated Massachusetts speech, Louisa turned to her daughter and the letter. "You may go to your practicing, Georgia," she said, lapsing at once into her most affectionate parental tones. "Far be it from me to keep you from your piano. Music is still my life, too, despite the harried hours spent trying to help your poor father run this establishment."

"But I thought you said you'd share Mrs. Fraser's letter with me! And why do you sometimes call Papa by the name poor father?"

"Because the good man strikes me that way at times when all of this hotel management gets to be too much for him without me."

"Papa says you're a very good wife."

"That's exactly what I've always striven to be, Georgia. Your father's a good father and a well-meaning, morally upright husband, who also tries very hard." After glancing around the lobby of the hotel, Louisa broke the seal on Anne Fraser's letter, reminding her daughter as she did so that she'd read aloud unless or until guests entered the lobby, in which case she'd stop at once and expect Georgia to run straight to her piano practice upstairs.

"We're all alone now," Georgia said impatiently. "Read, Mama, read."

Louisa gave her daughter a teasing smile. "And here I thought you were in such a hurry to get to Mozart."

Smiling, too, Georgia said, "That's mean."

"Not mean, child. Your mother's approaching forty-four. She's just getting old and peculiar."

"Please read! All we know is that Mrs. Fraser is going to be able to move into the Bostwick house sometime, but not when. I want to know when!"

Since Georgia was behind the high counter with her now, Louisa hugged her. "I am being mean. A mean old sinner and that's because there isn't a Protestant church in all of Marietta where your heathen, Unitarian mother is welcome to take Communion. So, don't blame me."

"I like it when you tease, Mama, but I'd much rather hear Mrs. Fraser's letter."

"And hear it you shall. Right this minute." After scanning the first page of Anne's neat, spidery script, Louisa began to read.

"Hopeton Plantation
Near Brunswick, Georgia
In care of James Hamilton Couper, Esq.
10 December 1851

My dear Louisa,

This letter has been a long time in the writing, but I received definite word from Mr. Fred Bentley only a few days ago, and many plans needed to be discussed here before I could place a possible date for our arrival in Marietta. Lawyer Bentley's letters are as charming and gallant as his conversation, and now I know that, allowing a week or ten days for my new home to be cleaned and readied, including some small repairs, we may be able to move at least some of our belongings and ourselves into it around the end of March 1852, or at least by the first week or so in April. My daughters and I leave the coast about a week after New Year's on the steamer *Welaka* for Savannah, where John Couper holds a responsible position with your husband's young friends and former business acquaintances, McCleskey and Norton, and where my girls and I are always welcome for an indefinite stay in the comfortable home of Mrs. Robert Mackay on East Broughton Street. I am sure we will be with her and her two daughters for a month or so, but that will depend on when my son can leave his work to make the long-awaited train journey to Marietta with us.

I feel I know you well enough, Louisa, to say honestly that without my son, I could not possibly be buying this house. I will be dependent on his late father's pension from the British government and on monthly help from John Couper for our livelihood. There was only time before my beloved husband went away for me to have given him one son, but as Tennyson wrote of Sir Galahad, his 'strength is as the strength of ten.' Pete, Fanny, and Selina are the companions of my heart, but John Couper is my rock as I so often say. Even though only Pete and I have seen Marietta and the house, Fanny and Selina share our excitement and are looking forward to the move. As you know, John Couper and Pete have been the steady forces behind my decision to uproot myself and stake what future happiness I may find on being up there near you. Not only have I begun to pray for you daily, dear Louisa, but I think of you often no matter where I am or what I am doing. I will do my best to be more definite in my next letter, but right now, it looks very much as though Marietta's population will, come April, increase by four females. John Couper will, of course, visit us as often as his Savannah work allows. I have told Selina about your charming and talented Georgia, only two years or so younger, and Selina is eager to meet her. My middle girl, Fanny, will fit in with all of you, since a kind, agreeable nature is her greatest charm. And, Louisa, I am counting on you more than you realize. You may, I promise you, count on me in any way in which you find need of me in your busy life. May you, Mr. Fletcher, Georgia, your middle daughter, Eliza, and little Louise experience all the beauty and holiness of the coming holidays. I can only pray that you are looking forward to our coming half as much as I am. When I know definitely, I will write again, since we will hope to stop with you once more at the Howard House until the great day when we can at last move into our white-light house.

Your friend,
Anne Couper Fraser"

"Oh, Mama, they're coming!"

"Georgia," Louisa said, studying her attractive daughter's serious face, "I've never known you to be so pleased about anyone else's moving to Marietta. Certainly not about the comings and goings of our hotel guests. What is it about Mrs. Fraser that you like so? Or is it anticipation of meeting her youngest daughter, Selina?"

"I think Selina and I will be good friends. Oh, yes! But I just liked Mrs. Fraser. There's something about her that makes me think of her often during the day. She is awfully pretty to be older, but even when she's laughing or smiling, I have a strange feeling that she's sort of blinking back tears, too. Is that because I know her husband is dead?"

"You're a most perceptive girl, Georgia. I feel the same way about her, and I know that she and her beloved John Fraser were deeply, deeply in love. They stayed in love for all the years of their lives together, too, according to what she told me. But Pete also confided how much other sadness her mother has had to endure since he died. Not only both parents and a sister, but Anne's own firstborn daughter died too—her sister and daughter within two years of the time she lost Mr. Fraser."

"Oh, dear," Georgia whispered, in awe of such sorrow. "I'll be ever so kind and thoughtful with Mrs. Fraser, I promise. Could I ask you something?"

"Have I ever refused you, Georgia, when you need to know?"

"Are you and Papa deeply, *deeply* in love the way Mrs. Fraser and her dead husband were?"

Louisa kept her smile in place. "Your father is an honorable, hardworking man, Georgia. He and I have known each other since I was about your age or longer. He's not always interested in everything that interests me, but we do share music, books, and our total devotion to you and your sisters. And speaking of music, weren't you supposed to be at the keyboard long ago?"

Georgia sighed. "Yes and I'm going, but oh, Mama, talking to you makes me feel so grown-up and—intelligent."

"Thank you, my dear. Now, run along to your practicing."

"I like it that she calls the Bostwick house her white-light house, don't you?"

"The truth is, child, I like everything I know about Anne Fraser."

PART V

January 1852–
August 1859

Chapter 35

On Wednesday afternoon, January 7 of the new year 1852, John Couper took Miss Eliza Mackay's old front steps two at a time, and when Miss Eliza herself answered his knock, he was relieved.

"Come in, John Couper," she greeted him warmly. "I wish you knew how glad I am to see you this very afternoon."

Hanging his heavy cloak and top hat in her entrance hall, he grasped both her hands and asked why she seemed particularly pleased "this very afternoon."

"Because I'm all alone except for my servants back in the kitchen, and I need to talk to someone. Come on, it's warmer in my parlor."

John Couper seated the aging lady in her rocker near the roaring fire and then took a chair opposite.

"Nothing's wrong, I hope, Miss Eliza."

"Oh, son, with all my heart I hope nothing new has gone wrong in our poor, troubled country. Mark Browning hasn't brought my newspaper yet today, but he will when he can. I know both Mark's favorite statesmen in Washington—Henry Clay and Daniel Webster—are ill. We need those men."

John Couper gave her a quizzical smile. "You're not the typical Southern lady, are you, Miss Eliza? I hear a lot of talk in the firm where I work, you know.

285

Mostly, since I've barely turned nineteen, I keep still and listen, but Southern businessmen are more and more rankled that the South is coming to resemble a Northern colony."

"I know. And women aren't supposed to have opinions on such things, but the equality of our region and the states to the North must be clung to. I own some people, but I'm against the spread of slavery into our Western Territories, and I'm old enough to want the Union of all the states preserved."

"You sound like my Uncle James Hamilton Couper. He's a big slave owner but a strong Unionist. Mrs. Mackay? I came here today for two reasons—aside from the pleasure of seeing you again. May I speak freely?"

"John Couper, you already know that's a rule in this house. I hope all our guests can always feel free to say whatever they want. I admit I worry some about keeping all our states together, but one of the surest ways to break us up is for people in both regions to stop speaking freely and honestly together. I do hope you're not going to tell me your dear mother can't visit Savannah again before she moves to Marietta!"

"Oh, no, nothing like that. She and my sisters should be here when the *Welaka* docks tomorrow. They're all looking forward to time with you, and one of my reasons for coming today is to thank you from my heart for your kindness to my mother during all these lonely years while she's had to move from one friend's home to another. She's always seemed so much more cheerful after a visit with you."

"This time I'm just going to listen. I know she's bound to be the proudest mother anywhere because of your swift rise in your business firm, my boy. And you say you've just turned nineteen?"

"Yes, ma'am. Last month, in fact. Maybe I should tell you first that my sister Pete and I are really behind Mother's move to Marietta. I put a lot of stock in my sister's judgment, in spite of her sometimes impetuous ways. She's been old enough through all of Mama's many sorrows to have observed her, not only as her mother but as a woman struggling to hide her hard grieving for the sake of the children—all of us. Pete and I planned the initial trip to Marietta because, thanks to my friends the Wilders here, I became convinced that not only everyone's health, but Mother's shattered heart will be better up there in that splendid weather."

"I'll certainly miss her visits, but so many people speak of Marietta's temperate weather, fine water, and clear air, it will be a comfort to Anne knowing her children are likely to be healthier up there. More and more Savannahians go up every year just to avoid fevers here, you know. You've made a wise decision, John Couper. Did you ever have any doubts?"

"No, ma'am. And, of course, I'm going by train with Mother and my sisters when it's time to make the trip. I'll stay as long as I think she needs me. Mr. McCleskey and Mr. Norton are most understanding of the responsibility I have."

"And how blessed your mother is to have you!"

"No young man ever had a more important mother than I have, Miss Eliza."

She laughed a little. "I don't think I've ever heard a son use that expression before. Any mother would swell with pride to be called important."

On the edge of his chair now, looking directly at her, John Couper said, "I—I need to say something to someone outside my immediate family, and I've chosen you. I want you to know that from the day we lost my father—and I was only a small boy then—I've had one purpose in my life. That is to take care of Mother, to do everything possible to give her back at least a little of the pure joy and happiness she knew with my wonderful father." He saw tears well in Miss Eliza's eyes and added, "My father was a very hard man to lose, Mrs. Mackay. He and my mother were in love from the first moment they met, you know. I don't have his charm, but at least I can help see to her material needs. I mean to help her buy the house up there she loves so much."

"Have you seen the Marietta house?"

"No, but if Mother likes it as she seems to now, it's fine with me." He smiled. "She calls it her white-light house, you know. Since the day we buried Papa, she's clung to the hope she seems to find in—light. I'm not as poetic as Mama, but I have always seemed to understand why she's needed light to cling to. But she can tell you about the house. That's part of the reason she's so glad to be spending a month or so with you." His smile faded. "That's not what I wanted to talk to you about."

Her kind face gave him the courage he needed to ask her if she and his mother had ever discussed the question of slavery. "Does she talk to you about it at all? There are so few people with whom anyone can speak freely on the subject."

"We've discussed owning people, yes, son."

"Then you know my father was against it." She nodded. "I don't think Mama ever thought much about it until Mrs. Fanny Kemble Butler came to St. Simons before my father died. She's said very little to me, but Mother owns twenty-one people. There are only three cabins on the nine acres around her Marietta house. We, like most others over the past few years, have had little money. Mother is going to need more than she now thinks once she's moved up there. I know she needs new clothes. So do my sisters if they're to make the right impression in Marietta. Of course, Fanny is an expert seamstress and Pete can tutor some, but Mama's going to have to agree to permit me to sell and rent out some of her people. She can take only Eve and June, Mina and her daughter, Flonnie, Big Boy, and Rollie to look after her up there. I know my mother, though. She will *not* want to sell a single person or even rent anyone out, Miss Eliza."

"And you want me to talk to her about the necessity of doing both. Is that what you're driving at, John Couper?"

"Yes, ma'am. It would relieve me a lot if you could see your way clear to do that while she's here. I'm happy to say that Mama has already found a Marietta lady, Mrs. Louisa Fletcher, the land-lady at the Howard House hotel, who seems to be as fond of her as my mother is of Mrs. Fletcher. I'm deeply thankful that she's found someone she likes so much, but—"

"But, outspoken Louisa Fletcher is from Massachusetts and deplores slavery. She and her husband, Dix Fletcher, both come from the North. I know them slightly. She's a glorious singer. I've heard her often here at Savannah's Christ Church. He sings too, I believe,

although they are very different persons. Louisa has definite opinions. The Fletchers lived here for several years, you know, until his
cabinet-making business burned."

With an almost sly grin, John Couper said, "I confess I hoped
you knew them. Mrs. Fletcher especially. Mother's so attached to
most of our people, I'm going to have some trouble talking her into
letting me do what I must do with part of her property and—"

"And you think I can convince her to listen to you first before
she listens too intently to Louisa Fletcher?"

"Something like that."

"I can't promise anything, John Couper. I think I must warn
you, though, that where my heart is concerned, I might just be
almost exactly where your mother is when it comes to selling people—or renting them out." Miss Eliza thought a minute, then said,
"Your mother is a sensible woman, though, John Couper. And
would never want to be a burden to you in any way."

"I know that."

"I also hope you know you mustn't allow all you're doing for
her to come in the way of living your own life."

He grinned. "Miss Eliza, Mama *is* my life these days."

Chapter 36

Late on Monday, February 23, by the time Anne and her children had changed trains at the town now being called Atlanta, Anne wished impatiently for Eve, who, with June, Big Boy, Rollie, Mina, and Flonnie, had to ride in the Negro car at the rear. Trying to tidy her hair with one hand while she held a small looking glass from her portmanteau in the other was nearly impossible, especially with all the jerking. They'd been in this car for only several minutes, but the train had chugged to three stops in the night darkness—black except for the frightening showers of sparks that blew about the ladies' car where they rode. Burning chips and splinters scattered in the wind along the length of the entire train, blown from the wood fire that powered the engine and the wood-burning stoves providing heat in the front and the back of each car.

Seated near the front of the coach, Anne felt her face alternately singed and chilled, depending on how much time had passed since the conductor last fed the stoves with fresh wood. She felt grown to the stiff, unyielding seat of the Western and Atlantic ladies' car as she'd felt grown to almost identical seats on the Central of Georgia and then the Macon and Western, all through the exhausting, muscle-bruising day since they'd boarded this morning in Savannah just after first light.

Only twenty miles left to travel north and she would be in Marietta. John Couper's regular, cheering smiles buoyed her, but her boy, seated now beside her, looked so exhausted she could have wept.

John Couper could, of course, ride with her and the girls in the ladies' car since he was their escort, and Anne was somewhat relieved to have had a few minutes with Eve on the platform in Atlanta when they'd all changed trains there.

"We gonna git to Mar'etta any time now, Miss Anne," Eve had said with her best smile. "June say it ain't but 'bout twenty miles left. Why you don't make up your min' to think hard 'bout all we got to be thankful for, till we gits there. Think 'bout you havin' your own house to go to soon."

Anne scooted her body to a slightly more comfortable position on the hard seat and began to try her best to mind Eve. She could certainly be thankful for Miss Eliza Mackay's promise of daily prayers for them all as they worked to settle into their new surroundings. She was grateful for Miss Eliza's reminder that Anne would now have her first real chance to learn to live through the second part of her married life without John. Able, at least, to make her own decisions. She gave silent thanks for that, but why had a one-day train trip so exhausted her? So exhausted all of them? Even young Selina had dark circles under her eyes. Were they so weary because they knew this was the real wrench? The last severance from their beloved coast? Their last good-bye to St. Simons Island, with John's dear body left behind in the tree-shaded churchyard at Frederica along with her parents, her sister, and her Annie? But didn't she believe, as she had the day she'd said good-bye to John at his graveside, that he knew about the white-light house in Marietta? And if John knew, didn't Papa and Mama and Isabella and Annie also know?

Eve was right. She should be sorting out the good things. Even the rattling screech of the train wheels and the shimmer of excessive heat, which she could actually see reflected in the oil lamp of the railroad car, reminded her that just a few years ago the more than three-hundred-mile journey from the Georgia coast to Marietta by stage would have taken anywhere from three to five days, depending on the condition of the roads. The train was bringing her there in only one long day.

When the car lurched to a stop that could have knocked Anne off the seat, John Couper held her, kept her safe. She could be forever thankful for her son, who would always—even so far away in Savannah—find a way to protect her and Pete and Fanny and Selina. All three girls appeared to be napping now. She was thankful for that, too, even though Pete was forced to share a seat with a huge woman whose body was unpleasantly odorous.

John. If only there had been a way for John to make the journey with them, even their numbers would have been even. She and John could have shared a seat, John Couper could have sat with one of his sisters, with the other two girls together.

At the very moment when counting her blessings seemed to bring a sense of John's presence, her heart ached because for every day of the rest of her life, with John gone, their family would be uneven.

Anne's very life would be uneven.

Then, over the clanging bell in the night, which meant more screeching of metal wheels on metal rails and still another stop, she could have sworn she heard John's voice again as she'd heard it when she stood beside his grave for the last time: *"Oh, Anne, you're going to love the white-light house!"*

Over and over and over she heard it through the next jerking, scraping stop; then as the train pitched forward again into the night, she thanked God that at the end of this trip, she would not have to hunt for a home. They had one. Anne Fraser once more would sleep at night and plan meals and place her own things around in a house that would be hers. She would again be able to write in her diary at her own desk in her own room.

And maybe equally important, she already had at least one friend in Marietta. This very train, within half an hour, could—if there weren't too many more stops to take on wood, water, one or two passengers, a crate of chickens—pull into the Marietta depot. And the depot was just a few steps from the Howard House, Louisa Fletcher's home and their home, too, until the longed-for day when they could move into their own house to stay.

"Want to put your head on my shoulder, Mama, and grab a few winks?" John Couper asked. "We should be there soon now."

"Yes, Son. Yes, I think I'd like very much to do that."

HER HEAD RESTING ON JOHN COUPER'S WIDE, SLENDER SHOUL-der, the reassuring pressure of his hand as he did his best to hold her steady against the lurches of the train, sent Anne's thoughts to the painful subject she'd tried throughout the whole trip to avoid. Not one bit reconciled in her own mind to what John Couper vowed they had to do, she saw the puzzled, even frightened faces of her people, who had served them all for much of their lifetimes, come before her. Where were they now? How were Tiber, George, and Peter, three of the men John loathed buying all those years ago at the Savannah slave market? Big Boy, Rollie, Mina and her daughter, along with June and Eve, were going to Marietta with them, but the others had been rented out and not even together, not even to the same plantation. Tiber and George were rented at a dollar and a half per day to the owners of the plantations responsi-ble for the upkeep of Frederica Road back on St. Simons. Since Horace Gould headed the group, at least she knew Tiber and George were not being mistreated. But someone in Savannah had rented Peter, and a man in Augusta was working a dozen or more of the Frasers' longtime field hands, and— She stopped thinking about it. Trusting John Couper had never been anything but natural to her. That must not change now. The boy was doing everything he knew how to do in order to better her life. He was even going to send her ten to twenty dollars a month from his sixty-dollar salary from McCleskey and Norton toward the monthly house payment of thirty dollars they would have to make. No mother could ask for more. Few received as much.

"All our people are your property, Mama," he had reasoned. "Everyone makes real estate transactions by making use of personal property."

True. Anne certainly knew that, but she could almost hear John's comments—comments that would sound much like those of Fanny Kemble Butler or her new Marietta friend, Louisa Fletcher. Miss Eliza Mackay had confirmed what Anne already knew: because Louisa Fletcher came from Massachusetts and held strong opinions about almost everything and was a Unitarian—as was Fanny Butler's friend the late Dr. Ellery Channing—Louisa did not approve of owning people.

"What do *I* really think about the idea?" Anne asked herself again. Long ago she'd lost count of how many times she'd asked that question, and right now, longing for her familiar, comfortable routine with Eve, her answer was no clearer. Maybe no clearer than it had ever been.

The train was slowing, its wheels screeching again on the narrow tracks. John Couper took his arm away and leaned toward her. "Mama? I think we're there! This must be the Marietta depot. Look out the window."

She looked. Surely the expression on her face had to show a mixture of relief, gladness, but some anxiety. "Oh," she said. "Yes! Yes, Son, this is the Marietta depot. Only it's so dark in the Square beyond it, I can't really see much, can you?"

"Enough to know we've made it this far, at least," he said with a soft, comforting laugh. "I just hope Mr. Dix Fletcher's still up and behind his Howard House lobby counter. I, for one, am already thinking about a nice, clean bed!"

NOT ONLY DIX FLETCHER WAS BEHIND HIS COUNTER WHEN JUST after midnight, the travel-worn guests reached the Howard House. His wife, Louisa, was also there, wearing a pretty plaid silk dress and a smile of welcome. Anne felt especially warmed when her new friend met her halfway across the lobby, arms outstretched as though they'd been friends for years.

Louisa lost no time with introductions. She presented her husband to John Couper, Fanny, and Selina promptly and reintroduced Anne and Pete. When Eve, June, Big Boy, Rollie, Mina, and Flonnie entered the lobby laden with valises and boxes, Louisa began at once to direct them upstairs with full instructions about finding the three rooms reserved for the Frasers. Anne longed for a few minutes alone with Eve before she had to leave for the quarters reserved for Negro servants and so was more than grateful for Louisa's excellent, adept management of the arrival.

"I'm so glad to be with you at last, Eve," Anne said when Louisa had said a quick but warm goodnight. "You know where everything is packed and I don't."

"Ain't no reason you need to know when Eve knows," the servant said, doing her level best to be cheerful, even though Anne realized how exhausted she must be. The ladies' cars were palaces compared with where Eve and the other people rode. "You sit yo'se'f down an' rest, Miss Anne. Eve have what you need tonight unpacked and laid out in no time at all. Miz Fletcher, she done got bof hot an' cold water right here waitin' fo' yo' bath."

"It's going to be the quickest sponge bath in history. Pete's going to be here any minute. Between us, we'll get ourselves ready for bed. If you really want to please me, you'll just find a nightgown and my robe and slippers and go straight to—wherever you and June will sleep tonight."

"Dey be a cabin out back of the hotel for us niggers." In what seemed like seconds, Eve whipped out Anne's nightclothes and laid them as neatly on the hotel bed as though they were already in their own house together again. "How long you speck it will be till we kin git in our own place, Miss Anne?"

Holding up her arms for Eve to unfasten the hooks at the back of her travel shirt, Anne sighed. "Heaven only knows. Two weeks, maybe even a month. I meant to ask Mrs. Fletcher, but I was scared to find out, tired as I am tonight."

"What you skeered ob?"

"I thought you were going to speak better English once we got here."

Eve's smile flashed. "Dat begin tomorrow, Miss Anne. You see."

"All right, but don't forget. And"—she held out her hand, which Eve took timidly—"thank you."

"Pshaw, you thank me for one lil ole nightgown, Miss Anne?"

No. I thank you for being—Eve and for being here with me. I hear Pete in the hall. That girl can't be quiet even when she's exhausted and it's going on one o'clock in the morning!"

"That's our Pete, Miss Anne. An' Pete, she be fine jus' like she is." At the door, ready to leave, Eve said, "You an' me, we's gonna be jus' fine too. You see Eve be right." Giving Anne one more smile as she opened the door to Pete, Eve added, "You see how good Eve talk by in de mornin', too. Good night, Miss Anne."

"Good night, Eve. Try to have a *good* night. Pete! For goodness' sake, come on in. If I don't get in that bed soon, I may be too old to make it all the way across the room! I hope you thanked Louisa Fletcher for hurrying us off to bed so fast. Did you?"

"I did," Pete said, not pouring but literally dumping hot, then cold, water into two washbowls. "And Mama, guess what?"

"Right now, I couldn't guess anything."

"Mrs. Fletcher told me to tell you she'll have a surprise for us tomorrow morning. She seemed really happy about it, too."

Chapter 37

UP, BATHED, AND DRESSED BEFORE SIX THE NEXT morning, Louisa Fletcher enjoyed the unusual spectacle of her normally solemn husband who today was actually smiling, as pleased as was she at Louisa's "surprise," which was saved until after the Frasers were revived by a good night's sleep.

"You'll be able to move into your house sooner than anyone expected," she said as she and Dix sat with them at their Howard House breakfast table. "Lawyer Bentley came by right after noon yesterday with the news that since one of the sons of the Bostwick relatives occupying it off and on during the past year is entering school in the North, the house could be cleaned, repaired, and all ready for occupancy two or at most three weeks ahead of the date for which anyone dared hope. My dear Anne, you will be moved into your own house within three weeks, I'm sure. Just in time to see all your lovely dogwood blossoms burst into bloom! When do you have to return to Savannah, John Couper?"

"My employers are generous men. They've given me a full month away from work." He turned to his mother, his handsome young face aglow. "Mama, do you realize what this means? Not only will you get to watch the dogwoods come out, you'll see me in full action going about the business of getting my beautiful mother settled and happy in her very own home. Now, aren't you glad I urged Uncle James Hamilton to crate and send our furniture a little early? I may even still be here when the big old heavy desk Grandfather Fraser gave you arrives. We can decide together where to put it. Mrs. Fletcher, this is great, good news! Thank you so much."

"Yes, Louisa, oh, yes!" Anne gasped, her face radiant.

"Don't thank me. Be grateful to the messenger. I honestly believe Mr. Bentley had quite a lot to do with helping the temporary tenants make up their minds to go early. He's a splendid gentleman. John Couper, you can certainly feel safe leaving your mother and all her affairs in Lawyer Bentley's capable hands. The house is partly furnished, though. You're not shipping too many heirloom pieces up from the coast, are you, Anne?"

"Our beds, Louisa," Anne said. "We all wanted our own beds. John's old kneehole desk, books, and, of course, the handsome old Fraser piece from my father-in-law's London house." No one could have missed the adoring look Anne then gave her son. Louisa certainly didn't miss it. "Oh, John Couper, you could be here with us in our new home for a whole week!"

Happier than she'd felt in years, Louisa looked at Anne's three daughters, looked slowly from one to the other. Pete, her flaming red hair still a bit tousled from the long sleep, seemed about to burst the bonds of ladylike behavior. Quite evidently, Anne thought so too, for she said quickly, "Pete, no! Don't jump up to hug anyone. We're still in a public place. Just sit there and be a lady. Like your younger sisters."

Louisa gave the youngest, Selina, a warm smile. The child was wearing a grin and looked awestruck. And Fanny, the quiet, middle daughter—the least attractive physically of the three sisters but truly good, Louisa was sure—had tears of pure joy on her face as she blew a silent kiss in the direction of her mother. Louisa herself could only laugh. And in her laughter was so much delight that even her husband, Dix, was studying her face as though he'd never seen anyone quite like her before.

Sweet, silent Dix, Louisa thought. The man means so well. If I didn't know him as I do, I'd swear he's working at containing his own pleasure this minute at the sight of such a happy family as the Frasers. Of course, he said nothing beyond, "I trust you will all be contented in your new home." Then, as he so often did, Dix fell silent for a time, examining his hands in his gentle, awkward way. "I work with my hands, Mrs. Fraser, as I'm sure you know. That is, I did at one time. I'm a cabinetmaker by trade. Louisa isn't exactly the kind of lady one might expect to marry a craftsman, but I'd like to make an offer. If there's anything—anything at all I might build for you once you're moved into your new home, you have only to let me know."

With all her heart, Louisa wanted to hug her husband. She didn't, of course, but along with Anne and John Couper, she praised his offer and assured them all that "whatever Mr. Fletcher may build for you will be letter-perfect. I urge you to accept his offer. He's an expert artisan and had his cabinet and lumber business in Savannah not burned to the ground some years ago, he'd still be making his extraordinary pieces."

FOR THE NEXT TWO WEEKS ANNE SPENT HER TIME SHOWING SE-lina, Fanny, and John Couper the charming, prospering, newly chartered city of Marietta, sorry they had all missed the elaborate celebration held earlier this year, 1852, on the day the village of Marietta became the city of Marietta. In the Fletcher carriage, driven by June because Louisa's driver, Elmer, was needed at the hotel stables, they drove about the countryside, spread picnics, inspected the new buildings and grounds of the Georgia Military Institute, and at Pete's insistence, drove out to Oakton, where John Couper's Savannah friends the Wilders lived when they were not in Savannah. Pete had stayed at Oakton before her mother came to Marietta.

"Mrs. Wilder's so in love with Marietta, I'm sure she'll move here permanently, even though John will have to make the train trip to Savannah often," John Couper said. "The lady adores this place, Mama, and once you get to know her, you'll understand why."

"You sound as though you still have to convince me to move to Marietta, Son," Anne laughed. "I'm here and under all the circumstances of my life right now, there's no other place I'd rather be."

ONCE THE FINAL PAPERS WERE SIGNED AND THEY GAINED POSSES-sion of their new home, the days flew by until it was nearly time for John Couper to return to Savannah.

The day he was handed the notice that several large crates were at the Marietta freight platform under his name was a day Anne would never forget. She was overjoyed at the sight of her son, flushed and excited as he directed the removal of Father Fraser's huge old desk from a heavy cart into the light-drenched parlor of the new house. It was a sight she would be able to see again any-time she called it up. Anyone strong and young could have done what John Couper did, but his act had meaning for her beyond explanation to anyone. She held it close.

"There's no other place for it, Mama," the boy laughed as he stood back to size up the look of the tall piece against the inside wall of the spacious living room. "So stop bragging on me. It's just too big to go anywhere else in the whole house! Sorry we had to remove that nice old ornamental piece from the top of it, though."

"I'll brag all I want to, John Couper," Anne laughed, "but even my son couldn't think of a way to raise the ceilings. Anyway, it's a good omen. To me, Father Fraser's cherished desk actually looks better there than anywhere else."

Both hands on his mother's shoulders, the boy looked deep into her eyes. She could feel his look, not unlike his father's in the old days when John was trying to win a point with her.

"You're going to be all right here, Mama," he said, his voice solemn. "I'd give anything if I didn't have to go back to Savannah at the end of this week, but every minute I'm away I'm going to remember you with the expression I see on your beautiful face this minute. You're a courageous, strong lady. I'm ever so proud to be your son." When she said nothing, he grinned down at her. "It's no wonder my father was so hopelessly in love with you. You're not only strong, you're truly beautiful. Didn't he call you beautiful Anne?"

Feeling her face flush with pain and joy, Anne said, "Yes. But he was often a very biased man. In many ways you're—you are more like him every day, John Couper. I want you to remember that always. I want you to be more like him—more and more and more like him. Even sometimes stubborn. He was, you know."

"I know I seem stubborn to you because I'm insisting that we have to rent out or sell most of our people. We do have to, Mama. I signed the papers today for the dozen or so who'll be working on the state railroad. I wish I earned more money than I do, but considering my age, I feel McCleskey and Norton are most generous with me."

"They're not generous at all. They're just good businessmen and they know how valuable you are to their firm."

"I told you I've given myself a new goal. Within three years I mean to own my own mercantile business."

"John Couper! You're not yet twenty!"

"Both my employers are still in their late twenties. As Eve would say, where is it written down that a man has to be any particular age to own his own business?"

She laughed. "Nowhere. Your father would call you an original."

"He would? Why?"

"Because he was your father and because you're his son."

SAYING GOOD-BYE TO JOHN COUPER ON THURSDAY, MARCH 25, the very last day he could catch the Western and Atlantic from Marietta to head back to Savannah, was an impossible ordeal made possible by Louisa Fletcher herself.

"I know you wondered who on earth would be knocking at

your door at this early morning hour, Anne," Louisa said when Anne opened her wide front door, "but I know what day it is. Your handsome son leaves today. I've brought Elmer and our carriage. Won't it help some if you and the girls can go along to the depot with him? I thought it might give a—well, a kind of party atmosphere to what could be somewhat sad for you."

"Louisa, Louisa, you are a friend! Thank you. June was going to take him in the dray we rented to bring the remaining crates here from the Howard House, but you've saved the day. Surely for John Couper's sentimental mother."

"Only another mother can understand the sharpness of saying good-bye to a child, even when that child will someday be back for another good visit. I do like to believe that you and I rather understand each other, Anne."

Chapter 38

BY EARLY MAY THE SPRING GREEN SHEEN, WHICH spread across every gum and hickory and dogwood and pine standing across the nine acres on which the Greek Revival house sat in its majestic simplicity, had burst into white blossoms of dogwood, ivory magnolia, and chartreuse pine blooms. To Anne's feasting eyes the blossoms seemed only to heighten the multiplied spring-into-summer greens, more visible each day when Eve drew back the bedroom draperies.

"Morning, Miss Anne," Eve whispered eagerly almost every day. "Look out the window. We still here! You an' me's still here in our own scrumptious place. Wake up yo' sleepy eyes an' look for yourself. It ain't no dream. Eve an' June, they startin' to git their brick cabin all straight, an' the new flowered curtains you an' Fanny make for me looks prettier every day they hangs there!"

Eve, Anne supposed, would eventually vary her almost rote morning greetings, but she really hoped not. Anne liked her days begun on the throaty melody of Eve's pure delight, not only in the light-filled beauty of the big house—Anne's very own—but in Eve's *brick* cabin. "Do you suppose you'll ever stop calling the house where you and June live your brick cabin, Eve?"

"No, ma'am, 'cause I never, ever dream that Eve

an' June they have a real brick house. Why you didn't tell me my cabin be made outa bricks like me an' June was rich folks?" Her good smile flashing, Eve turned from preparing Anne's bathwater. "This be a happy day, Miss Anne. You seem 'bout zactly like your ole smilin' self now that we finally here, an' Eve plan to keep you that way." Mixing hot with cool water in the huge, hand-painted porcelain bowl on the washstand, Eve asked, "Why you ain't said something 'bout me?"

"What am I supposed to say about you?"

"Don' I be talking good now that we lives in Mar'etta, Georgia, 'mongst the high-up folks?"

"Oh, I'm sorry! Every day I've meant to tell you how proud I am of you. Will you forgive me?"

"Yes'm. June, he don't seem to mind neither. In fact, he tell me last night arter—after—we done got in bed that he felt like he married to a Ebo queen!"

"Are there Ebo queens?"

"How Eve know that? Eve ain't no Ebo. She jus' love the groun' one ole Ebo walks on!"

"I know, and sometimes I wonder if you have any idea of my downright joy that you and June still have each other. Do you know how glad that makes me?"

"Co'se I know," Eve said, sponging and rinsing Anne's back, then drying it quickly because the morning was chilly, even in May. "I also knows I shoulda lit a fire in this room. How I keep forgettin' it get cold in the night way up here?" Reaching for one of the new, warm undergarment vests Fanny and Pete had bought yesterday right out of a regular store down on the Square, Eve said, "Put this on, Miss Anne. A genuwine store-bought vest keep you good an' warm till the sun come out."

"What makes you so sure the sun's going to come out? I know these bright, white walls make it seem light anywhere in this house, but I'd swear I heard it raining just before you opened my curtains a while ago. The trees are dripping this minute. See for yourself."

"The sun, he comin' out later, though."

"How can you be so sure about everything?"

" 'Cause June, he say so."

While Eve hooked the back of her bodice, Anne mused, "Do you remember how you and I used to tease my John because he was always wrong when he tried to guess the weather?"

"Yes'm. I remember. Mausa John, he never wrong for you, though, Miss Anne. Even when he foolin' you 'bout something, he be right for you. You ever thought how safe you are now?"

"Safe?"

"Safe, 'cause from now till you an' me gets to heaven, you can't ever lose Mausa John again. Someday, Eve gonna need you bad, 'cause someday, him bein' fifteen years older than me, Eve gonna lose June—jus' like you lose Mausa John. But you ain't never gonna have to say good-bye to Mausa John, not ever again. You ever think of that?"

After a silence, Anne said, "No. I—I guess you're right, though. How old is June now?"

"He be a lot older than Mausa John was when you lose him. You an' me's in our fifties."

"Do you have to remind me of that?" Anne thought a minute. "June must be—Eve, his hair's as white as snow, even though he looks like a man in middle age. But do you realize June is nearly seventy years old? Oh, we could neither one ever do without him!"

"Someday we gonna have to, Miss Anne. Eve, she done settle that within herse'f."

"How? Tell me how a woman who loves a man the way you love June can ever settle a thing like that? Eve, I haven't settled it within myself—and John's been gone nearly thirteen years!"

Eve's eyes brimmed, but she stood very straight. "It be different with Eve."

"What on earth do you mean by that?"

"A lot of your trouble settlin' yourself was not havin' a home of your own no more. It cause you trouble tryin' to find a place to lay your head, Miss Anne. That will be decided for Eve. Eve belong to you. You the one says where Eve lib after June, he gone to heaven."

Anne frowned as she studied the woman's expressive face.

"What are you telling me, Eve? Are you saying that by some means it won't be as hard for you to lose June? You can't mean that!"

"No'm. I don' mean that. June, he take half of Eve jus' like Mausa John take half of you."

"Then what do you mean?"

"I mean where I lives will always be settled for me. You do that."

"Eve, it isn't right for you to go confusing me after all these years. Why do you keep doing it?"

Swiping tears from her face, Eve answered in a voice that told Anne nothing. " 'Cause it be true. You owns Eve's whole life now. When June take part of it away, you still own what's left. Looks like you'd know that, Miss Anne."

"But I also need to know if that's good for you or bad? Does it comfort you that you and I will always be together?"

"Where would Eve go without you?"

"I suppose that's the only answer I'm going to get."

"Yes'm." On her knees, Eve ordered, "Stick out your foot so's I can put on your stockings. Dat be the only answer you gonna get, 'cause it's the only one I knows." Finished with the stockings, Eve got up. "The more I talks to other nigger womens 'roun' here, specially the ones that sticks their chins in the air when they reminds me *they* is 'free people of color,' the more I wonder if belongin' to you really be good or bad." The sly grin came. "Today, it be good! June, he say the sun come out after noon an' I got me a real brick house an' you got you a white-light mansion an' we be—us. That good, ain't it?"

"I might have known you weren't going to give me a straight answer," Anne said, tossing a light woolen shawl around her shoulders. "How often do you talk with other people of color?"

Eve only shrugged and changed the subject. "What time you reckon your new Mar'etta friend, Miss Louisa Fletcher, get here to take you to the shops on the Square? I know you be eatin' your breakfus with her at the hotel she live in, but you needs at least one cup of coffee before you goes out on this chilly morning."

"No, I don't. Mrs. Fletcher will be here any minute and that only gives me time to say good morning to my girls before Pete starts Selina's lessons. I have a little money today. John's pension came in the mail yesterday. Is there something you and June need for your brick house? I can try to find it in one of the shops while I'm out with my new friend."

"How come you call her your new frien'? We done been livin' here nearly two months now an' anybody knows to listen to you an' Mrs. Fletcher talk you be real frien's with her."

Anne smiled, then sighed. "I suppose you're always going to be nosy."

"I speck so." Eve was smiling, too. "If it have to do with you, Miss Anne, it my bi'ness to nose 'roun'. I likes Mrs. Fletcher jus' fine."

"I'm sure she'd be relieved to learn that. And I do thank you for helping me dress."

"You ain't got to thank me all the time. You never used to do it. Eve help you jus' the same, either way."

"I know, but if I feel like thanking you, I believe I'm free to do it. Don't you?"

Eve's grin was both impish and affectionate. "I'se free as any nigger ever be with you, too. You might say I'se also a free person of color, 'ceptin' I don't stick my chin in the air ober nothin' but my brick house! I ain't met one that calls herself a free person of color that got a brick house."

"Well, you do and you're also hopping from one subject to another as though you're just trying to mix me up. I asked if you needed anything for your house. Could you bring yourself to answer me?"

"Scuse me," Eve said, still grinning. "I didn't mean to do wrong. I would like to have a strip of some kind of string or ribbon to tie back my new curtains, so when June's sun come out later like he say it do, all that white light you loves kin git into my kitchen too. Don't spend much ob Mausa John's money, though. Pete, she tell me you got only enough to pay for yo' house."

"A yard or two of ribbon or shiny cord won't cost much," Anne

Chapter 39

DURING MOST OF THE FIRST MONTHS SPENT AT THE white-light house on its rise of land in Marietta, life was hectic and noisy, even at times confused as—according to Anne's means—workmen came and went, making minor repairs even while she and her girls attempted to do at least a small amount of entertaining. In fact, there had been no escaping it, because most of the warmhearted, genteel ladies of Marietta paid call after call welcoming Anne and her fatherless family to town.

"I know they're being kind," Pete complained one hot, almost airless August morning, "but wouldn't you think someone would pass the word that we're just not settled yet, Mama?"

"That isn't one bit ladylike or neighborly of you, Pete," Anne said as Eve refilled their glasses of cold tea while Anne rummaged through her bedroom desk.

"Neither is it ladylike to add that in my opinion, part of their neighborliness is just plain old curiosity about us, but I think it is. What on earth are you looking for, Mama? I thought you invited me to have some tea with you up here in your gorgeous bedroom."

"I did invite you and if you have to be so nosy, too, I'm just looking for my diary. I'm ashamed to say I haven't even laid eyes on it since the first week we lived here. I certainly do not deserve to be called a diary keeper. I'm not."

Pete laughed and so did Eve. "Who call you a diary keeper, Miss Anne?" Eve teased. "You just tell me an' Pete who call you a name like that and we give them a piece of our tongue."

"It's no laughing matter, and someday when I'm dead and buried, Pete will be sorry to see all those blank pages that tell nothing about any of the good times or bad times in our new place. Not even one name of a lady who's called, not the name of a single carpenter, nothing."

"I'll know the name of every lady who called," Pete said, her blue eyes twinkling, "and the way I'll know is to check the town census because I'm sure everyone has been here at least twice!"

"I've always meant to keep that diary current," Anne said, "as a kind of memorial to my well-bred mother, for whom you're named, young lady, and I'll thank you very much if you'll stop making fun of me—Rebecca!"

"Watch yourself, Pete," Eve said with a grin. "Miss Anne, she don' call you Rebecca lessen she mean bi'ness."

Pete set down her half-empty glass, got to her feet, made an exaggerated curtsy, and strode toward the door. "I can take a hint and so can Eve. I just saw you find your diary in the top drawer of your desk, Mama, and we're both leaving you alone with your memorable thoughts and entries. Come on, Eve. Mina needs us to help her shuck all that beautiful shoe-peg corn I picked from my magnificent garden this morning."

"How you know she needs us? What Flonnie doin'?"

"Cleaning my bedroom and I don't want her disturbed, so I volunteered our help. Follow me." When someone knocked briskly on the front door downstairs, Pete said, "Jiminy cricket! Now, which one of the ladies do you suppose that is right in the middle of what is supposed to be a work morning?"

Without being told, Eve grabbed one of Anne's freshly laundered day dresses from the clothes press and had it partly unbuttoned and almost ready to slip on when Anne stopped her. "No.

You answer the front door, Eve. I'm perfectly capable of putting on my own dress. I suppose you're not changing, Pete."

"That's right, Mama. I'm already bathed and wearing exactly what I mean to wear all day long. But run on, Eve. I'll help her highness."

Busily changing from a negligee to a crisp, much-mended blue day dress, Anne warned, "I don't need any help, Pete, and don't you dare try to do one thing to my hair. Eve's already fixed it." Abruptly, Anne began to smile and look around the spacious, comfortable bedroom. "Oh, Pete, Pete, just look around us!"

"I thought you were in a hurry."

"I am, but except that we do have lots more company than we ever had at Lawrence or Hamilton, I want to tell you something. I'm beginning to love this house in the same way I once loved Lawrence. And you know something else? I'm sure your blessed father loves it too. Callers or not, I've promised myself that when one of these hopeful feelings comes over me, I'll take a minute to savor it."

Pete's long, slender arms were around her. "Mama, savor away! Savor all you want to. You deserve it. And even though he owes me a letter, I'm going to write to John Couper this very evening and tell him exactly what you just said. He and I so longed for you to be happy here. That is, as happy as you can be without Papa."

"Pete, have you any idea how I thank you and your dear brother for giving me just the nudge I needed to move up here? And do you realize I must be getting shorter every year I live? When you put your arms around me, my head rests quite comfortably on your shoulder—just as when John Couper holds me in his arms."

"Is John Couper as tall as Papa?"

"No. No, but he's like him in so many ways." Anne laughed softly. "Not as outwardly impetuous, but it was impetuous for him to urge me to uproot myself and come here to live. He really surprised me."

Pete patted her shoulder. "Was it impetuous of me? I'm the one who visited Marietta first, don't forget."

"I'll never forget that, but no, I expect you to be daring. And darling, very little you do has surprised me in years." She smoothed her old blue dress. "Am I presentable?"

"No matter who's down there this minute, Mama, she won't be half as lovely as you are—every minute."

Louisa Fletcher was downstairs. Eve had just seated her in the parlor and was heading back to Anne's room to give her the good news. "I know you glad it be Miss Louisa Fletcher come to call, Miss Anne. I tell her you be glad an' relieved, too."

"I just told Pete she hadn't surprised me in years and now I'm telling you the same thing, but Mrs. Fletcher will understand exactly what you meant by being so forward. Now, you and Pete are supposed to be helping Mina in the kitchen. So scoot!"

"We scootin', but it look like you want to know Miss Louisa she got a look on her face."

"What on earth are you talking about?"

"If she don' have somepin good to tell you, Eve gonna be mighty surprised. She grinnin' all over."

"Louisa, my dear," Anne said as she held out both hands to her friend. "I was sure that bright August sun made this room seem so light, but I think now it's your smile! Has something wonderful happened for you? For Dix? For the girls?"

After a quick embrace, Louisa said, "Probably the most wonderful thing in all the world has happened, and I could almost not take time to finish those dreary hotel accounts before rushing straight here to tell you. If I'd thought a telegram would have reached you before I could, I'd have sent one!"

"Louisa, what on earth?"

"I know I've never come right out with it, but Anne, I all but hate being a hotel landlady, and although he'll never come right out with much of anything, my poor Dix hates being the landlord in someone else's establishment."

"Then your husband is tired of the hotel business, too?"

"Oh, I think he'd like owning his own hotel, but, yes. The poor man stays worn down from such heavy responsibility. In Savannah, you know, Dix owned and operated his own cabinet and lumber business until the dreadful fire. It looks very much as though we're both going to be set free."

"My dear, if that's what you want, I'm happy for you, but you and Mr. Fletcher are so successful at it. Everyone who stops there speaks of your splendid management and hospitality. We chose the Howard House over the Marietta Hotel for my first visit here because it was recommended all the way down in Savannah, and mainly because of 'those lovely Fletchers.' "

"I know, but Dix and I lived in Savannah for something like fifteen years. Savannahians are biased in our favor"—Louisa laughed—"except for the slavery hotheads. But Anne, aren't you one bit curious about how we're making our escape from behind the counter of the Howard House lobby?"

"Of course I'm curious. Just trying not to be nosy."

"My dear husband, Dix, is going to be appointed a United States Marshal for Cobb County!" Still laughing with delight, Louisa began to applaud her news. "I expected you to look puzzled at the thought of Dix as a U.S. Marshal. That is why you're looking so perplexed, isn't it?"

"Frankly, yes. The man's so soft-spoken and quiet."

"And—tough."

"Mr. Fletcher is tough?"

"All my life I've risen before dawn. First as a child, forced to help my widowed mother with my younger sister and the housework, later because I loved to study in solitary quiet. But if you doubt my husband's firmness, you should have heard him lay down the law to me last year because now and then after a long day at the hotel, I slept until first light!"

Now Anne laughed. "That's almost more than I can believe. When will you be leaving the hotel?"

"Oh, I doubt we'll live anywhere else. Not for a while anyway, but Anne, my beloved friend, I'll have time during the day for us to shop, to take walks, maybe even to make short trips here and there, and all exactly when we want to do it."

"You'll have so much more time with your daughters, too," Anne said. "Have you told them yet? Is Eliza too young to understand what a treat it will be to have you free?"

"I have said not one word to any person in the entire city except you, and I beg you not to tell even your own daughters."

"Oh?"

"It isn't that I don't trust them. It's just that the whole idea sounds too good to be true, but once Dix is back in Marietta from Macon later this month, the appointment as marshal—if God is kind enough to let it be true—should be safely in Dix's hand. Then we'll have a party to celebrate. Dix seems quite pleased, not only with the chance to become a United States Marshal but with the whole idea of having been selected to attend the Macon convention, too."

"Louisa, dear, you're so excited you've forgotten to say a word about a convention! I take it Mr. Fletcher is to be a part of the Whig nominating session."

Louisa's lovely laughter came again. "Anne, forgive me! I am indeed excited, and yes, Dix will be attending the Northern Conscience Whig Convention in Macon on the eighteenth of this month. I think he's going in a lost cause, from his viewpoint. Dix and those meeting with him are Winfield Scott men. They'll name Scott as their nominee, I'm sure. I'd much prefer Daniel Webster, but he'll already have been nominated by the Third Party Convention the day before Dix even attends the Macon gathering."

"You and your husband disagree on nominees?"

"Nothing serious and I don't even bother to try to convince him. He's so closemouthed, it's impossible, really, to have a true discussion with the man. Both Scott and Webster disapprove of slavery. As does Dix, of course. I just happen to be a great admirer of Daniel Webster. I always prefer true statesmen in politics to military men, anyway. It does seem to me gentlemen in general regard women as lacking in any understanding of government." She laughed. "You and I won't live to see the day, Anne, but they could just find out how wrong they've been. Let them make a few more messes comparable with the Mexican War. They'll find out. Men call women tricky, but even tricky actions spring from the mind and not from gun muzzles."

"Louisa, I do agree. If God created human beings with brains, why isn't it better always to use those brains ahead of the trigger finger? Why, I've always wondered, do we have to have so many political parties? Won't the Whigs end up powerless when they can't even agree about the North and the South? What is this new faction people are beginning to talk about—the Republican Party? I'm ignorant about so much of politics, especially now that as John's widow, I'm a British subject, but I've heard rumors that the Republicans are growing stronger in the North."

"Would you be interested to know what I think?"

"Of course."

"I predict—but only to you, Anne, since my dear husband is so flattered to have been selected to attend the Northern Conscience Whig Convention—that the Whig party will vanish one day and the Republicans will take over."

"You mean there will be only two political parties?"

"Something like that. As long as there is an American South, there will be Democrats, I'm sure, even though they are divided at best—for and against the Union, for and against the evil institution of slavery." Louisa paused. "My dear, do I offend you by speaking my mind so bluntly on the subject of controlling the very lives of other persons? You—you simply don't seem like a slave owner to me."

"Well, I am."

"But at least we can talk about it and remain friends. Look, I did not come here to speak of freeing the colored among us. I came to gloat and share my joy in the prospect of my own freedom— mine and Dix's—from the bondage of being innkeepers. Poor Dix took over the management of the Howard House only because of losses in Savannah. He's seldom mentioned despising it. He's too much a taciturn New Englander to complain, but I know the man. He's hated the unending burdens of innkeeping as much as I do. Besides, it is an honor to have been appointed a United States Marshal."

"You aren't worried that he might be imposed upon by whoever takes over the management of Howard House if the two of you are still living there?"

Her most joyous smile lighting the intelligent face, Louisa tossed her dark head. "We have absolutely no plans, and even that is pure relief!"

"Well, early next year you both have at least one night's social plans. I simply cannot put off my daughters' desire to give a fairly large dinner party. We've set no exact date yet, but without you and your kind husband in attendance, I'm sure I'll never be able to boast about our very first real social function. Say you'll come, dear Louisa."

"Of course we'll come. You're wise to wait for winter, though. It will be much cooler then and the handsome cadets will be on hand in full force at the Georgia Military Institute. I have to keep an eye on Georgia constantly when they are here, or she's at a Howard House window signaling them with her waving blanket. Well, I shouldn't be surprised, I guess. Selina does it from your house, too! But she's nearly sixteen and Georgia's only fourteen."

"Louisa, Louisa, how often do you stop to realize the weight of responsibility we each carry as the mother of three daughters?"

"Not often enough, I'm sure. But I'm equally sure that the goal of my life is to carry that God-given burden with the greatest care I can muster. It is a burden for any mother. But oh my, what tender burdens our girls are, Anne."

"I'm sure it's no secret to you," Anne said after a moment's thought, "but I do envy you."

"You envy *me?* You with this lovely house and Pete old enough and sensible enough to share the responsibility of her younger sisters? You with as splendid a son as any woman ever had? I could easily envy *you*, especially for Eve. She's not only a superb servant, her devotion to you is such that any woman would be green with envy. You have everything, Anne!" Louisa's broad, pleasant face looked abruptly stricken. Her mouth fell open, then uncharacteristically closed again as she went toward Anne, arms out. "Oh, my friend, my friend. Or are you still my friend after such a thoughtless, insensitive outburst?"

Anne smiled a little, but the smile was warm. If anyone in the city of Marietta knew Louisa Fletcher was truly sensitive, it was Anne. Louisa had simply not thought about John at all. Handsome and strong in his Royal Marine uniform, he looked down at them this minute, but to Louisa Fletcher, John would always be a stunning, slightly arrogant, strikingly good-looking portrait hanging on the parlor wall.

"Don't keep me waiting another second, Anne," Louisa begged. "I must know at once that I'm forgiven. I—I don't think I forgot about your beloved late husband. I just think I've seen clearly for perhaps the first time in my whole life that my way is more or less to reckon apart from Dix. Unlike you and your John. Oh, I cherish my husband. I admire his goodness of character, his industry, his unblemished faithfulness to me, his adoration of all three of our children, but—"

"But you don't really love him?" Horrified at her own blunt question, Anne added quickly, "What I meant to say is that when you think of your life, your deepest personal life, do you think of yourself rather apart from him?"

"*Do you forgive me?* I certainly intend to answer your question, but not with a shred of a barrier between us, Anne. Am I forgiven for having been so thoughtless? Your daughter Pete, the very first day I brought you to this house, made it plain to me that the love you and her father shared was not ordinary married love. But I have no excuse whatever for what I said. Please, please say I'm forgiven! What you and your John had together must have been most unlike what otherwise devoted couples share."

After a tender embrace, Anne whispered, "I forgive you, but I also understand what you're telling me about you and Dix now. And, Louisa, it changes nothing. If anything, we're even closer."

"You really don't envy me, do you? Many women do and I

know full well why they do." Louisa thought for a minute. "So many women in this small city would give almost anything to be able to trust their husbands as I've always trusted Dix. Not only to be faithful to me, but his self-control in all areas is—" She broke off with a soft laugh. "Well, the man's self-control is not only an amazement to me still, it can be quite maddening as well. You know how stimulated I am by good conversation. I can't tell you how long it took me to realize that when Dix just didn't answer one of my questions, he meant to be telling me to use my own good judgment." She laughed again. "I honestly think I'm still learning how to interpret some of his grunts, to remember to look up at him when he merely nods assent or shakes his head in disgust."

"But he's always so kind and agreeable."

"And he also seldom forgets a promise. Only this morning at breakfast he asked again if you've decided about needing him to build you a new bookcase or a table. Perhaps even new cabinets. He really wants to give you something to celebrate your new Marietta home, Anne. My husband meant his offer quite seriously, I assure you."

"I don't doubt that for a minute. But leaving the hotel and undertaking new work will mean his time will be limited, won't it?"

"Not according to Dix. Actually, he thinks he may have more free time once he's back from his political errand in Macon next week. And Anne, I hope you won't mind this, but when my husband and I were at your delightful family get-together the other evening, he made a splendid suggestion. Perhaps no one else would be rude enough to come right out and tell you, but your daughters are of the age when dancing is highly important, and the wide, original pine boards in the floors of your parlor, dining room, and entrance hall don't make the best dancing surface. My husband would be so pleased if you'd permit him to lay a good, smooth, hardwood floor on top of the one already there before you have your first big party. Have I offended you?"

Anne's eyes lit up. "Offended me? Far from it, Louisa. Pete and Selina have brought up those uneven floorboards every time we talk about giving our party. But isn't that an enormous job? And won't the materials for hardwood floors be costly?"

"No, and this will show you how seriously Dix takes his offer to do something that will really welcome you to Marietta. You know how much my husband likes and respects Mary and Edward Denmead, I'm sure."

"I do indeed," Anne replied.

"Edward Denmead has begged Dix to allow his lumber yard to supply the best hardwood for your new floors if you'll permit my husband to supervise their installation. Dix has two available carpenters and needs only two more men to help them out."

"I can supply two men. Neither is young, but both are totally reliable. Eve's husband, June, is already experienced, and my other man, Rollie, once my husband's blacksmith, has turned into quite a repairman. They'd be honored to help out—*if* you're sure all that extra work won't be an imposition on Mr. Fletcher."

"Then it's settled," Louisa said, getting to her feet to go. "If it were proper for women to lay bets, I'd wager almost anything that your acceptance will actually make Dix smile, so that even with little practice in translating his moods, even you will be able to see for yourself."

Walking arm in arm with Louisa to the front door, Anne said—her voice thoughtful, serious, almost solemn—"There will be a way for my children and me to thank you for the huge part you've played in helping them bring at least a semblance of wholeness back to their mother. I don't yet know what that way will be, but there *will* be one, Louisa."

"Don't you see you've brought wholeness to me, too, Anne? I wasn't unhappy when you reached Marietta, but I wasn't complete, either. I suppose I won't be entirely happy until some church welcomes me to the Holy Communion table simply because I'm a Christian."

"Louisa! Do you mean St. James doesn't allow you to take Communion at its altar?"

"I'm a Unitarian, Anne. I want to remain so. That makes me an outsider to this Episcopal parish."

"But you sing at St. James almost every Sunday!"

"I know. I sing for God, though. For the God of love." After a soft laugh, Louisa added, "St. James's rector doesn't agree that God loves and welcomes us all, especially Unitarians." She glanced at Anne's hall clock. "I must get back to the Howard House with the happy news for Dix that you welcome his new hardwood floor. That Dix and I love each other in the *inclusive* love of God is our strongest bond."

"Dix can't receive Holy Communion either at St. James?"

"No. But the dear man will be touched by that inclusive love in the very fact that you so welcome his idea of a smooth hardwood floor over these wide pine boards. You and Dix and I will at least know that we will dance because of the all-welcoming love of God on that new floor. It will be only among us. Dix will be so pleased to be included in our secret."

Chapter 40

"WAKE UP, MISS SLEEPYHEAD," EVE SANG OUT AS she flung back the winter curtains so that Miss Anne could have her first look in years at real, honest-to-goodness snow covering their well-kept nine acres of land and every bush and tree June, Rollie, and Big Boy tended. "Open your eyes an' look out de windah! We got us snow for New Year's Day. An' Eve brung your breakfus. Mina, she say she send you a New Year surprise!"

As usual, Eve noticed, Miss Anne had slept her nightcap off to one side, but the big smile on her face was like a light shining into Eve's heart because her beloved mistress had opened her eyes *with the smile.* Miss Anne had never fooled Eve when that certain smile had to be worked on. This one didn't. Surprise raisin muffins on her tray from Mina, plus the surprise of a newly fallen snow, plus John Couper's coming this very morning, plus its being the first day of the new year 1853, guaranteed that the smile would shine first thing.

"Oh, Eve, pull both curtains wide open so I can have a good look! Do you remember back when we still lived at Lawrence when Papa and John got so Christmasy from one little dab of snow, they dumped tons of pine and cedar and holly branches into poor Mina's kitchen? Their load was so big, we had to burn half of it in our fireplaces. Then you and I made fragrant little pillows out of the leftover needles."

Eve's smile flashed. "I sure do 'member an' I kin still feel how them pillows scratch, too! Mausa John an Mausa Couper, they bof go all the way whatever they do."

She checked Miss Anne's smile again. It hadn't faded a bit at the mention of her dead papa or her dead husband. The smile was still there and Eve's heart felt lit up from it. Only Eve had known how worried her own mind had been that moving all the way north to Marietta, away from the Island Miss Anne loved so much, might stop that smile. But there it was, and Miss Anne looked twenty years younger because of it. Pete and John Couper had been right, Eve thought to herself: It might for sure bring their mama to life again, just having her own house and property to live in.

"I remember the first time John and I saw snow together. He'd grown up with it in Scotland, but he never stopped being amused at me because when we were married, I'd seen only two or three light snows in my whole life!"

Eve turned from pouring Anne's breakfast coffee and stood facing her. "Mausa John, he sure like to laugh. And that 'minds me, Miss Anne, I been keepin' count ob somethin'."

"What?"

"June tell me today that I kin add one more day to my count. Big Boy, he cry ever mornin' we been in Mar'etta till last week. Me an' June we figure he ain't cried all this week between Christmas an' today, New Year's."

Miss Anne was staring at her as though dumbfounded. "Big Boy's been crying daily because he can't go fishing up here?"

"Yes'm. Tears roll down his big ole face every day 'cause he miss dem fish an' his skiff an' some kind of riber. Big Boy an' Rollie, they eats breakfast wif me an' June in our cabin. He done cry sometime while we sittin' at my kitchen table—till this week."

"Well, tell me, does he hate the work he does up here that much? I know he was Papa's fisherman all his life, but—"

"June, he say jus' las' night he had some hope now that he won't die of old age before he see Big Boy smilin' while he pull weeds outa your flower beds. June, he think once Big Boy's seeds starts to bloom, he git to like growin' flowers almost as much as fishin'.''

Eve placed Anne's tray before her and stood back as she'd always done to watch her mistress's face for the sign that Eve had made a good pot of coffee that day.

After one sip, Miss Anne grinned up at her. "Your coffee's delicious, Eve. Thank you. And can you truly believe that John Couper could be here in something over an hour from now if his train isn't late because of the snow?"

"Lil ole siftin' ob snow like that, Miss Anne? Anyhow, you done got it fix so's he don't need to wait for a ride from the depot. You got Miss Louisa holdin' a carriage for that boy."

"I didn't do it," Anne said, taking a huge bite of one of Mina's buttery raisin muffins. "It's not polite to talk with food in my mouth, I know, but my sweet Louisa Fletcher volunteered a carriage for him."

"Even if she forgit, he come on shank's mare. Dat boy gonna see his mama no matter what. Ain't nothin' gonna stop him gettin' here to wish you an' his sisters a Happy New Year!"

"I know. I also know I'm getting one of these delicious muffins because my handsome son's coming. Mina wouldn't think of not having a basket of his favorites waiting. I'm sure she made up extra dough so John Couper's will be so hot the butter swims. Oh, and when Mina bakes his batch, be sure she makes enough for June, Rollie, and Big Boy, too."

"Yes'm."

"Here, sit down on the bed with me and eat one of these. I'll be too stuffed to have breakfast with the girls if I have them both."

Still standing beside the bed, Eve said, "I done had one. Mina, she done slip me one in de kitchen while I'se waitin' fo' daylight to wake you up."

"Well, have another one, and bend your knees and sit down on this bed beside me. These muffins are just too good to let cool off."

Eve broke hers in two and popped a sizable bite into her mouth. "Oh, dey be good, all right. But Mina, she skin me alive if she ketch me eatin' one of yours."

"Is something wrong with your knees?"

"No'm. Somepin wrong with yours, Miss Anne? You plumb forget I'm a whole year younger than you."

Miss Anne gave a little laugh. "Hush up and sit down."

"Eve got work to do. It be purt near eight o'clock, an' even if John Couper's train late comin', he gonna git here befo' you done let me help you bathe an' fix your hair. I got orders from Pete."

"What orders from Pete?"

"She want me to be sure you looks young an' happy an' as purty as John Couper 'members you lookin'. Them two takes full credit fo' gittin' you to move up here to this fine house. Now, lemme get that hot water cool off some for yo' bath."

"Oh, Eve, sometimes since we've lived here in Marietta, I feel so spoiled!"

"Why you feel spoil up here?"

"I guess because I know poor Louisa Fletcher not only has had to work hard at the hotel, but that she bathes and dresses herself every day of her life."

"She don' believe in no slabery."

"For goodness' sake, that's why I feel so spoiled! Louisa's a real lady, too. It just doesn't seem right for you to carry hot and cold water all the way up those steps, bring my breakfast coffee every morning, and treat me as though I were the duchess of something."

Eve thought a minute, then decided her mistress's mood was good enough to give her the smile Eve knew would really puzzle her. The smile that had always puzzled her so much, Miss Anne seemed to want to smack her or beg to be told what the smile truly meant. So, with *the* smile on her bright-skinned, regal face, Eve said, "Well, Miss Anne, you an' me does things some different from the way other people does." The smile was gone before Miss Anne's question was asked, and Eve went on. "I know you's some downhearted 'cause Miss Louisa's husband, he don't get the new floor laid before John Couper get here."

"Of course I'm disappointed, but that beautiful flooring—all of it—is an outright gift. We couldn't afford to put down a new hardwood floor if our lives depended on it. Beggars can't be choosers, can they?"

"June, he say Rollie an' Big Boy bof ketch on how to fit an' nail down them floorboards. He speck Rollie to learn, but good an' kind as Big Boy is, ain't nobody, even June, thought he'd ever learn how to do more then fish."

"Is the water ready for my bath? I've got to get dressed for the big arrival," Miss Anne said, throwing back the covers. "Maybe if the weather warms up some, John Couper can take Big Boy fishing in the Chattahoochee River while he's here. You've got me feeling so sorry for the man, I wish you hadn't brought it up in the first place."

"Don't fret 'bout Big Boy. He smilin' lots more these days an' dat man think so much of you, Miss Anne, ain't nothin' kin make him grin like seein' *you* ack happy again!"

ANNE AND THE GIRLS HAD ALMOST FINISHED BREAKFAST IN THE dining room when they heard a harness jangle and the rattle of a carriage drawing up in the lane outside.

"Mama, he's here!"

"Pete, you're yelling the way you did when you were a little girl," Anne said, hurrying after Selina and Fanny toward the front door.

"Why not?" Pete demanded. "He's the only brother I have, and I guess the moment's close enough now so I can tell you John Couper has a big surprise for you, Mama."

"What surprise?" Fanny scolded. "You didn't tell *me*."

"Me, either," Selina called, jumping over a bare space in the new hall floor between oriental carpets they'd laid yesterday, so the carpentry work wouldn't look so unfinished. "I want to open the door for John Couper, Mama," Selina demanded. "I want to be the one!"

"All right," Anne laughed. "But do open it. I can't wait one more minute to look at him!"

And there he was, his dear, smiling face more striking than ever with winter frost coloring his cheeks. John Couper would, for a few days at least, no longer have to try to comfort and counsel her by letter. The handsome young man was actually beaming up at her from the path that led to her front steps, laughing, shouting light-hearted orders to Louisa's driver, Elmer, who almost never smiled but was smiling today. An unfamiliar boy of ten or twelve was there, too, and had plainly ridden from the hotel with her son in the Howard House carriage. Louisa had insisted on the carriage. No doubt the strange boy worked at the hotel where the Fletchers still lived. What difference why he was there? What if Elmer had shown himself able to smile after all? Weren't they all laughing and shouting "Happy New Year" and hugging? Weren't they all, except Elmer and the strange boy, acting like happy, laughing idiots at the soul-deep joy of seeing one another again after so many months?

After John Couper had reassured them for the second time that they had enjoyed a fine train trip from Savannah, the strange boy agreeing eagerly, Pete asked, "And do you like all this snow we have today, sonny? You must have come from Savannah, too. It certainly wasn't snowing there, was it?"

For the first time Anne looked closely at the boy, who was smiling at her now—almost, she thought, as though they knew each other. Pete had asked about the snow, but the lad answered with his eyes fixed on Anne's face.

"I like the snow just fine," he said, "although I've only seen it stay on the ground once before in my life. And no, there was no snow in Savannah when Uncle John Couper and I boarded the train."

Anne stared at the boy as though she saw a ghost. In a way she did. Except for the definite cleft in his chin—John's cleft—he was as much like her daughter Annie as a boy could be like his mother!

The slightly built, sweet-faced lad with John Couper must be Annie's son, John Fraser Demere. The baby Anne hadn't laid eyes on since his father, Paul Demere, came to Lawrence to take him out of her arms and care only months after blessed Annie died bringing the infant into the world.

Something needed to be said, but no one uttered a word until

Selina asked, "Mama, who *is* this boy?" Her question went unanswered.

John Couper, unable to miss seeing what his nephew's arrival had done to his mother, was steadying Anne, his face anxious. "Mama, I—I didn't do this intentionally. I swear to you, I had no idea until his father brought him to my door in Savannah that John Fraser was anywhere close by. He isn't the surprise I wrote about, Pete. I have another one, aside from Fraser here."

Finally, Anne whispered, "Fraser?"

"Yes, ma'am. Most people call me Fraser," the lad said, patting Anne's arm. "I'm so sorry, Grandmother. The very last thing I'd ever want to do would be to upset you. I thought, and so did Uncle John Couper, that you'd be kind of glad to see me."

"Oh, I am, son! But John Couper, couldn't you have sent a telegram?"

"Never mind that, Mama," Pete said, almost scolding. "We're all glad you're here, Fraser, but we're all going to catch colds if we don't get in the house by Rollie's good fire. Look at us, standing here as if it was summer. I don't think we'll ever learn how to live up North!"

"Pete's right, as usual," John Couper said. "I'll go dismiss the driver. Fraser can help you inside where it's warm, Mama. I know I made a big mistake surprising you like this. I guess I'm not all the way grown-up yet, eh?" He gave Anne his melting look. "Can you forgive me? Can you all forgive me?"

"Sure, Brother," Pete said. "But you did write me you had a surprise, and of course we thought—"

"I do have a surprise," he said, again assuming his role of man of the house. "Another one aside from Fraser, but not out here in the cold. Inside now. Inside—all of you!"

"Take my arm, Grandmother Anne," young Fraser Demere said, his smile warm. "I've learned to mind Uncle John Couper. I'll be honored to take you in to the fire."

Anne did her best to smile at the boy as she slipped her hand into the crook of his elbow. Her smile, she knew, had no warmth in it.

Chapter 41

IT HAD BEEN ALMOST TWO DAYS SINCE JOHN Couper turned Anne's world upside down by bringing her only grandson, John Fraser Demere, with him from Savannah on New Year's Day. She stood at her bedroom window, looking out at patches of green-brown where the snow had melted. She only half saw remaining clumps of ice drop from tree branches and bushes into the yard, and she failed to check tears that kept flowing as though her blessed Annie had just died—again. It was as though she'd had no chance to grieve until now. In September of this year 1853, young Fraser Demere would be twelve. Annie would have been gone twelve long years. Yet the first pain-blurred days after they'd buried her firstborn rushed back now in such agonizing immediacy, Anne honestly wondered how she'd endure the remaining days until John Couper would leave and take the lad with him. Adding to her agony, as always, she rejected even the idea that her son would have to leave her again.

Her pride in John Couper knew no limits today. It had never known any, but just last night he had sprung his second surprise—the one he'd promised Pete in a personal letter: All financial arrangements had been made, and sometime next year, before his twenty-second birthday, John Couper Fraser would become the owner of his own Savannah mercantile business!

Her heart swelled with joy for her son, but as she stood looking out at her snow-covered acres, the joy was matched by fresh grief for her daughter Annie.

Cold wind seeping in around the bedroom window did not cause her sudden, hard shudder. Her failure to show any real sign of affection toward Annie's boy, since their first glimpse of each other, shook her with a shame foreign to the Anne Fraser who lived her life for her family, who had so adored the tiny, warm bundle left in her arms when Annie went away forever.

Oh, Annie had tried not to die! How she had struggled to stay with her infant son, her young husband, Paul Demere, whom beautiful, tender, peace-loving Annie had—Anne could now finally admit—truly loved. To his mother-in-law, Anne Fraser, despite his efforts to establish some form of friendship after Annie's death, Paul Demere was still the epitome of arrogance and insensitivity. As she saw it, he had robbed good, sweet-tempered Annie of her very life in order to assuage a selfish passion.

"Dat be enough, Miss Anne," Eve ordered from across the room where she'd been standing silently beside Anne's freshly made bed, evidently reading Anne's unspoken thoughts. "What you thinkin' is *bad!* It ain't fittin' for you to hold them thoughts. *Stop it, Miss Anne.* You hear me?"

Whirling to face Eve, having forgotten she was there, Anne cried, *"What?* Who gave you permission to shout orders at me?"

"Where it written down that Eve not allowed to save you from yourself? Where that written down, Miss Anne? You ain't never threaten to sell me, but Eve can hear thoughts when you thinks 'em, so don't you dare think such a thought again. You mad enough to think it, but don't you dare speak it!"

Weeping openly now, Anne cried, "What did *you* just dare say to me?"

"Eve your property. Because June be gittin' old, Eve the most valuable piece of property you got. So, I ain't skeered. You ain't gonna git rid of Eve. Even when you so filled with fury at what you done you yell it out at me, Eve gonna shield you from hurtin' yo' poor self no more! Answer me a question. Dat boy, Fraser, he been here almost two whole days. You done give him even one hug in all dat time? An' don' tell me I ain't talkin' so good now. Eve know when she talk good or bad. Jus' like she know when you *think* good and when you think bad. You been thinkin' *bad* dis morning!"

For a long, long moment Anne stood, her back turned, silent, locked in a struggle to untangle the knots deep inside herself. With her own John Couper and the boy she had loved so tenderly as an infant both under her roof, there should have been no struggle whatever. There should be only joy and merriment and gratitude to God. Instead, Eve, the one person on whom she depended most next to John Couper, was giving her, deservedly, the sharpest, cruelest piece of her mind. Eve knew her so well, she could tell all the way across the room exactly what Anne had been thinking. Had somehow caught her ugly, secret accusation that young Fraser's father, Paul Demere, had caused sweet Annie to die!

"Mausa Paul Demere, he don' kill our good Annie. He done jus' what any man do when he love a woman like he love her. He didn't straddle her an' rape her like my poor mama got raped by dat mean white man I know be my earthly father. Annie, she *want* Mausa Paul Demere to do jus' what he done. Annie, she wasn't named Annie Fraser no more. She name Annie Fraser Demere, 'cause nothin' would do that girl but marry the one man she love an' dat be good lil Fraser Demere's papa!"

"Hush!"

"Why you want me to hush?"

"Because I said to, that's why."

"You wants me to hush 'cause you knows Eve be speakin' de truf, an' I knows the white way to say truf, too. You wants me to be somepin I ain't. But dumb I ain't, neither. Effen anybody know you want Eve to ack high 'n' mighty an' say *truth*, it be Eve. Eve part white, but Eve also part nigger. Today, Eve speakin' de *truf* to you an' the quicker you admits it, the easier you poor heart gonna be. It ain't really me that matters, though, Miss Anne. It be dat poor boy. Hab you hug young Fraser Demere even once?"

Anne waited. Waited. For one of the few times in her life, she could think of nothing to say to Eve—nothing kind, nothing sharp, nothing. When her servant crossed the room and laid her hand almost gently on Anne's shoulder, she could only breathe a silent prayer that Eve would keep talking just in case she hit on something that might give Anne the courage to admit that she had not yet given the boy even one small hug.

"You know you wants to hug him, Miss Anne."

Already Eve had said the right thing! "Yes. Oh, yes. He's—Fraser's so like her. Isn't he, Eve? Isn't the lad the picture of his mama? Those pale blue eyes, round face, pert little nose, and did you notice that when he's curious or doesn't quite understand, he wrinkles his forehead just the way our Annie did?"

"Yes'm. I notice. I also notice you done dug 'roun' till you find you a way to own up to all dat thick, black, bitter sludge down inside you where our sweet Annie still battle to live. She needs still to lib in her mama's heart, but not in all dat bitter!"

Eve might just as well have struck her. Anne turned like a wooden puppet and staggered to her little rocker, sure that Eve would rush to her side. Eve did not move.

"Take that back! Say you're sorry. Eve, I'm—I'm *not* bitter! Christians aren't bitter. Christians don't allow themselves to be bitter. How dare you?"

"You want I should lie to you instead?"

"Don't you ever let me catch you lying to me. I suppose you have often, but don't let me catch you doing it."

"You jus' spoutin' words now. Open yo' heart an' let dat bitter drain out, Miss Anne. De boy, Fraser, he keer 'bout his own papa. Don' you 'member how you love Mausa Couper, yo' papa?"

"Don't ever mention my father in the same breath with Paul Demere! Is that clear?"

"What be clear is I best git outa dis room till you simmer down to where we kin talk like—like friends."

"Don't go," Anne cried. "I just need a little time. You know we'll always be friends."

Without another word, Eve left the room and shut the door behind her.

🕊 🕊

EVE NOT ONLY RAN FROM HER MISTRESS'S ROOM, SHE RAN OUT OF the house and hurried along the path beyond the grape arbor out back toward her own cabin, begging the Lord as she went that June might be finished chopping wood for Mina's kitchen and that he was sitting as she was picturing him every step of the way, by their own roaring fire warming himself. She needed him to be sitting there, the steady light of June's spirit in his big, protective body ready, as always, to ease away her troubles. Ready, as always, to listen about Miss Anne, no matter how foolish Eve sounded, even to herself, as she poured out her heart to the man who would—even from heaven one day—go on being her shelter. "An' June, 'cause morning to night he ack like a man ob God, be gonna fly sure to heaven one day." Eve, however, permitted herself to think only about June when she thought of that day. To think about herself still trapped in grief on the earth and June in heaven with the light all around him was the only way she could let herself reflect on it. Oh, she could consider June's joy, but in no way could she allow her mind even to flick over herself when she would have to be torn in half as Miss Anne was torn when Mausa John went away from her.

Outside their cabin door, she stopped to listen. June was there all right and he was singing. Singing his favorite Sea Island slave song, his rich, dark baritone voice rolling out the rhythm so that Eve, even with patches of snow still on the northern ground of Marietta, could almost see the light and shadows again the way they fell only over St. Simons Island—could see them plain as day because June was singing.

> *"My God is a rock in a weary land*
> *weary land*
> *in a weary land*

My God is a rock in a weary land
 Shelter in a time of storm.
Ah know He is a rock in a weary land
 in a weary land
Ah know He is a rock in a weary land
 Shelter in a time of storm."

She'd heard June and the other St. Simons Negroes sing that old song with the African rhythm a hundred times, but each time the depth of June's own faith somehow set him apart—even from Eve. Once more his voice held her just outside their door in the shivery cold—she'd run out without a cloak as though they all still lived down on the warm coast—waiting, *feeling* around inside her own heart for a faith to match his. Lord knew she needed that kind of faith today after the way she had hollered at poor, torn-up Miss Anne.

June could help. Eve could count the times on one hand when the big, muscular, dark-skinned man had failed to think of something to soothe her, to straighten her out when she'd run to him with her troubles or what Miss Anne called her smart-alecky nature.

When June stopped singing with ever so many verses left in the song, Eve went inside and straight into his open arms to settle in his lap.

"You singin' better all de time, June, but I'se sure gittin' cold out dere eavesdroppin'. 'Sides dat, I needs a kiss."

After he kissed her, she snuggled almost as deeply into his good, low chuckle as into his big arms. "You s'posed to be choppin' wood," Eve whispered, stroking his clean-shaven cheek.

"You s'pose to be takin' keer ob Miss Anne," he said, a grin still on his open face.

"Hush," she ordered and jumped up from his lap.

"What you mean, hush?"

"You swears you not be born wif a caul ober yo' face. What you doin' readin' Eve's mind?" Hands on her hips, standing above him, she said flatly, "I done be takin' care ob Miss Anne an' dat's de trouble! June, I done make 'trouble in a weary land' for Miss Anne an' for me."

"You steppin' in God's shoes agin, Evie?"

"Don't you accuse me of dat!"

"I didn't accuse. Jus' axed. You a woman of faith almos' as strong as your beauty, Eve, but you does try to walk in God's shoes wif Miss Anne an' dat ain't right. It not only be wrong, you can't do it. Ain't nobody kin make dat work. God's shoes don' fit nobody but God Hisself. What you done say to Miss Anne now?"

"I didn't say nothin'. I jus ax a question. I seen you meet up wif her grandson, Fraser Demere, when he done come on dat train from Savannah wif John Couper an' you shook his han' an' smile an' let the boy know he was welcome here in Mar'etta wif us."

"Well, ain't he? He be our sweet Annie's son. De boy she die to bring into de worl'. What you talkin' 'bout, Eve?"

"I ax Miss Anne had she even hugged de boy."

"What she say?"

"It not what she say. It what she stood there thinkin' in her bitter mind an' heart."

"You call our good lady—bitter, Evie? I'd be 'shamed."

"She be bitter. You knows I kin hear her mind goin' almos' as plain as I hear her mouth. She ain't give dat po' boy one hug an' he done be here almost two whole days!" Standing, both fists clenched in agony and pity, Eve whispered, "June, I gotta fix Miss Anne's heart some way. She still hate Mausa Paul Demere. She ain't never like dat man, an' I see now she push her way through the pain ob losin' sweet Annie by leanin' on her hate for the man Annie love wif all her pure heart. I gotta fix it, June! Some way I gotta fix Miss Anne's black bitter, 'cause one day I gonna lose you an' Miss Anne she be all I got lef'."

There was nothing new about June's long silences. Eve had known them from the beginning of their love for each other. From the long-ago day of their marriage when, in the parlor at old Cannon's Point, they had jumped over a broom, Eve dressed like a queen in a dress Miss Anne had given her. He was silent now.

"You tryin' to git in God's shoes, June? Sometimes God be so silent, Eve could scratch Him!"

There was nothing new about June's good chuckle when almost any other person on the earth would have flared in fury at what she had just said.

"No, Evie," he said. "I ain't in God's shoes, but has you look at my white, wooly head lately?"

She tried to grin. "How I look at you an' not look at yo' white head? You so han'some, how I not look at you, June? You 'bout to play some kind ob trick on me?"

"No trick. Dis white head mean, though, dat June, he done lib more'n fifteen year longer than Evie. Once June hab dark Ebo skin an' dark Ebo hair. Now, June got only dark Ebo skin. An' in dem years past, he done learn that Miss Anne, like a lotta other humans, gits *hate* tangled up wif *hurt*."

"What you mean, ole man?"

"She don' hate Mausa Paul Demere. He jus' happen to be in the way when the biggest hurt ob all come to Miss Anne's heart."

"You tell me it hurt her more to lose sweet Annie den to lose Mausa John, her lover?"

June only shrugged and went on studying the way the blaze licked around the green oak logs in the roaring fire he'd built.

"Answer me!"

"I'm ponderin', Evie. No. It don' hurt her no more to lose sweet little Annie, but it hurt her as much I reckon. You an' me cain't neber know 'bout losin' a chile. You got to let Miss Anne sort it all out herself. It might could be she know so much pain when we bury Mausa John in de churchyard, she didn' hab no room to mourn sweet Annie so soon afterward. One thing sure, her pain ober him be different from her pain ober sweet Annie, but she a good lady. Miss Anne, eben if you don' believe it, she knows de Lord jis as good as you knows Him, Eve. Just as good as I knows Him."

"Ain't nobody knows Him good as you, June!"

The soft, velvety chuckle came again. "You sure does lak to try to walk in God's shoes, Evie."

Tears from nowhere began to stream down Eve's cheeks. "Don' leab me no time soon, husband! I—I ain't ready to take the burden ob dis whole family on my shoulders yet wifout you."

"I ain't aimin' to go nowhere, woman." He laughed softly again, and his arms were already out when Eve jumped into them.

"Den, you jus' gotta stay wif us a long, long time, ole man. A long, long time!"

Chapter 42

ALONE IN HER CORNER BEDROOM ON THE MORNING
of January 3 of the new year 1853, Anne stood again
at her favorite front window, trying her best to come
to a decision. Through all her years, making decisions had never been hard. She would be fifty-six on
January 11, eight days from today. Much of her life
had already been lived. What a time to turn wishy-
washy, to feel afraid of doing the wrong thing, to be
unable to see clearly, especially when what tormented
her this morning centered on her dead daughter Annie's only child, Fraser Demere—downstairs now
with her own children, pretending, at least, to be having a good time singing with the others while Fanny
played the pianoforte.

Pretending? The boy, Anne knew, was not at ease
as he should have been, and it was her fault that he
wasn't. He'd evidently counted the days until his father could send him to Savannah to visit his uncle,
John Couper, and the two of them had made the surprise trip to Marietta during the holidays when John
Couper could leave his work. Neither boy had
dreamed that their surprise would bring her anything
but joy. Anne herself had longed for over eleven
years for the chance to see Fraser again. Well, she
thought, the lad is here now, and I'm moping as
though I lost his blessed mother only yesterday. She

felt as though something living inside her had been covered over, buried along with Annie way back in 1841, and only now, with the arrival of the boy whose birth had taken Annie's life, was torn open again.

During the precious few months in which Anne had kept and cared for the infant in the Lawrence cottage, she had grieved normally for her daughter. But the day young Paul Demere, John Fraser's father, came to Lawrence and announced that he was taking the baby because he'd found a new wife, Jessie Sinclair, Anne felt that everything vital—even her painful grief over Annie—had been stopped dead. Eve declared that Anne couldn't bring herself to make her grandson truly welcome, even now. Never mind that he was Annie's own; he was also the son of the man Annie married, the young, slender, arrogant Paul Demere. Even though he was from a fine St. Simons family, Anne had never liked Paul. But did this give her license, after all these years, to be cool toward the youngster who was trying so hard to merit her attention?

The decision grating on her frayed nerves this morning would normally have been easy. The Edward Denmeads, Louisa Fletcher's friends and now Anne's, had invited the whole family to Ivy Grove, their spacious Greek Revival home at the edge of town, where John Fraser could ride a fine Denmead horse to his heart's content along the miles of bridal paths that wound about Ivy Grove's eighteen hundred acres. With all her heart Anne liked the Denmeads, pioneer settlers in Marietta. Edward Denmead was one of the leading contractors for the Western and Atlantic Railroad. She'd have liked them if for no other reason than that their exquisite taste in the arts had made them genuine admirers of Louisa Fletcher's superior singing voice. "It was the Denmeads, bless them," Louisa would laugh, "who convinced Dix and me to visit Marietta. Just think, Anne, without them, you and I might never have met each other, and what would we do without our friendship?"

Anne agreed. Louisa Fletcher, with more free time now that her Dix no longer managed the Howard House, was daily more important in Anne's life and might well want to go with them to Ivy Grove.

"Then why am I having such a time deciding whether to drive out to the Denmeads with the children today?" she asked aloud into the empty room. "*Why?*"

Her light blue eyes brimming with tears, Anne turned abruptly from the window and, from habit, especially when she needed comfort, sank into her familiar little wooden rocker. *Where on earth was Eve?* Part of Anne needed her desperately. Another part, leaden with what surely seemed almost like fresh grief, felt relief that the servant was nowhere nearby. Eve's very presence could force Anne to be truthful. Even with herself. And truthful was what she wasn't sure she wanted to be this minute. Eve would force her to face the ugly guilt she felt because she had not been able to show affection for her grandson, John Fraser. And Eve just could be right.

"Am I guilty?" she whispered. "Eve's already accused me of it and she's sometimes right. No! I won't have her right. Not this time. I have not been harboring bitterness toward Paul Demere for all the years my Annie has been dead. Christians don't harbor bitterness! And most of what Eve knows about Christianity I've taught her. I won't have her preaching at me. I hold no bitterness toward Paul Demere. I just—don't like him. I never thought him good enough for Annie and that's my privilege to this day. Paul Demere didn't surprise me one whit by marrying another woman before my daughter's tombstone had settled. He did exactly what anyone would expect a selfish, spoiled young man to do. Eve can't be right this time. And why does it matter so much to me that she even thought such a dreadful thing about me? She and I are supposed to be friends. Even so, she's still my servant. I still own her. She certainly doesn't own me!"

A light, though insistent, knock at her bedroom door startled her.

"Go away, Eve! I don't want you in here right now. Go away!"

The knock came again, still light, but also still insistent. It can't be Eve, Anne thought. Most of the time, she doesn't even knock.

"Who's there?"

"I'm here, Grandmama," the boy's voice called. "I have something to show you. Aunt Pete said it was all right to knock."

The odd, dead weight of what felt like grief held her as though chained to the chair. "John Fraser?"

"Yes, ma'am. I have something to show you. It's—it's important to me to show you first. None of the others have seen it yet."

As though she weighed three hundred stone or were a hundred years old, Anne pushed herself up out of the little rocker and went to open the door. "Good morning, John Fraser. Do come in," she said, hearing the flatness in her own voice.

With Annie's smile, showing "her" slightly crooked front tooth, Fraser said cheerfully, "Do you know you're the only person who calls me John Fraser, Grandmama?"

"Well, no, I guess I didn't know that. But you were named for your grandfather, Lieutenant John Fraser, my beloved husband. It has always pleased me very much that you were."

"My mother gave me his name, Papa says. He likes it, too, though, because Papa liked Grandfather Fraser so much."

"Yes," Anne said. "My husband always seemed to be fond of your father."

"I know he was. Papa's told me lots of times that they always got along fine together."

"Take that chair, John Fraser. You've grown so, my little rocker's too small, I'm sure."

His smile—Annie's smile—came again as he sat down in the armed brocade chair across from her rocker. "I don't think I'll be a big man like my grandfather was, though. Papa says he was really tall and broad-shouldered. I'll be more like Papa, I think. But I'm pretty strong like him too."

"I'm sure you are," Anne commented and thought critically, I am just *commenting*, not really conversing with this boy. God forgive me and help me.

"It must have been pretty hard for you losing Grandfather Fraser and then my mama in such a short time."

His surprising identification with her two heartbreaks coming so close together startled her so that for an instant she could think of nothing to say. Finally, she managed the inevitable question, "How do you know so much about me? I mean, how is it a boy your age has even thought of the short time between—my losses? My dreadful losses?"

"Oh, I didn't figure it by myself. Papa told me that even though you've had to watch so many of your loved ones die in just a few years, having my mother and my grandfather die must have been the hardest of all for you."

Anne gasped. "Paul Demere told you that? Your father actually told you that?"

"Yes, ma'am. That's about the only way I'd know it, I guess. We moved to Camden County before I was a year old, so I haven't had much chance to talk to anyone but Papa about either my mother or you."

"No. No, I guess not." Anne fumbled for something else to say. "I—I never knew your stepmother, the Sinclair woman. My friend Mrs. Thomas Butler King had met her a time or two, but—"

"Miss Jessie is a pretty nice lady."

"Miss Jessie? Do you call your stepmother Miss Jessie?"

"Yes, ma'am. That's what Papa likes for me to call her. He says I only had one real mother."

"He does? Your father says *that?*" After an awkward silence, she spoke again. "John Fraser," Anne began, failing in her struggle to return the boy's smile, "you must forgive me if I seem slow, if I have trouble following what you're telling me, but your father took you away from me when you were far too young to remember your real mother—"

"She was your namesake," the boy said pleasantly, as though he liked the idea. "I'd give almost anything if I could remember her. Just anything about her would help a lot, but I guess I was only a few days old when she died."

"That's right," Anne said, tears again filling her eyes. "You were only a little over three days old."

"You were surely good to take care of me the way you did. With a broken heart and all. Papa told me your sister, who would have been my Aunt Isabella, had died, too, only a few months before Mama did."

Anne tried not to stare at him, but each new revelation about

Paul Demere was like a bolt of lightning. Eve must not be right, declaring as though she were almighty that Anne had allowed herself to carry bitterness all these years against Paul Demere! Eve had even gone so far as to hint that her mistress had never truly allowed herself to grieve over the death of her daughter as much as she needed to grieve, because she was hiding behind that bitterness—until now.

Stop such thoughts, Anne scolded herself, at least until the boy's no longer in the same room. Those pale blue eyes of Annie's are watching your every frown, seeing the tears. Fraser did have Annie's light blue eyes—Anne's own eyes, John always liked to remind her.

"Papa vows my mother was a peacemaker. He says Aunt Isabella was kind of that way, too. Sometimes he tells me I go too far being a peacemaker, though. That men aren't supposed to be sweet-natured all the time. That a man has to show his own strength."

"I—I never thought of your father as being too sweet-natured. Do you know what he really meant by a man's showing his own strength?"

"Not exactly, I guess. He says I sometimes give into people when a little iron in my spine would help a lot more in the long run."

"I see."

"You don't like Papa very much, do you, Grandmama?"

"Whatever would make you say a thing like that?"

"Oh, he told me. He says you didn't think he was good enough, gentle enough, for Mama."

What Anne said next stunned her more than it could possibly have stunned the boy. "You must always remember, though, son, that your mother loved your father with all her heart. Did he tell you that, too?"

"Yes, ma'am."

The amazingly mature, thoughtful boy had startled her again. Anne unexpectedly found herself wondering what manner of woman Jessie Sinclair must be to have worked such seemingly miraculous changes in Paul Demere. Or *had* she worked a miracle in the very nature of the once arrogant, selfish young aristocrat? At that moment, while young John Fraser sat politely waiting for her to say something else, Anne was overcome with a desire to know more about Jessie Sinclair Demere. But if her Annie had been unable to smooth some of the cocky, self-absorbed edges off young Paul Demere by her innate goodness, what had really happened? One thing Anne was still not ready to accept was that Eve's accusation that her mistress went on harboring bitterness against him could possibly be true!

Having spent much of her life around growing children, Anne knew the lad was waiting—waiting impatiently, no doubt, as children did, especially boys, for her to speak. But she was stuck, grounded, as a small boat gets stuck on a sandbar, for a way around her continuing annoyance that Eve just might be correct after all. Why did that matter so much? Because it was Eve, in light of what the boy was telling her about his father, who had shown herself to be so smart?

Had the two women, servant and mistress, been somehow competing with each other for all their lifetimes? During their childhood years, while the white master's daughter and the half-white slave girl had merely been good playmates, Eve had certainly been able to climb a tree faster than Anne could, had even found her lover, Ebo June, before Anne found John Fraser, had almost condescendingly explained true love to Anne although Eve was a whole year younger.

What did any of this nonsense have to do with Anne's own responsibility to bring this strange, surprising conversation with her grandson to a satisfactory conclusion?

"Grandmama?"

Anne jerked her thoughts back to the moment, to the courteous, lovable boy. "Forgive me, John Fraser. I—I must be getting old. My mind was far away, I'm afraid, dwelling on ridiculous things."

"That's all right, ma'am. I'm probably the one who needs to be sorry for interrupting your morning like this. I do hope you're going to decide to ride along with us out to the Denmeads today. Are you?"

"I'm—not quite sure yet. Ivy Grove's a beautiful place, and they're such likable people. Does it matter a lot to you whether or not I go?"

"It does, yes, ma'am. Especially since Uncle John Couper and I have to take the train back to Savannah so soon. I surely do like to be with you." His smile was disarming. "And I did knock on your door a while ago for a special reason. I have something important to show you if you have a few more minutes to spare me."

"Oh, yes, son, we have all the time we need right now. I'd love to know what you want to show me before you show anyone else! It makes me feel quite special."

"Good," he said, getting to his feet. "I'm pretty sure you've never seen it. At least, Papa doesn't think you have."

"Your father doesn't think so?" Anne asked, thinking the question to be as stupid as it sounded.

The boy was rummaging in an inside pocket of his woolen jacket, giving her his tenderest smile as he did so. Then he took out what appeared to be an oval-shaped gold-framed picture but quickly put it behind his back. "I carry what I'm going to show you everywhere I go. I even sleep at night with it beside me on a table. It's my treasure. Papa gave it to me on my eighth birthday, and I could tell by the look on his face that if he'd gone to a shop and paid about a thousand dollars for a present, it couldn't have meant as much to him as this does. I guess I'll remember that day and the look on his face for as long as I live!" The sunny smile gone, the boy said, "Shut your eyes and hold out both hands, please."

"Shut my eyes?"

"Yes, ma'am. You're about to see the most beautiful sight anyone ever saw. At least, that's the way I feel about it."

Eyes closed, Anne, still seated, held out her hands as he carefully, tenderly, laid the small object on her open palms.

In a reverential whisper, the boy said, "Now you can look, Grandmama."

Anne opened her eyes, and there before her was an almost perfectly painted miniature of her firstborn, Annie, the more lifelike because the pale blue eyes showed the lovely young face about to break into the familiar smile that never failed to lift the heart of anyone blessed enough to have seen it. Anne's abrupt intake of breath was followed by a silence so long she could feel the boy's eagerness for a response.

"I—I know you're waiting for me to—say something, son, but —but I can't seem to." Tears wet Anne's cheeks. "Did your father say when it was painted?"

"On their honeymoon in Philadelphia," the lad said, beaming. "He carried it with him wherever he went until the day he gave it to me. Was there ever a face as beautiful as my mother's face?"

"Never. And I had the joy of looking at it from the day she was born until— For twenty-four years I could actually look at that face, feel the blessing of that smile. Oh, John Fraser, I am, of all women, most blessed." And then, unable to help herself, she began to speak directly to her own firstborn child. "Annie, oh Annie, I hope you can hear me because for the only time since you left me, since you *had* to leave me, I feel a kind of—peace. Dear Annie, I'm almost afraid to say it, for there has been so much unpeace in me. So much that Eve swears I've been bitter! And maybe she's right. Maybe I should even tell her she's right. Can you hear me, Annie? Your resentful mother was the first person to call you a peacemaker, and now look! Look at the peace you've given me after all these years. . . ." John Fraser was still standing beside her, the same smile waiting to break over his face so like Annie's—Annie's smile on a young boy's face. Tears streamed from her eyes now, but she felt herself begin to smile, too, looked straight at her grandson, held the framed picture in one hand, and reached toward him with the other.

Taking his grandmother's hand, he asked, "Do you think she heard you talking to her?"

"Yes. She heard me, son. If she didn't, then all we believe about God and being with Him when we leave this earth is wrong."

Still smiling, the boy said firmly, "It isn't wrong, Grandmama. My papa's sure she hears me when I talk to her, too."

The thick, seemingly impenetrable wall between her and Paul Demere was beginning to crumble, but enough of it still stood, had stood for so many years, she felt too new and foreign for a quick acceptance of the doubtful fact that Paul may really have faith in God. Of course, she hoped he did. This tender boy with a face and heart so like Annie's needed a father in touch with the Eternal, but her response came slowly.

"I guess I never thought about your father's faith," she said. "My Annie, your mama, knew about it, I'm sure."

"Oh, yes, ma'am. Papa will tell you that to this day, he couldn't have kept on living without her if he didn't know for sure she was right with God. And that they'd see each other again someday. He told me that after she died, he might have stopped believing anything if it hadn't been for this picture of her. That's the reason he wanted me to have it for my very own."

Anne leaned back in her little rocker, exhausted, yet somehow beginning to rest. "I see. John Fraser, thanks to you and your sweet mama—and to your papa's kindness in giving his only picture of her to you—suddenly I see so much more than I ever thought I'd see!"

The old Maxwell clock struck from the downstairs hall. The boy laughed softly. "Say, did you have any idea I'd been up here with you for a whole hour? Uncle John Couper must have sent for our carriage by now. You will go with us out to the Denmeads' house, won't you, Grandmama?"

Anne jumped to her feet, arms out. "If you'll let me give you the kind of hug you should have had days ago, nothing on this earth could keep me from going! You and John Couper will be leaving me again in such a short time, I don't intend to miss another minute of being with both of you." As her bitterness flowed away in the boy's strong arms, Anne knew she could now make her peace with Eve.

Chapter 43

THE WHOLE FAMILY SQUEEZED INTO WHAT HAD BEEN the Bostwick carriage, cared for by Big Boy as he cared for the team that came with the house. Beaming, the big man headed into Decatur Street and drove toward the Square, young Fraser riding in the high driver's seat beside him. Once Anne had made up her mind to go along with the children to the Denmeads' for dinner and a day at Ivy Grove at the edge of town, she simply had to let herself hope that Louisa would be free to go with them.

"It's awfully short notice, Mama," Fanny said from her seat beside Pete across from Anne, John Couper, and Selina. "Don't get your hopes too high that Mrs. Fletcher can go with us."

"Hush, Fanny," Pete scolded. "It's so good to see Mama with high hopes, we'll just believe she *is* free to go and that's that. I'll run in the Howard House and tell her what's afoot for the day. She isn't working anymore since her husband was appointed marshal last year. After all, the Denmeads are the people who invited the Fletchers to Marietta in the first place."

"You don't need to tell us that old story all over again, Pete," Selina complained. "We know it. They invited her on a visit to Savannah, hoping she could sing some Sunday in Marietta's St. James Church. We also know she does sing at our church almost every Sunday, and anyway, Pete, sometimes I get tired hearing you make all the decisions in this family."

"Well, somebody's got to make them. John Couper, you and I know the whole point of our being in Marietta is for Mama to be happy again, and she and Mrs. Fletcher are like peas in a pod. You'll have a much better day if she's along, won't you, Mama?"

Before Anne could answer, Fanny mumbled, "I'm just trying to be practical. Where's Mrs. Fletcher going to sit?"

"I don't think Fanny wants anyone else but family along today," Selina said.

"That's not true!"

"Well, Mama always wants Louisa Fletcher, and I can talk her into coming along. Rein the horses over in front of the Howard House," Pete called to Big Boy. "Mrs. Fletcher will be glad to take their buggy. She can drive her and Mama. That lady handles horses with the best of them."

Before Pete, still the tomboy, could jump out, Anne called, "Wait for me, Pete. I'll go in the hotel with you to invite Louisa."

"Don't get out, Uncle John Couper," young Fraser called as he, too, jumped down from the high step, hand out to help his grandmother from the carriage. "Come on, Grandmama. I can hold you. I'm strong! Papa taught me how to help ladies from a carriage step. Careful now."

As Anne walked beside Pete toward the entrance to the Howard House, she said, her voice confidential, "I want you to know Fraser and I went a long way together when we talked in my room earlier today. I need to tell someone that I've—misjudged Paul Demere all this time. Thanks to his son, I feel I've lost almost all my bad feelings toward him. I was wrong."

She felt Pete squeeze her arm. "I know you were, Mama, but you have to forgive yourself."

"Yes."

"The truth is you just never liked Paul. All the rest of us liked him fine. I know Papa did. You didn't for a reason that's no one's business but yours." Nearly a head taller, Pete looked down at her mother. "In your eyes, there wasn't a man on earth good enough for Annie."

"I don't know why you and Eve have to be so smart!"

"Eve knew, too?" Pete asked.

"Yes, she did."

"Mama, are you going to admit to her that she and I were right? That at least some of your heartache was because you'd blinded yourself to even the possibility of a good streak in Paul Demere?"

Because Louisa was coming toward them across the hotel lobby, Anne only whispered curtly, "Maybe I will and maybe I won't, Miss Know-it-all!"

"How do you do, Mrs. Fletcher?" Pete said, using her most ladylike manner. "We're invited to the Denmeads for dinner and it would mean everything to Mama for you to come along."

"What my daughter meant to say, dear Louisa," Anne said, "is that it would mean a lot to us all. To the Denmeads, too, I'm sure."

Louisa's good smile never failed to lighten Anne's spirit. "Well, I'm not a working woman any longer. Why not? My husband has a business appointment for dinner anyway with Mayor John Glover. Yes! I'd love to go, but is there room in your carriage?"

"I'm afraid not," Pete said. "I thought perhaps you could drive Mama out in Mr. Fletcher's buggy. I know what an expert you are."

Louisa laughed. "Flattery will get you anywhere you choose to go, dear Pete. I'd be honored to drive your charming mother, my new best friend! The buggy's ready to go. My husband won't need it, though. He'll be glad to walk."

THOUGH WITHOUT MUCH WARMTH, THE JANUARY SUN WAS CLEAR and bright as the two women settled on the buggy seat, both bundled in heavy cloaks. Louisa drove deftly along Canton Road in the direction of the Denmeads' place on the outskirts of town.

"I thought sure there'd still be patches of snow when we reached the edge of town," Anne said. "There aren't. I don't see a single place where it hasn't melted."

3333333

Louisa looked at her friend. "Anne, you didn't invite me to tag along to discuss the weather, now did you?"

"No. I need to tell you something truly important. At least, I feel it's going to be very important to me from now on."

Louisa listened intently as Anne told her in some detail of the meaningful, sweet time she'd shared with her grandson this morning and, as though she was showing her a rare treasure, handed her the miniature of her daughter Annie, which the boy had insisted his grandmother keep until time for him to leave.

"I had only a silhouette of Annie in profile. Just seeing this almost perfect likeness of her face again means—everything," Anne said, seemingly unmindful that tears rolled down her face.

The Fletchers' horse knew the way to Ivy Grove, of course, so Louisa studied the lovely face in the portrait with great care. "Anne, Anne," she said at last, "I admire you more than ever for having lived through a single day without this beautiful, tender daughter."

"I haven't lived through a single day with any grace," Anne said in her honest, direct way. "Even my servant, Eve, knew I was making everything harder by staying bitter toward Annie's husband, Paul Demere. The truth is, I never liked him, so I blamed him for her death in childbirth. Of course, I flared at Eve for accusing me of such a thing." And then she surprised Louisa by adding, "It—it might not be so hard from now on, though. This is the important part, Louisa. My grandson, only eleven, somehow found a way to melt my icy bitterness toward his father. You see, the boy let me know, by showing me that lovely miniature his father arranged to have painted of her on their honeymoon, that Paul Demere *wants* young Fraser to keep my Annie fresh in his memory. That's the only likeness Paul owns of her. He gave it to the boy. Fraser also vows his father wants him to call his stepmother Miss Jessie—not Mother. Oh, Louisa, mothers can be quite unreasonable. It's still hard for me to admit, but I have been. I have been! I'd give anything if I could ask Annie's forgiveness."

After a moment Louisa said, her voice tender, "Annie forgives you. You'll just have to remember that she now lives in the very presence of the Forgiver. God is a veritable artist at forgiving. He created forgiveness. Where would we all be if He hadn't?"

When Louisa returned the miniature to Anne, who placed it carefully back into her reticule, Louisa asked, "Will you keep me posted? I think it might help if you simply tell me now and then as we live our days as friends—as special friends—that you are remembering that Annie has already forgiven you."

Anne said nothing but reached to give Louisa's arm a squeeze.

For the distance of a quarter mile or so, they rode along in silence. Finally, Anne said, her voice far steadier, "Thank you. Thank you. I'm sure I'm ready for our day with the Denmeads now."

Chapter 44

THEIR VISIT WAS NOT ONLY PLEASANT, THE CON-
versation with the Denmeads at dinner challenged
Anne so much, she found herself steadily glad that
Louisa was there too. At the first opportunity, perhaps after John Couper and young Fraser had said
good-bye on Saturday morning, she intended to have
a real talk with her best Marietta friend. Heaven knew
she would need to keep her own mind occupied after
the boys left, because this time she would be saying
good-bye to her son for at least six months and to
young Fraser for longer than she dared face.

Except with Louisa, Anne had not ventured to
discuss one word about politics or even broach the
subject of slavery with any of the new friends she'd
made. That the political atmosphere in Marietta was
unlike the position on the coast—as unlike as night
and day—she had no doubt from the start of her new
life. No one had told her, but she guessed that the
Denmeads of Ivy Grove probably owned more slaves
than did anyone else, not only because she'd seen
some of their people that day but because the
Denmeads owned more than eighteen hundred acres
of land. Still, at dinner she had heard both Mary and
Edward Denmead declare themselves to be Unionists,
declare their faith in the singular vision of the United
States forefathers.

Of course, as Anne well knew, not every Unionist necessarily believed that slavery was wrong. After all, her own brother James Hamilton, one of the largest slaveholders in a slave-owning county down on the coast, believed staunchly in the union of all the states and reminded her, the last time the two had talked, that she mustn't allow her unforgettable friend Fanny Kemble to convince her that everyone in the North was an abolitionist. "That, dear Sister, is far from the truth. I'm in correspondence with an antiabolitionist Northern Whig gentleman who declares that the abolitionists mean to agitate until Southerners are driven to madness—the madness of secession—at which time there will be plans to free all Negroes. Men such as my New England correspondent dread that, because he believes that if slavery is outlawed, the Union cannot endure. Like me, he is a strong Unionist. Seek no simple answers, Anne. There are none."

Anne remembered her brother's words because he so seldom discussed politics with a woman. She had felt honored; yet now, living a whole new life, she was oddly annoyed with herself for having been honored in such a demeaning way. On the coast, for much of her lifetime the troublesome issue of owning people had almost seemed natural to Anne. Oh, Papa and Thomas Spalding despised it, but both were large slave owners anyway. Fanny Kemble Butler herself had vowed to Anne that Anne's father, Jock Couper, "turned to jelly when I brought up the ugly subject in his presence. Still, in his good heart, he knows his tyranny over the lives of his Negroes is against the will of God. Only God Himself is fit to be a master."

These disturbing, yet somehow freeing, thoughts had been crowding Anne's mind as she rested alone in her bed at the end of such an eventful and stimulating day. The children—John Couper, Fraser, and all three girls—were outside cutting dark, shiny, green magnolia leaves at Eve's insistence and, of course, under her direct supervision. She and Mina had decided that dinner tomorrow, and each day before John Couper and Fraser must leave Marietta, had to be a celebration, which to Eve meant decorating the house with fresh greenery cut, of course, under her eagle eye.

Anne had watched them all for a few minutes. They were having a good time and, except for Pete, seemed totally involved in their project. Because Pete kept looking up at Anne's bedroom window, as though something weighed on her mind, Anne went to bed. Pete was so smart she equaled Eve at times in the almost weird way she had of sensing her mother's most private thoughts. Pete's life in Marietta was, so far as Anne could tell, not exactly exciting for a young woman in her late twenties. She had met no young man who appeared to interest her. As always, she hated to sew and scoffed at fancywork of any kind. Her eldest daughter's one mission seemed to be seeing to her mother's happiness. I wonder if I need to worry about Pete more, Anne thought, as she turned down the coverlet and plumped the bolster before stretching out on her bed.

Still able to hear the children laughing from outside in the big yard, she assumed the footsteps on the stair must belong to Mina or her daughter, Flonnie, come to discuss something about tomorrow's celebration dinner already in progress in Mina's big kitchen.

When Pete appeared in the open doorway to her room, Anne made no effort to hide her surprise. "Pete, how on earth did you get up here? You were in the yard cutting branches only minutes ago!"

This time Pete's devilish grin did not conceal that she was plainly worried. "It was easy, Mama. I just did what we always do. I used the stairway. It leads right up here from the hall downstairs."

"You sound like Eve."

"Teasing you?"

"No, being a smart aleck. But enough of that. What's worrying you?"

"Does something have to be worrying me just because I came to talk to my own mother? You weren't asleep, were you?"

"Far from it. We had such stimulating dinner conversation at the Denmeads' today, how could I fall asleep? I was—thinking. And oh, Pete, isn't there a lot to think about? Aren't things different up here in Marietta from the way they are on St. Simons or in Brunswick or even in Savannah?"

"You mean the way people up here look at slavery and even the Union?"

"I thought you were mighty quiet during dinner at Ivy Grove."

Again the grin. "Why, Mama, I'm always quiet and ladylike, aren't I?"

"Be serious. I need to talk to you, too. Did I talk too much today about knowing such a famous lady as Mrs. Fanny Kemble Butler? Oh, I forget she isn't calling herself Butler anymore since her family tragedy—the divorce. She's just Mrs. Fanny Kemble now."

"I'm surprised she still calls herself Mrs., aren't you?"

"No, she has two girls. She must hope the Mrs. will keep the tongues from wagging. I haven't heard from Fanny in years, but she's probably still performing in different places all the time and doesn't want her daughters to pay more than they've probably already paid because of her divorce."

"That old Mrs. helps clean up a woman's reputation, I guess. I know people—some of them—give me funny looks up here for not being married so far up in my twenties."

"You only imagine that."

"Is it really true that Mr. Pierce Butler divorced her because she couldn't bring herself to believe in owning slaves?"

"Pete, you've been taught all your life not to use the word *slave*."

"I know it. Papa and I used to laugh about it together."

"You and your father laughed about it?"

"Sure we did. You said at dinner today you certainly do remember how Papa disapproved of slavery."

"You used it again!"

"And I'll probably keep on using it. People are different up here. You know the Denmeads are strong Unionists, but they have to own a lot of people to work all that land and keep that big house."

"Your uncle James Hamilton believes in the Union, too. Not all planters who own people are what they're now calling disunionists. Oh, Pete, are things getting worse in our country, or does it just seem that way because people talk more freely about it up here?"

"We haven't run into any Southern fire-eaters yet, thank heaven. Do you think we have, Mama?"

"I hope not! Of course, that's hard to know for sure in Marietta. The people are successful in the main with an apparently bright future. I'm sure there may be a few of what you call fire-eaters, but those we've met are so cultivated and genteel, most would consider it bad taste to bring up anything so controversial, I'd think. Wouldn't you? Marietta folk seem not to want to rock the boat."

"I'm not as smart about people as you are," Pete said, frowning. "Mama? Are we Unionists?"

"Because of your father, dear, we're British subjects."

"I know, but does that keep us from having an opinion about all this secession talk we keep hearing and reading about? Didn't your favorite newspaper man, Mr. Robert McAlpin Goodman, tell you one day when he called on us soon after we came here, that more and more Southern men besides the late old South Carolinian John Calhoun are plumping for the South to secede from the rest of the country? I know Mr. Goodman hates the idea. And writes about how bad he thinks secession would be. You must want the Union to stay together, Mama, or you wouldn't read Mr. Goodman's writings the way you do."

"I come by my love of the Union naturally, Pete. Your Grandfather Couper believed with all his heart in it. So did your father."

"I know Papa did. He told me himself."

"You actually talked about the Union with your papa, Pete? You were only fourteen when he—left us."

"I know how old I was. But Papa wanted me always to try to protect you where slavery was concerned. He knew you'd grown up with slavery."

Anne stared at her. "Protect me? Did he take the time to try to explain things like that about me—to you? I know, loving St. Simons as I did, longing so to come back to live there with him, I made it hard for him. Which, of course, forced the sweet man, no matter how he hated it, to become a slave owner himself. And oh, my dear girl, your father was indeed a totally sweet man. An unselfish, considerate, kind man. I wish I had been far more unselfish with him."

"Don't wish that, because if you'd stayed with him in London, I might have one of those snooty British accents."

"Why do you have to make a joke about everything?"

"To keep myself sane, I guess. Heriot Wylly picks flowers. I make jokes. Most of which poor Fanny doesn't understand. Did you know Fanny's a secessionist?"

Startled, Anne sat up in bed. "*What?* I never heard of anything as foolish as for you to say a thing like that about gentle, submissive Fanny!"

"I can be pretty foolish when I try. But I'm honestly not trying where my little sister Fanny is concerned. We may not have met a fire-eater socially, Mama, but Fanny's getting sweet on one, and he's got her completely sold on the idea that the South can secede from the rest of the country and do just fine with slave labor. Fanny's so taken with him, she'd believe anything he told her."

"Who, Pete? Who is this young fire-eater your sister's supposed to be interested in?"

"His name is Buster Matthews and he works down at the Denmead flour barrel factory. I think he splits white oak for staves. Not exactly a flaming success as a citizen, I'd say."

"But where did Fanny meet him? And how do you know so much about all this?"

"Fanny doesn't dare worry you with anything. John Couper and I have told her we'd put one of old Sofy's hexes on her if she did or said one word that might keep you from being happy."

"But you've seen to it that I found out anyway. Pete, I never know when to take you seriously. You are more like your father every day where your humor is concerned."

"Good! But this isn't humor. And I took the chance on telling you right out because I think Fanny should stop seeing this young man. Mama, he's an out-and-out secesher!"

"Where did you ever get a word like *secesher?*"

"It's used around here. I even saw it in print the other day in Mr. Robert McAlpin Goodman's newspaper."

"Well, I didn't, and he's such a cultivated gentleman, I can't imagine he'd use a word like that. It isn't even a real word."

"Well, he used it. Of course, he was making fun of Southern hotheads who want to leave the Union, but—"

"Pete, this has gone far enough! What did you say to Fanny when she told you about this boy?"

"I told her she could do a lot better."

"But did you tell her that her father—your father—even as a British subject, believed we should keep the Union together?"

"No, because she started to sniffle. I tell you, Mama, Fanny may be falling in love with him."

Sitting on the side of the bed now, Anne demanded, "I want you to tell me at once why you've decided in your almighty wisdom that you needed to tell me when you made such a point of keeping Fanny quiet about her real feelings for this boy?"

"Because I'm not Fanny's mother and he's filling her full of a lot of trash about how God put a curse on Negroes because they're the descendants of Ham or some such stuff. The curse is the reason they have to do all the hard work for white people."

"That's just plain ignorant."

"Of course it is, so now do you see why I told you? Fanny needs you to order her to stop seeing him ever again."

"I have no intention of doing any such thing! Fanny is as well-born as you, Pete, and I trust her completely. Your sister isn't exactly a beauty, and she simply needs some extra guidance because I'm sure she must feel uneasy sometimes for fear she might not have as many suitors as you and Selina do."

"What suitors have I got?"

"At least your dance card was filled at the last party we gave, and with that glorious red hair, you'll never lack for suitors, Pete. If you do, it will be because you drove them away yourself."

"If I do, Mama, it's only because I'm so smart. Young Bobby Stiles, Mrs. Eliza Mackay's grandson who lives over in Cartersville, told me I scare young men away because I make them feel dumb.

That's as good a reason as any for staying single—which I certainly mean to do."

"Pete, you still don't imagine yourself in love with Anna Matilda King's little son William, do you? Darling girl, he was only a child when he died that day on St. Simons. You were a mere child too!"

"I think that's my business, Mama. Don't you?"

"I guess it is. I just hate to think how much you could miss."

"I know about you and Papa. What the two of you had doesn't happen a lot, though. Can't you just be grateful for your own perfect love and let me be—me?"

"Yes, Pete. I promise never to bring it up again. And Fanny will soon forget about this young wood splitter of hers. You'll see. I asked a question of you a while ago and you didn't answer. Did I talk too much at dinner today with the Denmeads about knowing such a famous lady as Fanny Kemble? If I did, that's the worst taste."

"Of course you didn't. You do know her. I'd guess a lot of ladies wouldn't even admit that now that she's divorced, and according to what we read in that Savannah paper right after Grandpapa Couper died, Pierce Butler wanted the divorce because she hates slavery. I know I used the word again, but you might just as well get used to that, Mama."

"I'll try. My heart still goes out to poor Fanny Kemble. I don't think I've known another mother with such love for her children as she has for her daughters. Pierce Butler even demanded that she see them only now and then. If her dislike of the evil institution—as she calls our owning people down here—costs her that much, I sometimes wonder if I believe anything as strongly myself. Oh Pete, I wish I understood more. I'd give almost anything to understand how something like that could break up a family!"

"It's going to break up a lot more families, too, Mama," Pete declared. "Even right here in conservative, self-satisfied Marietta. You mark my word about that."

"Pete, don't say such things. Don't even think them."

"Do you really prefer that the subject of slavery not be mentioned? At least it's discussed up here right along with politics of any kind. To me, that's a lot healthier than the way they skim over it on St. Simons. Papa used to say they tried to ignore it, or pretended it was natural for everybody, or boasted about how good they were to their people."

"I'm surprised you didn't say slaves again."

"I'm not being mean about it to you, Mama. Papa also told me you hadn't really given it any thought one way or another because you were born into the ugly system."

"Even you can't say Eve and I aren't real friends!"

"Wait a minute," Pete said, taking Anne's hand in both of hers. "You and I can't let it come between us. I've never put it into words before, but I'm pretty sure I agree with Papa about slavery. Papa and Mrs. Kemble. It won't come between us, though, will it? Promise?"

Anne tried to laugh a little. "I promise. I don't think I even have a choice because I honestly don't know where I stand on the subject. In a different place because I loved your father. I do know that much. In a different place from where I saw things as a child— before I met Fanny Kemble or your wonderful father. But if my life depended on it, I couldn't explain exactly how I feel about owning Eve. I couldn't do without her, but that's all I know."

Chapter 45

Two months later, at the very moment Anne heard Pete call her name from downstairs, she was pinning into place the delicately twisted gold brooch John had sent from London before they were married. The brooch she had hurried to show Anna Matilda even before she told her parents that along with the brooch had come a letter from John asking her to marry him. Now, when Pete hurried into the room waving a note from Anna Matilda, Anne sat smiling as though she'd just won a private guessing game.

"Look at you, Mama. You haven't even mentioned your childhood friend Mrs. King for such a long time, I thought sure you'd be surprised that I brought a letter from her! And don't put on polite airs with your own daughter. I don't need to be here when you read it. I can wait to find out the St. Simons gossip."

With that, Pete hurried back downstairs, not at all surprising her mother because Pete seemed always to be in a hurry. Anne sat down in her little rocker and even though she knew Pete was out of hearing, called her thanks anyway before breaking the seal on Anna Matilda's thin, single-page letter.

15 March 1853
Retreat
St. Simons Island, Georgia

My dearest Anne,

This will be very brief since I am packing and the place is in a turmoil today. But there are days when I still miss you so much, I find I simply have to let you know of my sudden change of plans. My beloved husband's letter reached me from California only yesterday with the exciting news that he and our son Thomas Butler, Jr., will be arriving soon in New York City and long for the children and me to meet them in Philadelphia for a real reunion. After he and our son have been away in California for nearly three long years, what a reunion that will be! I've had no news of any planned visit by you to the Island anytime in the future, but did want you to know that we will be far, far from Georgia. Thank heaven for trains! Because Thomas Butler, Sr., is Thomas Butler, Sr., our immediate future plans are, of course, still a mystery. But oh, Anne, he and our son are both well and I am, in spite of my many complaints about being left here with so much responsibility, feeling selfish indeed. I am so, so grateful just knowing that, God willing, I'll really be in my husband's arms again. Will write again from the North.

Yr forever friend,
Anna Matilda King

Postscript: I have just learned from Caroline Wylly Couper that her son Hamilton will share rooms in Savannah with your splendid son, John Couper, who will, I'm sure, be a superb influence on his cousin Hamilton. As you may guess, I am a bit anxious until I know that my husband will come back here to Retreat with us and not, because of his many railroad and other business dealings, have to be away from his own home again.

The pin from John—his late mother's pin—didn't quite suit Anne when she had finished placing it on her dress, and as she tried again, with Anna Matilda's letter read only once, she struggled as always against the old, still-sharp desire to be with John again. Not that she envied Anna Matilda. She felt nothing but happiness for her after such a long separation from Thomas, but it was still hard not to be able to share every shred of news—good or bad—with her own absent husband.

SUMMER WAS CERTAINLY WARM IN MARIETTA IN 1854, BUT NIGHTS cooled down enough so that Anne could at least imagine the breezes off Kennesaw Mountain whispering that they, too, could go on helping her make the transition into her new life without John. Even in the tiny city of Marietta, where she had never awakened beside the dear body in the bed beside her, there had been times when he seemed closer than breathing. She wondered often if Anna Matilda had ever felt her Thomas that near. Since Anna Matilda's letter early in the year, explaining to Anne that she hadn't communicated over Christmas because she was so distraught that Thomas Butler, Sr., had felt the need to travel to Texas on railroad business instead of home to St. Simons Island, Anne had been increasingly worried about her friend. How disappointed she must have been to drive along the picturesque live-oak-lined lane into Retreat Plantation alone with her children instead of knowing the joy of finally having Thomas again beside her.

The long, sunny summer days passed rather quickly into fall 1854. And although his work kept John Couper in Savannah, in late July he had spent almost a week in Marietta, full of excited talk about his own new business and how homelike it seemed to have his cousin Hamilton sharing rooms with him.

"You'd be surprised what a difference it makes too, Mama," he told Anne, "just knowing that when I miss you especially, I can now visit Aunt Frances Anne. I think it's made life a lot better for Menzies, too, having his mother right there with him."

"Does Menzies see much of his brother? I know James is at sea much of the time and that Frances Anne can go for weeks, even months, without seeing the boy."

John Couper's good laugh was more like his father's every day, Anne thought. "I guess I shouldn't laugh," he said, "but old James is not what one could call an elevating influence—even when he's in town. Menzies is as unlike his brother as any two men could possibly be, Mama. You must know that James has always been hard to pin down. I even find him hard to talk to, and I don't just mean his rough language. He's just different from the rest of the family somehow. James seems to be almost embarrassed that his brother is such a well-respected boy. I know it's no laughing matter. I'm sure it isn't to poor Aunt Frances Anne."

"I know why you're laughing, though. There isn't much else to do, I guess. But Menzies, with his wonderful sense of humor and good nature, certainly helps compensate for the heartache James causes their mother."

Grinning at her, John Couper asked, "Can you imagine my spoiled cousin Hamilton Couper actually cleaning our rooms while I'm up here with you this week? He vowed he was going to do just that. But good Miss Eliza Mackay promised, the day I left for Marietta, that she'd slip Emphie over to my place just to make sure the cleaning really gets done."

"I hope you see as much of Miss Eliza as you can, Son. I can't even remember the dozens of times something she's said in years past still helps me. That great lady has a straight, uncluttered path to God."

"Besides that, she's good company," John Couper said. "I expect I drop by the old Mackay place at least twice a month. We're all hoping the yellow fever passes us by this fall, but I'll try to see her more often from now on. I think even the squares in Savannah would seem empty without Miss Eliza's being there."

Chapter 46

ON A MILD SEPTEMBER MORNING IN THE FALL OF 1854, a few days after a fire had burned an entire block of businesses, Louisa Fletcher sat reading her mail in the dining room of the Howard House. She and Dix still lived there while he made certain that he'd found the exact tract of land he meant to begin farming, at least as a hobby. Three of the four letters spread before Louisa were from Savannah and all bore frightening news, even worse than Marietta's fire. Since the always dangerous month of August, sickness from the almost annual siege of yellow fever had begun to grip Savannah. All but six thousand of the eighteen thousand inhabitants of the town had fled to Savannah River plantations or farther inland.

One of the letters was from kind, thoughtful Miss Eliza Mackay. Her single-page note was written just before she and her daughters left for Knightsford, Mark Browning's Savannah River plantation, a reasonably safe distance from the city where people were seemingly well one day and deathly ill or dead the next. Two letters told of how the priests and ministers in Savannah churches were exhausted and falling ill one after another. Miss Eliza left it up to Louisa whether and how much to tell Anne.

Louisa sat staring into space, wondering how she could bring herself to tell Anne that John Couper, on whom she depended minute by minute, had been back in Savannah, in dire danger, since August. Should Louisa even tell her? She had no real choice. After all, telegrams and the railroad had so speeded up communication between the two cities, Anne would soon know anyway. Better that she hear the dread news from someone who truly cared for her, who would stand by her no matter what happened.

And then she was stunned to see John Couper, his face drained as white as chalk, standing in the doorway that led to the hotel lobby, his eyes searching the dining room as though looking for a familiar face.

"John Couper," she called, "here I am!"

As the young man hurried toward her, she got to her feet and embraced him as though he were her own son.

"Something's terribly wrong, isn't it, John Couper? Please sit down and I'll order some cool tea."

"Oh, Mrs. Fletcher! Your face is like an angel's from heaven to me right now. I need your help. I have dreadful news for my mother and she's so fond of you and—do you have time to go with me to her house? I know she'll need you there. She's told me how close the two of you have grown to be and—"

"Who's dead in Savannah, John Couper? I was just reading my mail, and three letters told of the yellow fever epidemic! You look pale, but you're not ill, are you?"

"No. No, I'm all right, Mrs. Fletcher, but my first cousin, my father's brother's son Menzies Fraser, is dead. Mrs. Fletcher, I saw him on Liberty Street right outside his rooms only day before yesterday! He was fine, ruddy-cheeked, laughing. He was taking a surprise to his mother, my Aunt Frances Anne, one of Mama's closest friends from childhood. Mrs. Mackay's Hannah had baked a chicken for Menzies and Aunt Frances Anne. He was hurrying back to his rooms with it to surprise his mother. Such a good-natured, charming fellow. Menzies Fraser didn't have an enemy anywhere. He—he looked so healthy and full of life and then he came down with the fever and now, that fast, he's—dead! In his grave at Laurel Grove . . ."

This fine young man needed her now. He had left for Marietta almost as soon as his cousin—his friend—had died. Why? To break the tragic news to his mother himself? Something was expected of Louisa this minute. She prayed for wisdom and felt her prayer answered almost at once. "John Couper, my dear boy, did you come here yourself to allay your mother's fears about you? Did you come yourself so she would be sure you're all right?"

"I know it looks foolish but, yes. And somehow I don't really think you consider me foolish for having come. This yellow fewer epidemic is so widespread, Mrs. Fletcher, anyone can sicken and die. If young, healthy Menzies could die, anyone can!"

Of course, Louisa thought. He needed an older person to tell him he'd done the right thing by making the train trip. And, of course, it would help Anne to see him healthy, though pale and shaken over the sudden loss of his cousin, his close friend. "You did exactly the right thing, John Couper, and it so happens I was going shopping this morning, so a buggy is harnessed. I beg you to take it and go straight to your mother."

"Should I have tried harder to get Aunt Frances Anne to come with me, Mrs. Fletcher? I know she needs to be with Mama. They've always been so close."

"Where is your aunt now?"

"With Miss Eliza Mackay at her friend Mark Browning's plantation house out on the Savannah River. She's fairly safe there, I think—they both are—from the fever."

"I've heard often about how much your mother thinks of Mrs. Mackay. I'm sure she'll be happy to know Menzies's mother is with her. Miss Eliza can help, if anyone can. She's learned how to live without so many loved ones. Come along, John Couper. If you like, I'll ride with you to your mother's house. One thing is certain, though. Anne must not even consider going to be with her sister-in-law Frances Anne. She's here, away from the danger of fever. We must keep her here."

❦ ❦

As soon as Anne learned that Frances Anne was with Miss Eliza, she calmed down. The heartbreaking news of Menzies's death affected her in a way only Pete could make clear to the others. Anne didn't weep or cry out. In fact, she fell abruptly silent as she sat in her bedroom with Louisa, John Couper, and Pete.

"Don't just sit there staring at her," Pete pleaded with her brother and Louisa. "Can't you both see that this is just one thing too much for Mama? We came up here to escape sickness and death and tears and more grief. For a mysterious reason our mother certainly doesn't deserve, it's all following her here. Give her some time. Don't try to comfort her or think of a way to make her say something she may be sorry for later."

"You know you're much better off right here, don't you, Mama?" John Couper asked, as though Pete had said nothing.

For what to Louisa seemed an eternity, no one spoke. Then, straightening her shoulders, Anne said in a voice so unlike her, Louisa couldn't believe her ears: "That's enough, John Couper!" Anne almost shouted. "Your sister spoke the truth when she warned you not to force me to say anything I might be sorry for later. Do you hear me? Not another word!"

From downstairs a loud banging at the front door brought Anne to her feet as though someone had jerked her from her little rocker. "Who is that?"

"I'll go down and find out," Pete said, heading for the door.

"No! No, Pete. You're so sane and sensible today, I want you here with me. John Couper can find out."

Louisa knew at once that Anne had hurt her son, so she gave him what she hoped was a bracing smile when they exchanged quick glances just before he left his mother's room to head downstairs to the front door.

Then Anne did another surprising thing. She followed the boy into the upstairs hall. Through the open bedroom door Louisa could see her friend lean over the stair railing, plainly eavesdropping. Nothing, she thought, could be more unlike Anne Fraser!

The woman's voice booming from downstairs left no doubt in Louisa's mind who was making the unexpected call. It could be no one but the fire-eating woman who thrived on nourishing trouble between longtime Marietta friends, especially those who for various reasons happened to be on opposite sides of the secession question. Louisa knew that the Fletchers' good friend Robert McAlpin Goodman had told Dix he almost feared Beaulah Matthews, because he knew of no fire-eating citizen in town with as much capacity to cause trouble as a proslavery, anti-Unionist woman. Louisa knew Beaulah Matthews was one of the more dangerous because she was one of those deluded citizens who insisted that if a person believed in the union of all the states, he or she was bound to be an abolitionist.

"So, you're her much-discussed only son," Beaulah was saying in her strident voice.

"Yes, ma'am. Are you and my mother friends?"

"I'd say we'd better become friends if things keep going from bad to worse as they've been doing for the past several months. One reason is that my son, Buster Matthews, a staunch and loyal Southerner, intends to marry your sister Fanny. That is, unless she's bitten by the germ of Unionism as I keep hearing is the case with your mother and your red-haired sister. Where do you stand where your native country is concerned, young man?"

"I—I didn't come prepared to discuss politics, madam," John Couper answered politely. "We've just had a death in the family back in Savannah. My first cousin, who was one of my best friends, just died of yellow fever. There's a terrifying epidemic in Savannah."

"Oh, I know! Almost everyone has fled the city and those left behind are ill. Excuse me, young man, but I must be going! I certainly didn't come here to be exposed to—a dreadful disease! Tell your mother I called, please?"

Louisa had heard every word, and, of course, so had Anne. The door banged shut and Beaulah Matthews was gone.

The front door had no sooner closed than Anne whirled to face Louisa and Pete in the upstairs hall. "I don't want that woman in this house again! Do you understand me, Pete? She is never to set foot inside that door as long as she lives."

"Mama," Pete said as though she was speaking to a small child, "you're upset over poor Aunt Frances Anne. You can't just take it out on old Mrs. Matthews, no matter how much she ruffles your feathers. Fanny hasn't said a word about marrying her dumb, hot-tempered son, Buster. I don't believe it."

"Well, you'd better believe it," Anne snapped. "Fanny told me herself yesterday. It would break her father's heart—her Grandfather Couper's too—but your quiet, seemingly submissive sister is a strong Southern sympathizer."

Louisa had stood quietly beside Anne at the top of the stairs, saying not one word until now. "But my dear Anne, this is a free country. There are so many persons in Marietta who *do* blindly sympathize with what they call, almost reverently, the Southern Cause. Your daughter Fanny is a thoughtful girl, and even though her father was a British subject, it's perfectly possible that she does hold such anti-Union feelings."

"Possible," Anne said, "but Louisa, you know it's not plausible!"

"Perhaps she's been influenced by Buster Matthews. His mother, as difficult and obstinate as we may find her, is, like us, a citizen of a free country. You and I both believe in that country. We just want it to stay together as one. And nothing, believe me, can divide families and friends as can politics or religion."

Anne turned abruptly to look at Louisa. "Louisa, Louisa, can you ever forgive me? If anyone knows what it's like to be shut out by those who profess to follow the same God of love, it's you! There's no one more faithful in church attendance than you, and our own minister can't or won't allow you to partake of Communion with us. I'm so, so sorry I let my rage show. I'm a slave owner too! And owning slaves is supposed to be part of faithfulness to the twisted Southern Cause. We should all be thinking only of poor Frances Anne Fraser in her dreadful grief. We should be thinking only of her and—oh, I'm surely not strong enough even to go on breathing in the face of such tragedy." Suddenly she almost screamed out John Couper's name. "Son? Where are you? Are you still standing alone down there in the entrance hall?"

"Yes, Mama," the boy called, taking the stairs two at a time until he was beside her, holding her close in his arms. "Here I am. And I'm fine and healthy. You don't have to worry about what you'd do if you lost me. I'm right here. I'll always be right here to look after you."

Anne clung to him. "Yes. Yes, you're here now, but any day I'm sure you'll tell me you have to get back to Savannah to look after your own business. Don't, John Couper! Don't tell me that. You said he was fine and healthy one day and the next he was still and cold and buried in Laurel Grove Cemetery. John Couper, I must go to Savannah. I know—I *know* Frances Anne needs me."

"Mama," Pete said, "Aunt Frances is with Miss Eliza Mackay. As wonderful as you are—and you're the most wonderful mother anyone ever had—even you couldn't be of more help than Miss Eliza is. You can write to her. Even if you only say you're praying for her, that will help somehow. If it doesn't, then God just isn't doing His part in any of this!"

"And Mama," John Couper said, "I'm not going right back to Savannah. We may be a little short of money for a month or so, but almost everyone, businessmen included, have left the city. Rest your heart, Mama. I promise you I'm not going back to Savannah until I know the worst of the epidemic is over. Don't you believe me?"

"Yes, of course I believe you, Son. I've always believed every word you've ever said to me. Now, Louisa, I don't think I can endure another minute without writing some kind of note to Frances Anne. Will you excuse me?" She reached to touch Louisa's arm. "And forgive me? And pray for me and Frances Anne?"

Chapter 47

FOR PETE, WRITING TO ANY MEMBER OF HER IMME-
diate family had never been difficult. She didn't consider it a chore. And surprising even herself, she had
grown so fond of Fraser, her sister Annie's child, during his visit to Marietta that writing to the boy had
become almost second nature. She had always liked
children enough to know how to play with them and
to make them laugh at her antics. But with young
Fraser, everything was different. She made no bones
about how much she enjoyed what had come to be
regular correspondence with him. Even her usually
solemn sister Fanny broke down now and then and
teased Pete about the boy.

"I declare," Fanny said one November morning
as the two strode—because Pete always strode—
toward the post office on the Square hoping, as everyone hoped these days, for news of what Mama
called the trouble, which seemed to be spreading. "I
never saw you so fond of any child before, Pete. You
and young Fraser Demere have a regular case on
each other. He writes to you almost as often as you
write to him."

"What's wrong with that, pray tell?"

"There's nothing wrong with it, for goodness'
sake. It's just that you're always saying how glad you
are that you don't have to be tied down looking after

small children and worrying about them the way poor Aunt Frances Anne has always had to worry about our cousin James. He's the only child she has left now to care for her in her old age."

"I'd just as soon you didn't talk about that, Fanny. Have you ever seen anything outside our immediate family hit our mother so hard as Menzies's sudden death? We've watched her go through so much, sometimes I think I can't stand to look at her sad, pretty face again. I honestly think if she didn't know Aunt Frances was with Miss Eliza, she might try to go smack into all that sickness in Savannah just in case she could find a way to help Aunt Frances."

"Oh, I don't think she'd do that," Fanny said.

Surprised at how definite Fanny was all of a sudden, Pete asked, "And why not, Miss Know-it-all?"

"I don't know anything for sure, but our mother isn't stupid. I overheard her tell Miss Louisa Fletcher just yesterday that she'd been through so much herself in the past few years, she'd only make matters worse for Aunt Frances if she tried to talk to her. Mrs. Fletcher was here to tell Mother she felt sure her husband was going to buy the Breakfast House down by the tracks from Mr. Glover. I guess there was little or no damage to the building from the fire back in September, and people flock there to eat breakfast when the trains stop."

"I thought Mr. Fletcher was thinking about becoming a farmer."

"I guess he can do both, Pete. Businessmen are making a lot of money in this town these days, and it seems most business deals are paid off a little at a time. Mr. Fletcher will have until 1859 to finish paying Mr. Glover for the Breakfast House."

"I just wish we knew a way to get our hands on some of the cash that keeps flowing around. You know how Mama hates buying on credit."

"You did a lot of eavesdropping during Miss Louisa's visit yesterday, didn't you, little Sister?" Pete asked.

"I'm a good listener."

"And I wonder if you ever forget anything!"

The letter from Miss Eliza Mackay in Savannah came on Friday, December 8, 1854, just after Anne had finished a tearful admonition to Fanny and Pete, making it plain that there would be no decorations or any other kind of celebration or gift giving this Christmas out of respect for Aunt Frances Anne's fresh grief over Menzies, who had been in his grave a little less than three months. Pete picked up the letter for her mother at the post office when she'd walked there hoping for some word from her favorite, young Fraser Demere in Florida. There was only Miss Eliza's letter, though, and Pete tried and failed to smile at her own disappointment. Fanny was right more often than anyone expected and had continued to tease her older sister because of her unusual attachment to their sister's child.

"I don't see anything wrong with enjoying Fraser's letters to me, and heaven knows there's been little enough to lift anybody's heart around this house since we heard that Menzies had died. It's a good thing John Couper finally let us know the doctors who survived the fever believe the epidemic is over. At least no one's died this week. I was really worried that Mama herself might get sick worrying about John Couper's going back when he did."

"Well, I didn't get sick," Anne said, surprising them from the parlor doorway. "And I suppose this is a common subject to be discussed these days every time my back is turned."

"You didn't mean that to sound as cross as it sounded, did you, Mama?" Pete asked.

"No, of course not and I'm sorry. Did you girls go by the post office?

"Pete did," Fanny said. "And she brought a letter for you from Miss Eliza Mackay in Savannah."

"Well, give it to me, Pete!"

"I suppose Selina's down at the Fletchers'," Fanny said. "I was hoping she'd be back by now to help me with the darning."

"She's at the Fletchers' talking boys with Louisa's daughters,

I'm sure," Anne answered absently while breaking the seal on Miss Eliza's letter. "I do hope Mrs. Mackay's written a full report on poor, heartbroken Frances Anne."

"Wanta read by yourself, Mama?" Pete asked.

"No. Stay, both of you, but I will scan what she's written, alone first, if you don't mind." For a minute or so, Anne's eyes flew over the still-firm, clear handwriting, and then she gasped. "Oh, no! Dear Lord in heaven, not this too! Pete! Read it aloud. I—I can't!"

Pete grabbed the letter and started reading.

"My dearest Anne . . .

I have never written a harder letter, so forgive the brevity and I'll get right to the point of it. Your sweet, shattered sister-in-law Frances Anne has just been devastated by still another blow. Her older son—the only remaining child—was killed in what people are calling a drunken brawl three days ago on the waterfront. The papers say James and two German sailors, ashore from their merchant ship only two days, began with merriment that ended with poor, hapless James Fraser found floating face down in the Savannah River. I beg you, Anne, to ask your girls to join you in praying that I will find some small words of comfort for Frances Anne. At least, that she may be given something of her old, courageous will to live. The woman at times seems so full of despair and sorrow over her dependable son Menzies's death, it is almost as though she hasn't room left to grieve for James, whom she loved greatly because of the boy's prevailing, enormous need of constant help. Frances will, I know, pass through many stages of grief this time, and only our loving Lord can sustain her. One thing is certain, Anne, she does not want you to come to her. She loves you too much and feels her crushed heart could not endure watching you work at trying to comfort her. I ask you to believe that I fully agree with her and urge you not to beg to come.

Your friend,
Eliza McQueen Mackay.

Postscript: James was buried in Laurel Grove beside Menzies.

Your fine, rosy-cheeked son, John Couper, was a pallbearer and I know sends his love to all of you there, as I send mine. Frances seems more strongly attached than ever to John Couper now that he is the only living male member of your family to carry on the name Fraser."

Chapter 48

MISS ELIZA MACKAY CONTINUED TO WRITE OCCA-
sional notes to Anne, but despite trying to participate
with her girls at the various Christmas and New
Year's social events in Marietta, Anne carried a heavy
heart for Frances Anne into the late fall of the next
year, 1855, and wrote more often than ever to John
Couper.

"I probably only clutter his busy life with my incessant pleadings for word of his aunt, but I go on
believing that your brother understands and doesn't
dread still another letter from his mother. Do you
think I'm fooling myself, Pete?"

"Mama, I don't see how any young man could do
more to prove to you that he lives his life around
concern for your well-being. Don't you hear from
him at least once a week?"

"Yes, yes, I do. It's just my worrywart heart. The
boy's written faithfully. And how he's tried to reassure me that Aunt Frances Anne is doing all she can
do under the circumstances to live her life. I do wish
she'd agree to spend the remainder of the year with
Miss Eliza, now that they can all live in town again.
I'm sure being in a completely strange place at the
Brownings' Knightsford was hard for her, no matter
how beautiful it is out there on the Savannah River.
As do a lot of coastal people, she feels comfortable

and at ease in Miss Eliza's home on East Broughton Street. That wise old lady and both her daughters have a way of making everyone feel so welcome, even needed."

"I think they do need company. Two spinster sisters and an aging widow can soon rattle around in a big old house like that. And poor old William Mackay has gotten so fat and moody, I hear, he's not much company anymore."

"I don't think that's very nice, so don't repeat it."

"I have no intention or reason to repeat it to anyone. Mama? Is Aunt Frances Anne really going back to St. Simons to live at the old Wylly place with her odd sisters Matilda and Heriot?"

"You know she's written only once—that sad, heartbreaking letter pouring out her false guilt because she can't seem to grieve for poor dead James the way she goes on grieving for Menzies."

"I know. You must have read us that letter a dozen times. And I think it's pretty normal for her to be that way. Menzies was her— John Couper. She relied on him to be on hand to take care of her for the remainder of her life. Does Mrs. Mackay think Aunt Frances Anne is going to try life at the Village with her sisters?"

"Yes, she does. They're both difficult for Frances Anne, but they're family. When you're a little older, you'll understand that."

"What do you mean? I'm almost thirty, I'm an old maid and I do understand. I understand a lot more than you sometimes think, Mama."

Anne grinned a little. "Yes, I imagine you do. In fact, I hope you do."

"Well, I do, although I'm not quite sure whether your hope for my understanding is for your sake or mine. But, never mind. One thing I know. No one can depend on Heriot for anything beyond fresh flowers from her gardens, and if I had to watch Margaret Matilda Wylly sitting in that chair of hers on the porch watching for any chance visitor who might come out their road, it would depress me more than poor old fat William Mackay could ever do. I'm sure you're right about family, that Aunt Frances will eventually go back to St. Simons to live at the Village, but that's when I'll increase my prayers for her, believe me. She doesn't need more gloom. It's gloomy enough shopping now and then on our own Square here since our second fire last month. All Marietta businessmen seem to think about is opening new businesses and making more money. When on earth do you think they'll get down to setting up our own fire company?"

"Who knows, Pete? I don't think there's a single woman in town who doesn't know we need one. Even strong-headed Mrs. Matthews was going on about it last week. Between tirades against the Union, of course. You know I haven't gone once to the Square since this fire. Does it really depress you to do our shopping?"

"You bet it does. If Selina and Fannie weren't so boy-happy, it would depress them, too, but Marietta loves its social life as much as it loves money, and those two don't seem to think of much else but off-the-shoulder dresses and billowing evening skirts. Our Square is our showplace, or it was. Now those burned shops and the charred remains of the Marietta Hotel, along with all the other blackened buildings, would depress anybody but my two sisters. All Selina can think about these days is finding something new to wear. She doesn't really surprise me, I guess, but my usually sensible sister Fanny does, and Fanny's ready to go shopping with her every time Selina gets the urge."

"Well, surely there won't be another fire anytime soon, and if even one businessman has a grain of sense, he'll agitate until something is done about getting our own firefighters and some decent equipment."

"Depressing or not, I have to go to the Square right now," Pete said, "for some more binding tape. And about those businessmen and a new fire department—do you want to bet?"

"No, I don't want to bet, but if we have another fire, help will have to be brought all the way from Atlanta, and that's twentysome miles!"

Chapter 49

ANNE WAS GROCERY SHOPPING IN THE ALMOST RE-
stored Square with Selina, Fanny, and Pete when
Louisa Fletcher reached the white-light house late in
the afternoon on the fine, though windy, spring day
of April 13, 1857. Louisa stood alone in Anne's elegant parlor while Eve prepared to serve tea. Mina had
just baked cinnamon buns, and the spacious house
was filled with their mouthwatering aroma.

Louisa, who always needed to watch her ample
figure, made one more effort to rearrange her wind-
blown hair before a long, gilt-framed looking glass on
the wall that faced the spot where hung the handsome
painting of Anne's late husband, John Fraser, one fine
hand holding the striking bonnet of his Royal Marine
uniform. Louisa was extremely fond of Eve and
looked forward to her return with or without cinnamon buns.

"You lookin' at Mausa John, ma'am?" Eve asked
from the doorway to the parlor, a large silver pot of
tea and a generous supply of buns gracing the tray
she carried. "He be one fine-lookin' gent'man, Miss
Anne's Mausa John, an' how dat woman did love that
man!"

Beaming, Louisa turned to Eve, her nose wrinkled
with joyful anticipation of Mina's fragrant buns. "Oh,
Eve, I do know she loved him. She's talked and

talked about him to me in the five years you've all lived here. In fact, each time I enter this room, I feel I should greet the handsome gentleman myself."

"Mausa John, he like that. I bet he's laughin' right now, if we could only hear his voice. He a big man for laughin' an' singin'. An' Miss Louisa, he sing better'n any bird. I reckon she done told you the name of their favorite song."

"Was it 'Drink to Me Only with Thine Eyes'?"

Eve smiled. "I knew she done tol' you dat. An' if you don' think I'm being forward, I oughta tell you never, never to sing that song where she can hear you. I knows you sing like a bird, too, an' Miss Anne, she love your singin' at church, but she ain't never allowed nobody to sing or play their song since he went away from her all them years ago. You thinks me forward for tellin' you never to sing it?"

"Eve, Eve, haven't you caught on by now that I know way down in my heart what close friends you and your Miss Anne really are? Haven't you guessed that unlike so many people here, I don't consider conversation with you as anything but good and welcome? That you and I simply exchange ideas much the same way your mistress and I do?"

"The same as you and Miss Anne?"

Louisa laughed a little. "The same, and I'd wager that if the two of us had more time to talk, we'd both find out that we agree on far more than meets the eye." Then she looked directly at Eve. "You must know that I'm the object of much criticism in this town because I let it be known that neither my husband nor I believe slavery is God's will for anyone. If he presses on with his notion to begin farming out at Woodlawn on a small scale, I'm sure Mr. Fletcher will have to own a few people, but although I guard my tongue at all times—or try to—I will not be in agreement even if I manage to stay quiet. Now, does it make you any more comfortable with me knowing how I really feel on the subject?"

"I reckon so."

"Don't you know?"

"No'm. You see, I'se been owned all my life, but by Miss

Anne an' nobody else." Eve smiled. "That do make a big difference."

"Yes, I'm sure it does. At least, I know you're really Anne's
friend and that you have a wise as well as beautiful head."

"Thank you, but I knows that. An' you kin let your heart rest
where Miss Anne's concerned. Even after I loses my June—an' he
be gittin old—I promise you that Miss Anne, she have full use of
my good head." With no show whatever of pride, Eve added simply, "You right that Eve got plenty of wisdom for whatever her an'
Miss Anne got to face on any tomorrow."

"I really count on that. Did you know?"

"Yes'm, I know 'cause I know you one Mar'etta lady dat love
Miss Anne for herself, not just for her family roots. Looks like you
feels the same 'bout Mina's buns, too."

"They're delicious! Even without that tasty cinnamon icing, the
buns themselves are masterpieces." Louisa went on joyously with
her tea and buns. "And doesn't the house smell wonderful? Even
with a separate kitchen out back, I could smell this tempting aroma
all the way in here. Please tell Mina her buns are a huge success,
Eve, and that I—"

Without a word, Eve had slipped across the parlor to a front
window. "You smell sompin besides cinnamon buns, Miss Louisa?"

The sudden urgency in Eve's voice caused Louisa to look up at
her. The tall, lithe mulatto woman had pulled back the curtains and
was yanking at the window, trying to open it.

"Eve! What's wrong? It's so windy outside, any more breeze in
this room will cool my tea and buns. You're frowning. Is something
wrong out in the yard?"

"Sniff, Miss Louisa! Give yourself a good sniff an' you'll smell
more than Mina's buns! Come over here an' sniff good!"

Beside Eve now at the open window, Louisa caught the sharp,
pungent whiff of something burning outside. The wind was
stronger than before, and branches on Anne's lovely magnolias
were whipping in it wildly.

"Eve, there's another fire! Dear, compassionate Father in
Heaven, protect us somehow! Pray, Eve. Pray!"

"I'se already prayin', Miss Louisa. My June, ole fool that he is, already headin' toward the Square! Big Boy right 'longside him. I sho' wish Rollie hadn't been hired out to the Denmeads. They could use his hep right now."

"But June's an old man! And by the look of that wind, it isn't only the Square in danger—that fire could spread to every residence in town!"

"June be ole, but so's his white head. He won't do nothin' crazy. Big Boy'll look after him. It's Miss Anne and Pete an' Selina an' Fanny I'se worried 'bout. They all be down there in that Square!"

"Dear Lord," Louisa half prayed, half addressed Eve. "And the whole town of Marietta sprawled here at the foot of the mountain right in the path of that wind and without anything to fight a fire except men's muscles and buckets of water!"

"God done make one miracle, 'cause Mina ain't made a peep from back in her kitchen. If she knowed they was a fire roarin' down on the Square, she be hollerin' an' runnin' 'roun' like a chicken wif its head cut off. Mina goes crazy wif fear over a fire!"

"It appears to be Colonnade Place burning—sending up those huge, thick puffs of smoke. And Eve, look how that smoke's whipping around! Eve! Where are you going? Big Boy will take care of June. You said so yourself."

"June ole an' wise. It be Miss Anne an' the girls I worries 'bout," she cried, flying out the door and across the yard. "Don't you try to stop me, Miss Louisa," she called over her shoulder. "I aim to find my ladies somewhere an' bring 'em home!"

Through the heavy smoke and gathering darkness, Eve found June first, his bent but still-strong shoulder forming part of a bucket brigade, and then she saw Big Boy about nine men down the line of pickup firefighters.

"Don't worry none, Eve," Big Boy gasped, without missing a beat with the next bucket held out to him. "I done fin' Miss Anne an' her girls. Done sent 'em packin' off toward home. It be dark soon. But you pray, hear? Pray Miss Anne an' the girls gits there and also that the firefighters from Atlanta git chere in time to help us. We ain't gonna hold out much longer. Pray, Eve, pray!"

Hurrying as fast as her aching legs would take her up Decatur

Street toward Miss Anne's house, Eve realized that until tonight she
had never thought about simple, good Big Boy praying. It was dark
now, so that the leaping flames from the burning shops and stores
and nice Mr. Denmead's warehouse and the post office and the
Howard House were lighting the sky for miles around. She prayed.
Oh, how she prayed. And felt a new strength rise within her from
somewhere. Somewhere? she asked herself. From God. From Sweet
Jesus. Because Big Boy was praying too. Never again would she
think of the huge Ebo as a backward child. From now on, Big Boy
would be what he really was—a godly giant. Somewhere in the
Bible it said, "Except ye become as little children . . ." Ebo Big
Boy was the right kind of little chur'n. And if only she could find
Miss Anne, she'd gladly confess she'd made a mistake and thought
chur'n instead of *children* as she was supposed to do.

And then, over her own tangled thoughts—as tangled as Miss
Heriot Wylly's had ever been—she heard the distant beat of many
hooves. Heard it over the yells and whistles and cries of men shouting orders to each other as they worked—borrowed slaves along
with the town's men of stature and means—hauling, carrying,
throwing, scooting furniture, bags of wheat, cotton, and huge barrels out of the crackling, blackening warehouses, away from the
flames and into the street. But that steady beat of hooves could
mean only one blessed thing, an answer to the prayers of every
person within sight of that ugly fire that was changing the village of
Marietta forever. The prayers for help from Atlanta's fire company
had been heard. The company was heading toward Marietta. Their
crying to God had been heard and He was sending help.

"Eve! Oh, Eve, here we are! We're hitting for home as fast as
we can go. June's all right. I found him. How did we miss seeing
you before now? Eve! It's Pete. Mama and the girls are with me and
we're all right."

Then Miss Anne's arms were around Eve, and without one in-
kling that she may seem forward to do it, Eve was holding Miss
Anne in her own arms . . . holding her, holding her, rubbing her
poor back, murmuring aloud to Sweet Jesus some of the almost
painful gratitude she felt to have found her loved ones at last. . . .

WITHIN A FEW WEEKS, A HUE AND CRY WENT UP ALL OVER TOWN at the prospect of the actual receipt of Marietta's first very own hand-powered fire engine, delivered from Atlanta, where it was built.

It arrived on Canton Road near the Square, where it would be housed in an all-brick building and manned, in case of another emergency, by the town's own fire company. The bell was late arriving, but when it did come, the city celebrated in the midst of the charred ruins left in the Square by the third, and worst, fire yet. Everyone, even practical Pete, who thought such tardy pomp and pretention ludicrous, attended the ceremony.

"You might just as well go and enjoy yourself, Pete," Selina told her sister excitedly, struggling into the new Swiss muslin Fanny had just finished. "This is going to be a different kind of celebration. It has to do with progress in Marietta."

"Progress, my foot. If ever I saw the barn door closed after the horse was gone, this is it! And your new dress is going to brush against some old burned-out crate or sidewall just as sure as anything. You and Fanny are both dressed to a fare-thee-well. What are Fanny and Mama doing outside in their good clothes?"

"Gathering flowers and leaves. Haven't you heard? We're going to decorate the new fire bell so it will look really festive and show our civic pride in it."

"Sometimes I can't believe this town even though we live right in it. Any old excuse for a social event, but don't worry, I'm going too, and I'll applaud and cheer with the best of them. Are we meeting Miss Louisa Fletcher at their new hotel?"

Selina giggled. "Miss Louisa would love hearing it called a hotel in the condition it's in right now. Mr. Dix Fletcher closed the deal with Mr. John Glover at least two years ago just for the old Breakfast House. How long do you suppose it will be before all those thirty-two rooms he's adding will be finished?"

"So we can jump right in and begin giving parties there?"

"Well, sure. When Miss Louisa gets through supervising it all, the Fletcher House will be perfect for parties of all kinds!"

"Of all kinds is right," Pete said mockingly. "Anyway, we have to celebrate the new fire bell first, and I'm sure Mama and Fanny have enough flowers by now."

Chapter 50

THE YEAR 1858, DURING WHICH MARIETTA WAS RE-building after the fire, was so hectic and busy for Louisa Fletcher that she was both glad and sorry she had finally given in to her long-held desire to keep a daily journal. Her husband, Dix, was now in the process of paying off his indebtedness to John H. Glover for the purchase of what had been called the Breakfast House, and Louisa was in the midst of the final chaos from Dix's extensive remodeling of their new hotel, now called the Fletcher House. It fell to her to purchase furnishings for the added thirty-two guest rooms. She still had no love for innkeeping, but, being Louisa, she was of no mind to leave the exterior of the newly redone building in the hands of anyone but herself. The Fletcher House would offer the best accommodations and food, and its very shape and look would add to the elegance and beauty of the town. With all the extra duties, plus her regular work as landlady, she resented the number of blank pages in her journal. More than anything else, Louisa loved to write, especially reviews of each new book she devoured.

Slipping through her entries, or lack of them, her usually dependable sense of humor helped quell her irritation over the unfilled pages. She smiled a bit to herself as she scanned her journal's entries early in the year 1859. Seldom had she failed to commend herself for having kept her vows about improving herself: She had kept her resolution to cease complaining about how much she hated hotel life, and her gratitude was growing for the gift of Anne Fraser's friendship.

"I love Anne as though she were a member of my own family," she had written in January 1859, "and although Dix's passion for life in the country out at Woodlawn, his eighty acres at the edge of town, and my own love of city life drive me to the brink of annoyance, I doggedly work at teaching the children near Woodlawn because a seemly wife obeys her husband. It is teaching me to be a better Christian, and I thank God I have Anne Couper Fraser as my best friend. She has learned to live with the loss of so much of her life, I am kept on guard over my own soul's impatience. I now know I can share anything with Anne and still count on her support of me as I struggle to grow spiritually."

Many pages were also given to the interesting quandary among the members of her immediate family because one of Marietta's most prominent and wealthiest gentlemen had fallen head over heels in love with her beloved eldest daughter, Georgia. No one, not even Louisa, could find a single flaw in the suitor, Mr. Henry Greene Cole, except that he was twenty-three years older than Georgia! The man was even a strong, sensible Unionist, which, of course, pleased both Louisa and Dix, especially now that the normally clear, clean air over Marietta was thickening daily with ugly talk of how greatly the South would prosper were it only to secede from the Union.

Aside from these high political qualifications, Mr. Cole, a kind and thoughtful gentleman, was the owner not only of the newly rebuilt Marietta Hotel on the Square, but of countless valuable tracts of land in Cobb and many surrounding counties. He was educated and had come south from New York as a well-paid civil engineer during the construction of the new rail systems, heavily responsible for the continuing prosperity of Marietta. Georgia, Louisa's journal made clear, was so in awe of Henry Green Cole that her feelings bordered on downright fear. His tender, minute-by-minute consideration of the pretty twenty-one-year-old girl won her over, though, and they were to be married at St. James Episcopal Church on August 25 of the year 1859.

"With three eligible daughters, Anne," Louisa told her friend one late January afternoon as the two sat in the Fletcher House parlor, talking through one of Louisa's rare free hours, the winter sun still high in an almost cloudless sky, "it won't be long until you'll be facing the excitement, joy, *and* anxiety over their futures that I now face with my daughters."

Anne laughed a little. "Don't be too sure. Selina, my youngest, yes. With the new Georgia Military Institute in session now, I fully expect her to find her one and only any time."

"And she's a beautiful girl!"

"Thank you, but the only one of the three for whom I have much hope of a happy marriage is Selina. There isn't a sweeter, more amenable child anywhere than my Fanny, but let's face it, Louisa, she's no beauty. And so far the only young man who's shown her any attention is Buster, that dreadful Matthews boy with the impossible mother. I honestly couldn't wish anything to come of that. I love Fanny too much."

"Of course you do! He's a boor, Anne. Not only because he's one of those fire-eating secesher, as Mr. Goodman calls them in his paper, but Fanny can do a lot better than that smart aleck. Only a mother could love him, *if* the woman known as his mother is capable of any measure of real loving." She laughed dryly. "I don't sound like a Christian at all, do I."

Then their talk shifted to Pete. In some detail Anne told Louisa of the tragic day she and Pete, while Pete was still a small child, rode frantically from their home at Hamilton Plantation on St. Simons to the Kings' Retreat when Anne's closest childhood friend, Anna Matilda King, sent for her to come quickly to help with her sick child. "Nothing would do Pete but that she had to ride with me. We rode hard, both of us praying all the way, and the girl, not quite eight then, was in a panic that truly frightened me. You see, Louisa, I don't expect marital happiness ever for Pete because, as self-contained and opinionated as she's grown to be, she swears she loved, and will always love, young William Page King, her best playmate."

Louisa stared at her. "And you believe she still feels so strongly about a little boy? I take it he died that day."

"Yes. Well, the next day, as I remember. It broke his mother's heart for certain, but also Pete's little heart. And it seems not to matter at all that she's nearly thirty-four now. She shuts me up every time I mention anyone's courting her by reminding me that her one real love is still that little fellow. About the only added explanation I ever get from her is when she grins that tomboyish grin and reminds me that no one ever climbed a tree as William did!"

"To this day?"

"To this day. It seems they signed some kind of lifetime pact."

"Anne, Anne, you have lived through more than your share of losses by death, haven't you?"

"I just don't know. I've heard of people who have had more losses than I. Perhaps none that left deeper scars. I only know that I pray daily it has come to an end now that we're up here. Then I see my blessed sister-in-law's stricken face—Frances Anne's face now that her son Menzies, on whom she depended as I depend on John Couper, is gone too."

"And, in the same year, her firstborn. Was it James?"

"Yes, named for my Scottish father-in-law, James Fraser. I believe Frances Anne when she writes that she can't find room to grieve for James. Menzies filled her life. James was not what anyone would call a—good boy."

"Do we love one child above another, Anne?"

"I've never thought so. But perhaps all mothers fight admitting it, even if it's true."

"Similar, I guess, to my own conflicts when I try to differentiate in any way among my own feelings about my three living girls and the three small daughters who died while Dix and I still lived in Massachusetts."

Louisa reached to touch Anne's hand. "At any rate, I want you to know that from today on I'll be joining you in your daily prayer that news of even one more death doesn't reach you up here. Believe me, Anne, I truly care and so does our loving Lord. When sorrows pile up, the human tendency of us all is to—wonder. Even to doubt that He cares. But He does. Oh, my friend, He cares. The sparrows that fall to the ground do not have a corner on our Father's love and notice and caring."

THE VERY NEXT DAY, FRIDAY, JANUARY 28, PETE brought Anne's mail from the newly rebuilt post office. On top of the small stack of letters was one in a handwriting so uneven and broken, it was barely recognizable as Anna Matilda's. Anne remembered what Louisa had said about our inevitable times of doubt that God truly loves as He claims. And then she began to read.

> Anne, oh Anne,
> How can I write this? My beautiful son, Thomas Butler King, Jr., is gone from me. . . . The doctor says an aneurysm took him. I'm so confused, I can't imagine how—or why. My friend, I had to let you know first because this can be the death of me. My handsome Butler . . . Butler, named for his father, the one man I've ever loved. Anne . . . Anne, what will I do now? Nothing fills the void. Butler, my splendid Butler, is gone. As we laid his dear body in Christ Churchyard, I thought—and I still think—this can be the death of me, too. He was the jewel of my life. I long to follow him.
>
> But I am your friend,
> Anna Matilda King

Her mind, body, and heart feeling wooden, Anne still insisted on the girls' attending the long-anticipated winter ball to be held at the Georgia Military Institute in February, and she wouldn't hear of their canceling a dinner dance planned at their own Marietta home in March. She even helped them dress for the ball and took part as hostess when their young guests arrived for the dinner party. Anne canceled plans to attend a community picnic in the park at the center of the Square and could tell Louisa honestly that she had done well to keep walking around. Every painful pang of homesickness and longing for St. Simons, which had tormented her through the final months in London with John before they returned to the Island to live, had come rushing back. Had not a letter from Anna Matilda's husband stopped her, she would have made the trip to St. Simons to be with her longtime friend in this new, terrifying grief.

"Our son, not quite thirty, seems to have taken the life of his mother with him when he went," Thomas Butler King, Sr., wrote Anne in the letter whose plain intent was to beg her not to come. "In her condition, I doubt that she could converse even with you, her closest friend."

When her own John Couper wrote, pleading that she not try to make the journey, urging—almost ordering—her in his gentle way to stay in her white-light house for all their sakes, she agreed.

Then, in the same mail with John Couper's letter from Savannah, Miss Eliza Mackay added another heavy burden to Anne's heart. Anne knew, as did everyone who read the short but neatly written script, that Miss Eliza had told her sad news as lightly and gently as a brokenhearted mother knew how. Over and over Anne wondered how, in the name of heaven, she would endure this, too, so long and so deeply had she herself leaned on Miss Eliza Mackay, who wrote:

> My dearest Anne,
>
> It is with the heaviest heart that I write these lines to you, even as I apologize for their brevity. As I sit here—I believe it is August 7—five long days since we buried our beloved William, my long-suffering son, my solid comfort and solace through even the tragedies of his own sorrow-filled life. The only comfort, except the Presence of God now, is the sure knowledge that William is, at long last, back with his sweet wife and children, who went down when the steamship *Pulaski* took so many lives long ago. Mark Browning and his dear wife, Caroline, are, of course, my stays now, as are both William's sisters, but my peace comes from

the certainty that William is united with his own three loved ones. William fell down our steep stairs from a heart attack on the morning of August 1. My blessed Mark Browning was with me.

Your friend always,
Eliza McQueen Mackay

At the end of some days lately, Anne had found solace in the very act of going each night to her own spacious bedroom on the second floor of her beloved house; had felt deep in her bones that maybe, just maybe, enough time had passed now so that she would learn how to snuggle down between clean sheets in Eve's carefully made bed and truly rest—even without John's strong body beside her. After all, he had been gone twenty years last month. It was now August 1859, but most Marietta nights cooled off so that sound sleep was usually possible. It had come to be all right, with little or no adjustment required on the mornings when Eve was a bit late getting there to open her draperies. After all, June had reached such an advanced age, he often slept until long after daylight.

Eve.

I had better be getting myself in hand, Anne thought on the morning of August 31, when her little filigreed bedside clock told her it was not only past daylight but nearly nine. One day Eve would arrive needing Anne as Anne had always needed her. June would be gone, and with all her being, Anne longed to be adequate to Eve's grief. Eve had loved June even longer than Anne had loved John. There was no comfort in the long-delayed realization that colored folk suffered the same pain, felt the same joy and sorrow experienced by whites. Anne had known this for a long time, and the very knowing had made her friendship with Eve deeper but also somehow harder, because it required more of Anne. Will I really be able to help Eve when she needs me most?

"Like right this minute?" she asked aloud in the empty room. "What's stopping me from getting up and drawing those draperies myself?"

Just when the blessed white light flooded the handsome room, she heard Eve's footsteps in the hall outside. Within seconds after the slender, still-beautiful mulatto woman entered the room, Anne knew something dreadful had happened. For a strange instant—a mere flash of time—Anne was back in the dream she must have been having on waking earlier. She not only could feel the hot, semitropical sun on her face, see the waving shadows cast by banners of Spanish moss hanging from giant St. Simons live oaks, but could actually smell the pungent, familiar, sharp odor of marsh mud and felt safely at home. Then her thoughts veered to her childhood friend Anna Matilda, in her own fresh grief over the death of her fine son, Thomas Butler King, Jr.

Trembling, Anne whispered, "Good morning, Eve. Is—June ill today?"

And when Eve's calm voice and almost normal manner told Anne that June had not been the reason Eve was so late arriving, she grabbed Eve's arm. "Then what is it? I'm not cross because you're late. After all these years I know there's a good reason, but something's wrong, Eve. I can tell by your face, the way you're working at keeping your voice calm. You—you have a knowing about something. What? *What?*"

"I be later than ever in my life, Miss Anne, 'cause of Pete. She must have had a knowin', too, 'cause she went so early to the post office for your mail." And then Eve handed her a single letter from St. Simons Island.

Anne grabbed the letter. "Since when did Pete start to have knowings?"

"She always had the gif'."

"I suppose your grandmother Sofy told you that."

"Yes'm. I sorry jus' to say 'yes'm,' Miss Anne, but I be here right with you for whatever wrote down in that letter."

"Not wrote," Anne corrected. "Written."

"Never mind," Eve scolded. "You better read it."

"I had such vivid dreams about St. Simons last night." Anne's voice was flat, toneless. "I must *not* allow myself to be homesick for that Island, Eve!"

"That's right. But read, Miss Anne. Eve right here."

Anne flared. "How can you possibly know I'll need you just

because of this letter? I don't hear from her often, but I'm almost sure that's Hannah King Couper's writing. Anna Matilda's daughter Hannah is married to my brother William Audley, you know."

"Yes'm. How I not know dat?"

Anne's hand shook as she broke the seal, and part of the letter was torn. "Now, look what you made me do!"

"I gonna let dat go," Eve said. "Read, Miss Anne. *Read.*"

The letter from Hannah was short—only one page—but one line blazed in Anne's eyes: *"Mama died from a broken heart.* Papa knows that. I know it. Everyone knows she lost whatever spark that was keeping her alive when we lost my brother Butler. People do die of grief. Mama died of grief, and this short note is asking nothing of you but your prayers for all of us who loved her so much. No one's life will ever be the same here again now that Mama, too, is lying in Christ Churchyard. She died August 22. We buried her the next day."

PART VI

September 1859–
January 1864

Chapter 51

IF ANNE HAD BEEN ABLE TO REACH ST. SIMONS IN time for the funeral service and burial of Anna Matilda King, Pete knew her mother might not have found the habit of looking for a letter from Anna Matilda so hard to overcome. But despite the improved train service between Savannah and Marietta, they hadn't even known her friend was gone until well after the funeral on August 23, 1859. And so, although Mama knew there would never again be a letter from Anna Matilda, Pete was aware that her heart ached painfully at mail time.

"I wish I could do something to help," Pete would say almost every day in September when she came home from the post office—and felt foolish saying it. "God just *has* to send something to cheer you —to help you through this bad time. Does it help at all that John Couper is now the paymaster for the officers of his Independent Volunteer Regiment of Savannah? Think how proud Papa would be!"

"I know, Pete. But I don't feel the same about anything military as your father did. If I could even imagine that killing could accomplish anything, I might feel otherwise. I don't. War leaves nothing but scars on both sides." Glancing up from her parlor chair at John's portrait on the wall of the bright, elegant room, her mother added, "Your tender father really only thought he loved the soldier's life. It was its color and excitement and pageantry he cared about. The parades and snapping flags. There was nothing in his whole nature to lead me to believe that he didn't hate the killing as much as I hate it. Now, Pete, don't argue with me."

"I'm not arguing! I agree with you all the way. But there is something about men that I don't think most women understand. We don't understand it because we don't have it in our nature." Pete tried a slight grin. "I seldom think I'd like to conquer anything or anybody. Do you doubt that?"

"Well, no. At least most of the time I don't." Pete could feel her mother studying her. "Pete, are you driving at something? Are you trying to find a way to tell me something in particular?"

"I guess I am."

"Then tell me. You're the only daughter I have with whom I can speak freely without being interrupted by word of a new style in ladies' capes or off-the-shoulder dance gowns. Your sisters are thinking of nothing but young men and dances these days."

Pete thought a moment, then blurted: "Did John Couper ever tell you he could be a secesher?"

"What a ghastly way to phrase a question!"

"Well, you know he's not only a member but the paymaster for the officers of the Independent Volunteer Regiment in Savannah, and you certainly know what the word *volunteer* means."

"It means that as with every other young man moving toward success in the old city, he joined a regiment when he went there. Miss Eliza told me all about how her husband sponsored the young Mark Browning when he first came from the North."

"Mama, John Couper's in a *volunteer* regiment! He's in it because he's—"

"If you use that word again, I'll—I'll—"

"You'll what? I was afraid he didn't tell you when he was here last. When he brought my much-beloved nephew, Fraser Demere, he told me himself not only that he joined of his own free will, but that should anything as insane as secession happen in Georgia, he would fight willingly for the South's Cause!" Pete hurried on. "I begged him to tell you himself. He said he would if he had a chance. I guess he thought he didn't. Or he saw so plainly how you'd take it, he didn't dare."

Pete's mother jumped to her feet and went to stand at a front window. Hurrying to her, Pete saw that she was crying almost uncontrollably. "Oh, Pete, Pete," she gasped. "Hold me! Please hold me. I've been so afraid that was true. I'm not stupid, you know. You and Eve just sometimes act as though I am."

Holding her mother, Pete asked, "Have you been talking to Eve about John Couper's being on the South's side?"

"No. No," Mama answered, checking her sobs. "I haven't talked to anyone but God—and now you."

"And Mama, don't you believe my brother when he vows he loves the military life the way our father loved it? I honestly think he's proud to have discovered that about himself. And if, as he says, Georgia is insane enough to secede from the Union, I guess I'm glad he does love it."

"Pete, why on earth would you say a thing like that?"

"For the same reason you'd say it if you thought a minute. I love John Couper and I want him to love whatever he does with his life. Mama, so do you!"

"I—I suppose I do."

"You know you do!"

"Yes, and I think it's touching that loving the military as his father certainly did makes the boy proud."

"Mama, you had a lot of bad times with Papa over that, didn't you?"

"I had—some, yes. In a way, I forced him to stop trying to get back in the British military by my longing so for St. Simons and home." She turned to look straight at Pete, the very inside of her heart on her tear-streaked face. "Your father must have truly loved me, Daughter. Selfish as I was, he did love me."

"Mama, you weren't selfish, nor was Papa. You were just— different."

"I know, I know. And I need you to tell me straight out if you really do agree with me about the insanity of secession. Pete, even as a British subject, your papa believed in the union of all the states. That nothing less could endure. Will you tell me what you really

402 ✣ EUGENIA PRICE

think—and do it, please, in a way that gives me room to believe you?"

"Mama, I swear to you I'm no secesher and I will never be. I love St. Simons Island every bit as much as John Couper loves it. My roots are there, too, as he kept reminding me about his. But I think it will bring a particularly wild, hopeless tragedy if the South breaks away. And Mama, it won't be just our family it divides, either."

"Hush! And don't ever talk like that again to me, Pete. Do you hear what I say? I know how Fanny talks, but only because of that dreadful Buster. John Couper can't be like that. He's my—rock. He's yours, too, and Selina's and Fanny's. We wouldn't be able to live without him! Even if I could find a way to keep breathing, I couldn't do it."

The sound of carefree laughter, a girl's and a boy's, came from outside the front of the house. "Mama!" Pete ordered. "Sit back down in your chair and get yourself together. Selina's coming up the walkway and she's got a tall, handsome cadet with her from the Georgia Military Institute."

"No!"

"Yes. And you can't let them see you with all those tears on your beautiful face."

"You're right, but what in the world would ever make Selina do such a thing? Without a word of warning or—"

"You, Mama. You've always told all of us to feel free to bring any of our friends to our home at any time. None of us would dream that you didn't mean it."

"I did mean it!"

"Then act as if you did. Dry your eyes and let me see that sweet, welcoming smile."

"I SWEAR TO YOU, PRETTY LADY, WHEN I MET AND FELL HOPElessly in love with you at Georgia Fletcher's wedding last month, I had no idea my heart had been stirred by such a wealthy girl! Your home is truly elegant. No wonder your mother likes it so much."

Clinging to the arm of the tall, brown-haired cadet, Selina laughed. "I agree with you that the house is a wonderful place, but you're dead wrong about the wealthy part! We're far from wealthy. I don't think my brother, John Couper, has told Mama yet, and maybe the sale isn't even final, but I'm sure he plans to sell some of our people in order to keep sending us money each month. He does, you know, or we'd lose this glorious house. John Couper and my sister Pete decided Mother had endured enough loss and grief on St. Simons Island, and both of them took things into their own hands. Our need of this house is far more than a mere roof over our heads."

"And you're sure Mrs. Fraser won't mind your bringing me here unannounced like this?"

"She won't mind at all. In fact, she's always urged my sisters and me to bring our friends home. I'll only be obeying her."

"Splendid. That may even give me a boost in her estimation." He grinned down at Selina. "And I promise not to tell her on our first meeting that I *am* hopelessly in love with you, Selina."

SEATED BESIDE SELINA ON A SMALL DAMASK LOVE SEAT IN THE parlor of the handsome Fraser house, George Stubinger, after Selina had made her fluent introductions—even to the serving maid, Eve —felt oddly at home. Selina's mother, Mrs. Fraser, was so pretty and well bred and charming, he was reminded of his own lovely mother back in Louisiana. George thought Anne Fraser so lovely, he felt almost disloyal to his mother because he'd always almost childishly believed no one had a mother as beautiful as his, Martha Jane. Sampling a cinnamon bun, George smiled at the startlingly attractive mulatto woman who was serving them.

"And did you bake these delicious buns?" he asked of Eve.

Pete, the tall, red-haired Fraser sister, let out a rather unladylike whoop. "You'd better not let Mina hear you say that, sir," she laughed. "Mina's the goddess of cinnamon buns in this house, and even Eve, who dares try almost anything, wouldn't risk her ire by trying to bake even one cinnamon bun, would you, Eve?"

"No, Petey," Eve said with her own disarming smile. "I meant to say 'No, Miss Pete.' "

"You did not!" Selina piped. "You never called her Miss Pete in your whole life, Eve, and no one needs to be proper around Mr. Stubinger."

"Selina!" Mrs. Fraser scolded. "That was a most impertinent thing for you to say on Mr. Stubinger's first visit to our home!"

"Forgive me," George said with a big smile, "but your daughter Selina and I have known each other since the Fletcher-Cole wedding in August, and what she said is not only true, but one of the reasons we're such good friends is her fine humor. She's teasing you."

"My children are all teases except for Fanny," Anne Fraser said with a somewhat forced smile. "Quite like their father when he was alive."

"Is that so?" George asked. "By the way, I believe I met your other daughter in the company of one of Marietta's real Southern hotheads, a man named Buster something. He didn't seem at all pleased by our meeting, but your daughter Fanny was most charming and friendly toward me."

"With Selina and me standing right there in the Square, too, she wouldn't dare be anything else," Pete said. "Poor Fanny's man friend is never charming. He's too afraid someone will think he's forgotten how to eat Southern fire, isn't he, Mama?"

"That's more than enough about Buster Matthews, Pete," Anne said, almost sharply. "We all know, Mr. Stubinger, that the best way to bring Fanny to her senses about anything is to let her think her own way through it. She really has an excellent mind and, unlike certain other members of this family, knows how to keep silent."

"She'd have to keep quiet with Buster around so much, spouting off about the evils of the Union and being a downright boor!" Selina's big eyes snapped. "But you know already, George, that except for Fanny, we're all Unionists. But it doesn't matter at all to you, does it?"

"That's a terribly presumptuous question, Selina," her mother said, then added, "but since you've already asked it and Mr. Stubinger is your guest, I'll be presumptuous, too. A straight answer to her question, young man, could save us much heartache later on. I presume you're a secessionist. Am I right?"

George smiled, revealing his strong, white teeth. "You're only partly right, Mrs. Fraser. My father's a doctor in New Iberia, Louisiana, and he does own our house servants. My sympathies are with the South, yes, but I'm no fire-eating secessionist. Selina tells me you moved to Marietta from the coast and that your family has always owned slaves. Sometime I'd love to hear why you're a Unionist now." The disarming smile broadened. "Am I being too forward?"

"Of course you aren't!" Selina said firmly. "Tell him he isn't being forward at all, Mama."

"My only son, John Couper Fraser, is, I fear, just about where you are in his thinking, Mr. Stubinger." There was a hint of sadness in her voice. "You'll find that Selina's family, except for Fanny, who has allowed Buster Matthews to influence her unduly, is in favor of preserving the union of all the states. Even my late husband, a British subject, felt strongly about the necessity of this country's remaining one. I'm afraid my beloved son, although he strongly favors the Union, would actually risk his life for the South's Cause, but Selina and Pete and I hate war for any reason. We can only pray that John Couper will come to his senses, although he's very proud of his Southern roots. Especially is he proud of being named for my father, John Couper, of St. Simons Island."

"And of Uncle James Hamilton Couper, too," Selina put in.

"He's rightly proud of both gentlemen," George said with conviction. "They're both known even in Louisiana."

"Well, Uncle James Hamilton is known abroad, too."

"I know he is, Selina. And you all have every right to be proud. But may I ask where your father, the planter John Couper, stood,

EUGENIA PRICE

Mrs. Fraser? And your brother Mr. James Hamilton Couper? Is he
a secessionist?"

"He is not!" Anne snapped. "Nor was my father. Both men
would be firmly with those Mariettans who pray that if things get
worse, Georgia will remain staunchly in the Union."

"I'm quite at home with your family, madam," George said. "I
would, along with your son, John Couper Fraser, enlist in the
South's Cause, but I pray there will be no need for either of us to
go that far."

For a few moments no one said anything, and then Selina's
mother smiled at George. "You can be sure everyone in this room
joins you in that prayer, Mr. Stubinger," she said sincerely. "And
will you add my otherwise gentle, sweet-tempered daughter Fanny
to your prayer? I loathe the cloud of enmity falling over this peaceful little city and wonder how I could bear Fanny's ever becoming
an active part of it."

Chapter 52

3 January 1860
Jasper, Florida

Dear Aunt Pete,

Before I get to the point of this letter, let me wish all of you happiness and health in the new year 1860. I know I wrote only last week, but I have had a little accident since and so am taking advantage of what I feel is our special bond. Letters are fine and I have kept and cherish every letter you've written to me, but I've tried for three full days now to get over my longing to see you and talk and laugh with you face-to-face and I have failed. I will be nineteen in September of this year, but I sound like a spoiled little boy, I know, when I beg you to think long and hard about paying me a visit here in Jasper. I do so want you to meet my stepmother, Miss Jessie, who has been so kind to me now that I broke one leg bone trying to climb a tree I should have left alone. I know you will like her a lot and my hope is that you will be able to convince my beloved Grandmother Anne beyond question that my father did not insult the memory of my dear mother by marrying Miss Jessie. Now, don't say anything about that to Grandmother because her attitude toward Miss Jessie when I was up there told me far more than she actually said. Our weather is fine here and you can reach Americus, Georgia, by train, then a stage to

Jasper. Do think about it and let me know soon how Grandmother received the idea.

My love to all there,
John Fraser Demere

Pete kept young Fraser's letter to herself for the remainder of
the month of January, through her mother's sixty-third birthday.
Of course, she wrote at once to Fraser, expressing her excitement at
the mere idea of seeing him again, and explained that it would take
a little time for her to work things out in Marietta.

He's a smart boy, she thought, as she walked toward home alone
after posting a letter to her brother, telling him about Fraser's invitation. She seldom wrote to John Couper on the sly, but Mama's
lingering animosity over Paul Demere's having married another
woman so soon after Annie's death still haunted Pete. Owning his
own business kept John Couper in Savannah for such long periods,
she felt more and more responsibility for helping their mother. She
thought often of seeing Mama's best friend, Louisa Fletcher, to ask
her advice about how to broach the subject of a Florida trip with
Mama. Seeing her would be easy now, since her husband had leased
the Fletcher House to a Mrs. Starr, and Louisa was no longer burdened with being a hotel landlady. Since August of last year, the
oldest Fletcher girl, Georgia, had been married to Henry Greene
Cole, the well-to-do owner of the prospering Marietta Hotel, where
Georgia and Henry and her parents now lived.

Pete was so accustomed to making up her own mind about
everything that she wondered at herself. Not for having written to
her brother for advice about a Florida visit, but because there was
another person she longed to tell. Eve. If anyone knew Mama
through and through, it was Eve, and more than any other colored
servant Pete had ever known about, Eve was apt to be outspoken
with her mistress. She cared that much for Mama, and if Eve
thought she needed guidance, or a scolding, she let fly. Some days
Mama fussed back at her, showing more than a spark of her own
mother, Grandmama Couper. Most days, though, the two—Eve
and Mama—ended up laughing together. Mama loved her lifelong

servant, and no one with a grain of sense could doubt Eve's devotion to her. It was obvious also that Eve was partial to young Fraser.

Even though Eve belonged to Mama, Pete found herself hoping that when dear old June died, as he likely would before Eve—he was now about seventy-seven—Mama would somehow find the strength and the wisdom to give Eve the support she would surely need when June went away.

Climbing the rise in the ground to the white-light house, Pete said aloud to herself, "Thank heaven, I've already been through my big grief over losing the person I loved most. I'm sure Mama and anyone else who happens to know about my feelings for my best playmate, William Page King, think I'm as peculiar as Heriot Wylly, but I guess I'm the one who knows myself. Until the day he died, I planned to marry William someday, so my big sorrow, like Mama's when Papa died or Eve's when poor old June dies, can't happen. Let them all think what they want to."

On the mild morning of March 21 of that year 1860, Pete sat blessedly alone on a train seat, staring out the window at flat stretches of farmland outside Americus, Georgia, on her way at last to Jasper, Florida, for a face-to-face visit with the Demeres, whose farm was just outside the small town. Leaving had been far easier than she'd dared hope. Mama had not only agreed almost at once that it would be fine for her to go, she had shown near relief at the idea. Was the still-attractive lady, who practically filled Pete's world, more peaceful down inside than Pete or any of the other children dared believe? She would never stop missing Papa. No one expected that. But slowly, surely, Mama was becoming her buoyant old self, and a calm acceptance had been added, which left her much less nervous, more willing to listen, less burdened by secret, hidden cares. She had even begun to speak of Annie rather freely, and by one action at the Marietta train station before Pete left, Mama proved her new self more clearly than any words could ever have done. She had pulled Pete to one side of the platform and handed her a small, square package for Annie's boy, Fraser. Pete knew it was the portrait of Annie, which the boy had left with Mama to keep.

Mama had so carefully wrapped the package in tissue paper tied with blue ribbon, Pete had no notion of opening it, but she knew what it was and fell to remembering her older sister, Annie—far sweeter, far more a peacemaker than Pete would ever be and no one knew that better than Pete. Annie would be overjoyed by the mere thought of Pete's journey to Florida at Fraser's urging. How like his mother Fraser Demere was! He'll be a peacemaker, too, Pete thought, surprised that she hadn't dwelt on that before now. Hadn't the boy sent for her to visit in Jasper so that Pete could see for herself what a good person his stepmother really is? Was he depending on his Aunt Pete to take a true picture of Jessie Sinclair Demere back to Marietta? After William's death, the thought of marriage had never tempted Pete once in all her thirty-four years. Was she harboring even a small longing now for a son of her own exactly like the nephew she'd loved on sight?

She stretched her long legs until her feet were under the seat ahead of her. Not ladylike at all, she mused. Dear Mama would remind me. Well, maybe she just did. I know, despite her coldness when Fraser first arrived in Marietta with John Couper over seven years ago, that Mama's heartbreak at Annie's death was heavier because she was deprived of caring for Annie's baby. Had Mama needed all this time since Annie's death to separate the two heartaches in her own mind?

WHEN THE TRAIN JERKED TO A STOP SOMETIME AFTER DARK, THE screech of metal against metal roused Pete from what had evidently been a sound sleep. At any rate, it took her some time to realize where she was, and her relief was great when she learned that within an hour they would reach a travelers' inn, where passengers going farther would board a stage for the final hundred and fifty miles to Jasper.

She grinned to herself as her mind pondered a perfectly useless question: Why, oh why, was the hardest part of a trip at the very end, when bones and muscles were already bruised and battered? She'd grinned, because until this moment, Pete Fraser had never made such a trip in her entire life. She'd only heard about those uncomfortable journeys that ended by stage. Well, she was making one herself now and for the first time felt a little nervous, because with a broken bone in his leg, the chances were that Fraser would be unable to meet her stagecoach. Would his father, Paul Demere, be there? Or one of Paul's other sons by Jessie Sinclair? And, outside of Fraser, who had begged her in two letters to come, how welcome would anyone make Pete feel?

TWO DAYS LATER, HER BODY ACHED ALL OVER FROM THE ENDLESS jostling miles by stage, but one look at her welcoming party in Jasper almost entirely eased her knotted muscles and her uncertainty about how she might be greeted.

Beside the roofed platform where the stage driver reined his team stood a tall, beaming, curly-haired gentleman—not Paul Demere—waving his hat as he hurried toward her, a smile so warm on his handsome face, Pete had the distinct feeling he already knew who she was.

"Aunt Pete! Aunt Pete!" The excited, cheerful voice came from a somewhat battered carriage reined near the stage stop. It was Fraser, a grown young man now, also waving and grinning from ear to ear.

"You must be my patient's beloved aunt," the gentleman said as he hurried to where Pete stood. "Fraser's leg is mending nicely, but somehow I'm sure, as his doctor, that with you here at last, he'll be able to throw away his crutch in no time. Miss Pete Fraser?"

His manner was so warm and welcoming, Pete had to laugh.

"Indeed I am, sir, and no one was ever happier to have reached her destination!"

Bowing, the gentleman said, "I'm Dr. Samuel Smith and—and"—he gestured toward the carriage—"my friend John Fraser Demere and I welcome you wholeheartedly to Florida. Why not go to the carriage so my patient can greet you properly while I collect your luggage."

"Fraser," Pete called, "don't try to stand up in that carriage! I'm coming, I'm coming. One broken bone in your poor leg is enough."

But by the time she reached the carriage, the young man had scrambled to the ground with his one crutch and was embracing her as though he'd been waiting a lifetime to see her again.

"Isn't Dr. Sam a fine fellow! I don't know what I'd have done without him. He doesn't have too many patients in these parts so he's given me lots of careful attention, and look, I can almost walk without a limp. He took off the splints nearly two weeks ago. I hope everyone is fine at your house in Marietta. John Couper wrote to me last week with the good news that the family's doing well. You—you're a dear to spoil me like this, Aunt Pete. All of us here are awfully glad you came."

"Well, that was quite a welcoming speech. You're talking more since you've grown up. Do you know who you remind me of? My own father!"

"I'm named for him."

"I know, and I brought something for you. Here."

She hadn't dared trust the cherished portrait of Annie to the top of the stage roof luggage rack and was still holding the carefully wrapped picture Mama had handed her for Fraser the day she left Marietta.

He took it eagerly. "What on earth could this be?"

"A present from your Grandmother Anne."

"And you carried it by hand over all that long train and stage ride?"

"When you open it, you'll understand why I did."

Fraser's sun-browned fingers were feeling the shape of the ribbon-tied package, and then he looked at Pete quizzically. "Grand-mama Anne sent my mother's portrait back to me, didn't she?"

"I'm not absolutely sure, but I think so, Fraser. And that just could mean far more than either you or I think right now."

"Would it be all right if I show my mother's portrait to Dr. Sam when he brings your luggage from the stage?"

"That's for you to decide, but I don't see why not. The man certainly seems to be fond of you. I'd think he'd be really interested to know what Annie looked like." She grinned at him. "Like you, actually. You both have the same pale, pale blue eyes. And you're a peacemaker like her, too."

"How do you know I'm a peacemaker, Aunt Pete?"

"You talked me into visiting here, didn't you?" Before Dr. Sam's long strides brought him all the way to the carriage, Pete whispered, "And I want you to be sure I'm wide-open to the idea of liking your stepmother Jessie."

"I know that. I know I can always count on you."

"And how do you know?"

"It's just something I've always known about you and me." With a big smile on his face, he called to Dr. Sam, "See? I told you my aunt wouldn't have the typical woman's pile of valises and boxes."

Swinging one medium-sized valise and two hatboxes up onto the carriage rack, Dr. Sam agreed. "The truth is, Fraser my man, I see nothing typical about your aunt. The amazing thing is that this confirmed bachelor is already at her feet. And feeling it's the place he'd most want to be." He turned to Pete, who had already climbed nimbly into the carriage. "Look at that, Fraser! Any other woman in the world would still be standing impatiently waiting for some gentleman to help her up the carriage steps."

Pete laughed. "Sorry, Doctor. I'm just not accustomed to hav-ing a gentleman nearby to help me." With that, she reached her hand down to give Fraser a boost up into the carriage.

Beaming proudly at Dr. Sam Smith, the young man said, "You see? My aunt helps gentlemen and she's good at it."

For a brief moment Sam Smith stood at the foot of the carriage steps, looking straight at Pete. Then, quite solemnly, he said, "I see she is. And I fully plan to remember that—always." With a quick smile, he lightened his voice. "That is, if the lady has no objection."

"The way you've helped me, I can guarantee she has none. Have you, Aunt Pete?"

"Not so fast, young man. Somehow I sense this conversation is running along on two tracks, and I'm not accustomed to that, either."

"Aunt Pete's different from other women, too, because she always says exactly what she thinks, Dr. Sam. You'll never catch her hedging behind pretty speeches the way other women sometimes do."

"And what I think right now," Pete said, "is that we'd better head toward the Demeres' place. I have no intention of pretending I'm not starved. I am!"

Chapter 53

TALL, ANGULAR JESSIE DEMERE, PETE DECIDED AS Fraser's stepmother met her with open arms on the wide front porch of their frame farmhouse a few miles from Jasper, Florida, was not plain, nor was she mystically lovely as Pete's sister Annie had been. Paul Demere, still clean-cut, slender, and charming, had obviously recognized both his and the infant Fraser's need for a woman in the house. If the obedient, sweet-tempered, gentle Fraser was any true sign, Jessie Sinclair Demere was certainly an outstanding mother. Paul had come for Fraser while the boy was still a baby. He had broken Mama's heart by taking him away, but that he'd placed the child in the care of a fine, intelligent woman Pete had no doubt.

Pete watched Jessie closely as she supervised Alma, the rangy young colored woman who served their delicious first meal, and she couldn't help marveling at Jessie's naturalness and skill with servants. Skinny, dark Alma, who had prepared as well as served the succulent roast chicken dinner, was as contented in her work as a slave could hope to be, Pete decided, not showing the smile at her own frank admission to herself that by now she almost matched Mama's friend Louisa Fletcher in her dislike of slavery. Pete had grown up among slaves, but she could no longer take their docility or their seemingly easy laughter at face value.

Seated at the dining-room table were four of the six children born to Paul and Jessie Demere. In addition to the youngest, Francis, being fed by his nurse, there were Sinclair, who, according to Fraser, was sixteen, and Paul, probably fourteen, and their one, talkative sister, Pauline, about seven. The other two boys were visiting playmates that day on a nearby farm.

"Our neighbors have a fair-sized creek," Sinclair said, and Clarence and William would rather have a hook in the water than eat their catch." Paul made a grown-up, condescending face. "That is, when my brothers can get a catch."

"I can fish, too," Pauline chirped. "Can you fish, strange lady?"

"Miss Pete isn't a strange lady, Pauline," Jessie said easily. "She's your half brother Fraser's very own aunt."

"How?" Pauline wanted to know. "She isn't my half aunt, so how can she be Fraser's aunt?"

"Never mind," her father said in his firm but gentle way. "When you're old enough, you'll be able to get it all straight."

With an exaggerated sigh, the inquisitive seven-year-old said, "You sure have to wait forever to be old enough for anything. Are you married, lady? And how come you have such red hair?"

"No, Pauline," Pete said. "I'm not married and I guess I got my red hair from my grandfather, John Couper, who lived on St. Simons Island up in Georgia."

"People who live in Florida don't think much of Georgia," Pauline said, stuffing her mouth with chicken. "I wish Dr. Sam Smith had come for dinner when he brought you in Papa's carriage. Why didn't he come, too? Don't you like him? We all like him."

"Pauline, dear, you mustn't be so nosy," Jessie said.

"Yes, little Sister, and anyway, Aunt Pete just met Dr. Sam at the stagecoach stop. She doesn't really know him as well as we do yet," Fraser said easily. "Isn't that right, Aunt Pete?"

"Yes, it's right, but I already know I like the doctor a lot. And I certainly understand why Pauline wishes he'd come for dinner."

"I thought Pete was a boy's name," Pauline said. "I never heard of an Aunt Pete in my whole seven years!"

"That's enough, Pauline," Paul Demere said, looking at Pete with a sly grin. "My son Fraser told me what your mother did, Pete. I'm quite touched by her generosity." Then Paul explained to his wife, "I gave the only portrait of his mother to Fraser a few years ago, and proving his heart as generous as Annie's, he gave it to Annie's mother, Mrs. Fraser, when he was in Marietta some time ago."

"Mama cherished it," Pete said, "but she wanted Fraser to have it as his very own."

"I don't see why Dr. Sam didn't come for dinner." Pauline pursued what was evidently her main concern. "I know he must have been hungry. Even if he doesn't have very many patients, he works hard for the ones he does have, and he told me once when he and I were having a picnic out under the sycamore tree that he was never as happy as when he had one of Mama's chicken dinners and a bottle of wine to wash it down."

"I guess I neglected to warn you how much Pauline likes to talk," Fraser said to Pete. "You'll just have to excuse her."

"I don't think she needs to be excused," Pete said. "How does a little girl learn if she asks no questions? And I think she has every right to know that her good friend Dr. Sam will be back after a while."

"Dr. Sam's coming back to see us today?" Pauline all but yelled her delight.

"I hope it's all right with you, Mrs. Demere, but I told him it would be fine if he dropped by again later today after he's delivered someone's new baby." Pete turned to Pauline. "That's the real reason he didn't come to dinner," she explained. "The new baby was due and he needed to be there."

"You're pretty nice after all, strange lady," Pauline said warmly. "May I be excused from the table, Mama and Papa? I know that's the new Robinson baby because Mrs. Robinson's been sticking out something fierce for a long time. If I'm excused, I'll run to meet Dr. Sam!"

"You're excused, Pauline," Jessie said. "Just don't go too far if you don't see the doctor coming soon." To Pete, after the child left the room, she added, "You're patient with our only daughter, Miss Fraser."

"I like her a lot. And I hope I didn't overstep my place as a houseguest by agreeing that Dr. Sam might call on me this evening. I really can't imagine what made me do that! I realize I should have spoken with you first, Mrs. Demere."

"Wouldn't we both be happier if I became Jessie to you and you Pete to me? And you're free to invite anyone you please to this house. Paul and I are so, so glad you're here." She laughed softly. "And weathering our daughter's table talk so well."

Pete laughed. "Think nothing of that, please. I grew up with my mother's trying to calm me down at the table. And I'd love it if you and I used our first names with each other. My real first name is Rebecca, but probably because I was so noisy as a child, I've always been called Pete. Actually, Mama has always told me my father liked the nickname Pete so much that he was going to name me Peter had I been a boy."

Beaming proudly because he was so fond of his Aunt Pete, Fraser said, "The truth is, Dr. Sam already calls her Miss Pete, doesn't he, Aunt Pete?"

AN HOUR OR SO LATER, PETE WAS SITTING BY THE PARLOR WIN-dow in the Demere farmhouse, pretending to read, when Dr. Sam rode up on his big brown horse with Pauline behind him, clinging for dear life to his clean white shirt. Within seconds Pete was on the front porch, completely forgetting that a young woman was not supposed to act so eager to see any young gentleman she had just met.

Well, she thought, making herself stop at the top of the steps that led to the porch, I'm not all that young anymore and certainly not in the habit of receiving gentleman callers.

"Did you deliver the new baby, Dr. Sam?" she called, fully

expecting talkative Pauline to answer her, which she did. Yes, the new baby was there and it was a boy.

"Why don't we all go swing?" Pauline almost shouted, reminding Pete still again of herself as a child.

"Swing, Pauline?" the doctor asked, feigning surprise that she had even thought of such an unladylike diversion. "I've come to call on Miss Pete, sweetheart, and that means you think of something else to do."

Pauline wilted. "I suppose I'm too young to be a part of your call."

"No, not too young, but don't you think Miss Pete and I need a little time alone to get acquainted? After all, you had dinner together."

With another of her exaggerated sighs, Pauline gave them both a long look, turned, and ran abruptly toward the rope swing.

"I must say, Doctor, you're as skillful with seven-year-olds as with newborn babes. Does this come naturally to you?"

Revealing attractive though slightly overlapped white teeth, Dr. Sam laughed as he took her arm and headed them toward a narrow path that led through a scattered stand of cabbage palms and gum trees beside Paul Demere's flourishing patch of tomato plants.

"You must be tired after delivering that baby. Will we find a place to sit down near here?"

"I think I remember an old live oak up ahead, but at least we're alone—and together. Am I dreadfully presumptuous to be so glad about that?"

"I suppose not. In fact, I'm rather relieved too. Everyone here is new to me except Paul Demere, and when I knew him, he had eyes only for my lovely sister Annie, Fraser's mother."

"I know. But don't sell his present wife short. She's a remarkable lady."

"No one has to convince me of that," Pete said. "Jessie's already done that herself."

"Why did you come all the way to Jasper, Miss Pete?"

"Because I've loved my nephew, Fraser Demere, since the first moment I set eyes on him. He's devoted to his stepmother and wanted me to know her. That's enough for me."

"Young Fraser's devoted to you, believe me, and he's also counting heavily on your convincing your mother that Jessie Demere is as fine a woman as he believes her to be."

"Mama's heart's still broken over losing my sister Annie. I don't mind telling you—and I don't think I really need to tell you—that Mama still resents both Jessie and Paul for marrying so soon after Annie died trying to give Paul a son—Fraser. Within a few months Paul appeared at our door on St. Simons Island and took the baby away from Mother."

"I know. Jessie told me herself."

"Jessie?"

"She's like that—direct, sensitive to the feelings of others. All these years during which she's borne Paul Demere six more children, she's known of your mother's heartache and of her bitterness toward her."

"I consider that impertinent," Pete said firmly.

"You won't, wonderful lady, after I remind you that your nephew, Fraser Demere, and I have been close friends for much of his life."

Pete let her shoulders slump a little. "Fraser has known for a long time that Mama's been bitter toward Jessie and Paul, hasn't he?"

"Yes. And you know perfectly well that's one of the big reasons he so wanted you to visit here. There's really no need for you to pretend about anything with me, Miss Pete." As tall as Pete was, Sam could actually look down at her when he smiled his melting smile. "I don't intend to pretend with you just because we just met and it's probably considered proper. I—I think I loved you before we met, though, Pete. Do I need that Miss? May I call you Pete?"

With a startled laugh, Pete said just above a whisper, "I guess I loathe pretense more than anything else. Please do call me Pete. But also don't make me suffer any more shock at myself."

"You're shocked at yourself?"

"Yes, I am! I've never spoken so plainly to a gentleman in my entire life. I'm not sure I like doing it. It—gives me a strong feeling that somehow I should take myself in hand. I don't think I've known this giddy feeling since the day we were on a picnic at Kennesaw Mountain up in Marietta and I decided to let myself go and run down a fairly steep mountain path—so fast I couldn't stop."

"And did you like the way that made you feel, Pete?"

"Yes, but I didn't like myself for liking it. All my thirty-four years, I've been disgustingly proud of my ability to control my feelings."

"And do you know why that made you proud?"

"Of course I know!"

"Why?"

"Because when I'm in control, I feel—safe."

Sam stopped walking, took her by the shoulders, and turned her toward him. "I think that surprises me more than anything else either of us has said in this rather surprising conversation."

"Why does it surprise you? Any woman needs to feel safe."

"Forgive me for being blunt, but I just plain don't believe that about you. You're not any woman, Pete."

"What am I?"

"You're—well, you're Pete. And to me that makes you different from any other woman in the world. I've known for a long time that if I ever had the good fortune to meet you face-to-face, you would be unlike anyone else—anywhere. You see, I've been far more than just interested in you since young Fraser came home from his trip seven years ago to Savannah and to Marietta. He told me you were not like anyone else. Are you anything like his own mother was?"

"Annie? Heavens, no! She was all beauty. A near angel. One would never have guessed we were sisters."

"As I expected," Sam said, "the lad loves you because you're altogether—you."

"Well, I certainly love Fraser. In fact, since we've both lost our sanity in this conversation, I may as well tell you that for the first time in my life, I almost long to have a son, if he could be like Fraser."

"Are you telling me the truth?"

"Have you ever known such an appealing young man?"

"No, I haven't. And I've long ago lost count of how many times I've had the same wish—for a son like Fraser." His smile came again. "At least we have that in common. And the loss of our sanity. Both of which I like. To prove it, here comes another wild question: Pete, have you ever loved anyone?"

"No. I mean—not since I was a child, and you will think I've taken leave of my senses. But I did love an Island boy who died when we were both children. Until—until—" She broke off abruptly.

"Until what, Pete?"

"You have gone too far, sir. I require at least a small amount of sanity in my friends."

"That's odd," he laughed. "So do I. But I can wait. Not always gracefully, but I *can* wait."

Chapter 54

WHEN SHE LEFT MARIETTA IN MARCH 1860, PETE had every intention of beginning the return trip at least by mid-April. She not only hated to miss the violets that spread their purple wonder across Mama's front yard, but fully expected to be more than ready to leave the Demere house within a month or so. It was now May fifteenth.

All those half-formed plans had not taken into account the pure joy of knowing that almost every day she would have at least a few minutes alone with Dr. Sam Smith. Being Pete, this both intrigued and annoyed her. Yet, she had to admit that even though Fraser teased her about Dr. Sam, after a time the intrigue began to win out. She no longer minded her nephew's teasing. Her guarded but definite change of attitude registered plainly with the boy, whose extraordinary good looks never failed to cause Pete to think of his mother *and* of Paul Demere. Fraser was slight like Paul and had Annie's pale blue eyes. And although she was only his stepmother, something about his highly sensitive nature and good humor was very much like Jessie Sinclair Demere, whom Pete liked enormously.

"Do you know something, Jessie?" she asked as the two sat over a second cup of coffee one May morning. "I'm still here—taking up sleeping space in poor Pauline's bed every night and causing you extra trouble—as much because of you as Fraser. I like you. I just plain like you and I'll miss our talks together when I've gone home."

Jessie touched Pete's hand. "Then we're even," she said with her appealing smile. "I've wanted you to be my friend since the first day you and your mother visited at the Caters' on St. Simons back when I was a hired governess. I envied your glorious red hair, and you always seemed so sure of yourself."

Pete frowned. "No more. Haven't you noticed? I'm anything but sure of myself these days."

"Are you in love with Dr. Sam? He's in love with you, and the man believes, almost with the certainty with which a child believes its mother, that both of you have simply been waiting for each other all these years."

"And do you believe that, Jessie?"

"I believe Sam means it with all his heart. He's a fine doctor, struggling to practice in the wrong place. He's a lonely man, too. Pete, don't you believe it?"

"Do I believe him or do I believe we've been waiting for each other?"

"I'm not quite sure. But except when he fails to leave his wine bottle alone, he's a most dependable, trustworthy, truthful man. And never, never has he neglected a patient because of his tippling. That tells me something important about the man. He needs more focus to his life, more of a reason not to dull the pain of his uselessness."

"I think if anyone else used that word *useless* about him, I'd resent it. I don't with you because I know you had a reason for using it. Please tell me."

"He's anything but useless! Still, the effect on him is the same because much of the time when he's just waiting between patients, he genuinely *feels* useless."

"And then he drinks."

"I could weep over him sometimes, Pete. I've never seen him out of control or even acting foolish. He just reaches for a glass of wine, as he says, 'to kill the pain.' As I've said, he's very lonely."

"And that makes me feel as though you're somehow blaming me!"

Jessie laughed. "Well, I'm not blaming you, but he does need a reason for living."

"For—living?"

"Yes. Both his parents are dead. He has no brothers or sisters. His medical practice is his life, and we're just so sparsely populated around Jasper. Has he talked to you much about Marietta?"

"Too much! At first I talked and talked about the bright prospects anyone in almost any line of work would have in a growing, prosperous place like Marietta—until I caught on. Jessie, how would I or any other woman know the real reasons he keeps asking about life up there? I know he doesn't earn a decent living here."

"Wait a minute, Pete. Not so fast! If you're even hinting that Sam is an opportunist, forget it. He is not. I'd swear to that."

"He proposed to me last week," Pete ventured, almost shyly. "Marietta is growing by leaps and bounds. He could build a good practice there. I can't help thinking of these things."

Jessie looked at her for a long time, then said, "You do keep on surprising me, Pete."

"Why?"

"Because I happen to know you'll be thirty-five in November and you should recognize—I think any woman with a mind like yours would recognize—when you're being lied to. I knew Paul thought a lot of me, but I also knew he needed a mother for his infant son, Fraser. It so happened that I loved him enough to marry him and take my chances on giving him such a good life, he'd eventually love me. Pete? Don't you believe Sam loves you for yourself?"

After a moment Pete said, "If I told you how little I know about men, Jessie, you wouldn't believe me anyway. The truth is, I don't know at all whether he loves me for me or not. Laugh if you like, but when I was a child, I pledged myself to marry my best St. Simons playmate. Then he died before he was seven and I was less than eight."

Jessie stared at her. "Pete, have you stayed faithful to that childhood pledge all these years?"

"Yes, I have. And I sincerely thank you for not laughing at me. I've told almost no one. Mama knows and John Couper and my sisters. None of them laughed at me, either. I don't know what they think about it, but at least they didn't laugh. I guess everyone decided simply that it's something old Pete would do."

"I couldn't laugh at anything so touching. Could I ask a bold question?" When Pete nodded yes, Jessie asked if she'd told Dr. Sam about her childhood playmate.

"I was afraid you'd ask that. But, yes, I told him. Of course, he said it only made him love me more."

"I believe that, don't you?"

"Oh, Jessie, I don't know what I believe! I've done fine as a spinster all these years. Mama and John Couper and my two sisters seem enough for me. Do you believe that?"

Without any hesitation, Jessie said, "Yes, Pete. I most certainly do believe that. But you're missing so, so much without children of your own."

"Maybe."

"Take it from me, you are missing so much. And I see so plainly how deeply you're attached to your nephew, Fraser. Wouldn't you—"

"Yes!" Pete blurted. "If I thought Sam and I might have a child half as lovable as Fraser, I would really be in a quandary. But how does one ever know? Sometimes children only bring trouble. And what if there's a war soon? There could be. Mothers suffer more than anyone except sweethearts when a young man has to go to war. All this glory stuff when a young man is sent off to bleed and die for some geographic boundaries makes me sick! Mama and I both hate war. And every bit of me is revolted at the idea of anybody's son being used as cannon fodder!"

"Pete, you and I have come to be fast friends, haven't we?"

"I believe we have."

"Will we remain friends if there is a war between the North and the South? Is it true that there are a lot of Unionists in Marietta? Are you one?"

"I wondered how long we'd be able to avoid the subject, Jessie. Yes. I'm all for keeping the Union and so is Mama. And yes, there are Unionists in Marietta. Men don't plant large tracts up there the way you do here." For a long moment, neither spoke. Then, Pete went on. "Sam asked me the same question almost as soon as I got here. With all my heart, I want to believe him. He claims he's also a Unionist. Vows that's one reason he's so interested in Marietta as a place to practice medicine. Do you believe that?"

"I know it. He and Paul get into an argument every time the subject comes up. That's why it's been possible for you and me to avoid it until now. Marry him, Pete. At least the ugly trouble can't come between you and Dr. Sam!"

Chapter 55

ANNE HAD MISSED HER DAUGHTER PETE EVEN MORE than she feared the day she and her other two girls saw her off at the railroad station, headed for Jasper, Florida.

As close as the two friends had grown, Anne even had trouble telling Louisa Fletcher how concerned she had become during the nearly two months Pete had been away. Even as she tried her best to give Louisa an honest opinion of Dr. Samuel Smith, who accompanied Pete home over the long, difficult miles, she felt inadequate to the telling. Seated at a secluded corner table in the dining room of Henry Greene Cole's large Marietta Hotel, where Louisa and Dix were now living, Anne could tell Louisa was doing her level best to help. Louisa knew exactly how Anne had missed Pete, how she had come to depend on her daughter's company, her honesty, even her willfulness. Pete was being willful about Dr. Samuel Smith, though, in a way even her own mother didn't understand, and as Louisa saw it, a way Anne definitely did not accept.

"How do you know I don't accept it?" Anne asked her friend. "The truth is, I don't know whether I accept Pete's strange behavior or not. I don't even know that I'm not just imagining that she's acting unlike herself."

"I can tell you if you promise not to give me that icy look."

"Louisa, I never mean to give you an icy look. How could I? You're my best friend."

"And you're mine, but best friends can upset best friends, even when it's the last thing intended. This will probably upset you, but aren't best friends supposed to help at a time like this? Over and over I've asked you to tell me point-blank when I forget and let my rancor spew toward Reverend Benedict when his refusal to allow me to take Communion hurts in a deeper way. I can't imagine our Lord turning any of us away just because we're not communicants of a certain church, so some Sundays I confess I am hurt more than others. But because you are my best friend, I trust you to tell me when I let it show too much."

Anne smiled ever so slightly. Then, with an edge to her voice, she said, "But I don't expect you to act as though you understand why Reverend Benedict is so pigheaded. You expect me to understand why Pete is suddenly at Dr. Sam's feet. Don't deny it. He's a nice enough young gentleman, but I don't understand and I'm not sure I even want to!"

"I must admit that's true honesty, Anne."

"Who would know better than her own mother that Pete just isn't the kind of young woman to plunge into something as serious as marriage without giving it great thought ahead of time."

"And who says the girl is even considering marriage?"

"I say it because Pete just does not do anything halfway!"

"Anne, don't you believe Pete when she still insists that she made that long trip to Jasper, Florida, to set your heart at rest about the woman Paul Demere married?"

"In part, yes. She also went because she's so deeply fond of Annie's boy, Fraser Demere."

"And does that really alter a single fact in this whole thing? It seems to me that both Pete's reasons for going show only affection and real caring for you." When Anne said nothing, Louisa went on. "I'm going to ask an impertinent question right now. One you may not care to answer or even to face. One you certainly won't like."

"And has that ever stopped you in the past?"

"No, but I flatter myself that I've earned the right because of our friendship."

"True."

"Did your daughter Annie ever really know how much you disliked and disapproved of the man she chose to marry?"

"Where did you ever get the idea that I disapproved of Paul Demere? There was no finer family anywhere in coastal Georgia than the Demeres. Old Captain Raymond Demere came over with James Oglethorpe, was granted his fifty acres of rich land by the Crown, and built a fine house—Harrington Hall."

"I'm not talking about his pedigree, and you know perfectly well I'm not, Anne. You didn't like Paul himself."

"Did I ever say I didn't in so many words?"

"No, but I do know you by now, and it was clear that even Fraser, your grandson, knew how you felt about his father. I could tell that when he visited here from Savannah with John Couper." Louisa laid her hand over Anne's. Anne's hand flexed briefly as though she was about to jerk it away. Then her fingers closed over Louisa's and squeezed hard, clinging, the gesture all but begging for help.

Finally, Anne whispered, "My daughter Annie was so sensitive to me—to everyone—I suppose she did know how I felt down inside. But does it matter now what she knew? I'm not about to make the same mistake with Selina. I tell her over and over how much I like her young man, George Stubinger—and I do like him. I'll be able to welcome him warmly as my son-in-law."

In an effort to put Anne at ease again, Louisa began to tell her of the exciting plans she, her married daughter, Georgia, and her son-in-law, Henry Greene Cole, were making at the Marietta Hotel for the all-important Fourth of July social season to be centered around the Georgia Military Institute. "Here, at my son-in-law's hotel, we'll be serving dinner to a hundred people, and, of course, since Georgia thinks no one else can do it, I'll be the one to see to all the decorations. Examinations begin July 10, continue all week, and everything will culminate in the College Grand Ball."

"A hundred people are invited to the dinner? For heaven's sake, Louisa, who all will be there?"

"You and your daughters, undoubtedly, since this is George Stubinger's final session at school. Then all the other cadets, plus the new military company known as the McDonald's Guards, plus certain specially invited citizens. I've decided to decorate the tables with fruit, evergreens, flowers, and carefully arranged banners. It isn't the end of June yet and the hotel is already filling up with out-of-town folk. Requests for rooms are pouring in." Louisa broke off her half-complaining narrative. "Anne, forgive me! You're not listening anyway and why should you?"

"Oh, but I am listening, Louisa. And your willingness to take on so much extra work in order to help Georgia's husband in such a huge undertaking shows me far more than mere words that, unlike me, you'll go to almost any length for Georgia's sake. I know how much you dislike hotel business—you and Dix both. You must be happy your husband has hired someone to manage the Fletcher House."

"Yes, I certainly am!"

"But here you are diving in again because Henry Greene Cole owns this hotel and you mean to see to it that his huge influx of guests want for nothing. The Fourth of July festivities will be perfect, because you're not as spoiled and selfish as I've always been. Louisa, help me with Pete, please?"

"You don't like Dr. Sam either, do you, Anne?"

"I think I do like him, a lot. And that's what puzzles me so about myself! He's only five years older than Pete. His profession, heaven knows, is an honorable one. He seems to adore her, and although I find it very hard to believe, I feel Pete loves this man. I'm just so taken aback, I guess, because I felt so sure I'd always have Pete right beside me for the remainder of my days. How could she change so completely in such a short time? It's just so unlike Pete!"

"Unlike Pete as she really is, or unlike the image you've built up for her all these years? I've never quite understood, Anne, how you could honestly believe that an attractive young lady—even your tomboy daughter—could really remain faithful to a childhood pledge made so many years ago when both she and the little King boy were only children."

Anne had been clinging to Louisa's hand. Now she released it and leaned back in her chair. She smiled when she spoke, but her words were firm, to the point. "Louisa Fletcher, sometimes you make me angrier than anyone has done in all my sixty-three years!"

"I know I do."

"Then why do you go on doing it?"

"I'm your friend, Anne. I sincerely want to help you as you've helped me so often."

"When have I really helped you? I can't think of one single time!"

"Then you're not thinking straight. You've helped with two big, hurtful problems that come to my mind. The first was the day you convinced me forever that you loved your handsome husband, John, despite the many differences between you. From that moment to this, because you'd told me that, I've been more content with the equally numerous differences between Dix and me. In my heart, I had blamed him all the years of our married life for not liking to discuss, as I do, the books he's reading, for seeming to refuse to use his rather good mind except on business matters. I made it easy to allow him to bore me at times! No more, thanks to you. I now find a measure of real fulfillment from being his devoted, loyal wife, as different as we still are. The other heartbreaking problem I've faced, as you well know, is the ugly, cruel fact that the rector of St. James Episcopal Church, where you and I worship God together, refuses, because I'm a Unitarian, to serve Communion to me."

Anne, listening intently, asked, "But how on earth did I help you with that, Louisa? Reverend Benedict still refuses you Communion."

"You told me in your straightforward way that Reverend Benedict was robbing you, too, by refusing Communion to me. You may not fully understand why that helped me so much, Anne, but take my word for it as I took yours."

"Oh, Louisa, what will we do if we're separated? I know Dix means for you to move out to your farm at Woodlawn someday. What will I do if we can't see each other for weeks at a time? I do depend on you so much!"

"And you know you depend on having Pete right in the house with you, watching over your every change of mood, listening for your laughter, seeing to your needs. You know these things all blend into what you're calling your mysterious dislike of Dr. Sam, don't you? At least your resentment that he came into Pete's life."

"Yes, I know all that. And I also know that I dare not depend on anyone but God. Only He won't change, because change is not in His nature. And, Louisa, I'm so worried about the changes in our country. Do you think there's going to be a war? Will the Federal government, in which we both believe, attack us if the Southern states secede? Even John Couper's loyalty is with the South. Not vindictively so, but I'm struggling to accept the fact that since he's paymaster for his Savannah regiment, if there is a war, my only son will fight against the beliefs of both his parents. Louisa, please, please tell me why that is? No one, not even my fine, dependable son, could possibly love St. Simons Island any more than I do!"

"You don't seem terribly upset because your Fanny's sympathies are with the Rebels down here. Do you know why that is?"

"No. If I'm honest, no. I suppose because she isn't John Couper."

"Is that the only reason you can think of?"

"I guess so."

Louisa straightened her plump shoulders and tried to smile. "Will you just listen to us, Anne? We're crossing all kinds of bridges before we come to them. The Southern states haven't seceded yet! Unless wise, truly patriotic Mr. Lincoln is elected President, perhaps they won't. If he is elected in November, maybe he can bring some reason to bear on all our problems."

"I'll turn your premise back on you, Louisa. Is that the only reason you can think of that might keep us from what could be ghastly bloodshed?"

Louisa looked out the hotel dining-room window onto the busy Square outside, where women were shopping, drays were rumbling by, citizens of Marietta were going about their daily affairs as though the whole world were at peace. "It's the only reason I can think of right now, Anne."

Chapter 56

Twenty-three-year-old Selina Fraser, her long, dark curls shining in the light cast by dozens of candles burning in the polished brass chandelier overhead, floated onto the ballroom floor of the Marietta Hotel in the arms of her very own cadet, George Stubinger, whom everyone present knew to be her intended. To Selina, the entire evening had kept her large, dark eyes near tears because it would be her last with George for a while. Yet close behind the tears lay pure, young joy. A bittersweet evening, she thought, and made a mental note that the word *bittersweet* would, for her, always typify tonight.

What would this enchanted night mean a year from now to her older sister Pete, waltzing in the arms of her Dr. Sam? Who can ever tell about Pete, Selina thought, and dismissed both her sister and her —her what? Her intended? What had Sam and Pete whispered to each other throughout these unforgettable hours? No matter, she decided. Whatever Pete does with her life will be definite, will bear the stamp of Pete's total approval. Pete always knew her own mind. Well, so did Selina this night. So did Selina forever. She had every intention of one day becoming Mrs. George Stubinger, and the intention left her breathless with delight and gladness.

"When this last waltz is ended, sweet Selina,"

George was saying, his lips close to her ear so that her whole body thrilled to his touch, "there will be a private buggy awaiting us outside in the Square. I intend to have you all to myself until the very last minute."

"A private buggy, George?" she gasped. "In all this crowd, how in the world did you manage that?"

"By thinking ahead, Little Girl."

Little Girl had become his favorite, secret name for Selina, and when his arm tightened around her tiny waist, she wondered how her next breath could possibly come, so intense was her love for this tall, gentle, brown-haired young man who seemed to love her as deeply as she loved him.

"Our private chariot was engaged two whole months ago," he boasted on his infectious, happy laugh. "And Little Girl, I must ask you to promise me something."

"Anything, George. Anything."

"Once we're in our chariot, not one more word about when I may be called to fight for our beloved South. I've heard too much talk of war all around us—even in the midst of this glorious evening. You know where I stand and I know where you stand, so—"

"If you know where I stand with either the North or the South, George, you know a lot more than I know. I just don't think about any of it. Even when Mama and Pete get into one of their Unionist tirades, I just close my ears to them. I don't think about anything except how much—oh, how much I love you! And when I do allow myself a quick thought of anything so ghastly as war, I know only that I don't want you to go, for either side."

He laughed again. "But you have no intention of allowing any of that to come between us. Is that still true? You declared it was true only last night when I called at your house right after my last examination was behind me."

"George, the impossible can't happen! Nothing could ever come between you and me! *Nothing.*"

"Then why won't you marry me before I have to leave tomorrow for Louisiana?" He held her away from him just far enough to look into her deep, dark eyes. "Why, Selina? Why won't you send me away a whole and happy man?"

"Because I'm sure all this war foolishness will be settled soon. On the day I stand beside you and vow my love forever, I want every cloud in the sky to be gone. That only makes sense, doesn't it?"

"It makes *ideal* sense, yes. But life is never entirely ideal, Little Girl."

"I know. That's what Mama and Pete are always telling me, but I do my own thinking and I insist on a clear, blue sky above you and me—forever. You don't really want to deprive me of the pure joy of making wedding plans, do you? Maybe Mama's right. Maybe men just don't realize what ecstasy a woman knows in planning the last, tiny detail of her own wedding. Mama's right now and then, and if she's right about that, I'll just have to forgive you."

"YOU ACT AND TALK JUST LIKE A MAN WHO HAS SOMETHING UP his sleeve, Dr. Samuel Smith," Pete said, grinning up at Sam as they both waved briefly in the direction of Selina drifting in her dream world, as Pete called it, in the arms of her young cadet, George Stubinger.

"I'm not as young as these cadets in attendance on their fair ladies at the Ball tonight, Miss Fraser, but I'll wager we all have similar appendages up our sleeves, even those of us out of dress uniform."

"I think that's supposed to be funny," Pete said as though she addressed a small boy. "I'm not laughing. I wish you'd talk sense more often, Sam. Nonsense is fine in its place, but I'm getting sleepy and I promised a little six-year-old friend of Louisa Fletcher's, whose parents are staying at the Marietta Hotel, that I'd take her horseback riding early tomorrow morning."

"And miss my last breakfast at your mother's house?"

Pete stopped waltzing to stare up at him, a sensation she both adored and disliked since she'd always been tall enough to look down at almost everyone. "Your—last breakfast at our house, Sam? What in heaven's name are you talking about?"

"I think I've had free board and lodging quite long enough, my glorious Pete. I've found a small house, and I move into it tomorrow about noon. Your mother's splendid Eve has already promised to be there in plenty of time to hang my new curtains at the windows, just as soon as I pick them up at the shop in the Square where I ordered them." On a not very carefully smothered laugh, he added, "Do your feet hurt along with being sleepy, Miss Pete? This is the last waltz of the evening, and two people in love as we plainly are should be drifting about the room on a roseate cloud of romance!"

"Who says we're in love, sir?"

"We do. You and I say so."

"You may. I haven't mentioned it all evening."

"To my deep, heartbreaking chagrin, I might add."

"When did you decide to stop staying at our house, Dr. Smith?"

"The day I knew I'd never be going back to Florida, especially not to Jasper."

"And when, pray, was that monumental decision made?"

"The minute I went over the figures given me by Dr. Setze, who assures me that should I open my own medical practice here in Marietta—watching my *p*'s and *q*'s so that I don't run myself too deeply into debt—I'll be earning ample money within a year to support not only myself, but my striking, red-haired wife, too!" He whirled her adeptly away from the crowded dance floor and said seriously, "Pete, my wonderful Pete, you're going to love our little cottage. It's only four years old and cries out for nothing to make it perfect except the touch of a talented, capable woman—you!"

"July's a dreadful month for a Grand Ball," she said abruptly. "It's getting awfully warm in here. Will you bring me a glass of cold lemonade, please?"

"Another glass of lemonade? You didn't tell me, woman, that you're addicted to lemonade. Of course, one may as well be, since Mrs. Dix Fletcher decreed her prohibition against anything else more interesting. I marvel at these cadets, don't you? I thought young people enjoyed kicking up their heels a bit at the end of school. Didn't you think so, Pete?"

"I think you're talking a lot, Doctor," she answered coolly. "How many times have you and my sister Fanny's boorish friend, Buster Matthews, the Southern fire-eater, visited what appears to be an innocent bowl of lemonade?"

"Only the three times you already know about, my dear. And only while you were dancing with your mother's friends—Mr. Denmead, Dix Fletcher, and his son-in-law, the wealthy Mr. Henry Greene Cole."

"I suppose you think I didn't see you arranging with each of those definitely older gentlemen to ask me," she snapped. "I'm not a social butterfly, Dr. Smith, but neither am I stupid. Did you have a drop of whiskey in your pocket, or did you spike your lemonade by the courtesy of Mr. Rebel Buster Matthews?"

"I'm not a social creature, either, Miss Fraser. That's a lasting bond we have in common. But are you always such an alert watch-dog?"

She gave him a long, hard look. "Will you take me home, please, Doctor? I certainly don't want my mother to be worried. Furthermore, no gentleman—no *sober* gentleman—calls a lady any kind of dog! Not watch or otherwise. I want to go home *now*, sir."

KNOWING HOW DISAPPOINTED LOUISA WOULD BE THAT ANNE missed seeing the splendid table decorations she'd arranged at the Marietta Hotel, Anne nonetheless stayed home to nurse one of her sudden headaches. Eve, of course, insisted on staying with her. Because Anne knew Eve's usually dependable common sense deserted her when she was, for any reason, deprived of looking after her mistress, she tried her best to act pleased to have her faithful servant there.

"You never desert me, do you, Eve?" she asked idly, laying aside the book she was reading in the vain hope that Eve might take the hint and go to her own place with June. "And don't get careless with our ages again and remind me, as you did last week, that you and I have been friends for over sixty years. It's bad enough to be sixty-three, but that's all I am. You're sixty-two and I'm sixty-three, even though you look about forty!"

"What difference that make?" Eve wanted to know. "If Mausa John could see you this minute, he'd still call you his beautiful Anne. You be beautiful to Mausa John and to me till the end of the worl', Miss Anne. An' Eve's place allus be right beside you. Specially when your heart be troubled like it be tonight."

"What on earth does that mean? What made you say I have a troubled heart tonight especially?"

" 'Cause Eve know your heart better'n anybody know it. Petey, she go way down to Florida to see Mausa Paul Demere's second wife so's to be able to tell you she a fine woman, but she trouble your heart instead by findin' herself a man. Miss Anne, troublin' your heart be the las' thing Pete eber mean to do."

"Stop it! Shut your mouth before you say something you'll be really sorry for, Eve!"

Eve's large brown eyes filled with tears when she said, as soft as a whisper, "You ain't never tol' Eve to shut her mouth before in your whole life, Miss Anne."

"I know! But don't say another word because I—I just can't be responsible for what I say to you tonight, Eve. Do you hear me?"

"You holler so loud the peoples could hear you down at the Mar'etta Hotel. It be time for *you* to hush, Miss Anne. You hear me?" Eve jumped to her feet from the parlor rocker where she had been sitting. "Hush up an' listen. I hears a horse an' buggy comin' up our lane. You hear it? It be Pete acomin' home early."

"How could you possibly be so sure of that? I suppose you have one of your knowings?"

"More likely Petey she got one ob her knowin's 'bout you, Miss Anne."

"There's nothing to know about me. This is all being hatched in your head."

At the French doors now, Eve said over her shoulder, "I sure couldn't hatch Pete comin' home early wif her man. Dey out dere."

"Watch your speech, Eve!"

"I busy watchin' Pete climb down outa that buggy all by herself. Dr. Sam, he ain't even helpin' her."

"That's just habit with Pete. She still isn't accustomed to being helped with every little thing she does. Eve, is Pete smiling at the doctor?"

"No'm, she ain't. She—isn't."

"Turn around and look at me and listen. I have no intention whatever of being selfish and cross with Pete the way I was with my poor Annie when she fell in love with Paul Demere. I want you to back me up in that. I expect you to help me convince Pete that if she's absolutely sure she loves Dr. Samuel Smith, she should marry him. Eve—Eve, are you listening to me?"

"I doin' more than listen. I thinkin' back *wif* you, Miss Anne. You 'memberin' this minute that if your mama or your papa tried to stop you and Mausa John from marryin' each other, your whole life would be ruint. Ain't dat what you thinkin'?"

"Yes. Yes and trying to swallow the whole idea at once. Are you satisfied?"

"When I sees or hears you turn Pete loose to do what her heart tell her to do 'stead of what her mama tell her, I be satisfied, Miss Anne. An' "—Eve reached her hand toward Anne—"I also be downright proud ob you too!"

"Oh, Eve, this may sound silly, but I want you to be proud of me. . . ."

"Yes'm. I certainly be downright proud, Miss Anne. An' even if Fanny, she marry that no-good Buster man, you an' me, we be all right together. You an' me, we always be—just fine, Miss Anne."

At that moment Anne heard the front door close. She and Eve stood listening, one as interested as the other, Anne knew, to find out if Sam came inside the house with Pete.

"I'll relieve both your minds," Pete said from the front hall. "I'm alone. There's no one with me. The festive affair at the Marietta Hotel was just that—festive. For everyone but me, that is."

"Pete," Anne asked, "what are you saying? We know the doctor brought you home in a buggy. Eve saw you out the French doors, but I'm surprised to hear you say you didn't have a good time."

"Well, don't be surprised, Mama. In fact, you and Eve can save yourselves a lot of confusion if you'll quietly accept the fact that confusion belongs to me right now. And only to me. I know good old Pete has no right to be confused, but she is and if you insist on talking to me about Sam, you'll both have to wait until morning."

"But Petey," Eve said, her voice firm, "you mama ain't gonna try to stop you an' Dr. Sam from marryin' up. She done change from the way she used to be wif Annie an' Mausa Paul Demere. She just want you to be happy in you heart."

"That's enough, Eve," Anne said, not unkindly. She was too aware of Eve's loyalty to her, too touched by her eagerness to back Anne in her new resolve to allow the girls—all three—to live their own lives. "Thank you, Eve, and I hope Pete is taking you seriously. Eve's right, Pete. I've—changed. I've never seen you this way about any other man. If you love Sam, you must marry him, child."

"Child!" Pete snapped the word. "Since when have I become a child? I'm the one who's always supposed to know her own mind at least a year ahead of time!"

"Don't talk smart to your mama, Petey," Eve ordered.

"If she's so changed, why not?"

"Sound to me like you the one dat's change," Eve said, half to herself.

"Maybe I have! For every day of my life since Papa died, I've bent every effort to smooth the way for Mama. I've thought of almost nothing else. Now I'm thinking about *me.*"

Anne took a step toward her red-haired daughter. "Oh, Pete, how dreadful for you! Please tell me how I can make it up to you?"

"If I knew what to tell you, Mama, I would. But I don't know because I don't know myself anymore. I know I'm supposed to, but I don't. One day I'm spinning like a top and the next I'm me again and that's all I can say because that's all I know. I know I'm being ugly, I know I look ugly—my face must be as red as my hair—but until someone introduces me to me the way I really am, I'd be ever so grateful if you'd both just be still and let me go to bed."

Chapter 57

By November 1860, Dr. Sam Smith had lived alone in his newly purchased cottage for some four months, with Pete making daily visits as she helped him select new paint colors for the walls and saw to the fitting of fresh slipcovers. Pete was not adept with a needle, but she knew what she liked and Sam insisted their tastes were identical.

"If you only knew how I look forward to the welcome sound of your special knock on my front door, Pete," he said when he'd hurried to greet her on the showery autumn morning of November 6— presidential Election Day, which people North and South viewed with far more than the usual curiosity about the name and party of the man who would be President of the United States for the next four years. If their sympathies lay with the Union, they prayed for victory for the tall, craggy man from Illinois named Abraham Lincoln.

If, as did most coastal planters and large slave-holders all over the South, they believed the South's only hope lay in breaking away from the Union, they prayed to the God who agreed with their politics.

"I always believed that man was made in God's image," Pete said as she and Sam sat together in his porch swing. "Now, it looks as though some Americans believe they can remake God in their image. It scares me, Sam, when I even think of how many people in Marietta will vote for John C. Breckinridge or John Bell because they favor the South. Have they all forgotten that we fought a war to win freedom for all Americans? It hasn't been that long ago. Sometimes I can't believe how fast people forget!"

"I can't believe you came by to see me today just for a history discussion," Sam said, grinning at her as he held her hand in his. "Would you like to know, ma'am, what this student in your history class got from today's lesson?"

Pete could never resist his smile, so she smiled back. "If I have to know, yes. What did you learn, Master Samuel Smith?"

"Nothing new, really. But I've been reminded once more that there is no reason under the sun why you and I shouldn't be married right away. Look, lady, you wouldn't even have to worry about your husband's going to war! He's too old. We're even on the same side in this trouble. You like my little house, I love you with every fiber of my being, so what do you say, Pete? You know I'll ask again every day!"

"Yes, I know, Sam."

"Which should also tell you how completely I trust you, Pete. If a man ever put himself at a woman's mercy, it's I with you."

"You're no more at my mercy than I am at yours."

"Explain that, please, ma'am."

"Why do you think I walk or ride these four blocks every day?"

"You've been helping with my slipcovers."

"I hate to sew and fit things!"

"Then why do you come every day?"

"One thing that's never crossed my mind is that you're stupid, Dr. Smith. I come every day because I think I love you with all my heart!"

He stared at her. "Pete!"

"I love you, Dr. Sam. I was sure I'd never love a man as long as I lived on this earth, but I love you. I'm here because I can't find a way to get through a single day without looking at you."

She was in his arms now, clinging in the exact way she half

hated, because the thought of any woman clinging to any man irked her. "I love you, dear idiot. And if you don't know it by now, then you are an idiot. The very fact that I'm here this minute would prove it to you if you weren't so thick in the head."

"But I am thick in the head, Pete. Why is this minute different from any other?"

She pulled away to look directly into his face. "Because I walked out of our house and headed this way in the rain, leaving poor Mama alone with that old hatchet face, Beaulah Matthews."

"What's she doing there?"

"Paying a proper call, I'm sure she'd say, but the truth is that she couldn't let this day go by without using her sharpest knife on Mama because it's Election Day, and Mama's made a point of letting her know that she and Selina and I are praying Abraham Lincoln will win the presidency."

"Why in the world would an intelligent lady like your mother even let the old witch find out about her political leanings? I'd even lie outright to keep Beaulah Matthews in the dark about mine."

"That's the difference between you and Mama. Mama has always come right out with what she believes or does not believe."

"But it would be so easy just to steer old Beaulah in the wrong direction, since your family's roots are on the Georgia coast, where almost no one will want Lincoln elected."

"My uncle James Hamilton is for him because he believes in the Union. If Grandpapa Couper were still alive, he'd be a Lincoln man. That's enough for Mama. Whatever her father believed, Mama did too. Still does. And I don't think she's allowed you to forget that my papa, a British subject, also thought it would be lunacy to break up the Union."

"I'm sure she's told me that a dozen times. Somehow I get the idea that each time she tells me, it helps her in a strange way."

"I guess I'll never quite get over Mama's telling you such personal things, Sam. It took years, but she does talk about Papa to my sisters and me now, but it's usually something quite casual. It's as though she still has to keep a separate world that's only for her and Papa. It really touches—and puzzles—me that she tells you her private thoughts. When we talk about the Union or try to persuade Fanny to believe in it, Mama never mentions what our father believed about the Union or slavery. I think she talks to Eve about how he hated the whole idea of slavery."

"Has Eve ever told you she does?"

"You don't know Eve very well, do you. She would no more tell anybody else a word about any conversation with Mama than she'd fly off the side of Kennesaw Mountain."

He smiled. "I love your exaggerations. How about another one? How much do you love me, Pete?"

"More than I should," she answered solemnly. "Far more than I should allow myself to love you."

Then she was in his arms again, his mouth devouring hers, and for too long, Pete returned his kisses. On her feet suddenly, she kissed him again, holding his face in her hands. When he began to try to say something to her, she held one open hand hard across his mouth and ordered him to be quiet. "Don't say another word, Sam. Not one word, please! I don't know myself like this and I'm not at all sure I should even be here. I know that old hatchet face is giving poor Mama a hard time, and if you try to stop me from going straight home, you'll be sorry."

WITHIN FIVE MINUTES FROM THE TIME PETE DISAPPEARED FROM his sight into the rainy morning, Sam was doing what he'd vowed he would not do again if only she would keep on visiting him every day. He was drinking alone. As had been true for the past year or so, he could not help drinking too much if he was the only person in the room.

The darkened cork, stained from the port in the tall bottle, made its usual welcome, comfortable sound as he removed it, poured a water glass half full, and felt every nerve and muscle in his body loosen even as he took a long, deep whiff of the familiar ruby red liquid.

A woman like Pete Fraser would—*did*—drive a man to drink,

he thought, feeling lighter in his mind already just knowing the glass of port was there with no one in the room but Sam himself.

As the first long drink began to warm his stomach and ease his mind and his body of the longing for Pete's strong presence, he began his now habitual rationalizing: "If I'm a real doctor," he said aloud, "I ease the way for my patients in pain. Somehow I find a means to do that for other people, so why not for me too? Every man needs a woman beside him for comfort, for respite from pain. I've found the strongest woman in the world and I need her beside me for all reasons, and she just hurried home to Mama. How does even a strong man—and I'm anything but strong—learn to live without trouble when the woman he loves makes him feel like a helpless boy? And why don't I feel helpless when she's in my arms?

"I'm strong when I'm holding Pete," he said into the empty room. "Because she's warm and vital and strong and smells clean and fragrant with the scent of rose water. Pete knows herself, knows *why* she's so staunchly in favor of keeping the Union, because she had to become enlightened."

Pete didn't happen to be born in the North as he was, into an abolitionist family that never owned a single slave for any reason— had no need of even one. Not so with Pete's family. Her father had been an unwilling slave owner, a coastal planter. Still, Pete could give you reasons—one, two, three—why she now believed so strongly in the union of all the states. Could quote from the speeches of Abraham Lincoln, using his flowing, musical lines much as a preacher uses the Scriptures as proof texts of the points he is making.

A small pool of red wine spread across the little walnut table Pete had polished only yesterday until it shone. He had poured another drink too fast and missed the rim of the water glass. If Pete were still here in the room, he wouldn't lose control of his thoughts and actions so quickly. Pete could keep him focused, transform the jellylike thoughts filling his brain into points one, two, and three.

Without her, he lost control of his own thoughts. Without Pete, nothing was as it should be. Nothing was as it could be if only she would agree to become his wife. . . . With God's help, he would find a way to convince her that together both their worlds would somehow right themselves like kites in a good, strong wind. Strong was the key word. No matter how often he refilled his glass, he knew that much. Pete was strong. Everything he didn't know, she knew, and would always know.

A COPY OF ROBERT McALPIN GOODMAN'S NEWSPAPER UNDER her arm, Pete let herself into their house totally unmindful that she had tracked in mud and freshly mowed grass blades left behind by Big Boy and June when they used the big scythes on the front yard yesterday. The headline in the paper had so startled her that every ounce of common sense vanished until she heard her mother call. "Pete, for pity's sake, look at your feet! They're caked with the horrible up-country red mud!"

"Oh, sorry, Mama. Blame your friend Mr. Goodman. Look! Just look at that headline in his newspaper! Things are far worse than we thought. It says here that Howell Cobb, President James Buchanan's Secretary of the Treasury, has left Washington and is headed back to Georgia, vehemently advocating secession! Did you expect that, Mama? I certainly didn't." Pete turned a page in the newspaper. "And here it says there's a rumor that South Carolina may have a big meeting in about ten days to decide whether or not it will secede!"

Pete's mother sank into a chair, her face stricken. "She vowed she knew something that would show up in our paper soon. Over and over with that smug look on her face, she kept saying that."

"Who, Mama? Old Beaulah Matthews?"

"Yes. You knew she was here when you fled to Dr. Sam's and left me stranded alone with her. Pete, is something wrong? That wasn't a bit like you to do that."

"Wasn't it? I'm sure I'd have no way of knowing because I just plain don't know *me* anymore. I don't know what I think, what I want to do, or what I don't want to do. Maybe I've spent too much of my life trying to decide what's going to be best for you or for Selina or, until she took complete leave of her senses and fell in love with that mean-spirited Buster Matthews, for Fanny."

"Have I been that selfish with you, Pete?"

"Yes. I mean no. See? I don't know what I mean. Until now, I lived a simple, pretty uncomplicated life. But I honestly don't think you can depend on me anymore, Mama. I know John Couper would give me one of his lectures for saying that to you, but I'd be lying if I said anything else." For a few seconds Pete studied her mother's still-pretty but now deeply troubled face. Pete had blabbed too much and knew it. How could she think of a way to change the subject? "What do you think old hatchet-face Mrs. Matthews meant when she said something would be turning up in the newspaper soon? I know Governor Brown may call a session of the Georgia legislature if Lincoln is really elected. I know all those Southern hotheads will stir up the Southern states to secede as South Carolina may want to."

"You don't know that, Pete. Mr. Goodman's newspaper only says it's a *rumor* about South Carolina's seceding. One thing we can be sure of is that Mr. Goodman will print nothing about which he isn't absolutely certain. You just saw Sam. What does he think will happen?"

"We didn't talk much about the country or politics or war or anything. Mama, all he wants to talk about is getting married to me!"

"And what about you? Do you talk to him about that, Pete?"

"Not much, I'm afraid. Today, if you want the truth, I mostly kissed him right out on his front porch in the swing without even checking to see if anyone was passing his cottage!"

THAT NIGHT, AFTER THE GIRLS WERE ALL IN BED, ANNE OPENED her inkwell and began what seemed, at least, like an extremely important letter to John Couper in Savannah.

My beloved son,
    It's quite possible that your mother has lived most of her life as a widow behaving like a spoiled, selfish child, and before I

write another line, I beg you to forgive me and to do all you can to convince your sister Pete that I see the folly of my ways and want desperately to change.

I will do my best to make all this clear to Pete, but she is already confused in her own life and I am having difficulty following her problems, as seems true with her too. For now, I want you to know that I am at last aware of how doggedly you and Pete have tried, since your father left us, to help me mend my own brokenness. In the main, you have both succeeded and I am forever grateful. I am not writing any gossip or news of Marietta, because this is only a plea for forgiveness and to beg you to be totally honest in your reply. Eve has not mentioned having one of her knowings, but I expect it any day, since my own worry grows by leaps and bounds for the future of our country. Oh, John Couper, I suppose you will see action if anything so insane and terrible as a war comes. I am not even asking you that now. I am just praying that you believe I want to change my selfish ways and become the kind of mother you and Pete deserve me to be.

My love always to you,
Yr Mother,
Anne Couper Fraser

Chapter 58

WITHIN DAYS AFTER ANNE MAILED HER SON'S LETter to Savannah, he had answered it, but not as a son writing to his mother, she thought. More as a careful parent addressing an offspring. With the utmost respect, he literally ordered her never, never to ask forgiveness again from him or from Pete. "Forgiveness cannot be in order," he had written, "when there is nothing anywhere to forgive. You have always been the world's best mother to us all, and anything we may have tried to do for you is the very least we could do in view of your worth to us."

As the news spread with certainty from one part of the nation to another that Abraham Lincoln of Illinois would be the next President, state boundaries in the South became backyard fences over which neighbors talked and buoyed one another with the seemingly unshakable conviction that the North would falter in no time and never, never dare to bully the entire South. John Couper even wrote that "plainly, there is a shortage of courage at the North, and they would never dare attack more than one Southern state at a time." This belief was growing so strong in the Southern states, Anne was afraid to broach the subject even to Pete or to Eve. Instead she held it in her own heart, firm in her personal conviction that such an idea was pure bluff and not

even worth the irritation she felt each time she heard it mentioned.

The agony in her mind, which far exceeded the irritation, came
from another part of her son's letter, in which he told her gleefully
how much he had enjoyed his latest and lengthiest assignment at
Fort Pulaski as paymaster for the officers of his regiment. "I'm
rather proud of owning my own business but now know that at last
I have found my real place in life, Mama, and it is in the military,"
he wrote. With a mixture of joy and panic, Anne thought of John,
his father, who certainly thrived in the military life above every
other.

"Nothing scares me so much," Anne told Eve morning after morning through the winter and into the early spring of 1861. In
fact, she and Eve spoke of almost nothing else any time they happened to be alone after the arrival of John Couper's letter in which
he'd written so glowingly of his newly realized attachment to his
volunteer regiment. It almost angered Anne that Eve usually said
nothing in response. "Don't just stand there staring at me like that,
Eve! Nothing could be worse than for my only son to feel as his
father felt about—that life! Somehow I've made my way through
the loss of his father, but if there is a war now and I lose my boy,
I'll—I'll lose my mind."

"You ain't gonna lose God though, Miss Anne, no matter
what."

"That's a glib thing to say!"

"What glib mean?"

"It means—thoughtless. Something you just blurt out without
really thinking first. It's a word you should know because you can
be masterly at it."

"Mos' of what I say to you don't need to be thought about first,
Miss Anne. I say zactly what I believes to you an' ain't nothing you
can do to change Mausa John Couper from what he be. He be his
papa's son jus' like he yours."

"And what's going to happen to me if there is a war and John Couper gets hurt or killed? What? Have you thought of a good glib answer to that?"

"No'm, not yet. But gimme time. Somepin come to me."

"I suppose you'll get one of your knowings."

"Maybe. Maybe not. You know, though, whichever way. An' ain't I done tol' you me an' you gonna be just fine?"

"I'm sure you have, but there's nothing in this world I hate so much as I hate war, Eve. Nothing but heartache and sorrow and suffering ever comes from it. No one wins. Everyone loses."

"That don' sound much like the Miss Anne I been gettin' used to lately. Look how you done change with Pete. I ain't seen one sign that you means to spoil her happiness in lovin' Doctah Sam. An' not only Pete, but Fanny too. You even does yo' bes' to act polite when dat ole hatchet face, Miz Matthews, she come by to rub your nose in the latest gossip, good or bad, 'bout the South. I be proud of you the way you been lately. I aim to stay that way an' pray you keep on growin' up!"

"Well, all I can say is—good luck!"

AT BREAKFAST ON THE MORNING OF MARCH 6, 1861, ANNE'S discomfort at finding herself alone with her daughter Fanny brought sure signs that one of her old sick headaches was returning. For months, because of Fanny's Southern sympathies, being alone with her beloved daughter had come to be something to avoid when possible, and it shamed Anne as a mother almost unbearably. That shame was more than she could endure today, especially with a throbbing head Fanny was sure to detect. Fanny, the born nurse in the family, was not only the one daughter who knew how to help her mother's bad headaches, but the one daughter for whom Anne's heart ached most. Was Fanny's undeniable plainness enough to cause such pain to a mother's heart, Anne had asked herself again and again lately, or had Fanny really changed? Gentle, quiet, submissive Fanny had begun to sneer or grin, evidently hoping to hide her pure delight at any shred of bad news about the future of the Union—the glorious Union, as dear Louisa Fletcher called it—which, Fanny vowed, "would never be united again." Any news that showed a strengthening of the Confederate States of America, as Southern states that had already seceded along with South Carolina now called themselves, plainly cheered Fanny. She smiled at the mere mention of what to her was good Southern news, and it was a smile her mother did not know, could not recognize as part of her tender, loyal girl.

Fanny's delight on March 4, the morning Abraham Lincoln's inauguration was to take place in Washington, had torn especially at Anne's very soul. It had driven home the ugly truth that she and her family no longer lived in the United States of America. It was still sickening to believe that Georgia, on January 19, had voted overwhelmingly to secede!

"Don't look so downhearted, Mama," Fanny said as she stood behind Anne's chair, rubbing the back of her mother's neck slowly, soothingly. "You know your headaches only get worse when you're upset. And mark my words, once old Lincoln is actually the President, things will get better and better for us down here. It doesn't matter really where your loyalty lies, because you're a born Southerner and the South is where you live. And don't forget, the South is already ahead of the North!"

"What on earth are you talking about, child?"

"We had our convention and we already have our President, the Honorable Jefferson Davis. Even Mr. Alexander Stephens, once a Unionist, sees which side his bread is buttered on and is now the Vice President."

"Fanny, you're hurting me!"

"You've got to let your neck muscles loosen, Mama, or your headache will never get better."

"Sometimes I don't think you care a fig about me—whether my head aches or not. How can you hold yourself so stiff and distant and apart from the rest of your own family?"

"Because I believe what I believe and I'm the only true Southerner in this house anymore. What makes you think you and Selina and Pete aren't the distant ones? You've always taught us to stand up for what we really think, and I wonder a lot what John Couper would say if he could hear you and Pete yammering on about the glorious Union."

"I did not teach you to sass me and I won't have it. Do you hear?"

"Yes, I hear, and I have to tell you something. Now seems as good a time as any. I—I miss you, Mama. I miss you and Pete, and although she thinks mostly about whether her intended, George Stubinger, is safe and still planning to marry her, you've got Selina believing she's a Unionist and I miss her, too! Turning against all we've ever known or thought in our family, ignoring your heritage, you've built a thick, high wall between us, Mama, and I miss you so much, sometimes I cry myself to sleep at night."

Anne got quickly to her feet, pulling away from Fanny's skillful hands. "And I suppose you think I don't know Buster Matthews's mother tattles to you every time she and I have a conversation! Has Buster asked you to marry him yet? I want an answer, Fanny. Has he?"

"Well, not in so many words. I mean, he hasn't gotten on his knees yet in that formal way, but—"

"But you just take it for granted that he will. Is that right? Don't you sense in your deepest woman heart that he's just stalling? That he's feeling satisfied with himself for now because he's found a way to come between you and your family by turning you into one of those unthinking Southern hotheads? Fanny, you're thoughtful— at least you've always been—and obedient, and you're anything but stupid. Please, please, dear child, begin to use your good head. I know it makes you furious for me even to mention his name, but Abraham Lincoln was right when he said 'a house divided against itself cannot stand.' Families can't either, Fanny. Please, please come back to us!"

When, in response to her plea, Fanny simply turned without a word and left the room, Anne sank back into her breakfast chair and began to weep.

Chapter 59

ON THE MILD SPRING MORNING OF APRIL 15, 1861, Anne stood at her bedroom window, looking down across the purple-spattered carpet of spring green grass and deep purple violets spread across her front lawn behind the picket fence June and Big Boy had just whitewashed. In the midst of so much beauty, it simply could not be, she thought, that every snatch of conversation and every letter held the dark threat of what could be a ghastly war between the North and the South of the once proud Union of the states. She looked out from her corner window on the second floor of her haven, the gracious, dear place she and her girls still called the white-light house, the place in which Anne had finally found the security for which she'd longed since the day they had been forced to leave the dangerously dilapidated little Lawrence cottage on St. Simons Island to move, at the convenience of their host or hostess, from the home of one friend or family member to that of another.

Just remembering St. Simons Island reminded her of the latest letter from Caroline, her brother James Hamilton Couper's wife, with its disturbing news of the possible fate of so many of Anne's faithful St. Simons people. "If war does come," Caroline had written, "James Hamilton said at dinner yesterday that he planned to bring all the remaining Negroes from Lawrence and Cannon's Point here to Hopeton to work and live, heaven only knows where."

As the sentence from Caroline's letter crossed her mind, Anne caught her first glimpse of her own Eve down in the yard with Anne's best Marietta friend, Louisa Fletcher. The two were making their way toward the house while stooping here and there to add to the mounting bunch of violets Eve carried in her flat, reed basket.

"Could there possibly be a more peaceful sight?" Anne asked aloud into the empty bedroom. "My two beloved friends—each cherished in her own separate way—Louisa Fletcher and Eve. And my handsome lawn surrounding my own comfortable house. But all of it—my two friends and my house and my violets and my spring grass—seem to be waiting. Waiting, not just for summer when the only enemy will be too much hot sun, but almost surely for the most fearful enemy in the world—war. No, God! Not in the United States, not in Georgia, not in my lifetime. Not war, God, without John to protect me, to tell me what he's thinking, to listen to my fears and complaints and the panic in my voice when I dare to let myself think that our son, our only son, John Couper, could be one of those young men being shot at! And he will be because he's a man and because he holds the perplexing belief that simply because he happened to be born in Georgia, he'd somehow be a traitor if he didn't throw his precious life into the danger."

Her eyes could see only the silent, peaceful panorama of the world waiting outside her house, but her heart had eyes, too, and there she could picture the ugly, bloody, noisy chaos of battle John had told her about during the years before he realized that she had nothing in her makeup to tolerate the thought of killing even for what could be considered a good cause. No one—*no one*—could ever convince Anne that either the North or the South had a good cause for war. Trouble could be settled another way between angry factions. As long as sane persons agreed to talk to each other, they could find a peaceful means of settling their dispute, and even her blessed husband, John, had never been able to persuade her otherwise.

Out beyond a big pine tree, Eve and Louisa were moving closer to the house, their basket now piled with violets—for her, she knew, because both women were keenly aware of her torment now that she knew her son seemed to have taken to the military life every bit as strongly as had his father. John Couper was her rock in the troubled land that lay all around her. With each letter she could depend on finding at least twenty dollars "for house purposes," as he put it, or word that he was sending her rice or flour or some other necessity that now cost so much in Marietta's stores.

Most painful of all, John Couper was her only male child, and the gift of a son to John had been her proudest achievement in life. Pete knew how much John Couper meant to her, but Pete had heartache of her own these days trying to make up her mind to marry or not to marry Sam.

Still watching from her bedroom window, Anne couldn't help thinking that the two women—Louisa, short and somewhat pudgy, and Eve, tall and statuesque—could not have differed more in appearance, but to her they were alike because she would stake her own life on their loyalty to her.

Suddenly, she needed almost desperately to be with these two women who were filling their basket with flowers until it was nearly running over—as both their great hearts ran over with love for Anne and for God. The two were smiling now and looking toward the house, evidently not seeing Anne at the open bedroom window. When she called their names, they appeared for the first time to notice her and motioned for her to come outside.

When Anne joined her friends at the top of the wooden front-porch steps, she could tell from a close look at Eve's face that despite their playacting, something was terribly wrong.

"But I don't understand," she said, addressing them both. "I've been watching you two picking violets for almost a quarter of an hour, talking together, even laughing now and then. If something's so wrong, and I'm sure it is from the way you both look now, for heaven's sake, tell me!"

"It done happen, Miss Anne," Eve said, her voice thick with dread and concern.

"What?" Anne demanded. "What's happened?"

"You tell her, Miss Louisa," Eve said. "You know all this war stuff better'n I knows it."

"Eve's right," Louisa said, taking a step toward Anne. "Somehow these violets, pretty as they are, seem a bit silly now. War, Anne. Oh, war hasn't been declared yet, but it will be. It's all the South's doing, of course, but they did it. It's really war and nothing good can possibly come of it!"

"Stop talking in riddles, Louisa."

"I don't have many details, but sometime in the black of night —I think about four-thirty in the morning on April 12—the South fired on Union-held Fort Sumter at Charleston. The bombardment kept up most of the next day until around late afternoon of the thirteenth, when Major Robert Anderson, in command at Sumter, surrendered. It's begun, Anne. Eve and I foolishly hoped our little offering of violets might help you some. I now see it was just that —a foolish hope."

Without a word, Anne sank to the top step and buried her face in her hands.

"I go fix the flowers, Miss Louisa," Eve whispered. "Dat be what Miss Anne she want me to do."

"Yes, Eve. I'm sure it is, and I'll stay right here with her for as long as she needs me."

THE LAST THING ANNE VOWED TO LOUISA, RIGHT AFTER THE well-meant but now pathetic presentation of masses of violets, was that she would not burden her girls with her own load of fear and worry over John Couper. She broke the vow almost at once by refusing to dine with her daughters for the remainder of the month of April. Reluctantly, Eve brought her meals to her in her room upstairs.

"You know I gonna climb them steps with every meal," Eve said, "but it be bad for you. You fixin' to kill yo'se'f from hunger an' den where we all be wifout you? You ain't eat enough all this time to keep a bird alive!"

"I'll eat when I can," Anne said. "It's just that I can't seem to make sense of anything until I've heard something from John Couper. He always writes to me every week. This time it's been a whole month, Eve!"

Standing at the bedroom door with the untouched tray of food, Eve said, "I knows. I knows, Miss Anne. An' I don' know nothin' else to say."

"Good. Then don't try."

A FEW MINUTES LATER EVE STOOD ALONE DOWNSTAIRS, JUST outside the dining-room door, trying to make up her mind what to do. The spacious dining room was oddly silent. Selina, Fanny, and Pete sat at one end of the long table, but no one spoke. *How I gonna think this through with everything so still?* Eve wondered as she stood there holding Anne's untouched dinner tray. Then she knew and, being Eve, set immediately about doing what she'd just decided.

"Gimme dat newspaper outa yo' pocket, Petey," she almost ordered as she set down the tray.

"What newspaper, Eve?"

"Dat Mister Goodman paper 'bout de South declarin' war on de North over in Montgomery, Alabama."

"I'll do no such thing!"

"Then I go get June's copy."

"June's got a copy of that paper? The one telling about President Jefferson Davis giving his approval of that Confederate congressional bill declaring war between the United States and the dumb old Confederacy?"

"Yes'm. His friend Johnson the barber saves the paper for him."

"What for?"

"I reckon you think June can't read. Think again, Miss Petey. You be the one dat promise me you won't do nuffin to add to yo' mama's heartache. It ain't right to keep any scrap ob news from her, an' from now on, Eve be the one that decide what Miss Anne know and what she don't know 'bout!"

Instead of flaring at her as Eve expected, Pete gave her a genuinely puzzled look. "You—you really think it's been wrong of us to keep the news story from Mama?"

"It ain't only wrong, it be mean. Now, you gonna give it to me so's I kin let her read it herself or is she gonna read June's paper?"

Looking a little sheepish, Pete reached into her day dress pocket for the crumpled piece of Goodman's paper. Without a word, she held it out to Eve, but before Eve could take the article, Pete quickly stuffed it back into her pocket.

"Give dat to me," Eve ordered, "or else take it right upstairs yo'se'f an' let me stan' there while you give it to Miss Anne!"

"Well, aren't you getting uppity, Eve?" Fanny fairly snapped, something she seldom did, even during these days of standing apart from the others in her family as the only Confederate sympathizer.

"No, I'm not just gettin' uppity, Miss Fanny. I speck I allus been dat way. I just made up my min' to begin to act like I really be Miss Anne's friend."

Chapter 60

ANNE WAS UP BEFORE DAYLIGHT ON THE MORNING of May 23. It was too early for Eve to come. The bedroom was still chilly from the night hours even though no wind blew, and as it had been for two weeks, the air outside her open bedroom windows was mild. Anne's whole body shivered anyway as she sat alone, one candle burning beside her on the writing desk. She just stared at her diary, still unopened because she knew not one word had been written on its pages since the day she learned the South had declared war against the North. Had she scribbled anything, it would not have been worth reading because she could only have written "still no word from John Couper. Still no word from John Couper in Savannah. God help me. Still no word from my son."

The soft, rapid knock at the bedroom door was as quiet as a whisper, but, her heart pounding as though John Couper himself were standing right outside in the upstairs hall, Anne leaped to her feet, threw open the door, and heard herself say, "Oh, it's you, Pete! I hope I don't look too disappointed. Come in, dear. I —I somehow imagined it was your brother knocking."

"In a way it was John Couper, Mama," Pete said gently. "Look! Here's the letter you've been waiting

for. I got home too late to give it to you last night. So here. See
what my brother has to say."

Anne unfolded the page and read aloud.

> "Dearest Mama and girls . . .
>
> It's happened at last. I'm sure you know by now that the President of the Confederacy, the Honorable Jefferson Davis, has finally declared war on the United States. Well, he has, and after all
> these months in a volunteer regiment, I am enlisted now in the
> great and glorious Cause as a first lieutenant in Captain John
> P. W. Read's Light Artillery Battery for the duration. I know this
> news will make my little sister Fanny happy. I'm not so sure about
> the rest of you, but I pray you will go straight to God, Mama, and
> let Him guide you in your loyalties as well as in your all-important role as our beloved mother. All over Savannah's military
> population there is a new sense of purpose and zest for living. It is
> as though we have all been given a potent spring tonic. God's will
> is so evident: We can only win our freedom as a separate country,
> and in His infinite wisdom, I expect Him to honor my mother's
> prayers and that her heart and excellent mind will open to the
> rightness of the Southern Cause. I send my everlasting love to
> you, dear Mother, and to all three of my sisters. I now fully
> understand why my father so loved the military life and expect
> that I will find a lifetime of valued work and satisfaction in the
> same life he loved so dearly. No more business worries. My silence has been so long because of our extremely full calendar
> these past weeks. I will write again when I know the date I am to
> leave for the front lines in Virginia."

When Anne looked up at Pete, she saw more fear and agony
than she ever expected to see in her strong daughter's face.

FANNY WAS SORRY IF SHE SEEMED MORE CURT THAN USUAL AT
breakfast the next day, but so much had begun to happen in Marietta in the few days since word reached there about the new Confederacy's declaration of war with the United States, Fanny simply

did the best she could to contain her delight and enthusiasm. Heaven knew it was hard at best to stay civil around her mother and sisters, with all three of them sick at heart and worried about John Couper instead of being proud of his spirited Southern stand. Usually Fanny let Pete and Mama do the writing to her brother, but she had actually written to him herself yesterday, so that he would know firsthand that at least one member of his immediate family was standing by him in his decision to lay down his life if need be for the blessed place of their birth.

She had tried and failed to convince Mama, Pete, and Selina that they should join most of the other women of Marietta in making garments, baking cookies, rolling bandages, and planning social activities for the Confederate soldiers who were rapidly swelling the ranks of General Phillip's Brigade, an ever-growing encampment of Confederate soldiers six miles or so from town, out the Atlanta Road.

"Whatever John Couper needs, he'll feel free to let us know," Mama had said sternly. "He won't be depending on the ladies of Marietta for his comforts or necessities, Fanny. You do as you choose. I've always wanted all my children to use their own good minds, to follow their own consciences. Go every day, if you can find a means of getting there, to General Phillip's encampment, watch your splendid Buster march and drill to your heart's content. But do give us the right to our own opinions in this dreadful war to come."

"Oh, Mama," Fanny could still hear the whine in her own voice, "I wish we all agreed on this, don't you?"

"My dear girl—and you are my dear girl—don't you dare try that whine of yours in order to sway my thinking. I don't want us to argue. We're too well bred for that! But I want a clear understanding. You are entitled to your opinion. Pete, Selina, and I are entitled to ours."

"I'd do almost anything, Mama, if I knew how to keep your approval the way I once had it. I don't. You don't like Buster. You don't like his mother. I love him, and most of the time I like Mrs. Matthews just fine. And I'm glad you feel the way you do about everyone's right to her own opinion. I certainly have mine." After a deep sigh, Fanny said, "I just wish I could think of some other really important way to help the—Cause. Don't you ever feel even a little bit of longing in yourself to help John Couper and his fighting friends, Mama?"

"Of course I do, but I also know which side has the good Cause."

"But the ladies of Marietta are going to cook a festive dinner and give each soldier a New Testament before they go marching off to the train depot next week. Don't you want to be part of that? Don't you just long to help the boys who, like my own brother, are willing to die for our country?"

"I'm a believer in the United States of America, Fanny, and that's all there is to say now. If we're not together as one country, our entire economy will perish and then where will we all be?" Her voice wavering, Fanny's mama added, "I'm too torn up to argue anymore at all. And as long as you're living in my house, you'll mind your tongue. Do you hear me?"

"Yes, Mama, I hear you. And I'll mind my tongue, but I'll also be searching for a place where I can contribute still more to—to *my country's* Cause!"

AFTER THE LARGE AND FESTIVE DINNER IN HONOR OF THE CON-federate soldiers in General Phillip's Brigade, the yelling, confident, laughing boys piled into the waiting train coaches, their New Testaments in their pockets. After fond good-byes to friends, sweethearts, and family members gathered to see them off to battle in Virginia, lustily singing "Dixie," they took their leave.

Fanny's Buster Matthews was not due to depart Marietta for two weeks, but she was at the depot hoping at least to see him and to find a chance to tell him something that might cover the humiliation she felt because neither her mother nor her sisters were anywhere to be found in the crowd of high-spirited well-wishers.

"I'm so sorry, and I know Buster will be, too, that he didn't have an opportunity to speak to you alone, dear girl," Beaulah

Matthews said in what Pete called her squishy, sweaty-handed way. "The boy will be heartbroken, I'm sure, but at least you and I know he's on God's side in this struggle. And God looks after His own. We'll both have ample chance to be proud of Buster just any day now. Please do tell your mother she missed a spirit-lifting spectacle here at this heartwarming occasion. Her lack of concern over you, with your intended due to leave on a life-and-death mission soon, is more than my mother's heart can take in! But, sweet Fanny, you *do* have Buster's mother, who means to stay very close to you come what may."

"Thank you, Mother Matthews, but I hope you don't think my mother is being hard-hearted. I know you and I think she's on the wrong side, but she cares about the Confederate boys. The minute she heard General Phillip's Brigade had gotten so large that it needed extra fresh provisions, she sent our June and Big Boy with every chicken and egg and fresh vegetable we could possibly spare. Don't forget, my only brother—and I guess Mama loves him more than anyone else on earth—is enlisted now in the Confederate Army, and Mama watches every day for a letter from her grandson, Fraser Demere, telling her he's enlisted in some Florida regiment. It's bad enough on you and me, but at least we're on God's side with the Confederacy and bound to win in just a matter of weeks, according to Buster. Poor Mama's just torn in so many directions."

BECAUSE SHE STILL WORRIED ABOUT DISOBEYING ONE OR ANOTHER of her own mother's instructions, one early June morning Anne forced herself to catch up on her diary. So much was happening. Too much—too much of it filled with anxiety and worry and downright fear, but she dipped the new steel-nibbed pen into her old inkwell and began to write.

Today is Monday, June 24, 1861. So much has taken place, I'll never get it all down here, but *if* after this dreadful war is ever over, someone has a mind to read these pages, I must try.

I've lost my way in calendar dates, but back in April, when the Confederacy attacked Union-held Fort Sumter, the new President, Abraham Lincoln, called for seventy-five thousand volunteers, which call caused Virginia, North Carolina, Tennessee, and Arkansas to secede, a sure sign that the tragedy grows larger. Other families, like ours, will surely be split apart. Then, toward the end of May, the capital of the Confederacy moved from Montgomery, Alabama, to Richmond, Virginia—to me, another frightening sign because the military installations are so heavy there. And also closer to home for me, reading a short letter yesterday from my beloved John Couper froze the blood in my veins! He is being moved from Savannah to Richmond in Captain John Read's Company of Pulaski Guards. God in heaven, multiply this mother's heartache, this grandmother's heartache (I do expect any day to learn of the enlistment of my sweet grandson, Fraser Demere), by thousands upon thousands and in your great wisdom send us all healing. My lovesick daughter Selina waits daily to learn that her beloved George Stubinger has also been sent from Louisiana to the far more dangerous Virginia. Selina, wanting the romantic wedding she has always dreamed of, persuaded George to wait for the war's end (he is a Confederate and so, like my own John Couper, feels cocksure the end will come quickly!), but I tremble for the suffering that may lie ahead for Selina because she waited for the trouble to end.

I know well that my dear Fanny, led so far astray from her family by her unpleasant, pushy Corporal Buster, might chance to read these pages, but my concern over her is based on a mother's fear that she might allow herself to be rushed into marrying that odd boy simply because other young couples are rushing into marriage. Is it possible that rather plain daughters sense their mother's pain because their choice of a husband is sometimes limited, as is my Fanny's?

I must stop writing since I hurt unbearably (the hurt never stops) because Fanny's loyalty is with the rebellious South after a lifetime lived in the presence of one of the proudest Americans of them all—my father, John Couper, her grandpapa. How Fanny's rebellion against all he believed about the Union must torture him, even though he is somehow free of earthly heartache! Does her life, so different from her family's life, ever bother Fanny?

What I wouldn't give to know a little of what she confides to that stubborn, brash Matthews boy! Fanny tells me nothing, which, in a way, is worse than knowing too much.

Anne closed her diary and stretched out on her bed to think. Fanny, she was sure, was out at General Phillip's Brigade encampment on the Atlanta Road right now, probably off somewhere with the fire-eating, bumbling Buster, if he had any free time from drilling and rifle practice. Selina was also planning to marry a Confederate soldier, George Stubinger, someday. Why didn't that upset Anne as Fanny's dreams of marrying Buster distressed her? Selina had acted, at least, as though she agreed with Pete and her mother on the Union's worth, but did Selina take anything seriously that didn't wear a uniform? And did she care that much which uniform? Fanny's serious side—wider than a mere streak—always made a far deeper impression on her mother than Selina's cheerful frivolity did. Anne couldn't have explained why, but it was true. And why did she somehow never truly worry about Pete, so obviously in love with a man who drank too much—so much, in fact, that people were talking now and marveling that he could carry on a successful medical practice as he surely did.

I don't worry so much about Pete, she thought, because she's too strong in her own right. I do worry, however, because such a strong woman can fall into the trap of believing she can truly help even a man who drinks too much. But Pete? Pete wasn't only strong, she was also wise. Besides, Anne had only to remind herself how much she, Pete's mother, also liked the charming, gentlemanly Dr. Sam. A man with real humor can always be brought to his senses, her John used to say. She would go on believing that about Sam because she had to.

She sat up on the side of her bed. "There's no room left in me for worry over Pete. My dear, dear son is encamped near enough to the enemy lines to hear them shout roll call each morning—within easy gunshot of each other. Selina, as long as George Stubinger went on adoring her as he did, would find a way to turn any vicissitude into happiness, into romance. But John Couper's very life was in danger! And probably young Fraser Demere's too. And

Fanny, although she never neglected the smallest particle of her household duties, busied herself steadily with sewing, baking, rolling bandages—doing any menial task that came to hand so long as it helped the rebellious South and the unsuitable Buster!

"I know Fanny tells him everything," Anne said aloud, still sitting on her comfortable bed. "I'm getting more like my papa every day. Listen to me, talking out loud to myself in an empty room!"

"YOU STAY BUSIER THAN ANYONE YOUR AGE I KNOW OF IN THE whole town of Marietta, Georgia," Buster said as he walked with Fanny away from the usual afternoon crowd of townsfolk visiting the Atlanta Road encampment. "I don't see why you're complaining about what you do."

"Because sometimes it bothers me," she retorted in the half-teasing, half-bickering way she had been forced to learn in order to make Buster more comfortable when they talked. "It does seem that with my gifts as a nurse—and even if I sound conceited, I know I'm a good nurse—it seems as though I should be doing something far more worthwhile to help our Cause. You've been promoted to corporal now in General Phillip's Brigade. Isn't there a string you could pull, something you could do to help me find more work?"

When Buster only cocked one sandy eyebrow and grinned at her, she added, "That's no answer, sir! You know as well as I that once the real fighting begins, nurses will be needed everywhere, so don't act as though I'm a silly, mindless woman just because I want you to use your influence to get me appointed soon to some hospital staff!"

"Fan, you know being a corporal is only one notch above being a private. What influence do I have? I ain't got no way to help you or anyone else in this man's Army."

"Don't call me Fan and don't say ain't. Your mother wouldn't like hearing you speak in such a sloppy way any more than I like it."

"What she don't know don't hurt her none."

"What she doesn't know doesn't hurt her," Fanny corrected again. It had taken timid Fanny more than three years to work up enough nerve to point out mistakes in Buster's speech, but lately she thought she had finally caught on to the reason he plunged, off and on, into plain old cracker talk. Although Fanny defended Beaulah Matthews to her own mother and sisters, she believed she probably understood why Buster was rebelling at his mother's domineering ways, and she certainly saw why her own family looked down on the woman. But to Fanny there was something rather dear and almost pathetic about Buster's defiant manner. He could, when he felt like it, be funny and downright sweet, but more than once she had heard Beaulah Matthews bemoan the fact that poor Buster, before he joined the Army, worked with his hands splitting wood for barrels at Mr. Denmead's flour mill. Inevitably, when his mother criticized him, Buster crumpled, piercing Fanny's heart to its depth with love, flashes of understanding, even pity for the only young man who had ever singled out Fanny as "his girl," the only one who had ever asked her outright to call him "her beau."

Was it possible, she asked herself often these days, for a woman to love a man and look down on him at the same time? This minute as they sat together on an old fallen log, she knew it was possible. For most of the time today, he had been his difficult, flippant self, but now his head was suddenly in her lap, his face pressed against her breasts, and as she smoothed one light brown curl off his forehead, she knew that part of her really loved him.

"You are sure one smart young lady to have picked me out of such a big brigade of soldiers," he said. "Ma was so surprised, you could have scraped her eyes off her face when she found out I'd been promoted to corporal, but not you, Fan old girl. You're smart."

"Maybe so," she said, touching his curly hair again, "but I don't like being called old girl."

Without warning, he pulled her face down to his and kissed her full on the mouth, so hard he hurt her lips. "Maybe you like it, maybe not," he laughed, "but you're my good old girl, and someday when the war is over and I'm home to stay, you'll wake up some morning to find out you're my good old wife."

"*What?*"

"Any objections?"

"No, but I'm not particularly fond of the way you proposed! No woman likes just being informed about her marriage."

"You're not just any woman. You're mine and I guarantee you'll have a high-up job as chief nurse of some kind just as soon as Confederate hospitals are opened, because good old hot Southern blood has begun to flow!"

On impulse, she clasped his head in her arms and held him against her. "No, Buster! Your jokes aren't very funny at best and that was a bad joke. I don't want your blood to flow. Not ever. You're the only man who ever loved me in my whole life!"

With one big open hand, he did what she hated most—he mussed her hair so she'd never get it back in place without a looking glass. "What you just did to my hair is not funny!"

"Oh, Fan, for pity's sake, I was only playin'."

"My mother and father played a lot, but there wasn't any sharp edge to it. When they teased each other, it made all of us children laugh. If I did what I want to do right now, I'd cry! You're—I guess you're really a good man, Buster, but don't you know what tenderness is? Do you even know what it means? I know I'm plain *and* tender, but sometimes plain women make the best wives. No one has to tell me that my plainness is one of the main reasons your mother wants you to marry me. She knows a pretty woman with a hard heart, even though she's married, doesn't hesitate a minute to snatch a husband away from his wife."

Buster stared at her, his eyes filling with quick tears. "Who told you another woman snatched my father away from Ma?"

"Never mind who told me, and stop pushing me into corners so I have to soothe your ruffled feathers! Everybody in Marietta knows your father walked out on your mother when you were a little boy and left you both to fend for yourselves. I hate it that they know, because I hate it that such a dreadful thing ever happened to either of you. And I beg you to forgive me for telling you I even know about it. Buster, Buster, we'll have a good marriage. I'll be true to you and you'll be true to me, and anyway, we've got our devotion to the Cause in common. Don't you realize that I've risked having my whole family turn against me—except John Couper—because Mama and Pete and Selina are Unionists?"

When she forced Buster to look at her, his face was flushed and angry. "Now, I suppose, if your family puts you out of the house, you'll blame Ma and me for turning you into a Confederate!"

"We don't have sharp edges in our family. We may not agree on everything, but my family would never, never, never put me out of our home."

"No, but you don't see the real reason your ma's the way she is. She thinks the North will beat us into submission down here. Tell her I said to think again! Your ma's gonna live to see the day she hates the North!"

"Buster, what day? What day will that be?"

"The day they spill the good hot Southern blood of your precious brother, John Couper Fraser! Your ma worships the ground he walks on, but pretty boy that he is, he's shown himself to be a true Confederate patriot, and the Union would just as soon spill his blood as mine."

"Buster, no! Don't say such things."

In response, he grabbed her face in both his big hands and kissed her again, hard, without a single look at who might be coming along the cleared path just behind the fallen log. And then he laughed.

"Don't laugh, Buster!"

"We're all gonna be laughing down here in no time, little Fan. And anyway, you told me once that you thought I had a good laugh. I don't forget things like that, and you mustn't forget that within six months or less, them Northern privy rats will be tucking tail and running all the way to Canada. I hear courage is already running out up there. Once we get a chance at 'em, they won't know what's hit 'em. We'll still own our niggers, too, but we're gonna be free of the Union down here—you and Ma and me an' all our kind. We got a fine future, Fanny, and it's even gonna be all right with your ma, because she'll hate Northerners the way we do once they kill off your handsome brother, John Couper!"

Chapter 61

By the end of July 1861—halfway through Anne's sixty-fourth year—she felt far older but tried to stay busy with needlework and hours spent at the keyboard of her pianoforte, practicing difficult pieces of music she had put aside in her younger, carefree days. She also spent two or three afternoons a week with Louisa Fletcher. Louisa and Dix still lived at the Marietta Hotel in quarters adjoining those of their daughter Georgia, married to the hotel's owner—wealthy, influential Unionist Henry Greene Cole. Anne knew that balding, gentlemanly Cole was many years Georgia's senior and, according to Louisa, was kind and generous not only to Georgia but to the entire Fletcher family. It was impossible for Anne to imagine what she might have done without Louisa to help her keep her own balance. The two women loved to discuss books, and although it was more and more difficult for Anne to keep her mind on any subject for long, she thanked God daily for the comforting stimulation of Louisa's company and conversation.

Anne's world, her very life, was already scattered and changed by the war, even though no battle action had yet crossed into the state of Georgia. Marietta itself was so changed, Anne felt at home only inside her own house. Since earlier that month, the men of the city had agreed to close their offices and businesses at five-thirty each day to allow time for every man, young or old, to drill in the town Square—which they did daily as throngs of women and children watched from sidewalks and carriages. Fighting, though, had, insofar as she knew, been mainly confined to Virginia. John Couper was now stationed near Williamsburg, and his latest letter told her that her grandson, Fraser Demere, enlisted for a year in the Confederate Army, had just reached Richmond by train from Florida. There was great relief at the white-light house when Selina heard from her George Stubinger that he had escaped injury in the fierce early battle at Manassas, Virginia. He also said he'd chanced to meet, and make friends with, James Hamilton Couper's son Hamilton in the same battle. There was an opposing pull at Anne's emotions, though, when the Marietta newspaper declared the Confederate forces the winners, which would surely cause still more foolish boasting among Confederate soldiers that the Union armies would surrender in no time at all. Every scrap of news increased Anne's inner turmoil. There were even days when she would have given almost anything if her own sympathies were with her native South. Oddly, Louisa Fletcher understood this better than did anyone else except Pete, who shared her mother's convictions that the Union must, by some means, be restored.

Weeks inched by through the fall months as the trees turned gold and scarlet across Anne's nine acres of land. Eve, as usual, kept the house filled with artistically arranged pitchers and vases of colored foliage and autumn weeds and grasses. Anne often forgot to thank Eve for her thoughtfulness but could always count on Eve's knowing why she forgot.

"You don't suffer one pain Eve misses, Miss Anne," the still-lovely, ever more dignified mulatto woman kept reminding her. "When your heart hurt, Eve's heart hurt too. But at least we knows John Couper be all right an' livin' in fairly good shape over in Virginia. We kin give thanks for that."

Anne did give thanks daily, sometimes hourly, because even though she knew her son kept his letters as cheerful as possible, he did sound reasonably safe and in good health and seemed to be actually enjoying his life headquartered with his 10th Georgia Regi-

ment near Williamsburg. He was finding life good—so good that
Anne stopped reading on a certain page each time she passed
an evening going over every line of his letters. Her adored son
actually loved the military as his father had loved it, and the letter
telling her about his interesting social life in various Williamsburg homes was the one in which he vowed that after the war,
he meant to make a career in the Army and never return to business.

"We gotta think one day at a time, Miss Anne," Eve went on
reminding her. "Not two but one. You borrowin' trouble from tomorrow. Miss Anne, I needs to ax you something. Maybe it's none
of my bi'ness, but I knows in my heart that you go up against your
son, your daughter Fanny, an' who knows 'bout Selina now that she
so head and heart in love with a Southern soldier. But how come
you so strong in favor of the Union when you born on Sn Simons
the same as your chur'n—children—was. The same as John Couper
an' your gran'son, sweet Fraser Demere. I reckon it be plain why I
favors the North. All us coloreds do, but why you think you does
when it cost you so much?"

"What do you mean, it costs me so much?"

"You don' thinks Eve knows how your heart wrench in two
'cause you can only be sure of Pete?"

"You know too much sometimes."

Eve laughed softly, not at her, for the laugh showed only that
Eve hoped to be understood. "You be in your sixty-fourth year,
Miss Anne, an' dat mean Eve be in her sixty-third. You want I
should pretend to be dumb?"

"No, of course I don't. I want you to be exactly as you are, and
all I can tell you is that my precious father believed in the Union,
my brother James Hamilton does, my husband did. Miss Fanny
Kemble Butler certainly did, and she made the best sense to me of
anyone I'd met until I became friends with Miss Louisa Fletcher,
who's a Unionist too. I can't help acting on what I believe any
more than you can, Eve. Besides, it just somehow seemed right to
me for us to pay money to the good folk like Flora McLeod, who
was John's father's cook and housekeeper in London, and the others

who took care of us there. We didn't expect their pampering solely because our skin was white! Theirs was too."

After a short silence, Eve said firmly, "You knows you kin tell anything you thinkin' to Eve."

"Yes, thank God, I do know. And what I'm thinking is how much I long to hear from my brother James Hamilton. If only he would write to me! I admire him almost as much as I admired Papa, but I need him now to be more than my brilliant, practical, talented brother. I need him to be close, to share his heart, what he's thinking these days. I need him to hold me, to talk with me, to tell me I'm not an inferior mother because I can't bring myself to side with my own loved ones over what some call a merely political problem. I know what Papa would say. He'd say, 'It's more than a political problem. Daughter, this is a matter of life and death!' And Papa would be right. Oh, Eve, he would be right."

"You also reads Mr. Goodman's newspaper, like I does. June, he read it too."

Anne took a step toward Eve, a half smile on her face. "I'm so proud of you for teaching June to read."

"When somebody like you gives such a gif' to me, ain't I gonna pass it on to the man I loves?"

"I suppose you'll just go on to both our dying days surprising me, won't you?" Anne asked. "Did I answer your question about why I'm a Unionist even when my dear, dear John Couper could be killed in the cause of the Confederacy?"

"You answer me good. It be jus' like June says. He done splain it to me long ago. I jus' wanted to hear you tell me."

"All right, Miss Smarty, now you tell me what June really thinks of me for going against my only son after all he's done for me."

Eve's best smile lit her face and seemed to light her very soul. "June say one thing ain't nobody ever gonna learn be wrong. He say a thing an' it jus' keep on ringin' true. June, he throw back his white head an' say, 'Miss Anne, our Miss Anne, be the bravest woman North or South!' "

"Oh, Eve, thanks for telling me that. I think so highly of June as a human being, it—helps me. But I'm not brave at all. I'm just plain confused and lonely and scared."

THE WINTER DAYS MOVED ALMOST ARTIFICIALLY TOWARD CHRIST- mas, and it did matter deeply that there was Eve, who could be counted on to understand her. Except for Louisa and Pete, every white person she cared about—outside of Miss Eliza Mackay in Savannah—seemed to have been swayed in some measure to the Confederate side. Miss Eliza was Christian enough to care for the tragedy of both factions of the bloody Civil War. Anne's middle daughter, Fanny, had hopelessly sided with her almost pathetic Corporal Buster Matthews, now also in Virginia with the Rebel forces. Selina, her youngest daughter, didn't disagree in so many words but seemed now to hold almost no belief in anything beyond God's power to keep her true love safe in the midst of whizzing rifle shot and bursting bombs. Selina's life revolved around her charm- ing, Louisiana-born Captain George Stubinger, still writing her spirited, sometimes humorous letters, although he was obviously in almost daily danger. Anne had begun to wait each night for the helpless, heartbreaking sound of Selina's weeping because she had chosen to wait to marry George until the war was over.

Because there were painful, personal thoughts Anne felt could only be written in her diary, each page was scrawled with the hope that no one anywhere would ever read what she was compelled to write.

December 1861

What manner of mother am I? George Stubinger's latest letter reported some three thousand Confederate boys killed or wounded in only one of the two battles in which he'd already fought! And why is it so hard for me even to admit that poor Fanny's beau, Buster Matthews, writes a rather good letter. De- spite our disagreement, Fanny goes on sharing Buster's letters with me, and I wish I could at least let her know I've noticed his fairly cultivated writing. He, too, is somewhere in Virginia, not far from a place called Sharpsburg. How can I not fall in line with these brave young men my daughters love so much? How can I still cling to my resentment of Buster Matthews when word could come at any moment that he has been wounded or killed? Above all, how can I not agree with my only son, whose coastal plantation roots seem far deeper than my own—far stronger. Now we know that sweet Fraser Demere, Annie's boy, has also reached Richmond, as willing and eager to lay down his young life as is John Couper, in a Cause I simply cannot embrace. Could even my best friend, my lover, my beloved John, help me explain myself to myself? Why, when so many others with my background can change their minds from Unionism to embrace the Rebel notion that somehow it *is* acceptable to God for us to own another human being? Why, when it would save me so much agony, can't I see their point of view? I ask myself over and over. Did my John suffer this pulling apart when, for love of me, he was forced to become a plantation owner? A slave owner? I'm a slave owner this minute! I still own the people, down on the coast, not yet sold by John Couper or James Hamilton. I live in a splendid house partially bought with the proceeds of the sale of those people. I still own Eve and June and Big Boy and Mina, and all the while Eve begs me never to make her leave the security of my home. How is it possible to live as I live—a contradictory, stubborn old woman.

As had become Anne's almost daily custom, she found herself hurrying toward the Square to seek understanding and consolation from her friend Louisa Fletcher, who not only sympathized with her but agreed with Anne's loyalty to the Union. Hoping to calm her nerves a little so that she would not be a too difficult caller for Louisa, Anne took advantage of the pleasant December day and walked from her house to the Marietta Hotel. Still more panic arose in her when she realized that by the first of January 1862—soon— Louisa might be living temporarily in a spacious cottage with her married daughter and that they would no longer have easy access to the private talks Anne had come to depend on in the large, roomy hotel.

"You've come for help, Anne," Louisa said. "How I hope I can give it to you. I can tell by the terrible sadness in your eyes that something drove you here this morning."

"No, I'm ashamed of myself," Anne said, trying to smile. "Nothing special has happened, but I am such a bundle of contradictions some days, I can't be alone with myself. Will you think I'm completely crazy if I tell you there are times when I almost wish I could find an acceptable reason to change my thinking? I love my son so much, Louisa, I'm sure I'll die, too, if—if they kill him. And yet, I long so for our poor nation to remain one, I find any shred of news about a Union victory makes me feel hopeful. I shouldn't feel that way, should I? I'm a born Southerner. As are my children. Can you understand that I'm living with my very being torn in two?"

"You must believe I understand, Anne, or you wouldn't be here telling me this." Then, after a long, thoughtful pause, Louisa picked up a letter from the small table between their chairs. "I have a letter for you. I picked it up at the post office this morning and planned to bring it to your house before dinnertime." She handed the letter to Anne, then watched the expressive face closely as Anne scanned the elegant script on the envelope.

"Oh, Louisa, dear Louisa! I've been praying for a letter from my brother. I knew somehow you'd help me if I came to you today, but I had no idea of this!"

"You speak of it so seldom, but I'm sure, no matter how much you love your handsome house here, that you miss your Island far more than even I know."

Breaking the ornate seal on the letter, Anne said, "I do! I wake up some mornings and imagine I'm actually smelling that blessed, pungent marsh mud. May I read James's letter aloud to you, Louisa?"

"Of course you may, but do feel free to scan it yourself first."

"No! I don't want to read it alone."

Louisa frowned at the stark fear in Anne's eyes. "What is it, Anne? You look frightened and you haven't read a line yet."

"I'm frightened every time I open a letter from anyone these days. And James writes so seldom, there must be something wrong." Hands shaking, Anne smoothed the two pages over her knee and began to read aloud.

"My Esteemed Sister,

Since my time is, as usual, rather limited, I must tell you first that in spite of the chaos in our land this year, I am happy to report that Hopeton and the surrounding plantations will undoubtedly produce thriving crops.

However, everything I must write is not to be, alas, in such a cheerful vein. My own heart and that of my beloved wife, Caroline, are numb with grief and shock at the news just received from our eldest son's superior officer at Manassas Junction, Virginia."

Anne stopped reading, her chin trembling as Louisa could see her eyes dart ahead in the letter. Louisa went to her and threw both arms around her friend. "Something happened to your nephew Hamilton Couper, Anne? The fine young man who roomed with your son in Savannah? Don't feel you have to force yourself to read the remainder of the letter aloud. Just know I'm here with you. Oh, Anne, my sweet friend, I'm with you in all ways!"

"My God, Louisa! My God in heaven, it's—begun! These next lines in James's letter say that his handsome, brilliant son Hamilton wasn't killed in a battle. He died of typhoid fever sometime after he fought in the battle near Manassas—"

The bitter sound Anne made was neither a sob nor a laugh. Some ghastly, heart-tearing sound between the two, Louisa thought as she began to smooth Anne's only slightly graying hair in helpless, loving little gestures.

After a time, Anne whispered, "You always know, don't you, Louisa? Thank you for not saying a word. What is there to say? My poor brother. Is—is there anything harder than losing a child?"

Softly, Louisa said, "There's more to your brother's letter, Anne. Would you like me to read it to you?"

"Please."

"I believe you read all of page one. Here is what he says next."

"I seem to have lost my ability to think clearly. You know I allow a definite amount of time daily for making plans for the immediate future, but neither Caroline nor I can think ahead even for one day. We will have our son's body brought back to S. Simons for burial in the family plot at Christ Church, and if it appears that this area of the coast will be attacked, I do plan to move us to Troupville in southwestern Georgia for a measure of safety. The last time I was on St. Simons, there were seven or eight guns on the battery by Mr. Gould's lighthouse tower, two at the nearby Couper's Point battery, and five on neighboring Jekyll Island. It is estimated that there are about a thousand Confederate men on St. Simons and five hundred on Jekyll.

Our brother reports in a letter to me that he plans to move his family here to Hopeton soon, since there is now danger at your old home, Hamilton. Anne, I'm sure you'll want to know the end of William Audley's letter. He sends love and the promise of all their prayers for your safety there."

"Oh, Anne," Louisa said, "I can't think of a thing to say to you, but I'm so relieved you're here with me to learn this news. At least you can sense how much I care."

Chapter 62

LOUISA FLETCHER NOW SPENT MOST OF HER TIME IN the cottage Henry Greene Cole had provided for his family after his new manager took over at the Marietta Hotel. With Georgia and her two-year-old child in the house, too, Anne had very little time alone with Louisa. She walked there to spend a few minutes with her friend only when her agitated mood warranted it.

In her diary on Tuesday morning, April 15, 1862, Anne tried valiantly to substitute writing for a longed-for visit with Louisa. A letter from dear old Miss Eliza Mackay, which Pete had brought yesterday, filled her turbulent thoughts and heightened her unyielding anxiety, because each day might bring tragic news about either John Couper or her grandson, Fraser Demere, or—almost equally dreaded— some word of death or injury to Fanny's stubborn but oddly attentive Buster Matthews or Selina's intended, Captain George Stubinger. All were fighting in Virginia. How she would endure Selina's or Fanny's grief, should George or Buster be lost, Anne had no idea.

The news in Miss Eliza Mackay's letter, in the wavering handwriting of an ill old woman, was devastating. The letter was brief, because Miss Eliza was plainly not well, but each line stung like a whip's lash.

"I am not well enough for length," Miss Eliza wrote, "but my heart cries out for an understanding friend like you, Anne. Fort Pulaski, taken over some time ago by the Georgia Guards, has been bombarded with deadly new rifled cannon by the Union and recaptured. In the fighting, which deafened us all, two were killed. One was the sweet, cherished, only son of my best friend, Mark Browning. The boy was named Jonathan, and I am sending this posthaste to ask that you pray for Mark and for his wife, Caroline, both numb with grief and loss. Jonathan was married to a tender, sweet Cherokee girl named Mary, and they had a precious small son, Ben. I can write no more now except to beg your deeper understanding, since you also know the heartache of a war-torn, broken family. You see, Jonathan, like your son, John Couper, fought for the Confederate Cause, in which he believed wholly. So does his mother, Caroline, but his father, my longtime friend Mark, is a Unionist as are you and I."

Anne's own uneven, nervous scrawl in her diary blurred as her eyes filled with tears when she tried to pray for Mark Browning, for his wife, Caroline. For Mary, the little Indian girl she'd come to love during visits to Miss Eliza Mackay. No words formed, even in her heart, even though praying was less and less a trial since her own spirit had become almost helpless, or so it seemed, each time she tried to ask God to protect John Couper and her beloved grandson, Fraser Demere.

"I'm determined," Anne wrote in finishing the diary entry for April 15, "not to fill these pages with gloom, and the only way I know not to do that these shadowy days is to hope for the best and try for a real visit with Louisa Fletcher. I know she often takes charge of Georgia's little girl, Mary Warren, so maybe I'll find her alone watching the child today. Two-year-olds don't sleep nearly often enough, but maybe I'll be lucky. I can hope to sit with Louisa while the pretty little girl takes her nap. It was so good back in the days when Louisa and I could always find time just to be together in any of a number of rooms at the Marietta Hotel. Alas, as with so much else of a happy, daily nature, those times are gone, too, and heaven knows how long it will take methodical Dix Fletcher to finish building their new home at Woodlawn, the small farm they own in the country, since he insists on doing the work himself. Actually, I have a secret hope that once the house at Woodlawn is completed, Louisa, who much prefers to be in the city, can visit with me for a week or more at a time right here in my own treasured place."

HAVING CONFIDED THIS HOPE TO HERSELF, ANNE THOUGHT HER heart felt a bit lighter. In spite of the sorrow shared by Miss Eliza Mackay over the useless death of Mark Browning's fine son, Jonathan, there was a slight spring in Anne's step as she headed toward the Cole cottage on Washington, within walking distance of her Marietta house.

"Anne, my dear," Louisa said as she welcomed her at the Coles' cottage door. "I can't believe our good fortune! Mary Warren has been bathed, played with by her grandmother, fed, and tucked in bed to sleep—dare I hope—through a good long visit with you. I've so much to tell!"

"This is almost too good to be true," Anne said, laying aside her hat and gloves. "How I needed to be with you today!" Seated in a rocker across from the one she knew was Louisa's favorite, Anne plunged into the sorrowful news of Jonathan Browning's death during the Northern taking of Fort Pulaski. Then, after just the right amount of sensitive commiseration, Louisa began her story of which, wonder of wonders, Anne had heard nothing.

"I predict what I'm about to tell you will become one of the most unusual episodes of the whole war. I wish I knew how it will all end. I don't—no one does. The last I heard, the chase is still going on."

On the edge of her chair, Anne asked, "What chase, Louisa? You're so excited over whatever it is that's happened, you haven't even told me what it's all about.

"Twenty or so Northern soldiers, a group headed by a Secret

Service man named James Andrews, appear to have actually stolen the South's splendid locomotive called The General!"

Anne gasped. "Stolen a—*locomotive*, Louisa?"

"They did it right here in Marietta, too! At least, it seems they boarded the train here on the morning of April 12, three days ago, and pretending not even to know each other, rode as ordinary passengers as far north as Big Shanty, where—now listen carefully, Anne—they uncoupled The General, its tender and two boxcars, while the Confederate train crew was off the train having breakfast. I won't know any more details until my son-in-law comes home for his dinner in a little while, but I'm sure—I feel it in my bones—that those brave Yankee men were able to shake their pursurers. You see, Anne, the train's conductor, a Mr. Fuller, and several other Rebels gave chase—would you believe on foot and in a railroad handcar?" Louisa laughed. "They'll never succeed in stopping Northern men who have that kind of audacity!"

"Louisa, for goodness' sake, tell me more about this amazing feat."

"Well, as I said, after boarding the train here, the Unionists actually confiscated the locomotive and the cars at Big Shanty and were smart enough, Henry Greene Cole declared with his wise chuckle, to head north from there toward Chattanooga, Tennessee, the better to cut off Confederate supplies. And since there's no telegraph office at Big Shanty, which is some seven miles north of Marietta, there was no way for word to travel with news of such a daring feat." The smile left Louisa's face. "Forgive me, please! I know the tragic news in Miss Eliza Mackay's letter upset you, Anne, and that you're in no mood to laugh at the futility of this wild Southern pursuit of a huge locomotive. But I know in my heart that you're as strong in your belief in the Union as Dix and Henry Cole and I. It is good news for our side that these men performed such a feat, and I simply had to tell you about it."

"Don't worry that you told me, Louisa. It is indeed a marvelous story, and I'll be eager to know how it all comes out. It's just that my own contradictory thoughts go on plaguing me. Those Northern raiders, brave as they are, were making every effort to cut off supplies, some of which my son might have needed. May need now up in Virginia. My dear grandson, Fraser Demere, too. I know they have to cut off supplies to the Confederates, but as much as I believe in restoring the Union, my son and grandson are in the Rebel Army! You'll undoubtedly have to put up with far more chaos in me in the future, Louisa. Can you bear it? My heart fights my head. My head fights my heart. I keep myself torn in two."

Anne was so distraught with worry over John Couper and Fraser that she finally asked Louisa to stop trying to keep her current on the dragged-out attempts to capture and punish the men led by the daring Andrews. His flamboyant plan to steal a train had failed near Ringgold, Georgia, just south of Chattanooga, when The General ran out of wood and stopped, forcing the Yankee raiders to flee into the nearby woods. Although Anne had no curiosity about the details, Louisa added that some had escaped, but most of the twenty-two raiders were captured within weeks and taken to prison in Chattanooga.

WHILE THE FORMERLY QUIET TOWN OF MARIETTA WAS CHAOTIC with all manner of war work and with evidently little or nothing on anyone's mind but the shock and surprise of the daring theft of The General, Anne received one of the hardest blows of all. For years, beneath any turmoil or trouble in her life had run the sure knowledge that her treasured longtime friend Miss Eliza Mackay was in Savannah—always ready and waiting with welcoming love and sound, solid advice. Then, early in July, a letter came from Anne's sister-in-law Frances Anne Wylly Fraser, which left her painfully bereft. It was good to hear from Frances Anne because the two friends always allowed too much time to pass between letters. But Anne found it hard to believe the vast emptiness already settling inside her when she learned that Miss Eliza Mackay had died June 13.

"Now that I'm living in Savannah," Frances Anne had written, "I of course attended the services for our beloved friend Miss Eliza. Anne, we must both pray for everyone—and the number is large— who will miss her touch on their lives no matter how seldom they saw her. Just last week as I was sitting by her bed in the Mackay house on East Broughton Street, she told me how often she prayed for everyone who had been driven from their homes all along the southern coast. Miss Eliza will go on praying for us all. We can be sure of that, and it is very sad, Anne, that because of the Yankee forays up and down the coast between St. Simons Island and Savannah, almost everyone has been driven out."

A WEEK OR SO INTO THE MONTH OF SEPTEMBER 1862, JOHN Couper, now eager and waiting with his regiment for battle near Sharpsburg, Maryland, very near the Virginia border, surprised them all at his mother's house in Marietta by predicting in a letter that the Confederacy would never risk the enemy's freeing the intrepid Andrews and his fellow raiders at Chattanooga. He was right, because soon Henry Greene Cole, who had become friends with Anne mainly because he was impressed that she, a Southerner, had the courage to believe in the Union, informed her that the Union soldiers, by then known as the Andrews Raiders, were being held in quarters out of reach of their own people in Atlanta. Indeed, it was Mr. Cole who found out that the first Yankee raider to be hanged in Atlanta was James Andrews himself, the man Cole called "the bravest of us all, who had given his life in God's own Cause on June 7."

Fanny, packing to join the staff of a Confederate hospital opening at Ringgold, gave her mother an almost impudent look when she heard what Mr. Cole had said. "Excuse me, Mama, it isn't that I'm not sorry when even a Northerner is hanged, but I can't help being amused that every Unionist, including the ones in my own family, are so sure God is on the Union side."

When Pete told Dr. Sam how her usually quiet sister Fanny had sassed their mother, she shouted, "I flared, Sam! I *more* than flared. Mother has enough worrying her. Fanny made me wish I dared shake the dickens out of her right then and there!"

Chapter 63

CICADAS, PAUL DEMERE THOUGHT IRRELEVANTLY, didn't sing so steadily as a rule until after sundown. It wasn't quite sundown now, but they were singing—rasping steadily—on this late September evening, almost making harmony behind the sturdy clump of his galloping horse. Paul, now forty-two, was heading as fast as he could go along the sand and clay road, through a stand of tall pines and low, scattered palmettos, toward his farm just outside the little town of Jasper, Florida. He was obeying the last request he'd had from his only son by Annie Fraser the day in 1861 the boy boarded a train for Jacksonville, bound for Richmond. The day his cheerful, sensitive son, Fraser, left for war at not quite twenty, his cheeks rosy with health, his young, brave heart high with confidence that his revered South would "win this thing in just a matter of weeks." And then, Fraser had made his urgent request, the request Paul was doing his best to fulfill now. "One thing you must promise me, Papa," Fraser had urged. "I'm going to war with great faith in the rightness of our side. We will win because it is God's Cause. God's noble Cause. But it is war, and death does strike. Should you receive notice of my death, promise me on your honor not to read the notification until you're with

Miss Jessie. I don't want the burden of thinking you might read it alone."

Paul had promised, and in his shirt pocket he carried an official-looking letter from a Major Brown of the Confederate Army in Richmond, which he was certain held tragic news.

JESSIE KNEW, OF COURSE, THAT ON EACH RIDE TO TOWN, PAUL visited the Jasper post office. She knew he had been there today, but there was no way she could have known that the dreaded letter had come. Still, the look on her plain but expressive face showed that she'd been waiting, watching, in order to be there because he would need her as he'd never needed her before today.

Jessie could tell he had galloped his horse hard, but his slow, almost feeble appearance as he dragged himself up their front steps told her only that something horrible had happened.

As usual, when he reached the porch where she stood, he nodded a greeting, then said, "I—I need you, Jessie. I'm keeping a promise to Fraser by hurrying straight to you before I read this." From his shirt pocket he took out the letter and handed it to her.

Jessie glanced at the envelope and stood, holding it. "This is addressed to you, Paul dear."

"I know," he said. "But I promised Fraser I wouldn't read a letter like this without you beside me."

"You promised Fraser?"

"Yes. The day he left. It was July 1861, over a year ago. Why do you think he asked that, Jessie?"

For Jessie, it suddenly fit together. "He asked because he gave me instructions for you the night before he took the train. I have a promise to keep too."

"Fraser asked you to promise something—special?"

"It was more than asking. He begged me to tell him I'd do exactly as he said. There's a sealed letter from him to you, Paul, in the tray of his big trunk upstairs in his bedroom."

Paul stared at her. "My son got you to promise something he

didn't even mention to me? I know how devoted he was to you, Jessie, but—"

"Paul! How devoted he—*was?* Are you sure this letter is to inform you that—that our boy is—dead?"

"Yes. I somehow know." Tears streamed down his cheeks. "I also know you loved him enough to call him *our* boy, too." On a hard sob, he asked, "Come with me, Jessie. Come upstairs to Fraser's room and let's find his letter together."

They climbed the stair to the room young Fraser used, and within no time Jessie had found the sealed letter to the boy's father.

"I brought Major Brown's letter upstairs with us," she said, breaking the seal on the letter. "It was written near Sharpsburg, Maryland, dated September 24, 1862. Sit down here on the bed beside me, Paul. Would you rather know what Major Brown has written, or shall I read Fraser's special letter to you first?"

"Jessie, oh, Jessie, I *know* he's dead! I know it, but I can't bear to hear it yet! Please read my boy's note to me first."

"All right, Paul. This is what Fraser wrote."

"My dear Papa . . .

When you take me to board my train, I will beg you to promise to carry out a special request. Miss Jessie has already granted the request I made of her. For many years I have thought that my grandmother, Anne Fraser, and you have not always been close friends. Thanks to Aunt Pete and Uncle John Couper Fraser, I no longer believe this to be true. I felt sure when I was in Marietta that Grandmother Anne had discovered how much she had misunderstood you in the past. I now pray that you will send Miss Jessie to Marietta to tell my grandmother if you learn that I am dead. I do not expect to die, because I am going in full faith that this is God's Cause and a noble one—fighting for the freedom of my native land, the Confederacy. Men do die in war, though, from disease and guns. So Grandmother will not experience the pain alone of learning of my death, I would rest so much easier if Miss Jessie, my greathearted stepmother, was with her. Along with us, my grandmother has endured the loss of my mother and my grandfather, Lieutenant John Fraser, so adored by her, and so I want to cushion any further loss a bit if possible. My beloved stepmother, Miss Jessie, is one of the world's strongest, most sensitive women. Please know how deeply I love you both and trust you to grant my request.

> Signed, your loving son,
> John Fraser Demere."

For several minutes Paul Demere paced the room, fighting back hard, racking sobs. Then he stopped where Jessie still sat on Fraser's bed. "You told the boy you'd go to Marietta?"

"Yes. I'll go gladly. It may help Anne Fraser a little to see for herself how much I loved her grandson, too."

"Jessie?"

"Yes, Paul?"

"It certainly helps me that you know how much I loved Fraser's mother, Annie. From my heart, I thank you for that."

"I've always known, Paul, and I love you so much that what's left for me makes me happy every hour of my life." She waited a moment, then asked, "Don't you want me to read the major's letter to you about our dear boy?"

"No. Just glance at it, please, and let me know if he—suffered a long time before he died."

Jessie scanned the single page quickly, then, with her hand on Paul's, she whispered, "He didn't suffer at all. It was almost instantaneous. A bullet in his head. They don't think he even realized what happened."

WHEN EVE KNOCKED AT ANNE'S BEDROOM DOOR EARLIER THAN usual on Saturday morning, September 27, Anne's first impulse was to be as cross as she felt. Instead, she checked herself and acted on her newly made vow to remember that she wasn't the only anxious, worried mother and grandmother in the country. North and South, women—sweethearts, wives, sisters, grandmothers, aunts—were all suffering the singular pain always endured by those who stay at home when there is war. Trying her best to keep her new vow not to fall into a pit of self-pity had helped some. When she read letters from John Couper and Fraser Demere in which they reported their safety and good health, Anne found a special solace until she realized that anything might have happened to either of them while the letter was en route to her.

There was little any woman could do about thoughts like these, but at least she could try outwardly to fulfill her mission as mother to her girls—especially in the letters she kept writing to poor, misguided Fanny, now in Ringgold on the nursing staff of a Confederate hospital. Still, everything she did was *outward*. Too much of the time she felt as though she was playing a role, not fulfilling a mission.

Her determination held, though, even with Eve, who had barged in just when Anne had finally fallen into a deep sleep.

"Mornin', Miss Anne," Eve said too cheerfully as she jerked open the draperies to let in the now familiar slant of clean, white light—light that Anne prayed never to take for granted but sometimes was too worried to notice. "I got a surprise for you an' that the reason I'm here so early on a Saturday morning. Looky here!" Eve held out a letter.

Anne grabbed the envelope and clasped it to her breast because it was from John Couper. Then she demanded to know why Eve had waited all night to give it to her, since the train bringing mail from Virginia always came at night.

"June an' Big Boy jus' got it when the pos' office opened today. I waited as long as I could to give it to you 'cause you ain't been sleepin' at night. You want I should get the water fo' yo' bath now?"

"No! Don't get anything. I'm sure you've looked and know already this is from John Couper, so stay with me. We'll read it together. Sit down here on the bed and I'll read it aloud."

"Yes'm."

"Do you have to go on saying 'yes'm'? I don't feel as though I own you anymore. Can't you just say all right?"

Eve grinned at her. "All right, Miss Anne."

"It's short. Less than one page. And dated September 16, 1862."

"Dearest Mama and Girls . . .

Just a line or two so I can go to sleep tonight with a clear conscience. We go into battle tomorrow, as far as we know, and I need my sleep, but there is good news. I have just learned that my nephew, young Fraser Demere, is also to report for duty here in Sharpsburg, and since he is now a sergeant, I have permission to meet with him at the first opportunity after we have licked the tar out of those Yanks! It will be so good to see him again, and I will write as soon as I can and let you know exactly how Fraser is faring. My love to all of you. I have just watered and groomed my faithful horse, Bay Boy, and will probably be asleep before I'm settled on my pallet. More soon.

Your excited and confident son,
John Couper Fraser

P.S. If several days pass with no word from me, don't worry. It will only mean we are traveling and busy as frisky bees."

Anne took a deep, trembling breath. "Oh, Eve, Eve, it's good that John Couper and dear Fraser will have a chance to see each other, but dear God, hear us plead for their safety. Take care of them both, please!"

ANOTHER LETTER, THIS ONE FROM JESSIE DEMERE, REACHED Anne in Marietta before fresh word from either John Couper or Fraser Demere.

"A letter from Jessie Demere!" Pete said excitedly when she handed her mother the letter from Florida. "I think it's wonderful that she wrote to you. I know you never liked her, because she was the woman Paul married when Annie died. Can't you see this is going to help you over that hurdle, Mama? And goodness knows you've got enough hurdles to get over these days!"

"Stop spouting, Pete, and I'll see what Paul's wife has to say."

"Are you scared it might be bad news about Fraser?"

"Not really. Somehow I think Paul would have written anything like that to me. Hush and I'll read it. Then we'll know. It's not long," Anne said, unfolding the letter. "And I'll thank you, Pete, not to give me a lecture about my attitude toward either Jessie Demere or Paul. At least not now. The letter's dated only a week ago from Jasper, Florida. 'Dear Mrs. Fraser . . . This may seem impertinent and rude to you, but my husband and I came to the decision together, and there is nothing courteous to do but let you know at once that by the time you receive this, I will be on a train headed for Marietta. When I tell you why I must pay you this visit, I'm sure from what sweet Fraser has told me about you that you will agree Paul and I made the right decision. I should arrive in Marietta on October 8, which I believe is Wednesday. Most sincerely, Jessie Sinclair Demere.' Pete! *Wednesday?*"

"This is Tuesday, Mama. She'll be here tomorrow!"

"I know it's tomorrow. Go get Eve. Tell her I need my hair washed and that we'll put Mrs. Demere in Fanny's room. Eve will need to make the bed with fresh linens and dust the room well. Big Boy should also beat the carpet."

Chapter 64

WHEN WEDNESDAY, OCTOBER 8, ARRIVED, PERFECT
autumn weather came with it. An even clearer, whiter
light filtered down over the Marietta house Anne
loved so dearly, with just enough pale gold in the air
to remind her of how John always laughed because
she vowed the very air on St. Simons Island turned
gold in the fall. She smiled at the thought, despite her
minute-by-minute worry that Jessie Demere would be
making the long, hard trip from Florida only because
she had bad, maybe even tragic, news about blessed
Fraser. Sadness, worry, hammering anxiety, had come
to be like a steady drumbeat in Anne's head, so for
the instant it lasted, she welcomed her almost involuntary smile.

Pete and Selina were dressed and ready to meet
Jessie's train at the depot in town when Sam, who
insisted on escorting them, stopped his well-main-
tained though secondhand buggy in the lane before
the welcoming, shining house.

"You really didn't need to come with me, Selina,"
Pete said, turning to face her sister riding alone in the
upholstered buggy seat because Pete, as always, was
sitting up front with Sam. "You could have stayed at
home with Mama to keep her company, and you
didn't have to get dressed up to ride into town. I've
told all of you, no one ever needs to dress up for Miss

Jessie Demere. One reason I liked her so much is that she's so down-to-earth and natural—not dressy or fussy about anything. Sam, have you noticed how no one ever listens to me in our family?"

Sam's good laugh had its usual effect on Pete. Her heart sang because she loved his laughter, and it usually meant that he was truly sober. She had sniffed rather shamelessly when she kissed him first thing. He hadn't had one drop to drink. "No one listens to you, Pete?" he asked, all smiles. "Everyone listens to you because—"

"Because it's the only way to get you to shut up, Pete. And stop trying to boss us around," Selina snapped.

"Sam," Pete demanded, "tell her I don't boss anyone!"

"I'm all the way out of this little female fracas," he teased, "except to declare that you both look utterly charming this morning."

"Flattery will get you anywhere you want to go," Pete said.

"Well! If that's true, my gorgeous Pete, I want to go to the altar at St. James Episcopal Church within the hour and marry you."

"How in the name of heaven can you think of a new way to ask me to be your wife—every day? You do, you know. I don't even have to keep track anymore. I just know you'll think of something." Scooting closer to Sam on the driver's seat, she laughed. "And don't you dare stop. Don't miss a single day! Do you hear me?"

"If that isn't bossing, I never heard it," Selina snorted.

"Will it make you homesick for Florida having Jessie here?" Pete asked, her pert, handsome red head cocked to hide how much she cared about his answer.

"What if I do get homesick for Florida?" he joked.

"I'm not being funny," Pete answered sharply. "And don't think you can hide it from me if you are, because I'll know."

From the passenger seat Selina said, her voice suddenly sad, "We're all being so silly and really quite unfunny because we're all worried to death about the reason Miss Jessie's coming all this way.

It's dreadful news she's bringing. I just know it is. Eve knows it, too. She has one of her knowings. She told me this morning. Why, when Mama isn't even here, do we have to try to be funny and pretend we think Mrs. Demere's just making that ghastly trip up here to be sociable?"

On a sudden, deep sigh, Sam said, "I don't know, Selina. People just do dumb things sometimes."

Selina decided to stay downtown in case there was mail at the post office for anyone, but especially for her from her beloved George Stubinger. "I don't even know Miss Jessie yet and I'm sure Mama won't mind," she told Pete and Sam as she headed for the post office and they for the depot.

SAM AND JESSIE GREETED EACH OTHER WARMLY AFTER THEIR long separation, and a short time later, in the handsome parlor of Anne's house, Pete presented her mother to Jessie Demere.

The two women—Anne of medium height, older, and Jessie even taller than Pete, in her forties, with dark, penetrating eyes and black hair—stood looking at each other in silence for several seconds.

When Anne offered a chair to Jessie, Pete watched their guest for some indication of how she might direct their conversation. Jessie gave her no clue. Instead, she smiled at Pete's mother, held out both her hands, and made no effort to hide the fact that tears had begun to stream down her somewhat severe features. Severe? Pete surprised herself for even having thought of such a word to describe good, kind, likable Jessie Demere's face. But she had thought of it and seeing Jessie there, away from her own parlor and in strange surroundings, Pete did think Jessie's angular face looked almost severe—until her smile came.

"All the way here on that horrible stage and then on the train, I tried to think what I could possibly say to you when finally you and I were face-to-face, Mrs. Fraser."

Pete knew that her mother was masterly at being direct, but

until she saw the flinty look in the pale, pale blue eyes, she also knew that in all the years of her life, she had never seen Mama look *hard*—even cruel. Pete was sure that every one of her sisters—maybe even John Couper, too, although he'd been gone so much as an adult—knew that Annie's death when little Fraser Demere was born had somehow enshrined Annie in their mother's heart. Or maybe, Pete thought, recognizing her own jealousy of her dead sister for the first time, the sisters decided that Annie, because of her ethereal beauty and position as the firstborn, had always been enshrined almost as a Greek goddess whose very soul was considered celestial.

"And can't you remember what you decided to say to me when we first met, Mrs. Demere?" Mama was twisting the knife of her longtime resentment of poor, defenseless Jessie. Pete felt almost ashamed of her mother but struggled the harder to identify with her parent—to understand how it had hurt her for Paul to marry another woman so soon after Annie died.

"Please sit down, Jessie," Pete said, her voice too loud, her words as explosive in the quiet room as they were harmless, merely polite, in themselves. "One of Mama's best friends is her personal servant, Eve. Eve's going to serve us lemonade and probably Mina's delicious cinnamon buns anytime now. You'll like Eve and our cook, Mina."

That stupid spiel of hers, Pete knew at once, would only make things worse, more awkward. What on earth was she thinking of, suddenly blabbing about Mina and Eve? What must Mama be thinking of me? What must Mama be thinking, question mark! Why can't I just keep quiet when there's a difficult subject afoot? Sam's favorite method of hushing her was to remind her that she must undergo some kind of violent physical spasm if a spell of silence filled a room—even for a minute or so. Dr. Sam! Sam to her rescue again. Good old Sam. She could change the subject and talk about him. Jessie knew and liked and respected Sam from the years in Florida when he was the Demere family doctor.

"Dr. Sam, Jessie! I'm sure you're dying to know all about how Sam's doing in his Marietta practice."

Clearly distracted by Pete's irrelevant remark, Jessie turned to her, tried hard for a pleasant smile, glanced apprehensively back at Pete's mother, then said, "Why, yes, Pete. As soon as your mother and I have something resembling a—a friendly exchange, I'd be ever so glad to know all about Sam."

"I'm not really as dumb as that sounded," Pete said, her flushed face showing how embarrassed she felt for talking too much. "I will be thirty-seven years old next month. Wouldn't you think I'd know better? I—I've just been so eager for you to get here, Jessie, and you can be sure I'll do all I can to make you feel welcome, just as you did for me when I visited at your farm in Florida." As though she were seven instead of thirty-seven, Pete turned to her mother. "Mama?" she asked, almost pleading. "Mama, I think Jessie might like to freshen up after that long, cramped trip. Shall I show her upstairs to her room before Eve serves us?"

Mama, like Jessie and Pete, had been standing in the middle of the parlor. Without a word, she buried her face in her hands for an instant, then rushed to throw both arms around Jessie. Mama was not very tall, so she had to reach up to Jessie's shoulder where, with no explanation, she began to sob.

In seconds, as though she'd just managed to realign her own emotions, Jessie was embracing Mama, both women weeping together, clinging to each other.

When Eve appeared at the door bearing a large, laden silver tray, Pete shushed her with a finger over her own mouth. Have I just watched a miracle happen, Pete asked herself? Poor Eve, that tray must be heavy, but anyway, she's my witness. She witnessed the miracle, too.

A QUIET, SAD PEACE ANNE DID NOT EVEN TRY TO UNDERSTAND seemed to flood her very being as she still stood with her face buried in Jessie Demere's shoulder. She was no longer sobbing. Jessie was quiet, too, but they went on clinging to each other as though both finally realized why. Anne supposed Pete was watching them. Probably Eve, too, by now. More important, though, with all her heart Anne longed to say the right words to this tall, warmhearted, sympathetic stranger named Jessie Demere, the woman whose very name had pinched not only the courtesy but the humanity from Anne's heart for all these bitter, misguided years.

Anne tried to speak. No words came.

"I'm—sorry, Mrs. Fraser," Jessie whispered as the two still embraced, but without the former desperation. "Oh, because of so many reasons, I'm sorry to the depth of my being!"

Slowly, Anne disengaged her own arms and stepped back a little to get a better look at Jessie's plain but appealing face. "In the name of all that's good and holy, Mrs. Demere, *I* am the one who should be sorry." She touched Jessie's arm. "He—he's—dead, isn't he? My sweet, rosy-cheeked, tender Fraser is dead, isn't he?"

"It was his idea that I come here myself, Mrs. Fraser."

"My grandson, Fraser, sent you?"

"Exactly as if he helped me into that stagecoach in Florida and off the train here at the Marietta depot. I'm here because Fraser begged me to come. The night before he took his train to Virginia, he got me to promise that I wouldn't allow you to learn of his death —alone."

No one could eat even one bit of Mina's tasty buns Eve had served, but they sipped lemonade and seated themselves about the room, with no one needing the formality of offering a chair. In fact, Anne was grateful that Jessie seemed to be so comfortable with her and had pulled her chair close enough to touch Anne's hand now and then as slowly and carefully she told them all—Eve included— every word about Fraser's leaving. She read the contents of his letter to his father, and finally—with Anne fighting more tears and Pete sobbing from her own grief—they learned that the boy had been shot in the head and did not suffer at all.

"But Jessie, Pete, Eve, I'll never see that gentle, dear boy again on this earth! I guess no one ever learns how to accept those things as coming from God's hand. Does anyone ever—learn?"

"I lost my whole family," Jessie said after a time, "in a ferryboat accident not far from my parents' home in Nova Scotia. But I don't think anyone ever learns to accept such tragedies as coming from God, because I don't think God sends them."

Anne stared at Jessie. "Then who does send them?"

"Our precious Fraser was killed in a war men chose to fight. God knew there would always be wars because He knows man's nature. But *He* didn't send this ghastly war. Men who hold their own opinions in higher esteem than human life declared this war. 'God is love' according to the Bible. If He is love, Mrs. Fraser, how could He send something so terrible to shatter the lives of the human race He loves? He didn't send this war, but if we allow it, He'll make some use of it."

"Who told you that, Mrs. Demere?"

After a time, Jessie said, "I honestly don't know. Maybe it just came to me now. Why do you ask?"

"Because I'm almost positive a dear, dear friend of ours, Miss Eliza Mackay, said almost the same thing to me once. You and Miss Eliza didn't know each other, did you, Mrs. Demere?"

"No. I'm sure my husband knew of her. I believe there are Demeres in Savannah, and didn't Mrs. Mackay live there?"

"Yes, she did," Pete said. "But it wouldn't surprise me if God Himself told Miss Eliza and Jessie the same thing. I doubt that He ever contradicts Himself."

"But how could anything useful ever come out of such a tragedy as the sudden death of a tender, sweet boy like our Fraser?" Anne asked. "And what did you mean when you said God will bring something useful out of such a tragedy if we let Him? How can we *let* God?"

"I know only that I am almost forced to keep remembering *not* to allow myself to get comfortable in a mass of self-pity. That's at least one thing I can do."

Anne's shoulders slumped, then straightened as she looked directly at Jessie Demere. "Thank you, Mrs. Demere. Oh, thank you! Even I can do that much. I can also try to tell you that even my own adored daughter, Fraser's mother, could not have reared the boy to be more of a peacemaker than he was—*is.* Fraser is with my

Annie again now. He—he isn't dead and he's making peace right here in this room today, isn't he?"

"Mrs. Fraser, yes! Oh, yes. It would help me still more if you gave me permission to call you Miss Anne. If you'd please, please call me Jessie. We've missed so much not knowing each other all this time. May I call you Miss Anne?"

"No, you may not," Anne said with a real smile. "I want you to call me Anne. Miss Anne makes me feel old. And does your forgiveness toward me really go far enough for you to let me call you Jessie? Does it?"

"There's no more need for you to be forgiven, Anne. We didn't even see each other for all these years, so how would you know that Paul Demere never stopped loving your Annie? Had you known that, you wouldn't have disliked me so much, I'm sure."

Pete jumped as though something had scared her. "Jessie! What a thing to say! You're the mother of Paul's six other children. How can you say he kept on loving my sister and even imply that he didn't love you?"

Jessie grinned. "I didn't imply that, Pete. In Paul's way and with every bit of room he had left in his basically kind, good heart, he loved me, too, as the mother of his children. But the poor man struggled all this time with his own emotions because Annie was his first love. And I think he made it through his days because somehow, although we never mentioned it, he knew that I knew he *couldn't* love me the way he loved her. I did know it, and because everyone told me, including Paul, that Fraser was just like her, I got through my days too. There's another Scripture in the Bible to which I go on clinging. I think it's somewhere in the book of Isaiah and it speaks of 'beauty for ashes.' That's very real to me. Beauty can come from ashes. What Paul has left to give me has made my life—beautiful. Beauty *does* come from ashes, if we give it time." She dabbed at her eyes. "You see, I loved Fraser as though he'd been my own."

Chapter 65

JESSIE DEMERE TOOK THE TRAIN BACK TOWARD Florida on October 11, allowing herself only two full days to rest after the long, strenuous trip up to Marietta. Anne couldn't remember two more meaningful days than those spent with the woman she had stupidly allowed herself to resent for so many years.

Toward the end of October 1862, the citizens of Marietta were sending clothes, towels, and bedding to the busy Confederate hospital at Ringgold, where Fanny was now head nurse. Until Jessie's visit with the sorrowful news that Anne's grandson had been killed in the bloody battle at Sharpsburg, Maryland, Anne had found one excuse or another not to take part in Marietta's Confederate war effort on behalf of the wounded soldiers there. But then Louisa Fletcher told her that the medical director from Knoxville was in Marietta, looking over buildings suitable to be used as local hospitals. After a pause, Louisa reminded Anne gently, but firmly, that suffering was suffering whether North or South. Ashamed, Anne weakened. After all, her own son could end up in any of the growing number of Confederate hospitals! Surely, John Couper's mother, no matter how strong her political convictions, could find time to collect and help Pete deliver bedding and clothes for other Confederate boys in need after the growing number of battles being fought. The weeks during which the war seemed distant, because no battles had yet been fought in Georgia, were coming to an end.

"The medical director told Dix yesterday, when he tore himself away from his hammer and nails and our new house at Woodlawn long enough to pay a short visit to Marietta, that they were expecting six to seven hundred sick and wounded soldiers in about a week! It doesn't have to mean that you and I do not support the Union Cause with all our hearts, Anne," Louisa said. "It means that God has given us a chance to show that we have found His great love abundant enough to cover everyone!"

As usual, Louisa was right and Pete was right, too, when she finally became an active participant in collecting bedding. "I can't help doing it, Mama," Pete said, throwing her cape around her shoulders before leaving the house in a heavy shower because she'd promised an elderly Marietta lady to pick up some sheets and blankets before noon that day. "The war is spreading, Mama, and no one believes an end is in sight. They're fighting or getting situated to fight in Tennessee, Mississippi, Kentucky, Louisiana, and, of course, they're fighting terribly in Virginia. Come with me, Mama. I need help, and Big Boy is ready to take us in the carriage to make our bedding collection. You won't get very wet."

On a deep sigh, Anne said, "What difference could it possibly make, Pete, if I do get wet? Some of this bedding might help your brother. It seems as though Jessie Demere's visit has freed me, but I'm not at all sure I like being freed. Hiding one's head in the sand can be quite convenient at times. Oh, and call upstairs for Selina. She's young and strong and will be a big help to us. Bedding can be heavy to carry. And wipe that impish grin off your face! I know Selina's probably just claiming to be a Unionist to please you and me. After all, George Stubinger is a captain in the Confederate Army. Selina lives and breathes that young man."

BY THE TIME PETE AND ANNE HAD DELIVERED THEIR HOSPITAL bedding, Selina, who had eagerly accepted their offer of a ride as far as the Marietta post office, was already home—soaking wet but so beside herself with excitement and worry, she seemed not even to realize how drenched she was. Anne and Pete found her in the front hall, dripping with rain and tears. In her hands she clutched an already crumpled, damp letter.

"You got it! Oh, Selina, you received your letter from George, didn't you?" her mother asked.

"Yes, yes! Mama, Pete, he's coming here! George has been wounded and is probably right now on a train heading for Marietta. Oh, Mama, you don't think he's horribly hurt, do you?"

"What a question to ask poor Mama!" Pete scolded. "Didn't he tell you in the letter?"

"Just that he's feeling very downhearted because the Confederate Army can't use him anymore."

"Then he must be really injured," Pete said.

"Let's not jump to any irrational conclusions, Pete," Anne said sharply. "Your sister has enough to worry about. I remember way back when your father was wounded near the St. Marys River while he was fighting for the British in their war against us early in the century. Dear old Mr. James Gould made a special trip to Cannon's Point to let us know John was hurt. It almost killed me! I let my imagination run wild. He had a rather bad arm wound, but not mortal at all. Selina, dear, you must get hold of yourself. Captain George will need you to be strong when he gets here. When do you think that will be?"

"He wrote to me from a Richmond hospital that they were relieving him of all duty. Would they let him leave the hospital if he's so terribly hurt they had to relieve him of duty, Mama? Don't you answer me, Pete! You always say too much."

"Well, I have only one question. Are you going to marry him when he does get here?" Pete asked.

"If I could figure a way to take our rector, the Reverend Benedict, to the railroad depot, I'd marry him the instant he sets foot on Marietta soil!"

"John Couper has already written to Pete that it wouldn't be wise for her to marry now because the economy is worse than it's been since 1857, and wartime is no time for a fancy, expensive church wedding anyway," their mother said.

"Mama, a fancy church wedding has stopped mattering at all to me! All I want is to know for sure that I'm finally George's wife." Then, Selina turned abruptly to Pete. "When were you thinking of marrying Dr. Sam, Pete? You didn't say one word to me about it. I'm your own sister! I'd certainly think you'd want me to be your maid of honor, especially since Fanny's off applying bandages in Ringgold. When George and I are married, I want you to be my maid of honor."

"This is no time for an argument," Anne said. "Just try to think straight, Selina. Didn't George give you any clue to when he might arrive in Marietta?"

Selina scanned the last page of his letter quickly. "Yes! Oh, Mama, there's so little time, but still such a long time to wait. He says he should be here sometime in the afternoon of November 24."

"That's day after tomorrow."

"Yes," Selina breathed. "But that's still nearly two whole days to wait!"

ON THE MORNING OF NOVEMBER 24, EVE AND JUNE WERE UP earlier than usual. Because it took June longer to bathe, shave, and dress these days, he was up before daylight, shuffling and clattering around their cabin.

June was a man of such regular habits, it always frightened Eve when he deviated even a tiny bit. "You all right, June?" she asked, sitting up in their bed to get a good look at him. "How come you up befo' daylight? You ain't plannin' to go to the depot with Big Boy an' Miss Selina, is you?"

"Co'se I ain't," the old man said, taking the time as he always did to give her a big, almost toothless smile and a kiss. "You done tol' me S'lina made it plain she gonna meet Cap'n George by herself. 'Cept for Big Boy to drive 'em in de carriage."

"Miss Anne, she don' like that one bit," Eve said, rubbing her eyes. "She thinks it ain't hospitable for the whole family not to be there to help Selina, since her man be so bad hurt he done got put outa de Army."

"What Miss Anne reckon Big Boy do wif all them bulgin' muscles if not to help Selina's man?"

Out of bed now, beginning to bathe, Eve answered, "We ain't none of us got any zact idea how bad Cap'n George be hurt."

"Dat lil thing, she been known to faint dead away when she upset 'bout somepin," June answered, using his sharp razor around his chin.

"Not this time!"

"What you mean, ole woman?"

"I ain't ole an' Selina she got too much of Miss Anne in her to faint when her man he needs her! Miss Anne, she always been a strong woman an' now she stronger than ever 'cause she done growed up. You wait an' see."

June rinsed the lather from his kind, brown face and toweled himself. "Eve? Ain't no time at all till we gonna see all kind of bad, bloody doins 'roun' this town. Might even one white gent'man fly into another white gent'man 'cause one's fo' the Union an' one's fo' keepin' you an' me in bonds."

"We ain't in no bonds! Tell me, what we do wifout Miss Anne an' John Couper to look after us? Someday Miss Anne kin pay me ef she's got the money to do it, but ain't no place I aim to go without her, so hush 'bout yo' bonds! You an' Big Boy bof be bad off wifout Miss Anne an' me, an' wherever Miss Anne is, I be too!" She pulled on a pair of clean stockings and slipped her feet into her shoes. "You been seein' too much of that Barber James Johnson lately. He puttin' troublin' ideas in yo' white head."

"You jus' talkin', Evie. You forgit you ole man got a sieve in his head. I kin listen this way an' that, but I always knows what to let go through that sieve an' why I let's it. Barber Johnson's my frien'. He needs me to talk to an' I needs him. This be one big, bloody war an' if it has somepin to do with the colored, the colored oughta sort out every idea 'bout it. Johnson, he dead sure Pres'dent Linkum, he gonna fix eberthing for eber nigger wif some kind of free-dom proclamation January 1 next year. I sift dat 'roun' an' 'roun'. I neber stops thinkin' when Barber Johnson is preachin' at me. I knows how he favors the United States, but I also knows he'd like to be right in the middle of eberthing helpin' the Yanks." June grinned broadly. "You knows, Evie, how proud Barber Johnson be dat him an' Mr. Henry Greene Cole be good friends. I got me a feelin' dat between 'em dey hatchin' somepin to help de Yanks on de sly."

"Well, you stay out of all that," Eve ordered. "We got us a good home wif good folks an' I don' want no boats rockin' no-where! Now, lemme make you some breakfus. By the time we eats, because she's spectin company, Miss Anne'll be up an' ready for her breakfus, too."

A FULL HALF HOUR BEFORE GEORGE STUBINGER'S TRAIN WAS even due to pull into the Marietta depot, Big Boy did his best to keep up with Miss Selina without her knowing it. She seemed bent on moving briskly from the wooden station itself, along the bag-gage platform as far as she'd been told the train would eventually stop, although there was still no train in sight, no whistle blowing. The gentle giant of a man knew he stood taller and had wider shoulders than other colored men waiting for their white folk to arrive. But he had to be especially careful since Selina had been determined to come alone except for him, and many whites thought white women needed special scrutiny out in town alone with a colored.

Of course, Big Boy knew well that Northern folk in Marietta had little reason to understand the easygoing whites and Negroes down on the Georgia coast, where both Selina and Big Boy had grown up. Even Captain George, before he went off to war, had taken the time to admonish Big Boy, however kindly, that he should never, never go out in town alone with Mrs. Fraser, Selina, or the other Fraser daughters. "It's just not safe for you, Big Boy," he'd said. "A lot of people, no matter how much they believe in the Union, don't like that. In times like these, it's wiser to be careful before trouble begins."

Big Boy remembered smiling at that remark, because his mentor, June, had trained him well for all the years since his boyhood, when he first reached St. Simons Island as the property of Anne's father, John Couper.

THRONGS OF PEOPLE FROM MARIETTA AND NEARBY PUSHED toward the noisy, grinding, steaming train when it finally slowed. Most of them, Selina had already learned as they all waited, worried and impatient, were meeting the wounded who, like her George, were heroes from the bloodiest fighting so far near Sharpsburg and Antietam Creek on the border dividing Maryland and Virginia. Some, she noticed as she strained to find George among the bandaged, battered young men, were limping, some were crawling, others were being carried from the coach steps as their families and friends waited to greet them. Arms and legs were set with crude, makeshift splints of wood and wire, and all bandages were blood-soaked and encrusted. Every dressing needed to be changed.

Over her shoulder in the direction she knew Big Boy waited at a proper distance, Selina called, "Not George! Big Boy, George can't be so hurt!"

"June, he keep 'mindin' me to tell you to be brabe, Miss Selina, so be brabe, you hear? Big Boy right here to help wif Cap'n George whatever shape he be in. Be brabe, Miss Selina, be brabe."

"I don't even see him! You're a giant, Big Boy. Stand on your tiptoes and help me find George. And stop telling me to be brave. I'm not brave, I'm scared. I'm so scared of what he might look like!"

"But Big Boy an' June an' Eve an' Mina, we all help wif Cap'n George. You see. Go on be scared. Don't be 'shamed. If you scared, be scared. Big Boy right here wif you."

The words were no sooner out of Big Boy's mouth than Selina, looking hard for George's dear brown head, the graceful, swinging gait, stood like a stone statue staring at the thin, bent, bearded man who might have been fifty years old as he struggled, one twisted leg in splints, to stand in the narrow train doorway, his sunken eyes hunting for Selina.

"Get him, Big Boy! Go up those steps and help George! He'll never get down those steep steps without you to help him. Big Boy! Hurry, hurry!"

"You reckon they let me go right up to the cap'n?"

"Who cares? I say go help him. My family owns you, so go, Big Boy. You promised to help me."

"Yes'm. But you got to promise to be brabe, like June say. Look at you, Miss Selina, white as June's head an' shakin' all over! *You gotta be brabe.*"

Without realizing it, she had begun to tremble from head to foot and to sob so loud, Mama would have been embarrassed. "Oh, yes! I know I have to be brave. And if you'll just help George, I will be. You'll see, Big Boy. From now on, I'll be as brave as any other woman in this noisy crowd."

SELINA AND BIG BOY KNEW AT THE SAME INSTANT, ONCE GEORGE was helped down the train steps and onto the ground, that he not only limped pathetically—each step tossed his emaciated body from one side to the other—but the long hours of sitting on the train had so stiffened him that Big Boy would have to carry him like a baby in his arms. To George's humiliation, Big Boy carried him and lifted him up onto the carriage seat.

Selina could hear herself prattling but could not stop her incessant talk. Not one plan had been made with Mama, with the Episcopal rector, the Reverend Benedict—with anyone—but all of life had been turned upside down since her first glimpse of the shattered, crippled, broken young man, and it seemed perfectly natural now to hear herself say, "Just as soon as you think you can stand long enough for the wedding ceremony, George, we'll be married at St.

James. And even though Mama's friend Mrs. Fletcher says he's a crosspatch about allowing anyone not an Episcopalian to share Communion at the altar, you are Episcopalian so I know the Reverend Benedict will change whatever plans he needs to change to marry us. Oh, my darling, there isn't any money for a special wedding dress, but I don't need one anyway. I don't even need a veil, George. I just need to be your wife, and how I've prayed that you're being truthful when you wrote to me that you did understand why I wanted to wait until all this dreadful war is over. Now I only want to be your wife! Isn't that right, Big Boy, don't I talk all the time about how dumb I was not to agree to marry George before he went to war?"

A pitying smile on his broad, brown face, Big Boy turned on his driver's seat to look at them. "You sure is talkin' all the time, Miss Selina, I knows that! It look like you'd let de cap'n get in a word."

"I thank you, Big Boy!" George laughed. "You do a much better job controlling her than I ever hope to do. But this word I must get in, Selina."

"Oh, darling George, please, yes. Talk, talk, talk!"

"Does this lecture on the Reverend Benedict and no need for a wedding veil mean you're actually going to marry me anytime soon?"

"Well, I thought about day after tomorrow, November 26, unless you don't feel up to it."

"I thought about tomorrow, November 25," George teased.

"Nothing they did to you in those horrible battles stopped your making jokes. I'm glad! Oh, I'm so glad. Mama always said one of the reasons she loves you so much is that you make her think of my papa and his sense of humor. She vows he could even laugh at himself back in the days when he was first learning how to be a planter."

"I may have a sense of humor like his, but I refuse to laugh at myself. I want to be praised. I demand to be praised. I'm a Confederate war hero. And even if you are Unionists at your house, except for that fine, patriotic Fanny, off in Ringgold caring for other Confederate heroes, I want to be praised—by you—for my valor." His almost merry laugh ran under his talk. "Selina, are you still a Union sympathizer after what they did to me?"

"Oh, George, I probably never was one! It's always easier to agree with Mother and Pete, but all I really think about is you. And even though your poor body is all bruised and your leg is in splints, at least you're alive and you've come back to me. And, the most important thing of all is that we're *going to be married*—right away!"

Chapter 66

It took some urging by her mother and Pete for Selina to wait the two days until November 26 to marry George.

"Just because you're finally going to tie the knot," Pete said in her no-nonsense way, "there's no reason you, Mama, and I should not have clean hair. Tomorrow, the day you've been plumping for, is just too soon. And I know it's only going to be a small wedding with family and the Reverend Benedict, Louisa Fletcher, her daughter Georgia, who'll be playing the organ, Henry Greene Cole, Sam, and Eve in attendance. But I want clean hair and it takes nearly all day for my hair to dry."

"I agreed, didn't I?" Selina snapped. "I don't like it, but I won't cause any trouble over it because it's going to be an enchanted day. I'd give almost anything if Fanny could be here, too, but under the circumstances, maybe it's best she can't get away from her hospital long enough. I hate this war for a million reasons! Thanks to the war, my own brother can't even give me away. What right has Mr. Henry Greene Cole to decide he's the one giving me away?"

"Because he happens to be available and kind enough to do it," Anne said. "Smile, Selina. In their wonderful hearts, both your brother and your papa are giving you in marriage, and as much as you and your Captain George love each other, what could possibly spoil your wedding day? I do thank you for thinking of Eve. That woman is walking two feet off the ground because you invited her as though she's a member of the family."

"Well, isn't she?" Pete wanted to know.

"To us, of course she is. But I'm glad so few people will be there, because I know none of the guests will be horrified that a colored person is sitting right in the regular pews with us instead of upstairs all by herself in the servants' balcony."

"You don't think Mina and her daughter will mind that they aren't invited, do you, Mama?" Selina asked.

"Oh, no. Mina's going to be too busy back here working on your fancy wedding cake, and poor Flonnie's so shy, she'd probably throw up if she had to walk into St. James Church." Anne laughed. "That wasn't very nice of me, was it? But I'm sure everything is being done just right and for all the right reasons. You're certainly not marrying George because you want a gorgeous wedding gown and a huge, expensive wedding. You're marrying him for the only reason anyone should dare take such a big step—love."

AS USUAL, WHEN EVE TURNED THE LATCH ON THE FRONT DOOR of their brick cabin, as she insisted on calling the snug brick house in which she and June lived on the Marietta property, she wakened her aging husband.

And, as usual, at the moment of awakening, June gave a loud, sleepy snort. "Who dere?"

"Who do you think it is, you old sleeping dog?" After she kissed him tenderly on his snow-white, wooly head, she twirled around the floor in a little dance that made her long, green-striped cotton skirt stand out in a circle. "June, it was a beautiful wedding and I'll remember it as long as I live on this earth!"

"Talk nigger talk, Evie," he grumbled. "You done been wif dem fancy white folk all afternoon, but you home wif me now. You ain't got Miss Anne tellin' you to talk dis way an' dat."

"I'll talk anyway I please, sir, and thank you for not scolding me. It just might take me a few minutes to come down off my puffy cloud where I been with all that beautiful music Miss Louisa's daughter, she make on that church organ."

"You feel lak a po' country girl from some coastal far-off Island, lak I say you would, wif all dem white folk dressed up in dere wedding finery?"

"No, I did not. I felt—beautiful too. Miss Anne told me I looked beautiful. I fix up her ole blue silk for her to wear an' she look beautiful too. Miss Anne an' me we bof still got our looks, June. Ain't nobody kin say we ain't. You so white in the head, you done forgot how quick dis weddin' done happen! You 'member lil Selina's Cap'n George he come home from de war all shot up? When he walks or try to, he limps so bad ebery step look lak he gonna tip ober! But he tipped right up to that altar and took his place 'longside Selina an' say all the right words after the preacher an' now they married. Miss Selina, she now goes by the name Mrs. George Stubinger, but oh, dat girl be happy!"

Shaking his head slowly, June mumbled, "My, my, my, my! Jus' think, Mausa John's lil girl he usta call Eena an' whirl 'roun' his head, she done growed up an' got herself a man. Evie, I wonder how Mausa John, he take all this?"

"If I knows Mausa John, he be laughin' 'cause his curly-haired Eena laughin' too. M-m-m! How she do love dat man, Cap'n George!"

His mind not at all on what Eve was saying, June asked, "You hab to sit all by yo'se'f in the gallery at de church, Evie?"

"I did not!"

"Where you sit at de weddin'?"

"Right beside Miss Anne downstairs in a white persons' pew. I be Miss Anne's friend."

He chuckled. "Yeah. When ain't no other white person lookin'."

"You tryin' to spoil my day, ole man?"

June chuckled again. "No, Evie. But when Aberham Linkum sign his Emancipation paper, my Evie she kin sit right up in de pulpit wif de preacher if she's got a mind to sit dere. You knows it be almost to the end of November? Just December to come an' go an' all us niggers be free! Free to do as we please."

"You been talkin' to Barber James Johnson agin."

"Co'se I has! Barber James my frien', too. An' he keep up on eberthing."

"Except common sense. You got more common sense in your lil finger, June, den Barber Johnson got in his whole head. He jus' so high-'n'-mighty 'cause he be a free person of color dat cuts Mister Henry Greene Cole's hair while dey talks together in whispers an' Mister Cole so rich an' strong fo' de Union, Barber Johnson, he think dat mean he knows it all too. It don't. His yellow skin gonna be as black as yours eben after dat Proclamation be signed by President Lincoln. Ain't no black slave an' no black free person of color gonna live any different than now, an' none of 'em gonna live as good as you an' me lives right today!"

ANNE, PERHAPS MORE THAN ANYONE ELSE IN TOWN, FELT FRESH panic when early in March 1863, the militia was called out and Cobb County members were sent to Atlanta with orders to head south for Savannah to protect the Georgia coast. James Hamilton Couper had written of the Yankee guns placed on St. Simons, but somehow, until this military action began to take place, Anne had not been too upset. Now, the thought of armed men and still more guns landing on her once quiet, peaceful St. Simons Island sent shivers up her spine. St. Simons, her birthplace, the birthplace of all her children, stretched its year-round greenness off the coast for laughter and living and family warmth and beauty, not for war.

Louisa Fletcher was right, of course, when she reminded Anne that the militia from Marietta was too poorly armed for violent action. The men carried mostly ancient pistols, knives, even wooden pikes—anything they thought might stop the invading Yankee soldiers. But to Anne, war was war and she hated everything about it. Young, unfulfilled lives were cut down foolishly. Husbands, sweethearts, brothers, sons, fathers, could be killed or at least horribly wounded even by the makeshift, handmade wooden pikes. But Southern tempers had flared in fresh rebellion at the signing of the Emancipation Proclamation, in effect now since January 1, 1863. True, Anne could see little or no consequences from it, either good or bad, in Marietta. And she and Eve made jokes together about the unlikely situation in which two ordinary women—one black, one white—could be such close friends that without fail one of them came every single morning to prepare bathwater and see to the proper arranging of the other's hair, the condition of her clothing. Then, as the cool spring turned into warm summer days, word came that the threat to the Georgia coast had not been as severe as feared, the militia returned, and life really didn't change much after Emancipation for Anne and her friend—no longer her slave—Eve.

The frustrating change in all their lives came from the absence of clothing in the stores and the steady decline in the kinds and amounts of foodstuffs they could buy. Worst of all were the high, high prices of food still available in the once plentifully stocked grocery stores in the Marietta Square.

"I am painfully aware," John Couper wrote to Pete in late March, "of your acute food shortage and, more troubling, your shortage of money to buy what is there. But don't shake this letter for enclosed currency, because there isn't any. I've not told you, wanting to save you worry, but my trusted, faithful horse, Bay Boy, was shot dead under me during the bloody fighting at Sharpsburg in September of last year. I have had to part with three hundred fifty dollars of my own money for a new mount because the Confederate Army is slow with compensation."

Pete, who did most of the usually meager food shopping, decided not to tell her mother there was no money, then thought better of it and let her know. She'd find out from someone in town anyway or begin to think Pete a little mad for bringing home such a pitiful supply of food from the stores. No wonder, Pete thought, that Confederate President Davis issued a proclamation in April in which he literally begged Southerners to plant only food crops instead of cotton and tobacco.

Selina, who would not have complained audibly for herself, fretted a lot because George Stubinger forgot himself and put his longing for a cup of real coffee into words.

"Nobody's doing anything to help anyone in this dreadful war," Selina said again and again. "I've never been the Unionist you and Pete are, Mama, but I think I'm less so now. Oh, I'm not one of these prickly Confederate women, either. But nothing's working for anyone. George all but gave his life for the Southern Cause, and what did it get him? A permanently crippled leg, and now there's no way to get him even a cup of weak coffee!"

ANNE AND LOUISA FLETCHER SAW SO LITTLE OF EACH OTHER, IT frightened Anne. Daily, she realized how she had come to depend on time with Louisa to preserve her own balance. What, she asked herself again and again, will I do when Dix Fletcher has their new house at Woodlawn in condition for them to move in? He'd proudly announced to Louisa that even with his piecemeal work, he hoped to have the main rooms ready by summer.

The only spot where Anne found any real peace or respite from the nagging worries of all their days, the only spot where she rested, especially after reading aloud to George in order to give Selina a variation in her daily routine, was the place she kept the old Cannon's Point rocker—her second-floor balcony with its view of Kennesaw Mountain. If there was even a slight breeze, she could catch it out there.

The rocker had been Papa's favorite when she was a child. It helped her to sit in it now. At times she went out onto the balcony for only a few minutes to collect her troubled thoughts. What difference had it made, indeed, that President Lincoln had issued a Proclamation freeing the slaves! Perhaps it had changed many things on St. Simons, where there were far more slaves than in north Georgia, but she doubted it. Her sister-in-law Frances Anne wrote that whites lived in fear of a slave uprising. So far as Anne knew, so far as she'd been able to find out from daily searching Mr.

Goodman's newspaper, the Confederacy had decreed the Proclamation of no importance whatever. The rebellious states mentioned in the document paid it no mind. But Anne remembered Louisa's reminding her that the courageous act of Lincoln's had roused sympathy for the North in both France and England—and most British people did love defaming slave owners.

Anne knew the Northern United States truly feared that Great Britain might soon recognize the Confederacy as a nation. Lincoln had at least stopped that, Louisa was right to keep reminding Anne. Today was May 3, 1863. The very next month would be June, and Louisa would surely be moving soon. How, Anne asked herself once more, will I live my days without seeing her? Louisa's strong faith in God had almost always helped Anne through her dark, despairing times. As Anne tried to face the tragic truth that her beautiful grandson, Fraser, lay dead in an unknown grave somewhere far from Georgia, Louisa reminded her in her definite way that young Fraser was really with his mother, Annie, in heaven. Of course, Louisa was right. But Anne was a grandmother, who seemed unable to attain lasting comfort without Louisa at her side.

Even with the Fletchers living on the outskirts of the city, she could have Big Boy drive her out to Woodlawn when her need became too great. Anne leaned her head back in Papa's old rocker and tried to give thanks.

Chapter 67

THE NEXT MORNING A LITTLE BEFORE TEN, SAM, BE-
cause no patients were due until afternoon, stood at
the front window of his medical office idly watching
the halfhearted drilling that seemed to take place all
day long in the Marietta Square.

Suddenly his attention was caught by the running
figure of a portly, unfamiliar man who, just before he
reached the open door of the telegraph office, caught
his boot and almost took a bad fall on the sidewalk.
The stranger limped heavily through the door and
disappeared inside the telegraph office, evidently intent on sending his message as quickly as possible.

Full of curiosity about the content of that message, Sam stood there rubbing his chin whiskers,
wondering if there was any subtle way he might find
out in case the stranger happened to be a Confederate. Almost everyone in Marietta knew Sam as a
Union sympathizer, knew he had been born in New
York. Those who didn't know for sure savored the
gossip that indeed he was a Unionist. Some of these,
he felt sure, were patients of his—if for no other
reason than their own curiosity about him.

Every day since he'd stood as Captain George
Stubinger's groomsman in November of last year, he
had tried and tried to find the real reason Pete still
refused to set their wedding date. That she loved him

he had no doubt. He was so genuinely fond of her mother, he somehow couldn't bring himself to blame her for Pete's reluctance. Long ago his attractive cottage had begun to feel unnaturally empty. Since Selina and George had married, Sam's own misery had grown. He'd been so sure that their standing together at the altar of St. James as matron of honor and groomsman would move Pete toward the longing to stand with him at the same altar as bride and groom. It did not.

Still standing at his office window peering at the open doorway of the telegraph office, he tried to put Pete's quixotic ways to one side and focus his curiosity on the unusual sight of the stranger, who even now was surely sending an urgent message. Urgent? The way the man had hurried, twisting his ankle in the process, must mean a real emergency. Why? The man was dressed in ordinary travel clothing. There was no sign of the military, either Northern or Southern, in his appearance. He was certainly too fat for active service with either Army.

As Sam stood at his window, wondering whether to make a run for the telegraph office to ask questions or to stay put in case a much-needed patient came by, he saw three other men rush from the telegraph office, each stopping a different person on the street to deliver what certainly looked to be a surprising message. The men spreading the word spoke rapidly, pointing, gesturing this way and that, and those who heard scattered at once in opposite directions.

"Uh-oh," Sam murmured to himself when he saw one talking, gesturing man stop Buster Matthews's mother, Beaulah. Telling Beaulah was the same as hand-delivering the actual telegram all over town! Worse, because she could embroider more skillfully with her tongue than with a needle and thread. When he realized that people were yelling to each other on the street, he leaned out the open window hoping to hear what they were actually saying. Over and over, he heard the same four words: "The Yanks are coming! The Yanks are coming!"

By the time Beaulah Matthews and a hundred other Mariettans had repeated the words, the story had grown to terrifying proportions. In effect, the stranger had been sent on the morning train to telegraph Atlanta for help because the Federal cavalry was even now on the Coosa River below Rome, Georgia, just over the Alabama line, heading south into Georgia toward Marietta itself!

Marietta seethed with the news, and in such a small community, Sam knew it would quickly spread into the whole of Cobb County. "Federal troops are coming to burn the whole town," Sam's first patient told him breathlessly. "They might be here tonight, but surely by tomorrow!"

"I'm sorry, Dr. Sam," another patient, a lady who never really needed medical service anyway, said, "but I'll just have to rush right over and get my children out of school—take 'em home where they can feel safe with me. I hear all women and children are being told to stay inside their own houses."

"Every man in town will be out and hard at work in no time. Mark my word, Doc. I know you need the money, but I can't wait for no doctorin' today," a bachelor in his thirties informed Sam. "You best get your gun an' come on out too! The men are plannin' to garrison the courthouse and shoot down the Yankee devils just as quick as they start advancin' across our Square!"

Sam's thoughts had flown to Pete, but he was torn between knowing he should stay in his office, because someone was bound to be injured, and rushing to make sure Pete and her family were safe. Not knowing which way to turn, he just stood in his office and did nothing.

ON THE THIRD DAY AFTER THE ALARM SPREAD ACROSS THE ONCE quiet, peaceful county, Louisa—still staying at the Cole cottage because Georgia was expecting another child—met Anne on the street halfway to her house. Each was trying to reach the other because of the still-terrifying emergency gripping the town.

"Louisa, my dear friend," Anne said, grasping both her hands, "are things all right at the Cole cottage? I know there's been no sign of a Yankee invasion, but what about dear Georgia?"

"She's doing fine, Anne. The new baby could be right on time, and, bless Georgia, at least she has her man beside her. I know my romance with Dix is different, not as dramatic as yours was with Lieutenant Fraser, but I do miss Dix. I pray he's all right out there in the country at Woodlawn."

"Probably safer than those of us in town," Anne said.

"And you, my dear, are you able to sleep at night? I hear folks all over town say that they spend nights peeping out cracks in closed shutters, fearing every tree branch that moves in the wind and casts a shadow. Are you and Pete and Selina afraid without an able-bodied man in the house? I know Captain Stubinger would do all he could, but the poor fellow is so crippled. Henry Cole's barber, James Johnson, tells him that your man, June, insists your new son-in-law will never be well again."

Anne laughed a little. "There's no such thing as a secret in this city, is there? But June's right, I'm afraid. As for my being afraid at night with no able-bodied men around—no. Not afraid, I think. Just lonelier than ever. It's not in a woman's nature to depend only on herself, Louisa. It's in our natures to do all in our power to care for those we love—especially our children—but not to fend for ourselves."

"I'm not sure you're right about that, Anne. Your own actions and the way you've learned to live your life without a man beside you prove you wrong. You're the most resourceful woman I've ever known. I was quite sure you were safe through all our recent scare, but I left Georgia with her nurse just now because I found I simply had to tell you that while I'm still nearby. If this scare passes, and somehow I think it will, Dix says the house will still be ready to receive its mistress sometime this summer. You will visit me often, won't you, when we get our guest room completed?"

"As often as I possibly can, Louisa. You know how lost I'll be without you. Mina baked fresh buns. Please come have some with me now?"

"She uses precious flour and sugar to bake cinnamon buns?"

"I smelled the spice before I knew what she was doing. Anyway, I doubt I have the heart to stop her." Grasping Louisa's arm,

Anne said, "Oh, Louisa, do you think this ghastly war will ever end? Does anyone really think it will ever be over?"

"I see no sign of its ending. Nor does Dix. Nor does my son-in-law, Henry. You hear often from your son fighting somewhere north of us. Does John Couper think there's any chance it could end?"

"Sometimes I don't know what to think of my son's letters! Each one is sweet and considerate of his sisters and me. He cares so much for our welfare, but I've told you until I know you're sick of hearing it that the boy loves military life as much as his father loved it. He owns his own business but is ready to drop that if, after the war, he can only find a position in the Army. It breaks my heart. I struggle to accept it, but I don't understand it at all. I didn't with his father. Louisa, can't you walk on to my house for a good, good, long talk?"

"I wish I could," Louisa said. "Had I found you at home, I only meant to stay a few minutes. Henry Cole hires the best possible nurse, but he doesn't like it one bit when I leave Georgia alone with her. I'll come for that good visit soon, I promise. I don't suppose Pete's any closer to marrying poor, lonely Dr. Sam, is she?"

Anne sighed. "No, I see no sign of any change of heart or mind in Pete. It really isn't fair to Sam, in my opinion."

ANNE WALKED SLOWLY BACK TO HER OWN HOUSE, STILL UNABLE, even with all the tragedy and hardship in her world, to deprive herself of the inevitable joy of just looking at her handsome house. The light from the late spring sky was white-white today, and her white columns gleamed their graceful welcome as she went slowly up her path.

"I have this beautiful home because of my beloved son, John Couper," she said to herself. "Oh, John, my wonderful husband, John, I have this beautiful home because of *our* son. If only I could talk to you for just a few minutes, darling! I need your help so much with our daughter Pete. You always seemed to understand

Pete far better than I ever did. She made you laugh. She made all of us laugh, and could that be the reason I never expected Pete to be confused by anything? Did you ever think she would grow up and reach a place in her life when she truly didn't know what she wanted? Sam is so kind, so good to her. He loves her dearly. I'm going to be joining you someday not far off, John. How I want to know Pete is in good, strong, gentle hands. They won't be like yours, John. No man ever had hands like yours, but Sam's hands are healing hands. Gentle, healing hands. I do wish Pete could talk to you. Even if I can't, I'd gladly help any way I could to fix things so that Pete could talk to her father."

NEARLY A WEEK OF QUIET NIGHTS AND REASONABLY QUIET DAYS passed before most of the citizens of Marietta could believe that the Confederate cavalry had actually met and turned back what they were by then calling the Blue hordes from the North. Even the strongest Unionists among them—those who declared themselves publicly and those who kept their political loyalties to themselves— still feared an invasion of Cobb County, a few months ago a prosperous, growing community whose future appeared brighter every day. Any form of destruction in Cobb County seemed impossible. Even Henry Greene Cole, surely one of the staunchest supporters of the Union, had rejoiced inside himself at every Yankee victory on the battlefield, even those considered small and inconsequential to most. He had found it hard to believe that anything could happen to mar the safe, solid plans every businessman held for the area.

The telegram to Atlanta stating that the Yanks were coming changed his feeling of safety for Marietta. "I don't want a word of this mentioned to Georgia," Cole told Louisa Fletcher as the two shared breakfast the morning of May 10, the day Sam believed the Coles' new baby would arrive. "My wife must be spared every added fear, and we mustn't forget that God is good to have sent us Dr. Sam Smith to attend her. The man is, I'm convinced, a truly strong Unionist. We can trust him to understand how inflated rumors about Confederate victories in the field, or even the possibility of an invasion from the North in the vicinity of Cobb County, would upset Georgia." Finishing his almost tasteless coffee brewed from okra seeds, he added, "I'm sure Georgia told you, Mrs. Fletcher, that we plan to name our new child after the late, great, true Unionist, Daniel Webster, if the child is a son."

"Indeed my daughter did tell me, Mr. Cole. And how the country needs another Daniel Webster!"

The baby—a boy—was delivered without incident later that day and duly named for the great orator.

PETE LEFT HOME A LITTLE BEFORE NOON THAT DAY AND, AS usual, headed first for the post office, found nothing of consequence for anyone in the family, and—her mind already made up—went straight to Sam's office. She expected a handful of patients to be waiting but was happily surprised to find the outer room empty, so she walked in her determined way right into his private treatment rooms. They were empty too. Sam was nowhere in sight.

Annoyed now, she said to herself, "Pshaw! How dare he not be here today, of all days? How like a man! I thought he meant it when he vowed not a minute passed in any day when he wasn't longing to marry me!"

And then, while she stood, hands on hips, in the middle of his private office, she heard Sam's cheerful whistle as he took the stairs to his second-floor suite two at a time. Near the top, only an empty room away from where Pete stood, he broke into song, the comical lyrics of a new ditty called "Jeff in Petticoats."

> "Oh, Jeffy D!
> You flow'r of chivalree,
> Oh, royal Jeffy D!"

In an exaggerated Southern drawl, Pete demanded, "Doctah Sam Smith, I declare! How dare you sing a song that makes fun of our great Confed'rate President, Jefferson Davis?"

So surprised he could only stand and stare at her, Sam gasped,

"Pete! Pete, in the name of heaven, what are you doing here? How *does* a man compose himself in the face of a surprise as glorious as this?"

"I'll show you how!" she fairly yelled.

And without another word, both her arms were around his neck, and they stood in his treatment room locked in a long, deep kiss as unconcerned as though there was no danger at all that a patient might appear.

"Pete, Pete, how I do love you! You're a completely mad woman and I love the very ground you walk on. Could I please have just a spoonful of the dirt you walk on, gorgeous, flaming Pete?"

"No, you may not have even a spoonful of the dirt I walk on. You may have me, Sam! I opened my eyes today, looked out at the May sunshine, and knew I wanted to marry you—*now*. Not next week. Not next month. Now! Just as soon as whatever has to be done can be done."

"Pete!"

"My name is Rebecca after my ladylike Grandmother Couper," she teased, "but, you may call me Pete."

"That's good. Thank you, ma'am, because you're just not a Rebecca."

"Well?"

"Well what, Pete?"

"Do you or do you not want to marry me, sir? All this time I seemed totally unable to bring myself to leave Mama with John Couper off at war and Selina married to a man who'd give anything he owns to get back into the Confederate Army, but it isn't as though you and I will be moving to Prussia or Japan! You have a medical practice right here in Marietta, and my mother lives in Marietta, too. It also isn't as though Mama doesn't want me to marry you. She loves you like a son. Well, she loves you as much as any woman could love another son. Her life will always revolve around John Couper. I've known that for years. But you and I look fine being second-best. How many more reasons do I have to think of before you agree to marry me, Dr. Sam, sir? And where have you been this morning? Tippling a bottle of wine with some wastrel friend in celebration of our not having been invaded by the mean old Blue hordes?"

Pete had been half teasing. Only half, but thinking that the tone of her voice could not possibly hurt or anger him, Pete took his face in both her hands, then playfully kissed the end of his nose. Sam did not even smile. Instead, he locked his fingers around her wrists and pulled her hands away.

"That's the real reason you've been refusing to set a definite wedding date, isn't it? My drinking."

"Did I accuse you of drinking too much? Have I said one word about drinking?"

"No, but I happen really to love you, Pete. And I was hoping you had stopped thinking about my drinking too much because you loved me enough to control yourself."

For a moment Pete just stood there staring down at her own hands, which had so recently held his dear face. "Sam, I did come here to tell you I'm really ready to marry you. What else can I say? And I think you know me well enough by now to know that I don't say anything I don't mean. I want to marry you. We'll be so complete together, you won't need to drink. We need each other, Sam. I miss my beloved nephew, Fraser Demere, so much, I've honestly come to see that I do not want to go into my old age alone in the world. I can still give you a child. I truly want to do that."

"Have you told anyone else about—what you've just told me?"

"No."

"Why haven't you?"

"I don't confide easily."

"Not even to your mother?"

"Sometimes especially not to Mama. Her heart's broken over Fraser, too. Why should I add to all the sorrow upon sorrow the tender, gentle woman has already endured? Besides, I know my own heart and my heart is yours. Not Mama's. Yours. Proper suitors go down on bended knee to propose marriage. Do I have to do that with you, Sam?"

Despite the tension in the room, he laughed a little, and as always, his laugh shattered any tension between them. "Pete, dearest, if you want to take a chance on this old tippler, he must be some special specimen. I need you, too. I need your strength. I need you to help me see myself as—as I've always wanted to be. Pete, more than anything, I want to be upright and trustworthy and—sober. For you."

"For yourself, too?"

"Yes, for myself, too."

Chapter 68

ONCE HER MIND WAS MADE UP, PETE HAD NO TROU-
ble setting the date for her wedding—June 9, 1863,
with a prenuptial dinner party at the white-light
house on the afternoon of June 8. Again, as with
Selina's marriage to George Stubinger, there would
be no fuss and no expense for an elegant wedding
gown.

George Stubinger would do his best to stand as
Sam's groomsman, Selina would be Pete's maid of
honor, and, of course, the Reverend Benedict would
perform the ceremony at St. James Church. And if
their house normally seemed full of light, it fairly
shone during the happy days leading up to June 9.
Mina was crushed that there was to be no meat
course for what they were gaily calling a dinner
party, and it took her a few days to regain her usual
cheerful manner. But she was unable to grump
around for long because she was so happy for Miss
Pete. Even Big Boy felt downcast for a time because
he tried and failed to shoot a wild turkey or any other
manner of game in the woods outside the city, but he
soon regained his good spirits.

Pete's usual firmness and charm took over, and in
no time they were all laughing and enjoying Pete's
makeshift, wartime menu: canned sardines, crackers,
pickles, wine, and cake. That Miss Anne agreed to

take a chance on finding more sugar at one of the few grocery stores still open in the Square soothed Mina's ruffled feelings, even though she would be permitted to bake only plain sponge cakes with no fancy icings. It helped Anne's spirits when Louisa Fletcher seemed absolutely enchanted with the menu and thought it could become the most talked-about dinner party in town.

About midafternoon on June 8, guests began to arrive as carriage followed buggy and phaeton up the driveway to the white-columned entrance of the Fraser home on Decatur Street. Among them were the Denmeads, the Robert McAlpin Goodmans, Henry Greene Cole with his wife, Georgia, and Louisa Fletcher, whose husband, Dix, was unable to leave the crew of painters working on his new farmhouse at Woodlawn. Mrs. Slaughter, the widow of Dr. Slaughter, came; Beaulah Matthews was invited, too, because even Pete thought she might cause more trouble by being excluded than by being there in all her Rebel glory. Of course, the guests included the Reverend and Mrs. Benedict and a dozen or so other prominent Mariettans. Group after group of guests reached the festively decorated white house on its nine acres of well-tended land. As always, most of the conversation centered on politics and the progress of the war moving ever closer to the small, prosperous city of which they were all so proud.

Eve was helping Mina and Flonnie with the flower-decked table where their sardine entrée would be served, but she also made a point of watching Pete's every move—and Miss Anne's. Pete, the bride-to-be, had been standing alone with her mother, greeting her wedding party guests for over an hour. A full half hour had passed since everyone was supposed to have been served.

Dr. Sam Smith was nowhere in sight!

Eve was proud of her flower baskets, which adorned Miss Anne's lovely table, but again and again she rearranged first one bouquet, then another, all the time wondering exactly what Miss Anne was thinking as she stood loyally beside Pete, making the kind of small talk Eve knew she disliked, desperately trying to help fill the time. And, of course, awkward silences gave Beaulah Matthews the kind of talking chance she reveled in.

"I keep telling my son, Corporal Buster, that I'm glad and relieved that he chose not to be a doctor. Buster's away fighting for his beloved country, you know. But one simply can never count on doctors to be on time for a mere social event!" Her laugh was not merry at all. It was mean, Eve thought, just plain mean.

"I well remember," Dr. Slaughter's wife said so sincerely Eve gave her an involuntary smile, "that my dear late husband was two hours tardy for the christening of the baby of one of his best patients! I forget the nature of the emergency call he had, but what could the poor man do about any of it?"

Miss Anne looked relieved at the possible reason Sam was so late, and, of course, that relieved Eve some. I can do most everything she needs done, Eve thought, but I can't help her at all at a time like this.

"Oh, Mrs. Slaughter, I'm sure you're right that Dr. Sam's been called to attend a medical emergency," Miss Anne said firmly but not sounding a bit believable. Even her laugh sounded hollow when she turned to Pete. "You'll just have to get used to things like this, my dear. I'm sure this is only the first of your future husband's late arrivals."

The look on Pete's flushed face almost scared Eve. Pete had never been a beauty, but her well-bred, patrician face looked like a storm cloud, and Eve honestly couldn't tell whether she meant to run out of the room or let fly one of her spiels in the sharp-edged voice Miss Anne always declared too loud.

Pete neither ran nor spieled. She just went on standing straight as a pine, glaring at the closed front door of their house. A flurry of forced conversation kept everyone but Eve and Pete from hearing the rattle of a buggy outside, and evidently no one heard Sam's carelessly loud, plainly thick voice when he yelled for Big Boy to take his horse. "Over here, Big Boy," Eve heard him call out. "My charger is thirsty as a noble charger can be! Why, he's almost as thirsty as I am! Big Boy! Where are you?"

For a reason Eve could not have explained had she tried, she looked at Pete, who was for the first time looking back at her. Until this anxious minute, Pete had seemed to look at no one. She was peering, Eve thought, deep inside herself and doing her level best to tear out whatever she was finding there.

532 ✦ EUGENIA PRICE

"Sweet Jesus, help her," Eve breathed. "Ain't nobody kin help her now but You, Sweet Jesus!"

When the front door burst open and Sam barged into the spacious entrance hall, he was awkwardly swiping at his thick brown hair standing on end as though he'd ridden through a high wind—and he was laughing like a fool.

"Dat ain't no happy laugh," Eve muttered. "Miss Pete's man be so drunk he kin hardly stand on his two feet!"

A silence as thick as heavy cream filled the whole first floor. No one spoke. Beaulah Matthews coughed. Then Sam began to sing a snatch of the one song still forbidden in the Fraser home: "Drink to me only with thine eyes—and I will pledge with mine."

Didn't Dr. Sam know that had been the one song that would always bring back the cruel truth that Mausa John was dead? Eve longed to run to Miss Anne, to hold her close, to remind her that the doctor didn't know what he was doing. When a man gets himself that drunk, he drops the reins of everything and lets fly! What Dr. Sam let fly in that song was worse than any arrow right through Miss Anne's poor heart.

The uneven murmur of voices stilled, and in the dead silence, with Sam weaving back and forth on his shaky legs, only humming the forbidden song now, Pete stepped toward him.

"Sam," she said, her voice too loud because she meant to be heard by everyone present, "did you have an emergency call to make? Is that why you're so late to our wedding dinner?"

"Late? Oh, Rebecca, my love—am I late?" He fumbled in his waistcoat pocket for his watch, dropped it, began laughing again, picked it up, blew on the watch dial, and polished it elaborately on his sleeve. "Why, yes, Rebecca, my love. I had a dreadful 'mergency! One you'll never believe!"

"You're right, I won't," Pete said. "And you won't have even one more chance to try an out-and-out lie on me, Sam Smith!" She turned to take in the gathering of guests. "I've never believed in beating around the bush about anything, as some of you may know. So this announcement, painful as it is—painful, I suppose, to everyone except Dr. Sam Smith, who feels no pain at all right now—is final and this will be the end of it. Reverend Benedict, friends, there will be no wedding at St. James tomorrow or ever." Looking straight at her mother, Pete added, "Mama, I'm truly sorry. I know how you've looked forward to my finding the right husband. I thought I had. I now know I had *not*. I knew you drank too much at times, Sam. I didn't know you lied, too. And lies I cannot, will not, tolerate."

WORD OF THE CANCELED WEDDING SPREAD ACROSS MARIETTA AS rapidly as had the terrifying news that the Yanks were coming. That news had so far been proved false. This was not. Within days, Sam closed his medical office, sold his cottage, and was on a train headed north to his native New York.

Despite repeated entreaties, Pete refused to talk to him before he left.

"What am I supposed to say to people?" Anne kept asking her mostly silent oldest daughter. "We do live in a talkative society, Pete. People make up what they don't know. Can't you tell me something you'd like me to say to them?"

"You're not being fair to Mama," Selina scolded Pete.

"I know I'm not. But I don't care what anyone tells anyone. For the first time I let my heart rule my otherwise good head, so I'll just have to go on paying for it. And I will." Pete's normally strong voice broke. "I'm—too heartbroken to think of anything for you to tell them, Mama. I just know I did the wise thing, but even when a woman is wise, she doesn't necessarily erect a protective fence around her heart. I'll come out of this. But in the meantime, will you both pray and ask Eve to pray that somehow I'll find out before I die that—Sam's getting along all right?"

"But, Pete, darling," Anne said, "what about you? Are you going to clam up and suffer your own broken heart in silence?"

Pete waited a long time to answer. Finally, she said in a surprisingly soft voice, "Yes, Mama. I expect I will."

Chapter 69

ON THE MORNING OF JUNE 19, PETE FOUND HER favorite bench, directly across from what used to be the entrance to Sam's medical offices in the Square. As usual, she had been to the post office, and because she seemed to be finding some solace in solitude these days, she sat down on the bench and for only an instant allowed her imagination to deceive her into believing that any minute now Sam would hurry down the narrow stair and run to where she sat, still holding the latest letter from her brother, John Couper.

Imagination, she thought, is dangerous and tricky. Most of the time since Sam left town, she had found a way to blame her imagination for the whole fiasco. No matter how hard she tried, there was no other way to explain how she had ever permitted herself to think for one minute that she could do what no other woman had ever done—reform a man's drinking habit. Her shame at her own behavior weighed almost as heavily on her heart as did the loneliness without him.

How like John Couper, she thought as she broke the seal on his fairly thick letter, to write so soon after he'd received the news of her messed-up marriage plans. Her fingers trembled unfolding the pages, and because there had been so much talk of the Rebel troops moving north, she breathed a prayer of gratitude that her brother was evidently still in Virginia at a camp near Culpeper Courthouse.

My dear Pete,

Your latest letter, which came yesterday, both concerned and relieved me. I have tried not to interfere, but what I had heard from other sources causes me to believe that you did the right thing in stopping what could have meant terrible heartache. I am praying for your recovery inside your good self. I know it is hard. I was, as always, glad and relieved to learn that otherwise you are all well and reasonably comfortable there. Just knowing that my loved ones are well lightens my load here. For days we have had only torrential cold rain, but I seem to take it in stride if I know all of you are all right. We are on the move, but of course I cannot tell you our destination.

It is gratifying to me in the extreme to have such good news of the well-being of our beloved mother. God grant her life and health for many years to come. If Selina's husband, after being turned down by the Confederate Army because of his wounds, does join John Hunt Morgan's Raiders, she may wait long periods to hear from him, but even if he's taken prisoner, it is likely his life will be spared. Notwithstanding our foul weather, we are a very healthy company and glad not to have to march today in the rain.

It pleases me enormously that you are all proud of my promotion to captain. It simply makes my life better, and the extra money per month will help us all in these difficult times. All I ask is some good, heavy fighting for my battery, and if I escape death, the higher I will go in rank. You see, I have a pretty good opinion of my fighting qualities. This is because of my experience, as I am as much at home and as unconcerned on the field as I usually am in a lady's parlor. Many people talk of peace. Believe nothing of it! War must continue for at least two more years and maybe longer if we are to prevail. These are my predictions from the signs all around me. Remember them, and I think you will find I am right. The greatest folly the South can be guilty of is looking forward to peace, thereby losing its vigor and watchfulness. I do not believe, nor does General Robert E. Lee, that the Yankees will give up until we have invaded them and their states and made them feel what war is actually like. What do the people of New York City know of war? Most Northerners are as comfortable as ever, and until the wealthy of Yankeedom feel war as has the South, the fighting will go on.

The subjugation of the South is the only salvation for the North, and the South can never be subjugated! But it is harder than anyone thought to drive this into Yankee heads.

With much love to one and all at home, and never, never forget that a brother never had a stronger, finer sister than my dear Pete. I rest in battle because I know I can count on you to guard and care for our dear mother. Always, I am your deeply affectionate and devoted brother,

John Couper Fraser

May God continue to give us all the courage we need. It will be some time before you hear from me again.

Pete sat on her wooden bench for a long time just holding the pages of her brother's letter. It was already hot in Marietta at a little after ten in the morning, but she felt herself shiver, almost as though she were feeling the cold rain John Couper had written about. He hadn't mentioned their being on the move to the North, but with unexplainable pain, she *felt* him going away—far, far away.

Finally, on her feet, the letter tucked in her reticule, she stood for a long time looking across the street at the empty, darkened windows of Sam's offices.

Without even whispering the words, she asked herself if a man could ever feel the black sense of loss a woman knew when he left. She would give almost anything even to know where Sam slept last night. Did he feel the terrible loss? Could John Couper, her knowing, always helpful, sensitive brother, have any idea of the loss the last line of his letter left in her?

Her legs felt wooden as she began to trudge toward home. She was suddenly convinced that only Eve might truly understand, might even have one of her knowings. But Mama would be in her room waiting, as always, for a letter to one of them from John Couper. And for her brother's sake and Mama's, she must put aside her own helplessness and think—as brother and sister had always thought first—of Mama.

Chapter 70

IN EARLY SEPTEMBER, BIG BOY, DRIVING THE HORSE and buggy because he could go faster than in the family carriage, snapped the reins sharply for as much speed as possible, heading away from the city toward the Fletchers' new home at Woodlawn.

It was a dark, rainy day. Miss Louisa would be soaked wet by the time Big Boy could get her back to Miss Anne's house, but he knew the nice, friendly lady would pack a valise and come with him without a question.

"It got to be somepin bad," Big Boy told himself as the buggy careened and rattled its way over the already muddy road. "Dat Miss Louisa lady, she be mighty partial to Miss Anne and it won't make no difference at all to her that she just gettin' settled in her new house and is needed there to boss people with boxes an' trunks an' what Eve she say be some mighty nice furniture. Miss Louisa trusts me," Big Boy bragged to himself. "She come right along once I tell her Miss Pete she needs her to be with her mama when she read the letter she just picked up at the post office today. Giddap, Prince!" he called to the straining horse and reminded himself proudly again that Miss Louisa, she trust Big Boy.

"LORDY, MISS LOUISA, YOU SOAKED WET ALL OVER," BIG BOY kept saying to Louisa Fletcher, alone back in the passenger seat of the buggy. Big Boy urged Prince to trot faster despite the sticky red mud underfoot. "Yes, ma'am, you be wet, wet, wet!"

"I know, Big Boy, but if Pete says Miss Anne needs me, that means she does and I do thank you for dropping everything to come for me."

"Mr. Dix Fletcher, he trust Big Boy too. He let you come right wif me."

"Oh, my husband is extremely fond of both you and June. And he certainly knows how deeply I care about Mrs. Fraser. Do you have any idea what's happened, Big Boy? It must be something dreadful to upset Pete so much."

"No'm. I don' know nuffin'. Only dat Miss Pete, she holdin' onto a letter she mus' think got bad news in it."

"A letter for Miss Anne?"

"June, he teach me to read some, but I ain't seen de letter close-up. Miss Pete she be white as a sheet. De letter mus' be bad, bad, bad."

"I wonder where Pete is now? Did she go straight to her mother?"

"No'm. She say she got to be wif somebody to help *her,* so she stay out in de brick cabin wif Eve. Since Rollie be rented out, I got me a room upstairs in the same brick cabin where June an' Evie lives," he added proudly.

"I know. Oh, dear. It doesn't sound a bit good, does it? If Pete can't trust herself to be with her own mother, I—I'm really worried, Big Boy."

"Yes'm. I be worried too. Miss Pete she got the nerve to break up wif Dr. Sam right in front of all dem people, Evie say, so effen Miss Pete be askeered to be wif her own mama, dey be somepin bad."

"Had she opened the letter at all?"

"No'm. She just stan' dere an' hold it all bent up in her fist."

"How did Mama seem when you helped her bathe and dress this morning, Eve?"

"Lawd, Petey, you done ax me that a dozen times since you walk into my brick cabin," Eve said. "She seem all right. She talkin' a lot today 'bout your papa. I speck she dream about him again las' night. But it seem like the dream was a good one. Mausa John, he mus' have give her a good talkin' to. She vowin' hard to stay strong for his sake. Sweet Jesus, Petey, dat dear mama of yours she got to stay strong. Effen she don't, we all gonna pay."

Pete, who had been looking out Eve's window, whirled to face her. "I knew it! You've had a knowing, haven't you? You already know what's in this—this scary letter, don't you?"

"Why you call it scary?"

"Because it's from John Couper's close Savannah friend Major John Read. My brother's been in his Light Artillery Battery from the first. Why would Major Read be writing to Mama if—if something terrible hadn't happened to John Couper?"

Eve swayed a little, then only breathed her earnest prayer: "Sweet Jesus, we leanin' on You! We leanin' hard!"

"Tell me your knowing, Eve. I order you to tell me!"

"Eve be a free nigger now, Petey. Even Miss Anne she don' own me no more 'cept we belongs to each other in our hearts."

"I know, I know! But don't keep me dangling like this, please! I'm so scared. I'm so—so scared they've killed John Couper! Eve, if they have killed him, what will Mama do? What will you and I do—with Mama? Eve, this could kill Mama, too!"

Eve stood to her full height and with an authority in her voice Pete had never heard before, she said, "You forget so soon? Your Mama she done had a dream wif your papa last night. She done promise him to be strong. *Strong!*"

Pete fell more than sank into Eve's flowered armchair. "I know you're half-white, Eve. But I'm all white! And I can't believe in knowings and dreams the way you do. How do you do it? Can't you help me? I ran to you because I need help! I should be with Mama, but I'm not. I'm—afraid to be with her."

In a voice every bit as authoritative as before, but softer now and full of caring, Eve said, "I knows you're white, Petey, but dat don' need to keep you away from knowin's an' it don' need to keep you from holdin' on to the gift God give us all when He send dat dream about your papa to your mama."

"What does God have to do with dreams?"

"Everything! God give His children sleep, an' don' dreams come outa sleep, Petey? Don' you reckon God He know why Mausa John give dat message 'bout Miss Anne bein' strong? Effen John Couper be gone from dis earth, it mean he right wif both God an' your papa! Where yo' faith, Pete? We gotta han' in faith too. God's got His part in it, but we got ours."

ANNE WAS SITTING AT HER SMALL DESK IN HER BEDROOM, STRUG-gling because she had promised John in her dream to write something courageous in her diary, when she heard the buggy rattle up her driveway. Through the open window she could hear not only Pete's voice but Eve's, and—her heart leaped with joy—Louisa Fletcher was down in the front yard in the rain!

She hurried to put away her diary, its courageous entry unfinished, stooped before her looking glass to examine her graying hair, and rushed downstairs, only half wondering why Pete had been so long at the post office and counting the unexpected visit from Louisa only as a happy surprise.

AFTER GREETING LOUISA AND SLIPPING HER OWN DRY SHOES ON her friend's feet, she asked Eve to bring refreshments and led the way into her parlor, the room still light and cheerful even on this showery day.

"Mama?" Pete asked. "Why don't you sit down in your favorite rocking chair?"

After a little laugh, Anne chided, "Well, thank you very much, Miss Fraser. I am seldom received so graciously in my own parlor."

"Will Eve be long?" Louisa asked, struggling, Pete knew, to keep her normally pleasant voice steady.

"Not long," Anne said, a somewhat puzzled look on her face. "Why do you ask, Louisa? Surely you don't have to leave anytime soon."

"No, Anne, dear friend," Louisa again betrayed her own churning emotions. "I can stay as long as you—as you need me."

"Oh, good!" Anne's face brightened. "Could you possibly spend the night with us? Say you can! I do miss seeing you now that you and Dix live out of the city." Still standing, Anne hugged Louisa again. "Pete and Eve can both tell you how terribly I miss our talks."

"I miss you, too, Anne. And I miss being in town. But I do wish you'd sit down now. Your daughter Pete has—has a letter for you."

As though on an unmistakable signal, they all quickly took seats. Only Anne looked puzzled, but the sun breaking abruptly through the clouds outside caused her to smile.

"Look!" she said. "Look out the window. The sun has just come through. And Louisa, isn't this room filled with a magic light all its own?"

Her voice shaking, Louisa said, "Yes, Anne. Oh, yes. I certainly understand why you call it your white-light house."

"Have I ever told you what my dear, all-wise little son said to me about the shadows going away when there's enough light? It was the day we buried his father. The whole family was together on Papa's old Cannon's Point veranda. The lad was only six, but he knew how I loved the sunrise. So he said he guessed that when there was enough light, the shadows just go away. I always thought that quite remarkable for such a small boy." Anne turned to Pete. "Louisa mentioned that you have a letter for me, dear. It will explain that sudden burst of sunlight from outside if it's from John Couper. Oh, I hope it is! He warned us in your latest letter from him, Pete, that it might be a long time before we heard again." With a small smile at Louisa, she added, "It has seemed a very long time."

Pete held up the crumpled, still-sealed letter. "This—this isn't from Brother, Mama. It's—it's from his close friend and superior officer, Major John P. W. Read." Irrelevantly, she said, "It's—it's from Savannah."

"Well, open it. Open it and read it to all of us."

"Are—are you sure, Mama?"

"Why, of course! Eve's here now with our buttered bread. Eve and I both apologize for the meager fare, but you know wartime scarcities." As Eve served them all, Anne mentioned that she was sure they should all be grateful for enough flour and shortening to bake bread. Then she said, taking a small piece of bread from the tray, "Thank you, Eve. I wonder why Major Read is writing to me," Anne went on. "Do you suppose John Couper's had another promotion? Remember he wrote that Major Read was so proud when he was made captain."

"Mama, in the name of heaven, stop chattering! If I don't read this soon, I'll—I'll—" Tears began to stream down Pete's face because she had already glanced at the opening of Major Read's message.

"Pete!" Anne repeated her daughter's name. *"Pete!"* This time it was almost a scream.

Everyone in the room looked hard at Pete when she began to read, because her voice sounded so unlike her. Each word seemed pushed out.

"Savannah, 4 September 1863

My dear Madam,
    I have seldom been forced to write such a painful letter, but intelligence has reached me of the death of your brave and noble

son, Captain John Couper Fraser. I, as you doubtless know, was his commanding officer in the old battery from Savannah, but above all, I counted him my close, personal, trusted friend. He was mortally wounded in the thigh on July 2, in the battle of Gettysburg, Pennsylvania, where he was heroically leading his men in the most terrible artillery duel the world has ever known. . . ."

Pete choked on those words and began to weep too hard to read. Louisa took the letter from her at once and with tears glistening on her own face, continued, fighting her way through the words.

"In his fall, the Confederacy has lost one of her noblest sons and most gallant officers. His wound was too severe for him to go on living. We all knew that, but I assure you he had every possible care and kindness. Your son bore his sufferings as only the truly noble can bear them. He offered not one regret, because he had fallen in the defense of Southern freedom and independence. It was impossible to move him, owing to the serious nature of his wounds, and he was left in comfortable quarters with an ample detail of nurses and medical officers to care for him. Be assured, dear Madam, of our sympathies in the loss of so noble a son. We all regarded him as no less than a brother. Hoping that with divine assistance you may be able to bear your loss as a Christian. John Couper did not die until July 11, but suffered without a visible sign of complaint and knew from the first that his wounds would be fatal. It is my prayer that commendations do sometimes help at such sorrowful times and beg you to know that we regarded him as a brave, gallant, and generous soldier and one that was beloved by all who knew him. I feel as though I have lost my last and best friend."

Eve was standing beside Anne, a hand on her quiet shoulder. Pete fought to curb her sobbing. Finally, Anne whispered, "Louisa. Louisa, my—boy will—never come home—again." Her voice gained what might be called a firmness: "He won't come home again because—he can't. The only reason he won't be coming, Louisa, is that he—*can't.*"

For what seemed a long, long time, no one said a word. Then Anne looked up at Eve. "Now, Eve, take me up to my bed, please. And look after Miss Louisa because she's spending the night with us."

Chapter 71

LOUISA'S OVERNIGHT VISIT EXTENDED BEYOND three weeks before her daughter, Georgia Cole, appeared at the Fraser house bearing an urgent message from her father, Dix Fletcher.

"He's pathetic, Mother," Georgia said, holding her infant son, Daniel Webster Cole, on her lap as they talked.

"Have you been out to see your father?"

"With this feisty boy demanding my attention almost every minute? No, but he made a brief business trip into town."

"He's a beautiful baby, Georgia, and I confess I'm both ashamed and relieved that you didn't need me more than the two weeks I spent with you when he was born. Since you and little Webster are doing so well, I'm really grateful I can be here. Some days I fear my friend Anne Fraser may never come out of this strange world where she seems to live these days with her grief over John Couper. This ghastly, foolish war will leave its ugly scars well into the next century, mark my word. And Anne Fraser seems completely resigned to the fact that it will not only get worse for us here but will go on for another two years."

"Why is she so sure of that?"

"Her beloved son, John Couper Fraser, made the

prediction in a letter to Pete, probably written during his march to Gettysburg."

"Oh, Mother, how dreadful for Mrs. Fraser that he was killed!" Georgia held her own infant son close. "The poor woman must spend hours remembering him as he was when he was Daniel's age —all ages of his young life."

Louisa sighed. "I know she spends most of her time deep in her own thoughts. Do you realize that except to refuse food or agree to just a little of this and that, she doesn't speak to any of us?"

"What?"

"Never leaves her room. She bathes, allows Eve to arrange her hair, but except for a change of nightgowns, doesn't dress at all. She's—she's retreated, I fear, into those devastating thoughts of her son."

"I know I should go to her room for at least a courtesy visit. But I'm afraid of her grief. What would I say? And wouldn't it only make matters worse if she saw my son? I've never known what to say to heartbroken people. To anyone—weeping."

"She doesn't weep. I wish she could," Louisa said. "But she just lies there in her bed or sits in her little rocker and stares into space. Maybe you can visit her later. She won't even have a real conversation with Eve right now, and those two, you know, are far more than mistress and servant. They're friends. Eve's heart is broken, but she perseveres."

"From what I've seen of Eve, I'm sure she does. Mama? Say you'll go home to my father, please? He really is pathetic, not knowing which way to turn at this stage of settling the new house. He needs you to supervise putting up curtains, fitting slipcovers, arranging furniture. You know how helpless men are at all those things. Just be glad he's at home waiting for you and not off trying to win this war single-handedly like Henry! I know you and Father both think Henry's too old for me, but he's so kind and generous with the children and me. He's just away so much of the time these days. How I wish he hadn't given up his civil engineering, but the man's a truly dedicated American. The Union has no more loyal citizen than Henry."

"I know that, Georgia, and my blessing on your marriage to him still holds. Your father simply wonders about some of his business tactics. Down deep, he admires the man as I do. But my dear, where does he go? Why is he away so much?"

"I have reason to believe my husband has made at least one trip to the Federal lines at Chattanooga as a spy for the Yankees!"

"Do you know where Mr. Cole gets his information?"

"Yes. From James Johnson, the barber, the free person of color who not only cuts Henry's hair and shaves him but does the same for Rebel General Braxton Bragg and who knows how many others of the enemy! I should be ashamed of myself, Mother, but I eavesdropped on Henry the last time Johnson shaved him. And what I overheard was Henry exulting because he thought, that day at least, that he'd caused the Rebels to fail at Chickamauga because he paid Johnson five hundred dollars to take word to Union headquarters that Rebel General James Longstreet and his men were on their way by train to reinforce General Bragg at Chickamauga. I guess Henry did save the Union forces some time with this news, but they retreated anyway back to Chattanooga. I don't know, Mother, how anyone keeps all this straight, but I do know that at times my husband, as right as he is in his loyalties, seems determined to be a hero!"

Georgia's son had begun to squirm and fuss, which meant their conversation was ending. "Oh, Daniel, darling," Georgia said to the child, jiggling him on her lap. "I'm so glad you're too young even to understand any of this horrible war talk!" She turned to her mother. "He's getting so restless, I think you can see I'll have to take him home, but what word shall I send to poor Father?"

"That I'll have Big Boy take me back to Woodlawn tomorrow. But before you go, I need to know if the Rebels are still hauling and carrying beds and tables and other hospital necessities into poor Marietta's main business buildings on or near the Square. I wonder, oh, how I wonder when they're going to start bringing the poor wounded Rebel soldiers into town? I—I find I have a new sympathy for them. Everything's gone far beyond whether our side—the Yankee forces—wins or loses since Anne's handsome son, John Couper, was killed. He was a Rebel captain, you know."

Georgia handed the infant to Louisa while she gathered his little cap and a rattle she'd brought along. "I know Miss Anne's son was a Rebel. He always seemed so intelligent and rational, too. I guess I'll never understand how fine men like John Couper can't see that the South could never succeed as a separate nation."

Mother and daughter embraced and Louisa kissed the baby. "I just keep praying that one day we'll all understand the madness, Georgia. Assure your father I'm coming home sometime tomorrow. At least I have a head clear enough to put up curtains. Do visit Miss Anne when you can, my dear. She's so, so heavy on my heart."

"Didn't you tell me her youngest daughter, Selina, is expecting a baby early in 1864? That could help Mrs. Fraser so much, I'd think."

"Yes, Selina's baby is due in late January or early February, and you're right. It could help Anne some. Especially since Selina's husband, George, told me just last week that if the child's a boy, he'll be named John Couper Fraser Stubinger, but they're not telling Anne yet."

THE NEXT DAY LOUISA PACKED EARLY SO THAT SHE WOULD HAVE some time alone with Anne before Big Boy took her back to Woodlawn. Eve opened the bedroom door when Louisa knocked.

"Oh, Miss Louisa!" The bright-skinned woman stood beaming in the doorway. "Come in, come in! Miss Anne, she so much better today. She almost like her old self again, even to fussin' at me. She's gettin' strong! Just like Mausa John he told her she had to be. She done remembered her dream about him an' we been talkin' about it."

"Yes, Louisa, come in," Anne called from her little rocker by the window. "Eve's right. I am strong today. Even though I know all the horror and suffering and confusion in our once quiet city, I think I understand so much more. *So* much more."

Rushing to Anne's side, Louisa said, "What splendid news, my dear friend. You couldn't send me packing on a cheerier note. But what's brought all this on?"

"She been writin' a letter to her Rebel daughter, Fanny, this mornin'. I don' know what she wrote, but whatever it were, it sure make Miss Anne stronger in her spirit. Can't you feel it in this room, Miss Louisa?" Eve laughed. "Why, she even give me a good dressin' down first thing when I come to help with her bath. The water be too hot, then the water be too cold, an' 'stead of mindin', Eve like every word. It seem like old times."

As though Eve had said nothing, there was a strange, almost expressionless look on Anne's face, which Louisa did not understand. Eve was so happy that her mistress felt stronger and was asserting herself again, Anne's peculiar, puzzling behavior appeared not to bother her at all. Of course, Louisa thought, Eve is probably just being wise in her way—a way no white woman, maybe even Anne, could truly understand.

"Eve's right, Louisa," Anne went on almost as though she were talking only to herself. "I am stronger. And there's a reason for it. I'm just about to decide to dress and go out and lend a hand to my fellow Mariettans—Confederate sympathizers. Pete tells me so many people are leaving their homes here. Just packing everything they can squeeze into a wagon or carriage and leaving. The war is coming to Marietta, Louisa. And I'm also writing to poor Fanny. I haven't written a line to the child since we found out that her brother was murdered by the war. Not a word. Pete wrote to her, of course. So did Selina, but not her mother. Well, her mother is righting herself. And I'll be ever so grateful if you never say one thing more to me about the value of the Union. I'm a Southerner, Louisa. I allowed Fanny Kemble Butler and you—and even my blessed husband, John—to cloud my thinking, but I'm stronger because I'm learning almost to—to hate everyone involved with making war! Or even taking sides . . ."

Louisa took several steps back, away from Anne's little wooden rocker. "Anne Fraser! Do you know what you're saying?"

"Yes and I include President Lincoln. Lincoln and all his kind. They thought they were going to take Eve away from me too! Well, you can see they didn't. Eve and I are friends, and she will never, never leave me. She belongs to me. We'll take care of each other until we both die. But it's wonderful, Louisa, just simply wonderful to have the strength to think again about something besides my own heartbreak. Believe me, there's strength in beginning to see the truth about everyone. To be able to use my mind enough to see at last that no one's on the right side. Not the North, not the South. They're all wrong. Let them write their pro-Unionist editorials, but I won't be reading them! I don't intend to waste an ounce of this new energy on taking sides. And maybe today I'll even dress, and when Big Boy comes back from delivering you to Mr. Fletcher, I may have him drive me to the Women's Center and begin to do my part. Confederate soldiers are sons and brothers, too, and they need bandages and underwear, and there's always a need for refreshment when the troop trains come through. And anytime they'll start bringing the Southern wounded into the hospitals now being prepared. And I'll assist, but with God's help I will not take sides with the North *or* the South."

Louisa stood there staring at her, not knowing what to say next, except that she'd have to think over what Anne had just told her. "It *is* God's way to love everyone on both sides, but I haven't heard you say one thing about love, Anne."

Anne looked almost startled. "You're right, Louisa. I haven't, have I? But I think the reason I haven't is that I just don't know anymore. I love you, my children, Eve. But beyond that, I just don't know. Actually, I'm almost afraid to love anyone. I've loved so many people in my life, and so many of them have died. It seems a lot simpler not to care one way or another."

"I hear Big Boy's buggy outside," Louisa said. "I must go. According to Georgia, her father is in great distress without me."

Anne reached her hand toward Louisa. "Forgive my outburst just when you have to leave, but I do thank you for staying with me so long in spite of poor Dix. I suppose he's still as Unionist as ever, as I'm sure you are. Oh, why can't I stay off that subject entirely? I guess I'm not as strong as I thought."

"But at least you're thinking again. My prayer for you is going to be that you will take no action on any of what you're thinking until you've had time to talk a lot to God about all of it."

Chapter 72

SOMEHOW THE CHRISTMAS SEASON CAME AND passed. To Anne, the hardest part this year was the empty, hollow feeling she endured every time she realized that John Couper was gone forever. But doggedly she kept her composure and didn't break down once, even when she remembered her own John's beautiful voice singing "Silent Night." For the first time since her son's death, she found a way to smile when Selina recalled how funny her brother had looked with pillows stuffed into his trousers as, dressed to their image of Father Christmas, he handed out the gifts on that last Christmas they had all spent together at Lawrence.

But the holy season vanished into the new year 1864. A few friends called house-to-house according to custom, and at night, alone in her bed, Anne tried to thank God for having come as a tiny baby that first long-ago Christmas in Bethlehem.

Louisa's words came to her again and again, and as always, strength flowed from them: "Just think, Anne, Almighty God Himself bothered to come to earth to live among us—as one of us—to get into this mess right with us."

When the dark, terrifying mystery of what might lie ahead in the new year grew too heavy to bear, Anne remembered her own words to Louisa: "And I do believe He came, not to discover how helpless we can feel as mere human beings—He already knew that—but, Louisa, I believe He came so that we, all of us, could be absolutely certain that He knows firsthand. God knows from having lived through His own human life on earth what it feels like to be us, in the midst of everything."

Louisa had given her a big hug and told Anne that for the first time she felt new hope. That the signs were there, if only they all looked and believed. And then Louisa had laughed. "Didn't you almost faint last Sunday when the Reverend Benedict actually allowed me to take Communion with you and the other Episcopalians? That *has* to be a good sign!"

By the start of 1864, it was plain to any thinking person that Georgia was going to be one of the two main centers of the pain-filled struggle between North and South. Except for the brief, tragic foray Lee had made into Gettysburg in July 1863, the South had endured most of the bloodshed and agony of actual battle. But Vicksburg had fallen, and the Rebels had practically lost the Mississippi Valley last summer. Anyone could see the war was moving into Georgia.

Since the fall months of 1863, the Confederates had lost Knoxville and Chattanooga, Tennessee, and Rebel General Joseph E. Johnston had retreated with his Army to Dalton, Georgia. General William Tecumseh Sherman, victorious at Chattanooga, would surely be moving any day straight toward Marietta. Up to now, most of the action in that vicinity had only been raids. But when Louisa visited Anne early in January 1864, she vowed Dix believed that soon big guns would be thundering all around Cobb County.

"Do you still refuse to read the newspaper, Anne?" Louisa asked as the two friends said good-bye on Anne's front porch.

The grin Anne gave her brought a big smile to Louisa's open, intelligent face. "You're too smart, Mrs. Fletcher," Anne said. "Do you want the truth?"

"You and I have never settled for anything less, have we?"

"I still pretend not to read the news," Anne replied, a little shamefaced. "But my daughter Pete is too shrewd for me. I forgot last week and answered a question she asked with a fact I could not have known unless I'd been sneaking to read the *Macon Intelligencer,* our most reliable source of information since Mr. Goodman sold his Marietta paper. Pete caught me. Oh, Louisa, I don't want to hide behind pretending with you one minute longer. I'm—I'm still a Unionist. How could I have been brought up by my patriotic father, John Couper, and not be? That dear man remained to his dying breath a true believer in the *United* States. He loved every foot of his Georgia properties, he loved Georgia, but he did believe in American independence."

"He must have been a wonderful man, Anne. And wise. I'm sure he knew that independence is person-to-person within our country. Not nation-against-nation as the Rebels now insist." Louisa took Anne's hand. "My dear, I've just had a marvelous idea! I'm so downright pleased that we no longer have to tread softly around your political beliefs and mine, why don't you talk it over with the girls and make up your mind to visit me for several days out at Woodlawn? My dear husband has really built us a very comfortable house. The guest room is just about finished, and it would be so good for you to get away from the hectic activity in town now. It's still quiet and peaceful at Woodlawn. Say you'll come, Anne, please?"

"But Selina's baby is due next month. I'd never forgive myself if I was away visiting and the infant happened to come early."

"But isn't Dr. Setze, the late Dr. Slaughter's friend, looking after Selina? He's very good. When does he think the child will get here?"

"About the middle of February, and, of course, I'd leave Eve here to care for Selina's daily needs until then, but this grandchild is so special to me."

"Anne, your room at our place will be ready by the end of this month, January, so I'm going to expect you by then and you must promise to stay at least a week. You know Eve will send Big Boy to bring you right home if the big event occurs early. Promise?"

"Yes! Yes, I promise. The whole idea sounds happy. I'm tired, Louisa. I never sleep through the night anymore. And I'll want so much to feel well when the baby comes. I expect Selina will need me more then anyway."

BECAUSE JANUARY 31 WAS A SUNDAY, IT HAD BEEN AGREED THAT Big Boy would take Anne and her valises to St. James Episcopal Church and that she would then ride out to Woodlawn in the Fletcher carriage.

She and Eve were up early. Eve prepared a few changes of clothing for Anne—darning and mending "these old rags," Anne's term for her worn wardrobe. Even if clothing had been available in Marietta stores, she could not have afforded to replace even a hat ribbon.

The up-country air, which gave relief from the heat of summer and early fall, was icy cold now, even with the heavy carriage curtains drawn. Anne sat shivering in the seat beside Pete, trying to keep her voice light when she confessed to feeling her sixty-seven years more than ever since her birthday earlier in the month.

Pete pushed closer on the cushioned carriage seat as mother and daughter tried cuddling and laughing during their chilly ride to St. James.

"I'll miss you, Mama, while you're out at Woodlawn," Pete said, "but I know you'll be having a stimulating time with Mrs. Fletcher and you need that so much. I can just picture the two of you sitting before a blazing fire in her new parlor, poring over some formidable tome and exchanging eruditions."

"*Eruditions* is an interesting word," Anne laughed, "but it's been so long since your aging mother has had a creative thought, I can't quite imagine it now. I want you to know I'll be fine, though, Pete. And Eve will probably kill both you and Selina with kindness. George, too. That woman does have a soft place in her heart for Selina's good husband. It puzzles me sometimes how Eve holds her personal feelings apart from her quite understandable dislike of the Rebel Cause."

"I know. It's certainly understandable that she's all for the Yankees and Mr. Lincoln, who freed her, after all. George is, or was, a Rebel Army officer and by all accounts is still trying to rejoin his unit or any outfit that will take him, even Morgan's Raiders. But you're right. I marvel at Eve's attitudes, too."

"Eve has a very healthy mind. Don't ever forget that. And a bright one." They rode along in silence for a minute or so, then Anne asked, "If you'd heard anything from or about Sam, you'd have told me, wouldn't you, Pete?"

"Not only would I have told you, you'd have guessed right off because I'd immediately look ten years younger. Mama, I miss him so much."

"You're not sorry, though, are you? You're still sure you did the right thing? I do hope he isn't drinking anymore. He's such a fine, tender, good man."

"The finest, the tenderest, the best. And yes, I'm still sure I did the right thing. You need me to give you my full attention now even more than you did back then. But you know, dear Mama, your heartbreak isn't the only one. John Couper and I were partners in the business of taking care of our beautiful mother. I've lost my partner."

"Darling, I know! And God has given me a good nudge about being selfish, even with my grief. I know, I do know, that my heartbreak isn't the only one. But I'm going to ask God every day to be sure your brother knows what a superb job you're doing." She made herself give Pete a smile. "Why, I consider this much-anticipated visit with Louisa in her new home a direct gift from you! Without you, I wouldn't even consider leaving Selina so near her time."

ANNE COULDN'T RESIST A GLANCE AT DIX'S PROUD FACE AS HE drove their sturdy buggy around the last bend in the narrow dirt road, heading them toward his new house.

"It may not look like a dream come true," Dix said, slowing the horse to avoid patches of thin ice, "but for me it is." Anne had a good look at the country farmhouse—a story and a half with a spacious front porch, a steep roofline, and a kitchen separate from the main house for safety from fire.

"Don't worry," Louisa said, also acting proud, Anne thought, "because there will be a second coat of paint on the exterior, Anne. You've settled on white, haven't you, Dix?"

"Always wanted a good, sturdy, white farmhouse. White it will be," Dix said. "Our downstairs rooms are finished now, Mrs. Fraser, and although my permanently antislavery wife objects, I've bought two field hands and an industrious Negro woman who will attend you and the house. So, feel free and right at home. And welcome, welcome as our very first houseguest!"

"We have so much catching up to do," Anne said, "particularly with the sad news of war and more war. Right now I don't see any way out of it, although you do know, don't you—both of you—that while I don't feel happy about turning against the South as a native daughter, I want our country to be *one* country. How can we possibly live in peace if we're chopped in two? Look at Europe's history. Separate small countries fight each other for their own rights as they see them. We need each other—North and South—but how, how can the Union ever be brought about again?"

Dix looked at them with an understanding smile. "It wouldn't surprise me at all if the two of you figure out a solution while you're here with us, Mrs. Fraser. I know what a relief it's going to be for my wife to have someone to talk with who also reads and thinks."

ANNE AMAZED EVEN HERSELF THAT IN THE QUIET AND PEACE OF the country, she could sleep soundly all night. And the days flew past without her becoming anxious at the thought of having to leave the warmhearted companionship of her friend Louisa. They spent their days walking about the countryside, reading aloud to each other, and talking at length about seemingly every subject under the sun. For the first time Anne felt free to talk and talk about John Couper, knowing she wasn't adding to Louisa's burdens as she did when she talked with Pete. Pete, despite her own heartbreak over her ill-fated engagement to Sam, did her best to share Anne's burden following John Couper's death, but she was showing more and more strain in the days before Anne left for Woodlawn. Poor Pete had spent her life trying to shoulder her mother's sorrows. More than anything, the time with Louisa reassured Anne that because she could feel her own inner strength growing, she could, from now on, be the kind of strong mother Pete deserved. Selina, with a new child coming, would need her mother's strength, too, her full concentration. By God's grace, they would both have it, and with resolve returning, she would also find a way to bridge the chasm that had grown between her and poor Rebel Fanny when at last she came home again from her Confederate nursing duties.

"Anne, even though I'd so much rather live in the city, not cut off from human contacts as I feel here in the country, I must tell you that Dix's beloved country life is agreeing with you. Do you realize you look ten years younger? And you've been here only a week."

"I honestly think I feel younger, although I was trying hard when I came out here to accept that I'm no longer young or even middle-aged—that I'm going to be seventy in three years."

Bundled in winter capes, the two friends were sitting together on Dix's ample front porch over after-breakfast coffee. Anne dared not ask how they came by such a luxury. Suddenly Louisa sat up and listened.

"Anne, I'm sure I hear a horse and buggy coming this way. Dix went into the city early this morning, but he wouldn't be coming back this soon. Who could it be?"

They didn't have to wait long before Anne recognized her own family buggy with faithful Big Boy urging the horse from the driver's seat and waving vigorously to Anne as he clattered up to the path that led to the porch.

"Oh, Louisa, it's Big Boy! Something's happened at home. Something's happened to—Selina! Do you suppose even Dr. Setze guessed wrong? Do you suppose the baby's already here? Or—or that Selina's in trouble with the delivery?"

"We'll know in a minute," Louisa said, hurrying down her front steps toward Big Boy, who was now running from the buggy toward them.

"It be here, Miss Anne! Miss S'lina's new baby done come las' night late! Miss S'lina she be fine, though, Miss Pete say to tell you right off. But dey all wants I should bring you home jus' as soon as I kin get you there."

"Big Boy, are you sure Selina's all right? And the baby? Was the doctor there to bring the baby?"

"Yes'm. He be there, but you an' me's gotta bundle you up fast an' git you back home. Evie say Miss S'lina had a easy time of it an' didn't cry out but once when that lil one come right out into dis ole worl'."

"Is the new baby a boy or a girl?"

"Oh, it be a fine, strong boy, Evie tell June an' me."

"And have Selina and George named the boy yet?"

"Not that I knows 'bout, Miss Anne. He jus' be borned las' night."

LESS THAN HALF AN HOUR LATER, THE BUGGY RATTLED AND bumped over the rutted road toward Marietta. Anne was in the worn day dress she'd planned to wear when she and Louisa took a picnic into the woods later when the day warmed up. Her underthings, still damp from the washing Louisa's woman had given them earlier, were stuffed along with other garments into the valise. The sight of her rumpled clothing would make Eve fuss when she unpacked later, but they were on their way—Anne and Big Boy off together on still another drive to an important destination.

"You mighty quiet, Miss Anne," Big Boy called back from the driver's seat. "Ain't no need to worry. Miss S'lina, she just want her mama."

EVE, WHO SAW ANNE AND BIG BOY DRIVE UP, WAS WAITING ON the front pinestraw path when the buggy stopped. Calling Anne's name over and over, she returned Anne's quick embrace and then assured her that Pete was with Selina and that everything and everyone were fine, just fine, and that they all hated to drag her away from time with Miss Louisa and that she just couldn't believe how young and healthy Miss Anne looked.

"Dis be a big moment for S'lina," Eve added. "And she tell me to send you straight up to her room fast. I declare dat child she find it hard to believe she done had herself a real baby. And Miss Anne, it be the prettiest baby I done eber seen 'ceptin' when John Couper he got born to you!"

With Eve's excited words still ringing in her ears and in her heart, Anne hurried up the stairs and straight to Selina's room where, for a deep, love-filled moment, she leaned over the bed, just holding her own youngest child in her arms.

"Mama," Selina gasped, "you even smell fresh and sweet like the country! I'm so sorry to drag you away like this, but—no, I'm not one bit sorry. I'm just sorry my baby couldn't wait for you to finish your visit."

"Oh, Selina, don't be sorry about anything! Just let me see my new grandchild. Where is he?"

"With his proud-as-a-peacock father, both hiding from you in Pete's room until Pete gives them the signal to appear."

"And where is Pete? I thought Eve said she was with you."

"I'm right here, Mama," Pete said in her most mischievous voice as she stepped out from behind Selina's draperies where she'd been hiding, waiting for the chance to signal George.

Mother and daughter embraced and Anne chided, "This house will be home to two children now because Pete, you'll never really grow up, will you? Well, don't. I like you just the way you are, and whatever your signal is, give it to George this minute so I can see my new grandchild for myself."

Pete stepped into the upstairs hall and whistled shrilly on two fingers.

"For goodness' sake," Anne laughed. "I thought you'd forgotten long ago how to make that ear-splitting sound!"

"You'd be surprised at what I know that you don't," Pete teased, standing in the open doorway looking for George to arrive with the infant. "Like what you're going to find out in just a matter of minutes now, Mama!"

To Selina, whose hand she was still holding, Anne said, "I know dear George is just bursting with pride. I also know his poor leg keeps him from walking very fast."

"He'd better not try," Selina said with a smile. "He'll be carrying the most beautiful baby God ever created! Oh, Mama, wait till you see. I know all mothers think their babies are beautiful, but mine really is. He's going to look like a cross between Papa and my handsome brother."

"Have you given him a name yet?" Anne wanted to know.

"Wait! Just wait for all things. Don't be so fidgety, Mama."

"They're coming," Pete announced. "Blow the trumpets, someone."

Anne could hear the uneven thump of George's bad limp from the hallway outside Selina's room and, without realizing it, held her breath for her first sight of the gift she fully believed God had sent to her to help fill her suddenly empty life.

"George?" Selina gasped. "Oh, George, he's so good, isn't he? I haven't heard him cry once since Mama got here."

"Good morning, Mrs. Fraser," George Stubinger called, beaming but concentrating fully on holding the tiny bundle in his arms just right. "I guess you can tell I've never carried a new baby before!"

"George, you're doing fine," Anne whispered, straining for a glimpse of the tiny face under the corner of the blanket.

"Now, Mama," Selina announced breathlessly, "George has a real presentation to make to you."

"Indeed I have, Mrs. Fraser," George said, holding the baby out to her. "My lovely wife, Selina, and I want to present to you, with both our hearts, your grandson, whose name is, from this moment forward—John Couper Fraser Stubinger!"

Anne reached for the child, took him tenderly in her arms, looked down at Selina and up at George, then at Pete, standing at the foot of Selina's bed and beaming. When Pete could stand it no longer, she prodded: "Mama? Aren't you going to say anything?

Isn't that the most beautiful baby you've ever seen in your whole life?"

"Pete, there are times when—no matter how much I love words—there just are none." She looked at Selina, then at George. "Is this really true? Is he really John—Couper—Fraser—Stubinger?"

"He is, Mother Fraser," George said in his soft voice. "And we both hope—in fact, we've prayed—that our child, your grandson, will give you a happy, laughter-filled, real reason for waking up in the morning. . . ."

Then, lifting the corner of the blue blanket, Anne addressed her grandchild: "Somewhere in heaven right now, son, you have a grandfather, Lieutenant John Fraser, and an uncle, Captain John Couper Fraser. They are smiling and saluting you! Both are brave men. And they both salute you for being already brave enough to have come into this ugly, uneasy, battle-scarred place. Somehow you will give us the strength and the vision to find beauty in the world again simply because you're here in it with us. . . ."

PART VII

February 1864–
October 1864

Chapter 73

For the remainder of the cold, mostly over-cast month of February 1864, Anne's heart was some-what lighter, although there were signs and sounds all around Marietta that the war was indeed coming their way. Each morning she begged God for His protection, but she also gave thanks because right under her own roof she had a new, interesting, and extraordinarily beautiful grandchild to watch over and love.

Twice during the months of February and March Dix drove Louisa into town to visit Anne, and she further primed Anne's own joy in the new baby by freely showing her own: "This child is so unusually pert and pretty, I find it difficult to believe that he hasn't yet smiled at the sight of us peering down at him! But when a baby's face remains impassive like his for the first few weeks, there's no way to know just how handsome he'll be eventually. How can you wait for his first smile?"

"I just—wait, Louisa," Anne laughed, "but not very gracefully."

"Daily, sometimes many times a day, I thank God that you have a new grandchild, Anne. No one, no one anywhere but God, really knows what horrors might lie ahead for all of us in Cobb County! I know my little grandson, Daniel Webster, and his sister keep us all laughing between bouts of genuine fear and dread. My daughter vows that the Rebel officers bivouaced here watch her husband like hawks. Henry does allow his patriotic fervor for the Northern Cause to loosen his tongue. Evidently he is slipping information to the Yankee lines, and Georgia expects every day to learn that he's been arrested as a spy! Actually, Anne, I think Georgia's wrong. Henry's too smart not to curb his tongue when need be, but who can really tell where a man's pride is concerned? Do you hear the guns thundering near town at times? We can, out at Woodlawn now. And how I loathe and despise the hideous sound of them."

Anne knew it was apparent to everyone that there would be some property loss in Cobb County. Despite her rapidly returning Unionist sympathies, her heart went out to the men who had come as pioneers in the 1830s and, too old now to fight themselves, gave their sons to the Southern Cause and were expected to lose most of their hard-earned property.

Because of his own devotion to the Southern Cause, George Stubinger had come to know some of these pathetic older men and worried about them aloud until Anne had to curb her own distraction. In fact, George kept her and Selina and Pete upset much of the time during April, while spring was struggling to spread its green and flowery beauty outside. George seemed unable to accept the Confederate Army's refusal, because of his severe wounds, to let him reenlist. His restlessness had grown so unbearable to him by the end of May that he talked almost incessantly of joining the colorful, dangerous forces of Morgan's Raiders. Any man daring to do this truly took his very life in his hands. Some citizens were justifiably wary of John Hunt Morgan's troops, although most almost worshiped the daring young man because he alone could still offer men like George the glory of real service to the South. His lax requirements, somehow obtained from the Confederate Army itself, were far less stringent. That, of course, was why poor, wounded George would be allowed to join the Raiders.

Anne thought George selfish because of Selina and his new son, now called Johnny. George's shattered leg would not prevent Morgan's accepting him into his Raiders. But when possible, each newly enlisted Raider had to supply his own horse, and George's money from the Confederate Army no longer arrived each month. In fact, there were no funds for anything, and even the thought of poverty terrified Anne almost as much as did the sound of the guns coming nearer with every passing day. Since January, when Morgan had begun to assemble his Raiders at Decatur, George had been agitating to find out more about how he might become one of them. By the time Morgan had issued an emotional plea for men to join, a plea printed and reprinted in the papers, George evidently had made up his mind to become a Raider as soon as possible after the baby arrived.

Anne had been so preoccupied with little Johnny, the horror of George's decision didn't begin to keep her awake until May, when Selina told her he had already decided to sell his treasured heirloom watch in order to buy the horse he would need.

On May 10, in a letter from Hannah, her brother William Audley's wife, Anne learned that Hannah's father, her old friend Anna Matilda's adored husband, had died peacefully at Waresboro, Georgia, where he had taken refuge from St. Simons Island. The sorrowful news further depressed Anne's spirits until she realized that at long last, Thomas Butler King, Sr., and Anna Matilda were together again in a place where he would never, never say another good-bye. The thought of her once beloved birthplace, St. Simons Island, no longer gave Anne any solace. In her once peaceful house in Marietta, which had for years given her only delight, the increasing roar of the big guns and the turmoil in the wide, once prosperous and attractive streets of Marietta cut her off from St. Simons in a way understood by no one but Pete and Eve.

Without fail, Anne thanked God each day that with Fanny in Atlanta now for heaven knew how long, nursing wounded Rebel soldiers, she still had Selina and Pete and her new, healthy, almost constantly smiling grandson, Johnny. Miss Eliza Mackay had always believed that a thankful heart would remain a strong heart, and Anne had determined to be strong for the loved ones still with her.

As a result of her seemingly growing strength, Anne somehow found the courage to remain thankful even when Louisa appeared at her door just after breakfast on June 10 with the terrifying news that Henry Greene Cole had been arrested as a Yankee spy and immediately sent to Atlanta!

"My daughter is half out of her mind with worry, but somehow I feel a man of his stature won't be terribly mistreated. He must have boasted to the wrong person about his really splendid Yankee activities. I can't stay long enough even to sit down, Anne, so do forgive me. I must get back to the Cole cottage to be with Georgia."

Anne said good-bye to her friend, went straight to Selina's room where the baby was taking a nap in his little crib, and was struck by even more frightening news.

White as a sheet, Selina stood in the middle of the bedroom floor, staring at a letter. "Mama!" she cried before breaking into tears. "Sweet, gentle, kind George has gone! I was sure he was too considerate ever to treat me like this, but—he just left! He left, before I woke up this morning, to join John Hunt Morgan's Raiders in Decatur."

And almost as soon as Selina began to weep in her mother's arms, Eve appeared in the doorway, demanding to know what had happened.

When Anne told her, or tried to, knowing so little herself, Eve said, "It all be a part of the war, Miss Anne. Ain't no woman nowhere dat's gonna know for certain what any man be thinkin' when they's war goin' on. Somepin 'bout war make even nice men like Cap'n George act crazy! June, he be too old to do more'n hol' me close in de bed at night, but at least he too old to fight even if colored could. You know Mausa John, he be safe with God now an' I know June be home in our brick cabin. Ain't it time to let me fix up de baby so's you kin take him outside to git some air? You an' Pete an' me, we's got to keep on doin' the things we always do. We got us a baby to look after. Lil Johnny, he need his grandmama now."

Selina whirled to face Eve. "No! The baby's all right, Eve! I need Mama with me. Who gave you permission to order us around?"

In a calm, steady voice, Eve replied, "No, you don't need yo' mama, Selina. You got me. Eve she sit right here an' hol' you an' comfort you an we talk all you need to talk 'bout why Cap'n George he go racin' off to war when he don' have to go."

Selina's weeping calmed almost abruptly. "All right, Eve. I know you're right. I'm being a baby. I'll stop it right now. Go, Mama, and you and Johnny have a happy time out in the yard. There are all sorts of pretty flowers to show him. I'm worried half sick over George, but this is no time for me to act like a child. I have a child of my own now."

THE ONCE CHARMING MARIETTA STREETS ANNE HAD KNOWN were more crowded than ever with family after family fleeing for safety to relatives and friends. She had no thought of taking the baby far from the sanctity of her house and sat down on a garden bench near her white picket fence. With Johnny on her lap, she tried to remember other early summer days in the city where she'd chosen to live the remainder of her life. Even now, every balcony was arched by honeysuckle blooms, every garden, even with its owners too busy to tend it, bloomed in profusion, and the bright green of summer foliage adorned every shrub and small bush.

Somehow she would find a way to keep Johnny surrounded by the beauty remaining within her nine acres of Marietta land. She had just seen Selina act, with no persuasion from anyone beyond one short speech from Eve, as a grown-up woman. Her own youngest daughter had stiffened her mother's spine, and Anne vowed to keep it that way. Even with the soft, living beauty growing around her now, there was no way anyone could know how long nine acres of quiet safety might be found anywhere in the city, which surely lay directly in the path of the bloody, deadly war. Marietta, where elegant hotels and thriving businesses and warehouses had given way to hospitals, was now overflowing with wounded, moaning, heavily bandaged soldiers. Where pleasure seekers used to roam and idle away the time, soldiers now crowded about. Occasionally, a Rebel general, with his well-dressed staff, jostled for room on the streets with ambulance wagons bringing in still more wounded and suffering young men, some pitifully maimed, others sick with fever to the point of death. Anne knew from Louisa's reporting that the road between Marietta and Atlanta was jammed with long lines of canvas-covered wagon trains, all filled with supplies for Rebel General Joseph Johnston's Army, and everything was caked with mud caused by almost incessant rain.

Anne and her grandson had been outside in the fresh air among her flowers and honeysuckle only an hour or so when the rain, which had poured down into every June day, began again. She hurried the baby back inside the house and found Eve waiting, as usual, to give her a hand.

Selina had evidently managed to lie down and rest for a while, and for that, Anne was glad. In the cheerful atmosphere of her white-light house, even with rain pelting down outside, she knew the Western and Atlantic Railroad was running more trains than ever, bringing the sick and the wounded in droves to the little town. She marveled at the courage and endurance of Southern women who filled churches and warehouses, working as nurses as did her own Fanny in Atlanta. She had even heard that the Rebel Army had taken over some private residences emptied of their owners who had fled the danger.

Against Anne's wishes but for Selina's sake, Pete had kept up her daily walks to the post office, insisting that surely one day there would be a letter from George from—somewhere. It took Anne a full week to get Pete to admit that despite her strong Unionist sympathies, she, too, had begun stopping off at churches and warehouses to lend a helping hand with bandages and refreshments for wounded, lonely, homesick Rebel soldiers.

"How can I not do it, Mama?" Pete asked. "They're human beings too, and I pray every minute I'm with any of them that someone bothered to help John Couper when he needed it most. That someone was at least kind to him. I know my blessed Fraser Demere died instantly, and while I clean up blood in the hospitals here, I give thanks that he did. Can you believe that groaning, wounded boys are lying in stacks on counters in the stores in the Square, which have been turned into hospitals?''

Throughout the preceding month of May, Anne had been unable *not* to follow the frightening reports in the *Macon Intelligencer* of General Sherman's advance toward Marietta. No one doubted that he was leading his forces to Atlanta. Marietta lay directly in his path, and fear gripped the city as citizens read, along with Anne, the almost daily notices of Sherman's whereabouts: From Ringgold Gap, Tunnel Hill, to Catoosa Springs, Varnell's Station to Resaca and Dalton, Calhoun, Adairsville, Pine Log, Kingston, and Cassville. Then, by June 5, New Hope Church, Pickett's Mills, and Dallas.

Finally, there was the glaring news that Federal troops were in Acworth, Cobb County, less than twenty miles away! The streets swarmed with more people leaving Marietta by whatever means possible. Anne, unable to bring herself to desert her beloved house, was quick to believe what several people had assured Pete: through her marriage to John, Anne and her entire family *were* British subjects. They would therefore be safe if Northern troops took over the city, despite their deep-South origins, if they hung out a British flag. To buy what small amounts of food were in the stores, Anne and her daughters had been forced to sell some of their own clothing. Among the clothes they found pieces of cloth the colors of the British flag. Anne stitched them together by hand to form a flag they prayed was large enough for the invaders to see—thereby hoping to save their home.

Anne worked so fast with needle and bits of thread that the day Big Boy hung the flag from her upstairs balcony, her needle was still in it.

One big relief for Anne was Louisa Fletcher's moving, temporarily at least, back to town to give comfort and help to her distraught daughter, Georgia, who, Louisa vowed with every brief visit to Anne, looked old and careworn from worry over her husband, Henry Greene Cole, imprisoned in Atlanta now as a Yankee spy. "Georgia has truly shown herself to be a devoted wife," Louisa told Anne again and again. "The girl has never known real trouble, and the weight of this sudden catastrophe could make her ill. Of course, I mean to stay with her as long as she needs me. It is almost impossible for her to believe that because Henry had always felt free to express his Unionist sympathies in Marietta, with the Rebels in charge now, he has been declared a criminal! I have come to like and respect the man and believe him to be guilty of nothing more than talking too much, but no one in charge cares a fig for what I think, Anne."

"Louisa, I'm sure you're right, but it's neither poor Mr. Cole nor which side is in charge. The whole problem is with war itself!" Her eyes still filled at every thought of her own deep, personal losses of John Couper and Fraser Demere, and she begged Louisa's forgiveness when so much tragedy still hung over Louisa's life. "I suppose nothing looks familiar out in the county, does it?" Anne asked, hoping to move their cherished talk to a subject less painfully personal.

"Everything is different," Louisa said. "Always there is that ghastly roar of the big guns, but almost worse, Rebel General Joseph Johnston is so determined to entrench us against the Federals, our poor countryside looks as though it's been torn up by its very roots! Rumors abound that the Yankees will march straight into Marietta early in July, and this is the end of June! I loathe rumors, but as you say, Anne, my dear friend, it's all war and they may well be here by then. You and I, though, have no more to fear from them than from these Rebels who have taken over our lovely little city. Less, perhaps. We're known Unionists and that should save us."

"Yes," Anne said halfheartedly. "We're Unionists and I've been led to believe my British flag—crooked and handmade as it is—will also cause the Federals to leave my girls and me alone. Do you suppose it will, Louisa?"

"Who knows? It could well incense the Northerners because Britain has been so close to recognizing the South as a separate nation, but I'm sure just the exoticness of your being a British subject could help. After all, it's bound to strike them more favorably than does your deep-South birth on St. Simons Island!"

Anne tried to give Louisa a courageous smile. "Well, there's only one way to find out what the Federals will do to me and my family, isn't there? Wait until they get here and somehow try to contain my mixed-up emotions about their arrival. I'm a Unionist, but at least the Rebels have been somewhat courteous to most of us. Pete is helping out at the Women's Center now. They all know she's a Unionist, too. She insisted on Selina's helping her some. They also know about her. We'll just have to wait and see, won't we?"

Chapter 74

NEITHER PETE NOR SELINA SEEMED AT ALL SWAYED from their loyalty to the Federalist Cause. Pete especially stayed strong in her convictions that there should again be a United States of America. Neither daughter wanted Anne to come along with them and share in their strictly humanitarian efforts to bring some comfort and peace to the suffering Southern boys. So Anne waited through one anxious evening after another for them to return from their volunteer work among the Rebel wounded with fresh word of what might be going on in Cobb County—even in Marietta itself. She went on waiting through anxious days, lately rain-soaked, often until well after dark for their return from town.

"Both of you get right upstairs and into dry clothing," she ordered when they came back at twilight through a drenching rain on Friday, July 1. "Do you think God will ever take pity on us and stop this steady downpour of rain?" Anne asked, helping them out of wet, mud-caked cloaks.

"We'd better thank Him for the rain, Mama," Selina said before she went upstairs to see to Johnny. "Pete can tell you what we heard from one of the Confederate soldiers in our ward today. He said the horrible weather is making it harder for the Federals to take over Kennesaw Mountain, which we know they're trying desperately to do."

"Which side are you on, Selina?" Pete asked lightly. "Do we want the Federals to reach Marietta so we'll get a few more courtesies or don't we?"

Selina sighed. "I guess we do. Whether they're here or not won't make any difference where poor George is concerned. He's likely to be anywhere tonight. Why *doesn't* he write? I do hope wherever he is, it isn't raining like this."

"Is she allowing her love for George and her worry over him now to change her loyalties, Pete?" Anne asked when Selina had gone upstairs.

"Who knows about Selina, Mama? Anyway, don't worry. It will all just help her grow up. But we heard all day how the roads out in the county have turned into quagmires with all this rain and those endless lines of heavy supply wagons churning over them day after day. The Rebels are pulling out, I think."

"You do, Pete? Well, the papers declare General Sherman will be leading his troops into Marietta almost any minute now. And it has to be better when they get here. I feel so sure their enlisted men and officers will be kinder, more civilized."

"Not all Confederate officers are brutes, Mama. Neither my brother nor Fraser Demere ever showed anything but kindness to anyone, and you know it."

"Of course I know it," Anne snapped, "and we must not allow this terrible war to cause us to misunderstand each other. We're both just so tired, Pete. So, so tired. What I wouldn't give for a good talk with Louisa Fletcher."

"Oh, I almost forgot to tell you. Mrs. Fletcher is stuck out at Woodlawn now in all this downpour of weather. I ran into her daughter, Georgia, on the Square today. Her mother wants to be remembered to you. And the funny part of what Georgia Cole told me is that neither her mother nor her father has suffered much rough treatment at all from anyone at the Rebel encampment near Woodlawn."

"I don't see anything funny about that. Just strange—as strange as all the other madness around us."

❧ ❧

WHEN PETE CAME HOME LATE THE NEXT NIGHT, SHE FOUND HER mother waiting more impatiently than usual.

"Did something bad happen today, Mama? You look worried."

"I have been all day because I want to make it clear to you that when I said yesterday that I expected much kinder treatment from the Yankees when and if they get here, I didn't mean it to sound as though our Southern boys aren't mainly gentlemen."

Pete, tired as she was, laughed. "Don't fret, Mama. I know what an expert worrier you are, and I also know it makes you exaggerate. I also know no two men are alike—North or South. Forget it. Just try to rest tonight."

"You've always been short-spoken, Pete," Anne said, "but tonight you're almost curt. Are you keeping something from me?"

On a big sigh, Pete said, "Yes. Yes, Mama, I am. Johnston's Confederate Army, which has been trying to hold on to their good lookout post and the parts of Kennesaw Mountain they took, are hightailing it away from Marietta."

"*What?*"

"They're giving up. Retreating. The streets today were seething with activity while the Rebels loaded their wagons and headed down toward Smyrna. So far as I can tell, everything that belongs to the South, including the wounded, is being sent out as fast as possible. General Johnston sensed Sherman's plans to force him to come down from the mountain, so the Rebels tore up the Western and Atlantic Railroad tracks from the foot of Kennesaw Mountain into the city. I also heard they destroyed four miles of telegraph wires. Just after dark as I was starting home, both Johnston's artillery and troops began to move south."

"Pete! Were you just going to bed without telling me any of this? Am I such a nervous wreck you don't trust your own mother to keep control of herself at a time like this?"

"None of that. I'm just tired. So tired I could drop in a heap right here on the parlor floor. But now you know. I fully expect Sherman's forces, at least some of them, to be among us by tomorrow. Most Federals will be in hot pursuit of Johnston and his men, but they're paying us a visit first. For how long, no one knows. But Mama, they're probably pouring into the Square right now!"

The sudden, loud banging at the front door startled both women.

"Pete," Anne gasped.

"Yes, Mama. I heard it and I'll go see who's on our porch."

"In the name of heaven, Pete, be careful!"

"The way I feel tonight, I can promise nothing, Mama."

"Don't be afraid. I'm right behind you."

"I'm too tired to be afraid."

Still wearing her hospital uniform, Pete charged the front door, jerked it open, and murmured, "Good grief."

"Who's there, Pete?" Anne demanded.

"It's Beaulah Matthews, Mrs. Fraser," the plump, out-of-breath woman gasped from the porch. "Please, may I come inside? My heart's so broken, I can hardly stand up on this porch, and I practically ran the whole way here from the Square. The tragedy that's going on in our Square tonight is enough to send a weaker woman to her grave!"

"But we all know you're not weak, Mrs. Matthews," Pete said in her most scalding manner. "Of course you may come in. There aren't any savages living in this house. We're Unionists, but we're perfectly civilized."

"Pete," Anne scolded under her breath, then raised her voice. "Do come inside, Mrs. Matthews. What on earth's the matter?"

"Our splendid Confederate forces are skedaddling in retreat before that Yankee monster, General Sherman, and he'll come bringing his murderous troops with him and only God knows what's going to happen to us! Besides that, Mrs. Fraser—" Her usually strong voice broke and she began to weep. "Oh, Mrs. Fraser, they wrote me from near Petersburg, Virginia, that my boy, Buster, is nowhere to be found!"

"He probably got scared and ran away," Pete said flatly.

"Buster would never do that, but oh, the boy's been through so much, so much hard fighting. Why, he was even at Gettysburg last year in all that slaughter!"

"We—we know about Gettysburg," Anne said softly, but in full command of her voice. "My son, John Couper, died there."

"Oh, my," Beaulah moaned. "I'm sorry to learn that. I mean, I knew, of course, that those vicious Yanks got your boy, but I—oh, could I come on into your parlor and sit down just for a few minutes?"

Pete made an elaborate bow toward the parlor, where Anne and Beaulah Matthews took chairs. Pete stood. "Does my sister Fanny know about Buster?"

"Not that I know of," Beaulah said. "I've been too overwrought to write to that poor, patriotic child down there in Atlanta giving comfort to the real heroes in this war. I was hoping she'd written to you."

"Is that why you came at this ungodly hour?" Pete asked.

"I—I guess so. That and a slim hope that one of you might reach a—helping hand toward me. Buster's all I have! I don't have any family to turn to. I just need someone to say, 'I'm sorry you're suffering, Mrs. Matthews.' "

Politely, but without much warmth, Pete said, "I'm sorry, Mrs. Matthews." Then her breeding took over. "I really am sorry. So is my mother. Excuse me for being curt with you earlier. I'm just so tired."

"I understand, Miss Pete. They say it goes with red hair, lovely as it is. I felt sure, though, that you'd both grieve for the heartbreak and worry poor Fanny must be enduring. She does love my son. And I don't know when you left the Square, Miss Pete, but the sight of those weary, tramping feet of the South's brave retreating boys broke my heart all over again. One old man stood weeping openly on the sidewalk. I longed to comfort him. Poor Cobb County! My heart aches for every person living in our beloved county. Our defenders leaving and the heartless enemy taking over!"

"My heart aches for us all, too, Mrs. Matthews," Anne said firmly. "And I promise to pray for your Buster this very night. I know we don't see eye-to-eye on this war, but we're both mothers. We're all three women and I sometimes think women fall victim to the loss of their men in war beyond anyone else. Come back anytime you need to come. Pete and I will both pray, won't we, Pete?"

"Yes, Mama. If ever people needed prayer, it's now, all of us. North and South. Try very hard, Mrs. Matthews, to remember that God *is* in charge. I seem to forget it much of the time. But He is."

RETREATING CONFEDERATES TRAMPED THROUGH MARIETTA streets throughout most of the night. The once picturesque little city was filling up fast with blue uniforms as Sherman's Federals marched in. By 8:30 A.M. the next day, Sunday, July 3, General William Tecumseh Sherman himself was on the Marietta Square in the heart of the city. The regular Sunday sermon was being preached in most of the churches when Northern canvas-topped wagon trains loaded with Yankee wounded and supplies rolled into town, followed by the marching men of the Federal Army. Anne's church, St. James, had six communicants present in its pews. So far as anyone knew, no service anywhere was disturbed, and the worshipers continued to sing while the din of the invaders' boots and the creaking of Northern supply wagons sounded through open sanctuary windows.

During that first day of occupation, dozens of Marietta men, many of them too old to fight, were arrested and taken prisoner with no chance given them to communicate with their families. St. James Episcopal Church was broken into within twenty hours of the Yankees' arrival and robbed of vestments, large sections of carpeting, kneeling cushions, and quantities of books.

Early on Monday, few stores were open and what little they had was for sale at exorbitant prices. Pete made her regular trip to the post office in hopes of finding the long-awaited letter from Selina's George. She also hoped to buy sugar and lard. She had sold her cherished evening scarf for money to pay for any supplies she might find. Alas, there was no sugar and no lard. But, glory be, there was, at last, the letter in George Stubinger's handwriting!

Pete shoved aside whatever ladylike conduct Mama would expect her to conform to and all but ran the whole way from the Square to their house.

No one in the family could whistle or shout as could Pete, and she did both as she burst through their front door, clutching the letter, bellowing Selina's name.

Her sister's hands shook as she reached for the letter after a barrage of perplexed questions that no one could answer: "Mama," Selina gasped, "George's letter is from Illinois! What's he doing way up in Illinois? And where is Rock Island?"

"We'll know the answers, Selina," Mama said, "as soon as you've read what George wrote. So read, child, read!"

"All right, Mama, but I have to open it first." Selina broke the seal, and with trouble getting her breath, she read the scant one-page letter.

"28 June 1864

My dearest Selina . . .

I am a prisoner of war in Rock Island, Illinois, having arrived yesterday after I was captured at Cynthiana, Kentucky, on June 12. I have written one letter to you, but since I have heard nothing, I assume you did not receive it. Conditions could be a lot worse here, but any real man hates being a prisoner and I find myself worrying and wondering night and day about everyone's health back there—especially that of my new son, John Couper Fraser Stubinger. Is dear Mother Fraser still so pleased with his name? Do not write more than one single page to me in reply or it won't reach me, but I beg you to write soon.

Your loving husband,
Captain George Stubinger."

Her face drained of color, Selina said in little more than a whisper, "He's all right. He's far, far away, Mama, Pete, but he's all right!

How will I ever find a way to thank God that George is alive and at least as well as he was when I kissed him the last time!"

"You must write at once, Selina," Anne said, "and be sure to tell him we did not receive his first letter from Kentucky. And my dear, you can thank God by taking good care of you and of George's fine boy! We'll all do our very best to thank the dear Lord when we're together in church next Sunday. But God is not penned up in any church, as my blessed Louisa Fletcher says, and we can all begin right now to give thanks and smother George in prayer for his protection."

Pete took a step toward her mother. "Mama, I have something to tell you. You too, Selina. We won't be going to church together anytime soon. The Yankees are taking St. James over as a hospital for their wounded. I heard a man at the post office telling someone that they've already stripped it of its pews for firewood—the picket fence, too—and should be bringing in the more seriously wounded in a day or so."

"Pete, you made that up!"

"I did no such thing! It's true. Furthermore, the Reverend Benedict, along with other ministers in town, was ordered to read the prayer for the President of the United States. He refused and on Wednesday, July 6, he's going to be interrogated."

"By General Sherman?" Anne asked. "That was a silly question when we've been told the general has already left Marietta and is heading for Atlanta. But why are they interrogating our rector?"

"I told you. He refuses to pray for Mr. Lincoln! And as I also told you, no church services will be held at St. James. It's right now being turned into a hospital. If the Reverend Benedict continues to refuse to pray for Mr. Lincoln, there the hospital will stay and even Georgia Fletcher Cole can't get in to play her beloved church organ —maybe ever again. At least not as long as the Yankees are in town. And if the Reverend Benedict fails his interrogation, he'll be arrested and ordered to report every single day to Federal head-quarters. Martial law is already declared, too, and that means no men can be on our streets until the Yankees can be sure of their loyalties and issue them passes."

"Does that mean colored men, too?" Anne asked. "No, it can't. The Northerners are hard at the business of setting Negroes free!"

"That's just part of it, Mama," Selina said. "George told me before he left that freeing the slaves—I mean really freeing them—isn't the only reason there's a war. It also has to do with tariffs and a lot of other mean things Yankees do to Southerners."

Anne took Selina by the shoulders and turned her around so that they were face-to-face. "Selina, has your love for dear George turned you into a Rebel, too? It's your business if that's true. But I think Pete and I deserve to know the straight of things around this house."

"Answer Mama, Selina," Pete ordered.

"A—Rebel?" Selina asked. "I don't think so, Mama. I mean I really don't know. I don't know much of anything anymore except that George is alive and maybe he'll come home to me someday!"

Chapter 75

ON SATURDAY, AUGUST 6, JUST AFTER MINA HAD scraped together enough sweet potatoes, a bit of ham, and some turnip greens for what Anne insisted still be called dinner, a knock at the front door sent Pete running to open it.

To everyone's joy and relief, Louisa Fletcher stood there, a big smile showing her delight at seeing them all again.

"Do you realize it's been more than a month since I've been able to look at any of you?" Louisa exclaimed as she hurried after Pete to the parlor, where she found Anne, Selina, the baby, and Eve all waiting to greet and welcome her.

"Is that all?" Anne asked as they embraced. "It seems as though I haven't seen you, dear Louisa, in six months! Sit down, sit down. Eve will bring what we laughingly call okra brew, and you can tell us all about conditions at Woodlawn. Have you been visiting Georgia today? How did you get permission to come to town?"

"Which question shall I answer first?"

"None of them," Anne said quickly. "Just tell us if you and Dix have enough good food to eat out there. And we've heard so many horrible stories about the ill treatment by these Yankee soldiers. How's your Unionist heart faring?"

"I still believe Mr. Lincoln's right—'a house divided against itself cannot stand'—but it grieves me to admit we found the Confederate troops much more gentlemanly and accommodating. Oh, there are kind, considerate Northern soldiers, too. Just not as many. Dix has been in town almost every day since they occupied us because he has a pass to move about freely. Bless him, he's found a nephew among the Yankee officers, and now I am also free to come anytime I can. The nephew couldn't save our faithful old half-blind horse, Hunter, though. Dix was hauling a load of firewood into town for Georgia not long ago, and some rude Yankees simply stole one of his team and left him to make his way as best he could with one horse. Still, we have ample plain food to eat, and since Dix's nephew has now placed a guard at Woodlawn, they've stolen little so far. How are you ladies here in town all alone, without a man to look after you?"

"We get along," Pete said. "Selina, Big Boy, and I planted a huge garden, you know. I'm sure there'll be more than we'll need of every kind of vegetable for a whole year and some to sell—I hope! We have little money beyond my mother's pension from the British government, but thank God it still comes. It's a struggle to keep up our small house payments."

"We've—we've sold a lot of our clothing," Selina offered, a little embarrassed. "There are some things even Pete and I can't grow in the ground, you know."

"We mustn't do all the talking," Anne said. "I've missed you so, Louisa. Tell us everything and anything you know! We see almost no one. Most of our friends have places to go and enough resources to get out of Marietta. I don't really envy them. I still love my house. I wouldn't have it without my sweet husband's pension and John Couper's regular help before he was killed. My house comforts me in more ways than I could explain even to you, Louisa."

"Is there any war news, Mrs. Fletcher?" Pete asked. "Is Sherman still heading for Atlanta? Are they fighting there? We're sure we can hear distant guns barking when it isn't too noisy here."

"Yes, they're fighting all around Atlanta, and Dix heard yesterday that there are Yankee troops even in Macon by now. I suppose you know our fine old friend Mr. Robert McAlpin Goodman is thinking of going North with his family?"

"No! Somehow I didn't think he'd really leave us," Anne said.

"And my other news could be happy news for a change. Dix has learned that the Reverend Benedict will soon be paroled and let out of his house arrest at the Marietta Hotel. He's there now for his crime of refusing to pray for President Lincoln. Anne and Selina, I believe we can be hopeful that the rector will be allowed to come to our homes to baptize both your little Johnny and my grandbaby, Webster Cole, before he leaves for Canada under orders of banishment. Dix has already spoken to him and believes there's plenty of time for the baptism, because Reverend Benedict doesn't leave town until September 1."

"That would mean so much to Mama," Pete said. "The Reverend Benedict could use Grandmama Couper's silver tureen as a font."

"That's exactly what Georgia and I planned to suggest," Louisa said. "My old china soup tureen!"

Over their happy talk, everyone heard the hard, brisk gallop of horses in their driveway.

"Mama," Selina gasped. "I'm going to run upstairs with Johnny where he'll be safe!"

"What do you mean, safe?" Pete asked, heading for the front door as the impatient, loud knocking began.

"I don't know," Selina said, gathering up her baby. "I'm just scared every time anyone knocks at our door."

"That isn't just anyone, I'm afraid," Louisa whispered. "They sound like soldiers. I heard voices like those before Dix's nephew had the guard put around our house. You'd better hurry upstairs with the child, Selina."

"Louisa! Why would soldiers come knocking at our door? Surely they won't steal from three women living here alone!"

"It depends on what type of men they are, Anne," Louisa said, still whispering. She moved quickly to catch Anne's arm. "Don't turn around, Anne! Don't look out your French doors onto the porch!"

Anne looked anyway, and peering in at her was the young, steely-eyed face of a Northern soldier, his blue cap set at a jaunty angle on his blond head. "I'm glad Selina's upstairs. That young man would turn her blood to ice water! She'd be so scared of him."

The heavy banging kept up at the door until Pete opened it a little with the terse question: "What do you want?"

"I don't know what business it is of yours, ma'am, but I'm Provost Jack Allen, United States Army, and if you'll step aside, we're coming in to inspect the plan of your house. You've plenty of room outside here for our purposes, but we'll need sleeping quarters for our officers inside."

"What right have you got to come barging into our home? We're only three white women here and a tiny baby." Pete wasn't pleading. She demanded to know.

"The right of the Army of the United States, ma'am. And I advise you—all of you—to stop trying to hide behind that despised English flag hanging outside and to give us no trouble."

"Please, sir," Anne's voice *was* pleading, "what is it you want with us? What do you mean to do with us?"

"Nothing at all, ma'am, if you behave yourselves and do as we say."

With that, he pushed open the door and motioned five or six other soldiers behind him to come inside the gracious entrance hall. Provost Allen shoved Pete aside, and in seconds the front hall seemed filled with rough, rude young men. The soldiers stood for a moment, taking in the look of the house, and then Provost Allen counted aloud: "One, two, three, four." Selina had come halfway down the stairs. Louisa stood close beside Anne, giving the provost her most forbidding look.

"I thought you said there were only three white women here. I'm counting four, lady, with the one just coming down the stairs. Lying to me will not go well for you."

Louisa stepped forward. "Mrs. Fraser did not lie to you, sir, I'm a guest in the house. I live out of the city and am in town only for the day. My husband is Dix Fletcher. His nephew is an officer of rank in your Army. Our home in the country has a permanent

Federal guard to protect us from harm. I'm a strong Unionist. So is Mrs. Fraser and both her daughters present. Mrs. Fraser and her family are all British subjects and were strongly advised to display the English flag, having been assured that you would honor it."

"Whoever told her that, flat lied, ma'am. What I tell all of you is fact. Anyone knows that English sympathies have been staunchly with the South through all this, and waving a British Jack in General Sherman's face is like waving a red blanket at a bull. We're taking this property to use as a hospital for our wounded men, and no tricks of any kind will change that! We need everything growing in that fine, big garden of yours, too, and it's ours for the taking. So, no tricks or you'll all be sorry."

"But my daughter, Georgia, is the wife of Mr. Henry Greene Cole, sir," Louisa persisted. "Surely you know he's in prison— moved to South Carolina recently from Atlanta—arrested by the Rebels as a Yankee spy! You can't know so much without having heard of Mr. Cole, surely."

"The name's familiar, yes. We've heard of him. And the gentleman is indeed a true Unionist, but that proves nothing about the occupants of this house."

"Except that Mrs. Fletcher here is my best Marietta friend," Anne tried to reason. "I am trying to be truthful with you. Marriage to my late husband, a lieutenant in Her Majesty's Royal Marines, made us all British subjects, although I was born on St. Simons Island, Georgia. Can't you see, I'm trying to tell you the whole truth?"

Eve, who had returned from the kitchen with their okra brew, set down her tray and stood firmly and directly in front of Provost Allen. "She be tellin' you the whole truth," she said with authority. "Ain't it even stronger truth when she be born a Rebel an' turn to favor—our side? Mrs. Fletcher, she be Mrs. Fraser's best *white* friend in Marietta, but I be her bes' friend!"

For an instant the tall, imposing figure of Eve standing there confronting him caused Allen to take a step back, the better to look her over carefully. "Well," he said condescendingly. "Is that so? And what makes you think your madam might be on *our* side? I didn't know niggers had a side in this war! Oh, I know they all think General Sherman came down to save them, and it's true, President Lincoln freed them, but since when did niggers start to matter anyway?"

"We done always mattered," Eve declared evenly. "And I be as free as you ever thought 'bout bein'. Whatever you got in your head to do to my friend Miss Anne Fraser, you better take me into your plan, cause her an' me, we's gonna stay together forever an' ever!"

"But you're free now, black wench."

"Yes, sir! Free to stay wif Miss Anne if dat what I wants to do, an' it's zactly what I means to do. So you got me to deal with, too."

"Shut up, nigger," he snarled at Eve, then turned to the others who had clomped into the house with him. "Give the boys outside the signal to start. They'll know where." Of Anne, he asked, "How many bedrooms upstairs?"

"Four," she answered weakly.

"That should work out just right. I want you, lady, and your two daughters moved upstairs and out of our way down here within the hour!"

"*What?*" Pete shouted.

"We both speak English, I think," he replied. "And that means you, mother-in-law of Henry Greene Cole, are to get out of this house now!"

"You're ordering my guest to leave?" Anne gasped.

"Now! Whoever you really are—out! If you don't go right now, you'll pay a heavy penalty, lady." Turning to Anne, who clung to Louisa's arm, he barked, "That English flag must be torn down within the hour, too, or you'll pay more than a heavy penalty, ma'am. You and your daughters. Now, lady, the door! Out!"

Two soldiers steered Louisa toward the front door and out onto the porch in silence. Over her shoulder as she hurried away, Louisa said, "I'll do my best to come back, Anne. Or send help to you."

"Out!" Provost Allen yelled.

Through the wide-open front door, from the yard Anne heard the cracks of what surely were rifle shots: cracks, splintering wood, louder cracks, yells and shouts, and some of the shouting in such foul language, she felt faint and reached for Pete's strong hand.

"Are you firing on us from outside now?" Pete demanded.

Allen laughed uproariously. "No, we're just gatherin' firewood from the pretty pickets of your fence. Now, get your nigger workin', you white women work, too, because we'll be back in exactly one hour and we expect the entire downstairs to be open to us and emptied of all your personal belongings. Oh, are there any men on the place at all? Any niggers?"

"They be one very old, weak man out in the brick cabin," Eve offered. "An' one giant 'bout sixty. Dat be all."

"Is the old man sick? We don't need no sick old people to look after."

"No, he ain't sick. He just—old."

"Why do you need our house, a private residence, when every business and public building on the Square is empty and ready to serve as a hospital?" Pete asked.

Provost Allen laughed but completely ignored her question.

NOT UNDERSTANDING WHY EVE ORDERED HIM TO TAKE DOWN the English flag he had so recently put up on Miss Anne's second-floor balcony, Big Boy worked as fast as he could as the sad, help-less voice of his almost lifelong friend June sounded in his ears: "Why they do'n this to our lady folk, Big Boy?" June was still pleading for an answer when Big Boy hurriedly took the tallest ladder and headed for the main house, June still walking after him. "Why de very mens dat come down to free us wanta treat our lady folk so bad? Don't you let nothin' happen to 'em, Big Boy. Not a finger to be laid on Miss Anne, Miss S'lina, Miss Pete, or my Eve, you hear?"

Big Boy heard, all right, but as he ripped the small English flag Miss Anne had sewn with her own fingers from the spot where he had so carefully nailed it, his heart pounded wildly. Big Boy was scared. He was always scared of what he didn't know about, and nobody seemed to know anything about what the Yankee soldiers might be aiming to do. Nobody. Not even Miss Pete. Not even Evie, who always seemed to know most of everything that went on.

& &

IN EXACTLY ONE HOUR, AFTER EVERYONE—INCLUDING MINA, Flonnie, and Big Boy—had carried and carried, the Yankees came back in force to find Father Fraser's huge desk empty, Anne's fine china and crystal gone, the linen closet bare, and Anne's three favorite chairs removed from the parlor.

The Federals brought over a dozen more soldiers, who marched across the well-kept front lawn through the remnants of the broken and split picket fence, which Big Boy had given a fresh coat of whitewash just the other day. The troops were followed by a dozen or so drays piled with tents, blankets, a pitifully inadequate supply of mattresses, and one gun carriage bristling with weapons.

For the remainder of the afternoon, while Selina's infant screamed with discomfort from an upset stomach, Anne, her two daughters, and Eve knelt beside the front windows in Anne's bedroom on the second floor, peeping out at the nightmare that was turning their once lovely lawn into a military encampment. Dozens of tents were being raised and mysterious-looking tables set up in rows that not only covered the lawn, which had lain green and beautiful behind the picket fence they'd all loved, but stretched across Anne's flower beds and up onto the porch itself.

The Fraser women and Eve, huddled behind the draperies of Anne's bedroom windows, spoke almost not at all. Even Pete, who always had such trouble not talking, only growled what seemed to Anne to be the same questions over and over again: "How long do you suppose they mean to crowd us out of our own home like this? When do you think they'll start hauling in wounded soldiers?" No one bothered to try to answer. No one knew what to say.

Finally, when campfires began to flare across the yard, sending black smoke up and into the house through the open windows,

Selina started to weep. "Our lovely white picket fence, Mama! They're building fires out of our pretty fence to cook their meals!"

"S'lina, you make eberthing worse for your poor mama wif both you an' lil Johnny cryin' at once. Why didn't I bring some of my peppermint to make tea for Johnny? Even a spoonful or two of my mint tea help his lil stomach. Why I not bring it?"

"Because smart as you are, Eve, even you can't remember everything on an ugly day like this one's turned out to be," Pete scolded. "Stop blaming yourself. We couldn't have done any of it without you to help us. Selina, do you think Johnny might stop crying if you picked him up and held him for awhile? It might stop you from crying, too!"

Selina's teary voice was abruptly stronger. One more look out the window and she was too angry to cry. "Mama! They're stealing all the vegetables in our garden! They're picking the last of our good tomatoes and cucumbers—and my squash, some of it still blooming. And listen! I hear them in our chicken coop! The chickens are squawking something fierce. Oh, Mama, if only George were here, he'd know what to do."

"Well, he isn't," Anne said firmly. "Neither is your brother or your father. But God is! Try to remember that."

"Do you remember it, Mama?" Selina asked.

"I mean to."

"So do I, but most of the time I forget, or it really doesn't help at all. I'm so scared!"

The soldiers hadn't even paid them the courtesy of knocking on the front door when they came back inside, but Anne was sure that by now there must be about twenty men downstairs barking orders, cursing, calling out names, and grunting as they moved heavy pieces of the Fraser furniture from room to room.

Pete and Eve went to check the chickens, and Selina had no sooner left the room to settle Johnny in his crib when Anne heard an almost gentle, young man's voice in the hall outside her closed door. Heart pounding, she listened again over the continuing hubbub downstairs.

"Mrs. Fraser? Mrs. Fraser, I know you're up here, but could you please signal where—which room? I'm sure what I found will be most important to you. Where are you, Mrs. Fraser?"

Realizing suddenly that his slight accent was British, she felt a small wave of relief. Even though the Union Jack had evidently caused this trouble, the clipped, cultivated cadence of a British accent somehow calmed her a little. "I—I'm here," she called and startled herself by opening her bedroom door to a stranger.

The slightly built, brown-haired young man who stood there, immaculate in his blue uniform, cap politely in hand, was also holding the large framed painting of Anne's beloved John, which she and the girls had neglected to bring upstairs in their frantic haste to clear out the first floor.

"Oh, sir," she gasped, reaching to touch the portrait. "How did you know? This is my most prized possession—my dearest possession! It's—it's the portrait of my late, adored husband, Lieutenant John Fraser of Her Majesty's Royal Marines! I can't think why I would leave it downstairs out of my sight. Thank you! Oh, how can I begin to thank you for saving it, for bringing it up to me?"

"Shall I carry it into your bedroom, ma'am? And then, perhaps I can find a nail to fasten it to the wall."

Anne was touching John's face in the portrait now. The cleft in his strong chin, the plume on his handsome Marine bonnet, which he had been holding in his hand when the picture was painted. "How can I ever thank you? Please tell me how!"

"By trying not to hold the men with me in such low esteem. They've been fearfully rude to you and your daughters. I do apologize, but I assure you not all of us are haughty monsters, even though some have surely acted that way."

"I know you'll have to go back downstairs soon," Anne said, "but if you'll step into my room, I think we may find a nail in one of my dressing table drawers. My daughter Pete believes in hoarding nails."

Carrying the large portrait into Anne's bedroom, the young officer asked, "Your daughter's named Pete?"

"That's her nickname. She's the one with red hair. Such a help to me. Keeps me on my toes in all ways."

Hurriedly, the soldier did his best to center the portrait on the wall Anne chose, used one of his heavy boots as a hammer, secured the picture, replaced his shoe, and bowed. "I owe you another apology, ma'am. I should have introduced myself since I'll be staying in your house in one of the downstairs rooms. I'm Captain David Porter. My parents came to the United States when I was twelve. I'm a citizen now. And thanks to my late father's influence, I grew up understanding and revering the American love of liberty." He smiled—a smile Anne knew she could come to depend on—and added, "I doubt that it's necessary to tell you that I'm a great believer in the Union Cause."

"Yes, Captain Porter, I'm sure you are. I was born, along with my living children, right here in Georgia, but I've come to be a Unionist too. My Scottish father believed so in liberty for everyone, he'd be a Unionist were he alive." She glanced at John's portrait. "My late husband, although a British subject, would be staunchly pro-Union too." For a moment she allowed her eyes to linger on John's face. "I do thank you—I hope you know—for retrieving his portrait. No one can ever do a more wonderful thing for me."

A booming voice shouted David Porter's name from downstairs.

"I must hurry back down," he said, giving Anne a light, impulsive hug. "But remember my name. I'm a doctor and if you need me, I'll do my best to be of service." From the doorway he smiled back at her. "Those aren't just words, Mrs. Fraser. I want to be your friend. Partly because you're such a lovely lady, but also because somehow I think we'll come to understand each other."

He closed the door, and Anne stood looking at it as she listened to the quick, easy sound of his boots descending her stair. "He's—he's so like John Couper," she said aloud to herself and to John's portrait. "This young man is very like our son, dearest. David Porter is my latest gift from God. I hope you know! Oh, how I hope you know. . . ."

Chapter 76

LOUISA FLETCHER GREETED THE REVEREND BENE-
dict at the front door of the cottage where her
daughter lived with her year-old son, Daniel Webster Cole, and her four-year-old daughter, Mary
Warren.

"I'm sorry to be a bit late, Mrs. Fletcher," Benedict said as he entered the well-furnished house, the
Episcopal Book of Common Prayer in hand, "but my
poor wife is so tired from packing to leave for our
exile to Canada, I simply had to help her a bit before
I came to baptize the baby. "Oh, I see you have my
font ready. Good. My time is rather limited. We leave
the day after tomorrow, you know."

"Yes," Louisa said. "And we're ever so grateful
that you're taking the time to stop by. Little Webster
Cole's baptism has great meaning for his mother,
Georgia, and for me. My daughter will join us with
baby Webster any minute now. And I must tell you"
—she lowered her voice—"Georgia looks as careworn as she really is. She's so worried about Henry.
He's now been moved from a Confederate prison in
Atlanta to Charleston, South Carolina. Georgia can
no longer take him good food or clean clothing. It's
just too far."

"The war has truly cut us all into pieces, hasn't it?
I do wish I had been able to influence Mr. Cole

toward the South. Such a fine man to be imprisoned when his city needs him so. But, we disagree, so we must, in the face of such catastrophic events, remain true in our spirits—the spirit of love must prevail."

"There even you and I agree," Louisa said, "and I do thank you for allowing me a few trips to the Communion table with my fellow Christians at St. James toward the last."

Benedict cleared his throat, a bit self-consciously, she thought. "Uh, yes, indeed. I accept your gratitude, Mrs. Fletcher."

At that moment Georgia came down the hall from the rear of the Cole cottage, Daniel Webster in her arms. She and the Reverend Benedict exchanged a few words, and as he spoke, he was finding in his prayer book the ritual for the Holy Baptism of children, which he read in the weary, defeated voice of a man far beyond his forty years. At the proper time he dipped his fingers in the water in Louisa's china soup tureen, touched little Webster's head, was joined by the two women in the final prayer of consecration, and it was finished.

There were tears on Georgia's cheeks, but her face showed understandable pride because her son had smiled throughout, and Louisa couldn't help asking how many other babies were ever so well behaved.

"Not many," Benedict said, drying his fingers on a clean linen towel there for that purpose. "In fact, I fail to see how the Stubinger baby could have done anything else but scream and cry throughout his baptism day before yesterday."

Louisa took a step toward him. "Tell us, please, how are they faring at my friend Anne Fraser's house? It pains me to say this, but I was visiting when the Yankees first arrived there, and they forced me to leave."

"But they didn't harm you in any way, Mother," Georgia said. "They just brought you here to my house."

"No doubt," the Reverend Benedict said scornfully, "because of the arrest of your husband as a Yankee spy, Mrs. Cole."

"Georgia," Louisa said firmly, "it's well known that you and the Reverend Benedict do not agree politically. We all know that. I just need to be sure my friend Anne Fraser and her girls are doing all right now."

"As well as could be expected," he said, "considering the savage conduct of her most unwelcome houseguests from the North. During the few minutes I was there to baptize little John Couper Fraser Stubinger, I could not avoid noticing that they've set up their operating tables almost directly beneath Mrs. Fraser's bedroom windows, and it's no wonder at all that the Stubinger infant was frightened and unruly. I'd guess they hacked off at least one arm and one leg from wounded Yankee soldiers in the short time I was there! The poor soldiers—one of them, at least—screamed more loudly than the infant!"

"But don't they administer chloroform first?" Louisa asked in a horrified voice.

"I imagine so, but when that knife and the ordinary carpenter's saw they were using when I was there cut deeply, it must cause unbearable pain."

"Did you actually see them amputate an arm and a leg, Reverend Benedict? I find that hard to believe!"

"If you'd stop by this minute—two days later—I would be not at all surprised if the same arm and leg aren't still leaning up against Mrs. Fraser's lovely cedar tree. I did see them—freshly cut and bleeding—stacked beside a dozen or more other extremities. I'm sorry to have such indelicate news to report, ladies, but you asked. And I must be on my way to give my good wife the assistance I'm sure she needs with our final packing. We'll be leaving this poor, battle-scarred city for good day after tomorrow."

SEPTEMBER, USUALLY A PLEASANT AND WARM MONTH, IN 1864 crawled by in an agonizingly slow stream of horror, discomfort, noise, and pain-drenched ooze of despair for Anne and her two daughters. By the first of October, the daily ordeal of waking from a fitful night of struggling to sleep a few minutes at a time, between gasps of prayer for the suffering boys lying on the lawn and across the ruined garden of Anne's once comforting house, was taking its heavy toll. The choking self-pity Anne once felt as she lay alone in her bed asking God again and again *why* her rock, her loving, sensible, beautiful son, John Couper, had to die, gave way to sheer pity for the horribly wounded Yankee boys lying under her trees and losing their arms and legs through every day and night to the crude hacking of the Union surgeons, not only poorly trained, but more poorly equipped with surgical instruments, bandages, and makeshift sutures. Much of what they used to amputate legs and arms, even to attempt brain surgery, were improvised instruments, many of them made from Anne's own tableware.

"Some days, Mama, I honestly don't think I can live through one more hour of—all this," Pete said as she tried to swallow nasty gulps of bitter okra brew. "I know I pride myself on not complaining in my struggle to keep up your spirits, because that's what John Couper would want me to do, but if I'm honest, I know deep down that John Couper and my blessed nephew, Fraser Demere, are the lucky ones. They're—dead. They're escaping all this!"

"I know, Pete. I know. But we just have to go on thanking God that we both don't seem to fall headlong into such black despair at the same time. Have you noticed? On the days you're ready to give up as you are today, God finds a way to give me a dollop of new courage. It won't, it can't, last forever, child. I'm glad too that John Couper and Fraser are out of it, for their sakes, but God's mercy isn't in short supply. It never has been, it isn't now. Somehow, sometime, this will end."

"Yes."

"Is that all you can say—yes?"

Pete only nodded her tousled red head, then without warning and because she couldn't help it, threw her cup of hot okra brew across Anne's room, breaking the cherished thin china cup that had been Grandmama Couper's. "Oh, Mama, I'm so sorry," she whispered, big tears streaming down her usually composed, strong face. "I—I lost control and I hate not being in control of myself!"

"I know you do, darling. But tally your average. You have a

hold on yourself far more often than not. Without your brother, I sometimes feel I have only you to lean on."

Stooping to gather up the shattered pieces of the china cup, Pete muttered, "Thank you. Oh, thank you for saying that. Even though I no longer think it's quite true."

"What do you mean, Pete? Who else is there but you?"

Pete stood in the middle of the floor, still holding the fragments of china. She looked her mother in the eye and said, "There's Eve, Mama. I grew up as you did, feeling only a kind of affection for some of our slaves—at least, I took them for granted as my right. None of that is true with Eve or June or even Big Boy. Those three are our staunchest friends now."

"But Pete, they're not slaves any longer. Lincoln freed them."

"Yes, but how many owners down here paid one bit of attention to what he did?"

"I did," Anne said. "I not only paid attention but rejoiced with them. Eve and June and Big Boy all know they're free to leave anytime."

"But they're not. Where would they go? What would they eat? And anyway, Eve feels not only that she belongs to you, but that you belong to her!"

"I know. I'm very blessed, Pete."

A piteous scream from the yard outside the open window caused Anne to clamp both hands over her ears. "No more! I can't bear to hear one more boy scream in pain like that!"

"I'm feeling a little braver, Mama, but not like me yet. So, don't you fall to pieces."

"I won't. I promise." Anne tried a little smile. "It's not my turn to let it show today. It's yours, Pete."

"And I'm beginning to be angry, so that means I'm stronger. I just can't get over their using horsehair to sew up those gaping wounds and jagged slashes the surgeons make with your old carving knife. Horsehair, Mama! Imagine! Have you ever asked your Yankee surgeon friend, Captain David Porter, why they don't have better implements to work with?"

"He's your friend too, Pete. We can all count on David. But I don't ask him anything I don't absolutely have to," Anne said. "I don't want to embarrass him. And I shudder to think where we'd be without him."

"Without him and his two English friends. I don't blame you for thinking the English are superior people, Mama."

"Well, maybe not superior, but certainly, in my experience, kinder. It's no wonder our old friend Fanny Kemble Butler hated everything about slavery. Most of the English do, and have for a long time. Your Grandpapa Couper brought me up to be a staunch American patriot, and I surely still am, but in a way I'm rather proud to be a British subject too."

"You're a brave woman, Mama."

"I am?"

"It takes courage to be as strong a Unionist as you are when you were born on a plantation and grew up having everything done for you."

Anne smiled. "I thank you for bothering to tell me that. You are regaining your Petelike courage. I'm very, very proud of you. And not only because you agree with my Unionist stand. I'm proud of you because you're—Pete. And my daughter Pete is strong."

"Mama? I've been thinking a lot lately about how hard life must be for my sister Fanny, working day after day with such pitifully injured young men. She certainly doesn't write to us often."

"I don't think she has the time, and also, there's no way to deny that as with other broken families—taking different sides in this ugly war—Fanny has broken from us in a way."

"I know. But she's strong too. She just disagrees with you and me."

"And Selina."

"Who knows what Selina really thinks? That adorable baby fills all her thoughts, except for her worries about George in prison way up in Rock Island, Illinois."

"Maybe it's best that little Johnny does take all Selina's attention. Believing strongly in a troublesome Cause as we do is hard work, Pete."

Anne reached for Pete's hand and gave it a pat. "But we'll make it somehow, dear girl. God is still in charge."

"How can God bother to be in charge of anything as stupid as this war that breaks close families apart? He told us to love one another!"

"Yes, and He meant it. We have to believe that one day we will all love one another—again." She sighed. "That is, those of us still left on this earth."

Pete looked out the window at the seething, bloody scene in the yard below—a panorama of pain and suffering and gore—to which no one could grow accustomed. "We'll never forget little Johnny's baptism day, will we?" she asked with a shudder.

"You, at least, may live long enough so that sometime you can remember it without the background of those awful screams and the blood."

"Does your friend Captain David Porter know how many wounded and sick men they have out in our yard and on the front porch?"

"The last time I asked, I think he said about twelve hundred patients."

"It doesn't look as though they're that many from up here."

"Oh, but David says they have to lie on the ground behind the house under the trees and in your garden—waiting their turn."

"I hate to tell you this, but David will if you ask, I'm sure. There are at least twenty boys stacked like cordwood out back under the pecan tree. They died in the night."

"It's going to be hot out today, too," Anne said, her voice full of dread. "Will we ever, ever get the stench of gore out of our nostrils? Ever?"

"Papa always told me," Pete said, "not to worry about something we can do nothing to fix."

"He did?" Anne asked, almost hopefully.

"The most horrible-looking operating table down there, Mama, is a church Communion table, I'm sure. It's slimy with gore from who knows how many amputations! Just yesterday afternoon and this morning . . ."

Anne's sigh sounded old and heavy and her voice trembled. "How many?" she murmured. "Oh, Pete, how many?"

Then suddenly she staggered from her chair, a look of anguish on her beautiful face. When Anne grabbed her reeling head, Pete flew to her side. "Mama! Mama, something's wrong. Are you sick? Do you have a pain in your head?"

"Not my head, no." Moaning, she stooped and clutched her lower abdomen with both hands. "My—my stomach! There's such a pain in there, Pete! I—I haven't been eating right. Eve's been telling me there's been nothing in my chamber pot but wee-wee and—" She laughed a little in embarrassment. "She didn't have to tell me. I knew it!"

With Pete's help she lowered herself back into her chair.

"Don't try to get up out of your rocker. Just sit right there until I get back with Captain David. Promise? Mama, do you promise?"

"I—promise. I couldn't get up if I had to. The pain is—that bad, Pete. But don't take David away from some poor, wounded boy who might need him."

"I'll do what I think best!" Pete yelled back from the door. "You need him worse, and you're my mother!"

PETE FOUND DAVID PORTER JUST AS HE WAS FINISHING THE AM-putation of the arm of a boy who couldn't have been more than eighteen. His cries had reached Pete as she ran down the stairs and out the back door into the yard, where the Federal surgeons were operating on one wretched fellow after another.

She waited impatiently while David wiped blood from his hands and liberally sprinkled powdered charcoal into the freshly cut muscle, raw and gory, that formed the hideous empty socket where the soldier's arm had been.

"Pete!" David called to her. "Forgive me for calling you Pete, Miss Fraser, but your mother always refers to you that way and—"

"That's my name, Captain, and my mother needs you desperately! She begged me not to drag you away from some badly wounded soldier, but I'm scared. She has a dreadful pain in her stomach. Can you come upstairs and look at her, please, sir? *Now?*"

"Yes, I'll come, of course. But I should bring a senior surgeon with me for another opinion."

"Whatever you say. Only it's you she trusts. Just hurry, please *hurry!*"

Chapter 77

PETE RUSHED BACK UPSTAIRS TO HER MOTHER'S
room ahead of Captain David Porter, who was
searching for an older surgeon to examine the patient
with him. And when she burst into the room, she
found her mother writhing in pain, almost falling out
of her little rocker.

"He's coming, Mama. Captain Porter is coming,
along with another surgeon so that he can have the
benefit of his advice too." She couldn't understand a
word her mother was trying to say but was relieved
to see her still alive and trying to form words over
the agony of the intense pain. Moaning, even whim-
pering now, Mama kept reaching into the air, as
though seeking help or trying to find another hand to
hold. Pete knelt beside her, grasping one of her hands
—squeezed into a fist against the agony—and tried
hard to understand even one word. Finally, she realized that Mama was trying to call for Fanny, who
hadn't written in weeks, even to Mama. In a brief
exchange last week when Pete had run into Georgia
Cole at the post office, Pete learned that the Rebel
hospitals in Atlanta had begun to close at the end of
July, since Sherman's men had headed that way.

"They allowed them something like ten days of
grace," Georgia had said, "to move the more seriously wounded Rebel soldiers to other places. My

husband wrote that he imagined some of the nurses were staying on duty during the difficult move for as long as any suffering young man needed care."

Fanny would stay, there was no doubt about that. Even if the long estrangement from her own family and the disappearance of Buster Matthews hadn't yet begun to make Fanny see that Pete and Mama had been right all along to support the Unionist Cause, Fanny would stay to care for the sick and wounded. However silent her sister had been, Pete knew Fanny's tender heart, knew that she felt as called to nursing as any man of the cloth had been called to the ministry.

Pete realized that since August, when the Yankee soldiers had stripped the garden and taken their chickens, they had grown accustomed to being hungry. It was not just the gnawing pangs of having skipped a few meals, but the hunger that comes from inadequate food over a period of time, conditions that may have led to Mama's terrifying illness. If the captain and his two English friends, both privates in Sherman's Army, had not deprived themselves and sneaked portions of their own rations upstairs to the Frasers, Mama might even be worse than she was.

The light, quick knock at the bedroom door was like a blessing. Pete rushed to open the door to Captain David Porter and an older, stern-looking medical officer David introduced hurriedly as Major Jones.

Mama had grown a bit quieter and was bravely trying to sit up straight in her rocker, but her white face—still so pretty despite the severe suffering—let Pete know that she was having to work at not moaning.

"Mrs. Fraser," Captain David said gently, "it's David. This is a most experienced, fine surgeon, Major Jones. He's my friend and I wanted him to see you too." As he spoke, David's slender, sensitive hand lightly touched the painful abdomen and Mama cried out.

"You've found the right place, Captain," Major Jones said in his dry, professional manner. A man shrieked in pain from the operating tables in the yard below. Major Jones acted as though he'd heard nothing, and although Mama's warning hand was raised in protest, he gave the same spot another, firmer test. She screamed.

"Stop him," Pete ordered. "Why go on punching her right where it hurts the most, David?"

"We just have to be sure, Pete. If I may, Major, I'd like to volunteer my opinion."

Major Jones only nodded assent.

"It appears to me that the deprivation she's had to endure, the lack of wholesome food, has caused a severe concretion. What has she been eating, Pete, that might cause knots of fibrous material to form in her intestines?"

"Since she's a human being and not a cow, I'd guess it's caused by Mina's food stretcher. We tried to make a game of it, but because your men stripped our garden of vegetables, our Mina has been cooking the few turnip greens we've found with ordinary grass from the lawn."

"Concretions," Major Jones said. "The grass and God knows what else has formed into a hard ball inside her." He looked up at Pete and almost smiled. "You're right, Miss. Your mother isn't a cow, so her system doesn't know how to handle a diet of mainly grass and other fibrous materials. I'd say there could well be more than one concretion, Captain Porter. How old is your mother, Miss Fraser?"

"She'll be sixty-eight next January."

"In my opinion," Major Jones said as though he and David were alone in the room, "only an operation could save her life, and she's too old for that. Without surgery, I give her no longer than ten days to live."

Pete gasped, "David!"

"Steady, Pete. I thank you for your opinion, Major."

"My duty, Captain. And don't get any wild ideas. No man in his right mind would even attempt such an operation."

"Both of you stop discussing her as though she wasn't hearing every word you say!"

Major Jones, who hadn't even removed his cap, touched it in Pete's direction. "Of course, Miss Fraser. And I must get back down to the yard. The last time I was informed, there were five men with severe shrapnel wounds in their extremities, all necessitating immediate amputation. Time is of the essence."

"Thank you, Major," David said as the older man hurried to the door to leave.

"You're most welcome, Captain. But don't think of trying anything foolish."

"Yes, sir."

When Major Jones had stomped down the stairs, banging the front door behind him, David said, careful to include his friend Anne Fraser, "I don't intend to try anything foolhardy, ladies. But I do mean to do the very best I can, heaven helping me, to—" He looked straight into Anne's eyes. "I do intend to do my level best to make you well again, Mrs. Fraser. You see, I've grown to need you, too. I wouldn't be able to get through some of my harder days if I didn't know you were here, praying for God to guide my hands and my head. I'll be counting on your prayers again now. With your permission, I intend to operate on you this very afternoon, as risky as it will be at your age. Just as soon as Pete can get your giant Negro to carry a kitchen table up here."

Dumbfounded, Pete watched as her mother forced herself to sit up in her favorite little chair. Looking straight at David, she said in a hoarse whisper, "You can count on my prayers—again, dear David. God will hear, and even in the midst of these burned-out ashes that are my life now, He will find a way to—to bring beauty from them. You'll see."

"Mama! Sweet, brave Mama!"

"If I'm brave, Pete, it's because God has never failed to help me find that beauty too. I'm afraid, but He'll bring beauty out of— even this."

"Pete, can you assist me during the operation?" David asked.

"*Me?*"

"I'll need someone, you know. I dare not take a man away from the emergencies they're having down in your yard."

Pete looked wildly at her mother, then back at David. "My sister Fanny would be perfect to help you. I want to, but I'm not as strong as I sometimes seem to be. This *is* my mother!"

"Then think of someone else, please! I have to have assistance."

"When you go for Big Boy to carry up a table, get Eve," Anne whispered in a hoarse, tight voice that told Pete the pain was twisting at her again. "Eve will come. Just tell her—I need her—to be with me."

When Eve appeared on the small porch of her brick cabin, almost as soon as Pete knocked, her eyes were reddened and the lids swollen. It was her eyelids, Pete thought, that always gave Eve's face that oddly patrician look. She was sure Eve had been crying, but this was no time to ask what was wrong. Pete gave silent thanks when Eve agreed to come to Miss Anne's room immediately.

"I done finish wif what I'm doin'. If Miss Anne need me, Eve be there."

Too frightened to take the time to ask questions, Pete ran, long skirt flying, back to the house and was relieved when Captain David met her in the downstairs hall.

"I know your sister Selina has been worried because she hasn't heard from her husband up in Illinois, so I thought you might be better off going to the post office while Eve helps me with the operation."

"Can't someone among the medical staff help you? Eve loves my mother in her way as much as I do!"

"Someone else could help, but I'd feel a lot better about your wonderful mother's chances if I had Eve beside me," he said, his gentle voice solemn. "Eve's so quick and intelligent. Your giant black man has carried a kitchen table upstairs. I have the chloroform right here in this bag—and everything else I'll need. I may even have found enough fine silk thread for sutures. Go, Pete. I promise to do my very best to save her, and I also promise to pray you'll find the letter for Miss Selina."

As though she were nine instead of almost thirty-nine, Pete was so relieved at being told exactly what to do, she ran down the stairs toward the front door without looking back.

Until David called to her: "You'll pray for me, won't you, Pete?"

"Yes," she called up to him. "Oh, yes, David, I'll pray hard! Selina's praying, too. And our cook, Mina . . ."

WHEN DAVID QUIETLY ENTERED ANNE'S ROOM, SHE WAS STILL alone. Eve hadn't gotten there. As he knelt beside Anne's little chair, he heard her whisper as if to a third person in the room: "God's grace is never late in coming, John. If I don't wake up here in my white-light house, I'll be waking up with you again. Oh, my darling—with *you* again!"

In the remaining few minutes while he waited for Eve, David studied Anne's still-beautiful features and prayed silently that when his dreaded work was finished and she opened her eyes, he would once more be blessed to look at their lovely, odd, pale, pale blue. Then he would feel free to tell her that one of the reasons he had come to love her so much in such a short time was that he'd never seen eyes like Anne's except those of his own, dear mother, dead since David's tenth birthday.

The door opened almost soundlessly, and Eve stepped into the room. "Miss Anne, she won't leave me, too, will she, sir?" she whispered.

David drew her aside, beyond Anne's hearing, and spoke in a soft voice. "Not if you and I do our work well, Eve. She's told me about her friendship with you. I know she wants you here now. We have no more sponges left," he went on in his professional voice, "but I've brought some clean, soft cloth. Please just follow my instructions. Lift this cloth when I say, place it back over her nose when I tell you to and I'll drop on the chloroform. Just the right amount will put her into a deep sleep, and she will feel little or no pain. Be brave, Eve. Follow my instructions exactly, and pray for us all three."

BEFORE PETE LEFT FOR THE POST OFFICE, SHE STOPPED IN SE-lina's room to give her a brief report on their mother's condition, taking care to minimize the dangers so that her sister would not be unduly alarmed. We all still try to protect Selina as the baby of the family, Pete thought.

Captain David had told Pete it would take a while to finish the operation. Still trembling with the unaccustomed terror she felt because she had heard, with her own ears, Major Jones declare that Mama's chances were slim, she tried to walk slowly away from the house toward the Square and to the post office. Once inside the building, she forced herself, to use up some of the painful waiting time, to walk the length of the room thirty, then forty times before she even approached the iron-barred window to ask if there might be a letter for her mother or for Selina. Long ago Pete had given up on hearing from Dr. Sam, the man she had pushed out of her life because his drinking would surely have brought still more grief, not only to her but to Mama. Only Mama and Selina were likely to have mail from anyone, now that John Couper was gone, along with sweet Fraser and Mama's childhood best friend, Anna Matilda King. Uncle James Hamilton Couper wrote only now and then, describing the ever-present danger of attack on St. Simons. The chaos there seemed strange indeed, because the very name St. Simons, to Pete, still defined the word *peace*.

And although her heart raced some when she found that yes, there was a letter from Captain George Stubinger and, even more surprising, one from her long-silent sister Fanny—both addressed to Selina—she still would not permit herself to start walking home. Only an hour and fifteen minutes had elapsed since she'd promised Captain David to pray for him, for Mama, and for Eve. At least, she'd prayed and prayed that Captain David and Eve had administered the chloroform correctly. He couldn't possibly be finished yet. There wouldn't be any definite word about Mama, whether she would live to walk again through her beloved white-light house, blessing them all with her soft laughter and her beauty.

Pete, alone on a wooden bench in a spot clear of bird droppings, longed to see a familiar face—even in her state of nervous anxiety and fear over her mother, lying there on her own old kitchen table, bleeding and unconscious.

Suddenly, she was seized with an impulse to go home. At least to see Selina—to share her fright and to give her the letter from George for which she'd waited so expectantly.

From long custom, Big Boy and even Eve used the back door when they entered the house, but today as Pete came in sight of the front porch and yard strewn and stinking with still-unburied bodies of the dead and bloody from the amputations performed on the living, she saw Big Boy, his huge frame hunched in a kind of knot, sitting on the top front step waiting, she supposed, for some word of his beloved lady, Miss Anne.

All around Big Boy were soldiers in heavy bandages, some on crutches, and staff doctors, their once white coats stained and bloodsoaked. As usual, Pete pushed her way to the front porch, picking paths between filthy cots and sobbing or groaning or cursing sick men, almost as though she didn't see them. She gave vent only inwardly to the anger that inevitably rose in her when she thought of those empty buildings around the Square, which could easily have made far better hospitals than did their once quiet, clean, lovely home. It seemed cruel retaliation for displaying their pathetic homemade British flag.

"Big Boy," she said softly, standing on the step where he sat, head buried in both his hands. "Big Boy, have you heard anything about Mama? How she's getting along?"

Big Boy was weeping. "No'm. Ain' heerd nothin'. Just settin' here cryin' for June."

"June? Why are you crying for June? Where is he?"

"June, he die no more'n a hour 'fore you come to fetch Evie, Miss Pete. My ole frien'—be daid!"

"What?"

"Evie, she done wash him an' got him dressed an' laid out on their bed at the brick cabin."

"And Eve left his body alone to come to help with Mama?"

"Yes'm. Dat woman she love Miss Anne an' Miss Anne, she say, be still livin' an' breathin' at least. June be daid. June's big, old body be empty now."

Without another word, Pete ran into the house and up the stairs, first to Selina's room. It wasn't the time to cry or even to feel sorry for herself because she was so scared. It was the time to *do* something that would really matter. Selina needed her letter from George, and Pete had loitered long enough because of her own terror that Mama might die.

When Pete hurried into Selina's room, her sister was holding Johnny's bare feet up in the air, lifting his bumpy to put on a fresh diaper.

"Selina," Pete choked out her sister's name. "Let me do that. Look! I have something for you. A letter from George! And, addressed only to you, one from Fanny too."

Selina let the baby's feet drop and grabbed both letters as Pete took her place diapering Johnny. Before she broke the seal on the letter from George, she said, "Tell me about Mama, Pete! Have you seen her? I heard Captain Porter go downstairs a few minutes ago and assumed he had gone back to the operating tables in the yard, so he must be finished with Mama's operation. Is she all right? I was going to check on her but I was too scared. Who's taking care of her?"

"Captain Porter would have told you if anything was wrong. Eve's with her. The captain couldn't get anyone else to help him. And, Selina, I just found out June—died this morning. Just an hour or so, Big Boy said, before I got to their cabin."

"Eve must be a wreck! She loved that old man so much. But how did the surgeon dare leave Mama alone with only Eve? It scares me that George might be—dead or terribly sick, too. Bad news comes in bunches."

"Don't be silly. Just read his letter. He can't be dead or he couldn't have written to you! Eve would say you're talking like your bread ain't done in the middle. Use your head, Selina, and read."

"I can't stand it one more minute without knowing how Mama is!" Selina cried. "Go, Pete, please, and find out, then come right back to tell me. We can read Fanny's letter together later."

Relieved that Selina was behaving so sensibly, Pete thrust the freshly diapered baby into her sister's arms and rushed from the room.

Chapter 78

FROM THE MOMENT PETE STEPPED INTO THE UP-
stairs hall, she could hear the guttural, gagging sound
of her mother vomiting. No one had told Pete to
expect this! Did it mean that Mama was drawing her
final breaths?

Without knocking, she all but ran into Mama's
room to find Eve right with her, sitting on the edge
of the bed, holding a dishpan. For an instant, Pete felt
faint. She suddenly remembered that Eve had left her
adored June on their bed in the brick cabin Eve was
so proud of. How had Pete dared to desert Eve at a
time like this? For all the years of Pete's life, Eve had
been only good and thoughtful and always there
when Mama or any of her children—or Papa—
needed her.

To steady herself, Pete leaned for a moment
against the door, then went toward the big bed—the
bed where Pete and all the others had been born, the
bed where Papa and Mama had loved them into life
because of their deep love for each other, the bed
where Papa had died at Hamilton on St. Simons Island.

The hard, labored retching kept up, and Eve
spoke without taking her eyes from Mama's face.
"She be s'posed to do this," Eve said, her voice thick
from weeping, but not weeping now. "Dr. David he

say the chloroform make her do this." She was giving Miss Anne her full attention, holding the pan just so, dipping a clean cloth into a bowl of cool water, then wiping Mama's white, drained face over and over with her long, slender fingers, as gentle as a baby's breath. But firm, Pete knew. Eve did everything in a measured, firm way so that the one receiving her care knew that each gesture was important. "The doctor, he say she be terrible sick when she begin to wake up," Eve said softly. "It ain't but to be expected, Petie. Don' fret. Your mama, she 'bout to wake up. Then I find a way to get her off them bloody bed clothes an' get some clean ones under her an' over her. She been through so much, she might could be chilly later. Ain't nothin' you can do now. Come back in a little bit. She be more herself then."

Pete returned to Selina's room with the news that their mother had survived the surgery. "Eve told me we can see her soon," she said.

Selina was composed now. "George is safe," she said, "not even minding prison life too much."

"That's all I need to know. I really do care so much about your heart, little Sister. I know what torment it can be not to know about the one you love. But could you read just a little of Fanny's letter to me now?"

More obedient than when she was a child and the spoiled baby of the family, Selina kissed George's single page, then opened Fanny's short note and began to read.

"Near Forsyth, Georgia
10 October 1864

My dear sister Selina,

I am writing to you because I know you've never seemed as far away from me as Mama or Pete, because your Unionist sympathies are not as strong as theirs. I'm well, but exhausted and think I am having a painful change of heart and mind. Buster is a deserter from the Confederate Army and I haven't heard from him in weeks, so I know that chapter in my life is at an end. I guess I loved him because he's the only man who ever wanted me.

But I am lonely for my mother and my sisters! I can't say I have
become a Unionist. I'm too tired to know what I am, except that
I'm coming home sometime before Christmas if I'm ever told I'm
free to go. Mama has been faithful to write. Pete sometimes. But
they both hold my politics against me and I have no spirit left to
defend myself. I need all of you and want you to tell Mama and
Pete that I love them, and, of course, I love you and pray your
baby is well. I pray every day that you are all well, that you hear
often from poor George in prison at the North. As soon as I can,
I will let you know when I am coming home. Please do all you
can to convince Mama and Pete to be glad to see me.

Your affectionate sister,
Fanny Fraser."

"I've written to Fanny as often as I've found the time, with
these soldiers crawling and bleeding all over our yard and porch,
and I know Mama has written only that we send her much love and
concern. Fanny seems so sweet and docile, but she's really quite
prickly, isn't she? She's the one who turned against all of us over
this dumb war!" Pete had let her words spew out and wished with
all her heart that she could take them back. Mama might be dying
this minute and it certainly was no time for anyone to spew spiteful
things!

"I know you didn't mean to be unkind about poor Fanny,"
Selina said, pushing Pete toward the door. "Go find out if we can
see Mama now."

When Pete reached the hall, the acrid smell of burning cloth
was so strong, she suddenly felt a new sense of panic. They had
lived for so long, week after week, with the prickly fear that the
Yankees would set fire to their house, would, in a half-drunken
state, attack one of them, would try to hurt them. Some of the men
were drunk most of the time. It seemed to Pete that all of them
except Captain David and the two English privates, who had been
kind to Mama, were so foulmouthed that she found it impossible to
understand some of the ugly swearing. Somehow the worst among
them had the idea that all the Frasers were Rebels. David had made
the innocent mistake of telling the men that the Frasers had been

born on St. Simons Island in south Georgia, where almost every planter owned slaves. Didn't the "damned old Rebel," as they liked to call Mama, own slaves herself? And didn't that make her their enemy? At this moment, *they* were Pete's enemy in a way she hadn't felt before.

The stench of burning cloth was no longer just a stench! The curtains at the open balcony door were smoldering. Smoke must surely be visible down in the yard where Captain David was hard at work, busy with his deft, sickening labor of sawing off a young man's lower arm with Big Boy's carpenter's saw.

Pete went flying into Mama's room. Mama was still retching horribly as though she knew everything that was happening down in her once lovely, green lawn—as though one more scream from one more boy's throat rising to her open bedroom window might cause her to die because she was so tired of fighting. . . .

Then, as she was about to reach for Eve's bowl of cool water to douse the smoldering curtains, Pete heard heavy boots stomp up the stair and was relieved when Captain David burst into the room and grabbed the bowl of water before rushing back into the hall.

After he had put out the fire and returned to Mama's room, Captain David motioned Pete away from the bed and said, "I'm more than sorry that someone tried to set fire to the house with your Mama lying so ill on her bed. I'm sick about it. I've finished the surgery that took me away from your mother, and I won't leave her again now. I promise."

"Will Mama—live, David?"

"I can't be sure yet, but I expect her to recover almost entirely with the kind of care I know you and Eve and Selina will give her."

"My sister Fanny, the nurse for the Rebels, is coming home, too," Pete said, her heart swelling with relief at the thought of Fanny's skill and what it might do for Mama.

"As I expected, your mother's still vomiting, but she should be conscious within another hour," David said.

"Is she awake enough for me to call for Selina now?" Pete asked. "Shall I call for Selina?"

"Not yet. I imagine she's in a lot of pain, and that will get worse, but"—he stood looking down at Mama with what could only be called love in his eyes—"she's a remarkable woman. It's a miracle that she's alive after enduring what she endured in the midst of such noise and ugliness. It's truly a miracle, Pete. I know I performed the surgery, but it was God who gave her back to us. It's God's miracle." For a moment David stood looking down at Eve, then he laid his hand on her shoulder. "You're part of the miracle, Eve," he said. "Big Boy told me a little while ago—about your husband. You also gave God a hand with His miracle. Big Boy wants you to know, now that I've told him Miss Anne should pull through all right, that he's gone back to your cabin to sit by his friend June. Thank you, Eve, for having the courage to leave your dead husband to help God and me save Miss Anne's life."

Eve looked up at David, then at Pete. There were fresh tears flowing down her mellow brown face. "Pete can tell you, Doctor, that I done promise Miss Anne to be right beside her for the rest of her life whenever she need me. My sweet June, he don' need me no more. God He be takin' care of June now."

"And I'm sure June knows that his kind, beautiful wife has been a part of God's miracle today."

Suddenly, almost peacefully, Anne's vomiting stopped, and her heaving chest settled down to a fairly even rise and fall.

Weeping had never been easy for Pete. It had always made her feel stiff and uncomfortable. The tears now streaming down her face felt calming and good. If only Mama were awake to tell them what this miracle meant to her . . . Mama would know exactly the right words.

And then, so did Pete. "Eve? Captain David? Mama would agree that we've seen God's miracle, but she'd call it beauty from ashes."

David's expressive face turned to look gratefully at the sudden shaft of pure, white light that came pouring through the window of

Anne's room. "Beauty from—ashes?" he repeated, as though he needed Pete to make it plain again.

"Yes, David. Beauty from—ashes."

For a time the room was quiet, Anne was quiet, as though in a deep, healing sleep. Then, Eve said to no one in particular, ". . . beauty from ashes, and *the oil of joy for mournin'.*"

Afterword

Whether a miracle or a fortuitous twist of fate took place that long-ago day in Anne's white-light house, she did survive the highly risky operation performed by a young man who would have been considered her enemy by other Georgians—showing to me the high-arching scope of God's love. That she recovered is to most persons unbelievable, considering the primitive medical equipment of the time and the inadequate training of the doctors. In fact, my own doctor, William A. Hitt, who is not only one of my most perceptive and loyal readers but a reliable source of reference for me in research, agreed to my using the procedure as written only when I assured him that I had it all down in black and white directly from a letter written August 10, 1865, by Anne herself. It seemed to illustrate perfectly that God can and does bring beauty from ashes. General Sherman's men did try to burn down Anne's house, which punctuates the truth that not all persons and their motives are alike.

Since Anne lived to be sixty-nine and died not from the surgery but after a brief illness while visiting the home of her daughter Selina in Louisiana on May 9, 1866, almost two years later, she is buried in Rosehill Cemetery at New Iberia, Louisiana. Her grave, because of the shortage of funds almost everywhere in the South following the Civil War, was without a tombstone until recently. George Stubinger is also buried in Rosehill Cemetery; Selina, who died after she and her family moved back to Marietta, has a marked grave in Citizens Cemetery. As far as is known, Pete and Fanny are there also, but without markers.

The body of Anne's beloved only son, John Couper Fraser, was moved sometime during the intervening years from Crawford's Farm in Gettysburg, where he fell, to the Confederate section of Laurel Grove Cemetery in Savannah.

Anne's father, the still-revered John Couper of Cannon's Point, St. Simons Island, lies beside his wife, Rebecca Maxwell Couper, in the picturesque cemetery of Christ Church Frederica, as does her erudite brother James Hamilton Couper, his wife, Caroline Wylly Couper, and their children. Anne's childhood friend Anna Matilda Page King is in her family plot nearby at Christ Church with her husband, Thomas Butler King, Sr., and their several offspring.

Many, many persons contributed to the writing of this book and will be acknowledged in these pages, but the first name that must be mentioned is Frances Stubinger Daugherty of Marietta, Georgia. A descendant of Selina Fraser Stubinger, Frances is a great lady to whom I have proudly dedicated this book. Frances and Nancy Goshorn, my full-time researcher, spent many hours together here on St. Simons and in Marietta and became warm friends through their close and interesting work on *Beauty from Ashes*. Because of their work, I wrote the book armed with maps, charts, cemetery and military records, and family histories galore—most of which came to me because of the constant and enthusiastic attention of Frances Daugherty. Dedicating *Beauty from Ashes* to her sprang from pure joy and a grateful heart, and Frances's never-failing sense of humor sealed the decision. Here is your book, Frances, and thank you, thank you for so much.

Without one iota of hesitation, I can say that I could not have made my deadline on this manuscript without Nancy Goshorn, who not only handled the complex research but did it with almost unbelievable patience and cheer. One of the reasons I am still working as hard as ever at my advanced age is that Nancy works with me full-time on research with little or no thought of anything else. She did all the required reading for such complicated research—especially when my eyes began to cause trouble about a third of the way through—and proved her unfailing humor by battling my messy first drafts. Beyond this, she has somehow found time to search for the next story, which we will tackle as soon as I catch my breath. I have four secret weapons, despite my pacifist bent, and one of them is surely Nancy Goshorn, researcher par excellence and my real friend, personal as well as professional.

Of more importance than I actually realize, I suspect, is my "overqualified keeper" and full-time assistant, Eileen Humphlett. Eileen is absolutely needed even more than I can know, because *she* knows exactly how to keep just enough away from me so that I am able to hold the writing of each long book front and center in my often overloaded mind. Most who are close to me already understand that by nature I'm as vague as my lovable father ever was and that I despise detail and business. Not only does Eileen take care of all my bills and taxes, she handles most publisher and agent contacts as well as most correspondence and phone calls (some not easy to handle) and still goes on loving me without a hint of a "smother." I love being cared for, but I do smother easily with too much attention. One of the most original and energetic minds I've ever known belongs to Eileen Humphlett, and I live my days in amazement at her upbeat nature and uncanny ability to laugh at me and with me at all the right times. My publishers continue to rave about the perfection of my final typescripts, and we all have Eileen to thank.

I owe Dr. James Humphlett, Eileen's disgustingly handsome husband, a heart-deep thank-you despite his insistence on my paying off a dinner wager, even though it was the baseball strike and not their won-loss record that cut the Atlanta Braves out of total victory this year. So, thank you, Jimmy, not only for spending time in Marietta taking pictures for me of the various settings used in this book, but for acting as chief cook and bottle washer at home so that Eileen could devote her total time and energy to the final editing work on my manuscript in order to meet our deadline. More than you know, dear Jimmy, I thank you for being exactly as you are.

One of Eileen's best friends is *my* best friend with whom I share my house, my work, my problems, and my dreams. Most know she is Joyce Blackburn. I doubt that anyone reading this has a true idea of what this means to me, but Joyce, even after thirty-four years of having me underfoot morning, noon, and night, still believes in me

—as a writer and, more important to me, as a person. That Joyce, Eileen, and Nance share a special, sympathetic understanding is one of God's greatest gifts to me because hour by hour I benefit. Joyce and I revel in silence together, we love baseball obsessively, and we share the same concepts of God, real jazz, and politics. She is the only person with whom I can spend all my time and never even think of the word *fidget*. Let me say that I still believe in *her* and can't imagine my days without her.

I was blessed and made happy the very first time I met Jo Couper Cauthorn, to whom I dedicated *Bright Captivity*. But before she had time to read, or I to finish, this book, she died. To say Joyce and I miss her is ridiculous understatement, but we are thankful for the laughs we shared (and they were many) and for the touch of true beauty she left with us. Jo also left behind a special husband, Bob Cauthorn, treasured by us both. And to me she left a permanent impression of what it's like to have been a real Couper descendant. With all my heart, I hope Jo approves of this book.

My absolutely essential agent–literary manager and friend, Lila Karpf, calls Eileen, Nance, Joyce, and Sarah Bell Edmond my St. Simons Support Group. She's right. To try to thank Sarah Bell adequately is as impossible as thanking Joyce, Eileen, or Nance. Counting me, we're a quintet of love and goodwill and downright fun. We all share a faith in the same God, a real passion for baseball and liberal politics, and a mutual understanding one of the other. Sarah Bell takes care of our house, takes care of us, and is as possessive and concerned about the Atlanta Braves as we are. During the writing of this book, she has donned another hat: I now call her my liaison because she drops off manuscript, research material, and anything else needful from my desk to Nance and Eileen almost daily. How I ever did without her no one knows, and what we would do without her now that she's become our treasured friend, no one dares think. She and Joyce share such a special bond that to Sarah Bell, Joyce is "Miss Daisy."

Is it possible for two already close friends to grow closer although life's circumstances keep them apart? Yes, because Tina Mc-Elroy Ansa and I have grown closer during the past months while both of us were hard at work on our novels. Tina, one of America's truly fine novelists, glows with the spark that causes me to give thanks every day that she is a part of my life. I depend on Tina in far more ways than she is aware of. Just knowing she's down the Island in her dear house being Tina, for me and for her talented husband, Jonée, matters in a thousand wordless ways.

Nancy Goshorn joins me in thanking the following persons for their invaluable research assistance: At the wonderful Georgia Historical Society in Savannah, Director Anne Smith, Jan Flores, and Eileen Ielmini; at the Brunswick-Glynn Regional Library, Director Jim Darby, Marcia Hodges, Dorothy Houseal, Diane Jackson, and Jane Hildebrand; at the Savannah Public Library, Sharen Wixom; at the St. Simons Public Library, Frances Kane and staff; at the archives of the Coastal Georgia Historical Society, Director Linda King and Pat Morris, historian; at the Coastal Heritage Society in Savannah, Executive Director Scott Smith; also in Savannah, Jeff Fulton of the Ships of the Sea Museum and at Fort Pulaski, Talley Kirkland and John Kelton; Joe Thompson at the Wormsloe Historic Site; Curator Roger Durham, 24th Infantry Museum at Fort Stewart, Hinesville, Georgia; and Dennis Kelly at Kennesaw Mountain National Battlefield Park, Georgia.

One of the most likable and helpful persons of all my valued helpers is Buddy Sullivan, until recently editor of the *Darien News*, now manager of the Sapelo Island National Estuarine Research Reserve. Buddy's biggest contributions to Nancy and me, aside from his downright pleasant nature, are his fine, careful, fascinating writings—especially his excellent book, *Early Days on the Georgia Tidewater* (Darien, Georgia: McIntosh County Board of Commissioners, 1990). I could not have worked without it on this novel, and I will be depending still more heavily on Buddy and his excellent material for my next one, planned at and near Darien, Georgia. Thank you, Buddy. Thank you for caring enough to expend all that energy.

I do not feel a stranger in Marietta, Georgia, because through all the years during which I've appeared at autographing parties in the Atlanta area, citizens of Marietta have been most loyal to me. I make almost no appearances these days, but my ties to Marietta remain strong and altogether pleasant.

Two of my best friends, Mr. and Mrs. Fred Bentley, Sr., live in nearby Kennesaw, Georgia, and if you've read other Afterwords in my novels, you know that now and then (as in this book) I name a fictional character Fred Bentley. I am truly fond of the Bentleys, and Fred has been of great research help to me through one more novel.

Through the good graces of Frances Stubinger Daugherty, I have been fortunate enough to add new Marietta friends. The first who comes to mind is Anne Fraser's great-great-granddaughter, Page Sanger, who now lives in Anne's white-light house and was gracious enough to allow Nancy Goshorn and Frances Daugherty to see and photograph the house. I am well aware that my readers will want to do the same, but from my heart, I beg you not to try to do so. Page Sanger has been generous with us, so offer your thanks, along with mine, by not trying to invade her privacy. She is a charming lady and has been so kind to me, I would consider it a personal favor if she isn't disturbed. The house is in a section of Marietta now rather built-up and resembles the old house only slightly. I am grateful to Page Sanger, however, for approving and liking the jacket artist's concept of Anne's house in the old days. And for her kindness to us all.

Another descendant who helped by letter and photographs with this book—as she did with *Where Shadows Go*—is Elizabeth Zervas, who lives now in Calabasas, California. Thank you, Elizabeth and Page.

As an added fine result of Nancy's visit to Marietta and again through the kindness of my friend Fred Bentley, Sr., I have become telephone friends with two Marietta history authorities, Connie and Dan Cox, who are now in the process of publishing the actual journal of Louisa Fletcher, a favorite character of mine. Both have kept themselves available to me, and I'm deeply grateful.

Another valued friend I've acquired long-distance is the delightful Jean Cole Anderson, whose graciousness and enthusiasm have been far more helpful than she probably suspects. She is the daughter of Louisa Fletcher's grandson, Daniel Webster Cole, whose father, Henry Green Cole, remained a staunch Unionist for all his days. Fred Bentley told me that Henry Cole proved his love of the states as a union by offering valuable land for a burial place for both Yankee and Rebel soldiers. Alas, the offer was refused by the Confederates, so to this day his land holds only the remains of hundreds of fallen Union soldiers. Another most helpful lady is Mary Cole, who, with her husband, Bayard Cole (the nephew of Daniel Webster Cole), gave Nancy and me much important assistance, and we thank them so much. Our thanks go also to Iva Fleming and Grace Wilborn of the Marietta, Georgia, Welcome Center and to Jeanie Hunter, my Eileen's sister, who lives in Marietta and once more came to my rescue.

When I'm stuck in research on almost any subject—in novel after novel—I call, and am always helped by, Stephen Bohlin-Davis of the Juliette Gordon Low birthplace in Savannah. Thanks, Stephen, for having come through still again.

Always the more-than-willing gentleman-to-the-rescue has once more been our good friend T. Reed Ferguson, whose new book, *The John Couper Family at Cannon's Point*, I highly recommend (Macon, Georgia: Mercer University Press, 1994).

Of course, I remain thankful for the good interest and ready help of Dr. William Hitt, and with *Beauty from Ashes*, I also thank Dr. Mary O'Sullivan of St. Simons.

My continuing gratitude goes also for sometimes personal and always needed help and encouragement of too many close friends to list here, but I especially thank Charlene Tribble, Jimmie Harnsberger, Juanelle and John Edwards, Clara Marie Gould, Frances Burns, Lucy Annand, Mary Porter, Peggy and Dan Buchan, G. G. Greneker, Virginia Hobson Hicks, Agnes Holt, Mary Wheeler, Millie Price, Cindy and Mike Birdsong, Ana Bel Lee Washington, Faith Brunson, Neddy Mason, Eleanor Ratelle, Sara Pilcher, Bobby Bennett, Burnette Vanstory, Rosemary Holton, Theo Hotch, Dena Snodgrass, Ann Hyman and Patricia Barefoot. They will know why. As I hope will my amazingly loyal readers everywhere who, even during the times when they're waiting for a new book, go on writing the most encouraging letters any author could hope for.

By now, everyone at Doubleday—President Steve Rubin, who honors me by retaining for each new novel my dear friend and expert editor, Carolyn Blakemore; Marysarah Quinn, my designer of choice; Whitney Cookman, art director supreme; Rob Wood, artist for the beautiful jacket; Renée Zuckerbrot, my bright, careful, skilled in-house editor, who along with Eileen keeps the ball rolling in my behalf; the entire Doubleday sales staff, especially Bebe Cole, Ellen Archer, publicity director, Jayne Schorn, marketing director; and Emma, my dear friend who sets the welcoming tone at the house as capable receptionist—*everyone* keeps me convinced that I couldn't be happier at any other publishing house.

I am especially grateful to Steve Rubin for proving his value again and again by retaining, along with the editorial skills of Carolyn Blakemore, the superior copyediting skills of Janet Falcone. How I depend on Janet as I write to catch me in all the punctuation and factual goofs and inconsistencies in the manuscript. Another plus: Janet and I are really friends.

Carolyn Blakemore has been my cherished friend for years longer than I've been a Doubleday author. She works for herself now, and if Steve didn't retain her for me, I would. She is my ultimate judge when it comes to the often difficult construction of a big novel. Writing another one without Carolyn would be like breathing without air. You laugh at me, Carolyn, but you *are* "the greatest editor in the universe," and I stand by my extravagance. Thank you. Thank you.

It is said often these days that a good agent is harder to find than a publisher. I wouldn't know, because once I began to work with Lila Karpf, I knew I had found the best. Lila not only works hand in glove with Eileen on a zillion angles in my behalf, she *knows me,* believes in me, and I am of all authors most blessed to have her as my agent, my literary manager, and my friend as well. Thank you, Lila, for being you. And for being for me.

And yet another time, I empty my heart of both love and gratitude for every reader of my work. Without you, I wouldn't have the energy or the courage to keep going. Because of you, I am, after some rest time, beginning another book, and with every page rolled into my old manual typewriter, I'll be counting on each one of you.

E U G E N I A   P R I C E
St. Simons Island, Georgia